Birds in Our Lives

Birds in Our Lives

ALFRED STEFFERUD, *Editor*

ARNOLD L. NELSON, *Managing Editor*

BOB HINES, *Artist*

THE UNITED STATES DEPARTMENT OF THE INTERIOR

BUREAU OF SPORT FISHERIES AND WILDLIFE. • FISH AND WILDLIFE SERVICE

UNITED STATES

GOVERNMENT PRINTING OFFICE

WASHINGTON : 1966

Foreword

THE WEB OF LIFE IS LONG, strong, and wonderfully intricate. No thread of it can be cut or weakened without endangering the whole chain of life.

The web links the lives of people, animals, and plants in matters of food, shelter, and the space they need to live, grow, and have their being.

It links them also in the continuous cycle of generation and regeneration of life—life being, in the words of Sir J. Arthur Thomson and Patrick Geddes, "an enduring, insurgent activity, growing, multiplying, developing, enregistering, varying, and above all else evolving."

All parts of the web, the chain, the cycle are important. That they are important to man or unimportant to man is not a point here—man himself is part of the web of life, a small part of the abundant living complex.

The parts are diverse and without number. One is the invisible microbes that can multiply into millions in a few hours and can kill or enhance life. Another is the molds, one of which gives us the antibiotic penicillin. Or the tiny green plankton of the oceans. Or the wild grass that was tamed in America before the white man came to the New World and, as corn, has been grown in a form so changed that it cannot revert to its wild state. Or the 6 living species of horse (20 are extinct), the earliest prototype of which roamed the plains of North America 45 million or more years ago. Or man himself, whose life as man may have begun about a million years ago.

More and more we are coming to know that creatures once considered insignificant are necessary links in the multiplying, varying, evolving chain of life.

Bees, for example, insure the pollination and continuation of the plants they visit to get food for themselves and their young (and people and bears). The life of a bird touches the lives of birds, insects, fish, animals, plants, and people in many ways, as this book recounts. Grass does not ask itself how important it is, but in the end all flesh is grass. Forests grow in their ordained way; they do not say "Come!" or "Go!" to the creatures that seek food, shelter, rest, breeding places, and recreation in them.

We are coming to know more and more also about the findings and importance of ecology, the study of the relations of organisms and their environment. We appreciate more than ever that the conditions of pure air, sun, food, space, and so on that make good homes for birds (and many other creatures) also make good homes for people; a habitat in which one species flourishes is likely to be a good environment for other forms of life.

But we have changed the habitats of many living things, including ourselves, unmindful of the old precept that we cannot command Nature except by obeying her.

We see it everywhere: The streams we have polluted, the forests we have ravaged, grasslands we have plowed up, swamps we have drained, the asphalt jungles we have built, the air we fill with fumes and smoke, the expanses we have poisoned with insecticides—all in the arrogant conviction that we can command Nature to manipulate the web of life in favor of one of its parts—man.

We have gained something, of course, but we have also lost something. Much of what we have lost in space, natural environment, clean air, woods and parks and happy environment, we can never regain. It may not be too late, though, if in our getting we also get the wisdom of a truer perspective of life.

I suggest that in this technological, moon-reaching age we learn more about the interrelationships of all living things on our own planet and apply the knowledge of ecology we have.

In whatever way we state our purpose and goal—whether economic, ethical, political, social, or esthetic—the results can be measured in positive terms of conservation of natural resources, beauty and convenience of our cities and towns, the prosperity of our countryside, the health of people, and the assurance that comes with an appreciation of the unity of life.

Any of several avenues will lead to this knowledge and awareness—a study of molds or plants or horses or bees or many another living thing, including man, surely will lead one to an appreciation of the complexity, the oneness, the wonder of life. Birds, too. This book on birds, a book that considers birds as part of the web of life, I commend enthusiastically.

STEWART L. UDALL,
Secretary of the Interior.

Preface

Our aim in this book is to give a wide perspective of birds as they affect and are affected by people, other birds, and other forms of life and activities.

To tell properly this story of birds in our lives, we have tried to be objective, unbiased, and unselfish, however much some of us love birds and decry the harm people sometimes do them.

We know that some birds may cause losses and problems and inconvenience in some places in cities and on farms. We know that sometimes birds are unwanted, just as some plants, even lovely ones, may grow in the wrong places; then we call them weeds. We know that some people are not interested in birds and consider them unimportant in a larger view of things. All such matters we record.

But we believe the best way to achieve public support for sensitive management and conservation of birds is through a widening of public understanding of birds. When that is accomplished, we can move forward confidently to resolving the problems and fulfilling the needs we set forth.

It may be that through this book we will influence the attitudes and actions of individuals and some policies of governments, councils, and communities. But in no sense should any chapter, or all of them, be regarded as a statement of policy of any government or organization of which the writers are employees.

Many persons had a part in the production of this book. The names of the writers, whose contributions are beyond their usual call of duty and reflect their selfless dedication to the public welfare, appear elsewhere. We are deeply grateful to them.

We express our thanks also to Rex Gary Schmidt and to Luther C. Goldman for many of our photographs and for other services.

Timely and devoted help was given by Lansing A. Parker, Gustav A. Swanson, Samuel D. Robbins, James B. Trefethen, Laurence R. Jahn, Charles H. Callison, Chandler S. Robbins, Ira N. Gabrielson, and Clayton F. Matthews.

We are indebted to John W. Aldrich for his verification of technical details and standardization of plant and animal names.

Frank H. Mortimer and Clifford W. Shankland, of the Division of Typography and Design, the United States Government Printing Office, designed the format and layout of the book.

We thank Emma Charters, who prepared the index, and Gertrude King, Frances Kulla, Mary Lu Lammers, Ferne Mains, and Ellen Warren, who helped with many details, especially typing manuscripts and reading proofs.

Birds in Our Lives deals primarily with birds of the United States, but some authors have adopted a wider perspective. A desire to emphasize certain points and to make each chapter self-contained has meant a degree of duplication among some sections. Our goal of objectivity dictated that the writers should give their own viewpoints on several controversial points, even at the risk of apparent inconsistency.

We hope *Birds in Our Lives* will be as widely read and as meaningful as was its predecessor volume, *Waterfowl Tomorrow*.

Alfred Stefferud and Arnold L. Nelson.

Contents

In Nature's Scheme

Science and Husbandry

The Hand of Man

For Better or Worse

Answers To Conflicts

Working for Their Survival

In Perspective

PASSENGER PIGEONS

What Are Birds For?

AT THE END of a talk about songbirds I once gave in my hometown of Jamestown, New York, an old friend rose to ask a question of the kind a lecturer welcomes and dreads.

"Yes, but Roger," she began, implying that what I had said was all well and good but that I had overlooked a basic detail—"what are birds *for?*"

I paused before I tried to answer. What does a clergyman say to somebody who asks him to explain the reasons for religion? What does a teacher tell a boy who wants to know what good is reading? Or a parent, should anyone ask him to list the values of a baby to parents, the human race, creation?

Questions like these call on one to justify in a small budget of words the faith that is in him, his love for living things, and the place of even the commonest sparrow in a universe where life has been changing, evolving, and surviving or declining these uncounted years, regardless of terms like "useful" or "practical" or "beautiful" that men may apply to any of the myriad components of that life.

I began my answer with a comment Dean Amadon of the American Museum once made: "Man has always had a double interest in birds— on the one hand esthetic, personal, impractical; on the other, utilitarian."

Even stone-age man, I continued, took time out from his hunting to etch the forms of his feathered prey on the rocks or on the walls of caves, thereby giving us the first published ornithological figures. Man has worshipped birds, used them as symbols, and hunted them for food and adornment.

I went on about the practical, utilitarian importance of birds to us, thinking that a person who asks, "what are birds *for?*" expects an answer that stresses practical, rather than esthetic, matters.

First, birds and science.

Ornithology, the study of birds, has added greatly to our knowledge of other natural sciences.

It was certain finches that gave Charles Darwin a major clue to his theory of natural selection. Ornithologists ever since have been in the forefront of those who are unraveling puzzles long obscured in the evolution of new kinds of organisms.

Ornithologists were the first behaviorists in the modern sense. They developed such fundamental concepts as territory and imprinting. The relatively new science of ecology would not be where it is were it not for insight gained by watching birds.

And it was a birdwatcher, the late Rachel Carson, who, in her controversial book, *Silent Spring,* alerted many Americans to the dangers of residual pesticides in food chains, which might conceivably affect man himself.

Birds, with their high rate of metabolism and furious pace of living, demonstrate life forces perhaps better than any other animals.

I spoke then of ordinary dollars and cents—the effect of birds on the economy.

One example is sportsmen, who spend millions of dollars for boats, dogs, guns, ammunition, field clothes, lodging, and more. Birdwatchers spend millions also for binoculars, books, cameras, telephoto lenses, raincoats, boots, hiking shoes, knapsacks, and travel.

And we must not forget the hundreds of thousands of homeowners who buy birdboxes and feeders and who put out millions of pounds of birdseed every winter.

Or, I went on, consider the domestic fowl, the most valuable bird in the world. Its captive origins are lost in antiquity but certainly go back 5 thousand years to the earliest known cities of India. Descended from the red jungle fowl, *Gallus gallus,* which still lives wild in the bamboo thickets of southeastern Asia, it has been spread by man around the world. Fully 200 varieties are known, from the diminutive bantam to the useless but beautiful Onagadori, a Japanese fowl with a fantastically long tail. Some strains have been developed to please their owners' esthetic whims, but most birds have had a more utilitarian background.

When I was a boy, chicken was the special treat at Thanksgiving and Christmas. Today it has become one of our cheapest sources of protein. Nearly 2 billion chickens are raised as broilers each year in the United States, and the laying flock is nearly double the human population. Close to 64 billion eggs are marketed each year. The best hens laid only 50 or 60 eggs a year in early Roman times, but today's champions lay four times as many. The record is 361 eggs in 365 days.

The pigeon may have been a dooryard bird in the Near East more than 6 thousand years ago. Today it far outnumbers and far outranges its wild ancestor, the rock dove, which still breeds on the seacliffs of Europe. Whether it was first raised for food or as a message carrier or simply as an ornament is open to conjecture, but today a hundred or more varieties demonstrate the "plasticity" of the species—"evolutionary potter's clay." Pigeon racing is a major sport in many countries, and flocks in urban parks give pleasure to thousands of city-bound folks who must do their birdwatching from park benches.

The turkey, America's great contribution to bird husbandry, numbers perhaps half a million in the wild, where they are now carefully managed as a game crop, but farmers market close to 100 million turkeys each year.

There may well be more domestic mallards (mostly white varieties) in the world than wild mallards. In the United States alone, 11 to 12 million farm ducks are marketed yearly. The value to the economy of wild ducks, pursued by more than 1.5 million sportsmen in the United States, is far greater.

The millions of canaries behind bars represent a far greater population than ever lived in the Canary Islands, from where European seamen first exported them in the 16th century. The budgerigar, or shell parakeet, currently is the most popular

Rachel Carson, scientist, author, and ardent bird-watcher, wrote Silent Spring, The Sea Around Us, The Edge of the Sea, *and other notable books.*

4

cage bird, and the millions in cages match or exceed the millions that still swarm the Australian back country.

A large percentage of the world's bird species have been kept in captivity at one time or another, and hundreds have been bred. The aviculturists—those who keep birds in cages—are nearly as numerous today as the birdwatchers. Many zoos of the world display several hundred species to an admiring public.

Even the nests and excretions of birds have been of considerable economic importance. For a thousand years, the soft down of eiders has been harvested on some of the rocky islands washed by the North Atlantic. Some families in Iceland have tended their special eider preserves for generations, taking the first crop of clean down with which the nests are lined. The females pluck their breasts again to replace the warm padding around the eggs, which are then allowed to hatch without interference. The birds in these managed and protected colonies are said to produce a better hatch of young than their fellows on the wild moors.

To use birds' nests for warmth and insulation is understandable—but to eat them would seem most improbable. Yet that is what many orientals do when they eat bird's-nest soup. This delectable consomme is made by boiling down the clear, hardened saliva with which small cave swiftlets of southeastern Asia build their nests.

By far the most valuable wild bird in the world is the guanay cormorant, whose nitrogen-rich excrement—guano—is worth many millions of dollars yearly to the economy of Peru. In fact, during the third quarter of the past century, the guano shipped away for use as fertilizer on the fields of the world was worth about 2 billion dollars.

Today Peru uses most of this valuable phosphorus and nitrogen itself, and what had once been a mining operation, removing the accumulation of millenia, has become not unlike modern game management, wherein the harvest does not exceed

Once on many farms, chickens, our commonest birds, were hatched from eggs kept warm by broody hens; now automated hatcheries do it in a large industry.

The picture was taken in Georgia, but it could have been in many other places: A hunter and his dogs, standing staunch over some bobwhite.

replacement. We have no guano operations off our coasts, because deposits sufficient for commercial harvest can only accumulate in climates where rainfall is too slight to wash the smelly white substance from the rocks.

At this point, to bring out a broader aspect of the place of birds in our lives, I changed my angle of flight to survey some of the changes among birds and people.

Birds also are important because there are so many of them—something like 100 billion in the world. That is more than 30 times the present human population, but we must remember that 8,600 species (more or less) are involved. Of these, only one species, the domestic fowl, a satellite of man, exceeds him in number.

There was a time, however, when birds probably outnumbered human beings a thousand to one.

That was in the late stone age, a hundred centuries ago, when the human population, mostly in the Old World, may have been under 10 million.

Over the centuries, man has seen many species grow scarcer, some to disappear forever. How many he himself has eliminated knowingly or unwittingly is a moot question, but we believe that most of the 76 species, more or less, that have disappeared in the past three centuries, were hastened into the void of extinction by man.

We must keep in mind that extinction is also a natural part of the evolutionary process. Species arise, have their day (albeit, a long day, spanning thousands of centuries) and disappear—to be replaced, presumably, by new and equally attractive species, frequently their own evolved descendants.

This process of disappearance and replacement has gone on for millions of years, ever since the

6

primitive *Archaeopteryx* sank into the Jurassic mud. It may well be that the species of birds that we now have make up scarcely more than one-half of one percent of the species that have gone before.

Even so, the 76 species of birds that have disappeared within the past three centuries point to an accelerated rate of extinction, for which the burgeoning human race is largely to blame. The roster of recent extinction stands as a reproach to all of us. So does the long list of endangered species, which have populations of fewer than a thousand individuals.

Our conscience and our growing awareness of our trusteeship over Nature have led us to spend millions of dollars to manage what remains of our wild heritage. Controlled hunting of some game birds—grouse, quail, pheasant—undoubtedly will survive, even though our population doubles its numbers and doubles again, as it undoubtedly will.

Grouse, quail, and pheasants distributed over millions of American acres have a high reproductive potential, and some species can be easily managed. But what about the waterfowl? They must congregate where the water is, and, because of the drainage of wetlands where they breed, their numbers have been declining.

Hunting in North America and hunting in Europe have had different beginnings and have developed along almost opposite lines.

In the Old World, shooting was the privilege of the aristocracy, the landowners. The preservation of the game was therefore their responsibility. To keep the bag generous, the number of hunters was restricted.

We, on the other hand, always have regarded the right to hunt as everyone's privilege, and the term "poacher" is almost unknown in our lexicon. To adjust the "harvest" to the "removable surplus" (call it what you will), the bag limit was divided among the many.

Down, down have gone the limits on ducks within my own memory from 25 a day to 2 per hunter in some flyways. In a democratic society where we divide evenly, we must halve the crop per hunter whenever the gun pressure doubles. This gives us pause; some persons even predict that waterfowling may become impractical and may even go out before the end of the century.

That does not mean that our splendid system of bird refuges should then be done away with and the marshes drained and turned into onion fields. Those who find sport in shooting ducks do not do it merely for the target practice. Most of them really like ducks, and they would still want to be able to watch mallards or canvasbacks or geese come in over the marsh on a windy day. I was not surprised, therefore, when a survey on a famous midwestern goose marsh disclosed that a hundred persons came to watch the geese for every one who came to shoot them. On some weekends, a half dozen policemen were needed to direct traffic caused by the crowd coming to see the geese.

To me that is further evidence that we no longer look at birds in a merely practical way, a resource to be utilized, but rather as a marvelous end product of millions of years of evolution, which it is our duty to preserve.

As a healthy indicator of this trend, the Bureau of Sport Fisheries and Wildlife concerns itself with more than the gunner's bag. The Bureau recognizes that the birdwatchers in the United States far outnumber the active duck hunters. Its research and management program therefore includes nongame as well as game species. The Forest Service, an agency of the Department of Agriculture, recently set up a refuge to help save from extinction a songbird, the rare Kirtland's warbler. This 4,000-acre tract in the heart of Michigan's jack pine barrens is supplemented by two State refuges dedicated to the same purpose. When a monument was dedicated in 1963 to Michigan's unique breeding bird, 2 thousand persons gathered on the common at Mio for the ceremony.

Indeed, on no part of the earth, except near the South Pole, can a birdwatcher be bored, as James Fisher, a noted British ornithologist, points out.

"Birdwatchers," he says, "have many different drives and directions. Some like to work alone, discuss things with few. Some have lost count of the clubs they belong to. To be quite clubless is to be on the bank, with the streams of warm companionship, benign freemasonry, scientific criticism and encouragement, flowing ever more deeply by. . . .

"The brotherhood of the bird club has contributed more than a little to the cause of international understanding and friendship. Our hobby knows no more political boundaries than the birds. Its devotees exploit nobody, compete only in excellence and thoroughness, take little, give much."

Mr. Fisher reported that the first field club was started in Belfast in 1821. Today there are nearly 200 in Britain and Ireland.

No one has made a similar survey in North America, but the clubs and branches associated with the National Audubon Society alone number about 275, and there must be several times that many bird or natural history groups that have no such affiliation.

The history of ornithology in North America goes back primarily to Alexander Wilson and John James Audubon, but birdwatching was given strong impetus some years later by the American naturalist Henry Thoreau and his friends of the Sudbury Valley. Maybe the climate of thinking they sparked made birdwatching a respectable hobby in Massachusetts long before it became popular elsewhere in America.

I recall my own early adventures in western New York more than 40 years ago. My interest was kindled by a Junior Audubon Club in the seventh grade, but I was really a loner, and few people in town shared my enthusiasm for birds.

Today when I return to Jamestown I find a booming club, and a thousand people or more turn out to hear me lecture—and to ask questions.

The same metamorphosis has occurred in a thousand cities and towns across the land, as more and more boys and girls, men and women discover the excitement of watching birds, the most observable of the vertebrates, and go on to discover for themselves the wonderment in natural history and an awareness of the importance of conservation.

What are birds *for*? For that—if nothing else. The National Audubon Society alone sponsors five or more illustrated lectures a season in more than 200 cities, and nearly a million persons attend them. These film shows cover a wide field of natural history and wildlife conservation, but birds are the main interest.

Actually, I guess more than 2 million Americans are active birdwatchers, whose interests may vary all the way from the white-breasted nuthatch they watch at the feedtray to the most serious research. (Some behind-the-times people, as I well know, make fun of "birdwatchers" and use the term in snide derision, but I, for one, ignore them. Those of us who may feel sensitive prefer the words "birding" and "birder.")

Conflicts with birds are inevitable, of course. Their invasion of the airlanes is a case in point. Planes sometimes hit birds, which lack the speed to escape. Usually the birds get the worst of it, but many a plane suffers costly damage and occasionally one falls with a tragic loss of human life.

To live with birds may be a delight, or it may be a trial. Birds are a nuisance around public buildings, and a certain few species, profiting by the mass production methods of modern agriculture, have become what we might call locust birds, swarming by millions into croplands, where their depredations are serious.

The pest problem is largely manmade, a result of monoculture and the futile expectation that we can go on squeezing Nature for more and more production. We must go back to cultural modifications, back to such time-tested methods as crop rotation—almost abandoned since synthetic pesticides came to hand—and break up the size of our crop areas so as to reintroduce diversity.

Recently I was scheduled to lecture in a southern city. Before the lecture, I was informed that the community was to be sprayed with dieldrin because the entomologists had discovered the presence of fringe beetles.

In my opening remarks I said it was good to hear the local mockingbirds. Then, I added: "But you probably won't have them next week." A hush fell over the audience as I warned them that *Silent Spring* is no fantasy. It can happen here.

I was not able to stay to see what happened, but I learned later that 309 dead birds were picked up after the spraying on 300 acres. More than one bird for every acre—and I daresay they were only a fraction of the birds that actually were affected, because dying birds try to hide. The evidence was available because people were alerted; the side effects of most spraying programs go undocumented.

A boy who discovers (and leaves undisturbed) a cardinal's nest has a memorable experience.

It is ironic that a citizen is subject to a stiff fine if he shoots a robin or so much as picks up a dead robin on the highway and possesses it—yet with impunity he may use chemicals to kill off hundreds of robins and other birds.

Although large-scale destruction of songbirds is deplorable, I am even more concerned about those species that are at the ends of long food chains—particularly certain flesh-eating birds. A lifetime of bird observation in many parts of the world and in all 50 States has convinced me that a number of species are in grave danger. The situation of the osprey and the bald eagle is well known. Less well known is the plight of many of the other birds of prey.

What is most needed, as Charles Elton, the English ecologist, pointed out, is to bring about a gradual change of emphasis that will consider chemicals only one among many approaches to insect control. The long-run, ecological solution of this problem will bring Nature back into the act as the farmers' partner. We must use natural controls as much as possible, design new cultural methods, use chemical controls as a surgeon uses a scalpel instead of as a bludgeon, and develop biological controls for the major insect pests.

Meanwhile we must speak up and stop those who in their arrogance would make a biological desert out of our landscape.

We in a democratic society must develop ways to resolve the conflicts between birds and people. The biologist is the man to whom officials and the public turn for facts and guidance. But the final solutions may involve politics, economics, recreation, and ethics.

The truth of the matter is, the birds could very well live without us, but many—perhaps all—of us would find life incomplete, indeed almost intolerable, without the birds. In the words of Samuel Taylor Coleridge:

> He prayeth best, who loveth best
> All things both great and small;
> For the dear God who loveth us,
> He made and loveth all.
> —ROGER TORY PETERSON.

There are so many ring-billed gulls at Mohawk Island, Ontario, that it is known as Gull Island.

ARCHAEOPTERYX

Masters of the Air

ABOUT A HUNDRED years ago, workmen came upon a strange, incomplete fossil as they were digging in a limestone quarry in Bavaria. It had teeth and the long, bony tail of a reptile but the feathers and wing and leg structures of a bird. About the size of a crow, it seemed to have lacked the broad, keeled breastbone that supports a bird's flight muscles, and so very likely the creature, when it was alive eons ago, could only glide, not fly.

Scientists called this remarkable fossil *Archaeopteryx lithographica*—from the Greek words meaning primitive and wing and imprinted on stone.

Archaeopteryx was a clue that has helped us piece together the story of birds and answer some puzzling questions: Where did birds come from in the first place? How can you explain their presence over the world? How did birds master the air and so find the key to universality?

The story goes back to prehistoric time, in the Triassic period some 180 million years ago, when birds arose from a somewhat specialized group of reptiles that had long hindlimbs. This group gave rise to dinosaurs and also crocodiles, the only present-day reptiles having an ancestor in common with birds.

The avian line from this reptilian ancestor may have begun as tree-climbing forms, which first jumped from branch to branch on their longer hindlimbs and later learned to glide from branch to branch by using membranes stretched between the sections of their shorter and slightly flexed forelimbs.

As they gradually evolved the ability to fly farther, these arboreal forms acquired greater sailing surface through the expansion and fraying out of the scales on the trailing edges of their forelimbs and along the outer edges of their long tails.

These modified scales developed to become what we call feathers. At that point we may say birds came into being, for of all the physical features of birds, none distinguishes them more sharply from all other creatures than these outgrowths of the skin.

Archaeopteryx is the earliest known bird. The fossil remains of three of them have been found at different times. This creature of the Jurassic period, some 150 million years ago, may have been one of several kinds of similarly primitive birds already existing, but we do not know.

We know that one such primitive species, probably of either Eurasian or African origin, acquired the power of flight (that is, the ability to sustain itself in the air for indefinite periods by flapping its wings). We know also that from this stock many species began to emerge as they became able to reach and fill more habitats and niches.

This evolutionary process, which we call adaptive radiation, was slow at first but steadily quickened during the next 149 million years, through the Cretaceous and Tertiary periods. Birds in time inhabited all the earth's great landmasses and occupied most of their principal environments.

But as the continents separated, merged, and separated, as mountain ranges rose and were worn away, as the climates shifted, and as plant forms evolved, flourished, and vanished, so did the habitats for birds. The species that became so precisely adapted to one habitat or niche that they could live in no other disappeared when the habitat disappeared. More species were always evolving, however, to fill the new habitats.

The primitive birds became extinct through the

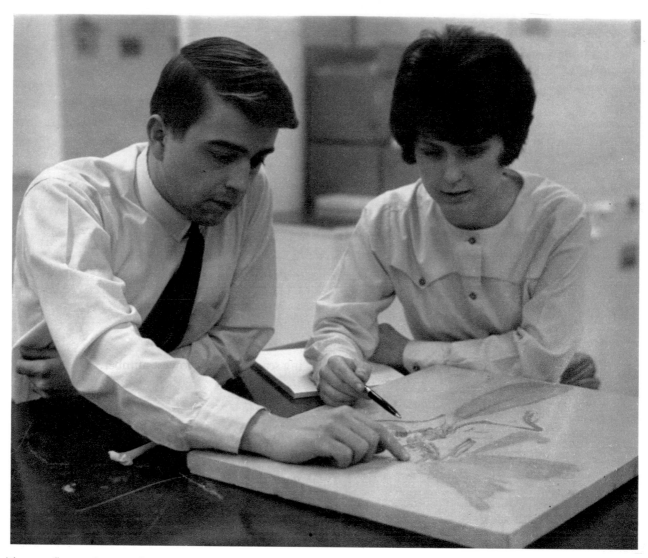

Two staff members at the U.S. National Museum inspect a casting of the fossil remains of Archaeopteryx, *forerunner of modern birds that lived some 150 million years ago. The casting is based on a specimen discovered in 1877 in a limestone quarry in Bavaria.*

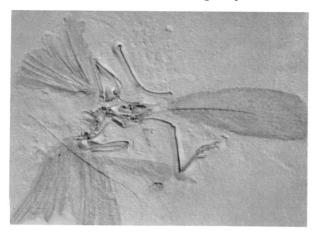

Cretaceous period, as did the dinosaurs and other great reptiles. The "new" birds began to look more and more like modern species, and many birds were recognizable by the end of the Tertiary as ostriches, pelicans, cranes, nuthatches, thrushes, and so on.

With the coming of the Pleistocene epoch, or ice age, about a million years ago, the abundance of birds in number of species attained a peak that has never been exceeded. This period of prehistory could have been called the Age of Birds, had mammals not already taken the ascendancy in size and aggressiveness to dominate the earthly scene.

Toward the end of the Pleistocene and the start of the modern epoch, about 15 thousand years ago, bird species began to drop out. Many more species were disappearing than were evolving. The decline of birds was underway. Man had not yet become a major destructive force in the avian environment. How and how fast that destructive force grows may determine how and how fast our 8,600-some species decline.

Most modern species of birds can fly and so can rove the earth, but each species is confined to a particular geographical range, which may be any area from several hundred acres to one or more continents.

A few birds are practically cosmopolitan. The barn owl occurs nearly everywhere except in the polar regions, New Zealand, and oceanic islands. The osprey is nearly as worldly. At the other extreme are the Kirtland's warbler, which nests only in a 100-by-60-mile area in Michigan and spends its winters on the tiny Bahamas, and several species that live the whole year on oceanic islands and archipelagos.

The ranges of different species overlap, so that in any one area there is an aggregation of species— an avifauna. Because the ranges of species rarely or never are identical, avifaunas are subject to marked variation. Ornithologists over the years have given considerable attention to the composition, comparison, and origin of avifaunas. It is still a challenging field for study.

To organize studies of living things and the habitats they occupy, ornithologists and other life scientists divide the world into six regions on the basis of the presence of birds, other animals, and plants.

The regions are:

Neotropical (South America, Central America, and the Mexican lowlands).

Australian (including New Zealand, New Guinea, and islands of the southwestern Pacific).

Ethiopian (Africa south of the Sahara).

Oriental (Asia south of the Himalayas and the East Indies, except New Guinea).

Holarctic (the rest of the Old World and North America, including the Mexican highlands).

Marine (all the oceans and seas).

All the regions have notable differences in their avifaunas.

The richest region by far in total number of species of birds and variety of unusual forms is the Neotropical. Here live nearly 3 thousand species, which represent 89 families. No fewer than 25 of the families are native to the region. South America alone has about 2,500 of these species— no wonder that it sometimes is called the bird continent. Ecuador, in northwestern South America, leads the world in the greatest number of different birds—altogether, some 1,200 breeding species.

The Ethiopian region has about 1,750 breeding species and is second to the Neotropical in total number of species.

The Australian region, with 17 endemic families, is second in different forms.

The other three regions are below the first three in total numbers of species as well as in endemic species—that is, species confined to the region.

The Marine region, which includes sea birds that do not live on land except during the breeding season, has the lowest number.

The Holarctic region, of which North America is a part, has fewer species and correspondingly fewer endemic forms than the other mainland regions, but most of these species are represented by greater numbers of individuals with generally wider ranges. The 700-odd species in North America north of Mexico include many that are much the same as species in northern Europe and Asia.

The North American avifauna today comprises elements from various sources.

During the mid-Tertiary period, North America was separated from South America by water gaps between islands and was connected to Asia by a bridge across Bering Strait. The climate in southern North America was uniformly tropical to subtropical at that time. Birds in the southern part of North America thus were partly isolated and existed in a favorable climate; they evolved into species that were highly peculiar to the area.

Then, toward the end of the Tertiary and in the early Pleistocene epoch, came the isthmus between North America and South America and the onset of a cooler climate. The result was a shifting of the ranges of birds and even the elimination of some species.

Among the more important North American groups that developed on the continent while it was isolated during the Tertiary are turkeys, wrens, thrashers, mockingbirds, waxwings, vireos, and wood warblers.

The hummingbirds, tyrant flycatchers, and the blackbirds or icterids evolved in extreme southern North America or on the mid-Tertiary islands (now Central America) and later moved northward. The loons, phalaropes, and a few other groups of birds are as much Eurasian in origin as they are North American. The cranes, pigeons, cuckoos, typical owls, kingfishers, crows and jays, titmice, and nuthatches reached North America via the Bering Strait bridge from Eurasia.

We cannot account for all groups of birds in North America. Grebes, herons, ducks, woodpeckers, and swallows, for instance, are so worldwide in their distribution that their places of origin are obscure.

Clearly, the North American avifauna has undergone many changes. So have all avifaunas. Sometimes we do not realize that they are undergoing changes all the time. Therefore we have to think of the ranges of most species as having fluid boundaries.

The instability of boundaries may be due partly to the tendency among species to invade new areas. Cyclonic storms may help or hasten resettlement by moving individuals to a different place, where they may survive and reproduce if the environment suits them.

Man has a part in it, too, when he transports birds on his ships. House sparrows reached the Falkland Islands on a ship that first stopped at a South American port, where the birds, attracted by sheeppens on deck, came aboard and remained until it reached the islands.

Nor are irruptions uncommon. For some reason, perhaps a failure in food supply, a number of northern species, such as hawk owls and boreal chickadees, suddenly in fall or winter move far southward to places where they do not normally live. They usually retreat northward with warmer weather, but the possibility always exists that a few may find suitable breeding areas without returning as far as the places from which they came.

We have seen several extensions of range in North America in the past few decades. The cattle egret has spread northward and inland from the Atlantic coast, following its arrival in South America from western Africa. The cardinal has moved steadily northwestward through the Mississippi Valley to Minnesota and the Dakotas. The house wren has pushed its breeding range southeastward into Georgia.

The expansion of the range of one species may

Soon this helpless, day-old, teaspoon-size bit of life will grow into a lively, lovely bluebird.

spell the decline of another species, into whose range it intrudes, by intensely and successfully competing with it. The spread of the starling westward through the United States very likely has greatly reduced the population of the red-headed woodpecker, whose hole-nesting sites it may usurp.

For this knowledge of our ever-changing avifauna we are indebted to hosts of birdwatchers who regularly report unusual birds in their communities to Audubon Field Notes, which is published by the National Audubon Society in collaboration with the Bureau of Sport Fisheries and Wildlife. Birdwatchers are encouraged to report their finds in order that we may have still better information on what is taking place.

Within its geographic range, a species usually occupies a particular environment or habitat.

It shares its habitat with other organisms, plant and animal, all of which are adapted to the prevailing conditions of soil, air temperature, moisture, and light. All the organisms in a given habitat collectively comprise a biotic community, since they show relationships to one another.

The biotic communities with which particular birds are associated are identified by their dominant types of vegetation. Some of the major biotic communities in North America north of Mexico are the tundra (alpine and arctic), coniferous forest, deciduous forest, prairie grassland, and scrub desert.

Within these major associations are a number of communities, such as lakeshores, marshes, swamps (bogs), fields, shrublands, and streamside woodlands, which are developing almost imperceptibly toward the major communities.

Where any two communities meet, more often than not there is an area of mixture and overlap, or ecotone, in which the birds and other living forms characteristic of these communities are intermixed and in which are additional forms that prefer this situation and seldom are found anywhere else.

When we study birds we are aware always of the importance of habitat or community in accounting for the presence or absence of species. We associate different species with particular environments—the red-eyed vireo with the deciduous forest, the grasshopper sparrow with the prairie

The red-winged blackbird, a common land bird, has flourished as forests and prairies have been converted to farms and the living conditions it seems to like.

grassland, and the verdin with the scrub desert.

When we travel northward on the continent or climb a high mountain, we expect a sequence of species as we pass through one environment after another—the olive-sided flycatcher in the coniferous forest, the white-crowned sparrow at the timberline ecotone, and the ptarmigan on the tundra.

We become conscious also of several significant aspects of ecological distribution.

Rarely is one species found throughout a community, even though it may be characteristic of that environment. As a rule, it occupies merely a niche, and to this it is adjusted in structure, function, and behavior as no other species in the same community.

The red-eyed vireo, for instance, lives in a treetop niche in the deciduous forest. The ovenbird lives on and near the forest floor. It would be unusual for the vireo to be seen on the ground or for the ovenbird to be found in the treetops. The vireo and ovenbird may appear to share their niches with other species, but none behaves exactly as they do or requires the same food, the same nesting sites, and so on.

Species of birds occur in greater variety and density in ecotones than in the pure communities that contribute to them. This phenomenon, called edge effect, is important to anyone who wants to see larger numbers of birds.

Edge effect is the result of a greater variety of vegetation—grasses, shrubs, and trees—which provides a greater variety of food and cover for birds.

For example, ecotones where field and forest merge have the plants characteristic of both field and forest and many additional shrubs. Thus they bring together birds of both field and forest, while attracting species that require either shrublands or a combination of trees, shrubs, and grasses.

Some bird species are adapted so strongly to a special niche that they cannot live in a different situation. If an element in the niche on which they depend is destroyed or seriously altered, they are more likely to disappear than to make an adjustment.

The everglade kite probably would disappear in Florida were disaster to befall the big freshwater snail, *Pomacea palludosa,* on which it feeds exclusively. It is likely that the Kirtland's warbler would disappear in Michigan if there were no groves of jack pines 5 to 8 feet high.

A good many species, on the other hand, are much more adaptable. Sometimes they are so widely tolerant of different situations that their precise niches are unrecognizable. The blue jay, black-capped chickadee, and cedar waxwing are so adaptable that we may find them almost everywhere in wooded areas throughout their ranges.

The species that restrict themselves to narrowly prescribed niches generally have small populations within correspondingly small ranges. The species tolerant of environmental changes and variations generally are mainly the ones that inhabit the transitional communities and ecotones; they have large populations and often range widely.

How many birds are there today? James Fisher has placed the number at about 100 billion, although he said it may be between 10 billion and 1,000 billion. Roger Tory Peterson has put the number of breeding birds in the 48 States at about 6 billion.

The most abundant birds are no doubt certain marine birds that inhabit vast areas with a seemingly limitless supply of food.

The guano-producing cormorant, or guanay, that breeds on desert islands off the Peruvian coast may be one of the most abundant. One island was

The emperor penguin is one of a few kinds of birds that have lost the power of flight. The hostile environment of McMurdo Sound, Antarctica, where the photograph was taken, is home to these birds of ice and snow. In the background is the New Zealand cargo ship Endeavor.

estimated to have more than 5 million adults and young. They required not less than a thousand tons of fish food a day. Mr. Fisher believes that the Wilson's petrel, a bird that spends most of its life wandering over the oceans, possibly is the commonest bird in the world.

Ornithologists are not certain as to the most abundant land bird in North America, but I think the red-winged blackbird may lead all other native wild birds. It breeds from the southern fringes of the arctic tundra to Central America. It is primarily a marsh bird, but it breeds in various upland situations across the continent. Wherever you travel by car in the summer, you see it on utility wires, seldom far from its nesting site in a grassy ditch, low shrub, or hayfield.

Roger Tory Peterson considers the red-eyed vireo the commonest breeding bird in eastern North America and the horned lark the leader in the prairie country.

In North America or elsewhere, the population of no present-day land bird even closely approaches the incredible numbers of the extinct passenger pigeon. A. W. Schorger believes that it totaled at least 3 billion individuals at the time of the discovery of America and may have made up 25 to 40 percent of the total bird population.

Accurate information on total populations of species is sparse. The species whose total numbers have been determined are those whose breeding areas are sharply restricted, completely known, and accessible for direct counting. Among them are the colonies of the North Atlantic gannet, which in 1939 were found to have 83 thousand nests— a population of 166 thousand adults.

We have the best figures for species with small populations. For example, the Kirtland's warbler, which breeds only in a small section of the pine barrens in Michigan, was estimated in 1951 to have 432 singing males or an adult population of fewer than 2 thousand.

It would be fine if we knew the sizes of the populations of all species, but the direct counting of individuals of most species generally is futile, because they are so numerous and widespread. Attention is better given to measuring the populations of all species in a given area and understanding their compositions and controls.

We usually determine the size of a population by direct counting, sampling, and applying indices.

In sampling, we cover a measured plot representative of a habitat (or a measured strip of successive habitats) systematically at regular intervals and count the number of species and individuals we see. Thereby we get an estimated numerical picture of the whole habitat or habitats.

In the application of indices, such as the number of birds observed per unit of time or distance, we determine the relative abundance of species in a population.

Estimates of bird populations in a limited tract may be made by calculating the ratio of banded to unbanded birds. For that, intensive, quick work is needed because the populations constantly are changing.

Censusing, the enumerating of individuals of a given area at a given time, is only a small part of the study of populations.

But more important than counting numbers is learning more about the various species themselves. It is a complex undertaking. It includes their reproductive rates; the ratio of age groups and sexes; the annual fluctuations of their respective populations because of varying physical factors of the environment (air temperature, precipitation, and so on) and biological factors (predation, diseases, food supply); and ways in which their populations are regulated or controlled over long periods of time.

Although populations normally show fluctuations in numbers of individuals per year, they are remarkably stable over a period of, say, 50 years, if their habitat is unchanged. Annual fluctuations are scarcely more than wrinkles in the long history of a population.

This study of bird populations has endless opportunities for investigation by professional and amateur ornithologists. It is of vital—"vital" meaning life-or-death—importance, for it is the basis for developing ways and means of conserving birds for the future.

So far, we have accounted for the origin of birds, their ages-long descent, and their presence and numbers in our lives. Now we come to birds as biological entities.

We look at them from two viewpoints: Crea-

Some hummingbirds, like the tiny black-chinned hummingbirds, a species that occurs in western North America, weigh only a fraction of an ounce.

tures which, in achieving a mastery of the air, are uniformly specialized, and creatures which, although uniformly specialized, are amazingly diversified.

Animals move from place to place by running, hopping, walking, crawling, swimming, gliding, and flying.

Among birds, flight is the principal means of locomotion, even though a few (ostriches, kiwis, penguins) in the course of evolution have lost the ability to fly. Therefore, we can recognize birds as birds because they are formed to fly.

The modern bird, like a modern airplane, is structurally and functionally efficient. It has to be to take flight, to stay aloft, and to reach its destination safely under the most adverse conditions.

I list six requirements for successful movement in the air.

Lightness is achieved by a covering of feathers ("the strongest materials for their size and weight known") instead of a thick skin; by loss of teeth and the heavy jaws to support them; by a reduction of the skeleton and by the hollowing, thinning, and flattening of the remaining bones; by a radical shortening of the intestine and the elimination of the urinary bladder; and by air spaces in the bones, body cavity, and elsewhere.

Streamlining also is achieved by the feathers, which overlap and smooth over the angular, air-resistant surfaces and provide bays, wherein the feet may be withdrawn.

Centralization and balance—so necessary for flight—are achieved by the transposition of all loco-motor muscles toward the body's center of gravity (leaving the limbs, like puppets, controllable by tendonous strings) and by the central position of the gizzard (the avian substitute for teeth) and other heavy abdominal organs.

Maximum power is achieved by the combination of exceptionally high, steady, body temperature for aerial maneuvers in all extremes of climate and weather; by feathers, which aid in conserving the heat; by increased heart rate, more rapid circulation of the blood, and greater oxygen-carrying capacity of the blood stream; by a unique respiratory system, which permits a double-tide of fresh air over the lung surfaces, synchronizes breathing movements with flight movements, cools the body internally, and eliminates excess fluids; and by a highly selective diet of energy-producing foods, which contain few indigestible substances to cause excess weight.

Visual acuity and rapid control are achieved by large eyes, which have a wide visual field and remarkable distance determination, and by a brain whose visual and locomotor centers are greatly enlarged and are capable of recording and transmitting nerve impulses with the speed of a seasoned pilot.

Birds range in size from hummingbirds to ostriches.

The smallest bird is the Cuban bee hummer, which measures 2.25 inches from billtip to tailtip. Fourteen of them would weigh no more than an ounce. The largest is the African ostrich, which stands 8 feet and weighs more than 300 pounds.

Among the largest flying birds are the Andean and California condors. They have 10-foot wingspreads and weigh 20 to 25 pounds. These giants, however, are exceeded in wingspan by the wandering albatross, specimens of which have measured about 11 feet from wingtip to wingtip.

There are limits to the size that flying birds may attain. They cannot be as small or as large as many other animals. Because they need a high rate of metabolism for supporting a high body temperature, flight movements, and so on, birds need sufficient food to maintain this rate and at the same time compensate for heat loss from body surfaces.

Theoretically, the smaller the bird, the greater its relative body surface and heat loss. Consequently, the smaller the bird, the more it must eat in proportion to size. Again theoretically, a bird smaller than kinglets and chickadees would have to eat all the time, night and day. Hummingbirds

These flightless Masai ostriches of northern Africa are only 3 months old. Some ostriches weigh up to 300 pounds when they are full grown.

can exist, small as they are, because they can lower their body temperature (that is, become torpid) at night or other times when they cannot eat. Thus they conserve energy.

The larger the bird, the faster it must fly to stay airborne: It must have bigger flight muscles for greater speed. That, in turn, means greater weight, as flight muscles are heavy.

Our larger birds have attained their size while retaining their ability to fly by developing a dependence on air currents. The largest flying birds, the condors and albatrosses, practically require winds and updrafts in order to fly at all.

Although we can recognize all birds as such, we find they have radiated in form and activities so they can live in particular niches in the environment.

Consider, for example, adaptations for locomotion and feeding. Some species customarily fly swiftly; others fly slowly. Some hover; others soar.

Some swim and dive; others wade. Some walk or hop. Others climb. To get food, some species probe in the soil, dabble in shallow water, scratch the ground, chisel holes in trees, make flying sorties, and so on.

These adaptations and others, always in complex combination, account for the different shapes of wings, tails, bills, and feet and differences in body shape, plumages and coloration, breeding habits, seasonal movements, and general behavior.

Or, to put it another way, thanks to adaptive radiation operating so vigorously in the descent of birds, we have some 8,600 different species.

Usually we think of birds in terms of species, rather than as parts of an ecological complex, or so many populations.

In doing so, we are paying particular attention to several aspects of their lives—the breeding cycle, food habits, longevity, seasonal migration, direction finding, and behavior.

The California condor is among our largest flying birds. Some of them weigh up to 25 pounds. Some may have a wingspread of as much as 10 feet.

I give a few details about some of them.

The main stages of the breeding cycle of most species are establishment of territory, the coming together of sexes, nest building, egg laying, incubation, hatching, and the care of young.

We have a vast amount of data on these stages, but still, surprisingly, we have comprehensive information on relatively few species. Work is proceeding on life cycles, but we still have a long way to go. Only for about 5 percent of our North American species do we know the size of territories; for about 10 percent, the average length of nestling life; and for about 20 percent, the average incubation period. For about 30 percent we have full descriptions of the sights and sounds that are a part of courtship.

As to food, I am fairly sure that for every kind of living thing there is at least one bird species adapted to feed on it in one way or another. Because bird species rarely are omnivorous, their food habits often are as good an indicator of species as their breeding habits are.

It now appears that the average age of a wild passerine bird—songbird—is 1 to 2 years; of a gull, 2 to 3 years. Some of the larger birds—albatrosses, for example—which have one egg per clutch and require 5 to 9 years to reach breeding maturity, have a much longer average life expectancy.

The average lifespan of a bird must not be confused with its potential lifespan, which is much longer. There are records of wild passerine birds living 10 to 16 years and of a wild herring gull living 28 years, but they are unusual or exceptional. It is not unusual, though, for albatrosses to live 30 years or more. Captive birds, of course, sheltered as they are from predation and other unfavorable factors of the natural environment, may exceed the normal life expectancy manyfold and live to astonishing ages.

We have learned about the longevity of wild birds mainly through banding, in which we put on a bird's leg a numbered aluminum band that will identify the bird when it is recovered. Each year more than a million birds are thus marked in North America, and about half a million abroad.

Why do birds withdraw from one region in the colder seasons and then return to it in the warmer seasons?

We do not know how and when seasonal migration originated, but we have a great store of knowledge on how it proceeds.

Very few species remain to be discovered and described. At least 98 percent of the bird species in the world are now on record in one way or another.

It would seem therefore that we have learned just about all there is to know about differentiation of bird species. Far from it. The new concept of biological species and the wealth of information that is coming from many workers in ornithology have given us new tasks in reappraising the nature and the status of species and their interrelationships.

All this emphasizes my point that birds are fascinating subjects for study and observation. Masters of an environment that man has conquered only by mechanical means, birds have delighted his senses, challenged his skill, and excited his thinking as no other creatures have or ever will.

—OLIN SEWALL PETTINGILL, JR.

Birds and Science

Know thyself. The proper study of man is man. If you accept those old precepts, consider what a study of birds can tell us about ourselves.

We sense in ourselves, for example, direct or indirect changes that we ascribe to heat, humidity, cold, sunshine, the amount and kind of food we eat, and other aspects of the environment in which we live.

Birds give us many illustrations of such physiological changes, which may or may not be clues to changes in our bodies or exactly comparable to them but in any event are interesting, suggestive of fruitful paths of investigation, and valuable to scientists.

Take the matter of cycles, an example of which is a woman's 28-day cycle of ovulation. In birds, an annual cycle is pronounced and easily studied. It includes the chorus of singing birds as they court in spring, its cessation in the summer, the raising of the young, the semiannual migration, the changing of plumages, and other seasonal phenomena. Such a cycle is present even in nonmigratory or resident birds in the warm zones, except perhaps among some in a tropical rain forest.

The seasonal cycle is not always a 12-month cycle. Large albatrosses have a 2-year cycle, the sooty terns of Ascension Island a cycle of 10 lunar months, and a number of tropical passerines a 6-month cycle.

What factors are responsible for these regular changes in the physiology of birds?

Part of the answer to this question we have

learned in the past 40 years, yet we are still far from a complete understanding.

The discovery of photoperiodicity in birds by the Canadian zoologist William Rowan, of the University of Alberta, gave us a big step forward. He showed that birds (particularly males) of certain species could be brought into breeding condition in midwinter when exposed to an artificially increased day length. The poultry industry has made good use of this discovery. Turning on electric lights in poultry barns has resulted in a notable increase in egg production.

Soon other scientists demonstrated that a rather elaborate chain reaction is involved: The light stimulus is transmitted by the optic nerve to the base of the brain (hypothalamus), which in turn releases some stimulus to the pituitary gland. The pituitary then produces a hormone, which circulates through the bloodstream to the sex glands.

It soon became clear that increasing the light was not the only possible stimulus, because, for instance, the Emperor penguin commences to breed in the antarctic autumn during decreasing light. Many desert birds experience a rejuvenation of the sex glands within 1 to 3 days after the heavy rains that herald the arrival of a season suitable for breeding.

Finally, D. Serventy and A. J. Marshall, two Australian ornithologists, conducted research that led them to believe it probable that in the slender-billed shearwater, a species breeding in Australia, the development of sex glands is largely independent of external stimuli and is controlled apparently by an internal "clock," or "calendar."

Many interesting physiological problems are associated with the annual cycle.

In many birds there is heavy deposition of fat just before the fall migration. More fat may be added in winter as insulation against the cold and as storage of food in case of blizzards. These physiological changes are likewise controlled by external and internal factors, and these factors are different in the fall and in the spring.

It is known that sex and thyroid hormones are involved in the control of the fat deposition, but the complete story has not yet been told.

Obesity being such a puzzling medical problem in man, it is possible that the studies in the deposition of fat of birds may lead to fundamental advances in basic physiology.

Another aspect of the annual cycle is moulting, the change of plumage. Almost all birds change their plumage at least once a year. Most birds have two moults each year, one right after the breeding season and the other one before it. Often there is an alternation between a bright mating plumage worn during the breeding season and a dull or hen-feathered eclipse plumage the rest of the year.

The change in color is determined sometimes by the sex hormones, as in the mallard and other ducks, and sometimes by pituitary hormones, as in some weaver finches. The thyroid hormone accelerates the growth of moulting feathers, but we are not sure what actually causes the moult. It involves an increase in the numbers of highly localized cells. The cells divide at a very high rate, while most surrounding tissues remain essentially the same. In contrast to a tumor, growth at all stages is completely controlled and fully patterned. How this control is exercised is another puzzle.

Birds differ from mammals and hence from man in numerous ways.

Their normal body temperature is several degrees higher than that of mammals. That fact alone affects nearly every aspect of the body's use of food. Birds have more efficient lungs than we do; all the air passes right through the lungs into the air sacs and there is no space for residual air that would lower the efficiency of breathing.

Sea birds—perhaps all birds—have a set of special salt glands, usually between the eyes and the nasal cavity, which enable them to excrete salt solutions at concentrations higher than that of sea water. They can quench their thirst by drinking sea water and get rid of the excess salt through the salt glands.

What we call a sense of direction in ourselves we call orientation in birds. It is a strange and wondrous aspect of avian physiology.

Take for example two species of New Zealand cuckoos, who leave their young to be raised in the nests of foster species. The old cuckoos start on their annual migration about 3 weeks before the young, who have nothing to guide them in their migration save the information they received in the genetic program contained in the germ cells. Yet these young, inexperienced birds fly with precision across hundreds of miles of open ocean to winter in the Solomons or in Fiji and Samoa and adjacent islands, all of them mere dots in the vast Pacific.

How can they do it? And why? Science can give some terms and hypotheses, but the ultimate analysis is still to be made. Since it is a collaboration between brain and sense organs that makes orientation possible, we must assume that the genetic program contains a detailed "blueprint" of the neural structures that make orientation possible.

That birds are "born" with an ability to choose certain directions during migration seems clear. But we still have questions as to the clues that enable birds removed from their homes by scientists, who study their homing instincts, to return to their nests. Very likely magnetism and gravitational forces are not involved. The sun may be involved in some way, yet the speed in which a released bird may start off in the home direction (often within less than 50 seconds) makes it seem improbable that the sun is the only source of the birds' clues.

This much, however, has been established: Some birds have an extraordinarily precise internal "clock," and in the sun they also have an excellent compass.

The feats of homing by displaced birds are indeed astonishing. A purple martin was removed from its nest in northern Michigan, was taken by car 234 miles south, was released at night, and was back at its nest in the morning—8 hours and 35 minutes later.

A Manx shearwater transported from the coast of Wales to Boston and released there returned to its nesting hole 3,200 miles away in less than 13 days. Since the ocean offers no landmarks and

The lesser scaup and other waterfowl species have glands that regulate the salt content of body fluids and enable the birds to live in marine situations.

since the return was far too rapid for any form of random searching, we must conclude that it used some set of precise clues in the environment.

The study of birds has revealed much about behavioral biology.

Pigeons can perform extraordinary tasks of learning when they are properly rewarded for giving the right answers. For instance, the sense of smell in pigeons is notoriously poor. Yet, when rewarded with food for making the right choice between two odors, pigeons learned to distinguish odors at amazingly low concentrations.

Birds also have been of value in the study of unlearned (that is, innate) behavior. Every species has its own patterns of behavior. Individuals of a species exchange species-specific signals with other members of the species. Learning contributes little to some of the behavioral elements, such as certain courtship movements. In other words, birds do their courting and mating as members of their species always have; they have not learned new ways to get a mate. No one has ever succeeded in training a bird to give the courtship display of a different species.

We would like to know much more about the components of behavior that perhaps can be modified by learning, the amount of variation among individuals of a species or a population, and the meaning of maturation—the physiological readiness for certain behavioral elements only when the individual reaches certain fixed age levels.

The possible effect of hormones is particularly important. Several scientists have demonstrated that certain activities in the breeding cycle will not be displayed until the proper level of a certain hormone has been reached or until that hormone has modified certain tissues or organs in the appropriate manner. The incubation patch, for instance, does not develop normally unless an estrogen and the hormone prolactin are present. The crop gland of pigeons grows under the influence of prolactin.

Ecology is the study of the interaction between organisms and environment. It touches human life in a number of ways. Ornithology contributes to our knowledge of our place in the world because birds are conspicuous, we can count them and identify them precisely, and we can capture them and release them after we have banded or marked them. Thus we can follow the movement of indi-

Dr. Wesley Lanyon, of the American Museum of Natural History, uses sound recording equipment in the Chiricahua Mountains of Arizona to tape bird calls and songs for behavioral research. He rotates the reflector until the call is monitored to its best fidelity.

Dr. Lanyon uses a sonograph to obtain visual descriptions of the notes in bird calls. The notes are fed into the sonograph as tape recordings and are reproduced on a graph; each note produces its own pattern.

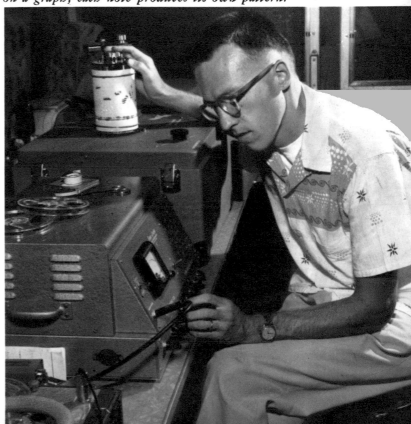

A male sage grouse in Harney County, Oregon, performs a strutting dance as he courts his mate.

viduals and study many facets of the biology of populations.

Birds are particularly good subjects for the construction of life tables in wild populations. An instance is the nature of predator-prey relationships.

The studies of several ornithologists have shown that birds are especially vulnerable to predators during periods of overpopulation and when they are weakened by disease. Each species of predator normally specializes on a different kind of prey, except when a prey species becomes superabundant, as during outbreaks of mice or lemmings.

The principle of competitive exclusion, already known to Charles Darwin, states that natural selection will favor differences in the occupancy of a niche—that is, in specialization as to food and habitat among species that coexist in the same area. We can deduce from it that birds and other animals may have a natural ability to select, after a dispersal phase, the species-specific habitat.

The selection of habitat is one of the many mechanisms by which size of population and dispersion of population are regulated. The phenomenon of territory—areas defended against competitors of the same species—is another one.

Discovered in birds by Bernard Altum, a contemporary of Gregor Mendel, and rediscovered in the twenties, it has led to deeper insight into the psychology and ecology of birds. Another mechanism that leads to the regulation of population is increased mortality of the young in large clutches and during periods of high population density.

These studies are of great indirect relevance to man in a time of an exploding human population. Problems like that can be solved only when we understand the interaction of factors and the basic causes. Since one cannot experiment with man, one must rely on other animals, particularly birds, for a clarification of the underlying principles.

Systematics, which deals with the recognition, description, and classification of kinds of animals and plants, has benefited from studies in the taxonomy of birds.

Since birds are so well known, we have been able to compare different populations of a single species and to analyze variations within populations.

As a result, we know more about the geographic variation of species in size, proportion, and coloration, various adaptive responses to climate and geography, which help our understanding of the

One of Dr. Lanyon's recording stars is an ash-throated flycatcher.

Vaccines for the prevention of sleeping sickness (encephalomyelitis) in horses are developed in chicken eggs. In this photograph a virus-filled embryo is being removed carefully under sterile conditions.

races of mankind. We have acquired a new concept of species, as arrays of variable populations, distributed in space and time. The importance of the local population as the testing ground of natural selection is particularly clearly shown by birds.

Hybridization is rare in birds with their highly developed species-specific courtship pattern, as compared, for instance, to plants.

We also know more about the colonization of islands and the mixing of faunas.

It has been possible time after time to determine the place of origin of the different faunal elements. All the native birds of the Hawaiian Islands, for instance, are the result of only about 14 colonizations, of which more than half derived from the North American Continent; the others came from the islands of Polynesia. Similar analyses have been made for Madagascar, New Zealand, New Caledonia, and Australia.

When North America and South America were isolated by a large water gap for 100 million years or so between the Middle Cretaceous and Pliocene epochs, some islands were stepping stones for intercontinental colonists such as hummingbirds, tyrant flycatchers, tanagers, blackbirds, and finches.

Yet the intimate mingling of these faunas did not occur until the Central American water gap was closed toward the end of the Tertiary. The analysis of the mixed fauna now occurring in Central America is leading to the development of new concepts and a better understanding of faunal histories. The colonists from North America and those from South America now mingle freely. The tropical rain forest is largely occupied by South American elements, such as toucans, antbirds, woodhewers, and puffbirds, while North American elements dominate the montane habitats and arid areas.

Charles Darwin, the great British naturalist who wrote *Origin of Species,* often referred to birds.

30

His studies of the finches in the Galapagos Islands bulked large in his thinking about evolution. Investigations since then of geographic variation have led to the theory that new species originate by a process called geographic speciation—that is, the development of reproductive isolation during geographic isolation of populations. Closely related species can coexist at one locality because they are reproductively isolated; they do not interbreed with each other.

This reproductive isolation is effected by so-called isolating mechanisms, such as sterility between species. Ornithologists, however, have shown that behavioral mechanisms are far more important in preventing the mixing of coexisting species than is sterility. Matings between mallards and pintails can be quite fertile, for example, but the courtship patterns of mallards and pintails are sufficiently different so that hybridization occurs only under exceptional circumstances even though the two species commonly nest side by side.

The study of such isolating mechanisms also has led to new interpretations of species-specific color differences, color differences between male and female, size differences in related species, the correlation between plumage color and song, and the study of behavior and competition.

All species must be well adapted in order to survive, but the pathways by which such adaptation is achieved sometimes are unclear. Adaptation often leads to convergence among kinds of birds with similar habits. So-called flycatchers in different parts of the world have become similar in morphology and habit after having acquired the ability to catch flying insects. The so-called finches are now believed to be a group of unrelated types with a cone-shaped bill. This bill was acquired independently in different lines of birds as an adaptation to a diet of seeds.

Birds have an increasing part in medical research. For instance, birds have malarialike diseases carried by avian plasmodia, and therefore they are useful in a preliminary testing of drugs that may be useful in treating malaria.

Birds also have been used for the testing of hormones. Their high metabolism and the high body temperature may make them interesting material for studies in comparative physiology.

Bird eggs are excellent material for the study of viruses and for the development of vaccines. The influenza vaccines, for instance, are produced from viruses raised in living bird eggs.

I merely mention, in passing, other fields of modern scientific research in which birds are studied or used: Neurobiology, geography, nutrition, research on enzymes and muscles, and game management. Indeed, we can well speak of the rediscovery of birds as exceptionally suitable material for research in many branches of biology.

Ornithology is basically a pure science rather than an applied science, but it is not science solely for the sake of science. Bird conservationists, superintendents of bird refuges and bird sanctuaries, aviarists of zoological parks, and raisers of cage birds and poultry are among those who put ornithological knowledge to work.

Whatever the task—whether it is to protect species in danger of extermination or to control damage caused by abundant bird populations—a reservoir of knowledge about the subjects involved is a basic need. If man would save birdlife from himself for himself, then, of course, he must know the ways and needs of birds.

Scientists do research because they want to explore the unknown and find the truth. Yet they are pleased if their findings benefit humanity. The work of scientific ornithology has already contributed a good deal to human welfare and there is every reason to believe that this will be equally or even more true for research that is still to be done.

—E. MAYR.

Literature and Arts

Birds and Fine Arts

THERE IS LASTING EVIDENCE on stone, in bronze, in song, in print, on canvas, and in practically every known form of creative art that man has been inspired by the beauty and charm of birds and the melody of bird songs as far back as the human record runs.

We know from pagan folklore, classic myths, ancient manuscripts, and the winged human figures in Greek sculpture and medieval painting that the heritage of the eagle and the dove was the dream of man for 5 thousand years.

Pieter Brueghel immortalized the fabled and fatal flight of Icarus in a masterpiece of painting. Erasmus Darwin, grandfather of the great naturalist, wrote of the Icarian fall from the sky into the Mediterranean waters:

> . . . . *with melting wax and loosened strings*
> *Sunk hapless Icarus on unfaithful wings:*
> *His scattered plumage danced upon the wave,*
> *And sorrowing Nereids decked his watery grave.*

Leonardo da Vinci designed a flying machine, but luckily for lovers of art, it never got off the ground with the inventor in the pilot's seat. Still the dream of flight by man persisted, and more than a century ago Alfred Tennyson wrote with poetic vision that he

> *Saw the heavens filled with commerce, argosies*
> *of magic sails,*
> *Pilots of the purple twilight dropping down with*
> *costly bales;*
> *Heard the heavens filled with shouting, and*
> *there rained a ghastly dew*
> *From the nation's airy navies grappling in the*
> *central blue.*

But Tennyson was a seer among singers, as Leonardo was an engineer among artists. Most painters, poets, and sculptors of the past thought that man would never soar higher than in flights of fancy to which the birds inspired them. Thus they gave us the favorite bird of Zeus, the eagle, carrying Ganymede aloft to replace the lamed Hebe as cupbearer to the gods and Zeus himself wooing Leda in the guise of a swan. They dedicated the owl to Minerva, the goddess of wisdom, and engraved figures of owls on some of their coins. They gave winged heels to Mercury and often portrayed Cupid equipped with wings as well as a bow and arrow.

Most of the winged figures in marble or on canvas are testimony that painters and sculptors borrowed from the birds to uplift and ennoble the human form. Take the statue that we know as the Winged Victory of Samothrace. There it stands, bathed in light, at the head of the great stairway in the Louvre, 23 centuries of ageless and enduring art.

But when we penetrate farther into the Louvre—or any other great art museum—we note a peculiar distinction that artists make in lending wings to the human form.

From the frescoes of Giotto down through the canvases of the pious medieval masters to the drawings of Gustave Doré for Dante's *Inferno* and Milton's *Paradise Lost,* the hosts of Heaven, the ministering angels, the seraphim, and the cherubim have the soft, lovely wings of birds, but Satan and his imps and attendant demons wear the mammalian wings of great bats, veined, hairy, hooked, and no doubt purposefully horrible.

In this way, artists definitely have put birds where Disraeli once said he stood with regard to a slightly different but at least distantly related matter, on the side of the angels. If the admirers of the Order of Chiroptera were organized, they might picket such pictures as "Unfair To Bats" or write indignant letters to newspapers denouncing the artists as unnaturalists.

It must be admitted, however, that birds are not often cast as the parties of the principal parts in great works of art. They appear more frequently as added decorations on canvas or in stone. Where carved or painted as lone figures, they usually are offered in the guise of symbols, such as the eagle for courage, the owl for wisdom, the dove for peace, and the hawk or vulture for rapacity. They have often served in literature as symbols, too.

When the ancient Greeks paid their drachmas to see and hear *The Birds* by Aristophanes, they well knew that they were going to enjoy a satire on human affairs and not a lecture on ornithology. All the birds of the fables of Aesop and La Fontaine were men and women in disguise.

Among the moderns, Maurice Maeterlinck was a naturalist as well as a poet and playwright, but his most popular production, *The Bluebird,* was not a bird biography but a touching study of human happiness for which the bluebird was the symbol. There was also Edmond Rostand who saw his *Chantecler* produced on the Parisian stage in 1910 with the great Lucien Guitry in the title role. But once again the fine feathers of the amorous and valorous Chantecler, the beautiful Pheasant, the stupid Peacock, the strutting Turkey, and the wicked Blackbird were just a cover for a presentation of human virtues and frailties.

Birds, however, have appeared simply as themselves in many famous paintings. The fact is that a full collection of these merely incidental bird portraits by medieval and Renaissance painters might have served as a good field guide to an astonishing number of the common residents or regular migrants over most of Europe. Indeed, a student can pick up some fine points about the wide distribution of certain species by scanning the paintings in the art museums around the world.

For instance, in the Kress Collection in the National Art Gallery in Washington there is a large canvas by Dosso Dossi titled, Circe and Her Lovers

WINGED VICTORY OF SAMOTHRACE

An eagle in marble, of the Hellenistic School, Egypt, about 200 B.C., is in the National Gallery.

in a Landscape. It depicts the island enchantress of Asia Minor and some of her ex-adorers whom she has transformed into various kinds of wildlife. They include three dogs, two deer, one hawk (species doubtful), one easily identified white spoonbill, and, of all things, a barn owl, a bird that is resident from coast to coast in this country. Dosso Dossi never left his native Italy. He must have seen the barn owl there. The bird student who wonders about all this and looks further into the matter will discover that the barn owl, like the osprey, is globe girdling in distribution.

In the Metropolitan Museum in New York is Sassetta's Journey Of The Magi, which shows the Three Wise Men of the East with their attendants on the way to the scene of the Nativity in Bethlehem. Sassetta had an eye for birds, too. Across the blue of the sky he painted six snow geese in line. In the lower righthand corner he has two European goldfinches feeding on the ground, and on a hill in the upper lefthand corner we find two of the common cranes of Europe, one feeding quietly and the other keeping a wary eye on the travelers below. Even at a distance they are clearly cranes, because the artist very definitely gave them the odd-shaped "tail assembly" that is the badge of the tribe.

Sometimes a bird in a painting plays a more important part than the artist had in mind when he was at work on it. The Uffizi Gallery in Florence has a painting by Raphael that was originally described as Virgin and Child with St. John, but—because the little St. John is depicted giving a pet bird to the Christ child—the famous work is now known as the Madonna del Cardellino or, in English, the Madonna of the Goldfinch.

In the Wallace Collection in Hertford House, London, a canvas by Melchior de Hondecoeter, a 17th century Dutch artist, shows a group of barnyard fowl with an added wild bird that many American enthusiasts would go miles to see in the depths of winter, a Bohemian waxwing, which is common enough in Europe but an irregular cold weather wanderer in the United States.

Gustave Courbet, a leader in the French realist movement, made at least two bad mistakes in his life. One was the tearing down of the Napoleonic memorial column in the Place Vendôme in Paris when he was a deputy in the French Commune in 1871. For that he was fined a total of 300 thousand

This marble gravestone, Girl with Pigeons, from the Island of Paros, Greece, was carved in about 450 B.C. The Metropolitan Museum acquired it in 1927.

francs when order was restored. The other was a painting he did about 6 years earlier when he was summering at Trouville, a popular French resort on the Channel coast. The painting shows a girl walking the beach with three dead black and white birds hanging from a stick she is carrying over her shoulder. Courbet titled the canvas La

37

Circe and Her Lovers in a Landscape is by the Italian artist Dosso Dossi (1479–1542). It is part of the Samuel H. Kress Collection in the National Gallery of Art in Washington, D.C.

This is a detail from the painting, The Journey of the Magi, by Sassetta (1392–1450). It is in the Metropolitan Museum of Art in New York.

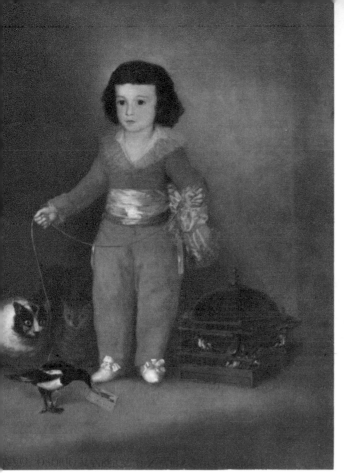

In this painting, Don Manuel Osorio de Zuñiga, by the Spanish artist Goya (1746–1828), the bird on a tether is a black-billed magpie, and the birds we see in the cages are known as European goldfinches.

Madonna of the Goldfinch, by the Venetian artist Tiepolo (1696–1770), is in the Samuel H. Kress Collection of the National Gallery in Washington, D.C.

Fille aux Mouettes, which, when the work was exhibited in this country in 1960, was changed to Girl With Seagulls.

A purist might challenge "seagull" as one word or overlook it as colloquial, but an ornithologist has to challenge the title as false in two languages. The dead birds hanging from the stick are not gulls but terns most plainly and definitely, the French for which is "sternes" and not "mouettes," as Courbet put it. The artist won many honors and awards in his time, but on this evidence he wouldn't qualify for an Eagle Scout badge in this country nowadays.

On the other hand, there were artists who were correct down to the last feather in painting game bags of duck, snipe, woodcock, and such after the hunt on some 18th-century baronial shooting ground. For that matter, where could you get a better painting of a black-billed magpie than the one the youthful Don Manuel Osorio de Zuñiga

Raid on a Sand-Swallow {bank swallow} Colony— "How Many Eggs?" was drawn by Winslow Homer (1836–1910) and printed in Harper's Weekly. Such scenes were common before we had protective laws.

Three canvasbacks, a watercolor by Frank W. Benson, was chosen for a migratory bird hunting stamp.

has on a string on the canvas that Goya did of the red-garbed Spanish boy and that now hangs in the Bache Collection in the Metropolitan? For good measure, Goya added two cats looking at the magpie malevolently and a cageful of European goldfinches seemingly contended behind bars.

Then there was Daubigny of the Barbizon School, who had a penchant for including colorful ducks in his paintings of the streams and ponds of the countryside below Paris. More recently there was Bruno Liljefors of Sweden, whose oil paintings of wildlife in general and hawks and eagles in particular won his convases places on the walls of museums around the world. Here in this country the waterfowl etchings of the late Frank Benson are as highly esteemed in the art galleries as they are by bird lovers and duck hunters.

Last and actually most important to modern or-nithologists and bird lovers are the "bird painters," whose patron saint or founding father was John James Audubon and whose followers are legion. For the record and for national field guides and regional bird books, they work mostly in water color, but some who have the time and talent go on to produce canvases that are pure art and that many museums are glad to have.

Among the notables in this field there would have to be mention of Alexander Wilson, the indomitable but eccentric and unfortunate emigrant from Scotland whose work really was the spur that started Audubon on his great career.

The "world's champion" modern bird portrait painter for the field guides of today is, of course, Roger Tory Peterson, who covers all continents. Others of more limited terrain but perhaps no less artistic talent—let's not go to law over this—would include Louis Agassiz Fuertes, Athos Menaboni, Don Eckelberry, John H. Dick, Rex Brasher, Peter Scott in England, Paul Barruel in France, and doubtless others here and abroad unknown to this amateur art critic.

One of the tourist attractions in Salt Lake City is a bird memorial. A little over a century ago the Mormons, whose religious beliefs kept them at odds with their Illinois neighbors, started an overland trek into the western wilderness to find a place where they could live their own lives in peace. After 2 years of hard travel, they reached the Great Salt Lake in Utah, which was then (1847) Mexican territory. The hardy Mormons cleared the land beside the lake and sowed grain for a crop that would be needed to keep the colonists from starving. Just when the grain was growing nicely, the fields were covered by an invasion of grasshoppers that swarmed to this unexpected feast of tender greenery. Starvation seemed in the offing for the Mormon tribe.

Out of the sky came one lone gull, then more gulls, and then thousands of gulls. They feasted on the grasshoppers and thus saved the crop for the grateful Mormons, whose descendants, in time, erected the memorial monument at which tourists and Salt Lake City residents gaze today. The Mormons didn't care, but those who are particularly interested in birds say that the avian rescuers were the California gulls that breed in the area. The four bronze panels on the monument that depict the story of the grain, the grasshoppers, the gulls, and the Mormons in bas-relief are the work of Mahonri Young.

In the Museum of Modern Art just off Fifth Avenue in New York City is a slim bit of statuary that caused a Customs Service dispute when it was brought to this country years ago. It's a thin, tapered cylinder of bronze that the sculptor, Constantin Brancusi, called Bird In Space and that he said was a valuable work of art. The customs agents said that it looked like scrap metal to them, and they wanted it assessed as such. As a work of art, it would be admitted free of duty. The case went to court. Amid some hilarious publicity in the newspapers for all concerned, Bird In Space was legally welcomed duty free into the country as a work of art.

Snowy Owl, by John James Audubon (1785–1851), is in the National Gallery of Art in Washington.

A golden eagle painted by Louis Agassiz Fuertes.

Roger Tory Peterson painted these whooping cranes.

Bird figures, of course, appear here and there in many sculptured works of art in stone or metal, but mostly as added attractions or decorative details. You can find them embroidered on screens and painted on porcelain. The jewelry trade offers miniature birds fashioned of precious metals and studded with glistening gems. Another great division of commerce offers bird figures pressed, molded, etched, or blown in the glass. Take your choice. There is no end to it.

In the field of music, the great Richard Wagner offers us the sight of a swan in Lohengrin, but luckily the bird is not permitted to sing. In Siegfried, however, we have the lovely music of the wood birds telling the hero, who understands their language after drinking the dragon's blood, the secret of the ring and the sleeping Brünnhilde. There is even more bird music in Igor Stravinsky's opera Le Rossignol (The Nightingale), as one might expect because the bird really plays an important part in the story. The same composer wrote the great ballet L'Oiseau de Feu (The Fire Bird) that was first produced by Diaghileff in Paris half a century ago and is still a favorite with the followers of that art.

The limpid grace and pure beauty of majestic swans gliding silently over quiet waters are delightfully described for us in music by two great composers in Le Cygne by Camille Saint-Saëns and Ein Schwan by Edvard Grieg, who, incidentally, may well have seen whooper swans on the river below the little house on the outskirts of Bergen, Norway, in which he wrote so much of his music. It must be admitted, however, that bird notes are scarce in operas, symphonies, concertos, and classical music in general.

It is just the opposite in the old ballad and sentimental song department. For more than two centuries, French cantatrices have been favoring their drawing room audiences with Le Coucou by Claude Daquin. We now sing Shakespeare's Hark, Hark, The Lark to the music of Franz Schubert.

A monument in Temple Square, Salt Lake City, Utah, commemorates the California gulls that arrived in 1848 in time to devour crickets that were destroying the crops of Mormon pioneers.

Pyx in the Form of a Dove, a 13th-century Limoges work in copper, is in the National Gallery of Art.

A false eagle, sculptured by West Coast Indians.

Who has escaped hearing parlor sopranos warbling Yradier's La Paloma (The Dove) or Sarradell's La Golondrina (The Swallow)? As children we joined the chorus telling how sweet Hallie "is sleeping in the valley and the mockingbird is singing where she lies." With piping voices we urged each other to listen to the mockingbird.

Tin Pan Alley in New York City produced a song dedicated to the whip-poor-will and another in praise of a red, red robin that came bob-bob-bobbin' along. There were other such masterpieces, but perhaps it is best to forget them.

Turn now to the field of literature, and we find birds at their best as sources of inspiration to those master builders of memorable lines, the poets. It is noteworthy that the first written verse in the English language was in praise of a beloved bird. It was a brief outburst that, according to Bartlett's Anthology, came to light about 1250 A.D. The first of its three verses ran as follows:

Sumer is icumen in,
Lhude sing cuccu!
Groweth sed, and bloweth med,
And Springth the wude nu –
Sing cuccu!

Centuries later, William Wordsworth asked himself the rhetorical question: "O cuckoo! shall I call thee bird, or but a wandering voice?" Elizabeth Barrett Browning paid poetic tribute to the familiar *Cuculus canorus* of the English countryside in her Sonnets From The Portuguese in these lines:

Remember, never to the hill or plain,
Valley or wood, without her cuckoo-strain
Comes the fresh Spring in all her green
*   completed!*

Shakespeare was a country boy before he went up to London to become the poet and playwright "not of an age but for all time," and his plays are full of scattered bird notes. He knew the birds of Stratford town and the farmlands around it. He was well acquainted with the sport of falconry and often used its technical terms in his dramas and comedies.

Listen to Othello when Iago has first poisoned his mind against Desdemona:

If I do prove her haggard,
Though that her jesses were my dear heart-
*   strings,*
I'll whistle her off, and let her down the wind
To prey at fortune.

Of the unnatural events that preceded the murder of Duncan by Macbeth a character in the play reports:

*   On Tuesday last,*
A falcon, towering in her pride of place,
Was by a mousing owl hawk'd at, and kill'd.

Petruchio, in The Taming Of the Shrew, says at one stage of the training of Katherine to be an obedient wife:

My falcon now is sharp and passing empty,
And till she stoop she must not be full-gorged,
For then she never looks upon her lure.

The page lent by the deluded Falstaff to Mistress Ford in The Merry Wives Of Windsor is hailed by the lady in this fashion when he comes on stage in Act III, Scene 3:

How now, my eyas-musket, what news with
*   you?*

An "eyas" is a young falcon, and the added "musket" put it among the smaller species. It is evident from all this and many more such lines in his plays that Shakespeare knew a gyrfalcon from a peregrine when the wind was southerly. He also knew "the temple-haunting martlet," the "ousel cock so black of hue with orange-tawny bill," and scores of other common species that filled the woods and fields around the Stratford he knew as a boy.

Even so, the play's the thing, and Shakespeare never wrote a play in which a bird appeared in a leading part. We have to turn to the field of poetry to find birds made immortal in literary masterpieces.

One of the early celebrants was the great Pierre de Ronsard (1525–1585), who wrote joyously of the feathered tribe in his quaint, old, unaccented French:

Dieu vous gard, messagers fidelles
Du Printemps, vistes arondelles,
Huppes, coucous, rossignolets,
Tourtres, et vous oiseaux sauvages
Qui de cent sortes de ramages
Animez les bois verdelets!

Times change, and so do languages and bird names therein. The "arondelles" of Ronsard would be "hirondelles" (swallows) in a French field guide today. The "rossignolets" of the 16th century have lost a couple of tailfeathers, too, and are now listed simply as "rossignols," better known to us as nightingales. On the other hand, the "tourtres" of the old poet (the same birds of which it is written in the Bible "The voice of the turtle is heard in our land") have spread their plumes a little and are now "tourterelles" to one and all. But the "coucous" still identify themselves as such in any language and the "huppes" remain just that in modern French though in English we call them hoopoes.

Seagulls, by the Swedish artist Bruno Liljefors (1860–1939), is in the National Museum in Stockholm.

Wordsworth's "ethereal minstrel, pilgrim of the sky," the *Alauda arvensis* of the ornithologist and the skylark of the English countryside, rivals the nightingale as an incentive to soaring flights of fancy by poets. Even American poets such as Edna St. Vincent Millay, Lizette Woodworth Reese, and Joseph Auslander, on first hearing the European skylark, burst into song themselves.

James Hogg, the Ettrick Shepherd, called it "Bird of the wilderness, blithesome and cumberless" and added some lines later:

O'er fell and fountain sheen,
O'er moor and mountain green,
O'er the red streamer that heralds the day,
Over the cloudlet dim,
Over the rainbow's rim,
Musical cherub, soar, singing, away!

Here is "A Lark is Flying," Jesse Stuart's homely, wholly American sonnet, from his book, *Man With a Bull-Tongue Plow:* [1]

The lark is flying in the morning clouds
And pouring forth the music from his breast.
And I have stopped my mules from harrowing clods—
(My mules are always glad to get a rest).
A song sings cross my pastures leafing early—
It sounds across the bottoms of green wheat.
These notes do not come from a small bird surely,
A small speck where the skies and hilltops meet.
The mules—if they could have some sense to listen—
Would please me better, but they fight the flies

[1] Copyright, 1934, 1959, by Jesse Stuart. Dutton Paperback Edition. Reprinted by permission of E. P. Dutton & Co., Inc.

45

And everlastingly keep trace chains jingling—
I strain my ears to catch the sound that dies.
The speck gets fainter—weaker grows the sound,
The mules and I must go on harrowing ground.

But the paean in praise of the song of the sky-lark that is best remembered and most frequently quoted, probably because it is required reading or even reciting in many schools, is the dazzling lyric of Percy Bysshe Shelley in 21 stanzas. That's a bit long for inclusion here, but the first and last stanzas are offered with the thought that they will stir fond memories in the minds of many readers:

Hail to thee, blithe spirit!
Bird thou never wert,
That from heaven, or near it,
Pourest thy full heart
In profuse strains of unpremeditated art.

Teach me half the gladness
That thy brain must know,
Such harmonious madness
From my lips would flow,
The world would listen then, as I am listening
*   now.*

Many are the poems about birds of many species. William Cullen Bryant gave us the familiar *To a Waterfowl* and *Robert of Lincoln*, who was so gaily dressed. Robert Frost wrote a sonnet about the ovenbird. Walt Whitman and a host of others waxed lyrical over the singing of the mocking-bird. John Burroughs wrote 50 lines of rhyme in honor of the Lapland longspur. Emily Dickinson was among those who praised the robin in meas-ured lines. She also added to the chorus in favor of the bluebird. Robert Browning wrote of the "wise thrush" that sings each song twice over:

Lest you should think he never could recapture
The first fine careless rapture!

Alfred Tennyson sang of the owl and the eagle and the swallow and addressed the European blackbird, which is a thrush like our robin, in this fashion:

O Blackbird! sing me something well:
While all the neighbors shoot thee round,

I keep smooth plats of fruitful ground,
Where thou mayst warble, eat, and dwell.

Some years ago on a visit to Cape Ann, that rugged headland jutting out 15 miles into the ocean to form the northern arm of Massachusetts Bay, the late T. S. Eliot wrote of the birds of the area as follows:

O quick quick quick, quick hear the song-
*   sparrow,*
Swamp-sparrow, fox-sparrow, vesper-sparrow
At dawn and dusk. Follow the dance
Of the goldfinch at noon. Leave to chance
The Blackburnian warbler, the shy one. Hail
With shrill whistle the note of the quail, the
*   bob-white*
Dodging by bay-bush. Follow the feet
Of the walker, the water-thrush. Follow the
*   flight*
Of the dancing arrow, the purple martin. Greet
In silence the bullbat. All are delectable. Sweet
*   sweet sweet*
But resign this land at the end, resign it
To its true owner, the tough one, the sea-gull.
The palaver is finished.[2]

Of all the wealth of verse directed at individual species, one of the shortest and best examples is the following tribute to the Baltimore oriole from the pen of Edgar Fawcett (1847–1904), who was an American playwright and novelist as well as a poet:

How falls it, oriole, thou hast come to fly
In tropic splendor through our Northern sky?
At some glad moment was it Nature's choice
To dower a scrap of sunset with a voice?
Or did some orange tulip, flaked with black,
In some forgotten garden, ages back,
Yearning toward Heaven until its wish was
*   heard,*
Desire unspeakably to be a bird?

The acknowledged masterpiece of poetry in this field is fittingly dedicated to the finest singer in the bird world, the nightingale. At least, that seems to be the majority opinion among those who love poetry and have had the exquisite pleasure of hearing it pour its lovely liquid notes over a moonlit landscape on its breeding grounds in England or on the Continent. Poets down the ages have paid homage to this plain, little, brown bird with the beautiful voice. There were fine poets among them, too, all the way from Quintus Horatius Flaccus to T. S. Eliot, but the supreme tribute came from one of the greatest of English poets, John Keats, in his cherished *Ode to a Nightingale,* of which just one of the eight inspired stanzas is offered here:

Thou wast not born for death, immortal Bird!
No hungry generations tread thee down;

The voice I hear this passing night was heard
In ancient days by emperor and clown;
Perhaps the self-same song that found a path
Through the sad heart of Ruth, when, sick for
*   home,*
She stood in tears amid the alien corn;
The same that oft-times hath
Charm'd magic casements, opening on the foam
Of perilous seas, in faery lands forlorn.

This was written in May 1819, when Keats was in a rural retreat not far from London and a pair of nightingales had a nest near his cottage. Out of the dusk came a bird song and out of the soul of a genius came a gem of lyric literature.

—JOHN KIERAN.

Tales Once Told

LISTEN, MY CHILDREN. A sage of the Paiutes is relating an offtold legend as the winter fires burn low and all is still, save the small sounds of the fire and the sleepy twittering of a grouse outside.

Listen, my children:

Long, long ago, all our world was under water—the woods where the elk, or wapiti, lives; the plains, where some antelope still race the wind; the chasm where the Colorado rushes. All, except the very tip of Kurangwa, the Mount Grant of the white man. There a fire burned, the only fire left in the whole universe.

Only a few Paiutes lived through the storms that brought the flood. They knew their last hope was the flame on the mountaintop. They knew they had to get the fire so their people could start life anew and make the world habitable again. But they were afraid. Winds made great waves, and wind and waves might grow so strong as to put out the fire.

But a storm-weary sage hen—grouse—flew by. She settled down on the tip of Kurangwa. She fanned her wings, and so kept the waves from washing over the fire. She paid a price for her heroism. So close was she to the waning flame that it scorched her breast. And that is why all sage hens have black breasts.

Listen, my children.

Now, far distant from the land of the Paiutes, a similar legend is being passed on by an old man of the Leni Lenape, the Delawares, who lived in the area that is now New York, New Jersey, Pennsylvania, and Delaware.

The old man's words may have been similar to those Daniel G. Brinton used in *Myths of the New World*, a book about the legends of the Leni Lenape and other North American Indians published in 1868:

"The few people that had survived had taken refuge on the back of a turtle who had reached so great an age that his shell was mossy, like the bank of a runlet. . . . A loon flew that way, which they asked to dive and bring up land. He complied but found no bottom. Then he flew away and returned with a small quantity of earth in his bill. Guided by him, the turtle swam to a place where a spot of dry land was found. There the survivors settled and re-peopled the land."

Many groups of people or races in many places have myths, legends, or lore about an all-submerging deluge. Birds figure in many of them.

That there was a flood of spectacular proportions is a matter of record. An account of a deluge like the one that occurred during Noah's time was written about some 2 thousand years before the beginning of the Christian era.

That story is engraved in cuneiform on clay tablets recovered from the ruins of Babylonia. It relates that a houseboat of arklike proportions was constructed by a chosen family so its members and a large, varied collection of livestock could survive.

The ark was at sea for about 7 days. It had no port of call and drifted along until it grounded on a barely submerged hilltop. It remained so anchored for another 7 days.

The cuneiform account then goes on to say that the ship's master freed a dove, a swallow, and a raven, which were to act as explorers. The dove and the swallow returned. Ever since, people have regarded doves and swallows as "good birds."

But the raven was never seen again. And ever since that day in the long-ago-and-far-away, it has been considered a less than admirable bird.

Indeed, the raven and all other members of the family *Corvidae* (jays and crows) were considered "Devil's birds" in the folklore of northern Europe. The magpie, another of the *Corvidae*, was thought to have Devil's blood on its tongue.

The European crow was said to visit the underworld each year in order to give the devil his due in the form of a tribute in feathers. This superstition may have related to the bird's moult in midsummer, the time of its supposed visit to the devil. At this season, it absents itself from its usual haunts and remains silent and mostly unseen until it has its new plumage.

The New World had a like superstition. It was applied to a bird of the same family. In the South, the blue jay (or jaybird) was reported as never seen on Friday, the day on which the jay was said to carry sticks and news of the world above to the devil.

The jay always completed its Satanic chores in time to be back on earth by Saturday. This was a day on which it was spoken of as being unusually gay and noisy. Its behavior was supposed to indicate that it was now as free as a bird for another week.

Indians in all parts of North America had many tales and legends about the birds they knew.

The Micmac, of the New Brunswick area, used to tell how the snowy owl laments the end of the Golden Age, a mythological time when man and animals lived in perfect amity. The Golden Age came to an end when the animals started to quarrel. The lack of unity so disgusted the god Glooscap, or Gotescarp, that he quit the area, announcing that he would not return until all differences had been settled. The snowy owl was so saddened at this turn of events that it cried in its almost raven-like tones, *Koo, koo, shoos*—its way of saying, "Oh, I am sorry. Oh, I am sorry."

The Tillimooks accounted for the small rise in the tides off the Oregon coast in this way: In olden times, the crow was endowed with a voice like that of the thunderbird—a mythical creature that could cause thunder and lightning and one depicted in aboriginal art as a huge bird with outstretched arms.

The thunderbird did not like its voice and considered it unsuitable for a being of its stature and abilities. It proposed an exchange of voices. The crow agreed, but only if the thunderbird guaranteed that there would be low water along the seacoast. That would make it easier for the Tillimook squaws to gather clams and other mussels.

The thunderbird agreed and quickly made the

The jays are mentioned in numerous legends and superstitions. This is a colorful blue jay.

water recede a great distance. The delighted crow at once ventured out onto the nearly limitless exposed sea bottom. But she became frightened when she saw the great variety of sea creatures left exposed in the wake of the receding water. She hustled ashore and begged the thunderbird to lessen the distance to which the water would recede. The thunderbird did so. And that is why, the story concludes, little sea bottom shows at ebb tide along the Oregon coast.

Still another legend comes from the Cherokees, once the largest tribe in the southeastern United States. This story concerns the wren, a bird sometimes paired with the robin in a protective way. In fact, the wren is supposed to have been in the stable when Christ was born. And there is an Irish saying: "The robin and the wren are God's two holy men."

The Cherokees, however, had no such high regard for the wren; they considered this bird a busybody. The wren, always designated as "she," was truly an early bird, according to the Cherokees. She, they say, got up at dawn, pried into everything, and called at every lodge in the course of her nosiness. All this bustle so early in the morning was to gather every bit of news to report at the birds' council.

An important part of the wren's newsgathering was to learn the sex of each newborn child. If she announced at the council that a boy had been born, the council lamented: "Alas! The whistle of an arrow! My shins will burn."

Such lamentation was understandable. The birds well knew that as the boy grew older, he would hunt them with his blowgun and arrows and roast them on a spit.

But if the wren-reporter announced the birth of a girl, all the council members rejoiced and trilled: "Thanks! The sound of the pestle! At her home I shall surely be able to scratch where she sweeps." The birds knew that as the girl grew older she would grind corn into meal, spilling some as she worked, and thus would provide food for them.

Many of the birds once believed capable of speech were, like the Cherokees' wren, small species. Some of them have been credited with always telling the truth. Our Biloxi Indians formerly be-

The raven is a bird of mystery in many legends.

lieved this of a tiny bird found only in the New World. This truth-telling feathered mite was the ruby-throated hummingbird, then, as now, a species that nests in the gulf coast area, as well as farther north.

Not so strange, really, that people once believed that birds could talk. As Solomon said (Ecclesiastes 10:20): "Curse not the king, no not in thy thought;

The Biloxi Indians believed the ruby-throated hummingbird had the gift of speech and truth.

and curse not the rich in thy bedchamber; for a bird of the air shall carry the voice; and that which hath wings shall tell the matter."

We have a phrase like it: "A little bird told me."

The Eskimos also had many myths. One of them was about Sedna, daughter of a chief, and the race-mother of the central Eskimos. Long ago, according to Eskimo folklore, Sedna was wooed by a fulmar, a common oceanic bird found in North America in the waters off islands of Bering Sea. The wooing was successful; Sedna was seduced by the fulmar's promises of a blissful life to come. She left the comforts of her father's lodge and traveled with the fulmar to a distant land.

Sedna soon learned that she had been deceived. Her fulmar spouse was unkind to her. The other fulmars resented and mistreated her. Her father, the chief, heard that his daughter was being cruelly treated. He journeyed to the land of the fulmars, killed her fulmar husband, and took his repentant daughter home. All the other members of the

fulmar village followed, uttering doleful cries. And this is the reason, so Eskimos used to say, fulmars, or fulmar-petrels, have such a mournful cry.

The common redpoll also is a resident of northern North America. A legend about it was set down for us in 1883 in *Birds of Bering Sea and the Arctic Ocean,* by Edward W. Nelson, who studied the ornithology and the ethnology of the Bering Sea area in the late 19th century.

Here is the way in which Dr. Nelson told the legend of the redpoll:

"Very long ago the whole of mankind was living in cheerless obscurity. Endless night hid the face of the world, and men were without the power of making a fire, as all the fire of the world was in the possession of a ferocious bear living in a far-off country to the north. The bear guarded his charge with unceasing vigilance, so frightful was his appearance that no man dared attempt to obtain any of the precious substance. While the poor Indians were sorrowing over their misfortunes, the redpoll, which at that time was a plain little wood-sparrow, dressed in ordinary dull brown, heard their plaint—for in those days men and beasts understood one another—and his heart was touched. He prepared himself for a long journey and set out toward the lodge of the cruel bear. After many adventures . . . he reached the place, and by a successful ruse stole a living ember from the perpetual fire which glowed so close under the breast of the savage guardian, and flew away back with it in his beak. The glow of the coal was reflected in his breast and crown, while his forehead became slightly burned. Far away he flew, and finally arrived safely at the home of mankind, and was received with great rejoicing.

"He gave the fire to the grateful people and told them to guard it well; and as he did so they noticed the rich glow on his breast and brow, and said: 'Kind bird, wear forever that beautiful mark as a momento of what you have done for us;' and to this day the redpoll wears this badge in proof of the legend, as all may see, and mankind has ever since had fire."

Along with the presumed power of speech, birds once were thought to have the power to prophesy.

Roman soothsayers practiced ornithomancy, a

form of foretelling the future by watching the movements of birds or studying their entrails.

The London Encyclopedia in the early 18th century commented thus on the meaning of the movements of birds in ancient Greek and Roman times:

"If flocks of various birds came flying about any man it was an excellent omen. The eagle was particularly observed for drawing omens; when it was observed to be brisk and lively, and especially if, during its sportiveness, it flew from right hand to the left, it was one of the best omens that the gods could give. . . . If the hawk was seen seizing and devouring its prey, it portended death; but if the prey escaped, deliverance from danger was portended. . . . The swan, being an omen of fair weather, was deemed a lucky bird by mariners.

"The most inauspicious omens were given by ravens, but the degree of misfortune which they were supposed to portend depended, in some measure, in their appearing on the right hand or the left; if they came croaking on the right hand it was a tolerably good omen; but if on the left a very bad one."

The belief that birds could foretell the future was not uncommon among North American Indians and apparently came into being without any foreign influence.

The Omahas and Indians of related stock once assumed that the whip-poor-will could reveal something of the future. It is a bird of eastern North America so nocturnal in its habits that it is known to most of us only by its call.

If they heard a whip-poor-will crying *Hoia, hohin?*, the correct answer was, "No!" If the bird then ceased its *Hoi, hohins?*, he who answered would soon die. If the questioning calls continued, it was supposed to be an indication of a long life to come.

The Utes of Colorado believed that the whip-poor-will was a god of the night and a magician. It could transform a frog into the moon. The Iroquois imagined that moccasin flowers—cypripediums—were the shoes of whip-poor-wills.

A great many other superstitions are associated with the noisy, persistent whip-poor-will. This bird of the night is reported as having been heard to call 800 times before quitting.

Most of these superstitions are connected with the bird's call, and many of them are of European origin. They were first applied to the nightjar, a relative of the whip-poor-will. It was only natural that the European settlers in North America transferred the superstitions about the Old World bird to that of a very similar New World species.

The first spring call of the whip-poor-will heard by an unmarried woman must have stopped her dead in her tracks. If no followup call came, she would have to wait another year for a husband. If the bird did not cease after the second whistled, three-syllabled call, she was doomed to remain a spinster.

A fast-thinking spinster could avoid an unmarried state by using another superstition associated with this bird. If she made a wish upon hearing *that* first spring call of the whip-poor-wills and kept it an absolute secret, her wish to be wedded would come true.

The call of the whip-poor-will was once thought

An Eskimo legend, illustrated in this painting, told how birds had flown men to the moon.

to have therapeutic properties. A man could rid himself of an aching back by turning somersaults in time to a whip-poor-will's calls. To ward off future aches of this kind, a man could practice a bit of preventive medicine. All he had to do was to somersault, synchronizing this bit of acrobatics with the calls of any handy whip-poor-will.

Such was not for men who liked to go to bed with the chickens or liked to lie abed after sunrise. For the whip-poor-will is given to calling just after nightfall and immediately before dawn.

Supposedly the call of a whip-poor-will near a house indicated death for one of the inmates. This is only one of many superstitions in which the presence of a bird means death.

A bird tapping at the window or flying into the house was thought to mean the death within a year of anyone living in the house. This belief may have come into being because a bird was once considered to be the "spirit of the spirit." In other words, it was one soul inviting another to join it, not on some flight, but in death.

The tapping of a robin at a window of a sick-room also portended the death of the person. A crow that croaked three times as it flew over a house was a sign that someone in the family would die. Jays that left a woods in flocks meant mortality or great famine.

People in Brittany, who had many superstitions, once believed that unbaptized children became birds. They flew through space until they were baptized by St. John the Baptist before the day of Judgment, when they then went to heaven.

Birds in all ages have been regarded as weather prophets—even today.

An old saying of sailors is: *So long as kingfishers are sitting on their eggs, no storm or tempest will disturb the ocean.*

Because some member of the kingfisher family is found on all continents and because sailors also have worldwide distribution, the kingfisher is a bird to which many a superstition applies.

It once was known as the halcyon. The European relative of the American belted kingfisher is the species of the legend of Halcyone. She was the daughter of Aeolus—in Greek mythology, the wind-god who kept winds in a cave on Aeolia—and the wife of Ceyx.

Ceyx was drowned on his way to consult the oracle of Apollo. Halcyone was so stricken with grief she threw herself into the sea. The compassionate gods changed the pair into kingfishers. Then Zeus, the supreme god, forbade the winds to blow 7 days before and 7 days after the winter solstice, the shortest day in the year. This interval coincided with the halcyon's nesting season, and in time these 14 days became known as the halcyon days.

Pliny, a Roman naturalist (A. D. 23–79), wrote of the birds and the season in this way:

"They (halcyons) lay and sit about midwinter, where dais be shortest; and the times whiles they are broodie is called the halcyon dais; for during that season the sea is calm and navigable, especially in the coast of Sicillie."

Another superstition regarding the kingfisher is reported by Sir Thomas Browne in *Vulgar Errors,* published in 1684. He wrote that the bird "hanged by its beak showeth what quarter the wind is by an occult and secret property converting the breast of the bird to that part of the horizon from whence the wind doth blow."

The halcyon is mentioned by Shakespeare, who wrote: "Disown, affirm, and turn their halcyon beaks/With every gale and vary of their master."

The fish-hawk, better known as the osprey, also was considered a weather prophet. Of it, Alexander Wilson wrote in his *American Ornithology* (1804–1814):

"They are sometimes seen high in the air, sailing and cutting strange gambols, with loud vociferations, darting down several hundred feet perpendicularly, frequently with part of a fish in one claw, which they seem proud of, and to claim "high hook," as fishermen call him who takes the greatest number. On these occasions they serve as a barometer to foretell the changes of atmosphere; for when the fish-hawks are thus sailing high in the air, in circles, it is universally believed to prognosticate a change of weather, often a thunderstorm in a few hours. On the faith of the certainty of these signs the experienced coaster wisely prepares for the expected storm and is rarely mistaken."

Gulls, man-of-war birds, swallows, and peacocks all were once held in regard as forecasters:

When man-of-war hawks fly high, 'tis a sign of clear sky;
When they fly low prepare for a blow.

When the swallow buildeth low,
You can safely reap and sow.

When the peacock loudly bawls,
Soon we'll have both rain and squalls.

The ancient Romans studied the condition of the breastbone of a goose to foretell weather and held:

If the November goose-bone be thick,
So will the winter weather be;
If the November goose-bone be thin,
So will the winter weather be.

Another couplet that applies to all birds is one that implies that the winterkill of big game may be heavy:

If birds in autumn grow tame,
The winter will be cold for game.

An article, "Birds of Ill Omen," by Alexander Young, in The Atlantic Monthly for September 1874, pointed out:

"Most birds were considered ominous of good or evil according to the place and manner of their appearance . . . . It is noticeable that this stigma has been affixed only to those birds whose appearance or voice is disagreeable and whose habits are somewhat peculiar."

Owls fit that description, although they are good neighbors because they help keep rodents in check.

As W. J. Broderip wrote a hundred years ago:

"Their retired habits, the desolate places that are their favorite haunts, their hollow hootings, fearful shrieks, serpent-like hissings and coffin-maker-like snappings, have helped to give them a bad eminence, more than overbalancing all the glory that Minerva and her own Athens could shed around them."

Although the owl was regarded in Britain and here as "a wise old bird," most writers considered the various members of this group as birds of evil intent. Pliny "denominated the owl as 'the funeral birds of night'." Spenser wrote that the owl "was death's dread messenger." It was generally believed in the days of castle warfare that owls perched on battlements meant a member of the family was about to die.

In the Welsh village of Llangynwyd as late as 1908, it was thought that when an owl hooted early in the evening from one of the graveyard yews, it was a sign that an unmarried woman had surrendered her chastity.

Parts of the owl were once thought to have strong curative powers. A medieval pharmacopoeia states:

"The feet of bubo (now the generic name of our great horned owl) burned with hard plumbago (woody herbs such as the leadwort) was held to be a help against serpents. If the heart of the bird was placed on the left breast of a sleeping beauty, it made her tell all her secrets; but the warrior who carried it was strengthened in battle."

This Old World bit of superstitious therapeutics appears in *The Long Hidden Friend,* a book printed in Carlisle, Pennsylvania, in 1863 and—in German—in 1819 in Reading, Pennsylvania, where a number of Germans had settled. Very likely the remedies and magic arts suggested in the book were practiced by the people of the area. One was a recipe for making a "sleeping-beauty reveal her secrets"—proof that more than a century ago, a "truth drug" was in use. The Carlisle book advises: "If you lay the heart and the right foot of a barn-owl on one who is asleep, he will answer whatever you ask him, and tell what he has done."

In *The Tribes of California,* published in 1877, Stephen Powers said that the now extinct Ashochimi, mountain dwellers, feared certain owls and hawks.

He wrote: "When the great white owl alights near a village in the evening and hoots loudly, the headman at once assembles all the warriors in council to determine whether Mr. Strix demands life or only money.

"If they incline to believe that he demands a life, someone in the village is doomed and will speedily die. But they generally vote that he can be placated by an offering and immediately set out a quantity of shell money (wampum) and pinole (dried, edible seeds), whereupon the valorous trenchmen

Owls figure prominently in legend and folklore as symbols of wisdom and as omens of evil and death. This saw-whet, a small owl, was photographed at the Malheur National Wildlife Refuge.

fall to eat the pinole themselves, and in the morning the headman decorates himself with owl-feathers, and carries out the shell-money with solemn formality and flings it into the air under the tree where the owl perched."

For the Pimas, Indians of the deserts of the Southwestern States, the owl had a spiritual significance. They believed in days gone by that at death the soul passed into the body of an owl. This owl-man association in death was explained by John R. Swanton, who wrote in a report of the Bureau of Ethnology in 1904:

"Should an owl happen to be hooting at the time of a death, it was believed that it was waiting for the soul . . . . Owl feathers were always given to a dying person. They were kept in a long, rectangular box or basket of maguey leaf. If the family had no owl-feathers at hand they sent to the medicine-man who always kept them. If possible, the feathers were taken from a living bird when collected; the owl might then be set free or killed."

Listen, my children.

The tale is told, and the telling is to explain, glorify, amuse, justify, instruct, challenge.

All peoples have their folklore, although some may call it something else—history, perhaps, or national heritage, or even science sometimes.

Folklore may be harmless, but it is well, I think, to distinguish between myth and truth. That is not always easy.

Folklore—prejudice—still attaches in places to birds like owls and hawks. The truth is that they, too, have their place in Creation.

From folklore stems our saying. "The goose hangs high." It used to be, "The goose honks high"—a reference to the belief that wild geese fly higher when the weather is fine or promises to be fine.

The truth is that wise management of land and resources is needed to halt the decline of some geese and other birds—to forestall a situation in which nobody will be able to say, "The goose honks high."

—WILL BARKER.

Birds in the Bible

"THE HEAVENS WERE OPENED, and he saw the Spirit of God descending like a dove, and alighting on him." In such words the Gospels record the Spirit of God descending from heaven on the occasion of the Lord's baptism and saying, "This is my beloved Son, with whom I am well pleased."

From the account of the creation in Genesis to the flying eagles in Revelation, more than 300 references to birds occur in the Bible. With reason: The ancient Hebrews were keenly aware of the birds (of as many species as are in the United States east of the Rockies) in the roughly 10 thousand square miles of Palestine. They had neighbors who attributed supernatural powers to birds, but the Hebrews believed in one God who created all living creatures. They saw living creatures as they really are. Birds gave them similes and metaphors that illumined their language and their thought.

They wrote and spoke of the majesty of hawks and eagles in the heavens, the eerie owls that stirred man's fear of darkness and the unknown, the dove with an olive leaf in its bill, the strange migration of quails, ravens that brought food to a starving prophet, the cock that crowed thrice in Jerusalem.

In Genesis we read:

"At the end of forty days Noah opened the window of the ark which he had made, and sent forth a raven; and it went to and fro until the waters were dried up from the earth. Then he sent forth a dove from him, to see if the waters had subsided from the face of the ground; but the dove found no place to set her foot, and she returned to him to the ark, for the waters were still on the face of the whole earth. So he put forth his hand and took her and brought her into the ark with him. He waited another seven days, and again he sent forth the dove out of the ark; and the dove came back to him in the evening, and lo, in her mouth a freshly plucked olive leaf; so Noah knew that the waters had subsided from the earth. Then he waited another seven days, and sent forth the dove; and she did not return to him any more."

Noah was following a custom of navigators from ancient times down to Columbus, who changed courses to follow the flight of birds released to indicate the direction of the nearest land.

Legend has it that the raven was pure white until it failed Noah and was punished by having its feathers turn to black.

The dove, the bird mentioned oftenest in the Bible, symbolized beauty, simplicity, and purity. In the history and religion of many countries, it is a symbol of peace and spirituality. Even before Christ, the homing instinct of a pigeon was recognized. When Ramses III became Pharaoh in the 12th century B.C., the news was carried all over Egypt by pigeon post.

We read also of Abraham. One night he heard a voice: "Fear not, Abram, I am your shield; your reward shall be very great." After showing the childless Abraham the stars in the sky as indicative of the number of his descendants, Jehovah told him to prepare a sacrifice of a 3-year-old heifer, a 3-year-old she-goat, a 3-year-old ram, a turtledove, and a young pigeon. For the rest of the day Abraham struggled to keep birds of prey from snatching the sacrifice from the altar (Genesis 15).

Abraham's travels took him along the migration routes of many species of birds. In the valleys of the Tigris and Euphrates, he would have seen ducks, geese, partridges, snipe, woodcock, francolins, and magpies. In desert country, he found other types. Crossing mountains and across the plains of Palestine, he must have encountered all the birds mentioned in the Bible.

When Abraham was about to sacrifice his son Isaac, Jehovah substituted a ram at the last moment. Isaac and his son Jacob became the fathers of a mighty people, who, as indicated in Leviticus, considered doves and pigeons as acceptable sacrifice offerings.

Abraham's great-grandson, Joseph, was brought to Egypt as a slave after being sold by his brothers to a caravan of merchants bound for the Nile. The perfidy of the wife of Potiphar, his master, put Joseph in prison in the company of the Pharaoh's chief butler and chief baker.

"And one night they both dreamed—the butler and the baker of the king of Egypt."

Joseph interpreted for his fellow prisoners the meaning of their dreams. For the butler, he pre-

St. John the Evangelist on Patmos, by Titian (c. 1477–1576). **The painting is in the National Gallery.**

This is how an artist of long ago pictured the dove returning to Noah's Ark with an olive branch.

dicted freedom in 3 days. As for the baker, who had dreamed that birds ate out of the topmost of three baskets of baked goods he carried on his head, Joseph had bad news—the baskets were 3 days, after which the Pharaoh would lift the baker's head from off his body. "And the birds," Joseph added, "will eat the flesh from you!"

In time there arose over Egypt a new king who knew not Joseph. Fearful lest the Israelites become more powerful than his native Egyptians, this new Pharaoh ordered all male infants of the foreigners to be thrown into the river. One infant, who was placed in a cradle and hidden in the reeds on the banks of the Nile, escaped death.

When the Pharaoh's daughter and her companions came down to the river to bathe they found this Hebrew child. The princess took the infant from the water's edge and decided to rear it as her own son. She named him Moses, which means "drawout," for she drew him out of the water.

Followed then the careful education of Moses by Pharaoh's daughter, which must have included

a proficiency in recognizing the scores of bird signs that are to be found among the hieroglyphics of ancient Egypt.

As a young man, Moses saw the native Egyptians worshipping such birds as the sacred ibis. Their god, Thoth, disguised himself as an ibis. The worship of this bird could be attributed to the fact that its favorite diet is scorpions and small reptiles. Other birds venerated by Egyptians included the vulture of Nekhebt, the falcon Horis, and the sun god Ra, who, in the form of a bird, was supposed to have hovered over the face of the waters and spread light, just as God's spirit hovered over the darkness as He said, "Let there be light."

Finally came the time, after plagues had visited the land of the Nile, when a mature and dedicated Moses was able to lead his people out of the hands of the Egyptians "unto a land flowing with milk and honey." Before long, thirst and hunger plagued them. Their hunger increased until "there went forth a wind from the Lord, and it brought

60

St. Mary Salome and Her Family, by Bernhard Strigel (1460–1528). From the Samuel H. Kress Collection.

The Annunciation, by Juan de Flandes (b. 1496).

quails from the sea, and let them fall beside the camp, about a day's journey on this side and a day's journey on the other side, round about the camp, and about two cubits above the face of the earth. And the people rose all that day, and all night, and all the next day, and gathered the quails."

Thus were the Israelites fed by the enormous flocks of Egyptian quails (coturnix) that migrate north in the spring and south in the early fall, traveling with the wind and sometimes, as they

did for the benefit of the Israelites, falling to the ground, too exhausted to fly.

Psalm 105: 40–41 also describes these miracles: "They asked, and he brought quails, and gave them bread from heaven in abundance. He opened the rock, and water gushed forth; it flowed through the desert like a river."

The use of birds for food is explained in Old Testament Law: "You may eat all clean birds. But these are the ones which you shall not eat: the eagle, the vulture, the osprey, the buzzard, the

61

kite, after their kinds; every raven after its kind; the ostrich, the nighthawk, the sea gull, the hawk, after their kinds; the little owl and the great owl, the water hen and the pelican, the carrion vulture and the cormorant, the stork, the heron, after their kinds; the hoopoe and the bat" (Deuteronomy 14: 11–18).

Then the children of Israel came to the foot of the jagged block of granite that is Mount Sinai. From the mountain the voice of Jehovah said to Moses: "Thus you shall say to the house of Jacob, and tell the people of Israel: You have seen what I did to the Egyptians, and how I bore you on eagles' wings and brought you to myself" (Exodus 19: 3–4).

Thus was given to Moses and his people the Covenant and later the Tablets, the Law, the Ark,

the Temple, and the Scriptures. And thus were eagles' wings established as a symbol of God's care for His people. All through the Psalms is found testimony to the protection given by God, who "shall cover thee with his feathers and under his wings shalt thou trust."

The eagles of Sinai lived on in the hearts of the Israelites, as evidenced in Revelation, where God's church in the form of a woman is saved by flight: "But the woman was given the two wings of the great eagle that she might fly from the serpent into the wilderness, to the place where she is to be nourished for a time, and times, and half a time" (Revelation 12: 14).

Elijah had prophesied a drought in Israel and in so doing had stirred up the wrath of King Ahab and Queen Jezebel. God's message was: "Depart

Elijah being fed by the ravens. (Reproduced photographically from an early Bible.)

from here and turn eastward, and hide yourself by the brook Cherith, that is east of the Jordan. You shall drink from the brook, and I have commanded the ravens to feed you there. And the ravens brought him bread and meat in the morning, and bread and meat in the evening; and he drank from the brook" (1 Kings 17:6).

References to the flight patterns and the nesting and feeding habits of birds abound in the Scriptures: The sparrow flutters. The swallow flits. The flight of eagles is swift. The dawn has wings. Clouds and snow are reminders of birds.

Among the many codes of conduct is an admonition to protect the nests of birds: "If you chance to come upon a bird's nest, in any tree or on the ground, with young ones or eggs and the mother sitting upon the young or upon the eggs, you shall not take the mother with the young; you shall let the mother go, but the young you may take to yourself; that it may go well with you, and that you may live long" (Deuteronomy 22: 6–7).

In recording the destruction of Edom, the prophet said: "But the hawk and the porcupine shall possess it, the owl and the raven shall dwell in it. Thorns shall grow over its strongholds, nettles and thistles in its fortresses. It shall be the haunt of jackals, an abode for ostriches. There shall the owl nest and lay and hatch and gather her young in her shadow; yea, there shall the kites be gathered, each one with her mate" (Isaiah 34: 15).

Jeremiah inveighed against the wickedness and disobedience of people: "Even the stork in the heavens knows her times; and the turtledove, swallow, and crane keep the time of their coming; but my people know not the ordinance of the Lord" (Jeremiah 8: 7).

Job referred to an order of birds that has changed little during 12 million years:

"The wings of the ostrich wave proudly; but are they the pinions and plumage of love? For she leaves her eggs to the earth, and lets them be warmed on the ground, forgetting that a foot may crush them, and that the wild beast may trample them. She deals cruelly with her young, as if they were not hers; though her labor be in vain, yet she has no fear; because God has made her forget wisdom, and given her no share in understanding" (Job 39: 13–17).

St. Jerome in the Wilderness, by Andrea Mantegna (Paduan School). From the Mellon Collection in the National Gallery of Art in Washington.

Many legends recount stories of birds as witnesses to the birth of Christ. One Scandinavian story describes the way the animals gathered around to adore the Lord and ever since at midnight on Christmas Eve have knelt, while the birds sing praises.

"And when the time came for their purification

63

The Nativity, by Juan de Flandes (1496–c. 1519). A part of the Samuel H. Kress Collection at the National Gallery of Art in Washington, D.C.

The dove of peace appears in this depiction of Christ's baptism. (From an old Bible.)

according to the law of Moses, they brought him up to Jerusalem to present him to the Lord—and to offer a sacrifice according to what is said in the law of the Lord, 'a pair of turtledoves, or two young pigeons'" (Luke 2: 22–24).

About 6 weeks after the Child was born, Joseph and Mary set out for Jerusalem to offer the sacrifice of purification. Actually, according to Leviticus, a lamb is required, but a provision in the law allowed the offering of two birds by those who are too poor to afford a lamb. So on this day in the reign of Caesar Augustus, Joseph walks, leading the donkey carrying Mary and her babe and a wicker cage containing two young pigeons.

Years later, Jesus pointed out to his disciples the constant care maintained by God for all living creatures: "Look at the birds of the air: they neither sow nor reap nor gather into barns, and yet your heavenly Father feeds them. Are you not of more value than they?" (Matthew 6: 26).

Later He asked, "Are not two sparrows sold for a penny? And not one of them will fall to the ground without your Father's will" (Matthew 10: 29).

Matthew wrote: "And Jesus entered the Temple of God and drove out all those who sold and bought in the Temple, and he overturned the tables of the money changers and the seats of those who sold pigeons."

And on that night, when He and the disciples had their last supper together, Jesus reminded Peter: "Truly, I say to you, this very night, before the cock crows, you will deny me three times."

Symbolic of peace in the Bible is the dove. Jesus taught His disciples to go forth and minister "harmless as doves."

Symbolic of strength is the eagle, to which there are references in 17 Biblical books, notably in Isaiah: "Even youths shall faint and be weary, and young men shall fall exhausted; but they who wait for the Lord shall renew their strength, they shall mount up with wings like eagles, they shall run and not be weary, they shall walk and not faint."

—EDWARD A. SHERMAN.

Birds and Words

Some of us, whether hawks or doves, forceful or peaceful, get up with the birds, swallow a quick breakfast—"not enough to keep a sparrow healthy"—and fly to the station, wondering why the old coot ahead of us doesn't drive more carefully.

We take a flyer to town, and note that the boss is watching us like a hawk as we mince pigeon-toed between the desks.

At lunch, we chicken out on a fellow worker's challenge to take the afternoon off for a round of golf, although we know we could certainly score a birdie or two and perhaps an eagle.

After a brace of cocktails when we return to the family nest, we feel light as a feather and free as a bird and cock of the walk. We may seem talky as a parrot to our wives and at times crazy as a loon—but on the morrow we'll be eating crow. And so to bed—also with the birds.

Sometimes we get the bird. We know what that means, but we may not know that originally this was a British expression, "to get the big bird," the big bird being the goose and the reference being to the hissing sound made by geese when excited.

Those of us who are entertainers know we get the bird when we lay an egg and for us, that week, no eagle will fly—there will be no payday.

We use other expressions. The cockpit of an airplane got its name from the pit into which cocks were dropped when two were pitted against each other. The term, to "show the white feather," comes from cockfighting, where crossbred fighting cocks often had white feathers and usually were defeated by purebred cocks having coats of solid black or red feathers. At the moment of defeat, the crest of the beaten cock would droop limply—and thus originated the word "crestfallen."

A somewhat more amiable sport gave rise to the word, "lark." In the time of Shakespeare, many people regarded the lark as one of the most toothsome items of game. Since larks are too small for hunting—at least with the weapons then available—they were usually trapped in nets. The nets were set out before daybreak, and the larks were enmeshed when they came down to feed early in the day.

It was not uncommon for young men and young women to join in the enterprise, and because their early morning activities sometimes were not wholly limited to trapping the birds, the whole business soon took on the aspects of an outdoor frolic, and larking became as popular as discotheques are today.

The wingless New Zealand kiwis gave their name to preflight cadets, who are known as kiwis until they solo.

Some birds, in Shelley's phrase, "never wert." Among them are Lewis Carroll's "slithy toves" and Cape Cod turkey—codfish, which got its fanciful name the same way, and for the same reasons, that a dish of melted cheese on toast came to be called welsh rabbit. And then there is Scotch woodcock, which simply consists of scrambled eggs heaped on toast spread with anchovy butter.

We have some special names for groups of birds. Just as we call a group of lions a pride of lions, we speak of a gaggle of geese, a cast of hawks, and a covey of partridges or quail. Most of these labels are obsolete now, but in days when hunting was a quest for food rather than recreation, such distinctions in the labeling of bird groups were observed carefully. A sord of mallards, bevy of quail, and wisp of snipe were terms of special meaning to the hunter of old. The true birdwatcher would speak of a nye of pheasants, a cast of hawks, and a watch of nightingales. Peacocks, appropriately enough, assemble in a muster, coots in covert, and larks in an exaltation.

The gull through the ages has been synonymous with a person easily tricked, cheated, or duped. Similarly pigeon—a bird not dissimilar in appearance to the gull—long has been underworld slang for a person waiting to be fleeced or plucked. The stool pigeon, though, is a bird of slightly different feathers. The stool in this case is a pole to which a bird is fastened in order to decoy other birds. The original stool pigeon in underworld slang, then, was a spy the law planted among outlaws.

The "cock" in "cocker spaniel" comes from woodcock, a small bird for the hunting of which this breed of spaniel was widely used.

Dozens of similes and analogies are related to birds: Chattering like magpies, hoarse as a crow, sweet as a nightingale, feather in your cap, crow's nest (of a ship), to crow about, as the crow flies, swansong, bird-brain, eagle-eyed, egghead, as welcome as a robin in spring, one swallow doesn't make a summer, robin's-egg blue, eggshell white, duck soup, to crane, to duck, goose flesh, loony, swan-necked, graceful as a swan, hawk-eyed, sparrowlike, soft as down, dove-tail, night-owl, gooseneck, cock-and-bull, cook one's goose, ducks and drakes, lame duck, popinjay, one fell swoop, talk turkey, roost, chicken-hearted.

A new term is birdiebacking. It was preceded by "piggybacking" (loading trailers aboard flatcars and transporting them by rail) and "fishybacking" (transporting loaded trailers by boat) and means loading trailers aboard airplanes. Other new terms very likely will appear and add their color to otherwise prosaic language—something like common as starlings, hopeful as kingfishers, persistent as whoopers, choosy as warblers, happy as canaries. The old terms serve us well, though.

You know many other terms of, by, and for the birds: Bluebird weather, wild-goose chase, black as a crow, weather fit for ducks, stormy petrel, free as a bird, feather your nest, a high flyer, the turkey trot, dead as a dodo, like water on a duck's back, light as a feather, cock of the walk, bird of passage, bird of peace, and bird's-eye view.

Maybe some of them will enlarge your view.

—WILLIAM MORRIS.

A Covey of Names

BIRD NAMES BRIGHTENED the geography of my early years. Our home was in Goosetown, a neighborhood with uncertain limits in La Crosse, Wisconsin. Residents of Goosetown were mostly first- and second-generation German immigrants, and the name apparently derived from the poultry pens that occupied many backyards.

Living in Goosetown carried a certain distinction. We believed we were more adept at sports and brighter and tougher than the kids who lived in other neighborhoods. When put to the test, our prowess and skills were not always supreme, but the occasional reverses did not mar permanently our Goosetown image.

Goose Island is one of numerous small, low-lying segments of land that share, with a tangle of sloughs and lagoons, the flood plain of the upper Mississippi River. In the years of my recollection, Goose Island embraced some 2 thousand acres, which were divided into seven farm units. From one of the farms my widowed grandmother, assisted by two bachelor sons, wrested a modest existence. The farm, which was about 10 miles by wagon road from La Crosse, served also as the vacation haven for city-dwelling relatives. We children, in particular, delighted in a week spent at the farm during the summer, and memories of the visits are sweet and vivid.

During the past three decades, the tide of progress has swept over Goosetown and Goose Island. The German immigrants who inhabited the former have long since been laid to rest. More recently, many of Goosetown's weathered clapboard dwellings have been razed to make way for the expanding La Crosse State University.

In the late thirties, Goose Island reverted to the birds. As part of a project to improve navigation on the Upper Mississippi, a lock and dam were built a short distance below the island. After the farmland was acquired by condemnation, most of Goose Island was drowned by the rising water. The 800 acres of nonsubmerged land are now administered as a county park and as a private conservation club. The island and its environs are within the Upper Mississippi River National Wildlife Refuge, and cranes, herons, and wild geese hold dominion over land and water.

The two places are unimportant geographically and historically. My justification for these personal recollections is that Goosetown and Goose Island illustrate several basic principles of avian toponymics.

The most obvious is that places named for birds are widespread and numerous. Within easy access to the homes of most of us there is undoubtedly a Duck Pond, a Gull Island, an Eagle Mountain, a Pigeon Creek, or a Swan Lake.

Another point illustrated by my homely examples is that bird names identify the intimate features associated with our lives. They are what George Stewart has aptly termed the "little names, known only to those who lived nearby, of ponds and swamps and creeks and hills, of townships and villages, of streets and ranches and plantations, of coves and gulches and meadows."

The "little names," including those derived from birds, generally have been bestowed by ordinary people like you and me, not by an official naming authority. Some names (Goosetown, for example) may be temporal and ephemeral. Others, by common consent and long application, become impressed upon our maps and landscapes.

In contrast, bird associations are rare among the "big names," those applied to political and administrative divisions and to the larger and more pervasive physical features.

Look at a map of the world or run your finger down a list of countries. The one name that appears to have a bird connotation is Turkey. This is, however, but the conventional (that is, English language) form of Turkiye, the official name of the

Republic. Moreover, turkeys are indigenous to the New World and were not known to Europeans until the name "Turkey" was well established. The name of the bird is said by some to derive from the "turk-turk" sound made by turkeys.

Then there are the Canary Islands, off the northwestern coast of Africa. An encyclopedia says the domesticated canary originated here. But wait: The birds were not exported to Europe until the 16th century, whereas the name "Canary Islands" (*Canaria insula*) was employed by the Roman historian, Pliny the Elder, as early as the first century A.D. We note, moreover, that *canarius,* the Latin word for dog, was applied because of the large dogs on the island. The sequence, therefore, is that the Canary Islands were named for dogs, and the yellow songbirds were named for the islands.

The name of another island group, northwest of the Canaries, does have an authentic bird association. In the early 15th century, the Portuguese navigator, Diego de Seville, discovered them. Because of the native hawks that he found there, he called the group the Azores (for *acor,* the Portuguese word for *hawk*).

Birds likewise are rare among "big names" on the map of the United States. Not a single State name has a bird association, but several States have bird nicknames. Delaware sometimes is called the Blue Hen State. Louisiana is nicknamed the Pelican State, "because the pelican is so frequently seen along the streams and other bodies of water throughout the State." The American eagle on her coat of arms accounts for Mississippi's designation as the Eagle State. Sage-hen State is Nevada's nickname, "because this fowl was formerly common throughout the State."

Of the State capitals, only Phoenix, Arizona, has an avian toponym, and hers is derived from a legendary bird. In Egyptian mythology, the phoenix was a fabulous bird that lived for 500 years and then consumed itself on a burning pyre. From the ashes arose a rejuvenated youthful phoenix, so the creature was, in effect, immortal. On the site of present Phoenix there was once a small settlement named Smith Station. When an irrigation canal company established headquarters in the vicinity in the late 1860's, the company sought a

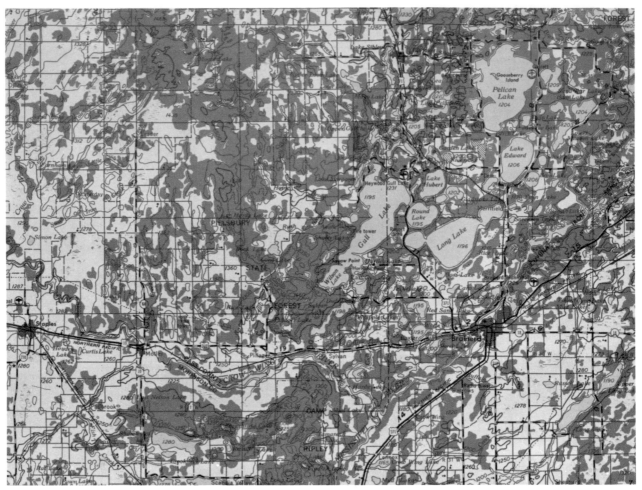

On the Brainard Quadrangle of U.S. Geologic Survey maps (Minnesota NL 15–4), appear a number of bird toponyms: Duck Lake, Crow Wing Lake, Crow Wing River, Swan Creek, Little Swan Creek, Loon Lake, Upper Loon Lake, Gull Lake, Upper Gull Lake, and Pelican Lake.

more colorful name for its headquarters. A classical-minded official suggested the name Phoenix because the new city would rise upon the ashes of the old.

Fewer than half a dozen of more than 3 thousand United States counties have names suggestive of birds. For at least two of the names the relationship is tenuous. The name of Crow County, Minnesota, is a loose translation of a Chippewa word meaning raven feather. Chief Black Hawk, the brave leader of the Sac and Fox Indians, was the source of the name of Black Hawk County, Iowa. Another Iowa county, Audubon, honors the famous ornithologist. Eagle County, Colorado, and Kingfisher County, Oklahoma, are probably true bird derivations.

It is not unusual that places named for the goose were common in our locality, for only the eagle, the turkey, and the swan surpass the goose as a source for avian geographical names. Goose toponyms predominate among bird names in a number of States.

An article in the July 1938 *Rhode Island Historical Society Collections* notes that "the humble goose, so often and so unjustly much maligned gave to Rhode Island more place-names than any other bird."

Similarly, in her *Nebraska Place Names,* Lillian Fitzpatrick wrote that, "among the wild bird life, the goose has given its name to the greatest number of lakes," with no fewer than eight Goose Lakes in Nebraska.

Erwin Gudde writes, in his *California Place Names*: "More than fifty geographic features in the State [of California], including a Goose Nest Mountain . . . were named because of the presence of this bird, so important as a food for travelers in the early days."

Henry David Thoreau recorded in his journal on November 30, 1857: "The air is full of geese. I saw five flocks within an hour, about 10 a.m., containing from thirty to fifty each, and afterward two more flocks making in all from two hundred and fifty to three hundred at least, all flying southeast over Goose and Walden Ponds. The former was apparently well named Goose Pond."

The goose even contributed to the nomenclature of our national capital. Draining the site selected for the District of Columbia was a stream variously referred to as Goose Creek or Tiber Creek. The former name, apparently considered inelegant, was dropped soon after the city was laid out—but not before the Irish bard, Thomas Moore, immortalized Goose Creek in a satirical verse. Moore, who visited America in 1803 and 1804, addressed the poem, in the form of a letter, to his friend Dr. Thomas Hume. Entitled "From the City of Washington," it reads, in part:

"In Fancy now, beneath the twilight gloom,
Come, let me lead thee o'er this 'second Rome!'
Where tribunes rule, where dusky Davi bow,
And what was Goose-Creek once is Tiber now."

Diverted from its original course and confined in a subterranean concrete conduit, Tiber (erstwhile Goose) Creek now flows, all but forgotten, beneath Capitol Hill and the House of Representatives' massive Rayburn Office Building.

The eagle surpasses all other birds as a source of geographical names. That is not surprising, for the American eagle has been our national symbol since 1782. Moreover, throughout history the eagle has been glamorized in story and legend as the king of birds, the symbol of freedom, an incentive to valor, and the pledge of victory.

As Francis Herrick has noted in his book *The American Eagle* (Appleton, 1934): "The eagle has come to possess a magic name . . . the grandeur of its flight into the clouds, its preternatural keenness of vision, its very feathers even, have stirred the imagination of men in every age and clime." The

The bald eagle has given names to numerous physical features and towns.

majesty of the eagle, he continued, "adds a touch of grandeur to the wild mountainside or rugged shore of lake or ocean which are his favorite abodes."

Nearly every State has eagle toponyms that identify physical features, towns, and cities. There are Eagle lakes, mountains, rivers, islands, forks, and buttes, without number. Among inhabited settlements are Eagle corners, villages, cities, bridges, mills, groves, stations, and squares, and many places designated only as Eagle. Variant name forms are New Eagle, Bald Eagle, Black Eagle, Red Eagle, White Eagle, and Golden Eagle and War Eagle, Eagleville, Eagleton, and Eaglette.

Except for the eagle, major inspiration for avian geographical names has come from the game birds. For good reason: The turkey, goose, duck, and swan are large birds and are easily observed. Their tendency to live and travel in flocks, their migratory customs, and their loud and distinctive calls serve to call attention to them.

An important reason for the popularity of game birds is their edibility. Turkeys, geese, ducks, swans, pigeons, and grouse were important food sources for the early settlers, who could not help

Swans, geese, turkeys, and ducks figure in many placenames.

but be aware of these magnificent birds. It was not uncommon to give bird names to places associated with hunting incidents or some unusual event or observance.

The wild turkey, which is native to America, has contributed much to our history, folklore, and nomenclature. Among the geographical names given by John Smith to features in Virginia was Turkey Isle in the James River, a short distance above Jamestown. It is probably the oldest of several hundred turkey names that dot the map of the United States.

Swans, among the most stately of birds, also have contributed liberally to our place nomenclature. Lakes, rivers, ponds, and creeks are most commonly named for this aristocrat of aquatic

72

birds. One of many Swan Lakes is located in Nicollet County, Minnesota. The county name is derived from Joseph N. Nicollet who, accompanied by John C. Fremont, led a government exploring expedition up the valley of the Minnesota River in 1838–1839. Nicollet's map and descriptive notes laid the groundwork for the geography of the Swan Lake region.

In his journal for June 19, 1838, Nicollet recorded: "We leave Middle Lake at 5 o'clock in the morning, and betake ourselves to Swan Lake by a zig-zag route to avoid the swampy places.... We stayed until 2 o'clock on the borders of this lake looking at its size and its wealth of islands, fertile and well wooded.... Some Indian families now occupy these islands living on wild rice, corn and a little hunting. These are the warriors who came to the St. Pierre with Sleepy Eye, whom we saw at the Sioux Crossing.... The good old mother of Sleepy Eye came herself on two staffs, to offer me as a present a swan just cooked and dismembered, that they were doubtless about to eat when they heard of our arrival."

Nicollet County's Swan Lake was visited in 1837 by George Catlin, painter of western landscapes. He was taken by the beauty of the lake and made sketches that were later incorporated into an oil painting, "Lac du Cygne" (Swan Lake), which is

Hundreds of places and geographic features, like this one in Virginia, were named after birds that were important to Indians or Eskimos or pioneer settlers. Goose Creek Chapel exists no more, but lovely Goose Creek still flows in Loudoun County, and there is a Goose Creek meetinghouse of the Religious Society of Friends in the village of Lincoln, Virginia.

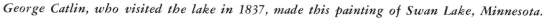

George Catlin, who visited the lake in 1837, made this painting of Swan Lake, Minnesota.

now in the collections of the Smithsonian Institution. The Swan Lake of Nicollet and Catlin is within Minnesota's picturesque "Land of 10 thousand Lakes." Within a radius of 50 miles are three other Swan Lakes, a Swan Lake Outlet, three Goose Lakes, two Crane Creeks, two Loon Lakes, and a Duck, Eagle, and Birds Eye Lake.

Because its habitat is more restricted and it is not desired for food, the gull has given its name to fewer places than have the aquatic birds I have mentioned. Along both our east and west coasts there are, however, Gull islands, points, coves, bays, capes, and inlets. Gull toponyms are most numerous along the Atlantic shore, and particularly in coastal New England. Their location off the northeastern tip of Long Island and adjacent to popular sailing and recreation areas has made Great Gull Island and Little Gull Island better known than most features bearing this specific.

The July 4, 1965, issue of the New York Times carried an account of two women ornithologists who spent a week on bleak and uninhabited Great Gull Island. Their purpose was to investigate, for the American Museum of Natural History and the Linnaean Society, an attempt by terns to reestablish a nesting colony on the island. A large colony of terns nested on Great Gull Island some 60 years ago. Decimated by hunters and egg collectors, the terns, as reported by the two birdwatchers, now are gradually returning to their former abode.

Pigeon and dove toponyms are outnumbered only by those derived from eagles, turkeys, swans, and geese. Most of the Pigeon rivers, creeks, coves, roosts, points, and runs in Eastern States were named for the passenger pigeon, which has been described as "the most impressive species of bird that man has ever known."

The small birds that brighten our surroundings with their gay plumage and cheery songs are recognized in only a sprinkling of American place-names. A careful search of the map will reveal a few Blue Jays, Sparrows, Cardinals, Wrens, Larks, and perhaps even a Goldfinch, Mockingbird, Whippoorwill, or Oriole that identify places of local interest or significance.

There are good reasons for the small number of songbird toponyms. Because they most often fly singly or in pairs and are of small size, songbirds are not readily observed. They are more hidden from casual view in their wooded retreats than are the large aquatic birds, whose habitats are open lakes, seashores, and marshes. Because they had little value as food, the songbirds likewise made slight impression on the early settlers. To the practical American colonists and pioneers, birds were of interest primarily if they were edible.

For the first several centuries after North America was settled, the small birds did not provide names for geographical features because they themselves were nameless. Early explorers and colonists found in America many new and strange birds. Those that resembled species native to their homelands were usually identified by the generic European name. The avian toponyms found on colonial maps, therefore, are of a general character and were derived from birds that resembled species familiar to the settlers.

Thus, Bird Creek and Swan Creek are the only bird names on the 83 plates of Christopher Colles' *Survey of the Roads of the United States of America,* 1789, the earliest United States road guide.

Augustine Herrman's 1673 *Map of Virginia and Maryland* includes only such bird toponyms as Great Egg Harbor, Little Egg Harbor, Turkey Isle, Turkey Buzzard Point, and Black Birds Creek.

The few bird names listed in Joseph Scott's *United States Gazeteer,* published in Philadelphia in 1795, are, likewise, of the same character.

Not until the 19th century were American birds scientifically studied and systematically named. There was so much territory to explore, and such a variety of birds to identify, that scientists on earlier expeditions could do little except collect and prepare specimens. Naturalists were notably lacking on many early western exploration parties. For want of such an expert, the Lewis and Clark Expedition brought back specimens of only three new birds. Two of these, Lewis' woodpecker and Clark's nutcracker, were named for the party's leaders.

Songbird toponyms are rare even in our National Parks and National Forests, where many names are of fairly recent origin. A careful scanning of the map of Yellowstone Park, for example, reveals only Chickadee, Nuthatch, and Tanager Lakes.

Yosemite Park has a Hummingbird Lake as well as a Vogelsang (German: *bird song*) Camp. In these as well as in other National Parks, duck, eagle, gull, pelican, swan, heron, and grouse place names greatly outnumber those derived from songbirds.

Few of the tens of thousands of lakes, ponds, and streams in northern Minnesota, Wisconsin, and Michigan are likewise named for the smaller birds. This is a particularly unfortunate omission when we note the multiplicity of Goose, Swan, Loon, Duck, Turtle, and Bass Lakes there.

The monotonous repetition, too, of Clear, Mud, Long, Round, Swamp, Dry, Big, and Rice Lakes in almost every county in these water wonderlands further suggests that the namers had a paucity of ideas. In Hubbard County, Minnesota, there is a series of Crow Wing Lakes, prefixed respectively with the ordinal numerals First to Eleventh. Within Michigan there are 40 Goose Lakes, more than 75 Long Lakes, and some 260 Mud Lakes. What a sad lack of imagination!

Most bird names, as I have suggested, reflect or record some specific incident, event, or association. For example, Eagle Lake, in Aroostook County, Maine, was so christened because it "was frequented by the bald eagle." Because of the number of turkeys in that vicinity in the early days, a stream in Hall County, Texas, was named Turkey Creek by the local cowboys. Condor Point, in Santa Barbara County, California, records the "onetime presence [in this region] of the California condor or vulture."

Naming incidents have not been limited to wild birds. Lewis A. McArthur relates that about 1870 a Mr. and Mrs. John Sims were on their way to have Thanksgiving dinner with Uncle George Frissel. Mrs. Sims carried her baby on one arm, and with the other she held a dressed goose. Crossing a small creek, the horse suddenly lurched, causing Mrs. Sims to loosen her hold on the goose, which fell into the water. Ever since that event, the brook in Lane County, Oregon, has been known as Goose Creek.

Associations resulting in bird names at times have been indirect or remote. David Starr Jordan in 1899 gave the name Ouzel to a creek in King's Canyon National Park, California, because "here

Ouzel Falls, Rocky Mountain National Park, Colorado, is named after the water ouzel.

John Muir studied the water-ouzel [or American Dipper] in its home, and wrote of it the best biography yet given of any bird."

Several years ago, William F. Barrett, a real estate developer, named a new community in Chester County, Pennsylvania, Black Swan Manor for the black swans he had become familiar with in Australia during the Second World War.

Names of physical features with a real or imagined resemblance to a bird or some part of its anatomy constitute another category of avian toponyms. A promontory on the west shore of Penobscot Bay in Maine is named Owls Head because it resembles the neck and head of an owl when viewed from the north.

Because its shape suggests a goose in flight, Goose Lake on Michigan's Upper Peninsula is so named.

Francois F. Matthes, onetime topographer in the Geological Survey, named Cockscomb Crest in Yosemite National Park because of its distinctive appearance.

The three spires of Eagletail Peak, Yuma County, Arizona, when viewed from one vantage point, suggest the tailfeathers of an eagle—hence its name.

Crowfoot in Linn County, Oregon, received its name from the pattern of intersecting roads that suggests the imprint of a crow's foot.

Feather Plume Falls in Glacier National Park,

A 24-foot, steel, 3,500-pound Canada goose welcomes visitors to Wawa, Ontario, Canada. Wawa is the Indian word for the Canada goose.

and many other similarly named features, reflect the feathery spray that hovers over many waterfalls.

Real feathers were the inspiration for naming Feather River in northeastern California. Don Luis A. Arguello, an early Spanish explorer, found wild pigeon feathers floating on the surface of the water and accordingly christened the stream Rio de las Plumas (Feather River).

Broken Egg Spring, in Yellowstone National Park, was so designated because "it is shaped like an egg set on end with the top broken off."

Another class of bird names has whimsical or legendary origins. Phoenix, Arizona, in the latter category, I have already mentioned. The legendary Greek bird, halcyon, during whose breeding period Zeus forbade the winds to blow, has also given its name to several places, among them Halcyon, in San Luis Obispo County, California.

In the category of whimsical names are Bird-in-Hand, Pennsylvania; Early Bird, Florida; and Starbirds, Maine. Cowpunchers who camped in the vicinity, and jokingly referred to themselves as "buzzards," are said to have named Buzzard Roost Canyon, in Gila County, Arizona. Similarly, Eagle Prairie, in Humboldt County, California, reportedly derived its name from an old settler who was locally known as "Old Eagle Beak."

In the West and Southwest there are a number of avian toponyms of Spanish origin, among them Isla da Alcatraces, or Alcatraz Island, in California. Alcatraz is a Spanish name for pelican. Gaviota (Spanish for sea gull) Canyon, in Santa Barbara County, California, was so named in 1769 by the Portolá expedition, because one of the soldiers in the party killed a gull there.

The wild pigeon (Spanish: paloma) is the name source for Palomar Mountain and Palomar State Park in California, as well as for related name forms in other States. Cordoniz, in Orange County, is the Spanish name for quail, California's State bird.

Little Egg Harbor, in New Jersey, was originally called Eyren Hafen by the early Dutch settlers because of the abundance of sea bird eggs they found there.

Some avian toponyms are of Indian origin. One of the more common is Wawa, the Ojibway word for the Canadian goose, which is perpetuated in

76

the names of Wawa Lake, Minnesota, and Wawa, Ontario. A 24-foot replica of the Canadian goose stands as a landmark near the entrance to the latter town. The Algonquin word for goose survives in the Rhode Island place-names Seekonk and Sakonnet. Chinati, Indian for blackbird, is the name of a town in Presidio County, Texas.

False or erroneous bird toponyms constitute another class. One reason for false bird names is the large number of personal names that are identical with names of birds. A list of avian toponyms selected from a map or from the index of an atlas may therefore include many that have no association with our feathered friends. For example, Hamill T. Kenny has suggested that some places called Buzzard may be corruptions of the German surname Bossert or some variant of it.

Likewise, few of the Robins and Robbins were probably named for the red-breasted songster. Phebe, in Perkins County, Nebraska, owes its name to Mrs. Phoebe Jack, the town's first postmistress. Andy Crow, early Oregon postmaster, is believed to have given his name to the village of Crow in Lane County. Famed Swans Island, in Hancock County, Maine, was named for Colonel James Swan, who bought the island from the State of Massachusetts in 1786 and built a mansion on it.

Lark, Texas, was not named for the songbird but for Lark Stangler, an early settler in the town. Peacock in the same State immortalized J. M. Peacock, the town's first postmaster. Peacock Spring, California, likewise has a human origin, having been named for trainmaster G. H. Peacock, a member of Lt. Joseph C. Ives' 1857 exploring expedition.

Even such toponyms as Goose, Hawk, and Pigeon may be suspect. Goose Creek, in Modoc County, California, for example, memorializes a German homesteader named Goos. Hawk, in Vinton County, Ohio, was named for one Wes Hawk. Joseph Pigeon, a member of Governor Evans' Council in 1705, gave his name to Pigeon Creek in Chester County, Pennsylvania.

These examples recall the old maxims that you can't always believe what you see and that, like fine feathers, an avian name may not always adorn a bird. The uncertainty concerning their origins is one of the interesting and challenging characteristics of geographical names. Tracing the source and development of specific names can, therefore, be a fascinating and rewarding experience.

Research on names in your own community will no doubt reveal a number of bird names as well as other distinctive groups of toponyms. It will also lead you through many delightful little byways of local history. As you advance and grow in your studies of place-names you may be invited to assist in selecting a name for some local feature. For naming is a continuing process that accompanies the growth of our Nation and of the many localities and communities of which it is formed.

Bird names, especially those of our many songbirds, comprise a rich and virtually untapped source for physical features not yet appropriately identified and for new streets and neighborhoods in residential developments. A recently opened community near my home includes a Thrasher Road and a Warbler Lane. If this idea catches on, our local maps may soon be adorned with such toponyms as Whippoorwill Walk, Meadowlark Drive, Tanager Hill, Mockingbird Grove, Sandpiper Beach, Cardinal Crest, or Hummingbird Gardens. We could do worse.

—WALTER W. RISTOW.

77

Birds on Stamps

I AM AN ORNITHOPHILATELIST. I collect postage stamps that picture birds. I started out, as I suppose all collectors do (whether of coins or paintings or glass), with a general interest—in my case, stamps. I soon learned I could not collect all stamps from all over the world. Besides, I became more and more interested in stamps closest to my work and training in biology.

Thus I became one of many topical collectors, about one-fifth of whom, I would guess, collect biological subjects. We are biophilatelists. (Every group and profession must have a high-sounding name these days.)

Almost one-half of the biological collectors collect bird stamps. Next in popularity are insects; many of those collectors have gone one step farther in specialization and limit themselves to butterflies and moths.

Others collect fish on stamps, wild animals, or plants (or only flowers).

I collect bird stamps from all over the world because the United States (or any other one country, for that matter) has issued very few—that is, aside from the duck stamps, which I discuss later. Strictly speaking, these hunting-permit stamps are revenue stamps and do not fall within the usual scope of philately, which is concerned only with the carrying of the mail. In a competitive exhibition, revenue stamps would not qualify unless there is a special class for them. The duck stamps, though, make an interesting collection by themselves. Many ornithophilatelists collect them.

The first United States stamp to show a bird was issued in 1851. It was one of two special carrier stamps to facilitate the delivering and collecting of letters. It shows a bald eagle.

Two regular postage stamps were issued in 1869 (a 10-cent and a 30-cent). Both show a bald eagle, although their formats are somewhat different.

Two stamped (embossed) envelopes were issued in 1893—a 5-cent and a 10-cent, which show the symbolic eagle with the heads of Columbus and Liberty.

A 10-cent registration stamp in 1911 showed the bald eagle. It was followed in 1934 by a 16-cent airmail special delivery stamp, which portrayed the bald eagle as it appears on the great seal of the United States.

The first United States stamp to portray a wild bird as something other than a symbol was issued December 5, 1947. It depicted a not wholly true-to-life great white heron, which shared the design with a map of Florida to publicize the Everglades National Park.

Our first postage stamp to portray a native bird accurately as a central theme was one of the three 1956 wildlife conservation issue stamps, which portrayed the wild turkey. The other two featured the pronghorn antelope and the king salmon. All three were designed by Bob Hines.

For the first time, we American biophilatelists were able to exchange interesting biological covers with our oversea friends who for some time had been sending us beautiful biological covers.

The wild turkey was followed on November 22, 1957, by the whooping crane on another wildlife conservation issue. Our hopes now were high that we might expect an example of American wildlife once a year, but the next four annual conservation issues were based on forest conservation (1958), soil conservation (1959), water conservation (1960), and range conservation (1961). The first pictured two small deer. The 1960 stamp showed two tiny wild ducks in flight. The artists who

ART FOR TURKEY STAMP

painted the original designs were Rudolph Wendelin and Elmo White, of the Department of Agriculture, and Walter Hortens, of New York City.

The only other central-theme bird to appear on stamps to date is that on the John James Audubon issue of December 7, 1963. It disappointed most ornithophilatelists, including me.

The stamp was beautiful and well executed, but the bird is not a native of the United States. The so-called Columbia jay is really the magpie-jay of Mexico and Central America. The choice of design was made by persons interested in art and obviously unaware that Audubon painted this plate from a mounted specimen and was misinformed about its geographical origin. The United States thereby became another country that issued stamps of wildlife not native to it.

A light Brahma rooster appeared on the Poultry Industry issue in 1948.

The American Bar Association stamp of August 24, 1953, was mildly interesting. It had a small, stylized owl, as shown in a frieze in the Supreme Court Building in Washington.

A tiny, stylized bird on the fence was part of an agricultural scene portrayed on the Future Farmers issue of October 13, 1953.

All other bird stamps of the United States (with minor exceptions) show the emblematic eagle. On July 4, 1942, the "win the war" issue was released. It featured a stylized eagle. Another eagle was shown on a 1946 stamp that reproduced the honorable discharge emblem. The Boy Scout issue in 1950 showed three scouts and a tiny, almost invisible stylized eagle on the scout emblem.

The bald eagle in flight on the 4-cent airmail of May 29, 1953, and on an airmail postal card is quite realistic. It has become a prized item in many collections.

A 6-cent, embossed airmail envelope in 1956 portrayed an eagle in flight. A highly stylized eagle appeared on the Steel Industry issue of 1957.

79

Bob Hines, who illustrated this book, puts the finishing touches on the final art work of the 3-cent postage stamp issued in 1957. An employee of the Department of the Interior, he is known for his wildlife paintings.

Three types of airmail envelopes in 1958 were surcharged with a stylized bald eagle to increase the value to 7 cents, giving rise to six catalogued varieties.

The St. Lawrence Seaway issue of 1959 shows a stylized eagle as the emblem of the United States and the maple leaf as the emblem of Canada.

The Malaria Eradication issue of March 20, 1962, shows the bald eagle as it appears on the great seal of the United States. On January 5, 1965, a 5-cent embossed envelope had the head and shoulders of a realistic bald eagle.

So, because only five native birds are portrayed on United States postage stamps, some philatelists have turned to collecting covers—envelopes—with post office cancellations bearing bird names. It is an interesting and inexpensive hobby with many possibilities.

Plain covers with nothing to detract from the postmark except the collector's address make an interesting collection. One can use removable labels for the address and collect the entire cover. Some prefer to eliminate the address and save space by mounting only the postmark and can-

celed stamp. This is accomplished by neatly cutting off and mounting the upper right-hand part of the envelope, which is standard procedure in collecting stamped (embossed) envelopes.

Some collectors prefer to prepare more elaborate and artistic covers. Appropriate drawings or water-color paintings of the bird are prepared on the left side of the envelope. Such an envelope is known as a cachet. Instead of the handmade drawings or paintings, some collectors use printed pictures, especially the popular National Wildlife Conservation Stamps. The killdeer wildlife stamp, for instance, is attached to the envelope to be postmarked at Killdeer, North Dakota.

You fit these prepared plain envelopes or more elaborate cachets with a medium-heavy, accurately fitted filler to assure safe passage through cancellation and the mails and send them to the postmaster of the appropriate office with a request that he mail it back to you. It is well to explain that you are making a collection of ornithological postmarks.

Among the towns named for birds are: Bob White, West Virginia; Brant, Michigan and New York; Crane, Indiana, Missouri, Montana, Oregon, and Texas; Crow, West Virginia; Curlew, Iowa and Washington; Eagle, Alaska, Colorado, Idaho, Michigan, Nebraska, and Wisconsin; Grouse, Idaho; Heron, Montana; Blue Heron, Kentucky; Jay, Florida; Blue Jay, California; Killdeer, North Dakota; Kingfisher, Oklahoma; Nighthawk, Washington; Osprey, Florida; Pelican, Alaska and Louisiana; Wren, Ohio and Oregon.

Among the combinations are: Brant Lake, New York; Brant Rock, Massachusetts; Buzzards Bay, Massachusetts; Grouse Creek, Utah; Hawk Point, Missouri; Pelican Lake, Florida and Wisconsin; Raven Rock, West Virginia.

Biophilatelists like these beautiful conservation stamps, which are issued in full, natural colors. The stamps show all kinds of wildlife and portray

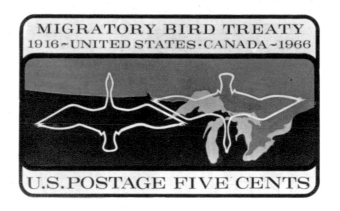

Burt E. Pringle, designer of an American postage stamp issued March 16, 1966, drew stylized Canada geese crossing from and to the United States and Canada to stress a main point of an important treaty.

Several of the postage stamps issued by the United States show the symbolic eagle. Other native birds represented on American postage issues are the great white heron, the rare whooping crane, and the wild turkey.

many birds. These stamps have no philatelic significance, however, except as they are used in the preparation of cachets.

Each year the National Wildlife Federation mails out sheets of these stamps to thousands of persons throughout the country. In return for the stamps, the person is requested to contribute at least a dollar to the federation in support of its conservation activities. As of April 1965, sheets were available from 1956 through 1965 at a dollar a sheet. Descriptive albums for each of these years were also available at 50 cents each. Looseleaf binders for the albums are available. A pricelist and order form may be had from the National Wild-

life Federation, 1412 Sixteenth Street, N.W., Washington, D.C. 20036.

An up-to-date *Directory of Post Offices,* Post Office Department Publication 26, may be purchased from the Superintendent of Documents, Washington, D.C., 20402, for 2.75 dollars. In it you can find many more places with names of birds.

The "duck stamps," properly known as "migratory bird hunting stamps" are prized by many collectors, although, as I have said, they are not philatelic items in the strict meaning of the word.

Most persons who collect biological stamps are keenly interested in all phases of wildlife conservation, and these stamps reflect such activities.

Migratory bird hunting stamps, popularly called "duck stamps," have been issued since 1934.

Furthermore, if you want to collect United States bird stamps, these are about the only ones you can get.

Remember this: One of the attractive and stimulating things about stamp collecting is that your albums are your own, and you can collect any way you want to. There is no set of rules and regulations. You collect for pleasure. You can include bird stamps and other related materials, such as printed pictures or newspaper reports of new stamps, as you see fit. Competitive exhibiting is, of course, another matter.

My albums contain 4 species of swans, 10 species of geese and brant, and 18 species of ducks on legitimate postage stamps of the world. Most have appeared since 1960, and nearly all since 1955.

The United States "duck stamps" portray 1 species of swan, 6 of geese and brant, and 19 of ducks. Of these, only 2 species of geese and 7 species of ducks are duplicated on regular postage stamps.

The Migratory Bird Hunting Stamp Act, passed by the Congress in 1934, requires that any person over 16 years of age who hunts waterfowl must have in his possession an unexpired Federal migratory bird hunting stamp in addition to his State hunting license.

The first such stamp was issued in 1934 (August 14), and 635,001 copies were sold. Thereafter, July 1 has been the date of sale. The issue of 1935 sold only 448,204; the 1936 issue sold 603,623; the 1937 issue sold 783,039; and the 1938 issue went a little over 1 million copies. I mention these figures because until 1942 the law provided that all unsold stamps must be destroyed. An act passed in 1942 permitted all unsold stamps to be turned over to the Philatelic Agency of the Post Office Department in Washington, D.C. This means that the issues previous to 1941 are exceedingly rare and bring a good price. The 1935 issue is the rarest, and mint copies catalogue at 25 dollars and used copies at 12.5 dollars.

If one is collecting them for the fine details of a miniature reproduction of the original artist's design, one must collect mint—unused—copies.

Legally, used stamps have the hunter's signature written across the face. Some collectors prefer this condition just as some collectors prefer used issues

The winning design of the 1966–1967 duck stamp depicts a pair of whistling swans, painted by Stanley Stearns, of Stevensville, Maryland. The annual competition for the series is sponsored by the Bureau of Sport Fisheries and Wildlife.

of postage stamps, since mint stamps have never carried a piece of mail.

I was told that on August 12, 1965, the issues of 1960 through 1965 were available from the Philatelic Sales Agency, Post Office Department, Washington, D.C., 20260, at face value—3 dollars each. All other issues are obtainable only from collectors or dealers.

If you are interested in the stamp design and are not too particular about perfect centering and such details, you can buy most of them for considerably less than catalogue quotations. The issues through 1947 had a face value of 1 dollar; those from 1948 through 1958 had a face value of 2 dollars. Beginning with the issue of 1959, the face value is 3 dollars, and the stamps are multicolored.

From an artistic standpoint, these hunting permit stamps are superior to most postage stamps. They are two to four times larger than most postage stamps and can therefore show more detail and habitat. Details concerning these stamps, including 4 x 5.5-inch reproductions of the original artists' designs, can be had from the Superintendent of Documents at 25 cents. Ask for Circular 111, "Duck Stamp Booklet of the United States Department of the Interior."

Here is a summary of these interesting stamps:
1934–1935   A pair of mallards dropping in.
1935–1936   Three male canvasbacks in flight over marsh.

The author of this chapter, Willard F. Stanley of Fredonia, New York, collects stamps that depict birds. He is publisher of Bio-Philately, the Journal of the Biology Unit, American Topical Association.

1936–1937 Three Canada geese in flight.

1937–1938 A flock of five greater scaup in flight over open water.

1938–1939 A pair of pintails over marsh.

1939–1940 A pair of green-winged teal on shore of marsh with five birds in flight.

1940–1941 A pair of black ducks in flight over rushes.

1941–1942 A pair of ruddy ducks with eight ducklings. (Interesting because, unlike most ducks, the male stays with the female and young.)

1942–1943 A pair of American widgeons (baldpates) on shore and a male dropping in.

1943–1944 A pair of wood ducks in flight.

1944–1945 Three white-fronted geese in flight.

1945–1946 Two males and one female shovelers in flight.

1946–1947 Five redheads; 1 female and 3 males on water with another male alighting.

1947–1948 Two snow geese in flight.

1948–1949 Two males and one female bufflehead in flight over reeds.

1949–1950 A pair of common goldeneyes in flight over three birds in the water. (Of two males on the water, one is in display.)

1950–1951 Two trumpeter swans in flight over land. (This was the first use of a completely protected species. The artist, Walter A. Weber, was the first to win the competition twice; see white-fronted geese.)

1951–1952 Two gadwalls rising from the water. (The artist, Maynard Reece, was the second to win the competition twice; see buffleheads.)

1952–1953 A pair of harlequin ducks flying above high waves.

1953–1954 Five blue-winged teal in flight over reeds.

1954–1955 A pair of ring-necked ducks in flight.

1955–1956 Two blue geese in flight.

1956–1957 A pair of common mergansers in flight over water.

1957–1958 Two male common eiders in flight over surf.

1958–1959 Two Canada geese in cornfield with five others alighting.

1959–1960 A Labrador retriever with drake mallard and ducks in flight. (The artist, Maynard Reece, is the first to win three competitions; see buffleheads and gadwalls.)

1960–1961 Pair of redheads and four ducklings swimming among reeds. (This is a puzzling design as the male does not habitually take an interest in his family.)

1961–1962 A mallard hen and eight ducklings in natural habitat.

1962–1963 Two drake pintails alighting with other ducks. (The artist, Edward A. Morris, was the first to win two consecutive competitions; see mallard hen and ducklings.)

1963–1964 Two Atlantic brant alighting in coastal waters.

1964–1965 Two nene or Hawaiian geese among Hawaiian lava flows. (A second example of a completely protected species.)

1965–1966 Three canvasback drakes in flight over open water.

Once you become really interested in collecting birds on stamps, sooner or later you are bound to turn to the stamps of the world. Every order of living birds is represented in my albums. The latest one was supplied by Ghana on December 14, 1964, with the issue of a stamp showing the blue-naped Coly or mousebird.

Counting only birds that can be reasonably accurately identified and are shown either as central theme or of secondary interest, my albums contain 500 species, representing 111 families and 28 orders. In a recent 12-month span, new issues provided 1 new order, 8 new families, and 95 new species. This breaks the record for any preceding 12-month period. The reason is that many countries have issued sets of native birds. In some instances, every bird in the set represented species not previously known to philately, and new families as well.

What the future may bring is anyone's guess, but one thing is certain—we ornithophilatelists will find much pleasure in trying to keep up with new issues. In doing so, we shall gain a wealth of information about the birds of the world. We can do this by our own individual investigations or we can associate ourselves with a study unit. If you are interested in such an international study unit, you can get information from the Biology Unit of the American Topical Association, State University College, Fredonia, New York, 14063.

Because of my interest in animals as a professional biologist, I organize my collection in a taxonomic sequence. This makes it easier for me to use my albums as references in my writing and editing of biophilatelic materials. My collection of birds now occupies five looseleaf albums, but they

Bird postage stamps issued by Canada feature migratory waterfowl.

Many countries have issued postage stamps in which paintings of birds are part of the design.

The Republic of San Marino has issued a wide range of colorful postage stamps that picture birds.

are bursting at the seams with the flood of new issues.

You can collect at least 6 identifiable species of penguins, 4 ostrich and relatives, the apteryx, 2 kinds of loons, 2 grebes, 5 albatrosses, 4 petrels, 3 tropic-birds, 7 pelicans, 5 boobies, 7 cormorants, 2 anhingas, 3 frigate-birds, a bittern, 12 herons and relatives, the hammerhead, the whale-headed stork, 7 true storks, 8 ibises and spoonbill, and 2 flamingos, representing 25 families and 12 orders.

My second album contains, besides the waterfowl I mentioned, 3 New World vultures, the secretary bird, 22 hawks, eagles, and Old World vultures, 16 "falcons," and the osprey. There are at least 6 "grouse," 8 "partridges," 4 pheasants, 4 peafowl, the jungle fowl, domestic chickens, 4 guineafowl, wild and domestic turkeys, the brush turkey, a curassow, and a chachalaca.

Moving on up the taxonomic scale, there are 5 species of crane to be sought, the kagu, 8 "rails," 4 bustards, 2 jacanas, 2 oystercatchers, 11 sandpipers and plovers, a sheath-bill, the skua, 5 gulls, 6 terns, the puffin, and a skimmer.

Another of my albums contains 24 families within 10 orders, and here we find the dodo and a solitaire plus 2 other extinct species, all issued by Mauritius. All draw our attention to the sad fate of many of our wildlife friends.

In addition, we have 3 sand-grouse, 19 pigeons and doves, 26 species of "parrots," the mouse-bird, 6 plantain eaters, 4 cuckoos, a coua, 4 identifiable owls, 2 nightjars, a swift, 6 hummingbirds, the quetzal, 5 trogons, 12 kingfishers, a tody, a motmot, 6 bee-eaters, 6 rollers, 2 ground rollers, 2 hoopoes, 9 hornbills, 3 barbets, a jacamar, 6 toucans, a honey-guide, and 10 woodpeckers.

My last album is devoted to the perching birds, or songbirds (order Passeriformes). Here there are 162 identifiable species. We start with an oven-bird, 2 cocks-of-the-rock, 3 New World flycatchers, the lyrebird, 2 larks, 3 swallows, a helmet bird, an Australian "magpie," 8 shrikes, 4 Old World orioles, a drongo, and 7 starlings. These are followed by 3 "crows," 5 jays and magpies, 2 callaeids, 14 birds of paradise, a waxwing, a palm chat, a cuckoo-shrike, 2 bulbuls, 8 Old World flycatchers, 8 Old World warblers, 13 "thrushes" (Turdidae), 2 mockingbirds, a wren, 4 "tits," a nuthatch, 2 creepers, 2 wagtails, a honey-eater, 9 sunbirds, 2 white-eyes, 8 New World orioles and blackbirds, a swallow-tanager, 5 tanagers, 17 "fringilids," 2 "estrilids," and 12 "ploceids."

By this time, the collector probably will have acquired a score or more of puzzling birds that will keep him exploring the world of birds, and probably corresponding with other ornithophilatelists here and overseas. By the time you read this chapter, there almost certainly will be many more on the new issues of the world's postal administrations. The chief regret probably will be that only 4 of these 500 species have been portrayed on the stamps of the United States.

With scores of countries issuing sets of postage stamps depicting all types of native wildlife, often in beautiful natural colors, it seems strange that the United States should have limited its postal portrayal to four native birds, two native mammals, and one native fish and completely overlooked native trees and flowers. This hardly seems consistent with the national interest in the scores of beautiful books focused on our wealth of native wildlife.

—Willard F. Stanley.

Clifford W. Shankland, a typographer and designer who lives in Falls Church, Virginia, works on his collection of stamps. His album of Israeli stamps, below, contains a number of attractive bird issues.

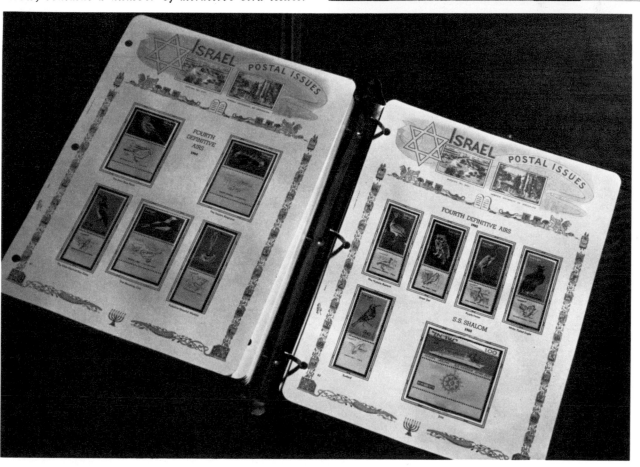

Birds on Coins

I LIKE TO HOLD IN MY HAND a small silver coin that was used to buy things in Athens almost 2,500 years ago. On one side it has the head of Pallas Athena, the Olympian goddess of wisdom, patron of the arts and of war, and guardian of Athens. On its reverse side is an owl, symbol of wisdom, luck, and victory, beside a spray of olive, signifying peace and prosperity, and a waning moon in memory of the battle at Marathon.

The coin, a tetradrachm (which originally was roughly comparable in usefulness to 20 of our dollars and which one New York coin dealer now will sell for many times that amount), links me

and the ancient Athenian who once handled it and tells me something of the aspirations and interests of the city-state in which he lived. If he were an Athenian soldier fighting in the epic battle against the Persians at Marathon, the owl told him that Athena was with him.

Just as Athena was associated with an owl, Zeus, the Jupiter of the Romans, who was foremost among the gods, was linked with an eagle; Apollo, with a falcon; and Aphrodite, goddess of love and beauty, with a dove.

Thus the eagle was preeminent on ancient— and later—coins as the symbol of might and freedom, the king of birds, and the bird of kings. It was believed sometimes that he lived with the gods on Olympus and was the bearer of Zeus' thunderbolt.

The eagle appears on the god's outstretched hand on silver coins of Alexander the Great. The Ptolemaic kings of Egypt used him in the designs of most of their coins. Fighting and victorious, he appears on some famous coins of Acragas in Sicily, which show two eagles on a hare or fighting a snake. Occasionally the eagle was used on Roman Republican coins, and after Augustus he frequently served to symbolize the Roman Empire.

Since then, he has served throughout the ages as a symbol of independent and imperial might. A "Roman" naturalistic eagle is shown, for instance, on a beautiful gold piece of the Middle Ages, struck about 1231 by Emperor Frederick II as king of Sicily.

In America, the eagle appeared in the late 17th or early 18th century on some tokens of New York; on cents struck in 1786 in New Jersey; on others issued in 1787 in New York; and in the same year in Massachusetts. The New York goldsmith Ephraim Brasher used an eagle design on a gold doubloon he produced in 1787. An eagle design was used also for early patterns of the U.S. Mint in 1792.

A naturalistic eagle within a wreath was adopted for the regular silver issues in 1794. An eagle holding a wreath in his beak—reminiscent of ancient Roman designs—is shown on 5-dollar and 10-dollar gold pieces of 1795 to 1797. A heraldic eagle design that followed was replaced with a somewhat stylized eagle with a shield on his breast and the arrows of war and the branch of peace in his talons. The Kennedy half-dollar of 1964 also has the heraldic eagle design.

A beautiful engraving of an eagle in flight by the great Philadelphia mint artist Christian Gobrecht in 1836 was used for patterns of silver dollars with the dates 1836, 1838, and 1839 and on cents struck in copper-nickel from 1856 to 1858.

For some time in the 19th century, an expertly mounted and magnificent example of the American eagle, which inspired the mint artists, was housed in a cabinet in the Philadelphia Mint. The bird, named Peter, had been a resident of the Phil-adelphia Mint for 6 years. He flew freely outdoors, always returning to the Mint. He died in an accident. He perched on a large flying wheel and was caught in the machinery.

The eagle designs on various U.S. coin series through the years are many and interesting. Usually he stands with wings spread, shield on breast, and an olive branch and arrows in his talons. On some, the tips of the wings point down to convey the idea of a perched, or "static," eagle. On others, the tips of the wings are raised, like those of a bird about to alight or possibly in flight.

On some of the 19th-century patterns for silver dollars, like those designed, for instance, in 1873, 1877, 1879, and 1882, the eagle is shown laterally and in a defiant position. This design was never adopted for regular coinage, however.

A powerful American eagle stands in profile with arrows and an olive branch in its claws on the 10-dollar gold piece designed in 1907 by Augustus Saint-Gaudens (1848–1907), the foremost American sculptor of his time. This type appeared on all 10-dollar gold pieces—"eagles"—struck up to 1933. The artist's intention was to use this design on the 20-dollar piece, but President Theodore Roosevelt, who took an active interest in the work on these coins, decided that, instead, an eagle in flight, also done by Saint-Gaudens, should be used for the 20-dollar piece.

An eagle perched peacefully with closed wings on the cap of a mountain, observing the rising sun, was modeled by Anthony de Francisci for the silver dollar struck from 1921 to 1935, a fitting rendering of the king of the birds for a coin symbolic of peace after the close of the First World War.

Many other eagle designs have appeared on U.S. coins. The series of commemorative half dollars, struck mainly during the early 1900's, was designed by prominent artists, among them Laura Gardin Fraser, who engraved the eagle in profile to the left on a half dollar commemorating in 1921 the Alabama Centennial. A facing eagle with open wings was designed by Edward Everett Burr for the half dollar marking the hundredth anniversary of the admission of Arkansas into the Union. These coins were struck with dates from 1935 to 1939.

Some U.S. coins have the eagle as a major element of design.

Henry Kreiss contributed a modernistic rendering of an eagle in profile to the right for the reverse of the half dollar issued in 1936 in commemoration of the hundredth anniversary of the incorporation of the city of Bridgeport in Connecticut. He modeled in 1935 a powerful design of an eagle standing left with closed wings for the Connecticut Tercentenary commemorative.

The half dollar commemorating in 1946 the hundredth anniversary of Iowa's statehood bears on one side the facing eagle as it appears on the State seal. The dies for the coin were prepared by Adam Pietz, a Philadelphia artist.

An eagle with open wings turned left—as it appears on the Illinois State seal—is shown on the reverse of the 1918 half dollar commemorating

Representations of birds appear on coins of many countries. One of the oldest, the 5th-century tetradrachm of ancient Athens, has an owl, which meant wisdom, luck, victory (top, middle).

the hundredth anniversary of the admission of Illinois into the Union. It was designed by J. R. Sinnock.

Other eagle designs appear on the Panama-Pacific Exposition half dollar, 1915, by the mint engraver Charles E. Barber; on the Stone Mountain Memorial half dollar of 1925, by Gutzon Borglum; and on the Texas Centennial coin, modeled by Pompeo Coppini and struck with dates from 1934 to 1938.

Eagle designs abound on the various private gold issues, struck during the California gold rush in 1849. They follow largely U.S. coin designs, but some, like the rare pieces the Cincinnati Mining

Dr. V. Clain-Stefanelli, Curator of the Division of Numismatics of the U.S. National Museum, and Mrs. Clain-Stefanelli, Associate Curator, assess the features of a new acquisition of coins.

and Trading Company issued in 1849, demonstrate originality.

The owl is the only other bird on United States coins. This ancient symbol of wisdom appears on the reverse side of 50-dollar gold pieces that were issued for the Panama-Pacific Exposition in 1915 and were designed by Robert Aitken. Appropri-

ately enough, a rendering of the head of Pallas Athena was adopted for the obverse side.

A great variety of birds, however, is represented on ancient, medieval, and modern foreign coins. During the Middle Ages, a beautiful artistic rendering was that of a falcon. It appears on a thin, large, silver penny, a so-called bracteate, struck in the name of Count Burchard II of Falkenstein (1142–1174), of whose family the falcon was the heraldic figure. It reminds us of people who found great pleasure in hawking.

In modern times, birds have appeared on coins mostly because they typify in some way the fauna of the particular country or sometimes the country itself. I list some of them.

BIRD OF PARADISE

German New Guinea 10 pfennig, ½, 1, 2, 5 mark, 1894; 10 and 20 mark, 1895.

BLUE CRANE

South Africa 5 cents, 1965.

CONDOR

Bolivia 1 and 2 centavos, 1878; and as part of the coat of arms on various denominations, 1864–1951.

Chile ½, 1, 2, 8 reales, 1838–1850, and on most coins issued since then. The 2 centesimos, 1964, bears, f.i., a condor flying to left.

Colombia above coat of arms, since 1839 on a large number of different issues.

Ecuador surmounting coat of arms, since 1844.

CROW

Japan 1 sen, 1938–1940.

DOVE

Cyprus 1, 5, 25 mils, 1963.

Griqua Town ¼, ½, 5, 10 pence, (ca. 1815).

Japan 5 sen, 1940–1943; 1945–1946. 50 sen, 1946–1947.

Papal Rome scudo, 1823. doppia, 1830. 5 scudi, 1846. Also, on many earlier issues as a symbol of the Holy Ghost.

Vatican City 5 and 10 lire, 1939.
5 and 10 centesimi, 1942–1946.
2 lire, 1950.
500 lire, 1958.
1, 2, 5, 10, 20 lire, 1962.
500 lire, 1963.
As part of coat of arms on many different denominations since 1942.

EAGLE

Albania 2 franka ari, 1926–1928.
10 quindar leku, 1926 (eagle's head).

Austria 100 kronen, 1923–1924 (eagle's head);
1 groschen, 1925–1938 (eagle's head).

Germany 3 and 5 mark, 1930 (evacuation of Rhineland commemorative).

Mexico on numerous issues since 1811.

The quetzal, known as the bird of freedom, is the national symbol of Guatemala. It is featured in the design of this one-fourth quetzal coin and on other coins minted in Guatemala since 1925 under authorization of a law passed in 1924.

Roman Republic	2 baiocchi, 1798–1799.
	various denominations from ½ baiocco to 40 baiocchi, 1849.
Sicily	1 grano, 1801.
	10 grani, 1801–1803.
	1 piastra, 1801–1810.
United States	many different eagle designs:
	1 cent, 1856–1858; 20 dollars, 1907–1933 (flying eagle);
	50 cents, 1916–1947;
	1 dollar, 1921–1935;
	10 dollars, 1907–1933.
	The heraldic eagle appears in different forms on the coins of Albania, Austria, Chile, Colombia, Ecuador, Germany, Italy, Panama, Philippine Islands, Poland, Romania, Russia, Siam, South African Republic, Yugoslavia, and other countries.

EMU

Australia	as supporter of coat of arms, on 3, and 6 pence, 1 shilling, 1 florin, 1910 and up to date.

GROUSE

Norway	2 ore, 1958, 1959.

GULL

Japan	1 sen, 1938–1940.

HEN

Ireland	1 penny, 1928–1937; 1940–1964.

HORNBILL

Zambia	1 shilling, 1964.

HUIA BIRD

New Zealand	6 pence, 1933 and later years.

KIWI

New Zealand	1 florin, 1933 and later years.

KOOKABURRA

Australia	1 penny patterns, 1919–1921.

LYRE BIRD

Australia	10 cents, 1966 (new decimal coinage).

MALAWI COCKEREL (*Austrolop cock*)

Malawi	6 pence, 1964.

OWL

Greece	5 and 10 lepta, 1912.

PEACOCK

Burma	1/16, ⅛, ¼, ½, 1 rupee, 1852.
	¼ anna, 1865.

PUFFIN

Lundy	½ and 1 puffin, 1929.

QUETZAL

Guatemala	as part of coat of arms, on many issues circulated since 1873.
	standing on column, on coins of 1925 and later dates.

ROOSTER

Cameroons	50 centimes, and 1 franc, 1943.
Celebes Island	1 kapang, 1835.
France	as additional symbol, on: 20 francs, 1850, 1851; 20, 50, 100 francs, 1878–1914.
	as main type, on 10 and 20 francs (gold), 1899–1914; 10, 20, 50 francs, 1950–1959.
French Equatorial Africa	50 centimes, and 1 franc, 1942, 1943.

French India	1 cash, 1836; ½, 1, 2 fanons, 1837.
Madagascar	50 centimes, and 1 franc, 1943.
Malacca	1, and 2 kapangs, 1835.

SEA EAGLE

Rhodesia and Nyasaland	2 shillings, 1955 (on fish); ½ crown, 1955 (surmounting arms).

SPARROW

South Africa	farthing, 1923–1960.

TITMOUSE

Norway	25 øre, 1958 and later years.

TUI BIRD

New Zealand	1 penny, 1940 and later.

TROPICAL BIRD

New Caledonia	50 centimes, 1, 2 francs, 1949; 5 francs, 1952.

WILD GOOSE

China	1 dollar, 1932 (three flying wild geese above sailing junk at sea).

WOODCOCK

Ireland	farthing, 1928–1937; 1939–1959.

WREN

Great Britain	farthing, 1937–1956.

MYTHICAL OR SACRED BIRDS

HAMSA

Cambodia	1 fuang (1846); 10 centimes, 1953; 10, 20, 50 sen, 1959.

PHOENIX

China	1 dollar, 1923; 10 and 20 cents, 1926, 1927.
Greece	1, 5, 10, 20 lepta, 1828–1831; 1 phoenix, 1828; 5 drachmai, 1930.
Japan	50 sen, 1922–1926 (bird of longevity); 100 yen, 1957–1958.
Korea	½ chon, 1906–1910; 1 chon, 1905–1910; 5 chon, 1905–1907.

ZIMBABWE STONE BIRD

Southern Rhodesia	1 shilling, 1932–1952.

The listing may induce some of us to form a collection of coins that show birds. For all of us, collectors or not, the list reminds us of the ideals they represent: The ancient owl, good fortune, victory, and wisdom; the dove, beauty, love, and peace; and the beautiful, rare, and legend-inspiring quetzal bird, the unending quest for freedom.

—VLADIMIR CLAIN-STEFANELLI.

Birds and Commercial Arts

AN ADVERTISING MAN once said that people's attention is attracted first by people, preferably adult, scantily clad females; second, cute, cuddly infants; third, man's best friend, the dog; and, fourth, birds.

Maybe so. At any rate, think of the places you see representations of birds—in porcelain, dress goods, Audubon prints, wood carvings, paintings, tiles, greeting cards, stationery, advertisements, draperies, airplanes, jewelry, architectural details (such as the 58 bird figures in the panels that decorate the facade of the National Wildlife Fed-

eration Building in Washington), and many more.

Think also, then, of the close connection between Nature, fine art, and commerce.

Years ago, cards showing birds in color were included in packages of tobacco, tea, baking soda, and other products. With each card, one received information about the birds and encouragement to collect and preserve these sets of cards. From such beginnings developed the basis for several fund-raising programs, in which birds provide interest and stimulus.

Developments have reduced the cost of color

Plastic panels are intended for home decorating.

All manner of items use birds in their design.

A mechanical bird in a gilded cage can turn its head, flap its tail, open its bill, and sing—after a fashion.

reproduction and have increased the output of calendars, prints, bird-identification books, and so on.

The use of figures and pictures of birds on ash-trays, platters, china, wallpaper, and stamps helped a great deal to arouse public interest in conservation programs.

Birds are popular subjects for hand-painted plates to be used for wall decorations.

Birds decorate all kinds of calendars.

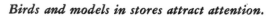

Birds and models in stores attract attention.

An exhibition of birds carved of wood was held in 1965 at Chestertown, Maryland, and attracted carvers from many parts of the United States.

Wood carvers need only a few simple tools but much time, patience, and skill in their craft.

Art objects are made in this country and abroad for the ornamentation of home and office. They are inexpensive or expensive, depending on workmanship.

Packets of sugar picture birds and ask people to help wildlife survive.

It is hard to prove that anybody has bought a Thunderbird, Skylark, or Falcon just because of the names, but it stands to reason that the "image" so carefully sought by advertising people is there—symbols of speed, grace, and beauty. Precedent also is there.

Graceful, well-designed radiator caps were the style some years ago. Among them was an eagle, whose wings rose and spread as the engine warmed. A quail in flight could be added to the 1931 Ford. A winged cap identified the Chrysler. Classic motor meters with spreading wings with the name Dusenburg emblazoned over a stylized eagle or an abstract bird form called a Dusen-bird provided the identity. The Thunderbird of Indian lore is familiar to this generation; it is on the rear trunk cover as a concession to modern design.

Several domestic airlines use bird designs as insignia on their aircraft. Others use bird names to identify grades of service. They are recognized by these names as frequently as by the names of their builders or operators. The Grumann Aircraft Corporation produced a series of amphibious airplanes, each model designated by such names as widgeon, goose, mallard, and albatross. We have become familiar with names like golden falcon, silver eagle, and others equally suggestive of maneuverability, speed, and regal beauty.

A major item of business is hunting decoys in the likenesses of ducks, geese, crows, and owls. For them, artists first provide models in appropriate shape and color, which are then produced in fiber, plastic, rubber, or wooden decoys hunters use. The gross sales of decoys in the United States are estimated at nearly a million dollars a year. Besides, many decoys are handmade by artist-craftsmen for sale at fancy prices to sportsmen and hunting clubs. Decoys and many other items, like cutouts or bird forms of storks, doves, egrets, macaws, and commoner birds, often are parts of window displays or are themselves advertising motifs.

Birds of pottery, china, glass, or wood, some of them inexpensive, some very costly, are popular for home decoration. Among them are mobiles, of thin sheets of brass, wood, tin, or paper; pewter ducks; surprisingly inexpensive bone china birds; carved horn birds; and delicate pieces made of seashells. Some are imported. All, I think, have some fitting place in a home.

—Rex Gary Schmidt.

Edward Marshall Boehm, widely known for his porcelain reproductions of birds, adds finishing touches to the eye of an ivory-billed woodpecker. He created this 54-inch work of art for an exhibition in London.

Beside a great horned owl is an earthenware owl made by Zuni Indians in Arizona for tourists.

A store in Washington, D.C., converted its main display windows into aviaries, in which birds from South America and Africa underscored the theme of a fashion show, "Fashion Takes Wings."

The Nation's Symbol

DELEGATES TO THE Second Continental Congress reassembled in the Pennsylvania State House after dinner on July 4, 1776, to carry on the business of organizing a revolution. During the afternoon, they signed the Declaration of Independence and dealt with many matters of less drama. Much was still to be done: The creation of a government, the conduct of a war, small tasks and large.

The Delegates empowered the Board of War to employ persons skilled in the manufacture of flints needed for small arms. They appointed a number of commissioners for Indian affairs. They voted money to pay for delivery of dispatches from Trenton. They authorized the Secret Committee to sell 25 pounds of gunpowder to John Garrison of North Carolina.

They also appointed Benjamin Franklin, John Adams, and Thomas Jefferson as a committee to bring in a design for a national seal.

The membership of the committee betokened the importance the Congress placed on the matter. Except for the absence of Robert Livingston and Roger Sherman, it was the same group that had drawn up the Declaration of Independence.

The need for an official seal was considered urgent. Inherited English custom and law demanded that the seal of sovereign authority be impressed on grants and charters to make them valid. The Continental Congress therefore felt the need of a device to verify its principal actions.

Franklin's committee went to work at once. It obtained the services of Eugene Pierre du Simitiere, a West Indian artist living in Philadelphia, and started the long search for a suitable design.

Du Simitiere thought the seal should contain the arms of the six nations that had peopled the Colonies. His design depicted the arms of England, Scotland, Ireland, Holland, France, and Germany. An eagle, like the two-headed Imperial German eagle, thus made its first appearance in a design proposed for the seal. His sketch showed to the left of these arms the figure of Liberty and, to the right, a uniformed rifleman with a gun in one hand and a tomahawk in the other.

Franklin, then 71, was in a more religious mood. His suggestion for a design, in his words, had "Moses standing on the Shore, and extending his Hand over the Sea, thereby causing the same to overwhelm Pharaoh who is sitting in an open Chariot, a Crown on his Head and a Sword in his Hand. Rays from a Pillar of Fire in the Clouds reaching to Moses to express that he acts by Command of the Deity." The motto offered was "Rebellion to Tyrants is Obedience to God."

Jefferson liked the motto, but he preferred a design that showed the children of Israel in the wilderness, led by a cloud by day and a pillar of fire by night. On the reverse side, according to a letter of John Adams, Jefferson suggested likenesses of Hengist and Horsa, "the Saxon chiefs from whom we claim the honor of being descended, and whose political principles and form of government we have assumed."

John Adams had another proposal, but he admitted it was too complicated and not original. He envisioned Hercules resting on a club. At one side, Virtue pointed to her rugged mountain and attempted to persuade him to ascend. On the other side, Sloth sought to lure him along paths of pleasure.

The committee accepted Du Simitiere's basic design with the European nations and their arms, around which were shields depicting the Thirteen

THE FIRST SEAL (1782)

THE SECOND SEAL (1841)

THE SEAL (1902)

The symbolic eagle dominates the Great Seal of the United States and is featured in the insignia of a number of American Government and private agencies.

Colonies. The rifleman was replaced by the Goddess of Justice. The Eye of Providence, in a radiant triangle, was placed at the top. At the bottom was the motto, "E Pluribus Unum," attributed to Jefferson. The reverse of the seal used

Franklin's religious scene and the motto, "Rebellion to Tyrants is Obedience to God."

The design was presented to the Continental Congress on August 20, the day that body heard the report of its committee appointed to draft the "Articles of Confederation and Perpetual Union." The proposal for a seal apparently failed to impress the Congress. It was tabled—for nearly 4 years.

The Congress revived the search on March 25, 1780. James Lovell of Massachusetts, John Scott of Virginia, and William Houston of New Jersey were appointed to bring in a design. Their offering, presented about 2 months later, omitted the eagle entirely.

The main features of their design were a shield with 13 diagonal stripes, supported on the left by a warrior with a sword and on the right by a figure representing Peace. The reverse of the seal showed the figure of Liberty. Again the Congress was not impressed, but the design contained a few elements that were to survive—a constellation of 13 stars, a single dominant shield, and alternating red and white stripes on the shield. The report also was tabled.

A third committee was appointed early in May 1782. Its members, Arthur Middleton and Edward Rutledge of South Carolina and Elias Boudinot of

New Jersey, promptly sought the assistance of William Barton, a resident of Philadelphia who had studied heraldry and had a facility in sketching and who was a brother of Dr. Benjamin Barton, the noted naturalist.

Barton submitted two designs to the committee. Both had a crested eagle, common in European heraldry. The major features were a shield displaying 13 stripes, a Doric column, and supporters of the shield.

His final design showed a uniformed American soldier and a maiden holding a dove. Barton's proposal for the reverse, which was largely retained in the seal eventually adopted, featured an unfinished pyramid of 13 tiers of stone blocks, surmounted by the Eye of Providence.

The report of the third committee, presented on May 9, still did not satisfy the Congress. Its Secretary, Charles Thomson, was asked to consider all previous proposals and to make his own recommendation.

Thomson used the eagle as the central figure and specified that it should be an American eagle. He placed a bundle of arrows in the right talon and an olive branch in the left. Above the eagle was a constellation of 13 stars surrounded by clouds. A shield on the breast of the eagle bore 13 red and white stripes in chevrons. In the beak of the eagle was a scroll with the motto, "E Pluribus Unum." Thomson accepted most of the features Barton had proposed for the reverse.

The revised design was returned to Barton. He changed the chevrons to vertical stripes and placed a field of blue above them. Thomson had an eagle rising in flight; Barton put it in a displayed position. He also specified that the right talon should hold 13 arrows.

The Congress adopted the jointly developed design on June 20, 1782, and by this act the American eagle became the national symbol.

In the approved seal, it still wore the European heraldic tuft or crest at the back of its head, but it was removed later. The earliest known use of the seal was on a commission dated September 16, 1782, granting authority to General Washington to arrange with the British for an exchange of prisoners.

Four years earlier, the State of New York had given the American eagle a prominent place on its

This monument is in Jamestown, Virginia.

The national symbol in a window grill.

coat of arms. Other States would later use the eagle in their seals—Pennsylvania, Mississippi, Illinois, Missouri, Arkansas, Michigan, Iowa, Oregon, Utah, New Mexico, and Wyoming. The seal of the District of Columbia also includes the eagle.

The selection of the American eagle as the national symbol did not please Franklin. He thought the turkey gobbler would have been a better choice. He admitted that the turkey was a little "vain and silly," but he credited it with being a true native of America and a bird of courage—an attribute he did not confer on the eagle.

In a letter to his daughter, Sarah, in 1784, Franklin expressed his feelings:

"I wish that the bald eagle had not been chosen as the representative of our country; he is a bird of bad moral character; he does not get his living honestly; you may have seen him perched on some dead tree, where, too lazy to fish for himself, he watches the labor of the fishing-hawk, and when that diligent bird has at length taken a fish, and is bearing it to his nest for the support of his mate and young ones, the bald eagle pursues him and takes it from him."

Franklin further described the bald eagle as a "rank coward" and said that even the little kingbird "attacks him boldly and drives him out of the district."

Many have taken issue with Franklin. The outstanding American zoologist Francis Hobart Herrick wrote in his book, *The American Eagle* (D. Appleton-Century Company, 1934), that the bald eagle is an expert fisherman in his own right and will not rob the osprey unless that bird is heedless.

He disputed Franklin's charge of cowardice: "[The Eagle] is never driven from the neighborhood by the little kingbird or by any other living being excepting a man armed with a gun," Herrick wrote. "To be sure, the doughty kingbirds trail after him whenever he crosses their vigilantly guarded nesting preserves; hawks and crows may be suffered to do likewise . . . whenever the eagle is not too much bored to turn and strike them down. . . ."

The regal golden eagle (shown here), and its cousin, the bald eagle, are protected by Federal law, but laws alone are not enough to assure their perpetuation.

The symbolic eagle is a prominent feature on many buildings. This photograph was taken in Baltimore.

History is generous in its judgment of the eagle and appears to be influenced more by the appearance and physical strength of the bird than with its natural habits, which sometimes do not match the ideals of human behavior.

More than 3 thousand years before the Christian era, the eagle was the guardian divinity of Lagash, a major city of southern Mesopotamia, near the head of the Persian Gulf.

The eagle was sacred to Zeus, god of the elements; shown with its talons sunk in a serpent, it represented triumph over evil.

To ancient Rome, the eagle was a symbol of victory and was emblazoned on the standards the conquering legions carried. It became the special emblem of Roman emperors and, after their death, the bearer of their souls to the stars.

The eagle became a Christian symbol of ascension and the symbol of St. John. It was likewise adopted as the emblem of Charlemagne, Napoleon, and Peter the Great. It was the emblem of the German Empire and the German Republic until the days of the swastika.

The eagles of the New World also were adopted as symbols of sovereignty. Mexico chose a crested species, the harpy, a bird distinguished by black and white plumage. The Aztec name for *harpia*

The eagle appears on American gold coins, silver coins, and gold and silver certificates. In the upper right is a silver dollar dated 1796.

was "winged wolf," a tribute to the hunting ability of this eagle.

North of the Rio Grande, the golden eagle was highly esteemed by all native North Americans. Daniel G. Brinton, an ethnologist, reported: "Its feathers composed the war flag of the Creeks, and its image, carved in wood, or its stuffed skin, surmounted their council lodges. None but an approved warrior dare wear it among the Cherokees, and the Dakotas allowed such honor only to him who first touched the corpse of the common foe."

The Natchez and other tribes regarded the golden eagle almost as a deity. The Zuni of New Mexico employed four of its feathers to represent the four winds when invoking the raingod.

In their idealization of the eagle, people have made it representative of power, courage, conquest, freedom, independence, magnanimity, truth, and immortality.

The world has 52 species of eagles.

Foremost among them are the golden, or moun-

We can no longer take the national bird of our country for granted. Positive action by all Americans is essential now to assure its survival in Nature.

The eagle appears on several United States internal revenue stamps.

tain, eagle, which is distributed in Europe, Asia, and North America, but confined mostly to the Rocky Mountain and Pacific coastal regions of North America; the gray sea eagle, of still more northerly range; and the American, or bald, eagle.

The bald eagle is sometimes confused during its early dark-plumage stage with the golden eagle, but you can tell one from the other in all plumages if you look at the feathering on their legs. In the bald eagle, the lower one-third or more of the shank is naked. The lower part of the leg of the golden eagle is completely covered with fine, closely set feathers.

The bald eagle is native only to North America. The species apparently mates for life. The parents are devoted to their young. The females are larger, as is usual for most birds of prey. The eagles build large nests, sometimes on a cliff but oftener in a tall tree, and use them year after year. New material is added each year until the tree falls or the nest crashes from its own weight. One nest observed by Mr. Herrick in Ohio was 12 feet deep and 8.5 feet across and weighed an estimated 2 tons. The female lays one to four eggs. The young are cared for at least 6 months.

The choice of the bald eagle as the American symbol appears to have been popular at the time.

The "Bird of Freedom" was pictured on buttermolds, blazoned on quilts, painted on chests, limned on gift plates, and used in many other ways.

The eagle first appeared in American coinage on a Massachusetts copper cent in 1776. The first coinage of American gold followed in 1795 in the form of "eagles," or 10-dollar pieces, and "half-eagles." In the 1797 issue of those coins, the design was nearly the same as the national seal. Quarter eagles were coined in 1796; double eagles (20 dollars), in 1849. The first silver dollar, struck in 1794, bore an eagle with extended wings, standing on a rock and encircled by a laurel wreath.

The die of the old seal had become worn by 1841, and a new one was ordered. The engraving was entrusted to Edward Stabler, of Sandy Spring, Maryland, who had cut many Government seals and had a reputation as a seal engraver. His new design, however, later was referred to as the "illegal seal." Stabler clipped the heraldic crest from the head of the eagle, but he placed only 6 arrows, instead of 13, in its right talon. He also made the red pales, or bars, on the shield twice the width of the white bars. There were many criticisms of the second seal, but it was used until 1884. In that year, the Congress appropriated a thousand dollars to prepare a third die.

The design was prepared by Tiffany & Co. of New York in consultation with a special committee led by Theodore F. Dwight, Chief of the Bureau of Rolls and Library, Department of State. The 13 arrows and the equal width of the bars were restored. The olive branch emerged with 13 leaves and 13 olives. The eagle remained without a crest.

The adoption of the bald eagle as America's symbol has conferred upon this majestic bird a special mantle of affection and meaning in the lives of 190 million people. The enacting clause of the law protecting eagles in the United States takes official recognition of this unique status:

"Whereas, by the Act of Congress and by tradition and custom during the life of this nation, the bald eagle is no longer a mere bird of biological interest but a symbol of the American ideals of freedom."

As the symbol of American Democracy and through the reproduction of its image on billions of coins and one-dollar bills, the likeness of the bald eagle has been spread to the most remote areas of the world, undoubtedly to a greater extent than that of any other living creature.

Americans are never far from the image of the national symbol. It is almost always on the person in the form of a design on currency. The eagle is honored by a perch at the top of flagpoles. It is used as an ornament on buildings and given a commanding position on bridges and other public structures. The eagle is used as an insignia on naval uniforms and as a water mark on Government bond paper. The highest rating a Boy Scout may attain is that of Eagle Scout. Business firms and athletic clubs incorporate the word "eagle" in the names of their organizations. And there is a wide resurgence in the use of ornamental plaques depicting the eagle for mounting over fireplace mantles and doorways.

In the official use of the seal, the likeness of the bald eagle is affixed to Presidential proclamations; to instruments of ratification of treaties; on documents granting authority to persons to negotiate and sign treaties and certain other agreements; to exequaturs, or documents of recognition, issued to foreign consular officers; on Presidential warrants for the extradition of fugitives; on the commissions of all Cabinet officers, ambassadors, ministers, and other Foreign Service officers; and to certain other civil officers. The seal is affixed to envelopes that contain letters of credence and recall and other communications from the President to the heads of foreign governments.

Despite the universal prevalence of its image, most Americans have never seen a bald eagle in the wild, and the chances of their doing so grow increasingly remote. The eagle is one of the victims of progress. Its habitat is polluted and reduced by those who care more for eagles on dollars than eagles on the wing. The most honored bird in America is in danger of becoming confined merely to zoological exhibits.

—Tom Evans.

The eagle adorns flagpoles and statuary. The Columbus Memorial is at the Union Station in Washington.

ROADRUNNERS

Symbols of States

TRIBES AND NATIONS have used birds as insignia or as symbols of supernatural guidance through all history. But in our country, native birds as State emblems are a new idea. Except for Louisiana, Maryland, and Utah, our States reached the twenties without benefit of State birds, although many had borrowed the national symbol, the bald eagle, for their seals and flags. Sparked by campaigns often led by State Federations of Women's Clubs, Audubon societies, ornithological societies, or school officials, most States have now made their choice.

Some have done it by vote of the legislature, some by Governor's proclamation, others by some sort of general balloting leading to an unofficial choice.

Motives behind these campaigns are different from those of the Second Continental Congress when our national symbol was selected. Perhaps the use of the word "symbol" suggests the difference, harking back to medieval heraldry. A bird of legendary powers, suitable for a battle standard and suggesting courage and dignity in civic affairs, has been thought to set the proper tone for a nation's seal or flag.

Few State birds would seem at home on a banner waving over a battlefield. They are more apt to be birds people like to see at their windowsill feeding station or commonly singing along road-sides.

Sponsoring groups often have used the choice of a State bird as a means of arousing general interest in birds and in conservation of wildlife generally. The common device has been a statewide balloting, perhaps with a few suitable choices indicated, either among schoolchildren or any of the public who can be persuaded to vote. With the authority of an impressive number of people in favor of a given bird, the sponsors then go to the Governor or the legislature with a plea that the choice be made official. This is like a popularity contest. It can foster publicity about birds, especially the final winner. The results are sometimes disappointing to those who hope that a distinctive bird, which will be especially appropriate to the State, will be chosen.

Some States have returned to the older heraldic ideas, finding a symbolically suitable bird of unique appearance and character, rather than a familiar dooryard visitor.

The pelican has appeared on the seal and flag of Louisiana from the earliest days of statehood. Presumably chosen by the first Governor, William C. C. Claiborne, it is appropriate ecologically and symbolically.

The pelican, a common and dramatic bird of the southern waters, also has an historic meaning in art as an allegory of Christ. It is in this guise that we see the bird as the State emblem—in the curious pose of a bird drawing blood from its own breast to feed the three young in the nest before it. The ancient belief that the pelican fed its young by its own blood, perhaps stemming from faulty observation of the bird's method of feeding by regurgitation, led to various legends that the bird restored its young by its blood after they had been killed and thus to a parallel with Christ's bringing salvation to man through the sacrifice of his own blood. This heraldic pose, known as "a pelican in her piety," has the old meaning of piety as filial devotion and thus in a wider sense epitomizes civic responsibility.

The brown pelican is listed as the precise species favored by Louisiana, although the birds on seal and flag are white.

The State bird of Maryland has been the Baltimore oriole by a tradition stemming from the 17th century, when the early colonists, and perhaps even Lord Baltimore himself, noted that it bore the family colors of the founder of the Colony. Described by Mark Catesby in his early work on American natural history as the Baltimore-Bird, it has ever since retained its standing in the State.

Utah's choice of the California gull also has been a matter of popular consensus since 1848, when the crops of the first pioneers were saved by the gulls, which came from their nesting areas around Great Salt Lake to eat the hordes of grasshoppers that had descended on the settlement.

Aside from the pelican of Louisiana and the gull of Utah, the only other water bird on the roster of State birds is the loon of Minnesota. Surely, I think, a more systematic selection would have given more places to the many attractive waterfowl and shore birds that have had such a large place in our history. Other large classes of birds seemingly most appropriate as emblems are missing also—notably the birds of prey, which include so many of our most valuable birds as well as those of striking manner and appearance.

Minnesota once had an unofficial choice, the goldfinch. The Minnesota Legislature appointed a commission in 1949 to consider a final verdict. This group, which included ornithologists, museum directors, and State officials, set up five excellent criteria:

"1. Since this is to be a distinctive trademark or insignia for the State, it should be a bird which no other State has as State bird.

"2. It should be fairly well known, though not necessarily abundant.

"3. It should occur throughout the State at least during the nesting season and preferably during the entire year.

"4. It should be a strikingly marked bird whose pattern, even in black and white, would lend itself well to use in insignia.

"5. It should have some special significance for Minnesota."

A vote, first only for schoolchildren, was enlarged to include sportsmen's clubs, other organizations, and interested citizens. A slate of eight birds was submitted by the commission: Pileated

The brown pelican is the State bird of Louisiana.

woodpecker, wood duck, belted kingfisher, kill-deer, scarlet tanager, rose-breasted grosbeak, mourning dove, and common loon. The voting was inconclusive. The schoolchildren chose the scarlet tanager, the most brightly colored of the eight, by a large margin, but no one else voted for it. The legislature found opinion so split that they took no action.

But the Minnesota Ornithologists' Union continued a campaign for the loon, and after several years of effort brought public opinion and the legislature around to their view. In 1961, the legislature passed bills making the loon official. Surely no other bird so stirringly evokes the spell of northern waters and wilderness.

If we consider the State birds as indications of the avian characteristics that have greatest appeal to people, we must conclude that bright color, me-lodious song, and a tendency to live near human dwellings are foremost.

Far and away the favorite, selected by seven States, is the cardinal. A map of those States defines the heart of the cardinal's range, which mostly is far enough north to make the presence of this brilliant bird in winter an especially striking and cheerful note in the landscape. From Illinois, Indiana, and Ohio, the roster swings south to include Kentucky, Virginia, West Virginia, and North Carolina.

Next in favor is the western meadowlark, whose buoyant song often is the most apparent sign of life in the far expanses of western prairie and

Connecticut, Michigan, and Wisconsin have designated a harbinger of spring, the robin, as their bird.

116

The mockingbird, a popular songster, is the bird of Arkansas, Florida, Mississippi, Tennessee, and Texas.

range. Its sponsor States make a pattern, too—from Kansas, Nebraska, and North Dakota to Wyoming, Montana, and Oregon.

The mockingbird long has been a token of the Old South. Five Southern States acclaim it—Florida, Mississippi, Tennessee, Arkansas, and Texas. If we are to judge the character of a State by its choice of bird, we would expect these five to vie in brilliance and versatility of speech and song (by day and night) and in determined and aggressive defense of their territory and tradition.

Three States, Connecticut, Wisconsin, and Michigan, have chosen the robin, one of our most familiar garden birds, whose song often is the first to awaken us on spring mornings.

A word of caution is appropriate here: State birds are not always here to stay. A study of old lists shows several changes, and presumably any State legislature may overthrow the decision of one of its predecessors. Many people, including the Michigan Audubon Society, would like to make such a change in favor of the Kirtland's warbler, a rare bird whose breeding range is confined to stands of young jack-pines in a few counties in Michigan.

The brilliantly colored eastern bluebird, a symbol of happiness, is the bird of Missouri and New York.

The wide-ranging American goldfinch is the State bird of Iowa and New Jersey. It typifies the agricultural lands of both areas.

The eastern bluebird, a gentle and confiding bird traditionally a symbol of happiness, represents Missouri and New York.

The mountain bluebird, the male vividly blue all over in contrast to the blue and rust of the eastern bluebird, nests in the high mountain meadows of the West and is an appropriate choice for Idaho and Nevada.

One other bird has been selected by two States—the black-capped chickadee. This ever-curious little sprite, sparkling with vim and excitement, enlivens the northern forests of Massachusetts and Maine and has won the acclaim of their citizens.

The Carolinas have been changeable in their choices.

North Carolina first designated the Carolina chickadee, seemingly an apt candidate. But this

This hardy, spunky charmer of the backyard feeding shelf, the black-capped chickadee, is the State bird of Maine and Massachusetts.

bird is known colloquially in the State by the old English name of tomtit, a word that had also taken on connotations meaning some little, insignificant thing. State legislators bristled when their homeland became known as the "Tomtit State," and they organized a vote among schoolchildren to find something more impressive. The cardinal won.

South Carolina first chose the mockingbird, but later switched to an especially suitable bird, the Carolina wren.

Historical associations may govern the choice.

Alabama, at the urging of its Ladies' Memorial Association, voted for the flicker, or yellow-hammer, since the Alabama soldiers of the Confederacy were known as "Yellow Hammers," the colors of their cavalry uniforms recalling this woodpecker's striking plumage.

Delaware went even farther into history and myth with its blue hen chicken. This was a term applied to Delaware soldiers in the Revolution, a compliment to their fighting ability based on a legendary blue hen, whose offspring made ace fighting cocks.

Several State birds are notable for the aptness, and uniqueness, of their choice.

The ptarmigan of Alaska, the cactus wren of Arizona, the California quail for its State, lark bunting for Colorado, willow goldfinch for Washington, purple finch for New Hampshire, and the hermit thrush for Vermont all bring to mind the distinctive landscapes of their States.

While the brown thrasher may not seem so closely associated with Georgia, its choice by a vote of schoolchildren gave recognition to a bird of handsome mien and eloquent song. Even more striking birds, unmistakable as emblems, are the scissor-tailed flycatcher of Oklahoma and the road-runner of New Mexico.

We sense a shift of influence from children to sportsmen in the choices of the ruffed grouse for Pennsylvania and the imported ring-necked pheasant for South Dakota.

The outcome of several campaigns for State birds surprised their sponsors.

In Rhode Island, garden clubs and the Audubon Society of Rhode Island undertook to promote an official State bird, the former choice of bobwhite having been just the result of a school contest. Four candidates were given wide publicity—the ruby-throated hummingbird, for the smallest State; the bobwhite; the osprey, the birdwatchers' choice; and the towhee, perhaps the State's commonest summer bird. At the same time, the poultrymen of the State had a bill introduced proclaiming the Rhode Island red chicken as the choice. They were prevailed on to add their candidate to the other ballot, but—with the wild-bird vote split four ways and poultrymen, many commercial interests, county agents, and the fans of the Rhode Island Red Hockey Club uniting behind the hen—the outcome was predictable.

As long as the wood thrush, a bird of woodlands, remains an appropriate choice for the District of Columbia, we may be sure that the green parks and residential areas of that central core of metropolitan Washington have not fallen too far under urban blight. It is indeed a "City in the Woods," where this shy bird's fluting song may be heard at dawn and dusk.

However fitting the choice, a State bird fulfills its purpose as totem or as advocate for conservation only if it is put to effective use by both State and private groups. Old ceremonial functions recede into history, but new possibilities await in teaching awareness of our natural world.

—SHIRLEY A. BRIGGS.

Sports and Recreation

WILLOW PTARMIGAN
NORTHERN SHRIKE

Hunting Is a Positive Thing

APRIL IN ALABAMA is a time of renaissance for all living things. The dogwoods bloom then, and the redbuds and azaleas. The pines get a fresh, new look from the tips of bright green that ornament the old color of last year's growth. Spanish moss festoons the live-oaks and beckons with every warm breeze.

Smells, too, limn the time and place: The sharp odor of pines, the perfumes of flowering shrubs, the heady pungency of freshly plowed ground.

And sounds. Spring is clamorous. Some of the tumult derives from the joy of living, as when children recess on a warm day.

But wild voices in spring have a serious purpose as well—to lure mates and to caution others of a kind who would preempt the home plot. And so every spring-seep and backwater has its chorus of chortling frogs; every hedgerow, its symphony of bird songs; every plum thicket, its whistling bob-white.

From deep in the woodlands comes the most thrilling and challenging sound of all—the reveille and taps a turkey gobbler sounds at dawn and dusk.

His drumlike call is defiance to other toms and an assembly note for his hens. His gobbling can be his undoing as well. It lets the hunter pinpoint his location. Then, with gun and turkey call, the hunter begins his vigil.

Such a prospect of bagging a gobbler took me to Alabama one creation day (as southerners describe a particularly lovely day) a few years ago.

Four times in early evening I and a skilled guide monitored the birds as they went to roost. Four times in early morning we hastened to the place.

The first hour I fought drowsiness. Then increasing discomfort made wakefulness easy. Mosquitoes hummed, but I neither slapped nor scratched. Pea gravel under my seat grew to boulder proportions. My legs turned to stone. Sounds behind and at the edge of my vision fought for attention, yet only my eyeballs turned to see.

Each morning, a gobbler answered our challenging call. Each time, a cautious tom advanced to the last line of shielding vegetation, then retreated unseen.

Each morning, a gobbler answered our challeng-the right or left and, with it, a variety of sounds to fire the imagination and tense the nerves.

And each morning, after several hours of excited anticipation, our quarry sensed something wrong. We returned emptyhanded.

Since that first trip, I have had this transcending experience four times in two other States. I have yet to see a gobbler over the bead of a shotgun, yet I count those excursions among the most satisfying and memorable in a lifetime of hunting. Yes, indeed, game birds offer the best kind of recreation, and a turkey gobbler in spring is the greatest challenge of all.

Why do men go hunting? Maybe we are led by a deep-seated predatory instinct carried forward in our genetic makeup from primitive times. Maybe

123

They are after the ring-necked pheasant, a bird so full of tricks it may foil the experienced hunter.

it is a learned response growing out of family associations, a form of play, or an expression of manliness. You may as well try to explain why men climb mountains, sail an ocean in a 13-foot craft, write an epic, or soar into space. Hunting, whatever the explanation, is a positive thing.

Whatever their reason, nearly 18 million men and women went in pursuit of game in 1965. How many centered their attention on game birds I cannot say, but very likely most of them hunted game birds if for no other reason than that a rich variety and wide distribution of species put them in easy reach of people throughout the country.

All told, 86 species are hunted legally in the United States. Resident game birds total 28 species, and every State has 2 or more. A few Western States claim the richest variety: Idaho has 11 species, and Montana, Colorado, and Washington each has 9. Parts of New England and the Southeast have two resident species, but hunters there derive reasonable satisfaction in what they have.

The sporty ruffed grouse and flashy ring-necked pheasant make up the pool of homegrown game birds in the Northeast. The parts of the Southeast that have a minimum of variety likewise have two of the best, the turkey and bobwhite quail.

The ring-necked pheasant stands in first place in terms of distribution and availability to hunters. It is a highly successful alien. It has done well since it was first introduced in the Willamette Valley of Oregon in 1881. Today, aided by many subsequent plantings, it is established in all suitable habitats in the Nation and is legal as wild game in 34 States.

Regionally, the principal continuous area in which the birds have not established at least token populations is the Southeast and the gulf coast from South Carolina to Louisiana.

What formerly were the central grasslands is the mother lode for pheasants today. In that rich land of corn and grain, the ringneck has found ideal conditions. Fewer than 500 were introduced into the northern prairie region before 1905. Many additional releases were made since in North Dakota, South Dakota, Nebraska, Iowa, and Minnesota. They flourished like the corn—even like weeds in a untended field. By the fifties, in fact, pheasants were almost a pest in some places, even though hunters took more than 82 million of them during that decade in the five States.

Without this showy Asian import, the outdoor scene would be the poorer. Consider the present range of pheasants: They are most abundant on farmlands in the northern third of the States. Before the plow and axe, the grasslands of the Northern Plains were well populated by greater prairie chickens and sage grouse, and the woodlands mainly by ruffed grouse. Modern agriculture changed that. The plains birds did not adapt themselves well to a farm environment. The ruffed grouse disappeared with land clearing. The ringneck occupied this transformed land and filled a sizable void. Today most hunters would not trade him for his predecessors.

Regardless of ancestry, the ringneck today is an all-American bird—tough, flashy, self-assured, persistent. Hunting dogs love him, but he will sneak and run and make a nervous wreck of a staunch pointer and lead a trailing dog out of the county.

Hunters love him, too, but I have seen hunters stand openmouthed and regularly miss the first shots of the season—the roaring flush and loud cackle are that unnerving. When surprise wears off, the big roosters are easy targets in their straight-away flight. With a few days of conditioning, there is no reason for a hunter to miss these lumbering birds, although I have managed to shoot around them.

All the virtues the pheasant has, the southern hunter sees in the bobwhite quail.

The bobwhite, an adaptable bird, has evolved into many races while occupying a range from the Rocky Mountains to the eastern seaboard and south into Mexico. In Washington, Oregon, and Idaho, breeding populations have grown from introduced stock.

The bobwhite is legal game in 34 States, but the hub of its wheel is the Southeast. There "the bird," as it is affectionately called, reaches its zenith in numbers. The open pinewoods of Georgia, palmetto grazing lands of Florida, cottonlands of Alabama, and croplands throughout Dixie, all are

Sharp eyes, keen hearing, and constant alertness make the turkey gobbler a wary bird.

the bobwhite's home. Generous bag limits and long open seasons reflect its prosperity and the keen interest of southern sportsmen.

There's only one way to shoot quail. That is over a pointing dog. To do otherwise is to corrupt what certainly is the most gentlemanly of all wing shooting. Bobwhite were made for pointing breeds. They lie tight for a bold-working dog. With the covey rise, they disperse just right for the working out of singles. They, more than any other game bird, have permitted the refined development of pointing dogs. They occur in combination with woodcock in parts of the South. The result: The sportiest of hunting for dog and gunner.

Ruffed grouse are hunted in 31 States. New England and the Lake States support the thriftiest populations, although the bird occurs throughout the deciduous woodlands of most Northern States and in hilly country farther south.

Grouse have a fast flight, like the bobwhite, and the explosive flush of the ringneck. That spells trouble for many hunters, but the snappy days of autumn and the lingering colors of Indian summer are compensations enough for frequent misses. If you should luck-out on a pair, you have the finest flesh that Nature has put on any game bird.

The ruffed grouse is highly cyclic, particularly in the northern parts of its range. It builds to great numbers every 10 years or so, and then declines rapidly to a remnant few. The how and why of it have intrigued research biologists for years; the prized bird continues to be the enigma of the North.

The turkey is legal game in 21 States, mainly in the East and the Southwest. Successful introductions in a few Western States give promise of extending the range of this trophy bird.

Hefted at arms' length, some of the big gobblers have gone 30 pounds, but, weighed fairly on a butcher's scale, the top size is more like 25. By either measure, the turkey is biggest of the game birds and, for my money, the toughest quarry of all.

This white-tailed ptarmigan, a bird of the high country, had his winter plumage when he was photographed in Colorado at an elevation of 2 miles.

Joseph P. Linduska and his favorite Labrador, Dan, are ready for action on the Eastern Shore of Maryland.

You cannot prove it by me, but successful hunters say a 12-gauge with number 2 or 4 shot is the best bet for fall hunting. In the spring, a called-up gobbler is best dispatched with number 6 or smaller shot in the head and neck.

These—the pheasant, bobwhite, ruffed grouse, and turkey—are the big four among resident game birds. Together they about blanket the country, and most hunters have access to one or more.

Other species add variety.

The Far West offers five kinds of quail—scaled, valley, mountain, Gambel's, and Harlequin (Mearn's). Strong flyers all, and fleet of foot as well, they eke out a living under arid conditions that would cause less hardy species to call it quits.

While these quail are happy in the desert sun, other prized game thrives at the edge of permanent snow.

127

A hunter sets out the "stools." Then he waits.

The rock ptarmigan is such a bird. In Alaska it lives mainly above timberline and on the bleak tundra of the arctic coast. There, on windswept slopes, it feeds on buds of birch and willow, shrubs that the severe climate dwarfs to a few inches. In Colorado you may hunt the white-tailed ptarmigan at the dizzying elevation of 2 miles or more. I did, and I puffed walking downhill. The oxygen is that well diluted.

Seven States still have sporting numbers of prairie chickens, a reminder at best of the days when market hunters trod virgin grasslands to bag them by the wagonload.

Sage grouse and sharp-tailed grouse can still be seen on the arid plains westward from the Dakotas.

Two foreign partridge have made a good go of it in this, their adopted country. The gray or Hungarian (hunkie to his intimates) has fit well into the grainlands in the double layer of Northern States from Wisconsin and Minnesota to Washington, Oregon, and Nevada.

The chukar, from India, has prospered better than well in some of the bleak and once birdless wastelands of the Far West. Goatlike describes chukars. They can make a living where no living exists. They weave through their chosen terrain of canyons, coulees, and steep hills with remarkable speed and agility. Their trail is always upward. You need a stout heart and willing legs to flush a covey.

Less well known is the chachalaca. A gallinaceous bird, it is related to all the species I have discussed. You would never guess it. Long and lean, it bears the dimensions of a magpie or a roadrunner. It claims few of the sporting attributes of the game birds. Even its voice has a predatory ring as it shrieks its name again and again from the tallest tree in a river bottom. It is mainly of Mexican origin, but a few spill over into a small district of the Rio Grande Valley in southern Texas.

Waterfowl are favored game to many. The 43 species that are hunted offer endless variety.

Some are highly adaptable. The mallard, for example, is equally at home in the ricefields of California, the marshes of Chesapeake Bay, and the cornfields of Iowa. When they migrate, they travel to all 50 States and are hunted in all but Hawaii.

The Canada goose in its many subspecies likewise is a willing traveler. It is a stranger only to our island State, although stragglers occasionally reach even there.

The pintail, which on this continent has the widest breeding range of any duck, is a favorite of hunters, particularly in the western flyways.

Other waterfowl are of restricted distribution, mostly because of their specialized food habits. Hunters on inland waters seldom see scoters, eiders, and brant, which favor oceanic environments.

New England hunters lean heavily on black ducks, of which fewer and fewer live in the South and West. Southern hunters have mottled ducks and tree ducks.

Mostly, however, the commonest species reach most parts of the country.

The numbers of waterfowl and of hunters of them go up and down. Water is the key. Most of the production of waterfowl is in the north country, and the main breeding ground on the Cana-

128

dian prairies is a fickle land. Some years are fat; rainfall is abundant. Some years are lean; they are years of drought.

We can measure the crop of ducks by the rain gage—and the number of hunters. In good years, 2 million bluenosed wildfowlers shiver in leaky blinds across the country. A few dry years cut the duck crops, and the number of hunters shrivels to a little more than a half-million stalwarts.

Good years or bad, however, few sports evoke the anticipation that wildfowling does. Day by day in spring and summer, the duck hunter looks anxiously to the north for reports on the brood stock, the rains, and, finally, the hatch. For weeks in early fall he busily repairs his decoys, boats, and gear. In October he hopes for an early Canadian winter to send the birds to his local marsh.

When it happens, the exodus from the North is like a giant weather front. From Alaska to the Maritimes and down to the northern tier of States, the birds begin to move in response to freezeup. As the leading edge of the feathered mass flows south, currents and eddies form. Mallards and pintails tarry over harvested croplands in the North to fatten on residues of barley and wheat. As the weather demands, they move into corn country and finally to ricelands and flooded pin-oak bottoms of the South.

Divers seek the lush aquatics of marshes, rivers, bays, and sounds. Their requirements for deep water hold them to major watercourses and sometimes draw them along a west-to-east diversion from the southward route.

Wherever they settle in, hunters wait. On Long Island Sound, Saginaw Bay, and Chester River, they wait for divers—scaups, redheads, and canvasbacks. A cold morning's work has gone into the hunters' preparation. They may need a hundred or more decoys to lure in the deep-water raft ducks. In potholes, sloughs, and shallow marshes, a dozen decoys may spell a come-on for a few mallards and teal and other dabblers. Elsewhere it may be pass-shooting from behind a fence row or haystack.

But wherever the hunters wait, the misses outnumber the hits. Their reasons or excuses always are the same—the birds were out of range or the hunter did not shoot far enough ahead of the speeding target. On fast-flying ducks, getting out in front of the bird (giving it enough lead) is important. And, of course, the limited killing range of a shotgun requires judgment in selecting shots. The hunter knows these two requirements for bagging ducks only from experience.

Sometimes the knowledge is slow in coming. I recall an incident on Chase Lake in North Dakota.

The wind was howling as it can only in that wide-open country, and the divers were flying with it. It was pass-shooting at its fastest. By midmorning I had run through a box of shells without scratching a bird.

Then came a long string of scaup. I pointed at the first bird, then swung forward for what I judged was a generous lead. Finally my first duck of the day fell out; it was the third bird back.

Yes, indeed, lead is the thing when the target is 40 yards out and hurrying along at 60 or 70 miles an hour. Then putting the shot on a collision course with the duck can be a job for a computer.

In migration and in their choice of nesting grounds, the geese are a breed apart from ducks.

Most of them are products of the arctic and subarctic regions, where water conditions are far more stable than on the drought-susceptible prairies. Geese therefore prospered well in the first half of this decade, while most ducks suffered from long drought.

Geese are even more gregarious than ducks.

The larger sized varieties of the Canadas particularly have strong colonial ties. That explains the separate populations that leave the total flock to appear with unchanging regularity on the same wintering grounds.

They are punctual. Nine years running I timed the arrival of a flock of 10 thousand at Remington Farms on the Eastern Shore of Maryland. Each year the forerunners arrive in the third week of September. Two weeks later the full flight is in.

The fall arrival of geese is something special for us who live within sight and sound of a wintering flock. It is always the same, even after living a long time astride a major concentration: When a skein passes overhead, we interrupt dinner, forget the roast in the oven, leave the sickbed (as I have done against doctor's orders), leave the Angus

Harold Hall of Cambridge, Maryland, puts finishing touches on a cock ring-necked pheasant he has mounted.

half fed to respond to this summons, to be thrilled again by this noble sight.

But our excitement at seeing the geese overhead is nothing compared to the excitement one feels when he crouches in a cornfield or peers from the rim of a pit blind. Life offers few experiences more dear and more keenly repeatable—maybe, just maybe, the longtime duffer's first hole in one, the young bridegroom's possession of his bride, a boy's discovery of "Lines Written Above Tintern Abbey," or seeing again, when the years grow small, the Manitou Heights where one dreamed and learned when the years were bright.

An 80-year-old friend who hunted geese for 60 years remembers—or so it seems—every goose he has ever taken. Now, palsied, he trembles uncontrollably. The sight and sound of a honker pitching to the decoys still unnerve him. But his eyes shine, and when the right moment comes to pick the near bird he is rock steady. He is young again.

In their annual migrations between breeding and wintering grounds, waterfowl tend to follow natural geographic features.

These paths of flight, flyways, include the two coastlines (Atlantic and Pacific Flyways); a broad strip marked generally by the Mississippi River and tributary waters (Mississippi Flyway); and a fourth area marked by the plains country east of the Rocky Mountains (Central Flyway).

Within these broad pathways, the birds seek waters and feeding grounds suitable to their interim needs while moving to their southern terminus. Some species—geese in particular—may make brief stops in traveling from breeding to wintering grounds. Snow geese, for example, sometimes move nonstop from James Bay to the gulf coast of Texas, a journey of 2 thousand miles in 2 days.

But whether the trip is lingering or direct, the routes are well known, and many favored way stations of today were equally well known to the birds (and hunters) of two centuries ago. These traditions of flight place waterfowling apart from other types of hunting, wherein the hunter seeks out the game. With waterfowl, the quarry comes to the hunter, who has long since learned of the favorite flight lanes and feeding and resting spots.

The result is what you would expect. Place-names of major concentrations of ducks and geese are as familiar to the wildfowler as are the names of major cities. Susquehanna Flats and Currituck Sound, Horseshoe Lake and Stuttgart, Lower Souris and Galveston Bay, Bear River and Klamath Basin—these are names to excite the wildfowler.

130

They identify as easily as New York City and Chicago and recall far more pleasant memories.

To the 43 species of waterfowl, you can add 15 other species of migratory birds now legally hunted.

There are rails and gallinules, chickenlike inhabitants of marshlands and wet areas. Shy, secretive birds of feeble flight, they flush close with legs dangling. Their labored movement makes them an easy target. As a sporty game bird, they leave a lot to be desired; so, also, the product that emerges from the frying pan or broiler.

They have their champions, who argue otherwise, but the fact is that the demand on them is so light as to make long seasons and generous bag limits possible.

In the group is the smallest hunted game species, the sora rail. At slightly over 2 ounces, it is about one-third the size of a bobwhite.

The coot may be considered as a member of the rail family, although by habits of feeding and flight it holds greater kinship to waterfowl.

There are also the common snipe and American woodcock and several migratory forms of upland habits—the band-tailed pigeon, white-winged and mourning doves, and the lesser sandhill crane, which divides its time between marsh and upland.

Of these, the mourning dove deserves special mention. It has the widest breeding distribution of any game species in the United States. It nests in 48 States and is hunted legally in 30. The estimated annual harvest of 20 million is greater than that of any other game bird.

Dove hunting can be the least strenuous of all shooting sports and the most difficult. Crouched in a fence row at the edge of a millet field or seated on a hamper at a watering hole, a hunter has little to do but to pick his shots. What shots! A dove pitching and rolling downwind can be an impossible target, and the hunter who fills a limit of 12 with a box of 25 shells can brag about it.

The changes of the past half century in farming methods, enlargement of farms, and uses of land have cut into game production in many sections. Yet at the same time game management has matured as a science to help offset losses.

We no longer can hunt out the back door, yet improvements in travel enable city sportsmen to reach the hunting hotspots perhaps a thousand miles away as never before.

A practiced retriever, such as this Labrador, is a helpful aide for any hunter.

Or, if they cannot because of pressures of business or the cost of a long trip, the commercial-shooting preserve, a recent development, may fill their bill.

On these pay-as-you-shoot tracts, the operator releases artifically propagated game birds on posted land. You can shoot as many as you want (or whatever you can afford) at a fixed price per bird. Many preserves offer a variety of species. On practically all of them it is possible to hunt at least mallards and pheasants. Some offer bobwhite, chukar partridge, wild turkey, and others.

The well-run operations offer challenging hunting in natural surroundings. Most of them maintain a kennel of good hunting dogs. The hunter need only deliver himself to the preserve and take to the field.

Their rapid growth attests their popularity. There were 756 in 21 States in 1954. Ten years later, the program had been sanctioned in 44 States, and the number of preserves had increased to 2,121, of which 563 were open to the public and 1,558 were maintained as private operations.

Sport hunting, always popular, is growing like the green bay tree. In the past two decades, the number of licensed hunters in the United States showed a growth of 80 percent while the population was increasing 43 percent.

Why? Our economy is growing. The standard of living is improving. There is more leisure time. Landowners have been helping to meet the demand for hunting while augmenting their farm income.

As an adjunct to the commercial-preserve-type of operation, more and more farmers are cashing in on natural game crops. The idea clashes with the concept of free hunting that many believe in, but the fact is that a goodly number of men and their sons are ready to pay for access to hunting and the services that are a part of such operations. Besides, an enterprise like this abets good game management among landowners.

Some regions produce good game crops as a byproduct of normal agriculture.

In South Dakota, for example, the ring-necked pheasant is the basis for a sizable industry as 50 thousand out-of-State hunters arrive each fall to share in the bounty. While there, they leave about 12.5 million dollars, a fair fraction of the total of 100 million dollars that makes recreation second only to agriculture in State income.

The benefits touch everyone—operators of eating places, motels, locker plants (which process birds at 50 cents to 1 dollar each), and landowners, many of whom fortify farm income by providing room and board and offering services such as bird processing.

Waterfowl can be a liability to farmers when they descend in untold thousands to glut on crops. They attract hunters, too, and the depredations are multiplied if there is no control.

But consider Lissee Prairie on the coastal plains of Texas.

Lissee Prairie touches elbows with the gulf coast, an industrial giant of rapidly expanding human populations. Between too many geese and ducks and too many hunters, the rice growers were at wit's end for years. Now the welcome sign is out. For fees of up to 15 dollars a day, hunters get a place to hunt.

The farmer has a means of regulating numbers of birds and compensation for his trouble and crop losses. Others in the community offer guide services, food and lodging, and facilities to meet the other requirements of hunters away from home.

The needs of the hunt are many. Altogether they make a giant industry.

A national survey of hunting and fishing in 1960 revealed that 1 billion dollars are spent annually on hunting. That includes only expenditures relating directly to the hunt and not the business generated in many directions.

One example that comes readily to my mind but perhaps not to yours is the enormous field of publications—newspapers, magazines, and books that in season or out lean heavily on hunting subjects and advertising.

The National Sporting Goods Association reported that consumer purchases of sporting arms and ammunition added 282 million dollars in 1964. But, as stated by E. B. Mann, editor of the magazine Shooting Industry, "that was only the small detonating cap that set off the powder that moved a mountain of business."

He added: "In 1964, 1,387 manufacturers outside the arms and ammunition industry produced and sold equipment for the hunter and shooting sportsman, and nobody knows how much shooters spent for the other gadgetry that goes with their sports."

The sporting firearms industry employed more than 20 thousand persons in 1963, had a payroll of 100 million dollars, and bought nearly 185 million dollars' worth of materials from other segments of the economy. Another 25 million dollars in sales were rung up by makers of handloading components and tools.

Automobile travel in 1963, for the purpose only of hunting, added to nearly 5 billion miles, and the cost was more than 310 million dollars. Suppliers of food, lodging, camping equipment, hunting apparel, public transportation, and boats for hunting use only reaped a total sales of 675 million dollars to hunters in 1963. Dogs, too. About 150 million dollars were spent on these working companions of the hunt.

No doubt about it. Americans are oriented to the outdoors, and sport hunting, with game birds as the mainstay, is one of the popular escapes from the stresses of modern living. In pursuing this healthful diversion, 18 million persons have invested in requirements of the hunt; that, with accessory needs, has built an industry bigger than that of any four spectator sports combined.

Sportsmen have been generous in their support of programs to assure that game supplies will not be diminished. Consider, for example, the hunter-sponsored Federal Aid in Wildlife Restoration Act. Since its inception in 1937, this excise tax on sporting arms and ammunition has put more than 250 million dollars into programs for research, management, and acquisition of lands for wildlife. These purchases now total nearly 3 million acres.

Sales of duck stamps since 1937 have amounted to more than 84 million dollars. Sales of State hunting licenses are about 70 million dollars each year. According to the National Shooting Sports Foundation, sportsmen invest 150 million dollars each year in programs to preserve the Nation's wildlife.

But mark well: Game management is never definitive to the point of serving hunters' interests alone. A marsh preserved for waterfowl is a marsh preserved also for dozens of nongame species. A marsh preserved for the hunter serves not only his purpose but the many nonconsumptive uses of birdwatchers, photographers, and others. In serving recreational purposes and supporting broad business interests, game birds have "selfish" custodians. They will not see their ranks depleted.
—Joseph P. Linduska.

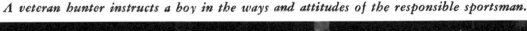

A veteran hunter instructs a boy in the ways and attitudes of the responsible sportsman.

To See; To Record

BIRDS ARE TO SEE, to hear, to store in memory. Many of us, even though an oculist tells us we have 20–20 vision, do not see all that we might and so miss the beauties of form, shape, color, size, and perspective that a sensitive artist and an experienced birdwatcher train themselves to see.

That you can do, too, and so enlarge your knowledge, alertness, and awareness of the wonderful world around you.

Try this: Look closely at the next pigeon or sparrow you encounter in a park or your yard. After a few minutes, when it is gone, see if you can describe it (as to a friend who asks you what you saw on Mulberry Street) in exact terms. Not that it was "big" or "rather small" or "a sort of dark color with some lighter patches someplace," but that it was 6 inches from beak to tail and medium gray all over, except for an inch-wide patch of dull white on its breast and black tailfeathers.

You will discover that seeing in this way with mind and both eyes wide open is fun and educational, whatever your interests—people, the trees you pass unseeingly every day, the waterfall you saw on your trip last summer, the carefully arranged flowers Aunt Emma had on her dinner table last Sunday, the fine points of the champion at the dog show you attended.

As to birds: After a time of careful looking at them, you will find (as have 10 million other birdwatching Americans) that you will want to see more and keep track of what you see. Binoculars, a camera, a notebook, and perhaps a taperecorder and phonograph records will help you do that.

A good pair of binoculars or birdglasses will multiply your pleasures by allowing you to make closeup, detailed studies. A 7-power binocular will bring the bird seven times closer and make distinguishing field marks seven times more obvious.

Think before you buy. Buy them from a dealer who will guarantee that the glass is free of defects and in perfect adjustment and that repair parts are available. Get the best you can afford. Treat them carefully. Then they will serve you a long time.

I recommend a prism binocular with central focusing, coated optics, wide field, and between 6- and 9-power magnification. To insure sufficient light, the objectives (the lenses farthest from the eyes) should have a diameter in millimeters at least five times the power of the glass. Thus a 7-power binocular (the most popular with birders) should read 7 x 35 or more.

For average birdwatching, 6- or 7-power magnification is enough. If, however, you want to view distant birds on extensive mudflats, say, or over wide bodies of water, 8-, 9-, or 10-power binoculars are preferable.

Some persons find it hard to hold steady any binocular above 9-power. For them, I suggest a supplementary telescope. Those of 20- or 30-power are most useful. Above 40 power, the field generally is too small, light is inadequate, and wind vibrations and heat shimmers may be too great. For sharp, steady images with a telescope, one needs a sturdy tripod—one that is sturdy enough to stop wind vibrations but can be adjusted quickly and locked firmly in place.

With or without binoculars, you will find your interest growing in birdwatching, a hobby that brings you companionship, a sharing of interests with friends and family, healthful exercise outdoors, and an outlet of many facets. You can choose the aspect you consider best suited to your temperament, disposition, inclination, and energy.

You may find full satisfaction in just looking and listening. You may want to know more about identification of birds, or birdbanding, or conservation.

Very likely you will wish to keep records of your observations of the migration, distribution, population changes, behavior, and classification of birds.

You may start with identification and details of the distribution and habitat preference for each species. You may like to keep a list of the birds you see and name. Some observers keep daily lists, trip lists, county lists, and a year list. Many shut-ins derive pleasure from keeping a list of the birds they see from their window or balcony. Each new bird visitor gives as much satisfaction as a new stamp does to a stamp collector.

Many persons use their first year list as the basis of a life list, an accumulation of all the species they have ever seen, with the place and date of each observation.

Another way to record your adventures in birding, train yourself to "see" more, and heighten your enjoyment is to take pictures of birds.

Every year more people do so. Recently I visited 44 States. In each, I met ardent birdwatchers of all degrees of experience using cameras of many types, from the very simplest and cheapest to elaborate ones with an assortment of lenses. On trips to choice places, such as the Everglades National Park in Florida, I have seen 25 bird photographers in a day aiming still and movie cameras at the exciting variety of birds feeding in the marshes along the Anhinga Trail.

Bird photography is by no means a sport for a select few or only for those who live in the country. I took my first picture of a bird, a king rail, near the edge of New York City when I was a sophomore in high school.

Far from the crowds and power boats, a birdwatcher explores the Ocmulgee River swamp in Georgia.

Hunting with a camera is a satisfying, captivating, year-round hobby, on which there is no closed season, no bag limit, and no protected species. You can go out when and as often as you want to. You can spend hours or just minutes stalking your prey and (unlike fishing, say) always get results.

When working in wilderness areas, far more knowledge of the outdoors, stalking skill, patience, perseverance, and capacity for exacting work are required by the photographer than by the hunter, who can bring down game from a distance.

Famous bird artists, like Roger Tory Peterson and John Henry Dick, say they get more fun out of bird photography than they do out of working on their paintings in the studio.

I add my own testimony to that: I work 12 months a year with birds and efforts to protect them, and my work brings me excitement, absorbing interest, and much happiness. Yet if I were asked to select the days that give me the greatest satisfaction, I would say the days in the field with my camera.

If you are already a photographer, there may be

This picture of wood ibis in flight over Everglades National Park, Florida, exemplifies the experience, skill with camera and film, and artistic sense that every good photographer of birds needs.

little new that I can tell you about equipment. If you are a beginner, I suggest first that you visit a camera shop and get their advice.

A single lens reflex camera with a sharp telephoto or lens of long focal length is most satisfactory, since it permits you to see exactly what you are getting right up to the instant of exposure. With it, you can determine whether the subject is large enough, the focus absolutely sharp, the background satisfactory, and the composition good.

Be sure that the camera you purchase has a wide selection of speeds and a long bellows expansion (or the equivalent) and permits the interchanging of lenses.

Selection will be governed by the size of the

The photographer used a neutral background to avoid distracting detail in this picture of parula warblers in Todd Wildlife Sanctuary in Maine.

negative or transparency you want. Many professionals insist on a 2¼ x 3¼ or even 4 x 5 negative, but that requires heavy equipment and expensive film. For good enlargements of black and white photographs, these larger sizes are by far the best.

Today, however, most bird photographers take color slides, using a single-lens reflex 35 mm camera with a telephoto lens. This equipment is generally light, and the film relatively inexpensive. Modern color film of this size is satisfactory for enlargements and is convenient for projection on a screen.

For the use of lenses above 6-power magnifica-

tion, a tripod is essential. Be sure that it is sturdy and easy to adjust.

Flash photography permits you to take pictures at night and in places where the sunlight is weak. Often the use of flash helps to reinforce daylight and illuminate heavy shadows. This artificial light can be concentrated to produce illumination many times greater than sunlight, so one can use fast speeds and small apertures, which seldom or never are possible otherwise. The faster the speed, the more motion it will arrest; the smaller the aperture, the greater the depth of field and overall sharpness of the image.

The kind of flash equipment you should get

Allan D. Cruickshank, of Rockledge, Florida, took this notable photograph of a common egret feeding its young at Galveston Bay, Texas. Capturing stories like this on film spurs the photographer to new tests of skill.

will depend on the type of camera you use, the speeds at which you plan to work, and the amount of money you feel you can afford. As in all purchases, be sure the one you select is manufactured by a reputable company and purchased from a trustworthy retailer. Double check to make sure it can be synchronized with your shutter and that there is some means of remote control.

You can get further help and advice from fellow birdwatchers and friends who use cameras. Books also will tell you many things that you will like to know. Your public library will have several on photography. My favorite—naturally—is *Hunting with the Camera,* published by Harper and Row in 1957 and written by me and several colleagues.

Motion picture photography of birds is just as easy, if not easier, than good still-camera work. Satisfactory equipment and film are generally more expensive, though.

Except for flight shots or sequences from boats and airplanes, never take motion pictures without mounting the camera on a sturdy tripod with a head that can be smoothly tilted and panned.

I recommend that you purchase the very best 16-mm movie camera that you can afford. Be sure that it is sturdy enough for rough field work, that it offers a wide assortment of speeds, and that you can use at least 1-, 3-, and 6-inch lenses. Models that permit direct focusing and composition through the lens, particularly while the film is being exposed, are most desirable. Most bird pictures will be taken with 3, 6, or higher powered lenses, but you need the 1-inch lens for most scenes and most human activities.

In still photography, black and white pictures are popular and widely used in publications; motion pictures of birds are now usually in color.

Since most birds are shy or difficult to approach, the photographer must often work from a blind or hide even when he uses telephoto lenses. Anything that conceals the photographer and does not frighten the subject may be used as a blind. In emergencies I have hidden in pup tents, cars, hollow trees, large boxes, canoes, caves, or shallow excavations covered with branches.

It is much more convenient, however, to have an ever-ready, light, easily erected, portable blind

A photographer took this photograph of an incubating California gull from a blind on Bear River National Wildlife Refuge near Brigham, Utah.

Birds, like this blue jay, also are inquisitive.

Birdwatchers have an enjoyable outing at Theodore Roosevelt National Park in North Dakota.

To get good pictures of birds, one needs—among other things—a sturdy tripod.

The wing prints of a crow gave Jack Dermid, of Wilmington, North Carolina, a chance to take an unusual photograph.

At the Lyman K. Stuart Observatory, Laboratory of Ornithology, Cornell University, students and visitors watch and photograph birds and hear the sounds of the birds transmitted from the pond into the observatory.

A portable blind is indispensable for the professional photographer of birds. The birds soon get used to it.

about 3 feet square and 6 feet high. A cheap, easy to construct framework consists of four uprights 6 feet high, driven into the ground at each corner of a 4-foot square and linked together at the top with galvanized wire. The base of the poles should be pointed so they may be driven into the ground more easily.

The cover should be opaque yet fairly light. I find bark cloth (used for slipcovers) most satisfactory. Green, gray, or brown colors are prefer-

able. The most easily constructed cover consists of two 17-foot lengths of yard-wide material sewed together to form a cross. Then sew three sides together to within a foot of the bottom. Use safety pins or preferably a brass zipper to close the fourth side or entrance. Make sure the cover fits snugly as the flapping of the cloth may frighten the birds. The pictures can be taken through a 24-inch slit on one side, partly closed by safety pins.

—ALLAN D. CRUICKSHANK.

143

BALTIMORE ORIOLE
CARDINAL
BROWN THRASHER
MOURNING DOVE

How To Attract Birds

IF YOU WANT TO ATTRACT BIRDS, bear in mind that wild birds seek only two essentials—food and protection. Their needs are simple but must be provided in the way that various species desire and require. If you follow a few rules you should have no difficulty in supplying what is needed for a start. Once you have gained a little experience, I am sure you will find the rewards so satisfying, inspiring, and exciting that you will want to expand your activities.

It takes little money—precious little when you consider the many hours of enjoyment you gain.

If you live in the country or in a quiet neighborhood with plenty of trees, attracting birds should be easy. You may need some ingenuity if you live in a town apartment or a treeless housing development. But if you really want to attract birds, almost any location can be made to serve.

Birds are active and spend most of the day seeking food. Usually most resident and migrant species in the neighborhood quickly locate suitable food placed out for them somewhere near their normal travel routes.

Grain foods are the simplest to place out and

attract the greatest variety of visitors. Mixtures are better than any single kind and may include milo, millet, wheat, sunflower seed, and many other good varieties. Breadcrumbs are fine, too, if they can be kept dry and protected from the wind, for they are light and more easily blown away than seeds.

Suet is effective in attracting such insect eaters as woodpeckers, nuthatches, creepers, and chickadees.

Tubes of sugar-water in season for hummingbirds and fruit, such as raisins, cut apples, and oranges, for waxwings, mockingbirds, and other berry-eaters, complete the basic all-round larder.

Here is a list of foods several groups of birds accept readily:

Woodpeckers: Suet, cracked nuts, corn.

Jays: Suet, cracked nuts, corn, peanuts, sunflower seeds.

Titmice, chickadees, nuthatches: Suet, cracked nuts, shelled and broken peanuts, sunflower seeds, breadcrumbs.

Mockingbirds, catbirds, thrashers, hermit thrushes, robins: Cut apples and oranges, currants, raisins, breadcrumbs.

Starlings: Cut apples, currants, raisins, suet, scratch feed, table scraps.

Blackbirds, cardinals, towhees: Sunflower seeds, corn, shelled and broken peanuts, scratch feed.

Juncos, finches, sparrows: Scratch feed, millet, wheat, screenings, small seed mixtures, breadcrumbs.

If you want to go to extra effort, you can prepare food cakes from any number of ingredients you very likely have on hand. You make them by scalding, or partly cooking, to a heavy consistency, coarsely ground grains (like corn or oatmeal) and adding eggs in any form, seed grains, chopped nuts, raisins, currants, or similar food and mix them with melted suet. Honey or other heavy sweeteners sometimes are added.

Such a preparation offers a varied diet and can be poured or pressed into holes drilled in food sticks, coconut feeders, empty dried sunflower heads, or preshaped molds, depending on the place you intend to put it. The suet helps protect the grain from wet weather and reduces spillage and waste.

A Carolina chickadee in winter feeds on suet held in a piece of hardware cloth. In cold weather, a fat-rich food, such as suet, is welcomed by chickadees, nuthatches, woodpeckers, and other birds.

To make a simple, inexpensive feeder, salvaged bottle caps are nailed to a foot-long piece of wood and a short length of picture wire is attached to it by two screw-eyes. Suet then is pressed into the caps.

Brownie Scouts display bird feeders they made to parents and leaders.

Sunflower seeds on a feeding station brought an evening grosbeak close to the camera lens.

A window feeder like this brings birds close. The pine tree near the feeder provides a perching place for the birds and a bit of shelter.

I suppose there are a thousand different ways to present food to birds, but the best ones are those that conserve feed, keep it available regardless of weather, and give the birds a haven safe from disturbance and predators while they eat.

The feeding devices themselves need not be elaborate or expensive.

One of the most successful feeders I know of consists only of a wide board with cleat rails. This platform is located on the window sill of a quiet study room of a country home. Flanked, but not hidden, by tall bushes and protected by an overhanging eave, this feeder is visited constantly by a great variety of birds and is a never-failing source of delight to those in the room. Breadcrumbs and grain foods are simply broadcast on the tray

through the window from a supply kept nearby in a small plastic bag. It is doubtful whether an odd length of a short board can be made to fill a more useful or enjoyable purpose. If sides, and back are provided, such a shelter makes an excellent feeder on a tree or post.

The more feeders you have, within limits, the better. Many people content themselves with one, not realizing the value of having many.

Several feeders are especially desirable wherever certain species or individuals tend to dominate and drive others away from a single source of food. Several feeders also serve to increase the number of species wherever a single location may not be ideal for all.

One woman I know had 23 seed feeders of vari-

Coconut shells can be made into useful feeders by sawing off one end, inserting a simple perch, and installing a screw-eye to fasten it by wire to a tree limb. These are filled with seeds and suet.

They clean out the bird-feeding shelter before they restock it with an assortment of food.

ous kinds scattered about the four sides of her home, accommodating as many as 75 birds at a time. What a riot of activity her place was when purple finches were in!

Another tip: You are missing half the fun if you are satisfied with merely attracting birds to within 25 or 30 feet. Bring them right up close. Even an English sparrow or starling becomes exciting at arm's length when you can easily see plumage patterns and individual variation in color. The pleasure of seeing birds at close range far outweighs the extra effort in bringing them near.

The trolley feeder is a way to draw birds from a distance to close ranges. It is a roofed tray suspended by pulleys from a taut line between your window sill and a tree or post. The feeder is serviced at the sill and pulled by a hand line to the far end, where birds are more apt to find the food and can become adjusted to feeding at it without fear. After the birds become accustomed to it, move it closer to the sill and repeat the operation until the birds are feeding close by. The trolley feeder is particularly useful, indeed essential, for attracting birds to second-story levels. But be careful of quick movements when you wish to enjoy birds close at hand, because they can see you well, too, and most species take alarm quickly.

The trolley feeder is but one example of the self-dispensing hopper type, which perhaps is the most popular kind for providing grains. The hopper feeder, stocked with an all-purpose balanced mixture of grains and seeds, attracts a wider variety of birds and feeds them more efficiently than a simple roofed tray.

If you want to see the birds from a particular window which looks out on a windy, treeless situation, you should have a revolving food house or "weather-vane" feeder. It is ornamental and practical. It is designed to swing with the wind, so that its contents are protected during stormy weather, when birds are apt to need food the most. It may be constructed with a hopper arrangement, but ordinarily it is only a tray with a roof on it.

A coconut shell with a generous hole in one end makes an attractive and efficient feeder. Fill it with chopped suet, cracked nuts, small seeds, or other suitable food. Suspended by a short twine from an eave of the house or tree limb, the coconut larder entices chickadees, titmice, and nuthatches. Starlings and sparrows, which some people do not like, seldom feed at such free-swinging devices.

Young people particularly like to fill and hang coconut feeders. A small can with a hole cut in the end may serve just as well, but a coconut feeder has a special appeal.

A small, rough log a foot or so long makes another kind of rustic feeder. Drill holes an inch or so in diameter in it and fill them with peanut butter, suet, or bird cake. Feeders of this type are usually suspended from one end on a tree limb, where they attract the same species of avian acrobats as the coconut larder.

An ordinary mousetrap makes a simple, effective holder for weather-resistant foods, such as suet.

The trigger wire and bait pan usually are removed, although this is not necessary. If it is used in winter, all metal parts should be painted, taped, or otherwise insulated so it will not adhere to the tongues of birds, which may touch it during subzero temperatures. The spring-loaded bar on the trap is then clamped over the piece of suet or food cake, and the feeder is fastened or suspended from a tree limb or post.

Do not overlook hummingbirds. These jeweled darts are easy to attract in season with artificial feeders. Attach a few strips of red or orange ribbon to a cluster of test tubes, in which you put a sirup of one part sugar to three parts water. Hang the tubes on a stake in your garden or among shrubs. If you are in hummer country and they are around, you will not have to wait long for action. One man in the Ozarks attracted 200 ruby-throats

An Oregon junco visits a feeding station in Benton County, Oregon.

at one time during the mating season; his large garden with feeders resembled a colorful parade with an air show in progress.

Once you get hummers coming, check your feeders often. Hummingbirds seldom approach a depleted feeder. In some mysterious way, they seem to know precisely when refills have been added. If you spend much time outdoors and can remain absolutely motionless (dark glasses will help to mask eye motion), hummers that are accustomed to your presence will feed from a dispenser you hold in your hand. One hummer admirer enticed a ruby-throat to feed while perched on his finger—but that comes only as a reward for much patience, constant cultivation of confidence, and elimination of all sources of alarm.

You and the children will enjoy watching birds drink and bathe. A watering facility is worth the extra effort. Water is second only to food as an attraction in many localities. In fact, in the hot, dry months or desert areas, water may be the factor that determines the presence and survival of individuals or populations.

The water you provide will appeal to a great variety of birds if you observe certain practices. Water should be kept clean and fresh. The birds should be adequately protected from predators—especially when they bathe. Birds with wet feathers are especially vulnerable to their foes.

Satisfactory watering and bathing facilities are usually more expensive to provide for birds than feeding devices but are apt to be fully as rewarding.

The pedestal-type bird bath is as good as any for the average location; if it has a small fountain, it can hardly be surpassed. Moving water has special appeal to birds, particularly if it is a bit noisy. The sound of moving water seems to draw tired migrants like a magnet.

Ground-level watering and bathing pools are risky for birds unless they are surrounded by an expanse of lawn. If perching or wading places are not provided, the value of such places to birds is not apt to be realized. But given lots of open space on all sides of the pool and at least one shallow edge—less than 3 inches deep—the deeper lilypond or fishpond can be made to serve birds safely, too, especially if there is a spray fountain near the shallow edge.

Once the basic facility is purchased or constructed, water can be provided all year long. Birds drink and often bathe in the winter if they have an opportunity. Some birdlovers place an electric heating element in the bath to keep the water free of ice.

It takes longer to attract birds by providing them with their favorite trees and shrubs than placing out food and water, but planting for birds has such great possibilities that every serious birdlover does well to keep birds in mind when he plans basic landscaping or makes periodic changes.

Actually, vegetation is basic to birdlife. The kind and abundance of plants you have in your neighborhood and about your home largely determine what kind of birds you are apt to attract to your window.

Directly or indirectly, plants supply birds with all their needs. Some plants have more value to birds than others. So, if birds are to be enjoyed fully about the home, an effort should be made

The man is installing a sheltered feeder on a stump in the yard of a suburban home. In subdivisions where developers are generous in sparing the natural trees and shrubbery, homeowners can expect greater variety and numbers of birds.

to plant the trees, shrubs, and other vegetation they like best.

Birds seek out trees and shrubs for food, protection, and nesting—but the needs of birds for these essentials vary by species and group.

Juncos, goldfinches, siskins, and most native sparrows depend largely on seeds for food. Mockingbirds, catbirds, and robins eat many fruits and berries. Insects comprise the staple diets of vireos, warblers, chickadees, woodpeckers, and nuthatches. Hummingbirds must have the nectar from flowers to live.

All use trees and shrubs for nesting.

A few plants have such a wide range of growing tolerances and attract so many kinds of birds that they deserve special consideration for planting almost anywhere in the more temperate regions of the country.

If you have a corner of your yard that is hard to maintain or a side facing vacant property, you will find that planting raspberries, blackberries, and elderberries—preferably in combination—will attract many kinds of birds. The resulting tangle is a welcome home to thicket-dwellers like catbirds, song sparrows, wrens, and thrashers, who live and nest in such places. The big attraction is the berries. More than 100 species of birds eat the fruits of these plants.

Ranking next in popularity with the birds, and of greater value in landscaping, are dogwood, sumac, redcedar, pokeberry, and mulberry. Because the mulberry drops its purple fruits readily, it should be planted where stains will not discolor walks or drives. More than 50 species of birds feed on these 5 plants, which can be grown almost anywhere.

Jewelweed and trumpet-creeper are among the favorites of hummingbirds.

Bird houses have been used since ancient times to attract birds by providing them with places to nest. Early colonists in North America saw how Indians hung gourds for purple martins on trees they had trimmed to bare stubs.

Our trend toward urbanization intensifies the need for nest boxes in cities and suburbs. Bird houses are useful to birds, a source of enjoyment to us, fun to make, and utilitarian: Watching a pair of birds nest and rear their young in a house

Gourds make natural-looking nest boxes for a variety of songbirds, including house wrens.

Boy Scouts Charles Littleton, David Miles, and John Littleton, of Troop 29 in College Park, Maryland, put up a wren box. The birds liked the home.

The box was the birthplace of a large family of wood ducks, which are cuddled close together (right corner), trying to escape the boatman's attention. Many States are helping this species by erecting nesting boxes.

The owner of a country store at Church Creek, Maryland, guaranteed his purple martin houses— one in front of the store was occupied by birds.

you made brings a special joy. The fact that most birds love insects and have extra mouths to feed during the gardening season is an added dividend of providing housing.

The house should fit the bird. Wrens select little houses tucked in close to bushes or low trees. Bluebirds like houses in sunny, open places and about 5 or 6 feet off the ground. Woodpeckers and nuthatches prefer their houses in trees or on the tops of high stumps. Purple martins, the only communal nesting neighborhood birds, will occupy multiple dwelling units.

More than 50 kinds of birds can be enticed to nest in a box if certain requirements are met. One family living in a country place of many trees, shrubs, and vines counted 17 species with about 40 nests in their yard, some in natural locations and some in artificial boxes and baskets provided for them. What a treat they enjoyed all spring, observing nesting activity, counting production, and watching parents and offspring!

An experimental housing project for birds by the Fish and Wildlife Service on a 3.5-acre plot in Maryland increased nesting from 7.6 to 26.6 broods an acre in 4 years. Your chances of having birds nest in your yard are much better if you put out several nesting boxes. You cannot always foretell which species will be abundant or scarce in your locality one year or another. But you will be in the best possible position to enjoy nesting birds and their youngsters if you provide each potential resident with more than one possible nesting site. The number of houses varied from 47 to 99 during the experiment in Maryland with 54 percent average annual occupancy.

It is unwise to have a large number of boxes constructed for similar species placed too close together. Birds usually insist on defending exclusive territories, especially against their own kind. Exceptions to this principle are tree swallows and the gregarious purple martins.

Houses should be well built, preferably of wood, and so constructed as to be rainproof, cool, and easily cleaned. Except for purple martins, whose houses can be painted white, it is best to treat nesting boxes with a dull green, brown, or gray stain. Smooth lumber should be roughened, grooved, or cleated on the inside of deep boxes to assist the young in climbing to the opening. Perches at entrances may be of greater help to enemies than to the residents.

That a house is not used the first season is no indication of faulty construction or improper placement. There may be more nesting facilities than the local population can occupy that year.

Houses should be located fairly low, say within reach of a man on the ground. It is wise to put them in a sunny place on a pole (with a catproof tin collar) instead of a tree. They should preferably face away from prevailing winds.

If you need more information—as to specifications for a bluebird house, for example, or ways to discourage unwanted cats, squirrels, and starlings from your feeder—I suggest you visit your librarian, who can refer you to books on feeding, planting, and building houses for birds. Natural

Purple martins like company when they raise their families. This simple house will accommodate eight breeding pairs. Houses must be made so they can be cleaned out when the nesting period is over.

history magazines often have articles on how to attract birds as well as advertisements to tell you about sources of supplies.

Local representatives of State fish and game departments, the Fish and Wildlife Service, and county agents often can give advice.

But do not put it off. Start now to prepare for the season ahead, whether it be time for planting, nesting, or winter feeding.

—Winston E. Banko.

The Christmas Count

EVERY YEAR in a thousand places in the United States and Canada some 15 thousand men and women and boys and girls, who love birds and the out-of-doors, take part in the Christmas count, whose purpose is to keep track of our changing bird populations.

The count is sponsored by the National Audubon Society and has grown steadily, until today it is the most exciting, stimulating, birdwatching event of the year for most of the bird clubs in the United States and Canada.

Twenty-five reports were submitted in 1900; in 1965–1966, more than 750 reports were sent to Audubon House.

To insure accuracy, rigid rules are followed. The count must be made during the Christmas period—12 or 13 days in late December or early January—as announced each year in Audubon Field Notes. It may cover only one calendar day. Each count area must fill or fit within a circle 15 miles in diameter. The circle is divided into sectors. Teams assigned to each sector spend the entire day trying to spot as many birds as possible within that area. Clubs making the most thorough coverage may have special boat parties searching for birds on the ocean, rivers, bays, or other waterways within the circle. They may even use airplanes as an aid in checking waterfowl carefully.

Dawn-to-dusk or longer counts are preferred. Those of less than 8 hours (except in arctic areas or at sea) are not accepted. As many good observers as a club can put in the field may participate. Two or three persons may cover some rural districts. Larger clubs may have 50 or 100 or more observers in their richest circle. Experienced leaders check all unusual identifications. Careful substantiating details are given for all birds that are unusual in a particular area at Christmas time.

Special owl parties may start one second past midnight and work until dawn, listening for owls and other nocturnal birds, each of which is marked on a map to avoid counting it twice. Other participants continue after dusk and may work as late as midnight, trying to add one more owl, goatsucker, or rail to the list.

Persons in all walks of life participate—merchants, students, scientists, housewives, physicians, clergymen, farmers, writers, civil servants. One of them, Allan D. Cruickshank, lecturer, editor, photographer, and instructor in ornithology, took part in his first Christmas count in 1922, when he was barely in his teens. Forty years later, he says he derives as much fun, excitement, and satisfaction as ever from this intensive activity.

A primary aim is to stimulate interest, yet every effort is made to insure reliability of the reports. The appearance of an out-of-range or out-of-season rarity is exciting but of little significance in itself.

The main contribution is that the annual survey indicates trends in the expansion or reduction of the range of a species, records great flights or invasions, and follows fluctuations or dramatic changes in populations. In the years ahead, the mass of data accumulated in the counts will yield an increasing wealth of information to the research biologist.

Only the more rugged watchers volunteer for the midnight-to-daybreak shift on a frigid night. (Others sleep—or try to—until 4 or 5 o'clock in the morning.) They then put on warm clothes and sturdy shoes, have a hearty breakfast, get last-minute instructions, and listen to the latest weather forecast, which may dictate some last-minute change in the sequence in which areas are visited. Each leader takes inventory of his maps, checklists, and lunch kit. He sees that his observers, especially the novices, have enough warm clothing, sharp pencils, and binoculars.

The leaders have been planning their attack for weeks. They have studied maps, summoned their cohorts, deployed field parties to scout their assigned sectors in advance, and established a communications network for reporting rarities and for keeping in touch with participants on the big day.

Let me, as leader of a party, guide you through some of the thrills of a midwinter day in the field—as I have done on scores of Christmas counts in the past three decades, from Maryland to the mid-Pacific, from New England to the Gulf of Mexico. (This time it will be near Ocean City, Maryland, but it could be elsewhere.)

I have a fondness for owls, whose haunts and habits are as poorly known to birdwatchers as their beneficial diets are to farmers. My friends expect me not to report back at night until I have several owls on my list. By going out before dawn, we have a good chance to hear a few distant owls if we can get far away from airports and arterial highways.

I drop off my crew at intervals of 2 miles or so, and by the time I circle back to pick them up one of us is sure to have heard a great horned or a barred owl—unless winds are high or the weather is threatening. Screech owls need a bit of coaxing; I imitate their quavering call for 5 minutes or so before we move on to the next stop.

If we are far enough south to be in woodcock country, we have arranged to be near brushy fields when the pale light of dawn first tints the eastern sky. If we do not hear their peenting or detect the music of their whistling wings in those few short moments, we may as well write off the woodcock as lost for the day's list.

Next comes the frantic race for thrashers and hermit thrushes. Before the woodcock have retreated from the approaching daylight, the silence is broken by a soft chorus of mewing and hissing notes, which are identified only by those who know hermit thrushes and members of the thrasher family. In barely 15 minutes, this chorus is gone, and the whole day's total for hermit thrushes may have been reached.

GREAT HORNED OWL

155

With the help of a boat and a skipper supplied by the Coast Guard, observers check numbers of sea birds during the Christmas bird count.

In the meantime, the recordkeeper has been pushed to keep up with the tally. Mockingbirds in all directions answer each other's loud, scolding notes; they can be heard for more than a mile. Cardinals and a host of sparrows fill the air with their characteristic chips. The experienced birders call off to the compiler the names of all the birds as they salute the dawn.

What's that? A pileated woodpecker! Except for the sapsucker, this is the only member of the family that we can identify by the way it drums. It would be fun to tarry a while and try to see it, but to do so would cost us several birds per minute in these precious early-morning hours. If we all remain alert, we may see one later in the day, without taking extra time. Right now, we are more interested in seeing *how many* pileated woodpeckers we can locate than in pursuing one of them to satisfy an individual's desire to lay eyes on this spectacular species.

There is not much real singing on a cold December morning, but by imitating the whistled song of a white-throated sparrow or a robin, we can often start a chain reaction that brings a few birds into song and causes hordes of others to respond with their typical call notes.

After a quick review of call notes, our carload of observers splits into three walking parties. At this point, a beginner is always assigned to work with a more experienced participant. The hiking routes are laid out as to cover the best woodland areas between 7 and 10 o'clock in the morning. Most birds of fields and ponds can be counted at midday after the forest species have become quiet and hard to locate.

Now, working singly or in pairs, and with the keenness of a forest animal stalking its prey, we strain our ears to pick up the faintest call of a distant kinglet, the leaf scratching that betrays a towhee or fox sparrow, or the cracking of cones that reveals the presence of a flock of crossbills.

As the morning wears on, a single chip will lead us to a whole flock of silent songbirds. We examine every bird in the flock in hopes of spotting something rare or unusual.

Excitement runs high when a strange or unexpected call note is heard. All else is forgotten until the stranger is identified. Sometimes it is nothing but a starling's imitation, a distant mockingbird, or an unusual call from a towhee. Or, it may be something more or less out of place—a field sparrow wintering in Massachusetts, a grasshopper sparrow or a Wilson's warbler in Maryland, an indigo bunting, or a Lapland longspur in Virginia.

At the appointed time, the driver picks up his scattered crew, and a composite list of species is assembled. Rarities are verified immediately.

After a brief coffee break, the party hurries off to cover sample areas of other habitats nearby. They comb the fields for sparrows, meadowlarks, blackbirds, and doves. They hike along the wood margins, which are especially productive of a variety and abundance of birds. They scan the skies for soaring hawks and vultures and the ponds and streams for ducks, herons, and kingfishers. The list grows. So does the appetite.

Finally it is lunchtime. If the weather is cold, we go to a warm restaurant to have hot soup with our sandwiches. If there is no quick-service eating place close by, we stay in the car or meet at a specified school or private residence for lunch so we can compile a preliminary list.

If the parties do not get together in person, they may phone in a progress report to headquarters

156

and in return receive instructions about missing species that require a special search. Or there may be a message that another party has seen the bald eagle from the other side of the river, so it will not be necessary to post an observer to watch for it. Or, the whole flock of six short-eared owls that had been spotted earlier in the week was seen at dawn, so our party need not take time to search for them at dusk.

Plans for the afternoon depend on the terrain, the availability of watchers, and the job to be completed. If the assigned sector is a large one, comprehensive and systematic coverage continues, and weary but still enthusiastic counters are detailed to slosh across muddy fields, wade marshes, or penetrate unbroken expanses of snow. If a sector is strategically located and small, such as a coastline or the only marsh or evergreen woods in the entire circle, we detail one or more persons to stand watch in a tract that was covered previously in the hope that we can find additional species.

Unless we are having a heavy rain or a snowstorm, we scale a firetower to search for hawks and to make a telescopic count of soaring turkey vultures. Such a count must be compared carefully with tallies from other party leaders to prevent duplication in the final records.

Most party leaders are familiar with their territories. For the Maryland counts, for instance, we assign the same leader to the same territory each year. His crew members may change, so as to familiarize observers with many different areas and different techniques of coverage. Basically, however, the same coverage is maintained from year to year. In this way, there is a better opportunity to detect actual changes in bird populations.

Midafternoon finds the observers inclined to drive more and walk less. The woodlands are dead. The wind has picked up. Watering eyes torment the patient telescope man on the exposed shore.

It is then that an observer may begin to think he has done justice to his own assignment and would like to visit a neighboring sector of the circle in the hope of spotting some rarity that a colleague has missed.

Such doublechecking of the most strategically located concentration spots at different times of the day increases the chances of sighting the rarer species, but it also cuts down the time we can spend in new territory, where every bird seen can be added to the day's list. Nearly all participants therefore are expected to remain within their assigned territories.

When crows in long, majestic lines begin to break the monotony of a silent landscape, it is time to put the evening roost-watch into effect. Even the beginner is pressed into special duty, wrapped in warm clothes, and stationed alone on a perch overlooking invisible pathways through the air.

Within minutes, the pathways will be filled with flock after flock of well-fed robins, mourning doves, meadowlarks, waterfowl, or blackbirds in huge, globular masses or in endless, undulating lines.

If, perchance, a vulture roost has been located, we detail one or two counters to get an exact record of the birds as they enter the roost.

Chandler Robbins, Edmund W. Stiles, (center) and Fred Scott (seated) tabulate the birds they saw during the 1965 count at Chincoteague, Virginia.

There are tense moments ahead. If a roost of robins or blackbirds has moved and the birds fail to appear at the expected position, there is energetic scouting to locate the new flight lines.

As dusk approaches, there are never enough counters to continue to keep track of birds going to roost; to check marshes for the evening calls of marsh wrens, snipe, and rails; to listen for woodcock; and to record the host of sparrows that chip so noisily just before they bed down for the night.

And before the sparrows and wrens become silent, it is time to listen for the great horned owls, which are generally the first of their family to hail the approaching darkness.

Finally, our hunger vies with the desire to add just one more owl to the list. Screech owls are harder to call up in the evening than in the morning, but we try for a few before we end our day.

Meanwhile, at hotels and restaurants and at the headquarters of bird sanctuaries across the United States and Canada, weary but jubilant birders are peeling off layer after layer of clothing and gathering in small huddles to compile the party lists.

The best finds of the day are not disclosed now, although the commoner species are discussed openly with members of the other parties. The oldtimers claim not to have done very well, but the grin of a beginner indicates that he is keeping secret some prize bird until it is time for the big compilation.

The groups of counters in Cocoa, Florida, for example, ask themselves: "Did we break the continental record?" or "Did we break 200 species?" The watchers at Wilmington, North Carolina, wonder if they have a bigger list than the counters in Charleston, South Carolina. The oldtime rivals of Ocean City, Maryland, and Cape May, New Jersey, compete with groups that cover Bombay Hook National Wildlife Refuge in Delaware and Chincoteague National Wildlife Refuge in Virginia. Similar competitions exist among closely matched groups in other parts of the United States and Canada.

Such rivalry is not the main objective of the counts, but it does much to stimulate the participants to put forth their best efforts throughout the long day. Each group aspires to beat its own previous record or to add a new species to the alltime

local list, but such happenings become less and less frequent.

While the field observers are at their evening meal, which very likely was prepared by the less energetic members of the bird club, someone may tell about the origin and history of the Christmas bird counts.

The first count was taken on Christmas Day, 1900 by 27 participants, who covered 25 areas. Among the first counters were such well-known ornithologists as Ralph Hoffman, author of early 20th century field guides; Lynds Jones, editor for many years of The Wilson Bulletin; Witmer Stone, author of the classic *Bird Studies at Old Cape May;* Alexander Wetmore, who later became Secretary of the Smithsonian Institution; and the originator of the count, Frank M. Chapman, Curator of Ornithology at the American Museum of Natural History.

Dr. Chapman's purpose in establishing the Christmas count was twofold. In the original announcement of the count, he pointed out that sportsmen had been accustomed to meet on Christmas Day, choose sides, and then "hie them to the fields and woods on the cheerful mission of killing practically everything in fur or feathers that crossed their path—if they could."

He urged readers of Bird-Lore (now Audubon Magazine) to spend part of Christmas with the birds and to report their count, together with locality, time afield, and weather conditions, for publication in the next issue.

Besides initiating a sport that would publicize conservation rather than destruction of wildlife, Dr. Chapman foresaw the value of obtaining a measure of winter bird populations against a yardstick of number of hours of coverage.

The growth of the Christmas count exceeded expectations. The number of reports increased nearly fivefold in the first 5 years, and it became necessary to limit the number published by setting up minimum standards of coverage, which in time were made more and more strict.

At first there was little sense of competition. The counters simply took a stroll for 2 or 3 hours and listed the birds they encountered. During the first decade of the count, no group listed more than 56 species—a total that by present standards would hardly be worth publishing except in the Northern States or Canada.

In the next 2 years, however, William Leon Dawson, author of three monumental State bird books, organized counts at Santa Barbara, California, that reached 76 and then 100 species. In the East, Ludlow Griscom and Leverett Saltonstall, later Senator from Massachusetts, found 70 species near Tallahassee on Christmas Day, 1911. From then on, bird clubs and individuals worked harder and harder to obtain lists that were representative of their areas.

Competition centered around obtaining a long list of species until 1948, when an incentive was created for placing more emphasis on the numbers of individual birds of each species. That was accomplished by publishing, as part of the Christmas bird count report, a composite list of all species recorded each year, together with the highest single count for each species and the name of the area that achieved this high count. This annual summary, first prepared by Robert E. Stewart, a biologist in the Bureau of Sport Fisheries and Wildlife, has stimulated observers to strive for a

In Denmark, a sheet of decorative stamps of birds, "Our loyal Christmas guests," has been published at Christmas for 100 years. Einar Holbøll, an artist, started the series in 1865.

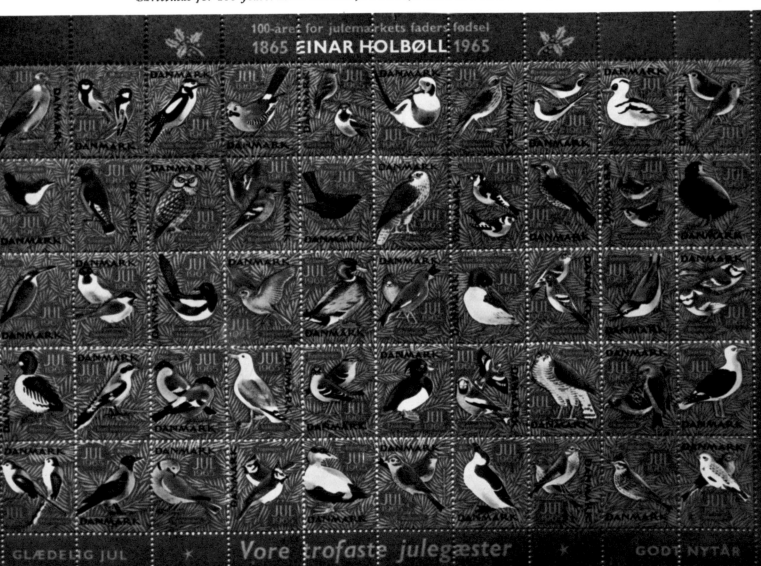

more representative count of each species rather than divert all efforts toward obtaining a long list of species.

In the first 13 years that followed initiation of the summaries, the total number of individuals recorded per year went from 9 million to 52 million birds and the number of observers increased from 3,670 to 8,928.

The annual summaries provide an easy reference to areas of high abundance for each species and to any drastic changes in abundance in the high-density localities. They also permit the reader to compare abundance of a species in his own area with abundance in an area of maximum density.

Finally, the hour arrives for the big compilation. The party leaders have finished tallying their totals, and the youngest counter has completed his assignment of collecting 50 cents from each participant to help pay for publishing the reports.

"Common loon," calls the compiler at Ocean City. There is silence. Then one by one the party leaders call out their totals: "Zero"—from all the inland sectors and from some of the tidewater parties. Finally a six and a two. Total, eight. Not good. The 16-year average is 14.

"Red-throated loon." Seventy-eight this year—well below the all-time peak of 292 in 1953, but nearly up to the highest count on the continent the previous year, which was 94 at Santa Barbara, California.

Down the list we go, species by species. Moans greet the confessions of the coastal parties that they missed the red-necked grebe and the gannet. But there are sighs of relief when we hear that a lone blue goose was found amid the flock of 700 snow geese.

The hawk totals cause concern. Both the sharp-shinned and the Cooper's hawk are down to one-third of their 16-year average—a decrease slightly greater than that recorded for the bald eagle.

Red-bellied woodpeckers are up to an alltime high of 116, more than 10 percent over our previous high for the species; the total therefore will be printed in boldface type for emphasis. Mockingbirds also reached 100 for the first time.

But as we go down the list, it becomes more and more apparent that this winter is a poor one locally for both species and individuals. We cannot pos-

sibly break our record of 150 species, and we will be lucky if we reach our average of 132. But we keep hoping. We wonder if the party that checks the blackbird roost will push our total of individual birds over the million mark. But no: The roost has moved outside the boundary of our circle, and grackles, instead of numbering in the hundreds of thousands, total only 8,600 individuals.

Although we know we cannot hope for a spectacular list, we listen with interest as species after species is logged in, as though we were hearing electron returns. Often a species will appear to be scarce in one party's territory but is above normal in other areas.

In an off year for northern finches, no one is surprised to find that crossbills and evening grosbeaks total zero and that purple finch and pine siskin are represented by only one and two individuals each.

We finally reach the last two species on the list, Lapland longspur and snow bunting. The longspur we seldom record, but the bunting is found 9 years in 10. We feel great disappointment when the Assateague Island party reports zero for both species. (Later we learn that our chief rivals, Cape May and Chincoteague, also missed the bunting.)

By custom, any species not previously recorded is saved until last. Such choice birds are always the subject of intensive questioning and documentation. If possible, other observers search them out the next day to substantiate further the occurrence. Often some rare prize has been captured alive and then dramatically brought forth before an incredulous audience as proof of correct identification. I have seen Ludlow Griscom pull a live dovekie from under his hat and other bird counters extract saw-whet owls from pockets or briefcases.

We at Ocean City found no new species in 1964. The cumulative species total remained at 189, and the day's list was an unimpressive 63 thousand birds of 124 species.

Disappointing? Yes, to any whose chief aim was to compile a big list. But to most participants the day was a big success—many memorable ex-

If a participant in a Christmas bird count sees something like this, Canada geese coasting in, he considers himself well repaid for his efforts.

160

periences, good fellowship, and the feeling that something worthwhile had been accomplished. No one had seen as many birds as he had hoped to, but the efforts of 25 persons had placed on record a sample count of the birds within our 15-mile circle—a count that may be referred to many times in coming years as scientists study our changing bird populations and take the necessary steps to assure preservation of our native species.

Each compiler copies his results on special forms and forwards them with his comments to the National Audubon Society for editing and publication. Every report receives the careful scrutiny of Allan Cruickshank, who has traveled nearly as widely as the birds themselves and who has an encyclopedic knowledge of bird distribution in the United States and Canada. Any bird reported outside its normal range must be well substantiated by details of the observation if it is to survive Mr. Cruickshank's editing.

The lists, with notes on weather conditions and coverage and the names of participants, are published in the April issues of Audubon Field Notes. Many of the highlights are brought out by Editor Cruickshank in his introductory pages, but most of the data remain to be digested.

All observations for the first 40 years were put on punch cards, and the abundance of each species was summarized by States and Provinces by Dr. Leonard Wing at the State College of Washington. This summary is a valuable reference to the occurrence and relative abundance of each species throughout much of its range.

The April 1950 issue of Audubon Field Notes gave a list of 20 publications based on the results of Christmas bird counts. In the first analysis, which appeared in 1914, E. H. Perkins discussed the changes in abundance of 10 species of songbirds in New York and New England. The greatest contribution of his study was to show that black-capped chickadees, which were believed to be sedentary, varied greatly in abundance from year to year. Periodic southward emigrations of this species were substantiated in later years.

Nowhere else in the world is there such a backlog of statistical information on the distribution and abundance of winter birds. The record already continues unbroken for 65 years. This makes it

possible to follow quite accurately the frequency and geographical extent of the cyclic invasions of northern birds, such as snowy owls, crossbills, redpolls, evening grosbeaks, northern shrikes, and red-breasted nuthatches.

Leonard Wing has used the Christmas counts to document the spread of the starling and house sparrow across North America. The spread of the house finch in the East and of the cattle egret can be followed in the same way. Dr. Wing also used the Christmas counts to map the relative distribution of the mallard and black duck in winter. These two species of similar habits and similar conspicuousness lend themselves nicely to such a comparison.

The Bureau of Sport Fisheries and Wildlife annually summarizes the Chistmas count figures for the mourning dove and the common snipe in order to obtain an annual index to changes in abundance. Only those specific areas that report one or more individuals of the spec'es in question are used in the comparisons, and the same areas are compared year after year. In all cases, the unit of comparison is not total birds, but birds per 100 party-hours of coverage for a certain State or group of States or Provinces.

The Bureau has other sources of information on population trends for these species, but data from the Christmas count are needed to complete the analyses. For instance, it is feasible to dispatch State and Federal wildlife biologists to make systematic counts of snipe in the major wintering areas of the Gulf Coast States and obtain an annual index to changes in abundance in the heart of the wintering area.

Snipe, however, winter in small numbers in some 30 Central and Northern States. This wintering population is scattered so widely that the cost of sending biologists to the field to obtain sample counts each winter would be prohibitive. Yet the total area involved is so large that the total number of snipe wintering in these 30 States comprises a significant portion of the entire population. Population changes in the northern parts of the winter range are not detected in any other way but through the Christmas counts.

As the Christmas counts comprise nearly the sum total of quantitative data on bird populations in North America for the years preceding the Second World War, many attempts have been made to analyze portions of the data, especially on a local or statewide basis. The investigator frequently has to conclude that there have been too few counts that have been continued over a long period of years, that weather conditions on the day of the count or counts he is studying mask many of the fluctuations he is trying to detect, and that many species are found in such small numbers that chance alone could account for the annual variations. Consequently, most "analyses" have been limited to tables of raw data, and only a few outstanding population changes have been demonstrated so far.

A few studies have been made specifically to "prove" preconceived notions or, more regrettably, to mislead the public deliberately regarding rate of decrease of some of our native birds. For example, by failing to take into account the continual increase in coverage and the increased emphasis since 1948 on counting individual birds, one can quote annual Christmas-count totals for almost any species and make it appear that the birds are on the increase, or are even undergoing a population "explosion."

One example: Figures were published in several agricultural journals to show an alleged increase in such species as the mourning dove, yellow-shafted flicker, robin, and cardinal during a period of intensive use of pesticides. Figures were grouped by 4-year intervals, and the figures used were the annual totals from all Christmas counts combined. It was stated that the mourning dove increased from an index value of 13,131 in 1949–1952 to 59,886 in 1957–1960 and that the robin increased in the same period from 41,214 to 367,733.

The author did not point out the extreme variability of the counts from one year to another. He did not reveal that in 1960, 86 percent of all the robins reported on Christmas bird counts were in a single roost at Nashville, Tennessee, or that the Nashville count had risen from 37 birds in 1959 to 800 thousand in 1960 and had dropped back to 11 in 1961. Such extreme annual variability in recording numbers of gregarious species must be taken into account in any significant appraisal of population changes.

Mourning dove populations actually did increase from a low in 1949 to a high in 1960 (from which they have subsequently decreased), but the rise as shown by other surveys was about 60 percent, not 350 percent as claimed. By comparing only those Christmas count areas that had been covered throughout the 12-year period and by correcting for the increase in party-hours of coverage, the Christmas count figures indicate an apparent rise of 135 percent in the mourning dove, or about twice the actual increase. This discrepancy is a rough measure of the extent to which Christmas counts during this period are biased by the greater effort expended in counting birds of common species.

The yellow-shafted flicker, which was quoted as increasing from 4,278 in 1949–1952 to 7,500 in 1957–1960, actually showed an apparent increase of less than 5 percent when corrected for hours of coverage and for continuity. If a correction were applied to compensate for the greater emphasis on counting individual birds, the net change in yellow-shafted flickers would show a decrease rather than an increase.

Looking to the future, as counting rules continue to become stricter and observers take even more seriously the desirability of uniformity of coverage from year to year, the Christmas bird count should become increasingly valuable as a means of showing trends in bird populations. These trends must be detected promptly in order that we may be aware in time of the effect on birds of one or another of our actions or programs, such as changes in the use of insecticides, growth of cities, draining marshes, and otherwise changing habitat.

In what other field of activity can one find thousands of citizens giving up a share of their Christmas vacation to spend a long, hard day—or more—in wind, rain, or cold, keeping detailed notes, supplying all of their own equipment and transportation—and even paying a fee for the privilege of participating?

Obviously there is compensation. The thrill of the unexpected, the comradeship, the satisfaction of aiding the cause of conservation, and the rejuvenation of the spirit, which is offered us daily by our Maker but which we so seldom take the trouble to accept.

—CHANDLER S. ROBBINS.

Falconry

FALCONRY is the art of taming wild hawks and hunting game with them. Hawks are predatory birds. They live off other birds and small animals; it is their nature to hunt. The training part, then, is essentially to teach the bird to return to its owner after a flight.

Many kinds of hawks can be trained. A falcon is one of a particular group of hawks, a group en-dowed with spectacular powers of flight, tractable, and responsive to training. It is therefore the tradi-tional favorite and the source of the term "fal-conry."

Many hawks that are not falcons also are trained for hunting—hence the sometime term "hawking." Generally, though, we use the terms "hawking" and "falconry" as well as "hawk" and "falcon"

164

synonymously as referring to all kinds of hawks and falcons for hunting. Just remember: A falcon is a hawk, but not all hawks are falcons.

The appeal of falconry lies in the excitement of the bird's flights and chases—the magnificent stoop of a towering peregrine falcon or the slashing, low-level onslaught of a scimitared goshawk. In no other form of hunting is the emphasis so much on the thrill and excitement of the chase and so little on the actual taking of the quarry.

Just as hunting with bow and arrow is more sporting than hunting with a gun, falconry is more sporting than the bow and arrow. In no other sport are hunter and hunted so evenly matched. Oftener than not, the quarry goes unscathed; in falconry there are no cripples.

Falconry is so old that nobody can say when it began. Drawings and statues in ancient tombs and ruins indicate that it was known centuries ago in Egypt and Mongolia.

I would guess that hunting with hawks or other birds began as a way to get food for the hunter's family.

Later, as falconry developed as a sport, peasants were restricted to hunting with "ignoble" hawks, such as the goshawk. Only noblemen could keep falcons.

Kings and noblemen trained the long-winged falcons solely for the sport and excitement of the aerial chase. The flight of a goshawk after a rabbit is not nearly so spectacular as the power dive of a noble, high-flying peregrine falcon as it stoops to challenge its winged victim. The low-flying, tail-chasing methods of the goshawk and its generally fractious disposition led to its being called an "ignoble" hawk.

Conversely, the falcons were called "noble" because of the sweep and grandeur of their high flight plus their amenable nature. I have long felt that the difference in training a goshawk and a falcon is almost comparable to the difference between training a cat and training a dog.

Falconry reached its zenith in the Middle Ages, when knighthood was in flower. Goshawks were flown by peasants and falcons by the aristocracy. Eagles, although not particularly useful for hunting, were reserved for kings.

Indeed, a mark of nobility was an eagle or fal-

con on the fist. The ladies of the court, too, were privileged certain smaller falcons, particularly the merlin falcon. Hawking parties were frequent social events.

So, in the storied time, the average person knew as much about falconry and its jargon as we today know about baseball.

Shakespeare was one. In "Romeo and Juliet," Juliet exclaimed: "O, for a falconer's voice, to lure this tiercel-gentle back again." We may not know what it means today, but in the Middle Ages it was completely meaningful: "Oh, for a loud voice with which to call my stray male falcon [Romeo] back again."

The jargon of falconry has many colorful and unusual words. To bowse means to drink. To feak is to wipe her beak after eating; to rouse, to shake her feathers into place; to warble, to stretch her wings. Jesses are the leather leg straps that are placed on hawks by their trainer. Bewits are the leather strips attaching the hawk's bells to her legs. The buildings in which hawks and falcons are kept are called mews.

The cadge is a portable perch on which hawks are carried afield for hunting. In medieval times, the man who carried the cadge usually was an older falconer and was called a cadger. This is probably where our word codger came from.

The decline of falconry in Europe from its peak of popularity was due largely to two developments—the invention and use of gunpowder and guns, which made the taking of game much easier, and the broad social changes that changed people's uses of their leisure time.

But the sport never died out in the countries where it had flourished. Always a small, dedicated group has carried the sport on.

John McCabe and his arctic gyrfalcon from Alaska. Once upon a time the most prestigious gift a king could give another was a gyrfalcon.

The late Colonel R. ("Luff") Meredith, once a pilot in the U.S. Air Force, has been called the father of American falconry. The gyrfalcon on his hand is a prized species among falconers.

An interest in falconry was born in America at the beginning of this century through the efforts of a small group of eastern falconers, led by Colonel R. Meredith. With him were Dr. George Goodwin, of the American Museum of Natural History, and Mr. Louis Agassiz Fuertes, the famous bird artist.

Colonel Meredith, or "Luff," as he was affectionately known to falconers, both in this country and abroad, is regarded as the father of American falconry. An Air Corps (later Air Force) officer, he loved hawks, and trained and flew them with great zeal. From the time of his graduation from the Military Academy at West Point in 1917 until his death in 1965, he traveled around the country with his birds, helping new falconers get started, and always making new friends for the sport.

Fuertes also helped the sport take root by his short but stimulating article on the subject in the December 1920 issue of National Geographic. His illustrations were exciting. Many of the older falconers who practice the sport were first attracted to falconry by Fuertes' story. I am one of them.

The first national falconry meet was held in Media, Pennsylvania, in 1938. About a hundred falconers and guests assembled from all over the country and flew their birds, among them powerful golden eagles and petite and delightful kestrel falcons. The event was the forerunner of meets now held every year. The 1964 meet at Centerville, South Dakota, was attended by several hundred falconers from the United States and other countries.

In 1965, the sport was thinly but well established in most States and Canada. In 1964, the Secretary of the Interior issued an amendment to the Migratory Bird Treaty Act Regulations, making it legal to use falcons for hunting all migratory game birds, including doves and waterfowl. This recognition of the sport by the Federal Government was a significant milestone. More than three-fourths of the States in 1965 provided for falconry as a legal means of taking game or unprotected quarry.

The North American Falconers Association is a national organization of falconers who practice this form of hunting, promote its acceptance as a field sport, and help conserve and protect the birds of prey.

166

It takes several years to learn the rudiments of falconry, even with the guiding hand of an experienced falconer. One cannot learn it from books. Time also is required to trap and train the hawks. Then, once trained, the birds require daily work of at least an hour for handling, feeding, and exercising. Few Americans can afford this effort. Falconry will never be a widespread sport.

All of the hawks must come from the wild, either as nestlings or as trapped birds. Hawks do not breed in captivity. Falconers, therefore, cannot raise their birds as a pigeon fancier breeds pigeons. This complete dependence on wild hawks for training in falconry demands of falconers an intense interest in the conservation and welfare of the birds of prey if the sport is to survive.

Two groups of birds of prey provide most of the birds used in the sport. They are *Falco* (true falcons) and *Accipiter* (true hawks). A third group, *Buteo* (buzzard hawks), contributes a few birds.

Falco is the most important. Any hawk in this group is spoken of as a falcon. Generally, because the peregrine falcon is the falcon most used in the sport, when one speaks of a falcon he has reference to the peregrine. In the strictest usage, the word "falcon" also means a female. The male falcon is referred to as a tiercel, probably because he is about one-third smaller than his mate.

In all birds of prey, the female is larger than the male, and therefore is the one most frequently trained. Hence a falcon or hawk is generally referred to as "she." Sometimes falcons are referred to as long-winged hawks because of their swallow-like wings. They all have large, black eyes and a thick, notched beak—features possessed by none of the other hawks or eagles.

Falcons are brilliant masters of aerobatics, and generally their quarry is limited to the birds they capture by sheer aerial skill. The best known members of this group in the continental United States are the peregrine falcon or duck hawk, prairie falcon, merlin falcon or pigeon hawk, and kestrel falcon or sparrow hawk. They are not large; they tend to be compact and streamlined. The peregrine

Major H. H. D. Heiberg, of the Potomac Falconers' Association and a resident of North Springfield, Virginia, shows off his peregrine falcon.

The peregrine falcon is capable of great bursts of speed and maneuverability and so can easily strike down a pheasant, even in full flight.

A boy begins to train his pet kestrel.

is about the size of a big crow. The kestrel is about the size of a small pigeon.

A rare falcon, the gyrfalcon, occurs in the arctic regions. It is prized in falconry, but not many are used because of difficulty in acquiring the bird.

The peregrine is a magnificent bird. Speed, power, beauty, nobility, all combine to make it one of Nature's most splendid creations. Some consider the eagle without peer. I question that. Not many years ago, I witnessed a duel between a haggard (mature) peregrine and an adult bald eagle.

The setting was the sand dunes of Cape Hatteras near the breaking surf of the Atlantic. The time was a wintry afternoon in late December.

The peregrine had perched on a snag of driftwood on the front beach, when the diving eagle appeared out of the gray overcast. Whether the falcon feared attack or whether she simply resented the presence of her larger adversary I do not know.

But instantly, her wings vibrating, she launched into a wide circle and rapidly scrambled for altitude. She was high above the eagle in a few moments. With a tight roll-over, she closed her wings and hurled down to attack. Her harsh screams filled the emptiness of the desolate setting.

An instant before the falcon hit, the eagle attempted a quick turn. He was too slow. Feathers floated in the air as the peregrine footed him hard. Up and over the eagle, the falcon quickly mounted. Again the powerful stoop. It reminded me of a large bomber under attack by a fast jet fighter.

Stoop after stoop by the pressing falcon soon brought the eagle closer to the sands of the beach. Finally, in desperation after being clearly bested in the air, the eagle sought sanctuary by landing among small dunes. The falcon roused in midair and climbed rapidly as she headed southward down the Cape.

Peregrines are at their best in falconry when flown at game birds, such as pheasants.

In a typical hunt, the falconer goes afield with his hooded peregrine on his fist. His bird dogs range ahead. The hood on the falcon blindfolds her and thus keeps her quiet.

When the dogs find a pheasant and point, the falcon is cast off—released. She commences to ascend in wide circles until she is high overhead. The higher a falcon mounts, the better bird she is said to be. Finally, when she has attained her pitch (maximum height), the pheasant is flushed from its hiding place.

In one tremendous, rocketing stoop, or vertical dive, the falcon hurls earthward to foot the pheasant with her talons as she blasts by. This thrilling stoop of the peregrine is the essence of falconry.

The second main group that is trained is the accipiter. Sometimes these true hawks are referred to as short-winged hawks, in contrast with the long-winged hawks, or falcons. They are the ignoble hawks of medieval history.

The principal American accipiters are the goshawk, Cooper's hawk, and sharp-shinned hawk.

These hawks have long tails and short, rounded wings, much like those of a quail or pheasant. The wings permit great bursts of precipitous speed. The oversize tail enables maximum maneuverability through dense thickets and forest.

Heinz Meng is getting his falcons ready for an automobile trip to a hunting area in New York. Hoods help keep the birds quiet during travel.

Accipiters also are called wood hawks, a reference to their favorite habitat. All are excellent hunters. Strictly speaking, one who trains and hunts these hawks is a hawker. He is indulging in the sport of hawking.

The largest and the one oftenest trained is the goshawk. Its top quarry is rabbits, although it may be flown from the fist at almost any type of small ground game, such as pheasants or squirrels.

On a cold, wintry, bleak day not long ago, I went hunting rabbits with Tawnee, my goshawk. It was the sort of bitter, overcast day I have grown to associate with goshawk hunts for rabbits. The cottontails had left the more open places and were now in dense thickets and overgrown fence rows.

Tawnee was keen as I carried her on my fist. The slightest movement in the brush caught her piercing eyes.

Suddenly, out from under the far side of a heavy brushpile darted a large cottontail. He headed for a thick growth of pines nearby. Off shot the goshawk, her bells jangling with each pounding stroke of her powerful wings. She was closing fast. The rabbit made it to the pines. His bobbing white tail disappeared quickly behind the trees. I felt sure that the goshawk would be thwarted by the thicket.

With incredible dexterity and only a slight slowing of speed, she hurled herself just inches off the ground up through the undergrowth. I could not see her then, but her bells told me she was still going. Suddenly there was silence.

Moments later, after I had fought and cut my way through the pines, I found her. Her wings and tail were outstretched on the ground as braces. Her mouth was open from exertion. In her talons was her limp quarry. It was a remarkable exhibition of perseverance and aerial skills.

The buteos, or soaring hawks, resemble small eagles in shape. They are broad-winged, soaring hawks. Often we see them wheeling slowly over forests and fields in search of rodents. Farmers sometimes call them henhawks, a term that disregards facts.

Buteos generally are not fast or agile enough to be particularly useful in falconry, with possibly one exception, the red-tailed hawk. It is almost as large as a small eagle. It has been trained with good success for rabbit hunting. It is less capable than a goshawk, but it can be counted on to provide exciting flights at rabbits. It is much too slow for any game-bird hawking.

The red-tail is an excellent hawk for beginners because of its stable disposition, tameness, and responsiveness to training. After a training period with this hawk, a neophyte falconer can go on to the more difficult goshawks and Cooper's hawks. Falcons should never be attempted until the very last.

Falcons are trained as hawks of the lure. The accipiters, buteos, and eagles are trained as hawks of the fist. The difference reflects the way in which each is flown.

Falcons are birds of the open country. They are never flown in woods—only in prairie-type country. Their flights are high and often far from their owners. To call them back, one needs a means that is clearly visible to the distant hawk. The falconer's lure provides this means.

The other hawks—the accipiters, buteos, and eagles—are trained to return to the fist after a flight. They do not fly high and wide as falcons do. Because they usually perch in the first convenient tree after a short flight, they are taught to return to the falconer's outstretched, gloved fist.

The training of all hawks has essentially two parts. First, the bird is tamed to accept a person as a friend. Second, it is taught the basic routine of returning to a falconer after flight.

Both are accomplished by the use of food as a reward. Food is the key to a hawk's training and handling. There is no training by reprimand or punishment, as with a dog. It is only through careful control of the bird's appetite that the bird can be flown and taught to return to the falconer after flights at game.

The taming of a hawk or falcon—or manning process, as it is known in falconry—is not difficult, especially if the hawk was taken from the nest. Falconers call such a nestling an eyess. Eyess birds usually tame much more rapidly than trapped birds, because they have not acquired a real fear of man. Eyesses tame easily, but they have drawbacks: They do not know how to fly.

Somewhere in the training procedure, therefore, an eyess hawk must get flight experience and learn the rudiments of the aerial maneuvers that a successful hunting falcon must be able to do. That takes time; most falconers feel eyesses are not worth the effort.

Furthermore, because eyess birds are so tame, they may acquire habits that falconers classify as vices. One, for example, is screaming. A hawk so addicted screams harshly and repeatedly at the sight of the falconer. She does so because she is hungry and associates the sight of man with being fed. Sometimes her screams are so unpleasant they cannot be tolerated. Then the falconer has to seek another bird.

The hawks most preferred for use in falconry are young birds that have left the nest. They must be trapped. A hawk that is trapped during its first year of life on its first fall migration is called a passager, or passage, hawk. Passagers are the ones falconers seek. The term "passage" derives from an old falconry expression, which considers a hawk on its first migration as one on passage.

A hawk that was trapped after it had moulted into the adult plumage—that is, more than a year old—is called a haggard. The terms "eyess," "passage," and "haggard," once assigned to a bird, stay with her, irrespective of how many years that bird may live in captivity.

Each year a falcon moults or changes her feathers. Once she does this while in captivity, she acquires the falconry term "intermewed." Thus an eyess falcon that has moulted is spoken of as an intermewed eyess. Passage and haggard birds similarly acquire the intermewed term after their first moult in captivity.

Most falconers seek their hawks during the fall migration. Their prime targets are the birds that

Dr. Heinz Meng and his peregrine falcon and springer spaniel pause after a pheasant hunt in New York.

were hatched earlier in the year and are now on their first passage southward. They have had several months of flying and hunting. They are already masters of aerial skills. They have not developed that total fear of humans that makes haggards (adults) much harder to train.

Most falconers also regard haggard birds as vital breeding stock. Hence, if haggards are caught in the traps, they are usually banded and released on the spot.

The commonest method for catching migrating hawks on the mountain flyways is called a bownet—a trap that was used for centuries in Europe. It is a small net, which is carefully concealed on the ground. When a hawk has been lured to its center by a bait bird or animal, the net is sprung by the trapper, who hides nearby.

Along the coastal beaches where peregrines migrate, the method of trapping is different. Once a falcon has been spotted, one of the trappers is quickly buried up to his head in the sand. A grassy headpiece with peepholes is placed over him. He wiggles his hands to the surface and is given a bait bird to hold. The other trappers withdraw. The fluttering of the bait bird attracts the falcon, and she usually comes winging over for an easy meal. Once she has alighted on the bait, the trapper slips his hands from the sand and secures the falcon by her legs.

When the hawk is acquired, the manning, or taming, process begins at once. It is done by carrying and feeding the hawk continually on the fist. After weeks of this, the hawk learns that her handlers are not harmful and will give her food.

The manning process is a continuous one. Hawks that are not handled every day soon get too wild to be flown free. A tame hawk, if left alone, will revert soon to its original wild state—sometimes in only a few days. How well I know! I once had a well-trained goshawk that got lost in the neighborhood for 2 days. By the time I located her, she had become so wild and unapproachable as to make her recovery impossible.

After a hawk has been manned, it is trained to return to its owner after being flown free. That is done by calling it back for food. Hawks must always be hungry when flown. It is in this phase of the training routine that hawks of the fist are trained differently from hawks of the lure.

Hawks of the fist, typically a goshawk, are taught at first to fly short distances on a stout cord (creance is the falconry word for this) to the outstretched, gloved fist for their food. Always a reward is given. As the hawk learns, the distances are increased until ultimately she will promptly return to the fist from 100 yards. Then the creance is discarded, and the hawk is flown free. At this point, she is ready to be started at wild game. Always, though, she must be keen—hungry—before being released.

The peregrine falcon is a typical hawk of the lure. Having been first manned, she is ready to start training to the lure. The lure is usually a leather object about the size of a flattened baseball, to which some colored ribbons or old pigeon wings are sewn so that the lure has an identity to the falcon. Attached to this lure are two leather thongs, which are used to tie raw meat to the lure. The lure then has a short line attached so that it may be swung in a circular fashion.

Each day at feeding time, the falcon's meat is tied to the lure. Then the falcon is allowed to eat from the lure. After a few feedings, she connects the lure with food. She will fly short distances to it the moment it is swung and thrown down on the ground. The falconer then picks her up from the lure. During all training, of course, the falcon is on a long line, or creance.

A falcon learns remarkably fast. In a week or so, she will take off at the sight of the swinging lure and fly hundreds of yards to get to it. Then she is flown free and may be tried at game.

Once trained to the lure, a falcon can see it at a seemingly incredible distance: She has amazing powers of vision.

Once I was flying a passage peregrine on a beautiful, sunny spring afternoon. Many thermal currents made it a perfect day for soaring, and the falcon strayed farther and farther downwind, as she circled upwards.

Soon she was just a speck in the blue sky. She faded in and out of my vision as she wheeled and turned just below the snowy clouds. A friend with binoculars kept her in view long after she faded from our unaided sight.

At this point, I became concerned that I might lose the bird and began swinging the lure. I hurled it high in the air and watched it fall some distance away in a field of alfalfa so deep and thick I wondered if I could ever find it again. Suddenly my friend exclaimed, "She's coming back!"

With the binoculars, he could see that she had given up her soar and was slanting toward us. In a few minutes we could see the diving falcon with her wings in that beautiful bent-bow arc so characteristic of a stooping peregrine.

Seconds later she skimmed over the field near us. Then she dropped out of sight in the dense alfalfa. I walked over, and when I picked her up, she had the lure firmly clutched in her talons. She must have been almost a mile away when she had locked on to the fall of the lure. Her extraordinary powers of vision were equaled only by her attachment to the lure.

Trained falcons and hawks are handled at least an hour every day. They are carried to keep them tame and fed on the fist. They are flown every day to keep them in good physical condition.

Falconry and the conservation of the birds of prey are inseparably linked.

Since all the birds used in the sport must come from the wild, falconry depends on keeping these wild resources. Falconers know that, and they work ceaselessly for the protection of these birds.

Protection means tolerance. Falconers therefore seek the cooperation of duck hunters in not shooting migrating peregrines, which are almost constantly exposed to duck hunters' blinds.

A few years ago, birds of prey generally were considered vermin, and bounties were offered for them. Now most States have protective laws, and the birds are regarded more and more as a valuable wildlife resource, subject to sound conservation management practices, like those for game-bird resources. Falconers support such management controls.

Falconers, however, cannot support absolute protection if such laws would deny falconers the use of the birds they need for their sport—except, of course, a species that may be threatened with extinction. In that case, falconers would be the first to urge total preservation.

Because many kinds of hawks and falcons may be trained in falconry, falconers would change to more available birds should any one species become rare and require total protection by law.

A promising idea is to develop a way to breed and produce hawks and falcons in captivity. A number of falconers in this country and abroad are actively studying the problem. Experience indicates that it is feasible. In a number of experiments, female hawks have produced eggs and then incubated them. But the eggs have been infertile. Falconers believe the problem of fertilization will be solved. When this is done, falcons will be raised in captivity, thus augmenting wild stocks and assuring availability of birds for training.

Throughout the ages, falconry has joined man with Nature's most brilliant aerial hunters. Beginning as a means of getting food, later practiced as an exciting pastime by medieval aristocracy, falconry in the 20th century is recognized as one of our more venerable heritages of the past.

ALVA G. NYE, JR.

Game and Ornamental Fowl

I RAISE GAME BIRDS as a hobby. I am one of the 6 thousand persons who hold permits of the Bureau of Sport Fisheries and Wildlife to propagate migratory waterfowl. I am one of the 2 thousand Americans who rear exotic birds for pleasure; for that, no permit is required.

My interest in natural history began as a boy. I kept turtle doves, guinea pigs, raccoons, opossums, box turtles, skunks, woodchucks, pigeons, domestic mallards, muscovy and pekin ducks, rabbits, and various snakes in our backyard in the urban community of Boiling Springs, Pennsylvania. An unused chickenhouse served as winter quarters. Wire enclosures were attached to it to provide outside runs.

My interest in hunting began when I was old enough to marvel at the rabbits my father would bring home after a day afield. When I was twelve, he took me hunting with him for the first time. What I learned then I have always remembered, although at that time I only dimly appreciated the lesson.

I was walking ahead, every nerve atingle, expecting something to appear from behind any tree.

At the very moment I least expected it, there was an explosion of leaves and a whirr of wings. For an instant I saw a plummeting ruffed grouse, which fast as a wink disappeared among the trees and over a hill.

I shot wildly. I turned toward Dad when I regained my composure and saw that he had not moved his gun at all during the entire exciting episode.

"Why didn't you shoot?" I asked.

"It's only a waste of shells to shoot at flying grouse," he said. "And even if you hit them, you ruin all the meat."

The point was that my father was a meat hunter, and I was of a generation that saw the beginning of change. In this new period, a hunter did not need to return with a full bag—his purpose in hunting is more therapeutic than materialistic. The pursuit of game is his declared objective, but in truth it is only secondary.

Now on my half-acre of landscaped lawn and water in pens in Boiling Springs, I keep American flamingos, fulvous tree duck, black-billed tree duck, black swan, black-necked swan, whistling swan, Pacific white-fronted geese, tule white-fronted geese, Ross' geese, emperor geese, bar-headed geese, Hawaiian geese, cackling Canada geese, Richardson's Canada geese, black brant, Cape Barren geese, ruddy-headed geese, South African shelducks, Australian Radjah shelducks, common shelducks, Hawaiian ducks, Laysan ducks, Mexican ducks, Baikal teal, falcated ducks, gadwall, European widgeons, American widgeons, Bahama duck, Chilean pintails, American pintails, common eiders, spectacled eiders, red-crested pochards, rosy-billed pochards, canvasbacks, redheads, ring-necked ducks, tufted ducks, greater scaups, maned wood ducks, Carolina wood ducks, mandarins ducks, Hartlaub's ducks, common goldeneyes, Barrow's goldeneyes, bufflehead, hooded mergansers, common mergansers, ruffed grouse, Himalayan monal pheasants, Indian blue peafowl, black-shouldered peafowl, red junglefowl, eastern wild turkeys, Lilford cranes, lesser sandhill cranes, Sarus cranes, demoiselle cranes, whitenaped cranes, East African crowned cranes, South African crowned crane, African gray parrots, yellow-naped

Two races of crowned cranes from Africa.

Amazon parrot, slender-billed cockatoo, scarlet macaw, hyacinthine macaw, Illiger's macaw, and Japanese sika deer.

I conduct special propagation projects with the tule goose, Cape Barren goose, Mexican duck, and Hawaiian duck—species that are on the list of rare or endangered waterfowl.

I have been making studies of controlled breeding methods for cranes, particularly Sarus cranes from India and our native lesser sandhill cranes.

This game farming—the mass rearing of game birds in pens for release in suitable habitat—is an outgrowth of gunning for sport. Many State game departments have established their own game farms in order to assure a steady supply of birds for restocking. I am one of the individuals who do it privately, under permit.

Many of the game breeders have become operators of preserves on which people pay a fee to hunt. The breeders rear the game and develop and plant their lands so as to provide the best habitat for game birds. The result is that there are still large sections of farmland, often near cities, where hunters can find sport and relaxation. The quality of the recreation on a well-managed preserve may be superior to that of free hunting, which in this day and age is harder and harder to come by.

Alongside game farming is another kind of bird husbandry—the keeping and rearing of birds for their grace and beauty. This aviculture began as a hobby, usually with pheasants, which lend themselves well to this kind of activity.

An interesting feature of those participating in the activity of aviculture is the fact that it is not limited to any one group of citizens. Any cross-section of Americans you wish to take will have birdkeepers in it—doctors, lawyers, teachers, preachers, ranchers, barbers, garbage collectors, and laborers, who are ardent aviculturists. When these persons with varied backgrounds get together at meetings and conventions, their common interest in birds unites them in an enthusiastic and congenial group.

They keep in touch with each other through a number of organizations. Many belong to various State groups. There are several large national associations.

Information regarding them can be had by writing to the following persons: Thane Earl, Secretary-Treasurer, American Pheasant and Waterfowl Association, Whitewater, Wisconsin; Samuel McCluney, President, North American Game Breeders and Shooting Preserve Asso., Inc., P. O. Box 312, Warrensburg, Missouri; Robert Landon, Secretary, The Canadian Ornamental Pheasant and Game Bird Association, Box 220, Simcoe, Ontario, Canada; George A. Allen, Jr., Secretary, International Wild Waterfowl Association and American Game Bird Breeders Cooperative Federation, 1155 East 48th South, Salt Lake City, Utah.

Two monthly magazines unite the bird breeders,

Jack Kiracofe, whose hobby is breeding waterfowl, displays prized birds, the tule race of white-fronted goose (left), Pacific white-fronted goose (right).

A Copper pheasant on the game farm of Harry Rohrer at Hagerstown, Maryland.

report on developments in the field, and tell people where they can buy, sell, and exchange stock. The magazines are Modern Game Breeding, Avicultural and Zoological News, 300 Front Street, Boiling Springs, Pennsylvania 17007; and Game Bird Breeders, Pheasant Fanciers and Aviculturists Gazette, 1328 Allen Park Drive, Salt Lake City, Utah.

Among the books about bird rearing that beginners may find useful are *Raising Game Birds in Captivity,* by David B. Greenberg; *Pheasant Breeding and Care,* by Jean Delacour; *Pheasants of the World,* by Jean Delacour; *Waterfowl of the World,* four volumes by Jean Delacour; and *Pheasants Including Their Care in the Aviary,* by H. A. Gerrits.

Breeding stock usually is obtained through purchase or exchange with other breeders. You can buy a pair of golden pheasants for about 10 dollars, a pair of wood ducks for 15 dollars, a pair of Malayan Argus pheasants for 500 dollars, Impeyan pheasants for 75 dollars a pair, and a pair of emperor geese for 200 dollars.

The price usually reflects the rarity of the species and the difficulty of breeding it. Permits occasionally are issued to aviculturists of proved ability to take specific rare kinds of migratory waterfowl for propagation purposes. The permits are issued by the Bureau of Sport Fisheries and Wildlife with very strict controls and stipulations.

A few of the more avid ornamental bird breeders arrange through foreign contacts with trappers and dealers to import desirable breeding stock. This is an expensive and risky procedure, but with good luck it can be successfully accomplished. The cost of these birds overseas is often quite small, but the air express and quarantine will raise the cost of several pairs of birds to several hundred dollars.

Most game breeders keep birds as a hobby and hope that they rear enough surplus stock to help pay the feed bill. The few who are making a living at it import great numbers of birds or purchase any bargains that may be available. Anything they have is for sale. The hobbyist sells only his surplus stock, and much of the rare and unusual therefore is not for sale.

Picture a beautiful lawn, landscaped with evergreens and shrubs. Across it, stepping sedately is a bird with a scarlet breast, an orange and black ruff, and a golden yellow crest atop his head. This is a male golden pheasant in a setting that brings out his beauty. He is only one of a number of species of pheasants that aviculturists keep as creatures of ornament.

Their attractiveness and colors range over the spectrum, and one can find a species to suit his taste with little difficulty. The usual outcome is a collection of many varieties: Several kinds of guineafowl from Africa; peafowl from India and Indochina; jungle and spurfowl from Asia; quail, cranes, and flamingos from around the world; and parrots from tropical lands.

Spacious, landscaped aviaries usually are provided in order to display the ornamental birds at their best. Special care and feeding form an important part in the keeping of these creatures, for part of the challenge is to provide conditions in which they flourish and reproduce.

An interesting fact regarding the rearing of birds is that they are adaptable to many circumstances. Some of the most successful breeders keep their stock in small enclosures in their backyards. The pens are usually a wire enclosure, either on ground or with wire floors. An effort is made to keep ground cover and various other plants growing. A suitable pen to house a pair of pheasants can be built for under 50 dollars.

Most feed requirements can be bought from local grain distributors. Chicken scratch grains are universally used and cost 4 dollars to 6 dollars per 100 pounds. Specially prepared crumbles and pellets for game birds and breeding and developing waterfowl are available at 5 dollars to 7 dollars per 100 pounds. Some breeders use fortified dog or trout feeds for keeping and rearing the rare sea ducks. These cost about 10 dollars per 100 pounds.

Several large milling companies maintain laboratories to provide specific feeds and medication for the game breeder.

Most successful game breeders collect the eggs from their birds and hatch them either in an incubator or under bantam foster mothers. Some of the incubator companies that manufacture equipment especially for the game breeder are Leahy Manufacturing Company, P.O. Box 269, 406 West 22d Street, Higginsville, Missouri 64037; American-Lincoln Incubator Company, New Brunswick, New Jersey; and The Humidaire Incubator Company, 217 West Wayne Street, New Madison, Ohio.

As the eggs hatch, the young are placed in some form of brooder, either with the bantam or with

These chicks are the offspring of the jungle fowl, the wild species from which chickens were developed.

an artificial heating element. It is essential to keep the young birds warm and to provide a commercial starting feed and water. They are moved to outdoor rearing pens, usually at 6 to 8 weeks, when they have matured enough to withstand the elements on their own.

Waterfowl are usually displayed best when ponds and pools are provided, but some species have been bred when only enough water for mating was at hand.

Permits to purchase, keep, propagate, and sell migratory waterfowl must be obtained before these birds can be bought. These permits can be secured by applying to the district game management agent of the Bureau of Sport Fisheries and Wildlife. It is usually necessary to also get a similar permit from the State game departments. It is best to write the State officials, since the laws vary with each State.

An aviculturist's life is always interesting. Everyone for miles around knows the bird enthusiast, and all the little bird orphans are brought to his door.

I know a lady in Minnesota whose hobby is birds. She became the foster mother of a loon chick. A loon is not the easiest fowl to cater to, for their diet is mostly minnows. Even a baby loon requires 3 dozen small fish a day, and each day's growth means that many more minnows. Soon she spent many hours catching minnows. In the fall, when the loon was grown, it rejoined its own kind and migrated with them—reward enough for the hours she spent to keep him fed.

A man in Illinois, 78 years old, has kept rare pheasants for more than 40 years. He attributes his health and age to his interest in birds.

A 90-year-old man in northern New York has raised quite a number of kinds of wild creatures.

An example of the type of pond private breeders build for their waterfowl.

His special interest has been the whooper swan, and he has been rearing them for more than 50 years. "Some folks tell me they dread to grow old," he told me recently. "I can't see it that way. I expect to spend my declining years as I have spent those behind me—spreading the gospel of conservation, especially as it applies to our vanishing wildlife."

A Pennsylvania surgeon took up birdkeeping many years ago for relaxation. He acquired a fine collection of rare birds. He became so interested that he led an expedition into the jungles of Guatemala in quest of the ocellated turkey. He returned, after considerable hardships, with a small collection of these rare birds, some of which he sent to zoological gardens. To bring the turkeys into captivity was only one of the difficulties. It became evident, after several breeding seasons, that the birds could not reproduce. Their eggs always were infertile. Faced with this problem, a zoo on the west coast enlisted the aid of a nearby university, and females were mated by artificial insemination. Fertile eggs were produced and a number of young reared. These second-generation turkeys reproduced naturally, and as a result a new and interesting bird, the ocellated turkey, is being displayed in collections.

Not all such undertakings end so happily. One hobbyist spent a great deal of time and expense some years ago to import a pair of rare Cabot's tragopan pheasants. He was successful with them and reared a group of young. Birdkeeping friends around the country were soon sending notes of congratulations. Then came a violent hurricane, which did no damage except to blow open the door to the pen of young tragopans. All disappeared without trace. That winter one of the adult birds died, and so ended a wonderful dream.

I have found that wild waterfowl are one of the most interesting and beautiful groups of birds for ornamental use. It is instinctive among gunners to turn over in their hands a wood duck drake they bagged and admire the colors of this beautiful creature. An acquaintance, who is a gunner, once said ruefully he wished he could breathe life back into the lifeless form he held in his hand.

The aviculturist very nearly has this power to create life. For, given a pair of wood ducks, he may rear as many as 30 young if he manages them properly. He has the pleasure of observing the devoted courtship of his woodies; the thrill, in time, of discovering the first cream-colored egg that has been laid; the joy of cupping in his hand the soft, downy, bright-eyed duckling; and the satisfaction of releasing, as many aviculturists do, the birds he has reared into the wild. He feels warm satisfaction, too, when he applies his knowledge to rear some rare species and induce difficult species to reproduce in captivity.

One man I know in New Jersey has a number of large, elaborately landscaped aviaries in which he breeds unusual foreign species, including the tiniest of hummingbirds.

The aviculturist is limited only by his own finances and imagination. He can observe birds as can no other birder, because birds in confinement lose much of their fear of man, although they retain their natural instincts and reactions.

I recall two male wood ducks I once had. They had been reared together as the only survivors of an early setting of eggs. They therefore had become attached to each other, ignoring the other waterfowl in the holding pen.

We place our birds, at breeding time, in the pens in a ratio of one hen for each drake. Our experience is that wood ducks normally mate in this fashion. Among the breeding drakes were the two males that were so strongly attached to each other. For a while it appeared that they did not want to have anything to do with the females, but finally we noticed that they were beginning to follow one rather small, shy female.

As it developed, they were satisfied to attach themselves to her alone, and they worked out quite a system. One male did all the courting, while the other did all the fighting. When another drake would show any interest in their wife, the fighting male would tear into him. The Romeo of the triangle would silently escort their mate to some quieter section of the pool. When the fighter suddenly would pause long enough to discover that he was alone on the field, he would go frantically in search of his companions.

This arrangement seemed to work out very nicely through the nesting season. When it was over, the males were content to desert their wife

An Amherst pheasant cock.

A flock of ornamental flamingos is kept at the Hialeah Race Track in Florida.

Breeders raise trumpeter swan cygnets in rather simple facilities that have an adequate supply of clean water. Birds so raised are for zoos, parks, and other public display.

and continue to enjoy each other's company into the fall and winter. The mate we had so carefully selected for the extra drake was won by another, more arduous male, who appeared very proud to go swimming about the pond with two females vying for his attention.

Aviculture has become a useful tool of wildlife management, as the pressure of our modern civilization has destroyed many of the natural habitats of our wild birds, insect-control methods have further jeopardized the natural productive processes of our wild creatures, and conservation methods of the past—the acquisition and maintenance of natural preserves and protection from gunning and other predation—are no longer sufficient.

One example is the work of the Bureau of Sport Fisheries and Wildlife at a propagation center on the Patuxent River in Maryland. Studies there seek to develop methods of reproducing under favorable conditions cranes, vultures, falcons, and waterfowl. The aim is to rear birds to be reintroduced into the wild flocks to bolster declining species.

The Swinhoe pheasant is a rather common species in private collections, but it has become rare in its native Formosa. Breeders in the United States and England have undertaken to raise numbers of these birds for return to their homelands.

Some private aviculturists and zoological gardens also are working on special programs to assist various State and Federal game management departments to preserve several rare and endangered species, such as the Mexican duck, tule white-fronted goose, masked bobwhite quail, and trumpeter swan.

The swan is a special interest of mine. To obtain hand-reared stock of this great, white, noble bird, Robert and Elizabeth Elgas, of Big Timber, Montana, my wife, Viola, and I went to Alaska in 1962. We also brought back the first spectacled eiders ever to be brought into captivity. The purpose of the trip—and several others to the Arctic—was to collect wild waterfowl to be used for research into propagation.

The whistling swan has never been induced to

breed under controlled conditions. This has been primarily because no hand-reared breeding stock is available. Hand-reared stock is a prerequisite for success with many species of waterfowl. The purpose of our trip to Alaska in 1962 was to obtain spectacled eider ducklings, whistling swan cygnets, black brant and cackling Canada goose goslings, and sandhill crane chicks. We hope, from the birds collected, to develop this breeding stock.

Unfortunately, since both Robert Elgas and I conduct our wildlife work as a hobby, we have responsibilities to our regular work. For that reason, we had to leave the tundra by July 4. The swan eggs had not yet hatched, and we had no equipment to handle them properly. It was necessary to improvise a method of getting them back to civilization. First we collected seven eggs that were advanced in incubation to a point near hatching, since these normally retain their heat better than ones at other stages. These we packed in a haversack lined with a thick layer of eider down. The swan eggs were transported in this fashion to Bethel, Alaska, the first stop on our return flight. Overnight, an electric heating pad was inserted into the haversack and, with the aid of a fever thermometer and by changing the controls on the pad, we were able to retain a sufficiently uniform heat.

The flight from Bethel to Anchorage was so long that we felt it necessary to find a better way to control the temperature. The eggs were distributed among the four members of the party, and each placed their complement of eggs beneath their insulated underwear next to the chest. One of the eggs which I received was "pipped," and the cygnet had cut a hole partly around the egg. It continued its work during the flight, and I felt the cap of the egg slowly forced open as it exerted that last effort to free itself from the shell. Gradually the warm, wet cygnet worked itself out of the egg against my chest. I leaned toward Viola, who was seated next to me, and said, "I've just become a mother." We then told Robert and Elizabeth, and soon all the other passengers were aware of my condition. This caused considerable stir among them. Later, after the cygnet had dried off a bit, I took him out and let everyone have a look at our newborn.

All the eggs withstood this unusual handling, and from them we reared seven healthy whistling swans.

The Elgas operate a cattle ranch along the Boulder River near Big Timber, Montana. They keep and raise wild geese as a hobby. Their collection includes 25 species of geese.

They also have hand-reared whistling swan, lesser and greater sandhill cranes, Sarus cranes, and demoiselle cranes.

Mr. Elgas is very much interested in all species of waterfowl and an expression he frequently uses when speaking admiringly of any kind is: "This is one of my favorites." His special interest is wild geese, however, and he has done extensive private research in this field. He has acquired a vast store of little-known knowledge about the wild geese of the world. It was primarily his research which led us to the nesting grounds of the tule white-fronted geese in Old Crow Flats, Yukon Territory.

Mr. Elgas' interest in wild geese has led him on other expeditions, at his own expense, into the arctic nesting grounds. He accompanied another companion, Eldon Pace, of Shubenacadia, Nova Scotia, in 1960 to Southampton Island to collect breeding stock of the Atlantic brant. Mr. Pace reared this small goose for the first time under controlled conditions in 1965.

Mr. Elgas reared two tule geese in 1965 from stock he had previously collected. This is the first authentic nesting and successful rearing of this rare goose in captivity.

—JACK M. KIRACOFE.

Birds in the Home

A N AMUSING little feathered migrant from Australia took America by storm in the midfifties. The parakeet had bright colors, winning ways, and an ability to mimic the human voice, and by 1956 one of every five American homes had one—more than 14 million in all.

It was something of a craze. Newspapers reported how lost parakeets got back home by telling somebody their names and addresses. There were talking contests for birds, parakeet hair styles and color schemes, entertainment by parakeets in barbershops and nightclubs, and parakeet rooms in restaurants. A parakeet entertainer in Atlanta was said to have earned 780 dollars. A bird was listed in the Chicago telephone book and had his own private line. Chicago had a school for parakeets.

For one in Miami Beach, a vocabulary of 400 English and Yiddish phrases was claimed. Another in Dayton could repeat chemical formulas and a condensed version of the, theory of relativity. Mellie, in San Francisco—so it was said—could recite the Lord's Prayer, the pledge of allegiance to the flag, and several nursery rhymes.

Parakeets are clean, neat, friendly, engaging birds. Domestic varieties come in various colors— yellow, green, blue, mauve, violet, chartreuse, gray.

Great flocks of wild ones swooped over the grasslands of Australia in the 19th century. People called them budgerigars—"beautiful birds." They are still "budgies" to many people. The first live specimens were brought to England in 1840 by John Gould, a naturalist, and they soon became favorites of aviculturists in England, Belgium, the Netherlands, and other countries.

Thousands were trapped each year in Australia and shipped to Europe and the United States. Finally, in alarm, the Australian government passed a law forbidding further export of the birds. By that time, this parakeet had been bred in captivity, and breeders and hobbyists had discovered a number of color mutations were possible.

The giving of parakeets as love tokens was popular in Japan until the Japanese government banned their importation in 1928. In fact, parakeets are sometimes referred to as lovebirds, although the true lovebirds are chunky little parrots with shorter tails; they come from Africa.

At the time the parakeet craze was cresting, other segments of the cage bird populations were relatively stable, except for a slight upswing in favor of the more unusual and exotic birds.

Canaries were in second place, with a population of about 4 million. Other popular cage birds were finches of various kinds, myna birds, Java sparrows African lovebirds, cockatiels, and members of the parrot family.

In the intervening decade, the number of parakeets has slowly leveled off. In the United States, about 7 million families had at least one pet bird in 1965—5.6 million had parakeets (about the same as in 1953); 1.5 million had canaries; and about 150 thousand had other exotic birds.

Each year, approximately 2.3 million birds are sold by retail stores and breeders. Prices for parakeets and canaries range from a dollar a bird to 10 dollars. Birds of unusual color cost the most.

Many cage birds live to be 11 and 12 years old, but the average life expectancy in captivity is much less—about 4 or 5 years for parakeets and canaries.

A sizable industry has grown up alongside the increased popularity of birds as pets. The ready availability of clean, balanced bird food and accessories has made it easy for people to own birds, especially canaries and parakeets, and to provide for their needs.

Parakeets eat nearly 100 times their own weight annually. To equal that, a man of average size would have to eat more than 45 pounds of food daily.

Into the preparation of the various dietary items

Boys sometimes make pets of crows.

for canaries and parakeets go more than 20 ingredients from several countries: Canary seed from Argentina, Australia, Turkey, and Morocco; rapeseed from Canada; cuttlebone from the Mediterranean, Gold Coast, and Japan; and various seeds from Iran, India, and the Netherlands. Until 1955, about the only seed ingredient grown in the United States was millet.

Total sales of bird seed and edible accessories are estimated at about 23 million dollars annually. Most of the feed sold is seed, although owners feed their pets a variety of other items. For parakeets, these include biscuits, condition food, and sprays of millet. Canaries supplement their basic seed diets with biscuits and conditioning food.

Parakeets and canaries require constant supplies of gravel, cuttlebone, and water. Gravel is needed to grind their food. Cuttlebone, which the birds peck at, supplies calcium. Both can be bought in packages.

About 12 million dollars' worth of nonedible accessories are sold each year. They include toys, mirrors, play yards, training aids, travel equipment, and a host of other items. Once you could buy a parakeet tote bag for 25 dollars (for taking a bird for a walk), a rhinestone parakeet sweater, gold and silver leg bands on which a bird's name and address could be inscribed, pants for parakeets that flew around the house, and even tiny coffins.

Bird cages (about 5 million dollars in annual sales) now are mostly functional affairs of metal and glass, but more elegant and fanciful styles, many of which are imported, can be had—split-level and ranch-style cages, elaborate Chinese pagodas, wrought iron and brass designs of contemporary styling, or period pieces.

These bird foods and accessories are sold in pet shops, variety stores, department stores, grocery stores, and drug stores.

All in all, cage birds are at least a 40-million dollar business in the United States.

Another part of the bird business is the breeding and selling of the birds themselves. Although most of the birds now popular as house pets in the United States originated in distant and usually tropical parts of the globe, they are now raised in Florida, Texas, California, and elsewhere.

For a while, the commercial importation and interstate shipment of psittacine birds were banned because of a fear of disease, but those Federal restrictions were relaxed in the early fifties. By then, the domestic raising of parakeets was well established.

Besides commercial breeders, thousands of amateur breeders throughout the country raise canaries, parakeets, and other cage birds as a hobby. There are cage bird societies, notably the American Budgerigar Society. Many cities have annual cage bird shows, in which hobbyists compete for prizes.

Cage birds have had a place in various research projects.

Parakeets, which as a species may be prone to

Parakeets and a friend.

Selective breeding has produced parakeets in a variety of colors.

tumors, have been used in studies of cancer. Their use as test animals in other phases of medical research has been recommended because they are virtually odorless and cleaner than rats and chicks.

Psychologists have found that the friendly personalities and amusing antics of parakeets make them useful in brightening the lives of emotionally disturbed individuals. At one time there was an organization called "Budgies for Recovery," whose aim was to provide the cheerful, little, talking birds for mental hospitals and lonely or chronically ill patients.

A study of behavior patterns of birds has been undertaken in the Department of Ornithology at Cornell University. There, in modern aviary-laboratory facilities, 13 scientists, with grants from the National Science Foundation and the National Institutes of Health, use modern techniques, such as time-motion photography, to conduct a comparative ethological study of parrot genus *Agapornis,* commonly known as African lovebirds. As a byproduct of their work, they have learned a great deal about the effects of early experience and genetics on the development of species-typical behavior.

The research may expand knowledge of the development of inborn and acquired behavior patterns in simpler animals and give clues to the complexities of human behavior.

Parrots were kept by the ancient inhabitants of India and Africa and have been favorite pets since the time of Alexander the Great (250 B.C.), when

the elegant Alexandrine parakeet was best known. In Nero's time (30 A.D.), the African species, particularly members of the ringneck parakeet family, became very popular. They were a high-priced luxury.

Columbus brought several parrots back from his first expedition to the New World. The Europeans were intrigued by the parrot's habits and abilities, and as late as the 18th century the possession of an exotic parrot in a costly cage was a status symbol.

Wild canaries are native to the Canary Islands and the Islands of Madeira, where they were first captured in the 15th century and carried back by sailors to Europe. By the early 16th century, these songbirds were prized possessions of many noblemen, and great ladies had their portraits painted with their pets perched daintily on their fingers.

Canaries were first bred for sale in Germany, and great singing birds were developed there. Canaries were imported to England in 1677 and have become a major hobby and business there. The British, who bred their birds mainly for beauty

Snowflake and Specks, canaries, sing along as Art Brown plays the organ on his Washington radio program.

of plumage and form, are among the greatest canary fanciers in the world.

The German breeders were the first to organize the sale of canaries on a large scale, and after the First World War shipped thousands of birds to New York. Importations from Germany were halted by the Second World War. American breeders then stepped into the picture, and the canary is now a naturalized, firmly established resident.

The little bird from the Canary Islands has been bred into about 50 well-marked varieties. The rollers, or German song canaries, are famous for their music, having been bred for their voices and trained by musical instruments and by other superior singing canaries. The St. Andreasberg is among the most famous of these breeds. Well-known English breeds include the Norwich, Yorkshire, London Fancy, and Scotch Fancy.

Who own pet birds? All kinds of people, to be sure. Bird ownership is highest among middle-income families with several young children. It is also highest in cities, particularly in the Northeast and on the west coast. The average parent in these bird-owning families is 35 to 40 years old, but many of the 12 thousand letters received annually by French's Pet Bird Laboratory, Rochester, New York, come from people, especially women, who are 60 to 70 years old.

All this is not surprising: Parakeets particularly are good pets for youngsters because they are hardy, affectionate, and amusing and need a minimum of care. Also, cage birds provide fun and companionship for older people, with a minimum of expense, care, and space. Apartment dwellers who have no room or facilities for larger pets can easily keep birds. Birds do not ruin the neighbor's grass, or terrorize the neighbor's songbirds, or need to be walked on cold nights, or bite the mailman, or scratch the furniture.

—Barbara M. Vayo.

Sunday at the Zoo

BIRDWATCHING is a popular hobby in the United States, but still ignorance of birds and their ways is just as pervasive among another large section of the population. Nobody knows these two forces better than the curator of birds in a zoo. His life is spent fostering intelligent interest and combatting indifference, and for both he employs the same powerful tool: Living birds in all their wonderful variety.

The Sunday afternoon zoo-goer may know a lot about birds (if only his local species) or he may enter the bird house merely because its open door is in his path, but it is the profession and pleasure of the man responsible for the collection to broaden the interest of the one and stimulate the curiosity of the other.

More and more, zoos are doing these two things, for the time is fast disappearing when zoo people are satisfied with exhibition alone. There is so much to tell about birds, so much to show, so many fascinating chapters in their life story that anyone can read if given a little help.

To the universal appeal of the bird as a living organism we owe the many brilliantly conceived and executed new methods of exhibition in this country and abroad—the "exotariums," the open, barrierless aviaries, new display concepts where birds are given the chance to live relatively natural lives and to demonstrate their specializations and abilities. Nothing takes the place of direct observations in the field; that goes without saying. But how many of us can give our lives to professional birdwatching?

We can do our birdwatching in a zoo, and it can be a rewarding experience. A fine collection of living birds affords those already interested in birds a simulated trip around the earth—conveniently and economically. In the presentation of beautiful creatures of natural worlds increasingly remote to increasing urban populations, a collection may offer anyone superb recreation and an education. Today the zoo is an urban outpost of wildlife and an advocate of the open door to the excitement of natural history.

Look about at the zoo—you may see a hummingbird from Ecuador, but a breath away a kookaburra from Australia, almost within reach a stately sarus crane from India, a European robin (so different from our own "robin"), or even an eagle from Africa. You will see, from our own countryside, thrashers, thrushes, warblers, and woodpeckers—all closeup and often within the span of a few unhurried glances.

Birds in zoos are generally well cared for today. Their diets are prepared scientifically, and their breeding requirements usually are understood. Longevity of birds in zoos is proverbial. Birds soon learn that man and other predators are fenced out of their exhibits and that man will not infringe on zoo-bird territory except to offer food.

At the Bronx Zoo, when a storm in 1950 broke a window in the large cage of three red-billed blue magpies from the Himalaya Mountains, the birds were frightened out into the wind and carried several miles away. They managed to find their way back to the cage, entered, and were waiting for their usual feeding the next day.

A crowned crane from Africa, whose clipped wing had grown out unobserved, once startled staff and visitors with unscheduled flights over the zoo, always returning to its original enclosure on the "African plains." This spectacular feat was relegated to second place by the majestic, and unexpected, soaring of a trio of horned screamers from South America high over a small exhibit at the St. Louis Zoo. These birds, too, returned to their enclosures.

Perhaps because they have learned they are secure, zoo birds, when given the opportunity, behave less secretively than they must in the wild. More and more bird behavior studies therefore are being conducted with captive bird collections. So much curious bird behavior has eluded description in the wild that even the casual zoo-goer may observe and take for granted facets of normal bird behavior that no scientist has yet recorded. Of course, many zoo birds interact with the visitor and this reaction, sometimes aggressive, is a compelling factor in the strength of the appeal and inspiration of a collection of birds.

Even the least analytical of zoo visitors watching the curious mutual dance of the black and ivory jungle mynas from Bali, the tail pump and flutter of the fabled quetzal of Central America, or the ridiculously menacing sideways cakewalk of the native killdeer cannot fail to be entranced by the obvious beauty, even if he is not challenged by the sometimes obscure meaning of bird posturing.

Constant movement and constant change help make exhibits of living birds especially satisfying recreation. They are always new, never dull.

In the zoo, as in the wild, birds are much involved in what they do. Unlike our tail-wagging dogs and the monkeys, they are less likely to invite comparisons with human qualities, and we are more likely to watch them for themselves.

More leisure time is not only a demand but also a fact of the 1960's—but, what to do with it? Forty-seven artists and amateur photographers were once counted at the six major waterfowl exhibits of the Bronx Zoo on a warm Saturday in July. The photo shop at the San Diego Zoo sold more than 135 thousand dollars' worth of film and photographic supplies in 1962. Zoo birds are a major attraction for amateur artists and photographers, and not a few professionals spend hours at their local zoo whenever the opportunity presents.

For the fortunate pet breeder or livestock farmer, there is a special fascination and pleasure in rearing animals. Some of this fascination seems to be attached by city dwellers to the births in their zoos. The announcement of a major zoo birth or hatching is sure to be followed by a swarm of newspaper reporters and photographers and, subsequently, by a deluge of visitors.

Because of the zoo's close rapport with the press and public, it becomes a center for the dissemination of wildlife information and a factor in the relations between bird and man. When an oil tank

A meal of oranges, bananas, and grapes is prepared for some birds at the National Zoological Park.

accident released oil into the Raritan estuary on the eastern seaboard, zoos in Philadelphia and New York were called upon to handle scores of oil-soaked waterfowl and to render advice to housewives and wildlife agencies in their efforts to save the birds.

New Yorkers call their zoo almost any time night or day to ask if something can be done for a pair of catbirds whose nest has been blown down in a storm, if a pair of woodpeckers can be kept from drumming on the eaves of their house, if the latest count of whooping cranes is up or down, and if peacocks will hybridize with guineafowl. (They will. At least one hybrid is on record.)

There is amazing confusion about what a bird is. Some zoo-goers have trouble accepting penguins as birds on their first visit to the penguin house, and many are surprised to learn that only birds have feathers or that ostriches do not fly. Innumer-

An outdoor flight cage at the National Zoological Park in Washington was completed in 1965.

Four species of pelicans are getting a meal of fish at the Bronx Zoo.

Penguins at the Bronx Zoo live in an enclosure that resembles Antarctica and is kept cold always.

A boy has his first experience with a duck at the Bronx Zoo.

able parakeet owners are distressed to learn, from a patient curator, that their pet's eggs will not be fertile unless the bird is provided with a mate. A casual walk through the zoo helps put flesh on sketchy concepts for even the most concrete-bound of urbanites, and the speed with which children grasp the challenging ideas of the assorted sights and sounds presented by a large bird collection and reach for the similarities and dissimilarities in ostrich and hummingbird, eagle and flamingo, is a delight to the naturalist if an embarrassment to the uninitiated parent.

As a longtime zoo-goer-watcher, I have been often amazed at the discernment of youngsters with no natural history education or field experience other than a day at the zoo. Such questions as, "Why do ostriches have feathers if they don't fly?" and the observation of a 6-year-old looking over a dozen species of toucans: "Mother, look, they all had the same father," no longer surprise me. The top honors in my book of subadult zoo

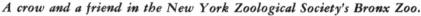

A crow and a friend in the New York Zoological Society's Bronx Zoo.

194

observations came from a 14-year-old farm boy from Crawford County, Missouri. After reading a sign in front of a cage of birds of prey, he came forth with his own rendering of the Conservationist's classic proposition: "If there used to be lots more huntin' and there used to be lots more chicken hawks and varmits, then chicken hawks and varmits ain't what's hurtin' the huntin'."

Although zoo visitors want to see the largest and smallest, the fastest and slowest, the most bizarre, and the most colorful birds, our familiar native birds usually form the best basis of comparison and appreciation for those who know them. So many people in New York are uninformed about birds beyond the ubiquitous pigeons, starlings, herring gulls, and English sparrows, that native bird exhibits at the Bronx Zoo have gained great popularity. They offer a challenge to become familiar with creatures that are "ours"—a part of the national heritage.

The informed zoo observer looks for and finds a world of startling parallels and surprising contrasts at the zoo. He is confronted, on one hand, by South American waterfowl which fly south to breed and, on the other, by North American birds which head south to winter. He cannot help but feel a sense of loss when he learns, in his first view of a great South American condor, that our California condor is comparatively as rare as the South American bird is common.

The lessons of comparative anatomy and physiology, even of adaptation and nutrition, lie in pleasant ambush at every turn of the zoo's walks. Here a hummingbird that finds it necessary to feed four times an hour during its active day and there a penguin stolidly moulting his entire feathered vestment with no food whatsoever for as long as 4 weeks. An anhinga, a pelican, a cormorant, and a gannet flaunt their adaptations and hide their under-the-feather relationship, while ostrich, emu, and rhea deceptively match adaptation and appearance without close kinship.

Led on by the simple fish or seed diet of stork or parrot, the zoo observer is confronted with the complicated mix for insectivorous birds and the special soup of the flamingos—a soup compounded not only to preserve life but also to preserve dietary-dependent pink and crimson feather colors. Zoo

visitors who have an opportunity to go behind the scenes soon realize it takes an extensive staff and a specialized technology to give proper care to a large, living bird collection.

The bird department of the Bronx Zoo, for example, includes a curator, assistant curator, headkeeper, assistant headkeeper, six senior keepers, eight keepers, and a secretary. More than 100 food items, from frozen shrimp and live mealworms to protein hydrolysates and vitamin concentrates, are employed in the daily preparation of a score of diets—often individually adjusted as substitutes for the diversified fare to which wild birds have adapted in nature.

Some captive rations are simple. Some are complex. Fish-eating birds usually can be fed fresh fish supplemented with vitamins and minerals, but insectivorous species are more demanding. A zoo dietitian can hardly march down to the corner supermarket and buy 50 pounds of assorted live insects (not even fresh-frozen insects) for his several hundred flycatchers, pittas, drongos, ant birds, woodpeckers, helmet-shrikes, and the like. Instead, he compounds a palatable mixture of meat, liver, eggs, and various meal, like a chicken mash supplemented with vitamins and minerals to provide basic quantities of essential proteins, fats, carbohydrates, vitamins, and minerals. The basic ration must then be further modified for specialized species. Then, by mixing live insects with the "insectivorous mixture," the insect-eating bird is taught to recognize his new ration as food. Sometimes this teaching process is difficult, and highly specialized birds must even be force-fed for a time and persuaded to eat with a variety of technical tricks. Some species, such as the chimney swift, which eats only flying insects caught on the wing, are so narrowly adapted that practical methods for feeding them in captivity have not yet been developed.

The deep roseate color of the American flamingo is dependent upon carotenoids the bird finds in the tiny molluscs, crustaceans, and worms it strains from the mud of lagoon bottoms. For years, zoo specimens deprived of these foods presented a sadly faded appearance. While it had been learned that flamingos would live and breed on a souplike mixture of various cereal meals, meat, and eggs, good practical color supplements had not been found. Eventually, it was learned that a carrot-oil concentrate or even fresh carrot juice contained carotenoids, which the birds could utilize to help color their feathers. Now zoos have red flamingos.

Hummingbirds are also fed on a special soup in captivity but only a few zoos show more than one or two species. San Diego Zoo has opened a new hummingbird aviary, where visitors are allowed to mingle with the birds. The Cleveland Zoo a few years ago became the first United States zoo to breed hummingbirds, but the most famous of hummingbird exhibits is undoubtedly the Jewel Room in the Bronx Zoo. There, in a series of small, attractively planted and brightly lighted, glass-fronted displays, hummingbirds have established remarkable longevity records. Several specimens in the air-conditioned, light-controlled exhibits have survived 7 and 8 years. One iridescent feathered gem, a Caribbean emerald-throated hummingbird, lived 10.5 years, a remarkable span for a creature of such high metabolism and quicksilver temperament. This bird lived on a blend of sweetened condensed milk, honey, beef extract, cereal baby food, liver protein hydrolysates, and vitamins mixed in water. It also received live fruit flies.

Food is only one part of bird care, however. Daily cleaning of zoo exhibits, preparation of new displays, introduction of new specimens, operation of incubators and brooders, hand rearing of chicks, and constant observation take most of a day in a bird department.

A curator usually begins his daily tasks by reviewing the collection with the headkeeper, walking from exhibit to exhibit. They note the need to move an overly aggressive bird or to consult with the veterinarian concerning health problems of individuals. A decision to obtain a new mate for that crane, to build an artificial nest for this stork, to prepare new labels, to replant an enclosure, to adjust a diet are all typical of an early morning curator-headkeeper dialogue. Keepers report problems and observations at each installation. The curator constantly notes observations on moult, behavior, and development in his notebook for future incorporation in scientific and popular articles.

Eventually, the curator gets to his office where

an international correspondence awaits him. Letters from ornithologists requesting information on the captive care of birds they are studying, a letter from a teacher who has found a hummingbird with a broken wing, a list from a collector in Ecuador, a note from a natural history club requesting a lecture, and so on. Meanwhile, his phone buzzes regularly with calls from people who wish information. He dispatches a car to the airport to pick up a touraco from Africa, gives a tour to a group of college students, consults with the zoo director on budgetary and planning matters and with the zoo's construction department on repair problems. Then he may dash out to observe the Jungle Stream exhibit, where a manakin is reported building a nest. Each day is hectic, and most days are stimulating for the curator of a large bird collection.

The largest bird collections in America exhibit from 800 to 2,800 birds of 300 to 800 species. Only the biggest, such as those in San Diego, New York, St. Louis, Chicago (Brookfield), Washington, D.C., and Philadelphia, have curatorial staffs.

Bird exhibits at zoos sometimes emphasize the practical aspect of aviculture. The material-minded can hardly ignore a jungle-fowl exhibit, where the ancestors of the domestic chicken are a living testimony to the power of selection. Even the esthete must marvel at the development of a delightfully edible egg-laying machine, capable of depositing 3 thousand eggs or more during its lifetime, from a tough little bird which would probably never lay more than 50 eggs during its entire life in the wild. The wild ancestors of domestic geese and the wild turkey are usually to be seen, and they demand from poultry consumers the sort of respect one might accord some prehistoric "common ancestor" of their various domestic descendants.

Behind each bird exhibited at the zoo lies a story of birds and men, sometimes dramatic but often simple and touching, for the zoo houses repaired waifs as well as daring captures. A window-washer once came to the Bronx Zoo carrying four small sacks. In each was an injured warbler rescued after a collision with one of the Empire State building's incredibly high window sills. Two were successfully nursed back to health and exhibited in the zoo's New England Garden for many years. An

A new building at the Bronx Zoo has a lagoon for flamingos.

These young trumpeter swans, a rare species, were hatched at the Philadelphia Zoo.

injured evening grosbeak was contributed by a Scarsdale cobbler, a Long Island banker drove in with a saw whet owl rescued from a cat, and a Bronx housewife contributed a killdeer with a broken leg (which later became the great-great-grandfather of a colony of zoo-bred killdeers).

A similar list could be composed by almost any zoo. These contacts often form the basis of a permanent wildlife interest for the bird Samaritan. Almost any zoo can tell at least one story of a hunter, out all day shooting, who finds a wounded bird on the way home, nurses it back to health, and takes pride in presenting it to the zoo.

The arduous expeditions of zoo bird collectors who have traveled to the ends of the earth in order to bring back specimens make up the most intimate of the sagas of bird and man. A broken leg, filiariasis, and 2 long years in the jungle were involved in Charles Cordier's successful capture of the elusive Congo peafowl in 1949 while he was working for the New York Zoological Society. The only imperial pheasants ever captured alive were acquired in Indo-China by Jean Delacour, first among the world's aviculturists, in 1925. Today, in American zoos, as elsewhere, all existing imperial pheasants are descended from this original importation. I, myself, brought back the first James' and Andean flamingos ever captured alive from a 1960 New York Zoological Society expedition to a lake 13 thousand feet high in the Bolivian Andes. These strange, high-mountain flamingos were viewed by more people during their first week of exhibition than in all previous history.

Today, zoos are beginning to act to meet a new and melancholy need—as repositories for the scattered population fragments of species which are facing extinction through man's agency. A Sunday at the Cincinnati Zoo in 1914 would have included a visit to see the last passenger pigeon. Had aviculture and attitudes been a little further advanced, the passenger pigeon might still be with us today, at least in zoos, for it was a species which could easily have been bred in captivity.

While maintaining vanishing species forever in "museum-zoos" is a grim and difficult prospect, it is quite possible that avicultural techniques will be useful in tiding a precarious population over a difficult period, or until new and suitable habitat has been developed or set aside for it. Mammals, such as the American bison, the European bison, and the Prjevalski's wild horse, are already profiting from such ultimate management. Unfortunately, some birds, among which is the bald eagle, are still difficult to breed in captivity.

At the zoo, surrounded by hundreds of species of birds, each different from others of its family and each intent on being its particular kind of bird, we human beings are likely to find a happy recreational escape from the artificial strictures of the manmade to the realities of a world evolved long before our advent and to become aware that wildlife did not evolve for us nor did it depend on us—as it does now. A door to the out-of-doors is opened, and we learn something of our world—and, perhaps, of ourselves.

—WILLIAM G. CONWAY.

In Nature's Scheme

COOPER'S HAWK
BOBWHITE

Raptors

Hawks and owls belong to two unrelated orders of birds that comprise many species and subspecies. They are readily recognizable as birds of prey, but they differ in size, structure, habits, and the habitats they frequent.

They have one important attribute in common. They live by killing and eating other creatures. Because they are predatory birds, or raptors, hawks and owls are controversial animals and demand a special sort of understanding among all of us.

To know how raptors fit into the scheme of things, we must first understand predation. To understand predation, we must measure.

As Lord Kelvin said, "When you can measure what you are speaking about and express it in numbers, you know something about it, and when you cannot measure it, when you cannot express it in numbers, your knowledge is of a meagre and unsatisfactory kind." This noted English mathematician, physician, and inventor was referring primarily to the physical sciences, but his statement is equally true of the biological sciences.

Knowledge of the role of predators in Nature, of the intricate relationships that derive from killing other creatures in order to live, is still "meagre and unsatisfactory," but advances in measuring animal populations have already led to a greater understanding of raptors. Although we may never express the interaction of this life and death process by mathematical formulas, we can quantify aspects of the phenomenon of predation, observe and interpret situations, and draw conclusions that will lead to more precise knowledge in the future.

The farmer who shoots a Cooper's hawk in the act of killing a bobwhite is not concerned with population phenomena, but he has made unconsciously a measurement, and he can express his knowledge in numbers: One hawk killed one quail. He may conclude on tangible evidence that Cooper's hawks kill game birds and are bad.

Such simplified gatherings and interpretation of data are not far removed from primitive times. The fact that one death awaits every life is a law without exception. Man has not questioned this fact, but perhaps in protest against it he has attempted to control it. He has made his own rules concerning the life and death of other creatures. They have not always been good or defensible rules. Generally they have been related directly to his own self-interest and to his own role of chief predator of the animal world.

Man's hostility toward hawks and owls probably began when he questioned their right to kill and consume grouse, ducks, or any other prey that might serve as food for himself.

In a highly competitive primitive environment of eat or be eaten, this was perhaps a justifiable attitude. As human beings emerged from hunting cultures into the more secure agrarian or pastoral forms of civilization, man's hostility to raptors only

increased. His ability to kill kept pace with his advancing technology. No longer just another animal in the community, man had the power to control drastically—to exterminate.

But understanding of the biological world also progressed, and science revealed the existence of a balance of nature, a dynamic ebb and flow of life regulated by natural forces. Man's rationale for exterminating raptors required re-evaluation. Here in the middle of the 20th century, hawks and owls are still persecuted. Sportsmen's clubs aid and abet local organized control efforts; farmers, landowners, and many rural dwellers too often repeat a smug cliché, "The only good hawk is a dead hawk."

We urgently need legislation and law enforcement to protect raptors. We also need intelligent policies to control them when necessary. For that, we need a knowledge of predation, a broad concept of life and death in Nature, and understanding and tolerance.

Enough has been learned about hawks and owls and the significance of their predatory acts over the past 50 years to give scientists a concept of raptors quite different from beliefs based on ancient prejudices.

Here we try to show the progress of scientific research as it relates to predation by raptors and so give the basis for the scientists' viewpoint. We attempt also to relate the growing body of biological knowledge to the old prejudices. We hope emotion and intellect eventually will be harmonized into public understanding and policy.

The question behind all others the research biologist asks in his search for truth about hawks and owls has had to be, "Is the killing done by raptors good or bad?" Not good or bad in the sense of human ethics or morality, but from the standpoint

201

202

of biotic balance, population dynamics, environmental control, and ultimately economic welfare.

This underlying question cannot be answered without first finding the answers to many related questions—without forming the body of biological knowledge necessary to support a "good" or "bad" conclusion. Without, in short, measuring. Let us trace this process and its background.

More than a hundred kinds of hawks and owls live in North America. They have large, powerful feet with long, curved talons for catching and holding prey and sharp, hooked beaks for tearing flesh. They are strong-winged, powerful fliers. Some are superb soarers. Some are speedy darters. Others are unmatched for combinations of speed and endurance.

The order of hawks and their allies includes the American vultures, Old World vultures, hawks, falcons, kites, ospreys, and harriers. We here exclude the vultures, because they are not primarily raptorial; they feed largely on carrion rather than kill live prey.

Owls are distinguished from hawks primarily by such obvious characteristics as forward-facing eyes, set in facial disks; large, seemingly neckless heads; and soft, fluffy plumage. Like hawks, they have hooked beaks and powerful feet and talons. Unlike the hawks, they generally are largely nocturnal.

The day-active raptorial birds are grouped into families.

The falcons usually frequent open country and are noted for speedy dives or stoops. They are distinguished from the other hawks by long-pointed wings and notched upper mandible. The ospreys are long-winged fish hawks. Structurally they are distinguished from other hawks by their reversible toe. The family *Accipitridae* includes such diverse forms as the eagles, the buteos, the kites, Old World vultures, and the accipiters. The accipiters, or short-winged hawks, frequent the woods. They can fly with great speed and control through brush and trees in pursuit of quarry. The buteos, or soaring hawks, are generally large, chunky birds with broad, rounded wings. They feed chiefly on small rodents and hunt from conspicuous perches, such

A family of barred owls at nest entrance.

as fence posts, dead trees, or telephone poles, or they circle and soar above cultivated fields.

The nocturnal raptorial birds are grouped into two families, the barn owls (*Tytonidae*) and the typical owls (*Strigidae*). The barn owl has a heart-shaped face, is almost worldwide in distribution, and is representative of the barn owl family. The small screech owl and the large great horned owl are familiar examples of typical owls.

From the time of John James Audubon in the first half of the 19th century until about 1930, American scientists were concerned primarily with recording the natural history of these raptors.

The work during this and earlier periods is summed up in Arthur Cleveland Bent's *Life Histories of North American Birds of Prey*. Here are compiled observations, reports, and field notes of hundreds of contemporary observers on the moulting, plumage, courtship procedures, nesting habits, egg dates, food, behavior, field marks, voice, enemies, winter habits, distribution, and migration of the many species of this continent's hawks and owls.

Only when the natural history of raptors was well documented could biologists turn their attention to gathering precise and more detailed information by employing quantitative methods.

Interest focused first on the food habits of birds of prey, because predation was a characterizing attribute and varied with species, geography, seasons, and even individuals of the same species.

This aspect of natural history demanded a great mass of data.

What, for instance, was the general diet of the short-winged hawks?

How did it differ from that of the buteos or soaring hawks? And how did their diet in turn differ from that of the eagles and the falcons?

How greatly did diets change with the seasons?—what are the major food items of the red-shouldered hawk in winter as compared with spring?

How important are pure chance or food preference in determining what raptors eat?

Size and specialized adaptations limit the prey a raptor can take, but within these evolution-imposed restrictions, what, if anything, guides predator-prey relationships?

Are some of these relationships based on the number of predators and the number of prey, and if so, can predation itself be expressed numerically?

W. L. McAtee, a biologist in the Biological Survey, analyzed the contents of the stomachs of 5,185 commoner hawks.

On the basis of the percentage of game species the hawks consumed in relation to the percentage of nongame or pest species they ate, he grouped the hawks according to their economic effect: Those whose feeding habits were definitely un-favorable to man's economic interests; those that could be tolerated; the neutrals; those more beneficial than injurious; the predominantly beneficial; and the almost entirely beneficial.

Dr. McAtee presented evidence that not all hawks and owls are detrimental to man's interests. He concluded:

"The capturing of birds may be judged much as are depredations on insects, that is, according to the economic tendencies of the forms involved, not all good nor all bad, but each case on its own

The Harris' hawk is one of the broad-winged, soaring hawks. It occurs in the Southwestern States and south-ward into Mexico, Central America, and South America. It feeds mostly on small mammals.

merits. It should not be forgotten, moveover, that checks on the multiplication of [nonraptorial] birds are part of the established scheme of things. Relieved of checks, these birds themselves might increase to an extent that would force man to reduce their numbers in self-defense."

The work of Dr. McAtee and others showed percentages of prey species in the diet of raptors. Now biologists began to ask new questions: Is stomach analysis the best method of sampling food habits? How can we get information that is more broadly representative of the birds' predatory life?

A relatively simple way to do this was at hand. Birds of prey eat some of the bones, hair, or feathers of their victims. This largely undigestible matter is formed into pellets and is disgorged, generally before the next feeding. Identification of the contents of pellets allows the scientist to get numerical evidence of the prey species eaten without killing the raptor. The feeding habits of a hawk or owl or a population could be studied in the field from season to season and over a period of years. Such evidence could be further supplemented with tabulation of food items brought to the young in the nest and from direct observation of kills in the field. Thus emerged a new era of investigation.

To determine whether hawks and owls were serious predators of the bobwhite in Georgia and northern Florida, Herbert Stoddard, an eminent wildlife ecologist and author of *The Bobwhite Quail,* analyzed the stomach contents and pellet contents of the raptors and recorded kills in the field.

His evidence showed that only the Cooper's hawk and sharp-shinned hawk were actually enemies of bobwhites in that area. Other birds of prey were either neutral or positively beneficial.

In discussing the marsh hawk, for example, Dr. Stoddard reported: ". . . Not more than four quail were discovered in approximately 1,100 pellets. . . . On the other hand, one or more cotton rats were found in 925 of these pellets. Since cotton rats destroy the eggs of quail, the marsh hawk is probably the best benefactor the quail has in the area. . . ."

By so balancing the food habits of the marsh hawk against the food habits of the cotton rat, Dr. Stoddard was able to reach a "good or bad" conclusion about the hawk—in this case, "good," because people value the bobwhite.

Later on, Paul L. Errington and F. N. Hamerstrom, Jr., when they were at Iowa State University, examined 4,815 pellets from great horned owls gathered from locations throughout the North-Central States. They found that cottontail rabbits and snowshoe hares comprised the greater part of this owl's staple food, but that this raptor also captured Norway rats, mice, muskrats, pocket gophers, waterfowl, and upland game birds.

The significance of their study was the attempt to correlate a raptor's food habits with the numbers and vulnerability of prey. They concluded that the great horned owl is an opportunist that captures whatever prey happens to cross its path when it hunts.

Dr. Errington's work intensified research on predators by bringing up these thoughts:

If a smaller area of land inhabited by great horned owls were intensively studied so that more exact numerical relationships could be established between available prey and prey taken, would new evidence come to light on the nature of predation? What would we learn if we studied simultaneously not one raptor species, such as the great horned owl, but the entire hawk and owl fraternity with respect to predation?

The great horned owl alone, it appeared, had little influence on major prey species—but would a collective population of raptors, each adapted to hunt different prey species at different times, show something different, perhaps the opposite?

Those questions led us to undertake a study of the ecology of raptor predation. We summarized our findings in the book *Hawks, Owls, and Wildlife,* published by Stackpole Co., Harrisburg, Pennsylvania, in 1956. The discussion that follows relies heavily on the results of that study.

We began with the belief that predation by hawks and owls is a complex natural phenomenon, that understanding of predation as a biological force can best be obtained by studying populations of both predator and prey, and that investigation had to be shifted from an individual or a species to an entire community.

We believed it essential to measure the year-round numbers, composition, and movements of

A pair of young sparrow hawks. They are a kind of falcon, have pointed wings, and a notched upper bill. They feed on large insects, such as grasshoppers, and some small birds and mammals.

a raptor population, as well as the types and densities of prey species, and the food habits of raptors as related to available prey.

A complex of such variables as weather, topography, seasonal changes in cover, and abundance of food that affect the vulnerability of the prey also would have to be investigated.

All this could be done best on a well-defined area of land where we could observe many of these elements at a given period of time and interpret them in relation to one another.

To understand our approach, visualize a farm, a favorite hunting site, or any stretch of familiar woods and fields. Imagine it multiplied to the size of a township (36 square miles).

In this area are cottontail rabbits, meadow voles, small birds, bobwhites, ring-necked pheasants, fox squirrels, and other creatures. These, taken as a whole, are the prey population.

In the same area are Cooper's hawks, red-tailed hawks, sparrow hawks, great horned owls, barn owls, and many others, which make up the raptor population. Each raptorial species is adapted to take a limited number of prey species inhabiting the township—no one raptor species can catch and kill members of all the varied species of potential prey, but the raptor population *as a whole* can do so.

How, then, does this collective population of raptors interact with the collective prey?

The activities of hawks and owls on the township form a pattern that helps us interpret this— the dynamics of predation. The raptors must seek and capture their own assortment of prey in order to live. Some of the prey must escape in order to survive, reproduce, and in turn furnish food for the raptors.

The interacting elements of this intricately balanced relationship combine to cause an aggregate effect on any given area of land and over an extended period of time.

What is the effect, and is it biologically or economically important?

To learn this effect, we set about first to find which species of raptor and how many of each were present on a specific piece of land over a long period. So we counted the hawks and owls throughout the seasons for 4 years on the 36 square miles of Superior Township, in Washtenaw County, Michigan.

By such systematic censusing, we discovered that during the winter the average population of raptors consisted of the following (in percentages): Buteos (red-tailed hawks, red-shouldered hawks, and rough-legged hawks), 28; sparrow hawks, 5; Cooper's hawks, 7; marsh hawks, 16; great horned owls, 13; screech owls, 18; long-eared owls, 3; short-eared owls, 10.

In the spring, the raptor population changed as winter residents migrated north and new arrivals moved in from farther south. When the nesting populations became established, the percentages were: Buteos, 37; sparrow hawks, 7; Cooper's hawks, 11; marsh hawks, 12; great horned owls, 11; screech owls, 21; long-eared owls and barn owls, 1; short-eared owls, 0.

We concluded from these figures that the buteos or "mouse hawks" were the predominant raptors on the area during all seasons. The percentages of short-eared owls fluctuated drastically from winter

to spring, an indication of the transitory habits of this species. The percentages of great horned owls and screech owls remained rather constant, reflecting the fact that these species were largely year-round residents. Most significant perhaps was the fact that the percentage of each raptor species in the population bore a direct relationship to the abundance and vulnerability of its major prey species.

For example, the fall and winter populations in 1941 and 1942, when meadow voles were abundant, were much higher than in 1947–1948, when voles were scarce, but there was little difference in the size of the spring and summer populations.

This illustrates the response of migrating raptors (particularly the short-eared owls, marsh hawks, and the rough-legged hawks) to an abundant food supply—in this instance, the meadow voles. The raptors were attracted and held here, as they are in other sections throughout the country, by available food. The size and composition of the hawk and owl population varied with the seasons and from year to year, but during the period of our study, an average of 145 raptors was always present in Superior Township.

During the four winters, an average of 98 raptors (a little more than one-half of them hawks) hunted over the 36 miles of Superior Township.

In the short transition period between winter and spring, the average number of raptors increased to 155, of which two-thirds were hawks and one-third owls.

During the nesting period of spring and early summer, the population averaged 131.

By late summer, after the young had left the nests, the number of all raptors was 238. This number fluctuated during the fall and dropped until it reached the low winter figure.

Now we had established seasonal and annual counts and arrived at some average counts representative of a 4-year period.

We concluded from them that numerous raptors were living in Superior Township at all times and at no time were the prey species free of predation.

We knew that our measurement of the numbers of raptors told only part of the story. We needed to know also how these birds were spaced throughout the township and how they moved: Were the hawks and owls evenly distributed? Did they wander indiscriminantly? Or was there some definite pattern to the location and movements of each bird of prey? How varied were the habitats over which they hunted? Was there overlap in hunting ranges and competition for food and space?

We discovered that theoretically an average of four raptors hunted each square mile of the township during the period we were there—one hawk or owl for each 160 acres. In practice, however, the birds hunted in the places where prey was most abundant and vulnerable and thus were concentrated where the hunting was good.

Parts of the township had no raptors. Some tracts supported a density as high as one raptor per acre for a time. Others consistently supported one raptor to every 20 or 40 acres. Within those tracts, they did not roam haphazardly or randomly in their search for prey. Each hawk or owl or each pair established a definite hunting range outside which it seldom ventured—the hawks hunting by day, the owls at night.

During winters when prey was abundant, there was overlap of ranges. When prey was scarce, hawks tended to defend their hunting grounds and keep intruders at a distance.

No conflict existed between the diurnal and nocturnal hunters, however. Owls hunted at night over the same land that hawks utilized during the day. This dovetailing of predatory pressure from day to night kept both diurnal and nocturnal species of prey in jeopardy from raptors. For some species of prey, such as the meadow vole, it meant a continual mortality from raptors 24 hours a day, day after day, year in and year out.

Young raptors or transients did not invade already established ranges of mature birds or resident birds, but either filled unclaimed territories between the ranges of established birds or emigrated off the area to establish themselves elsewhere, generally in less favorable places.

These self-imposed restrictions led to the distribution of hunting pressure so as to limit competition. It was a natural adjustment. It illustrates not conflict or competition but rather a built-in tolerance of one bird for the requirements of another. The result was maximum raptorial pressure on a wide variety of prey in all habitats.

Each year, as fall approached, the immature hawks and owls raised in the woodlots and fields of Superior Township grew restless. Most of the immature raptors and many of the mature hawks drifted and migrated southward. Some of the mature birds always remained in the vicinity of their nest sites—the red-tailed hawks and Cooper's hawks, a few of the sparrow hawks and marsh hawks, all of the great horned owls, and most of the screech owls.

Migrants, such as rough-legged hawks, short-eared owls, and marsh hawks, arrived from northern regions. Some stopped only temporarily. Others remained to establish hunting ranges and spend the winter. Each winter, the hawk and owl population of year-round residents and seasonal transients stabilized and showed little change in composition or numbers until spring, when the northward migration began.

These resident species can capture a variety of prey. Thus their diet (but generally not their numbers) changes with seasonal variations in the density of the different species of prey.

The transients are more specialized hunters. They depend on a few prey species—mostly meadow voles. These raptors, therefore, must move to new locations when their staple food becomes scarce. In contrast to the residents, their numbers change but generally not their diets.

All raptors are highly mobile, but the same species may be a year-round resident in one region and a transient in another, depending on the type and density of available prey and on the age of these particular hawks and owls—whether they are the young of the year or adults with established home ranges.

Specialized adaptations, migration, and mobility enable raptors to adjust their populations to those of the prey.

Is the opposite also true?

Does raptor predation definitely influence or alter the density and composition of a prey population? If so, how does this occur?

To explore this, we had to gather data on food habits. Thus the next step was to learn what the raptors captured and ate.

We determined the relative percentages of the major prey species in the winter diet of raptors by identifying 13,500 individual prey items from pellets. We determined the spring and early summer diet from 1,837 prey items recorded at raptor nests.

Meadow voles composed 83 percent of the diet of the raptor population in fall and winter but dropped to 30 percent in spring and summer. These mice are small, brownish-gray rodents with long fur, short ears, and small, black eyes. They inhabit narrow runways in moist grassland and multiply rapidly under favorable conditions. The small- and medium-sized nongame birds represented only 1.2 percent of the fall and winter food but rose to 37 percent during the warm months. Nongame food in the winter diet averaged 95.5 percent and game food 4.5 percent. In the spring and summer, nongame averaged 50 percent and game 50 percent of the raptor diet.

These percentages enlightened us concerning the feeding habits of a raptor population but did not in themselves reveal any basic relationship of predator and prey.

We could not evaluate raptor predation until we determined what animal species or prey groups

In defense of its young, this scrappy screech owl does the best it can to drive an intruder away.

were present and were hunted by this collective population of hawks and owls and measured what proportion of each was captured by the raptors present.

Enumeration and estimates of the major prey populations showed that in winter meadow voles were the most abundant prey. They occurred in densities as high as 140 per acre. White-footed mice and deer mice were second in number. Small birds were third. Game birds (ring-necked pheasants and bobwhites) were fourth; cottontail rabbits, fifth; and fox squirrels, sixth.

Spring migration raised the relative abundance of some prey species and prey groups such as small birds, and by summer the numerical relationships of the prey were altered further by reproduction. Now small birds were most abundant and meadow voles second, followed by frogs, snakes, and crayfish as a group, white-footed mice, game birds, rabbits, and fox squirrels, respectively. By late summer

A female great horned owl ready to do battle to defend her nest.

and early fall, however, meadow voles had surpassed all other prey species or groups in numbers and remained the predominant prey throughout the fall, winter, and early spring.

Now we have measured the raptors, determined what they ate, and estimated the relative abundance of the prey species and groups available to them. We concluded that raptor predation operates according to a definite pattern.

A collective population of hawks and owls hunts the available prey of any large area in such a way that each prey species or prey group tends to be taken in proportion to its relative density. This applied to predation in Superior Township in spring, summer, fall, and winter and can be expressed in numbers: If meadow voles represent 90 percent of the total prey available to raptors, white-footed mice 5 percent, small birds 4 percent, and game birds 1 percent, then meadow voles, white-footed mice, small birds, and game birds will tend to represent 90, 5, 4, and 1 percent, respectively, of the collective raptor kill.

The regulatory effect is quite evident here, since the most abundant prey groups absorb mortality in proportion to their abundance. This proportional mortality, besides reducing the collective prey populations, tends to give each specific prey group a fixed density in relation to all others in the prey category. This showed us not only *how* the prey was taken in relation to numbers but also *when*—an important fact to ascertain.

In Superior Township, winter prey sustained mortality from raptors unrelieved until after the middle of March, when the early passerine birds migrated north to augment the prey population. Even after the appearance of frogs, snakes, and late-arriving passerines, however, raptor pressures did not actually shift from the winter prey species.

Most adult raptors, both resident and transient, were hunting in the township by the middle of March. In fact, raptor pressure from early March to early April increased 50 percent above the winter pressure, although no important shift from winter to summer prey occurred. The winter prey species still constituted a major portion of the raptor diet from early March to mid-June.

The early March to mid-June period was critical for populations of winter prey. These overwintering animals, the adult breeding populations, sustained a 50-percent higher raptor population with its corresponding predation at a time when cover for these prey was at a minimum and when prey numbers had been reduced by the rigors of winter.

We need to emphasize the difference between "surplus" and "nonsurplus" prey animals in this context. We refer to the animals that start into a new annual breeding cycle as "nonsurplus."

A greatly simplified composite example based on data from Superior Township and other areas may clarify terms and concepts. Let us assume that a population of 300 thousand meadow voles in fall has been reduced to 30 thousand by late winter.

We know that can happen. Raptors account for a minimum of 80 thousand, or 27 percent, of the mortality. This, too, we have measured and know can occur. Disease, predation by mammals, starvation, inclement weather, stress, and other factors must then account for 190 thousand, or 63 percent. Taken together, these 270 thousand voles can be considered surplus, since relatively few had begun to breed.

The 30 thousand surviving voles are all potential breeders or nonsurplus animals. Most of them are sexually mature animals that will begin a new cycle of breeding. Some of them move to new home ranges. Nearly all become more active as breeding accelerates.

Occurring at a time when there is very little protective cover, this activity and movement render the voles highly vulnerable to half again as many hawks and owls as were present in winter. During the relatively short spring transition period, raptors take a minimum of 7,500 meadow voles, or 25 percent of the population that survived the winter. There is evidence that from early April until the middle of June they take at least an equal number. Perhaps 5,500 or 18 percent of the overwintering populations meet death by all other decimating forces. Nine thousand 5 hundred are left to breed, but even then they are not free of raptor predation. In a favorable year, this number may restore the original population level of 300 thousand, but generally the level remains suppressed for 3 or 4 years. Raptors appear to play a vital role in keeping it suppressed.

The important point is that the percentage of

mortality inflicted by raptor predation in fall and winter on the surplus voles in comparison to the percentage ascribed to other decimating forces is low, but the reverse is true with regard to the nonsurplus animals in early spring.

Any factor or force that causes greater mortality in the spring when breeding is getting underway can delay and reduce the production of a succeeding generation.

Raptors can and do prey on nonsurplus "breeders," and the time or the *when* of this predation is important. The heavy mortality imposed by raptors in early spring can reduce drastically the breeding stock of voles and other overwintering prey species. This appeared to be the situation in Superior Township.

A question of biological and economic importance that we may logically ask is: Can raptor predation have any real controlling effect when prey populations reach their peak or when (as in the case of some rodents) they attain plague proportions?

Generally, as the breeding season progresses, both prey and raptors multiply, but the prey multiply at a much greater rate. Continuous raptor pressure on the increasing prey populations, however, accelerates as the young hawks and owls begin to hunt. The young raptors in Superior Township had fledged by the first of August. The hawk and owl populations thereby attained maximum density when the collective prey population was annually at or near a peak.

In late fall and early winter, when small rodents attained their annual peak in numbers, migrating raptors halted their southward migration to take advantage of this abundance.

Let us examine another specific situation.

From the summer of 1957 until the spring of 1958, five counties in eastern Oregon experienced the most severe irruption of meadow voles ever recorded in the State and possibly in North America. Densities of these voles generally were in the hundreds per acre, although local popula-

Defense of nest was successful, for two alert youngsters fill the nest some weeks later.

tions may have reached 2 thousand to 3 thousand per acre in the peak period of November 1957.

During the fall and winter of 1957, exceptionally large numbers of hawks, owls, and California and ring-billed gulls were in the area, having congregated in response to the unusual density of prey.

The diet of the collective predatory bird population (gulls included) was almost entirely meadow voles. The total number consumed by thousands of gulls and raptors hunting day and night must have been enormous. Simultaneously, other natural controlling forces were at work on the voles—disease, lack of food, climatic factors, retarded reproduction, overstimulation of the adrenal glands, and perhaps others.

All the decimating factors, including predation, meant that only about 10 percent of the vole population survived to April 1, 1958. It is most significant that predation in these Oregon counties was at its highest during early spring and continued high through May and June.

Most scientists who have studied the meadow vole have concluded that the crucial period of the annual cycle is March to June. The fact that thousands of hawks, owls, and gulls were feeding on the breeding stock in the plague area at this critical time for voles, when other mortality factors had largely run their course, supports the view that raptor predation as a natural biotic control becomes most important in spring. It may also be that because of timing, predatory birds can be influential in modifying or controlling peak populations or plague irruptions of prey species.

To return to Superior Township, let us summarize the annual picture of raptor predation as brought forth in our study.

Raptor populations consist of both resident and transient birds. Populations stabilize at their lowest seasonal number during the winter, increase in spring with northward migration, reach their numerical peak in late summer after the young leave the nests, and fluctuate during the fall, as birds congregate in localities with high populations of prey and immature or transient birds migrate south.

At all times of the year, and year in and year out, raptors were present in Superior Township and exerted continuous pressure on the prey species.

213

During the years of our study, this pressure could be expressed as an average of 145 raptors, or 53 thousand raptor days per year.

Raptors concentrate and establish hunting ranges in areas where prey is most abundant and vulnerable. These ranges spread hunting pressure and limit competition.

By diurnal and nocturnal hunting, respectively, and by specialized adaptations for hunting, the hawk and owl population as a whole can catch and kill members of every species of the collective prey group.

The prey category is made up of game and non-game species; meadow voles, mice, and small birds are the most abundant. Relative abundance of prey species is altered seasonally by migration and reproduction. Game and nongame percentages in the raptor diet also vary according to season; non-game constitutes 95.5 percent of the fall-winter diet and 50 percent of the spring-summer diet.

Resident raptors are adapted to capture a wide variety of prey. Transients are more specialized hunters. Adaptation, migration, and mobility enable raptors to adjust their populations to the amount and kind of available prey.

Raptor predation tends to be proportional to density of prey species and is exerted primarily on populations of small rodents. Proportional mortality tends to maintain specific density relations of one prey species to another.

Raptor predation accelerates when prey populations reach their peak as migrating raptors move in to take advantage of unusually large numbers of prey.

Raptor predation does not operate solely on surplus or "doomed" animals. Its greatest influence is in early spring, when it is a limiting factor on non-surplus (overwintering) populations. The death of these survivors, before breeding, delays and reduces the production of a succeeding generation. In some, and perhaps many, instances, raptor predation is responsible for a critical reduction in the breeding stock.

We have presented some of the scientific aspects of predation by hawks and owls. What conclusions can the layman and the policymakers draw from them? Do they tell us whether predation by hawks and owls is good or bad?

It is evident that the number of ring-necked pheasants taken by a great horned owl or the bob-whites consumed by Cooper's hawks cannot be used as the sole indication of whether predation should be tolerated or hawks and owls eliminated.

If we understand and accept the biological facts as presented, it becomes apparent that the complex functioning of predation by hawks and owls fits into a still broader scheme of things.

This, too, must be understood if we are properly to evaluate raptor predation and ultimately pass judgment on hawks and owls as members of the animal community.

Animal populations are regulated by the relations between decimating forces and reproduction. The evolutionary process has produced an extremely delicate and complex balance between the reproductive potential of animal life and the environmental processes that inhibit it. Reproduction compensates for high or excessive mortality, and mortality similarly compensates for high reproductive rates. They serve as functions of one another.

A certain proportion of a prey population is annually doomed. This has to be because the reproductive abilities of the varied prey species ordinarily exceed the capacity of the environment to support the annual increases. The population ecologist expresses this by saying that the physiological expectation of life exceeds the ecological expectation.

We return to the meadow vole as an example. Shielded from the vagaries of the environment and given adequate food and shelter, a vole can live for several years. Under natural conditions, only an exceptional individual does so. Most of the meadow voles born in spring are dead before they have lived a year. In this respect they are doomed to die before their time. A similar fate awaits the young of passerine birds and many other types of prey.

The important thing is not that many individuals in a large population are doomed, but *how* they die—the manner in which Nature contrives, by their removal, to maintain population levels in harmony with the environment.

No single decimating force will play a dominant, controlling role at all times. In some situations, physical conditions—temperature, snow depth, moisture—impose a high degree of control. In others, biotic conditions, such as food supply, cover, disease, or predation, dominate. The failure of one of these basic regulatory forces to operate is normally offset by some other one.

The fact that seldom, if ever, is any single force independent of others, makes it difficult to determine the relative importance of each, but we do know that a combination of such forces is necessary to keep animal populations in check and that each must be evaluated with reference to all others. Raptor predation is one mortality factor or regulatory force that operates jointly to bring about environmental harmony.

Let us compare it with some of the others.

Raptor predation, as we have seen, is a highly mobile regulatory force that operates continuously to lower increase of prey in proportion to density of prey before more drastic but less steadily functioning forces (such as disease, malnutrition, or adverse weather) become effective.

Hawks and owls strike all components of the collective prey simultaneously and continuously. The other forces seldom, if ever, affect the total prey population at the same time but are confined to specific species. Disease may strike one prey; food shortage may strike another.

These natural forces are effective for only limited periods. Generally they are seasonal or of short duration.

So it is with most other decimating forces.

An exception is population self-limitation, imposed by the social intolerance of members in the population. It is not strictly a decimating factor, but it is another effective regulatory mechanism that operates continuously among all members of a prey population. It helps draw the line between surplus and nonsurplus animals by defining the living space of each individual or pair in a population. It is basic in determining the size of territories, and the size and number of territories define the size of the breeding unit.

Thus social intolerance limits population size by controlling reproduction but seldom directly eliminates individuals. Its function is to maintain a population density compatible with the habitat. Under certain conditions, raptor predation can cut into this pattern, temporarily reducing the size of the territorially defined breeding or overwintering populations. This can and does occur in early spring, when winter prey species are at low levels and highly vulnerable to raptors and other predators.

Social pressures normally force the surplus—generally the poorly adjusted or young of the year—into marginal and submarginal habitats. These surpluses attract raptors and are taken by them during the summer, fall, and winter.

As a suppressive force, predation does not reduce populations to very low numbers, as do epizootics or starvation. Moreover, the number of any single prey species accounted for may be far less than the number killed by a hard winter or a wet spring.

Sudden, drastic reduction in numbers temporarily releases a population from the pressures of control forces and thus allows its densities to increase again. This is a type of control characterized by excessive fluctuations in numbers from high to low levels.

Such fluctuations generally react harmfully with the habitat. In contrast, where raptor predation is dominantly operative, control is characterized by continuous and proportionate reduction that tends to keep prey population levels near a mean.

Drastic fluctuations in prey numbers are less frequent. Habitat damage is minimized or does not occur. The fact that predation operates as a steadily functioning force throughout the seasons, day and night and year after year, despite continually changing physical and biotic conditions of the environment, gives it a great advantage over population regulators that operate intermittently or only under special conditions.

Considering the distinguishing features of raptor predation—its continuous, simultaneous, proportional pressure on all members of the prey community—we see that it is a controlling force of particular effectiveness. In general, it can be labeled not only good but necessary.

We have traveled a long way from making on-the-spot judgment of a hawk that kills a quail.

Systematic accumulation of scientific data indicates that widespread and indiscriminate control of hawks and owls is undesirable.

Overpopulation of rodents, flocking birds, and other species attaining pest proportions in predator-controlled areas frequently have caused extensive damage to native vegetation, soil, crops, livestock, and other property or have become public health problems. The elimination of an important regulatory factor such as the raptors has undoubtedly contributed to such situations.

By opposing the forces of reproduction, raptorial birds help to balance prey populations with one another and with their total environment. This, in turn, helps prevent serious damage to the plant and soil environment.

Such damage is considered harmful, or bad, as far as man is concerned. Thousands of documented cases give evidence that entire crops have been consumed by overpopulations of rodents and rangelands have been nearly denuded of protective vegetation and thus left vulnerable to serious and widespread erosion.

Two researchers, H. S. Fitch and J. R. Bentley, of the San Joaquin Experimental Station, determined from experiments with range plots that three species of rodents—pocket gopher, ground squirrel, and kangaroo rat—totaling about 16 animals per acre could eliminate one-third or more of the annual herbage crop from open rangelands. The economic loss in crops and forage from rodents alone runs annually into hundreds of millions of dollars.

Today there are many districts where, despite adequate laws, the killing of hawks and owls by a growing horde of zealous and nondiscriminating hunters has almost completely eliminated the beneficial controlling effect of raptors on rodent populations.

It is at times best for man's interest to eliminate individual raptors or perhaps even to reduce the numbers of a particular species. That is not at all the same thing as destruction of an entire predator population.

A relatively large proportion of an abundant and widespread prey species can be killed locally by a single raptor species. When this prey happens to be valuable to man and therefore has been too heavily cropped, or if the prey animal is subject to particularly heavy environmental resistance, predation then very likely may become the condition limiting its increase. In such instances, temporary predator control is advisable if man is to reap a maximum harvest.

Where there have been artificially increased local densities of pheasants or bobwhites at game farms, and chickens or ducks at poultry establishments, however, relatively high losses must be expected unless these concentrations are given proper protection.

A farmer who keeps large flocks of poultry unfenced is bound to lose some to hawks and owls. But general destruction of raptors, with the attendant disturbance of environmental balance (to support substandard poultry raising and indefensible game farm practices) cannot be justified.

It would be unwise to provide legal protection for the horned owl, Cooper's hawk, and goshawk without provision for killing destructive individuals because it would then be difficult to control them in special cases when necessary.

Raptor control is necessary where populations of game birds are very low or are being established. In such instances, harmful predation can be anticipated, since very low or artificially formed prey populations are not secure in the environment. Predation on such animals is likely to be out of proportion to their numbers and can have a critical effect, because it tends to exterminate rather than regulate.

Actual extinction of animal life has occurred on some oceanic islands where rats have been introduced among island forms poorly adapted to cope with predators.

Conversely, the introduction of nonpredatory animals, such as goats and rabbits, on isolated islands where there have been no predators to check their increase has resulted in almost complete destruction of the native vegetation, extinction or reduction of native animals, and eventual decline of the introduced species.

The well-known catastrophic irruption of the English rabbit after its introduction into Australia and of deer in New Zealand—both islands having a dearth of large predators—are extreme examples of the damage that can be done before any natural decline manifests itself.

In all such cases, the remarkable adaptations of predators to prey, and vice versa, did not exist— heavy predation was alien to the balance that had evolved, and the sudden introduction of either predatory forces or uncontrolled reproductive forces created a disastrous imbalance.

216

When man disrupts Nature's mechanisms for regulating population levels or when excess populations of exotic or domestic animals are built up, temporary measures may be necessary to curb an expanding prey population or to control predators in an artificially created situation—but such measures should be finely calculated emergency operations and should be used only until more basic remedies can be applied.

Even such emergency operations should be moderate. When possible, they should be attained by re-establishing a natural balance between predator and prey.

Man, by concerted action and persistent effort, can and has reduced both wild rodent and raptor populations to critically low levels over wide areas, unaware or disrespectful of the fact that the checks and balances inherent in the natural relations between raptors and prey are the result of an infinite number of causes and effects that have evolved as animal life evolved.

Nature's system may not be perfect as it relates to man, but it operates impersonally and timelessly, and as yet appears to be far superior to any widespread control by man himself.

We must keep in mind that although man has greatly altered his environment and will continue to do so, his changes do not change or eliminate fundamental natural laws or processes.

To insist that man so drastically upsets the equilibrium of Nature that he must assume the full burden of controlling it is to overlook the fact that Nature has evolved over millions of years in response to changes—changes perhaps far more drastic and vital than any yet caused by man, although such changes probably were always more gradual than those man has wrought.

The force of raptor predation has adjusted itself over extensive regions to man's temporary disturbance of a natural environmental balance. Unless raptors themselves are eliminated, it may be expected to continue to do so and to function as a density-controlled regulator of prey populations.

This being true, we should try to utilize the force of predation. We should allow it to operate over the vast areas where we ourselves have little control and curb it locally only when there are strong reasons for doing so.

Let us conclude with a concept of raptor predation as a precise and powerful force that should be visualized in its ecological entirety: A force that man must recognize, not as an enemy in the form of "killer hawks" or "ruthless owls" tending to "steal" the rabbits or pheasants he could otherwise harvest, but as a force that he has only begun to understand; a force that is useful, essential; and a force that he should not eliminate.

Man can best manage raptor predation for his own ends if he does not disrupt it, for it is a vital component of the complex of forces that regulate animal numbers and influence human life.

—John J. Craighead and Frank C. Craighead, Jr.

Housekeepers

SOME BIRDS HELP US with our household chores. They tidy up after us and reduce the mountains of refuse, wastes, and garbage we make. Some species, such as the carrion-hunting vultures, work full time at scavenging. Many other birds merely supplement their usual diet with whatever dead flesh or edible refuse they find.

In North America and on its adjacent seas, the birds that consume natural and manmade wastes are the albatrosses, shearwaters, and petrels; brown pelican and frigate-bird; the vultures, including the California condor; eagles, certain hawks, and the caracara; jaegers, skuas, and gulls; the snowy owl; ravens, crows, magpies, Clark's nutcracker, and jays; the house sparrow; and the domestic pigeon.

The albatrosses, shearwaters, fulmars, and petrels are scavengers of the high seas. Their food is mostly plankton or larger forms of invertebrate life, but they readily follow a ship to pick up garbage thrown overboard from the ship's galley. Whaling ships attract large numbers of them as they search for bits of whale blubber, blood, and offal left from the processing of the whale carcasses.

The large, black-footed albatross, a common species in the North Pacific, has been called a feathered pig because of its voracious appetite. It can swallow a half-pound chunk of fresh shark meat in a single gulp.

Albatrosses are fairly common offshore along western North America but are rare in north Atlantic waters along the east coast. Only once in a while does one see yellow-nosed albatrosses along the eastern seaboard as they straggle northward from the South Atlantic.

Some of the smaller members of this group, shearwaters, fulmars, and petrels, are common offshore along both coasts. Their feeding habits are much the same as the larger albatrosses, and any floating garbage or carrion is a feast.

Most of the scavengers in this group are partial to animal fats, especially bacon grease. They can be attracted readily by hot melted bacon grease poured directly on the water or bits of bread soaked in bacon grease.

These birds seem to have a well-developed sense of smell, as they will move upwind—even in dense fog, when surely they cannot see far—toward the odor from bacon grease poured on the surface of the sea.

Birds of this group are the offshore scavengers of North America. Seldom do they come close to the shoreline. They spend most of each year at sea and return to land only during the breeding season. Many of them nest on islands in the Southern Hemisphere, either in the South Atlantic or South Pacific, particularly the islands off Australia and New Zealand.

The black-footed albatross that patrols the eastern North Pacific nests primarily on Midway and the other leeward islands of Hawaii.

Pelicans and frigate-birds are in another group.

The diet of the white pelican and the brown pelican consists primarily of fish and crustaceans, but the brown pelican is known to resort occasionally to feeding on bits of offal around fishing boats and piers. Once, at least, a brown pelican ate the bodies of birds and the flesh of porpoises thrown into the sea during the preparation of specimens on a museum collecting trip.

The frigate-bird, or man-o-war bird, a close relative of the pelican, gains much of its food by foraging on offal on the surface of the open sea or on water around piers, slaughterhouses, or sewers at the water's edge. The frigate-bird cannot land or take off from the surface of the water, and it must snatch up food in its long bill. Only the tip of the bill touches the water, and it picks up the bit of food with barely a ripple of the water's surface.

Frigate birds occur regularly over the tropical waters of the North American coast, especially around southern Florida, the gulf coast, and the west coast of Mexico. Stragglers occasionally wander far north along both coastlines of the United States and inland over the Mississippi Valley.

As scavengers, the vultures and condors are without equal. They are highly specialized for feeding on a diet of carrion. They also possess sharp food-locator senses. Most species locate food by sight, but some detect food by smell as well as by sight.

Vultures occur on most continents between the 60° parallel of latitude but are absent from the large landmasses of the East Indies, the Philippines, Australia, and Madagascar.

Vultures the world over have a superficial resemblance, but they form two quite distinct groups. The Aegypiine, or Old World, vultures are related closely to the eagles. The Cathartine, or New World, vultures of North and South America are a group quite distinct with no close relatives. The general resemblance of bare heads and necks in the two groups is purely adaptive, as both perform the same service as scavengers in the niches they inhabit.

Wherever they occur, vultures perform a service by consuming quantities of carrion and offal of all kinds. In many towns and villages, especially in tropical lands, vultures are the only reliable sanitation service. The dead carcasses of animals and offal of all kinds are eagerly sought after and quickly dispatched by these members of Nature's sanitary corps.

Their feeding activities are anything but fastidious. In some parts of the world they are quick to devour corpses.

Along rivers of India, bits of partly cremated human bodies from the burning ghats are devoured by the ever-present vultures as soon as they drift ashore. Members of one sect depend on vultures

CARACARAS

219

for the disposal of the dead. The Parsees near Bombay expose their dead on an iron grating in the dakhma, or tower of silence, to be consumed by vultures. The trees around the towers of silence on Malabar Hill in western Bombay teem with vultures and pariah kites, which wait for a Parsee funeral procession to arrive with a corpse.

In the part of North America that extends from northern Mexico through the United States and Canada to approximately 57° north latitude, three species of vulture are found—the California condor, the black vulture, and the turkey vulture.

The large and local California condor is so reduced in numbers—in 1964 it was estimated that as few as 40 individuals existed—that its range is restricted entirely to southern California. The condor (or, more correctly, its early ancestor) was abundant during the Pleistocene period and formerly ranged from British Columbia to Florida. The population and range of this great scavenger have dwindled until the remaining birds are close to extinction in the coastal mountains of southern California. Man and his encroachment upon the habitat of the condor have been its greatest decimator, and only the thoughtfulness of people can save it.

On the wing, the California condor is a majestic sight. It soars and glides over ridge and plain in a continuous search for carrion. The carcasses of cattle, sheep, and deer are its preferred food. Smaller ground squirrels and rabbits are eaten if they are abundant. That often occurs after poison grain is put out to eliminate rodents in places where livestock graze. Then the condors are a clean-up detail. They tolerate the poison in the carcasses pretty well, but the death of some condors may be due to the poisoning activities.

A report in 1965 by the National Audubon Society on the status of the California condor held that these giant birds do not lack for food. The numbers of cattle, sheep, and deer grazing in the foraging area of the condor were tabulated, and estimates were made as to their mortality. The researchers concluded that the carcasses of 3,840 cattle, 8,812 deer, and 525 sheep were available

The black-footed albatross (this one is on Midway Island in the Pacific) is a high-seas scavenger.

annually in the foraging area of the condor. If only 40 condors still exist, each, then, would have 329 carcasses a year.

Obviously, other factors must be taken into consideration in such computations. Every carcass will not be discovered by the condors. Other scavengers will compete for this carrion. A condor can gorge itself to a certain capacity. The report concluded that the California condor is not starving. Rather, the study stressed that the decline in numbers is due to actual destruction of the birds by wanton shooting and the pressure of human population on the condor's dwindling habitat.

The California condor, the Andean condor, the black vulture of the New World, and all the Aegypiine vultures of the Old World depend on their keenness of vision to locate food.

From its vantage point high in the sky, the hungry vulture keeps a sharp eye out for evidence of a carcass and for all its companions and competitors. As long as nearby vultures remain in their proper sectors, no carrion has been located. Let one member of the competition change its flight pattern and swoop earthward, however, and all the vultures in the sky are alerted. Food has been sighted. The scramble is on. All the vultures then will converge on the point and descend rapidly to the feast.

Many species of vultures often become conditioned to a constant source of food in a given locality, such as the offal dump of a slaughterhouse, and will tend to concentrate there.

The black vulture is essentially a bird of the New World Tropics, but it does range well within the borders of the United States. The species is abundant in the Southeastern States and is found as far west as southern Arizona and north as far as Missouri, Maryland, and southern Illinois, Indiana, and Ohio.

Unlike the other Cathartine vultures, the black vulture is a relatively sedentary species and prefers life close to people. It concentrates in large numbers in and about the cities and villages of the Southern States, Mexico, and tropical America, where it is often the only sanitation service and consequently is rigorously protected.

Frequently called carrion crows, black vultures are a common sight perched on rooftops, fence-posts, and walls or circling in a flapping, gliding flight high above a town. Whether perched or on the wing, they keep alert for the wastes of man. If the choice morsel is more than can be consumed by one vulture in one gulp, a free-for-all ensues, and a swarm of black vultures fights for possession of the food item. As each vulture tries to get its neighbor out of the way, the latecomer to the feast often is the one who is able to dart in and snatch the prize.

The black vulture is aggressive and pugnacious. It seems to prefer decomposed carrion, but it has been known to steal fresh meat from an outdoor butcher stall. Sometimes black vultures attack and kill newborn pigs, calves, lambs, and kids.

The turkey vulture is the most successful scavenger of them all—it can maintain itself in the great-est variety of habitats and thus enjoys a greater geographic range than any other kind of vulture.

The turkey vulture ranges from the Straits of Magellan at the southern tip of South America northward to the shores of Hudson Bay. In North America, it is migratory. It forages northward during the spring and summer and then withdraws to Central America during the fall and winter. Small numbers of individuals can be found throughout the winter in many parts of the United States wherever temperatures are not too low.

To locate food, the turkey vulture makes use of a highly developed sense of smell and keen vision.

Most species of vultures are gregarious, but the turkey vulture is a loner. It forages by itself except when roosting or concentrated at a discovered source of ample food. It is basically a low-

The frigate-bird flies low over the open sea and snatches bits of wastes with its sharp bill. Here a male is at the nest on Laysan Island in the Pacific.

Black vultures often concentrate in and about cities, where they commonly perch on rooftops. They are efficient and useful scavengers.

level forager. In its searching flight, it skims over crests of hills and sails down canyons, often only a few feet above the ground. It may sail swiftly below treetops through stands of vegetation and then bank sharply back on its course. Over level ground, it commonly flies a low-level searching course and frequently swoops upward to regain altitude.

Its low-level flight enables it to locate small items of food other vultures may miss. A dead rodent or the body of a snake, even though hidden in the shadows or deep grass, often is located first by its keen sense of smell and then by sight.

Field experiments have shown that the turkey vulture will not come to a large visible item of food, such as the carcass of a large animal, without first verifying by smell that it is not a decoy.

The black vulture appears to relish rotten offal of all kinds, but the turkey vulture prefers fresher food. The prey must be dead, however, to be acceptable. One time, the bodies of recently dead baby chickens were offered to captive turkey vultures during an experiment, but the vultures withdrew quickly when one of the chickens showed feeble signs of life.

The turkey vulture is timid and cautious. Timidity often costs it a meal. In places where turkey vultures and black vultures both occur, the latter often pays special attention to the foraging activities of the former. Although the turkey vulture may be the first to locate a choice bit of food, the aggressive and pugnacious black vulture frequently elbows the finder out of the way and devours the prize.

223

Wharves are among the favorite feeding areas of the herring gulls, opportunists that gather in places where organic wastes are plentiful.

Gulls, skuas, and jaegers also scavenge.

Gulls, especially the larger-sized species, are voracious. Of the dozen or more forms that are relatively abundant in North America, all will do scavenger feeding in varying degrees.

Gulls patrol the beaches of our coasts and are of great value in ridding them of dead fish, crustaceans, and other marine creatures the tide washes up. The dry sand above the tide line also yields them bits of hamburgers, hotdogs, and other remains from picnics.

Gulls often go considerable distances inland from the sea. Many species have adapted themselves to life in populated districts and show almost no fear of people. In many cities it is not uncommon to find them feeding in parks and school grounds. The birds become quite fearless and gather about the person feeding them, much like pigeons. A city refuse or garbage dump provides a banquet.

Near New York not long ago, 200 thousand herring gulls were found living off man's wastes; more than 50 thousand were seen near Boston. Consider the number of species of gulls, and you get an idea of the amount of refuse these birds remove.

Most gulls will accept almost all forms of animal matter. They locate food by visual means, either directly or indirectly, by watching the movements of other gulls.

Gulls can be attracted merely by pretending to throw something from a ship or pier. The gulls may be some distance away, but they will alter their course immediately and come in close to investigate the throwing motion.

Of less importance than the gulls as scavengers, but worthy of mention, are the jaegers and skuas. The pomarine, parasitic, and long-tailed jaegers and the skua are close relatives of the gulls and occur along both coastlines in smaller numbers than gulls.

Jaegers appear during fall, winter, and spring and obtain most of their food then by harassing gulls and terns. They force the gulls and terns to disgorge their own hard-won food by tenaciously pursuing their victims on the wing until the tribute has been extracted.

Much of the jaegers' food, however, consists of offal floating on the surface of the sea or cast up on the beach. The carcasses of dead porpoises, whales, and seals and garbage dumped from ships' galleys readily attract them.

The skua, larger than the jaeger, is a rare bird along our Atlantic and Pacific seaboards. When it does appear, it displays the piratical traits of its lesser relatives, the jaegers. It bullies gulls and terns to give up their food and often kills and devours the pursued birds themselves. It is fond of carrion and scavenges for food on the surface of the sea and along the beaches. Skuas have voracious appetites and can swallow enormous

The turkey vulture's excellent vision and keen sense of smell guide it in locating food. It plies the skies from the southern tip of South America to the shores of Hudson Bay seeking carrion.

Ring-billed gulls and a lone laughing gull (the one with a black bill) work over an ocean beach for scraps of food left by picnickers.

chunks of food, which sometimes make their throats bulge out larger than their heads.

Our national bird, the bald eagle, also is a scavenger. Possessed of powerful talons and a fierce demeanor, it delights in feeding on dead fish on beaches and shores.

The bald eagle is a sea eagle. It feeds extensively on marine fish, which its strong talons take on the surface of the water. It will let an osprey, or fish hawk, in its area do the work of fish catching. As the osprey rises with a fish, the eagle will make a fast sortie toward the osprey and cause it to drop its prey. Then, before the falling fish can reach the water, the eagle dives and secures it in midair.

Many species of birds and small mammals also are caught and devoured by the bald eagle, but it never passes up carrion in the form of mammal carcasses or dead fish on the shore.

Golden eagles also include much carrion in their diet. They have been known to drive condors, turkey vultures, and ravens away from a carrion meal. While these more timid birds wait at a safe distance, the eagle feeds uncontested until its appetite is satiated, and only upon its departure do the others return to the feast.

Most species of hawks prefer live prey, but some feed on carrion. The marsh hawk will return to a carcass too large to be consumed in one meal.

Laughing gulls follow the ferry to Ocracoke Island, North Carolina, to feed on scraps of food that may be thrown overboard by the passengers and the crew.

226

Albatrosses often follow ships at sea and feed on garbage thrown overboard. A pair of Laysan albatrosses is shown at their ancestral nesting grounds in Hawaiian Islands National Wildlife Refuge.

The common red-tailed hawk may eat carrion, but apparently carrion makes up but a small part of its diet.

The caracara, or Mexican eagle of Texas, Florida, and Mexico, scavenges offal and carrion. Vulturelike in its feeding habits, the caracara frequents known sources of carrion about slaughter pens and villages and often associates with black vultures.

Caracaras probably are the least fastidious feeders of all the scavengers. They feed on animal excrement of all kinds.

We have little evidence that owls resort to scavenging, except the large snowy owl of arctic and subarctic America. These large owls generally feed on live birds and mammals, but when hard pressed for food they will eat whatever dead bird or mammal material they can find. In northeastern Labrador, they may feed on bits of meat refuse near human dwellings.

Ravens, crows, magpies, and jays are omnivorous. Carrion and offal of all kinds comprise much of their diets.

Ravens are widespread in North America, especially in the subarctic regions of Alaska, Canada, and Greenland. In Eskimo and Indian villages there, the scavenging raven provides a good sanitation system. People therefore protect ravens.

They become quite tame and wander about the camps and villages much like chickens. They eagerly seek out the carcasses of seals, caribou, and whales before winter sets in. One whale carcass often provides food for a whole flock of ravens throughout the winter.

In California, the raven commonly feeds alongside condors and turkey vultures at the carcass of a sheep, cow, or deer. If food is scarce, ravens will readily steal the bait from trapper's lines. Lumberjacks of Ontario sometimes have to bury their lunch bags deep in the snow to protect them from hungry ravens.

The crow, like its larger relative, the raven, feeds on a wide range of food items, but carrion and wastes form a large part of its diet.

Crows and ravens are both exceedingly wary of people. Once the crow develops a feeling of security near a dwelling, however, it becomes quite tame. In many cities of North America, crows feed from garbage cans and patrol streets and parks for edible refuse.

In the Los Angeles area, crows have discovered the rich food supply to be obtained at drive-in theaters. Flocks of hungry crows regularly visit these sites early each morning and gorge themselves on popcorn, bits of hotdogs, hamburgers, and such that litter-bug movie watchers toss out of cars.

Both the American and the yellow-billed magpie depend largely on carrion, especially during winter and spring, when other types of food may be scarce.

Magpies, as well as crows, ravens, and vultures, habitually feed on the carcasses of animals killed on roads and highways by automobiles, which take a growing toll of birds, mammals, reptiles, and even scavenging birds as well.

Magpies, like jays, may store food, including the carcasses of small mammals, for future use.

Of the several species of jays in North America, most are known to resort to scavenger feeding whenever the opportunity presents itself, for all are well-known omnivores. The common gray jay, or "camp robber" of northern woods, eats any kind of meat, fish, or food left unprotected. It enters tents and cabins and will probe into opened cans, pans, and boxes in its search for food.

A bold bird, it often alights on the table at mealtime, stealing food from a plate or frying pan. Frequently it lands on the knee of a hunter or fisherman in hope of a lunch-time handout. They often damage the deer carcasses hunters may leave hanging in trees.

The Mexican jay of southern Texas, New Mexico, and Arizona is also credited with this type of feeding activity.

Jays that frequent the campgrounds of National Parks or National Forests of the United States and Canada are notorious scavengers and are well known to vacationers.

The Clark's nutcracker—a large, crowlike jay of the mountains of western North America—like the gray jay, commonly is referred to as "meat bird" or "camp robber" because of its scavenging habits about campgrounds. In winter when food is scarce, these birds readily come to houses looking for scraps from the kitchen.

The house sparrow is an active scavenger. It is essentially an urban species that likes places where people live. Time was when it fed on the undigested oat seeds in horse manure in city streets. Fewer horses have meant fewer sparrows, but sparrows remain a well-established species largely because they feed on plants, fruit, seeds, waste grain, insects, garbage, breadcrumbs, and other food refuse.

Domestic pigeons are well-known scavengers. In city squares and parks they feed on food given them or left them by their human friends. The good they do by cleaning up refuse is offset, though, by the nuisance they create by their untidy roosting habits.

That brings us to the admission, in conclusion, that the good scavengers do is not unalloyed: Some of Nature's sanitarians have harmful traits. Black vultures and turkey vultures that feed on carcasses on highways and airstrips, for example, may be a hazard to motor vehicles or aircraft; house sparrows may transmit various parasites harmful to poultry; the black vulture has a documented reputation for damaging or killing livestock. But, all in all, avian scavengers still help in urban sanitation. They tidy up the places we live and work in, and sometimes their cumulative effect is great.

—KENNETH E. STAGER.

HERRING GULLS

Some Birds Like Fish

THESE BIRDS have a special trait in common: Loons, grebes, albatrosses, shearwaters, tropic-birds, pelicans, boobies, gannets, cormorants, frigate-birds, herons, bitterns, ibises, mergansers, ospreys, eagles, gulls, terns, murres, puffins, and kingfishers.

They like fish.

You may hold that against them if you are a sport fisherman. You may think it is a good thing if you are a commercial fisherman, for often sea birds may help you find fish; or if you live in the Orient, and use birds to catch fish for you; or if you are a Peruvian and collect the guano of fish-eating birds for fertilizer.

230

Birds do not take many warm-water game fish, such as bass, sunfish, perch, and catfish. Herons and other wading birds do their hunting along the shallow margins of streams, lakes, ponds, and reservoirs and cannot get fish in the deeper waters.

Warm-water fish usually are in rather turbid water and therefore out of sight of kingfishers, terns, and other diving birds.

Birds get some nongame—or coarse or rough—fish along with others. These less desirable fish compete with game fish for food, prey on game fish, and feed on their spawn. Besides, the fish in warm waters may be overly abundant, and by removing young fish from crowded places the birds tend to improve fishing. We doubt, however, that their take has any appreciable effect on the general abundance of fish.

Actually, the birds are not very selective. Abundance, size, and accessibility determine mostly the type of fish they feed on. Sluggish, surface-feeding, or shallow-water fishes, which generally we do not utilize, are captured most easily and form the bulk of the fish birds get.

In New Mexico, Nevada, and Oklahoma, mergansers help reduce the numbers of rough fishes like gizzard shad and carp. Double-crested cormorants at Reelfoot Lake, Tennessee, feed mainly on rough fish, particularly gizzard shad.

Stomachs of cormorants collected in the North-Central States contained mainly tiger salamander, bullheads, and five-spined stickleback. About half of the food of cormorants in South Dakota was gamefish, and the rest was nongame fish and salamanders.

An examination of several pounds of remains under a nesting colony of great blue herons, within a mile of a lake in which game fish were stocked, revealed bones of only gar and carp. Eight great blue herons near a popular trout stream in western Montana had eaten 28 suckers, 15 frogs, 9 sculpins, 7 trout, a minnow, a mouse, and several large water beetles and dragonfly nymphs—insects that are destructive of small fish.

A study of the black-crowned night heron's diet showed that nonvaluable or destructive fish made up more than 37 percent of their food. Panfish comprised less than 13 percent; the rest was crustaceans, aquatic insects, frogs, and small mammals.

Trout fishermen damn the belted kingfisher—unjustly, most of the time. Actually, trout in streams are not very vulnerable to kingfishers, because most trout streams provide excellent cover with many hiding places. Chubs, dace, suckers, and sometimes sculpins often are common in trout streams, generally in larger numbers than trout. They are slower moving than trout and so are caught more easily by the kingfisher. These neutral or harmful fishes make up most of the kingfisher's catch in such streams. Since chubs and sculpins are destructive of trout spawn, the kingfisher does the

A black-crowned night heron and a common egret go after fish at Pea Island National Wildlife Refuge in North Carolina.

fisherman a favor by reducing the numbers of these fish.

Common mergansers, on the other hand, make inroads on trout and salmon when they are concentrated at streams. Along trout streams in Michigan, two investigators estimated the birds ate five trout a day, although in some streams the mergansers reduced the numbers of unwanted sunfish.

Mergansers are considered an expensive nuisance on restored lakes in Washington, where game fish predominate. The Washington State Game Department recommended a long open season on all mergansers some years ago in the hope they would be driven from the best fishing waters.

H. C. White, of the Biological Station at St. Andrews, New Brunswick, calculated that in 1 year belted kingfishers took 350 thousand young salmon, 50 thousand trout, and 40 thousand other fish from the Northeast Margaree River in Nova Scotia. The common goldeneye fed on young salmon in considerable numbers. The bald eagle sometimes killed large spawning salmon but ignored the young fish. Common, red-breasted, and hooded mergansers perhaps took a half million young salmon and trout from the Northeast Margaree.

In the Miramichi River in New Brunswick, salmon made up 46 to 91 percent of all fish eaten by common mergansers. Dr. White figured that a young merganser probably would take nearly 1,600 salmon juveniles and other fish before reaching its full growth.

Following years of unrestricted feeding by the birds on a tributary of the Northeast Margaree, Dr. White trapped 1,834 salmon descending the stream in the spring of 1937. The following spring, after a year of controlling the birds, when most of the kingfishers, common mergansers, and great blue herons were removed, 4,065 young salmon were taken—an increase of 121.6 percent. The number of large trout also increased. Intensive hunting by trained men to reduce the numbers of fish-eating birds is considered necessary to preserve the salmon runs in some parts of the Maritime Provinces.

On the Pollett River, New Brunswick, mergansers were controlled for 4 years. The result was an increase of nearly 500 percent in the number of suckers, chubs, dace, eels, and salmon. Salmon young increased four to five times in abundance and held this gain persistently.

Dr. P. F. Elson, of the Fisheries Research Board

232

of Canada, calculated that on streams like the Pollett, predation by mergansers is serious if there is more than one bird in each 15 miles of stream 10 yards wide. He estimated that 100 to 200 mergansers regularly visited the 10-mile experimental section of the Pollett each year and removed 75 thousand young salmon. Shooting of about half of the birds reduced the salmon loss to about 10 thousand a year.

In Alaska, however, an examination of 55 stomachs of common mergansers showed that few of the birds had fed on salmon eggs or fry, although salmon was plentiful and spawning had occurred just before or during the time the birds were collected.

Eagles, pelicans, cormorants, gannets, mergansers, and possibly penguins are among the birds that go after fish of commercial value. Gulls, terns, osprey, petrels, and albatrosses may take some.

Most of it is fish not used for human food—pollock, cod, and sculpins picked up as carrion on the beaches, spawned-out salmon, and remains left on the stream banks by bears and wolves.

Herring, a surface-schooling fish, may be taken alive in small numbers by gulls and other sea birds.

Most of the fish-eating birds of the Atlantic and gulf coasts probably feed on menhaden, which is not used for human food but for fishmeal and oil.

The brown pelican feeds on menhaden, mullet, and other coarse fish that school near the surface or live in shallow water. Assertions that it destroys food fish in Florida and Louisiana have been proved unfounded. The white pelican has been vindicated as a predator on commercial fishes in the West.

Although 35 percent of the food of double-crested cormorants in northern Minnesota and southern Manitoba was commercially valuable fish, the remainder included fish species that were predators and competitors of commercial fishes. In that area, these birds do their greatest damage by feeding on fish caught in pound nets. Cormorants also harm commercial fisheries on Lake Huron but probably less than is commonly believed.

Maine fishermen have called the double-crested cormorant a threat to the industry because it eats enormous amounts and disturbs impounded herring. Of 15 species of fish found in stomachs and regurgitations of cormorants in Maine, the redfish, winter flounder, pollock, butterfish, herring, mackerel, and alewife are commercially important. Few of the fish, however, were large enough to be marketed.

Birds swimming under water in pursuit of fish sometimes become entangled in nets. Oldsquaw ducks, for example, have been caught in fish nets set more than 130 feet deep. Commercial salmon fishermen on the west coast have killed western grebes entangled in their nets because they believed the birds were eating young salmon. Examinations of stomach contents, however, showed only herring, sea perch, codlike fish, blennies, and sculpin-like fishes. No remains of salmon were found.

In British Columbia, many salmon eggs are eaten by the common merganser. During the spawning season, the birds arrive in the creeks about dawn, feed upstream, and rest on rocks or gravel bars when their hunger is satisfied. They may feed again in the late afternoon and then depart for the sea. The gullets of some mergansers collected in the late afternoon were filled with salmon eggs, but very likely many of the eggs were not viable at the time they were eaten. Young salmon and trout also are taken at certain times and localities.

Large numbers of stomachs of mergansers in British Columbia disclosed fresh-water sculpin, sticklebacks, and such coarse fish as suckers, chubs, squawfish, and shiners. Because the sculpin preys on young salmon and competes with salmon and trout for the invertebrate food in streams, mergansers therefore may favor the production of salmon. Nevertheless, although common mergansers may not affect adversely the production of trout and salmon very much, some circumstances may warrant a reduction in the numbers of mergansers.

Since the birds feed only during low daylight tides and feed heavily on the wastage cast up on beaches during storms, the number of living herring eggs consumed probably is small. Gulls sometimes capture adult herring, but with difficulty.

Diving ducks, such as the surf scoter, greater scaup, white-winged scoter, common goldeneye, oldsquaw, and (less commonly) the common scoter and bufflehead, may feed on herring eggs under water. We see no reason for worry, though:

233

Herring gulls cannot pry open a clam, but they take them into the air and drop them on highways and other hard surfaces. This is what a bridge at Pea Island, North Carolina, looks like after gulls have feasted on clams.

An enormous number of eggs is lost to natural causes, and the annual take of herring along the Pacific coast by commercial fishermen is low.

The common murre, pelagic cormorant, red-breasted merganser, and (to a lesser extent) Brandt's cormorant, double-crested cormorant, common loon, red-throated loon, and arctic loon are said to feed upon adult herring during the spawning run. But this, too, is judged to have little effect on the overall abundance of the fish.

In the Pacific herring fishery, birds steal herring from loaded scows en route to the processing plants. Fishermen must cover the fish with netting to keep the thousands of gulls on the fishing grounds from making off with their catch.

Thus, although we have evidence that birds eat many commercially important fishes, the general effect on the fisheries in North American waters probably is slight. Osprey, gulls, terns, and the

Great blue herons have long legs and a sharp bill for fishing, which enable them to capture fish in shallow water. This photograph was taken at the Audubon Sanctuary, Vingtun Island, Galveston Bay, in Texas.

other sea birds are all worthy of protection except in local and unusual conditions. The common merganser is the most frequent offender and may need to be controlled in some localities.

In South Africa, only three species of birds are considered major predators of commercial fish. They are the cape gannet, the cape cormorant, and the cape penguin.

D. N. Davies, an authority on South African fish, estimated that the three species consume annually nearly a billion pounds of pilchard and about 150 million pounds of maasbunkers—about one-fifth of the average commercial catch. When the fish are abundant, it is unlikely that the birds have much effect on the commercial fishery, but when the fish are scarce, the birds may have a marked effect.

The birds are protected by law in South Africa because their manure—guano—is collected and sold to truck farmers. Dr. Davies, however, believes it would be more logical to control the numbers of birds and so make more fish available for direct human consumption. He recommends that the eggs be collected and destroyed.

235

Fish-eating guanay birds of Peru nest on San Lorenzo Island and leave droppings, which are processed and sold for use as fertilizer.

The guano industry of Peru is an example of the interaction of birds, fish, and man.

The accumulation of guano in the coastal islands of Peru is the result of a peculiar combination of physical and biological conditions. The upwelling of cold, nutrient-rich water from intermediate depths of the sea replenishes the supply of nutrients in the surface layer, where it is utilized by dense blooms of single-celled plants. The plants, principally diatoms, are filtered from the water by a small fish, the anchoveta.

Tremendous colonies of fish-eating birds are supported by the abundant fishlife. The feces of the birds, deposited on the nesting islands, are the guano of commerce, a valuable fertilizer. The dry climate of the islands keeps the nitrogen in the guano from evaporating and leaching.

Of the 24 species of birds on the islands, the main guano birds are the guanay or Peruvian cormorant, which has been called the most valuable bird in the world; the Peruvian pelican; and the Peruvian booby.

One estimate is that a hundred cormorants produce a ton of guano a year. On some islands, the cap of guano may be 100 feet thick—the accumulation of about 270 years.

More than 200 million tons of guano were exported to Europe and the United States between 1848 and 1875. At the close of the 19th century, as the result of long years of mismanagement of the industry and wanton destruction of the birds, Peru found her guano deposits reduced to the point that the country's agriculture was threatened.

The Compãnia Administradora del Guano was founded in 1909. The islands were made bird sanctuaries. The conservation program that followed was effective. The crop of guano was 24 thousand tons in 1909 and 5 million tons in 1961, of which 96 percent was of anchoveta origin.

Fishmeal, now the major product of the fishing industry in Peru, brought 71 million dollars into Peru in 1961, and provided work for more than 40 thousand persons.

One authority, Dr. Robert Cushman Murphy,

236

Concentrations of gulls and terns on the lower Potomac River often are associated with schools of rock fish and so fishermen use them as indicators of good fishing waters.

an ornithologist of the American Museum of Natural History, believes that the fishmeal and guano industries are incompatible. He has recommended that Peru's coastal waters be closed to anchoveta fishing until more is known of the consequences.

Scientists of the Instituto de Investigacion de Los Recursos Marinas, at Callao, Peru, have been studying the population changes in the guano birds in relation to oceanographic factors and the anchoveta fishery and have had no evidence so far that anchoveta fishing has seriously affected the guano birds.

A flock of wheeling, diving birds is better than map and compass—maybe even better than new, sophisticated electronic equipment—to some commercial fishermen.

Without birds, Hawaiian tuna fishermen would be unable to find the schools of skipjack that provide them with a livelihood and supply people with about 10 million pounds of food each year.

The tunas feed on shoals of small fish, which they crowd to the surface. Thus a table is set for the birds. While the tunas feed at the surface, the birds work low over the water.

When the tunas go deeper, the birds rise, spread out, and circle high, waiting for the tunas to resume feeding at the surface.

The fishermen, using pole and line and live bait, may land a ton or more of tuna during the 10 minutes the school is at the surface. The birds can follow the movements of the tunas even at considerable depth, so when the flock wheels and strikes out in a new direction, the fishing boat is not far behind. When the school surfaces again and the birds resume feeding, the boat soon arrives on the spot, live bait is again thrown out, fishing begins, and in a few minutes another ton of fish is brought aboard.

The size of the tuna school, the size of the fish in the school, and the depth at which the fish are swimming can be judged rather accurately from the kind, number, and behavior of the sea birds—if one knows what to look for. Certain species of birds behaving in a particular manner indicate a school of large yellowfin tuna to the experienced fisherman. Other behavior may indicate a school of mahi-mahi (dolphin).

A keen-eyed fisherman with binoculars can spot flocks of birds about 5 miles away—much farther than he can see the fish or their surface sign.

The flocks commonly sighted over tuna schools in Hawaiian waters may comprise more than 100 birds and are mainly noddy terns and wedge-tailed shearwaters. They sometimes include a few white-capped noddies, sooty terns, red-footed boobies, and Bulwers' petrels. Some flocks may be accompanied by frigate-birds.

The small islets near the main inhabited islands are breeding grounds for the birds and are closed to the public. The chain of the Leeward Islands—

237

which extends a thousand miles to the northwest, and includes Laysan, Lisianski, French Frigate Shoals, Pearl and Hermes Reef, and Midway and Kure Islands—are breeding places for several species of sea birds. These islands, except Midway and Kure, are part of a national wildlife refuge and are jointly protected by the State of Hawaii and the Federal Government.

Sea birds also are an aid in locating the small fish used as chum in live-bait tuna fishing. Then the birds compete with man for the same prey and with the tunas themselves for the small fishes or squids that have been driven to the surface and are attempting to escape.

In searching for bait fish along the coast of Baja California and in the Galapagos Islands, where it rains infrequently, fishermen look for the rocks on which the birds rest. The rocks usually are near abundant supplies of food (bait to the fishermen) and have a white wash of excrement that makes them stand out against a somber background.

Guides for locating tunas in the eastern Pacific include the frigate-birds and boobies, large birds that can be seen far off and are found working over offshore banks as much as 125 miles from the nearest land.

Shearwaters, petrels, terns, gulls, and tropic birds also point the way. On the inshore bait fishing grounds, pelicans, boobies, terns, and gulls are excellent indicators of the presence of fish.

The tethered cormorant has been the hired help of fishermen in China and Japan since the sixth century.

The fishing is done in rivers, lakes, and bays from small, light boats or rafts. Up to 2 years of training may be required for a young bird to become proficient.

Before the fishing starts, an iron ring or band of rattan is placed about the bird's throat to keep it from swallowing other than very small fish. In some places, about 15 feet of cord is attached to each bird. In others, no cord is used.

A skilled fisherman handles 10 to 12 birds at a time. He may cause the birds to dive and look for fish by giving a short cry, by rhythmically stamping his feet, or by striking the water with a pole.

When the laden bird comes to the surface, the fisherman may extend a pole to help the bird climb into the boat. Sometimes a dipnet is used to retrieve the birds. A 2-foot length of cord sometimes is fastened to the foot of each bird; to the other end of the cord, a float of bamboo or wood is attached. When the bird surfaces, the fisherman hooks the line and float and brings in the bird. He immediately forces open the bird's bill. Then, holding its head downward, he passes his hand along the bird's neck to make the feathered fisherman discharge its prize.

A cormorant may catch 100 or 150 fish an hour. It can work until it is 19 or 20 years old. As valuable possessions, the birds receive good care.

Fish also prey on birds sometimes.

Dr. K. F. Lagler, chairman of the Department of Fisheries, University of Michigan, estimated that northern pike annually cause the loss of 10 thousand ducklings on the Seney National Wildlife Refuge in Michigan. He recommended angling as the best way to control the fish, as long as it did not disturb the brooding parent birds.

The pike is a major predator on young waterfowl in the Saskatchewan and Athabaska River deltas, where the fish may take diving ducklings three times as often as young of the surface-feeding ducks. This predation may amount to 1.5 million ducklings a year, or nearly a tenth of the production of the deltas.

The alligator gar may do great damage to waterfowl in southern rivers and swamps. Of six large gar captured in Texas, four had remains of birds in their stomachs. One gar swallowed an anhinga that was roosting on a stick a few inches above the water. Live duck decoys have been taken by gars, and ducks downed by hunters have been lost to these fish.

Stomachs of goosefish, a marine coastal fish with an enormous mouth and slender, incurved teeth, have been found to contain remains of loons, grebes, cormorants, widgeon, scaup, scoters, mergansers, gulls, auks, and guillemots.

Cod take parakeet auklet, thick-billed murre, and cormorant. Bullfrogs prey on Baltimore oriole, phoebe, house sparrow, and olive-sided flycatcher.

At fish hatcheries, tanks, raceways, and ponds maintained outdoors for hatching and rearing fish offer concentrations of natural food that attract fish-eating birds. The fish, of a size birds like best, often are crowded in concrete raceways bare of any protective covering or vegetation. No wonder, then, that hatchery managers wage a battle with birds.

The fish are particularly vulnerable in the clear waters and confining tanks of cold-water hatcheries. They are less readily captured in the larger ponds and the more turbid waters characteristic of warm-water hatcheries. But the total loss to birds at the warm-water hatcheries is much greater because control and prevention of damage are easier at cold-water hatcheries.

The relative financial loss increases when hatcheries hold their fish to a larger size before stocking. The fish are exposed to predation longer, and when they are larger they are particularly attractive to such birds as the great blue heron and the osprey.

People try to get rid of the birds by frightening them with noise-making devices such as firecrackers, by shooting or trapping them, and by screening the fishponds to exclude them.

One year, hatcheries in nine Eastern States had to contend with 24 species of birds. The commonest offenders were the belted kingfisher, great blue heron, black-crowned night heron, and osprey. About 10 thousand birds were killed at the hatcheries.

A survey at 91 fish hatcheries of the Bureau of Sport Fisheries and Wildlife showed that 37 hatcheries had substantial bird depredation, 38 had a minor problem, and 16 had no problem. Forty-one of the hatcheries raise cold-water fish (salmon and trout); 39 raise warm-water species (largemouth and smallmouth bass, bluegill, pike, channel catfish, redear sunfish); and 11 raise both cold- and warm-water fish.

Among the cold-water hatcheries, 14 had a substantial bird-predation problem; 20, a minor problem; and 7, no problem. Sixteen of the warm-water hatcheries had a serious problem; 15, a minor one; and 8, no problem. Shooting or trapping was used to control the birds at 75 hatcheries.

Hatcherymen removed 2,450 birds from the 75 hatcheries in 1962 by shooting or trapping them or by some other method.

The kingfisher headed the list as the commonest bird predator at the hatcheries; 52 hatcheries removed one or more kingfishers in 1962.

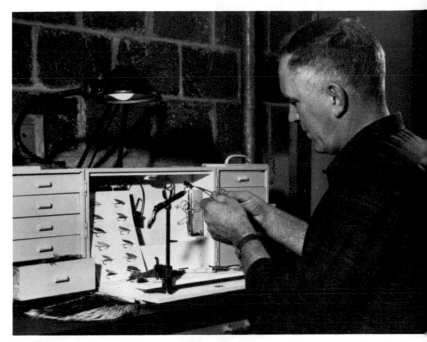

Feathers from a rooster, golden pheasant, guinea hen, mallard, turkey, wood duck, and peacock make a fly to be used in fishing for Atlantic salmon.

The great blue heron was removed from 38 hatcheries and was a problem at 12 others.

The 91 hatcheries include nearly all the Federal hatcheries, but they are only a small sample in comparison with the 492 State hatcheries and the more than 1,370 privately owned fish-rearing plants in the United States.

We would prefer to screen or fence tanks and ponds to exclude birds rather than shoot or trap them. At a number of stations, shooting and trapping have proved to be ineffective and costly.

For all but the smallest of rearing tanks, screening is too expensive and cumbersome to be generally acceptable. We need better screening techniques and a redesign of fish-rearing facilities.

All in all, in no instance have birds been known to contribute to the decline of the numbers of commercial fish, and in only a few special situations have they reduced man's take of sport fishes.

Both fish and fish-eating birds have value. Both are public assets. The headaches they may give us now and then do not warrant a major operation.

—JOSEPH E. KING and ROBERT L. PYLE.

239

Birds and Bugs

YOU HAVE WATCHED swallows, swifts, and nighthawks as they swoop in pursuit of winged prey. You have given up counting the trips parent wrens make as they take food to their young. You have observed the searching of treetop foliage by vireos and warblers and the intensive inspection of the bark of trees by nuthatches, woodpeckers, and creepers. You know, then, that birds consume vast numbers of bugs.

How vast is "vast"?

Scientists in Europe determine the amount and type of food nestling birds receive by putting rings around their necks for 20 to 60 minutes—not long enough to hurt the young ones—and so prevent them from swallowing the food their parents offer.

In this way, scientists in Germany examined more than 50 thousand samples of food from more than 12 thousand nestlings and concluded that insect-eating birds feed chiefly on harmful species, commonly in large numbers. Russian scientists learned that 73 to 80 percent of the food of starling and titmouse nestlings consists of harmful insects.

An American biologist, W. L. McAtee, carefully observed 100 acres of grainfields in North Carolina one week in the early spring and calculated that sparrows and goldfinches, which live primarily on seeds, were eating a million grain aphids a day.

S. A. Forbes, an employee of what is now the Illinois Natural History Survey Division, once estimated that birds killed at least 250 billion insects in Illinois annually. He based his figure on a guess that one bird on one acre destroys at least 20 insects or insect eggs daily.

That guess may be too low: In the United States in summer, there are probably two to four birds to an acre.

You may question that figure if you have

watched flocks of starlings fly into a city to roost at night or have seen several species at one time in your strawberry patch.

Indeed, it is not easy to measure accurately the numbers of birds or of insects in a given area in order to get a true picture of the effects birds have on a "normal" insect population. Practiced ornithologists can estimate resident populations of birds quite accurately, because pairs of nesting birds establish and defend definite territories and because they know the numbers of pairs that one or another habitat can support. Many "visitors" usually join the residents, however, and it is hard to estimate their numbers and the amounts of food they consume.

The only way to get a fairly reliable assessment of the effects of the consumption of insects by birds is to compare insect populations inside and outside an exclosure that screens out birds from part of a plot but allows insects to pass through. Such exclosures also help us determine the effects on crops by comparing crop development or defoliation inside and outside.

Exclosures have been found to be necessary to keep birds from taking laboratory-reared corn earworms that entomologists studying the chemical control of those insects put on the silk of ears in their experiments. However, little use has been made of exclosures in field investigations to learn in this very demonstrative way the degree to which birds control insects in specific situations or the results of such feeding.

Nevertheless, we do have many useful facts from studies of the food habits of common species of birds by Government biologists and others.

Examinations of the stomach contents of 890 eastern meadowlarks of the Southeastern States, for instance, indicated that 78 percent of their food was animal, of which grasshoppers and crickets were the most important items. The rest was vegetable material. Nearly 94 percent of the food of the Carolina wren was found to be insects; caterpillars, beetles, ants, grasshoppers, and spiders were taken in season. Forty-one cotton boll weevils were found in the stomach of a Bullock's oriole.

Cuckoos often eat 100 to 150 cotton worms at a feeding. Ninety-one May beetles were found in the stomach of a common nighthawk.

At least 66 different North American species of birds feed on the cotton boll weevil, 50 on the alfalfa weevil, 46 on the gypsy moth, 175 on leafhoppers, and 205 on wireworms. All these insects damage crops.

Although insects may make up as much as half the food of North American birds, the consumption of so many insects may not mean a substantial reduction in the overall insect populations or any great protection to crops.

The fact is that birds feed more or less indiscriminately on whatever they find and like, regardless of our interests in the matter. For example, aphids and their enemies, the larvae of the syrphid fly, may make a bird's whole meal. So we ask: How does such feeding affect the numbers of aphids? How does it affect the numbers of syrphid flies and the crops on which aphids feed?

Sometimes the feeding on insects may even lead to an increase in the numbers of their species, as when the ones eaten are diseased or parasitized and their removal prevents the spread of the disease to other members of its kind and the development of the potential parasites to attack them.

Even a stomachful of healthy specimens of a pest species could be meaningless in terms of crop protection. Insects consumed after they have finished their reproductive functions and they approach the end of their lives and those that would have died before long anyway (as in freezing weather) would not have contributed greatly to crop damage. But if an insect is not eaten by a bird it will likely be destroyed in some other way. In many different ways, Nature prevents an overabundance of most insects.

People who study birds and insects appreciate the importance of birds in helping to regulate insect populations. But they do not think of birds as the sole regulators. They think of them as part of a natural community—or ecosystem—that has many biological and physical aspects, which change constantly with time, place, stage of development, and other conditions. Any one of those factors may have a predominating influence on an insect population at a given time or place.

It will not do, then, to applaud one agent to the exclusion of others—whether a particular species of bird, a parasite that kills insects, unfavorable

Red-winged blackbirds also are beneficial and destructive. Their appetite for armyworms is as great as a child's liking for ice cream. Red-wings follow the plow and gorge themselves on cutworms, wireworms, and other pests. A short time later, though, they pull the sprouting grain. They are welcomed in hayfields, pastures, and fields of cotton and beans. But growers of rice, corn, and sorghum in many sections must make concerted efforts to protect their maturing grain from the blackbirds' depredations.

Birds that make such marks on both the credit and debit pages of crop ledgers cannot be given an unqualified evaluation of usefulness.

Pest eradication by birds usually is achieved only in local infestations. Birds are not sufficiently abundant to be more than one of the suppressive agents in widespread outbreaks.

Surveys in Nova Scotia in 1950–1956 indicated that hairy and downy woodpeckers reduced overwintering larval populations of the codling moth on tree trunks by 52 percent. At this level, other natural control agents were able to prevent the succeeding generation of moths from causing economic damage to the apple crop.

Woodpeckers are extremely adept in finding

weather, or some other factor, all of which are operating always in the ecosystem in a way to promote stability, to keep insects from increasing to outbreak proportions.

So, too, the usefulness of certain species of birds to agriculture may vary with the season or the crops being grown. During the breeding season, seed-eating and insect-eating birds alike consume large numbers of insects. In other seasons, some of these same birds may feed heavily on grain, seeds of weeds, berries, fruits, and other foods.

Orioles are the most active bird enemies of the boll weevil, a scourge of cotton. Orioles, though, can be destructive to blueberries, grapes, and other small fruits.

242

their prey. They seek out likely spots for cocoons and find the exact locations by tapping with their beaks. After locating a larva, the woodpecker either flicks the bark off or drills a hole in the bark and withdraws the larva with its barbed tongue.

Mountain chickadees destroyed 30 percent of the overwintering population of lodgepole needle miner during an epidemic in Mono County, California, in 1961–1962.

Woodpeckers have done much to reduce infestations of Engelmann spruce beetles, which breed in epidemic proportions when large numbers of trees are windblown and thus more susceptible to attack. Such a disaster occurred in Colorado between 1939 and 1952, when beetles destroyed more than 5 billion boardfeet of spruce. These losses finally were stopped by chemical control and natural factors.

Three species of woodpeckers—the northern three-toed, downy, and hairy—were of primary importance. They stripped the bark from heavily infested trees and fed on the overwintering brood of beetles. Beetle reduction by woodpeckers ranged from 45 percent on lightly infested trees to 98 percent on heavily infested trees. Thus the beetle populations were lowered to more normal proportions in many stands near the sites of the major outbreaks.

Less spectacular, but also of great economic importance, is the part other species have in helping hold a great many insect populations at moderate levels. Thousands of pests exist in our fields, orchards, and woodlands, but they are almost unknown to most of us because they never increase to epidemic numbers. When we consider the tremendous numbers of insects that birds require for themselves and their nestlings, we can appreciate how thoroughly they explore every nook and cranny for food.

We had a striking example in the Adirondacks of New York. An outbreak of spruce budworms threatened to increase to epidemic proportions in 1946 but subsided by 1948. An outstanding feature of this sudden turn of affairs was reduction in the number of budworms in the full-grown larval and pupal stages through the action of several factors,

A California gull with young.

This young prothonotary warbler is one of the millions of baby birds that must be provided with many kinds of insects from fields, gardens, and forests.

including parasites. Birds, especially warblers, accounted for a substantial portion. These little birds were busy everywhere, removing larvae from the protective webs that the insect spins on the terminal shoots of infested trees. Counts at one point showed that only 146 out of 600 webs still contained larvae. Four days later, the number was reduced to 48. By the end of the pupal period hardly any specimens could be found.

We two took part in investigations in northern Maine in 1949 and 1950 to find out the number of spruce budworms that birds destroyed on 40 acres of infested spruce-fir woodland. We removed as many birds as we could from the area in 6 weeks by shooting. We examined the stomachs of 737 birds of 45 species. The warblers had eaten by far the greatest number of budworms. Thrushes and sparrows were next. Wandering flocks of cedar waxwings and purple finches also fed extensively on budworms. Spruce budworms made up 21 percent of the food of these birds in 1949, but in 1950, when the budworm infestation was almost twice as heavy, 40 percent of the food was budworms.

Birds apparently consumed 100 to 300 full-grown budworm larvae or pupae per tree. During the late stages of development, the numbers of budworms declined much faster in places where birds were unmolested than in the experimental plot from which birds had been removed.

As a further check, budworms were put on small trees, which were covered with cages of cloth or coarse wire netting. Nearly all budworms on the trees fully protected by the cloth coverings completed development. But 25 to 36 percent of the budworms on trees less well protected by wire cages and 55 to 64 percent of the budworms on unprotected trees completely disappeared. The trees protected by wire were exposed to parasites and small predators. The unprotected trees were, in addition, exposed to birds.

Many investigations are being made in Europe as to the effect of birds on the numbers of forest insects. Scientists compare conditions in forests where birdhouses have been erected to attract birds with conditions in forests where such attraction is lacking. One such study was near Steckby-on-the-

Elbe, where infestations of the pine looper moth have occurred.

Regular samplings for pine looper moths over 33 years indicated that infestations of the pest remained low and little damage occurred in "attracted" forests, as compared with "unattracted" forests. Only one or two birdboxes to the acre were erected in the "attracted" forests. Most of the observations in Europe, though, indicate that many more birdboxes than that are needed for best results.

Experiments are being conducted on the feeding of birds to determine how to attract and hold them in specified areas. One interesting finding was that when fat is supplied to certain species of woodpeckers, their consumption of insects that overwinter under bark and in crevices is increased. After the birds satisfy their need for fat, they apparently are stronger and more efficient in seeking out more appetizing and satisfying food.

Several Russian scientists successfully colonized useful species—the pied flycatcher and the great titmouse—in forests where they did not occur naturally. They used three methods: Young nestlings were taken from the nests, fed in captivity, and moved when they were fully independent; bird families were moved intact; and adult birds only were moved. The transplantation of adults probably was the most successful.

Russian ornithologists have reported that populations of the gypsy moth were two to four times higher in a small section of woodland isolated from birds than in an exposed part of the forest not so isolated. The oak tortricid was controlled when 8 to 10 artificial nests, preferably starling boxes, were distributed per acre.

Scientists used to think that the number of birds that normally establish and defend a prescribed territory (usually one pair per acre) could not be increased on an area basis and that a population of more than eight pairs per acre was impossible. Now, however, it is known that populations of 25 or more breeding pairs to the acre can be had by a well-planned use of birdboxes, even without a mass increase in the numbers of insects.

That potential was demonstrated at the Patuxent Wildlife Research Center in Maryland, where 293 nest boxes were erected in 40 acres of open fields and along wooded margins. The boxes had three sizes of holes to accommodate various species.

Although the populations of hole-nesting species in the fields had been very low, 50 nests were established in the boxes in the first year and 77 in the second by house wrens, starlings, eastern bluebirds, Carolina chickadees, and yellow-shafted flickers.

Substantial and measured increases of certain desired species of hole-nesting birds have been made by many persons, who have discovered the most favorable style and placement of boxes.

They also have brought to light some highly interesting and unexpected facts: When only 40 percent of the boxes were unoccupied, additional boxes might attract additional birds. A concentration of boxes is necessary to attract semisocial birds. Woodpeckers would nest in a box for only a year. Male woodpeckers would roost at night in nesting boxes containing young and even defend them from their mates. Females required a separate roosting cavity where they normally roost alone.

It may be impossible to attract only the most useful birds. Warblers, which are open-nesting birds, and many of the cavity-nesting species are not attracted to artificial nests. Scientists in Russia reported that in 1953 only 3,821 out of 10,026 nest boxes were occupied by nesting birds and only 18 species were represented. Starlings, Old World flycatchers, European tree sparrows, redstarts, and woodpeckers are apparently the most frequently attracted species.

The most successful manufactured nesting devices used in Germany are made of a mixture of cement and mortar. Slightly different types are used for different species. Usually two to five structures are installed per acre. Some workers think that only two boxes per acre are useful, but the consensus seems to be that at least six per acre are needed to get the best results.

The erection, care, and maintenance of boxes on a large scale are expensive. In the intensively managed European forests, the use of birdboxes seems to have been justified at some times and places. In the United States, the use of birdboxes in forests is being evaluated by entomologists of the University of California. In 1962 they erected nest boxes in two study plots about 2 miles apart at Sentinel Meadow in Mono County. One plot was in an area

heavily infested with lodgepole needle miner; the other was virtually free of miners. Mountain chickadees used about three times more boxes in the infested than in the uninfested area. Although the use of boxes may prove beneficial in natural woodlands, the labor necessary to operate them in large areas will likely preclude their widespread use in the United States.

Chickadees, titmice, crested flycatchers, and flickers are among the few songbirds in this country that would nest in boxes in upland forests.

Nevertheless, tremendous acreages are being reforested in the United States, and well-planned ways to attract insectivorous birds to recreational sites and forest plantations are worth considering. A useful, interesting project for some boys' and girls' organizations, nature clubs, and others, may be to construct, install, and maintain nest boxes.

Other devices have been thought of to enlist more birds in the farmer's fight against insects.

One was suggested by Federal entomologists who surveyed celery fields near Sanford, Florida, and learned that the palm warbler, tree swallow, and red-winged blackbird kept the celery leaf tier under control in isolated fields and in fields adjoining woodlands. In solidly planted fields, where there was little shrubbery to provide protection, birds occurred in smaller numbers and did not reduce heavy infestations below the level of economic damage. The investigators suggested that much could be done to attract birds into such areas by planting small trees like the haw or wild plum along the ditch banks that intersected the celery farms.

In the Pacific Northwest, black-capped chickadees, ruby and golden-crowned kinglets, and red-breasted nuthatches go after the pear psylla. It may be worthwhile there to erect birdboxes to attract more birds.

In other places, too, concerted efforts to increase the number of wild birds in an area to protect a particular crop may pay.

Some farmers plow early in the morning so as to attract birds, which follow the plow and pick up exposed white grubs.

A great crested flycatcher adopts a nest box for its home. These birds skillfully catch many flying insects.

Some use is made of domestic fowls. Geese are sent out to combat boll weevils in cottonfields. Turkeys have been utilized to free rangelands of Mormon crickets and grasshoppers and so get fat on free feed. Grasshoppers were said to be an important part of the diet of about half a million turkeys raised in Utah in 1936.

Few exotic birds have been introduced into new areas specifically to control insect pests. Many of our worst insect pests are introduced species, but we have not introduced the bird enemies that help to control them in their native lands. The Indian

mynah bird was introduced into Mauritius in 1762, and is said to have controlled the red locust there, but that is the only such record we know about.

One of our introduced birds, the starling, is disliked by almost everybody, but starlings feed heavily on grubs of Japanese beetles. They probe the soil and hunt for the delicacies over every square inch of ground. In doing this they unknowingly spread the milky white disease—an important biological factor in the control of this pest. Entomologists have introduced the disease into many beetle-infested areas by inoculating soils

Laughing gulls betake themselves to farms when cultivators turn up the grubs, worms, and other animal forms they consume, to the farmer's benefit.

with spores. Starlings, after prodding treated soil or feeding on diseased beetle grubs, inoculate many new areas with spores that adhere to their beaks.

Very likely birds spread other diseases that attack insects. No one really knows, for instance, why the virus disease of the gypsy moth appears so suddenly at unexpected places or how the virus disease of the European spruce sawfly spreads throughout the vast territory it infests in only 3 or 4 years. Perhaps birds feed on infected insects and so spread the disease. This chain of events probably occurs repeatedly in Nature.

When we consider the role of birds in the ecosystems and their impact on other organisms, we are struck with their mobility, varied diet, differences in habits, and, above all, their remarkable independence.

This very independence, to be sure, makes it hard for us to employ all the characteristics of birds in our ceaseless struggle against noxious insects. We hear a great deal about integrated control, meaning a planned program to control a pest species by a combination of chemical and biological measures—mainly coordination of spray programs and use of insect parasites and predators.

We think more attention should be given to the use of birds in such programs: How, in a practical way, to encourage birds to police one or another crop, now that vast acreages are devoted only to wheat, or corn, or pasture, or whatever. How to make the most of hedgerows, plant cover, boxes, and so on for nesting places and concealment. Lessons can be learned in Europe, where insect problems are rarely as severe and where a high degree of ecological control of insects is in operation—although, we must point out, farms there generally are smaller and a wide variety of crops, grown in comparatively small plots, are separated by hedgerows, trees, uncultivated areas, and other barriers.

To sum up: Birds consume enormous quantities of insects. Within many ecosystems, or communities, of plant and animals, they have an important place along with other controlling agents and factors, in reducing insect populations. They consume large numbers in heavy outbreaks, but more importantly they may eat enough insects to hold potentially injurious species at such low levels as to thwart serious outbreaks. We value birds for their beauty. We value them also for their utility.

—Philip B. Dowden and Robert T. Mitchell.

Science and Husbandry

BLACK VULTURE

To Fly Like a Bird

A BLUE JAY MAY REACH a speed of 26 miles an hour for a few minutes and may go to an altitude of 2 thousand feet if the weather is good. The jet that takes you 3 thousand miles from New York to Los Angeles in 5 hours despite rain or cold may fly 20 times faster than the bird and 15 times higher. The 6-ounce bird (or another like him), though, is father of the giant.

The gestation period of human flight began in the mists of time, for man always has wanted to fly like the birds. Ancient myths tell of gods and heroes who flew through the air with the greatest of ease astride eagles, cranes, and ducks or in chariots powered by herons, doves, and peacocks. Daedalus and his son Icarus, one myth says, made birdlike wings of feathers and wax that helped them escape from King Minos of Crete. Poor Icarus, however, became too exhilarated and too ambitious and incurred the wrath of the gods; he flew too close to the sun, off limits for mortals, and crashed when the wax melted.

Chronicles of the Middle Ages abound in records of flying machines and attempts to fly with winglike surfaces attached to a man's arms, which were flapped after the manner of birds. These early experimenters, however, knew nothing of even the simplest principles of flight. Those who walked away from their crashes had ready explanations for their failures: The feathers they used came from the wrong bird; they had forgotten to provide a suitable birdlike tail; failure of the wind; the air was too damp. But men persisted in their follies and dreams, for whenever they looked up the inspiration of flying birds was always there to lure them on.

Then came Leonardo da Vinci (1452–1519) and the Renaissance, with the awakening of scientific progress. Leonardo, a Florentine, was a master painter, outstanding engineer, prolific student of man and Nature, universal genius.

Leonardo's plan was to study in detail the motions and functionings of bird wings in flight, find out their secrets, and then apply the knowledge to the design of flying machines.

He wrote: "A bird is an instrument working according to mathematical law, which instrument it is within the capacity of man to reproduce with all its movements, but not with a corresponding degree of strength, though it is deficient only in the power of maintaining equilibrium. We may therefore say that such an instrument constructed by man is lacking in nothing except the life of the bird, and this life must needs be supplied from that of man."

He planned a comprehensive study of all birds ("research" was not the word then that it is now) and intended to record his results in a "Treatise on the Flight of Birds." He would "divide the treatise on birds into four books; of which the first treats of their flight by beating their wings; the second of flight without and with the help of the wind; the third on flight in general, such as that of birds, bats, fishes, animals, and insects; the last of the mechanism of this movement."

The treatise as such was never completed, although Leonardo did begin the paper and wrote some 30 pages of it between March 15 and April 15 in 1505, when he was 53 years old. He carried on his studies of birdflight, however, with great intensity. Copious notes on his observations and deductions are scattered throughout his notebooks.

That scientific knowledge in his time was pretty elementary makes all the more amazing the accuracy of most of his conclusions on the nature of natural flight. Never before had such a clear and logical mind been focused on the basic problems of flight.

His sound understanding of the third law of motion, as later set forth by Isaac Newton, when applied to explain the lift of wings, is evidenced by Leonardo's theory of aerodynamic support:

"Since the wings are swifter to press the air than the air is to escape from beneath the wings the air becomes condensed and resists the movements of the wings; and the motive power of these wings by subduing the resistance of the air raises itself in a contrary movement to the movement of the wings."

In equivalent terms, he stated that the "movement of the wing against the air is as great as that of the air against the wing." He attempted to observe the flapping wings of birds in detail, but their speed was too great for even his sharp eyes to follow, and he was led to the erroneous conclusion that birds "swim" through the air by driving their wings downward and backward like "oars" to produce the required lift and thrust.

Applying his newly deduced law of action and reaction, he reasoned "that part of the movement which is made towards the earth checks the bird's descent and the backward movement drives it forward."

Others reached the same conclusion, for the fact that the cambered airfoil-like surfaces of birds' wings produce a large force normal to their direction of motion was not fully understood. That fact had to await its discovery several hundred years later by other students of birdflight, such as Horatio Phillips and Otto Lilienthal, whose pioneering research inspired the first successful flights of the Wright Brothers.

Still, Leonardo realized that "the hand of the wing is that part that causes the impetus," and that on the upstroke "the wing raised with swift movement remains filled with holes, and only rises with the impetus it has acquired, and this is renewed in the lowering of the wings, for the wing then reunites and presses one feather in beneath another . . . ."

In his designs of flying machines, Leonardo

Leonardo da Vinci (1452–1519), a Florentine painter, engineer, and student of Nature, contributed to man's knowledge of the flight of birds and aerodynamics.

planned to use the only source of power available to him—human muscles. Unlike his predecessors, though, he realized that the arm and chest muscles were inadequate for the task, and he made provisions for use of both arms and legs to duplicate more nearly the powerful pectoral muscles of birds. Entries in his notebooks suggest that Leonardo built and tested some full-scale flapping-wing machines, or ornithopters, but the results of the experiments were never recorded.

The great hope he held for the successful emulation of birdflight is evident in his final notation in the "Treatise on the Flight of Birds": "The great bird [his flying machine] will take its first flight upon the back of the great swan [Monte Ceceri near Fiesole in Italy], filling the whole world with amazement and filling all records with its fame; and it will bring eternal glory to the nest where it was born."

Leonardo da Vinci died in 1519 at Amboise, France, and his collection of notebooks with their records of his studies of flight and hundreds of other subjects passed into obscurity for nearly 400 years. In 1893, however, a large number of the original volumes were rediscovered and published. A translation into English by Edward MacCurdy

Paul E. Garber made this model of Da Vinci's proposed aircraft for the Museum of Science and Industry.

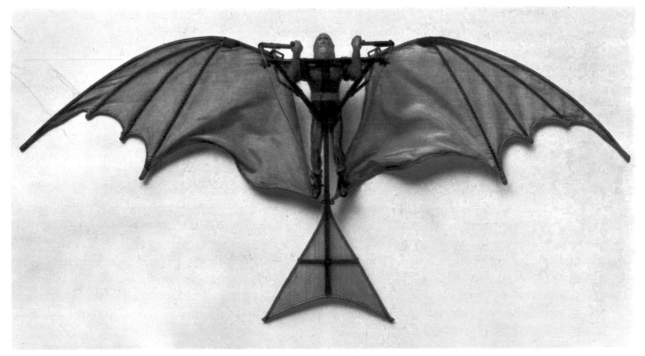

The brown pelican has a graceful flight pattern in marked contrast to its clumsiness on the ground.

Birds often fly in close formations, but amazing precision and maneuverability in mass flight mean they seldom, if ever, collide. These are royal terns at Cape Hatteras National Seashore, North Carolina.

A page from the notebooks of Leonardo da Vinci.

Centuries ago men dreamed of flying like a bird. A painting, a City on a Rock, by the Spanish artist Francisco de Goya (1746–1828), pictured men in flight.

was published as *The Notebooks of Leonardo da Vinci* by Reynal and Hitchcock in 1938.

An Italian mathematician, Giovanni Borelli, compared the relative muscle power and weights of man and birds and concluded in 1680 that it was impossible for a man to support himself by flapping flight unless his power output could be substantially increased. The Abbe Desforges d'Etampes in 1722 designed and constructed a muscle-powered, flapping-wing carriage, and in 1781 Jean-Pierre Blanchard tested a flapping-wing machine powered by both hands and feet. Neither was successful.

Two Frenchmen, Launoy and Bienvenu, in 1784 invented the first working model of the propeller (actually, the model was a helicopter) by attaching four feathers to the ends of two crossed sticks to form an airscrew. The model could raise itself with power from a spring. Thus, evolving from the simple observation that the bird's primary feather has a twisted surface, which creates considerable thrust when moved through the air, was born the airscrew, which proved so critical in man's later mastery of the air.

The most advanced work on flight to appear after that of Leonardo da Vinci was George Cayley's *On Aerial Navigation,* which was published in 1809 in England. It put the science of aeronautics on an organized basis for the first time.

Cayley, an enthusiastic student of birdflight, was convinced that the way to mechanical flight lay not in the extremely complex flapping-wing machines but in fixed-wing craft drawn by airscrews or propellers, a drastic departure from the previous notions.

He based his conclusions on intensive observation of natural flight and experiments with lifting surfaces in his laboratory. His designs needed a strong source of power to drive the propellers, and because the only possibility at that time was the heavy, cumbersome steam engine, no actual craft was built, and the importance of his work and conclusions was not generally appreciated.

Great strength and plenty of fuel reserves are needed to give this brown pelican the flap and kick to get off the water. The photograph was taken at fast speed—one-thousandth of a second—and with fast film.

Most investigators still believed the way to fly was to copy the flapping flight of birds, even if some sort of engine had to be used for driving the wings.

Observations of birdflight made it plain that the takeoff process required much more energy than steady flight through the air. Several inventors therefore released their proposed ornithopters from balloons so as to avoid the takeoff barrier. In 1812, for example, Jakob Degen of Vienna used a balloon to support half the weight of his flapping-wing machine. This ornithopter was designed to imitate the opening of the feathers in a bird's wing

Some birds, like the avocet, have long legs. Some have short legs. Some have long necks, and others seem to have almost no neck. Some have long, pointed wings, and some broad, rounded ones. So it is that the flight patterns of birds vary a great deal from one to another, depending on structure.

on the upstroke. The device produced some lift and might be considered the forerunner of the dirigible, but it was totally impractical and never actually flew.

Men continued to study birds to learn the precious secret of flight, but the wing motions were too complex and too fast for their eyes to follow. W. Miller in 1843 designed a flapping "aerostat," noting that the trailing edges of a bird's wing were quite flexible.

Therein, he thought, lay the total secret of their ability to fly. He planned an elaborate machine to utilize this principle, but we have no record that it was built or tested. Note, however, that the twisting of the bird's wing, as Miller apparently observed, does indeed have a critically important role in the mechanics of its flight; that Miller's machine could have reproduced the complex flexions is beyond reasonable expectation.

Lawrence Hargrave of Australia in 1891 produced what were probably the first successful models of ornithopters. These small models, powered by a tiny, compressed-air engine, flew well, but no attempt was made to produce full-scale versions because of the lack of a light, powerful engine.

Thereafter, active interest in mechanical flapping flight dropped considerably, for by then the more modern and scientific students of birdflight had determined that the successful attainment of mechanical flight lay in a different direction.

Cayley's idea of flight in fixed-wing machines was revived, this time by Count D'Esterno of France in this treatise, *On the Flight of Birds*.

D'Esterno was more concerned with duplicating the soaring flight of large birds by use of windpower than with development of powered machines, but his work indicated that the two basic requirements for flight, lift and thrust, could be treated separately with great resultant simplification of the overall problem.

Pierre Moulliard published a book, *The Empire of the Air,* in 1881. It gave the results of his extensive observations of birds, especially the larger soaring birds, which he had observed in northern Africa. It pointed out the advantages of separating lift and propulsion and inspired all the later investigators, particularly the Wright Brothers.

Jean-Marie Le Bris, a Frenchman, during some ocean voyages observed the incredible soaring power of the albatross, and on his return to France he constructed several gliders patterned after the albatross.

The basic requirements that had to be satisfied in order to accomplish mechanical flight were fairly well understood by 1890. In Germany, the experiments of Otto Lilienthal with gliders and wings had gained him world-wide recognition. His book, *Birdflight as the Basis of Aviation* (1891), presented new aerodynamic information, most of which came from his early studies of birdflight.

The science was not without poetry, or at least joy, as, for example, in the opening paragraphs of Lilienthal's book:

"With each advent of spring, when the air is alive with innumerable happy creatures; when the storks on their arrival at their old northern resorts fold up the imposing flying apparatus which has carried them thousands of miles, lay back their heads and announce their arrival by joyously rattling their beaks; when the swallows have made their entry and hurry through our streets and pass our windows in sailing flight; when the lark appears as a dot in the ether and manifests its joy of existence by its song; then a certain desire takes possession of man. He longs to soar upward and to glide, free as the bird, over smiling fields, leafy woods and mirror-like lakes, and so enjoy the varying landscape as fully as only a bird can do.

"Who is there who, at such times at least, does not deplore the inability of man to indulge in voluntary flight and to unfold wings as effectively as birds do, in order to give the highest expression to his desire for migration?

"Are we still to be debarred from calling this art our own, and are we only to look up longingly to inferior creatures who describe their beautiful paths in the blue of the sky?

"Is this painful consideration to be still further intensified by the conviction that we shall never be able to discover the flying methods of the birds? Or will it be within the scope of the human mind to fathom those means which will be a substitute for what Nature has denied us?"

In America, the first successful gliding flights in

Samuel P. Langley, onetime Secretary of the Smithsonian Institution and mathematics professor at the U.S. Naval Academy, spent hours studying bird flight and aerodynamics at the turn of the century.

Octave Chanute, another pioneer in the study of flight, was a contemporary of Samuel P. Langley. Both influenced the work of the Wright Brothers.

Orville Wright (1871–1948).

Wilbur Wright (1867–1912).

At Kill Devil Hills at Kitty Hawk, North Carolina, on December 17, 1903, Orville and Wilbur Wright made the first flight in a motor-driven, heavier-than-air machine and began a new era.

history had already been carried out in 1884 at Otay, California, by John J. Montgomery, but his failure to publish the results of his work kept it from making any appreciable contribution to the overall effort of the period.

Also in the late 1880's Samuel P. Langley, then director of the Smithsonian Institution in Washington, undertook a fundamental study of the basic problems of flight with a view to developing the basic principles needed to design an actual aircraft. The results of his brilliant studies, including his observations on birdflight, were published in 1891 in his *Experiments in Aerodynamics*. They provided a valuable technical basis for later investigators. After the successful flight of a large, steam-powered model in 1896, Langley undertook the construction of a full-scale craft, which was well designed aerodynamically but was unsuccessful in two attempted flights in 1903.

In 1894, Octave Chanute, a retired engineer and long-time student of flight, published a stimulating history of man's attempts to fly, entitled *Progress in Flying Machines*. Later Chanute and his assistants actually designed and experimented with a number of gliders that incorporated various wing designs. Chanute was an acute observer of bird-

flight, and many of his aerodynamic improvements were applications of the principles he had deduced from watching soaring birds.

Wilbur and Orville Wright ultimately made the first successful airplane flight on December 17, 1903, at Kitty Hawk in North Carolina. They began their study of flight around 1900 and got much of their early information on aerodynamics from Chanute and Langley. The brothers themselves were careful experimenters and observers of natural flight, and spent much time watching the soaring birds at Kitty Hawk. Their early realization of the need for precise aerodynamic control was generated by their observations of how the problem was handled by the turkey vulture.

Thus at Kitty Hawk, after centuries of toil and failure, man finally fulfilled his ancient dream to join the birds in flight.

It is ironic, though, that despite his intense study of birds, man did not really learn the basic secret of their flight, for the bases of birdflight remained mysteries long after man had mastered the air.

We who sit on a lofty perch of modern science cannot fault the pioneers for that: We can hardly expect that man could comprehend, much less duplicate, the miraculous mechanisms it had taken

Nature some 300 million years of judicious experimentation to evolve.

In reality, man conquered the air in much the same manner as the bird had done, by continuous trial and error. Only after man had learned the ways of the air by direct contact with its forces and had formulated this knowledge into the science of aerodynamics did he glimpse the true secrets of soaring and flapping birdflight.

As Orville Wright commented: "Learning the secret of flight from a bird was a good deal like learning the secret of magic from a magician. After you once know the trick and know what to look for you see things that you did not notice when you did not know exactly what to look for."

The countless clues and hints that man received from the birds in his long struggle for wings were no doubt critical factors in his ultimate success, but the greatest gift of the birds was the unceasing inspiration of their flight, which served to carry man onward through centuries of continuous failure and discouragement.

Clarence D. Cone, Jr., the author of this chapter, poses with a black-footed albatross and a model airplane to point up the relationship between the flight of birds and the centuries of study and trial and error and imagination and hope that preceded man's mastery of the air.

From a truly technical standpoint, only in the past several years have many of the phenomena of natural flight been fully investigated and satisfactorily explained in terms of aerodynamic theory.

Still, duplication of most aspects of birdflight by man is as much an impossibility as it was in ancient times. The aerodynamic principles underlying the static and dynamic soaring of birds have been extensively investigated in the past few years, and the results have yielded valuable information for application to the practical design of soaring planes.

Many motion-picture studies of flapping flight have been carried out since 1930, and the gross mechanics of this flight mode are well understood. However, little fundamental application of aerodynamic principles to the analysis of the wing forces and energy requirements has yet been made.

The aerodynamics of flapping flight, although involving the very complex phenomena of unsteady flows and aeroelasticity, nevertheless are amenable to aerodynamic analysis and further research on this important problem should indeed be carried out. Without question, there still remains a large number of significant and valuable aerodynamic facts which man can learn from the birds.

—CLARENCE D. CONE, JR.

In full rudder, with a full spread of wings and with landing gear retracted, this common tern is gracefully and accurately in command of where he is going.

Where Do They Go?

HOW DO WE KNOW that a certain northern waterthrush found in Venezuela one day had left Long Island, New York, 63 days earlier and had flown the 2,500 miles at an average speed of 40 miles a day? Or the origins and routes of the thousands of ducks and geese that migrate twice a year over the United States? Or that red-eyed vireos may make an annual round trip of 7,500 miles from one home to another on a pretty precise schedule?

We know those facts, and many more, from a system of putting identifying bands on birds in one locality, recovering the birds elsewhere, and tabulating the mass of data we thus get.

A small metal band is placed around one leg of a bird and closed. Each band has a unique number—usually eight digits—and a terse address or legend. A record is kept of each band as it is issued and when it is placed later on a bird.

The person who affixes the band records the species, the age and sex of the bird, the date and place of banding, and such other details as may relate to his particular study. He sends his records to the Bird Banding Laboratory of the Bureau of Sport Fisheries and Wildlife at Laurel, Maryland.

There, more than 13 million records of banded birds are maintained, and hundreds of letters arrive every week reporting the recovery of banded birds. Each report is acknowledged, and the person who did the banding also is informed of the recovery.

Systematic marking of birds for quick and accurate recognition began in Europe in 1899, when a Danish schoolmaster, H. Chr. C. Mortensen, used metal bands on the legs of storks and other birds in order to keep track of their movements. The method spread throughout European countries, where it is known as bird ringing, and to all continents, including Antarctica.

Long before that, John James Audubon, the eminent early American ornithologist, affixed silver wire to the legs of nestling phoebes. But the first important banding in North America was done in 1902 and 1903 by Paul Bartsch, of the Smithsonian Institution. He banded 101 young black-crowned night herons in the District of Columbia.

The guiding forces in organizing banding in the United States and Canada were Leon J. Cole and P. A. Taverner, both noted ornithologists. Their efforts led to the formation of the American Bird Banding Association. By the end of the First World War, the United States Bureau of Biological Survey recognized the importance of banding as a source of knowledge of migration and assumed the function from the association.

Frederick C. Lincoln was appointed in 1920 to set up and develop a single system of banding for North America. Only a few thousand birds were marked in the early years, and he and a secretary handled all the work in one small room.

The work expanded to keep pace with the growing numbers of birds banded by persons who searched for a better understanding of migration and the need for more facts on the longevity, composition by age and sex, annual mortality, life expectancy, and survival of populations of wild birds. One and one-half million birds were banded in 1964, the year that a new building was completed to maintain and process banding data by high-speed electronic equipment.

All the records now are stored on magnetic tape and are easily recalled and made available.

Bird banding is jointly conducted, and permits are issued through the Canadian Wildlife Service and the United States Fish and Wildlife Service; the band legend used is that of the latter.

Banding permits are issued only to qualified persons who are at least 18 years old, have a need for the technique to help solve a particular problem, and are endorsed by ornithologists, banders, and others. Generally, an outline of the proposed study is required. A desire merely to assist the two services in their programs is no longer sufficient, as it was when banding was in its infancy.

More than 2 thousand persons were authorized by Federal and State permits in 1965 to band migratory birds. Among them are school custodians, housewives, salesmen, lawyers, clergymen, and other highly qualified amateurs, who devote time and talent to studies of many aspects of avian dynamics, and professional workers, primarily biologists in conservation agencies, graduate students, and members of college faculties. Those in the professional group band mainly migratory game birds and species, such as blackbirds, that may pose some economic problem.

Banding in the backyard or places near home is done all year to sample migrants and to keep track of year-round residents.

A minister, for instance, one winter banded several thousand cowbirds and starlings he had captured in an old wire trap in his small backyard. Others do most of their banding on summer weekends and vacations when colonial nesters can be caught by hand and distant recoveries are probable.

A family team has visited islands in the Great Lakes and for many years has marked more than 20 thousand gull and tern chicks annually. A cabin cruiser is the base of their operations.

A husband and wife team bands 20 thousand birds—mostly passerine or perching birds—annually in North Dakota. They have a specially designed and equipped vehicle.

One man in Saskatchewan enlists the help of neighbors and acquaintances, some of whom telephone him from a distance. On short notice he has traveled all night in a blizzard to band a hawk or owl. We think of him as the annual banding champion for owls.

Others band only during migration periods. Teams of banders may journey far from home.

More and more banders are coordinating their efforts through studies referred to as Operation Recovery. Netting stations in the fall along the Atlantic coast from Nova Scotia and New Brunswick to Georgia were set up originally with the hope that one station would net a bird recently banded at a station to the north.

The effort expanded rapidly from 1955, and

263

More than 2 million bands annually are shipped to banders from the Bird Banding Laboratory.

major emphasis was shifted to studying the effects of weather conditions on migration. Banding records and bird weights (an indication of fat deposition) were used to aid in interpretation of migration data. The operation has spread to the Great Lakes, the Gulf of Mexico, and the west coast. At one station in New Jersey in 1963, a group of 47 banders captured and banded 31 thousand migrants, comprising 157 species, between August 2 and October 27. Many of them toil 2 months a year ageing, sexing, measuring, and weighing birds, recording fat deposits, and noting weather conditions.

Some of the first Operation Recovery reports away from the banding locations were of birds that moved to the north and east during the fall migration period—away from the direction of their winter grounds. The extent of such reverse migration was one of the surprises of the program. We now know that tens of thousands of songbirds fly northward in the fall on nights when winds are from the south.

Operation Recovery disclosed a pigeon hawk that had been netted in New Jersey and was picked up on the east coast of Florida. It also told us of the northern waterthrush that flew from Long Island to Venezuela, where it was live-captured by an American businessman in Caracas who had placed pink bands around legs of others to pinpoint local movements of individuals in their winter quarters. From Nantucket, Massachusetts, a Swainson's thrush arrived in northern Colombia in less than 81 days after departure.

Banding for 8 years by L. Richard Mewaldt, of San Jose State College, California, confirmed that some birds do return to the same wintering areas each year with marked fidelity. He also confirmed the ability of birds to navigate through unfamiliar regions and to return to their normal cyclic movements.

During the winter of 1961–1962, Dr. Mewaldt sent 414 white-crowned and golden-crowned sparrows by plane from San Jose to Baton Rouge, Louisiana, 1,800 miles away, where they were released. Twenty-six returned to San Jose the following winter, presumably after finding their way over previously unknown pathways to their nesting places in the Far North.

The next winter he shipped 660 sparrows to Laurel, Maryland, a distance of 2,400 air miles. Among them were 22 of the Baton Rouge releases that had successfully homed.

Again, these tiny sparrows displayed ability to navigate through unfamiliar places, for 15 birds returned to San Jose the next winter.

Noteworthy were four white-crowns and two golden-crowns that had completed the trip back to California from Maryland as well as from Louisiana. Natural mortality would be expected to account for 50 percent of the birds in a year—in this instance, 11 of the 22 birds released at Baton Rouge. Of the survivors, 6—more than half—homed.

Banding made Dr. Mewaldt's studies possible. It insured that every bird in the tests could be

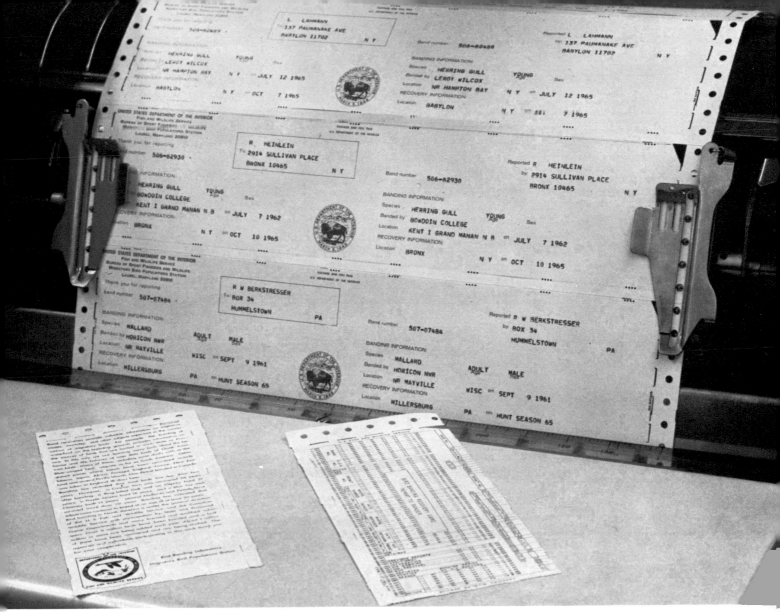

Reports to finders of banded birds and to banders are produced simultaneously by high-speed equipment. These card reports are separated by machine and mailed without further handling. The reverse side of each card in the foreground gives further information.

identified exactly—somewhat as fingerprints identify people.

One of the successful applicants for a banding permit in 1945 described himself as a practicing country physician who had studied birds in 48 States and in 26 National Parks, the West Indies, Mexico, and Canada. He set up a banding station in 1952. More than 400 thousand people from 50 States and 40 countries have since visited the Washington Crossing Nature Education Center near New Hope, Pennsylvania. The center is in the State Park where General Washington made his famous crossing of the Delaware on Christ-mas night, 1776. Legislative action in 1963 gave permanent status to the program, and the "Bird Doctor" and his wife—Dr. and Mrs. Paul H. Fluck—are in action every Saturday and Sunday afternoon. People come to see and learn. Children especially like to visit the center. One owl has been admired and petted by 100 thousand young-sters.

Bands for wild birds usually are made of alumi-num alloys. Most are of the cylindrical butt-end or split-ring type, because the band is placed around and closed on the leg above the foot. Birds of prey and a few others require a special locking

265

Information on punch cards is used as a basis for answering biological questions that come up in research on and management of birdlife.

High-speed magnetic tape equipment stores 100 thousand bird banding cards per reel and can produce them at the rate of 650 a minute.

type to prevent loss of the band. For long-lived species and those that nest on cliffs or frequent alkaline waters, the bands are of more durable Monel metal or stainless steel.

For special studies to observe individual birds or groups without recapture, other markers sometimes are added. They may be made of colored plastics and used as neckbands on geese, wing tags on robins, and leg streamers on blackbirds. Transmitting devices also are employed on a limited scale. Sometimes colored feathers are imped—attached—to make it easier to follow or recognize birds. Dyes also serve this purpose. Doves colored in Florida with picric acid were called flying oranges. (To relay the results of chariot races, the ancient Romans marked swallows with the colors of the winners.) With all such special devices, the official metal legband is applied also.

The cage bird trade uses closed or sealed bands for canaries, parakeets, and others. These bands are slid over the toes a few days after hatching.

In the early days of banding, the abbreviated

legend for Biological Survey, Washington, D.C., on the band might be read "WASH Biol Surv." On one group of bands, "Biol" was misspelled "Boil." A letter reporting the finding of a banded bird said: "I did what you said—washed, boiled, and served, and it was the toughest bird I have ever eaten." Perhaps it was an old crow.

Because finders of banded birds occasionally would telephone or telegraph collect, the terms "Write" or "Avise" were added to the band. "Avise" in Spanish, French, and Portuguese means inform or advise. Many migrants are taken in countries where those languages are spoken. Letters are received from United States citizens telling us we have misspelled "advise."

The reporting of the recovery of the bands is voluntary, but some finders ask for things of value in return for the band.

Some may report the number but retain the band as a souvenir. One person wrote us that he had taken a banded bird several years before and was letting us know now because he had since used the band on his domestic duck, whose fate was of interest to him. Occasionally people put bands on key rings. Several lost keys sent to the Bird Banding Laboratory were returned to the owners, whose names and addresses were traced through the letters they had written to report the band recovery.

Once we received a report of a large band found on a turtle. How did our band get on a turtle in Alabama from a goose shot in Saskatchewan by a person living in Oklahoma? Our reply said, in substance: "Your guess is as good as ours." Months later we had the facts: A Colonel in the Air Force had flown to Canada to hunt. On his return, he gave his son the band. The son gave it to a playmate, whose family later moved to Alabama and who banded the turtle there.

Another band was received from the Hon. Margaret Chase Smith, United States Senator from Maine. The details of the banded bird and our brief summary of the purpose and system of banding interested her, and she included them in the Congressional Record.

A letter from a Mexican boy in Baja California said he had taken a band from a mourning dove, a bird he often saw. This dove, he wrote, was special, since it was the only one that had a "silver" legband: "Just think, this little bird came all the way from Washington without the benefit of a train, plane, or bus ticket." The dove, however, was banded in California, but we do know from banding that some mourning doves move long distances south of the border—one from Iowa reached southern Colombia.

Not all of the bands are recovered and reported, of course. The size and kind of birds have something to do with it. About 30 percent of the bands put on geese may be reported. Fewer than one-tenth of 1 percent of the bands on warblers and other small, protected species may be recovered. Few reports come from the remote and tiny islands and atolls in the Pacific and from the Arctic. Another factor is the quick utilization of carcasses by predators. Also, hunters and other persons who shoot or find banded birds may not know the importance of the band and the reasons for reporting its recovery.

Banded birds from our hemisphere have been taken on every continent except Australia and Antarctica, on islands in the Pacific, and on Greenland, Bermuda, and the Azores in the Atlantic. Migrant, or wintering, birds have been recorded in every country of Central America and South America except Paraguay and in 28 of the 31 Mexican States.

Banding has shown that fall migration in North America generally follows a north-south direction but may be influenced by topography, weather, and feeding requirements. Birds move out of Alaska and Canada in untold numbers over pathways extending along the coastal areas, the Great Plains, and the Mississippi Valley.

Some migrants follow a diagonal course from the Northwest before turning southward along the Atlantic coast. Some populations from Arctic Canada follow the Mackenzie and Mississippi Rivers to the Gulf of Mexico. Others from the Arctic split off and veer sharply westward through the Northern States and across the Rocky Mountains to settle in the interior valleys of California. As migration proceeds southward, the pathways are compressed and have a funneling effect.

Birds that winter south of the border traverse the constricted landmass of Central America or take off over the Gulf of Mexico to Yucatan or

A close-up of a 2-millimeter leg band of the size used for the tiny hummingbird. The penny was put beside it to give a comparison of size.

A band is put on the leg of an immature least tern at Battery Island in North Carolina.

island-hop through the West Indies to reach South America.

Many species, from waterfowl to small warblers, have broad migration routes. The width of the route of the American redstart exceeds 2 thousand miles before various groups move into Mexico and other Central and South American areas or the Antilles. The opposite extreme—the birds with restricted or narrow pathways—is typified by the Ipswich sparrow, which nests only on tiny Sable

Island off Nova Scotia and migrates along the sand dunes of the Atlantic coast as far south as Georgia.

The shore bird family includes the familiar sandpipers and plovers. Of the numerous species that nest in North America, many leave the continent and winter in South America. The woodcock is one of the few shore birds that does not move south of the border.

The American golden plover makes long migrations to two separated areas but in fall uses an American pathway that differs from its spring route. From the tundra of Alaska and Canada, golden plovers move to the North Atlantic coast and largely follow an oceanic route through the Antilles before again flying overland to winter in Brazil and Argentina. The return is by way of Central America, the Gulf of Mexico, and the Mississippi Valley. The round trip is 15 thousand to 20 thousand miles. One was recovered in September on its southward journey in the Guadaloupe Islands, West Indies.

Another was on the move northward when it was found on January 30 in British Guiana. Another was taken in March in northeastern Texas. It had been banded as a chick on Victoria Island, Canada.

The golden plovers that nest in coastal Alaska and parts of Siberia fly as far as New Zealand and Australia. They stop en route at Pacific islands, such as Lisianski and Johnston, where plovers have been banded in October. A study of fat reserves of fall migrants reaching Wake Island indicates sufficient fuel—fat—for the 4-thousand-mile journey to their winter quarters farther south in the Pacific. When they stop for a rest on their return trip through Wake in April, they still have enough fuel to fly nonstop to Kamchatka or the Aleutians, 2,300 miles away.

The ruddy turnstone, another shore bird, is a circumpolar breeder. From the Arctic, the turnstones follow different routes to widely separated winter quarters. Those from the eastern Canadian Arctic and Greenland winter in temperate and tropical zones of the Old World. An adult female banded on the nest in Ellesmereland, Canada, was shot in Portugal. One that was banded in England was collected from the nest in Ellesmere. Still another, which left Iceland in January, was found in Greenland in May. Other groups of turnstones migrate along our Pacific and Atlantic coasts, but a third segment migrates to the Pacific islands, some going as far as Australia. Turnstones banded by the Japanese have been retrapped in Alaska. One that was ringed in the Pribilofs was picked up in Kamchatka.

Herons and egrets migrate far and wide. Banding has shown that the long-legged great blue

An ornithologist scales cliffs in the Badlands of North Dakota to band two young golden eagles.

herons reach 18 years of age or more in the wild and can exceed the speed limit if need be—one immature bird banded July 11 in Oregon was shot 19 days later in the State of Coahuila in Mexico. A black-crowned night heron from Ohio was recovered in Jamaica 17 years after it had been banded.

The Old World cattle egrets, which moved into the United States and Canada from South America, still may migrate to the West Indies and Central America. One even wandered to Colombia from Florida.

Little blue herons have white plumage during their first year. It is in this immature plumage that they migrate or wander the greatest distances. Many people from south of the border describe a white bird when reporting the band. A man in Peru, to whom we sent a report, wrote us: "Something is wrong. The bird I found was white—not blue, as you said in your report."

We find the greatest development of migration in cold and in temperate regions of the Northern Hemisphere. From those regions of marked climatic changes, birds move the greatest distances, as exemplified by the Arctic terns. Their breeding range is circumpolar, and when they leave North America, many fly across the Atlantic to southern Europe and thence south along the coast of Africa. Some may winter off the tip of South America.

Some common terns wander to the Pacific islands and join others that have their breeding area in the Old World. One from Michigan was shot in Hawaii. One that was banded in Saskatchewan was picked up in the surf of the Cook Islands.

The birds of prey and other land birds also can make long flights. The amazing travels of some of our hawks have been previously known through observations and collected specimens, but only through banding was the discovery made of the annual northward migration after the Florida breeding season of the bald eagle.

A retired Canadian banker, Charles L. Broley, banded more than a thousand eaglets in Florida. These birds dispersed northward over a broad area

A nesting colony of royal terns at Pamlico Sound, North Carolina.

in the United States and the Maritime Provinces of Canada. Eagle populations from the north, however, follow the usual migration pattern of wintering south of their nesting grounds.

Peregrine falcons migrate along each coast and through the interior from Alaska, Canada, and Greenland to South America. One that was banded in southern Greenland on August 4, 1941, was shot in Cuba on December 2, 1941. One captured as a migrant on October 4, 1961, on Assateague Island, Maryland, was shot in Argentina on January 5, 1962. A nestling falcon marked on August 2, 1952, in northern Alaska, was found dead in Argentina on December 13, 1955. The distance traveled between the two areas is about 9 thousand miles. The peregrine falcon had survived three round-trip journeys.

Many of the ospreys, which are a familiar sight around our bays, lakes, and streams, leave us for the winter and can be seen fishing in Peru and Brazil. Two that were tagged in Wisconsin sojourned in Colombia and Ecuador.

Other birds of prey, such as the owls, are not so highly migratory, but we have had long-distance band recoveries for a few species. A burrowing owl from Utah moved to Baja California, and two long-eared owls from Saskatchewan and Michigan also stopped in Mexico. Snowy owls move from the Arctic to the States some years when their favored food, lemmings, is scarce. A young snowy owl from Cambridge Bay, Canada, flew 3,500 miles to Sakhalin in the Soviet Union.

Chimney swifts often are noticed as they sweep in and out of chimneys by the thousands in the spring and fall. Suddenly one morning all are gone. Not until 1943 was the winter home discovered in Peru. A trader received 13 bands from Indians near the Rio Yanayacu. One each had been banded in Ontario, Connecticut, Illinois, Georgia, and Alabama. Eight had been banded in Tennessee. More than 500 thousand chimney swifts have been banded, but winter recoveries are still meager. Five other reports south of the border came in 1951 or later—all in Mexico during migration in April or September. Another Peruvian report came from Trujillo for one captured in a building on November 7, 1954; it had been banded at Memphis, Tennessee.

Swallows are familiar sights in the fall, perched on utility wires in tremendous numbers, like thousands of soldiers who have closed ranks and are at attention. But they, too, suddenly take off together, and their compass bearing can take them to Chile and Argentina. One was found in Brazil 11 years after it was banded in Wisconsin.

Banding tells us the journeys of barn swallows in some detail. A nestling from New York was shot on its return trip through Mexico on March 19. Another from Massachusetts was encountered crossing the Gulf of Mexico. One recovered in Bolivia on April 7, 1957, had departed the previous fall from Oklahoma. Another reported in 1935 in Bolivia had been banded in Saskatchewan in 1929.

A song that tells of the return of swallows to Capistrano refers to the ability of these birds to perform twice-a-year journeys with great precision. Reports by the press, radio, and television say that swallows always arrive at the old Mission on St. Joseph's Day, March 19, and all depart at the appointed hour on October 23, St. John's Day. Both cliff swallows and white-throated swifts have nested in the old ruins of the Mission San Juan Capistrano midway between Los Angeles and San Diego. These insectivorous birds feed in flight and migrate during the day and are less subject to delay by weather than are other migrants. Even though some migratory species tend to arrive and depart with small variation on either side of a given date, ornithologists have found that the swallows do not always live up to their press notices.

Warblers and vireos have various migration patterns. A few, such as pine warblers, winter in the Southern States. Some stop in the Antilles. Many winter in Central America. Others, notably the yellow warbler, sojourn in South America.

More than 400 thousand warblers and vireos have been banded, but total recoveries are small, and only a handful are from below the border. The most distant warbler movement shown by banding is that of a bay-breasted from Ontario to Colombia.

A bander in Pennsylvania refers to some of his red-eyed vireos as 10-thousand-mile travelers. Birds he has banded have returned to his banding station a year or more later, after completing a round trip of 7,500 or more miles each year. Far northern nesters from the forests of British Columbia would record 12 thousand miles to and from Peru.

More than 1.5 million sparrows of several species have been banded, but not many are known to winter south of the border. We know that some members of this family do reach South America, but banding does not show the full picture.

Dickcissels that nest in the United States occur in flocks of thousands in northern South America, but there is only one banding recovery—a fall migrant banded in Panama on October 18, 1963, was reported the following February in Colombia. More than 2 thousand north-bound migrants in the spring have been banded in Trinidad.

Other sparrow records of interest come from the Russians: A common redpoll trapped in the spring in Michigan was recovered the following spring in Siberia, almost 4 thousand miles away. Two snow buntings from Point Barrow, Alaska, also went to Siberia. A white-winged crossbill from Maine was taken when it came aboard a Soviet vessel in the North Atlantic near Sable Island, Nova Scotia.

An occasional banded bird in Russia has crossed the Atlantic and been taken in eastern Canada. One was a black-legged kittiwake, which was found in Newfoundland in 1937. An official of the Soviet Embassy in Washington once delivered to the Bureau of Sport Fisheries and Wildlife a letter from the Soviet Central Bureau for Bird Ringing with complete data on 26 American bands. We and the Russians have continued to exchange information. More than 400 of our bands have been reported to us by the Soviet Government. Most of the reports are for waterfowl, but 19 species are represented.

That snow geese banded in California in the spring and fall are recovered in the Western States and Canada is well known. That these geese represent migrants of at least two big populations was a discovery. Snows breeding on Wrangel Island off the Arctic coast of Siberia intermingle with thousands from Arctic Canada, once they reach the Western States in mid-October. The Russians estimate that as many as 300 thousand of these geese migrate each year to North America. Although the birds from Siberia winter mainly in

California, some have been taken as far east as Saskatchewan and North Dakota. Since 1960, we have come upon more than 500 snow geese that Russians had banded.

The pintail, the second most abundant duck in North America, is a champion globe trotter. One sped from Labrador to England in 18 days. Three months after leaving California, another arrived in the Cook Islands in the South Pacific, 4 thousand miles away. Two from Canada reached Japan. Wintering birds from Hawaii have scattered through our Western States, including Alaska, and western Canada.

We got more information about this fast flyer when Russians supplied recovery facts for more than 100 of our bands used in States west of the

On this map, the square figures mark the places where almost 5,000 young ospreys were banded. The triangles mark the places where the ospreys were recovered in winter south of the United States.

273

Mississippi and in Canada, Alaska, and Hawaii. Four of them had been banded as flightless young in Alberta and Saskatchewan.

Pintails are known to breed over a broad area in Russia, but we were not aware, until these Russian reports were received, that pintails moved regularly between the two continents. Band recoveries, of course, have documented that American breeders regularly migrate and winter over a big area as far south as the West Indies, Central America, and northern South America. Black brant, Steller's eider, oldsquaw, bufflehead, and even a mallard have reached Soviet areas from North America.

Blue-winged teals are among the earliest migrants to leave Canada and the Northern States in large numbers. Most have departed before the hunting season opens, following arterial routes southward through the eastern Great Plains and the Mississippi Valley. Many winter in South America. One rapid flyer covered 3,800 miles in a month from the Athabaska Delta to Lake Maracaibo, Venezuela, but it is not uncommon for this tiny duck to travel up to 3 thousand miles in 30 days.

Albatrosses, like other pelagic birds, spend most of their lives roaming the seven seas. We know from Samuel Taylor Coleridge's poem, "The Rime of the Ancient Mariner," the sailors' belief that bad luck befalls anyone who kills an albatross. When an acquaintance of mine shot one at sea, a whole series of mishaps followed: The ship's cook broke his leg, the fishing gear became fouled, and the ship had to return to port for repairs.

Banding has shown us that waterfowl, hawks, gulls, and terns may live 20 years or more. But some Laysan albatrosses have been found breeding at 32 years of age on Midway Atoll.

A biologist who has studied albatrosses for more than 10 years and has marked thousands of them, calculated the miles they fly. They clock 100 thousand miles quickly, and during their long lives some individuals may total 3.5 million miles.

We marvel that tiny hummingbirds traverse nonstop the 500-mile expanse of the Gulf of Mexico. Some believe that this is an impossibility for such a little bird, but studies in 1957 disclosed they have enough fuel for even greater flights. When they are ready to migrate, the ruby-throated hummer has an increase in migratory fat, and up to 40 percent of its body weight (about one-eighth ounce) consists of fat.

That the clapper rail is migratory was questioned some years ago. But banding of these coastal inhabitants showed that some of them are truly migratory. Rails banded in the marshes at Chincoteague, Virginia, were taken south along the coast to Georgia and northern Florida.

Sandhill cranes have been observed flying between Alaska and Siberia, but only since 1958 have wintering cranes been banded in Texas and in New Mexico so their movements could be traced. One from each State has been recovered in Siberia—perhaps the brightly colored plastic neckbands they had drew attention.

So we learn more and more about the mysteries of migration.

The sun and stars influence the navigation of day and night-time migrants. The glandular system prepares birds for migration. Lunar observations and use of radar indicate the magnitude and heights of migration, flight speeds, and directions.

Bird banding reveals the old age of some species and spectacular and unexpected journeys of others. It tells us that one bird from the Arctic tundra went to Africa, while his brothers and cousins traveled to Russia and South America—all contending with the weather and the many natural and manmade obstacles.

For more than 2 thousand years, the disappearance of birds in the fall was explained in part by hibernation. Swallows were thought to sleep in holes and other hiding places during cold periods. Some writers said birds sought refuge on the moon, which they reached in 60 days. Others believed that birds hid in the mud or under the water in streambeds. Some birds were credited with catching rides on the backs of migrant storks and cranes.

Strange as some of these ideas seem to us now, the idea of hibernation—rather than migration of some birds to warmer climates, persisted a long time. In 1946, a wintering poor-will was discovered in a torpid condition in California. The Hopi Indians seemed aware of this phenomena, for they called the poor-will "holchko"—the sleeping one.

No other bird species has yet been discovered that shows all characteristics of true hibernation, although swifts and others have been found in a torpid state. Hibernation is well known among mammals and reptiles.

At one time, students of migration believed that climatic conditions alone controlled the departure and arrival of migrants. Pioneering experimental work in Alberta, Canada, in 1925 with the slate-colored junco began a new approach to the study of factors influencing migration. This involved the correlation between increase of daylight (photoperiod) and enlargement of the reproductive organs. It was a logical beginning, for spring migration in part had been associated with the enlargement of the gonads.

The thyroid also was explored because of its relation to the metabolism of birds and the noticeable buildup of fat reserves in the fall and again in the spring. This fat accumulation does not normally occur in sedentary birds, and pre-migratory fat is a source of quick, easily utilized energy, as shown in studies with the white-crowned and golden-crowned sparrows and others.

Attention was focused on the pituitary gland, which affects the whole organism and particularly metabolism, sexual growth, and reproduction. Studies of the pituitary and of the endocrine system in general pointed to the relation between migration and the activity of the pituitary gland. Our knowledge of its exact part in migration is still incomplete, however.

Changes in photoperiods, fat reserves, and external factors, like temperature and food scarcity, all relate to the migratory phenomena, but they are not necessarily the same for species wintering in equatorial zones as for species wintering in temperate zones.

Simple visual observations have extended our knowledge of migration, particularly the migration of birds that move during daylight hours. We learned a great deal about night-time migration in the midforties when some 2,500 persons at 325 places between Canada and Panama spent more than 10 thousand hours watching migrant birds as they flew across the face of the moon. The study gave new insight into the magnitude of the fall exodus of birds, their varying altitudes and direc-

A Canada goose has just been marked with a leg band that will help biologists reconstruct its life story. The geese in the background await banding.

tions of flight, and the peaking of activity before midnight.

Still, despite all we know about migration from banding and in the other ways I mentioned, there is much we do not know. Perhaps we can learn more from the use of radar. Perhaps orbiting satellites will record and send back to tracking stations precise information of the movements of birds made possible by minute transmitters on the back or around the leg of a bird. Perhaps some other scientific marvel will disclose the "compasses," "barometers," and internal regulators that enable birds to chart their courses over untried routes and through many hazards.

But let us not sit back and wait for others. We can take our binoculars, notebooks, and bands and record events as they happen to add to our stockpile of knowledge. Computers are needed to sift and sort masses of data, but to most of us it is more satisfying to look at birds with our eyes, rather than through computers.

—ALLEN J. DUVALL.

Long, Long Ago

BONES OF BIRDS from places where people lived long ago help the archaeologist get a rounded picture of the culture and life habits of the prehistoric people he is studying. They can tell him a number of things: The kinds of birds that were captured; the importance of birds as food in comparison with mammals, fish, and shellfish; the seasons at which birds were obtained, thus indicating the time of the year the site was occupied; the climate prevailing at that time; and possible differences between the local avifauna of today and that of the period when the site was occupied.

Bird bones from archaeological sites also provide valuable information for the zoologist. They may extend the range of a species or show differences in the geographical distribution of species in the past and the present. They may indicate the former range of extinct species of birds and the approximate time at which they became extinct.

Bones in the places where prehistoric people lived tell of the birds they used as food. Their interest in birds is indicated also in paintings and pictographs, in bird figures engraved on bone and ivory artifacts, or stone, bone, or ivory carvings representing birds.

Complete skeletons of condors, eagles, and hawks buried in shell heaps in California are evidence of ceremonial practices connected with those birds in prehistoric times.

The modern California Indians had a similar practice that involved the ceremonial capture, killing, and rearing the young of condors, hawks, and eagles.

Burials of macaw skeletons in prehistoric pueblos in New Mexico show the high regard in which these beautiful birds were held. They are evidence also of prehistoric trade between the Pueblo Indians and those of tropical Mexico.

The methods prehistoric man used for capturing birds probably were little different from the methods of primitive men of later times. Traps and snares no doubt were the most effective means of catching birds on the ground. We know that flying birds sometimes were shot with the bow and arrow, for archaeologists have found the breastbones of cranes, geese, and other large birds in which are perforations made by arrows.

The Mesolithic hunters of Scandinavia also used a blunt-headed arrow for stunning birds without damaging their skins. The same device is employed by modern Eskimos and other northern peoples. Another weapon was the multipronged bird spear hurled with a throwing board, which also was a technique commonly used by the Eskimos.

The simplest method of capturing the larger birds was that of clubbing them or running them down during the moulting season when they were unable to fly. This was no doubt the way men of Paleolithic and later prehistoric times captured the great auk, the huge, flightless bird that finally became extinct around the middle of the last century.

Bones from Lower Paleolithic sites in western Europe show that the great auk formed part of the diet of Neanderthal man of the Mousterian period. Upper Paleolithic men engraved figures of the great auk on walls of the El Pendo cave in northern Spain. Bones of this bird have been found at numerous sites in western Europe; they date from the Upper Paleolithic, Mesolithic, Neolithic, and Iron Age.

In the Upper Paleolithic caves of France and Germany, the bones of willow ptarmigan and rock ptarmigan are far more abundant than those of any other species—evidence that these birds were an important source of food for the early cave-dwellers.

As Grahame Clark, a British archaeologist, has pointed out, ptarmigan most likely were caught in snares set in the snow, a practice still followed in northern Norway and Lapland. That would confirm other indications that the Upper Paleolithic caves and rock shelters were winter dwellings, a conclusion borne out by the paucity of ptarmigan bones at summer campsites of the related Hamburgian culture in northern Germany. As these sites contain the bones of young birds—swans, geese, and sea gulls—they must have been occupied in summer, when the birds were nesting.

The seasonal occupation of many other prehistoric sites has been determined on the basis of the bird bones they contained. I cite two examples.

Hildegarde Howard's analysis of bird remains from the Emeryville shell mound on San Francisco Bay showed that most of the bones were those of ducks and geese, which at present are winter visitors in the vicinity. There was also an abundance of cormorant bones, about half of them of young birds, which would have been taken from the nests in June and July. She concluded therefore that the site had been occupied continuously throughout the year.

At Muldbjerg, an early Neolithic site in Zealand, Denmark, J. Troels-Smith's excavations uncovered the bones of swans and various kinds of ducks that had nested in this swampy locality in June and July, as indicated by the presence of bones of barely fledged birds. The bones of bitterns and other migratory species pointed to the later part of summer. There were no bones of winter visitors among the migratory birds. From the evidence of the bird bones and of plant remains, Dr. Troels-Smith was able to show that people had lived at the site only during June, July, August, and September.

New Zealand has an important archaeological culture period named after a bird that was the principal basis of its food economy. It was the Moa-hunting culture, that of the first people to reach New Zealand from eastern Polynesia in the 12th century A.D. Landing on North Island with no cultivable food plants, these early Polynesians turned to hunting the moas, a now extinct order of birds, one of which, a huge ostrich-like bird, the great moa, stood about 10 feet tall.

There were about 19 species of moas on the North and South Islands. Moa bones have been found in the lower levels of archaeological sites on South Island but become less frequent in the upper levels, as these great birds decreased in numbers and finally became extinct. Moa bones were used for making awls, fishhooks, and other implements. Moa eggs were buried with the dead.

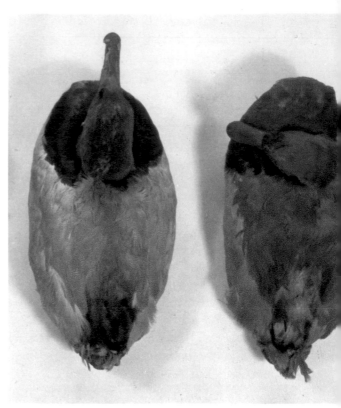

The Paiute Indians in Nevada used decoys in hunting waterfowl. They mounted skins of ducks (right) on floats made of tules. Some of the decoys (at the far left) had a handle on the underside. These examples are in the Smithsonian Institution and date from 1859.

This Eskimo mask from the Lower Yukon is in the Smithsonian Institution.

The Paiutes in the Southwest and other American Indians made fans of feathers.

278

A collection of several thousand bird bones, which I excavated at Eskimo sites on St. Lawrence Island near Bering Strait in 1929 and 1930 and which were studied by Herbert Friedmann, then Curator of Birds at the United States National Museum, provided interesting information on the birds that were hunted and eaten by these Eskimos over a period of some 2,250 years.

One of the sites was at Cape Kialegak at the southeastern end of the island. It had been occupied from the time of the intermediate, or Punuk, stage of culture of around A.D. 900 to the latter part of the 19th century. The other five sites were at Gambell, at the northwestern end of the island, and ranged in age from modern 19th century, through Punuk, to the Old Bering Sea culture of about 300 B.C.

Dr. Friedmann identified 45 species of birds in the collection. Ten were species that had not been reported previously from St. Lawrence Island: The slender-billed shearwater, cackling Canada goose, black brant, white-winged scoter, surf scoter, common merganser, wandering tattler, mew gull, red-legged kittiwake, and Kittlitz's murrelet.

The bones of Pallas's thick-billed murre were the most abundant at all of the sites.

Other birds that had formed an important part of the Eskimos' diet at all periods were the crested auklet, pelagic cormorant, Pacific common eider, king eider, paroquet auklet, short-tailed albatross, long-tailed jaeger, pigeon guillemot, and tufted puffin.

The absence of raven bones showed that in prehistoric times, just as today, the raven was regarded as a sacred bird by the Eskimos and was never killed.

The collection of bones from Cape Kialegak, though not so large as that obtained at Gambell at the opposite end of the island, included 11 species not found at Gambell: The whistling swan, cackling Canada goose, black brant, American pintail, spectacled eider, white-winged scoter, surf scoter, common scoter, common merganser, red-breasted merganser, and pomarine jaeger. These birds are rare at the western end of the island today and show that the present distribution of waterfowl on St. Lawrence Island is essentially the same as it was a thousand years ago.

A Pueblo Indian from New Mexico performs an eagle dance at the American Indian Performing Arts Festival in Washington, D.C., in April 1965.

One of the most interesting facts in Dr. Friedmann's study of the St. Lawrence bones was that the number of species and quantity of bones were much greater at the Punuk and later sites than at those of the Old Bering Sea period—evidently a reflection of new hunting techniques that were introduced in the Punuk period. The bird bo[...] and blunt-ended bird arrows both made their first appearance at this time; 256 bone and ivory bolas weights were found at the Punuk and later sites—none at the Old Bering Sea sites. It was no doubt the acquisition of this new hunting device, which is highly effective in capturing birds on the wing, that enabled the Punuk and later Eskimos to obtain so many kinds and such large numbers of waterfowl.

Very likely all primitive tribes ate birds and birds' eggs, and most of them have used feathers of birds for one purpose or another.

The Eskimos and other northern peoples, whose arctic territory is the breeding ground of countless numbers of waterfowl and other birds, have exploited their avian resources more effectively than have tribes of the temperate and tropical regions.

...bers, particularly those of eagles, have long been worn in Indian ceremonial events. Here Indians from Oklahoma perform a tail-feather dance at a White House reception in 1965.

The Eskimos and neighboring Siberian tribes are the only ones who wear tailored clothing made of bird skins. It is a coatlike garment, or parka, and usually is made of caribou skin but sometimes also of the skins of eider ducks, puffins, auklets, murres, cormorants, and other sea birds.

The Indians in the southeastern United States made mantles, cloaks, and blankets from the feathers of turkeys and other birds. Feather robes of a similar kind formerly were worn by some of the Indians of South America.

In most parts of the world, feathers were used mainly for decoration or in connection with ceremonialism and worship—as, for example, the feather prayer sticks, wands, and altar decorations of the Pueblo Indians and the down and feathers that many primitive peoples applied to their bodies when performing ceremonial dances.

Feathers were associated with symbolism and ritual in many parts of North America and among more highly developed peoples, like the Peruvians, Mayas, and Polynesians, were an indication of social rank or royalty.

The Plains Indians decorated the sacred calumet with feathers, birds' heads, or the entire skins of birds. Dried bird skins were carefully preserved in their sacred medicine bundles.

Eagle feathers were highly prized by almost all

American Indians. Their most notable use was on the elaborate war bonnets of the Plains Indians. With these tribes, the eagle feather was a mark of rank and military prowess, and only those who had performed deeds of valor could wear them.

Eagle feathers and horses were the standards of value and media of exchange, at the rate of about 12 feathers for 1 horse. Eagles were difficult to obtain, and their capture was attended by various ceremonial observances. The Pueblo Indians caught young eagles and kept them in cages as a source of supply for the downy plumage that was highly valued for ceremonial purposes.

Alaskan Eskimos and Aleuts embellished their gut-skin rain parkas and bags with little tufts of bright-colored feathers sewn in at the seams in parallel rows. The exquisite basketry of the Pomo Indians of California was decorated in the same way.

Featherwork reached its highest stage of perfection among the ancient Peruvians and Polynesians, whose beautiful multicolored feather robes, reserved for royalty, are works of art of the highest order.

To indicate the many kinds of birds primitive peoples used for food and the many methods they employed in capturing them, I give a summary account of Eskimo hunting practices, particularly those of the Polar Eskimos of northwest Greenland, described by Peter Freuchen and Finn Salmonsen in their volume *The Arctic Year*.

The Polar Eskimos, like those in other areas, hunt ducks, geese, and other large waterfowl by means of traps and snares, the bow and arrow, the bird dart cast with a throwing board, and, in earlier times, the bird bolas. For the Polar Eskimos, however, the most important bird is a little auk, the dovekie, which breeds in countless numbers on the rocky mountain slopes and which the Eskimos catch, like butterflies, with long-handled nets.

The dovekie is found only in the high arctic regions of the North Atlantic. It spends the winter among the drifting ice floes off western and southern Greenland, Labrador, and Newfoundland, and in May flies north to breed in northwestern Greenland, Spitzbergen, Jan Mayen, Franz Josef Land, and Novaya Zemlya. It does not occur in Canada or Alaska. It is estimated that at least 30 million

In Hawaii long ago, royalty wore red and yellow cloaks and Grecian-type helmets made of bird feathers. The kahilis, or royal insignia, at left and right are richly ornamented with feathers.

King Kamehameha of Hawaii wore this elaborate feather cape on public occasions when he was young. He gave it in 1839 to Commander Bolton of the U.S. Navy.

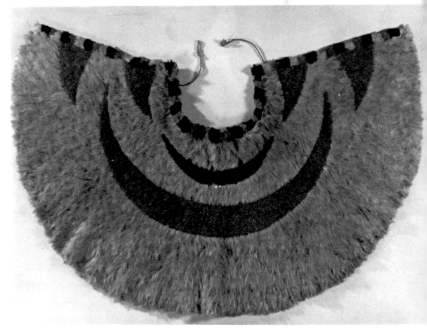

dovekies breed in northwestern Greenland from Melville Sound north to Etah.

The Polar Eskimos build low rock walls, behind which they hide and scoop the dovekies up with a long-handled net as they fly by. Often they get six or seven birds at one sweep. The Alaskan Eskimos on St. Lawrence and Diomede Islands use the same technique for catching the crested auklet. When the St. Lawrence Islanders catch the first few auklets, they do not kill them immediately but string them up on a line so that their fluttering will attract others.

Besides the dovekies that the Polar Eskimos catch and eat during the hunting period in late spring and summer, they store many others for winter food. The birds are killed as soon as they are caught and stuffed into a seal skin that has been removed in such a manner as to leave a thick layer of blubber on the inside. These seal pokes, called giviak, are covered with stones for protection against the sun; otherwise, the birds would become rancid as the seal blubber melted into oil in the summer heat. With the coming of cold weather, the bird-stuffed seal skins freeze solidly; preserved in this manner, they provide a welcome addition to the Eskimos' diet in winter.

Large numbers of dovekie eggs are collected from the crevices among the rocks, to be cooked and eaten. For a bird of its size, the dovekie egg is remarkably large. The Eskimos attach a special significance to this. When a girl baby is born, they hang the dried foot of a dovekie around her neck as an amulet, so that when she grows up she will bear large and healthy children.

Among Eskimos everywhere, the only birds of any consequence as a source of food, with the exception of the ptarmigan, are the sea birds—the small dovekies and auklets and many of the larger birds, such as ducks, geese, swans, murres, gulls, and cormorants.

One might suppose that the Eskimos would show scant interest in the many small passerine birds of little or no importance in their food economy. Not so, however.

Laurence Irving, of the University of Alaska, a biologist with anthropological interests, learned something that anthropologists who had studied the Eskimos had not suspected. He found that the Eskimos of Anaktuvuk Pass and the Kobuk River, Alaska, had a surprisingly detailed and comprehensive knowledge of the avifauna. They recognized accurately minute details of plumage and other characteristics that taxonomists use in distinguishing the species, and they had a definite and specific name for every bird, even the smallest.

The lively interest these Eskimos had for the smaller birds is shown by the names given them. Thus the Nunamiut Eskimos of Anaktuvuk Pass call the fox sparrow *Iklikvik,* meaning "tool box," from the quick rattling sound which the little birds make when scratching among dead leaves. The Nunamiut name for the gray-cheeked thrush is *Niviokruksioyuk,* meaning "goes after flies." The wheatear is called *Tikmiakpaurak,* or "little eagle," because of its rapid and swooping flight.

The many quaint and humorous names given to such birds show that the Eskimos had an intellectual and sympathetic interest in these small creatures and derived satisfaction in observing their activities, just as do birdwatchers everywhere.

In early times, before the magnetic compass was invented, birds were of great help in navigation and the discovery of new lands and islands.

Primitive peoples, like the Polynesians, and European navigators of medieval times could be assured of the existence of unknown land by observing the flight patterns of migratory land birds, which they saw flying out to sea and returning later in the season from the same direction.

Mariners on the open ocean could profit from a knowledge of the flying range of different kinds of sea birds that fly out to sea in early morning and return to their land base at dusk. By observing the direction in which the birds are flying at those times, they determined the approximate distance and direction of the nearest land.

On his first voyage of discovery, Columbus made his landfall by observing the flight of migratory birds. Toward the end of the voyage, he and his men saw enormous flocks of small land birds overhead, flying toward the southwest on their annual fall migration. Realizing that land must lie in that direction, Columbus changed his course to the southwest. A few days later, he sighted the Bahama Islands.

Samuel Eliot Morison, the noted American historian whose works include *Portuguese Voyages to America in the Fifteenth Century* (Harvard University Press, 1940), remarks that Columbus followed the path of the birds because he knew that this was the way the Portuguese had discovered the western Azores in 1452, as related by Las Casas:

"On the return passage they discovered the island of Flores, guided by many birds which they saw flying thither, and recognized that they were land and not sea birds, and thus judged that they must be going to sleep on some land."

S. Percy Smith, a New Zealand ethnologist and author of *Hawaiki, The Original Home of the Maori*, referring to the legendary discovery of New Zealand by Kupe from the island of Raiatea in the Tahitian group, says:

"Kupe had observed in his many voyages the flight of the *kohoperoa* or long-tailed cuckoo, year after year, always coming from the southwest and wintering in the Central Pacific islands. He and his compeers would know at once that this is a land bird and consequently that land must lie towards the southwest."

James Hornell and other writers think it likely that the Tahitians were led to discover the Hawaiian Islands by observing the seasonal migrations of the golden plovers that breed in Alaska and northeastern Siberia and winter in the South Pacific Islands.

According to the New Zealand historian, G. S. Parsonson, the daring exploits of the early Polynesian voyagers were in no small measure dependent on what they had learned from the flight of migratory birds. He wrote in 1962:

"In the subsequent search for land which their progressive penetration of Oceania and their new found dependence upon agriculture made necessary they must have relied to an increasing extent upon migratory birds, in particular the long-tailed cuckoo, the sooty shearwater, the golden plover and possibly also the godwit, whose flight, spread out over several weeks, they had long studied."

A more direct use of birds in navigation was the ancient and widespread practice of taking several "shore-sighting" birds on board the ship. They would fly in the direction of the nearest land when they were released.

Pliny, the old Roman writer, related that the method was employed by the seafarers of Ceylon on their ocean voyages 2 thousand years ago.

James Hornell, in an article in Antiquity in 1946, cites the following Hindu account of the same practice contained in the Dialogues of the Buddha of the 5th century B.C.:

"Long ago ocean-going merchants were wont to plunge forth upon the sea, on board a ship, taking with them a shore-sighting bird. When the ship was out of sight of land, they would set the shore-sighting bird free. And it would go to the East and to the South and to the West and to the North, and to the intermediate points, and rise aloft. If on the horizon it caught sight of land, thither would it go, but if not, it would come back to the ship again."

The Norse saga of Floki describes how Iceland was rediscovered with the help of ravens. In A.D. 874, Floki, a Norwegian navigator, set out to find the large island to the westward that had been discovered some 10 years earlier by a Swede named Gardar.

Floki took three ravens to guide him on the voyage. After sailing westward for several days, he released one of the ravens, which circled high in the air and flew back toward Norway. Some days later, he released the second raven, which flew high overhead and, seeing no land, returned to the ship. The third raven to be sent aloft flew to the westward and did not return; that meant that land lay in that direction. Floki continued westward, following the flight of the raven, and soon came upon the southeast coast of Iceland.

In the Biblical account of the Flood and the earlier Babylonian version of the same event contained in the Epic of Gilgamesh, in both of which ravens and doves are sent out to search for land, we have further evidence of the ancient practice of releasing captive birds to guide the mariner to shore.

—HENRY B. COLLINS.

Birds and Our Health

L OUIS PASTEUR, the great French chemist whose studies of bacteria led to the development of vaccination and pasteurization, was investigating in his laboratory in 1880 the tiny microbe that kills chickens with a malady known as chicken cholera.

He grew the microbe in a soup he prepared from chicken meat. He put small drops of the broth culture on crumbs of bread and fed them to healthy chickens. They all died.

In order to have fresh material every day, Pasteur had his assistants transfer his cultures to new batches of chicken broth. They would dip a wire loop into the teeming culture and shake the drop into the new broth. The next day this would be teeming with microbes.

After several weeks, the laboratory was cluttered with old bottles of broth, and it became necessary to clean up the mess. From some motive of curiosity, perhaps to see if the microbes were still alive, a few drops of the oldest cultures were shot into some chickens. As always, the chickens were in bad shape when he left his laboratory for the night. The next morning he was surprised to find these birds alive, alert, and normal. We do not know what his conclusions were. He left shortly for a summer vacation.

A month later, back from his vacation, he called for some new chickens to inoculate. Since only a few unused birds were available, he also inoculated those that had not died from the inoculation of the old cultures. The next morning, all the new birds were dead, but the ones that had recovered from the earlier inoculation of the old cultures were alive and happy.

Pasteur had discovered a method of making a vaccine, of taming his microbes so they would make the chicken only a little sick—but when she got better she could stand the big doses of his new cultures that ordinarily killed all his chickens.

This discovery has eliminated much human suffering and saved countless millions of lives. His work was a pivot point in the evolution of medicine from primitive mumbo-jumbo to the more factual approach of modern science. Our particular interest here is the place birds have had in the quest for ways to insure the health of people.

Disease was terrifying and mysterious to primitive man. Evil spirits were the cause of his ills, and to combat them a glomeration of hocus-pocus evolved, such as the use of birds as charms to bring back health.

For example, Welchmen once thought that if they walked around a well while carrying a chicken and praying they would transfer their epilepsy to the fowl. Parts of birds were used for centuries in making potions, medicines, and salves. The feathers of owls and eagles were an important item in the medicine bags of the American Indians' medicine men. Goose grease has been used as a salve since the time of ancient Egyptians and Chinese.

One thing that comes to mind when I think of birds and their connection with our health is the use of their eggs to identify disease-producing organisms and to prepare vaccines.

Many of the thousands of disease agents that occur in nature produce a definite reaction in the tissues of the embryo that develops in a fertile egg.

Scientists and technicians in laboratories therefore inject fluids, cells, or body tissues, that they suspect may be diseased, into the egg. Because they know what to look for, the effect (or none) on the embryo helps them diagnose many aliments of people and animals.

Because eggs react to some of the disease-causing germs, they are used in the commercial manufacture of many vaccines, including those for rabies and smallpox.

Chicken embryos are inoculated with the disease-causing organisms.

Like Pasteur's old broth cultures of chicken chol-era, inoculation into man of tissues of such infected embryos produces a mild form of the disease—mild but enough to stimulate the development of antibodies. People are inoculated with the vaccines to protect them from infection or to ease suffering and prevent death.

Veterinary public health specialists list more than a hundred diseases of animals in the wild that can be transmitted to man. Many involve birds. They are called zoonoses (pronounced zōa-nōsez). They include communicable or infectious diseases caused by viruses, bacteria, protozoa, and the larger parasitic worms. They may be spread by contaminated food, contaminated air, direct injection by a biting or blood-sucking insect, or by direct penetration through the skin.

Some of the diseases that affect birds are host specific—that is, they are confined to a particular species or group of species. Others are confined to birds. Others are shared with other animals and man. Most of the diseases of birds do not occur in man because man is not susceptible or because no opportunity normally arises for the transfer of the particular disease-causing organisms between birds and man.

Gary Knipling, technician at the Patuxent Wildlife Research Center, takes a blood sample from a duck for use in studies of malaria.

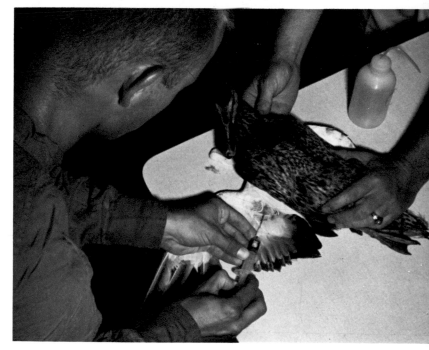

A malarial blood parasite is transmitted from one bird to another by blood-sucking blackflies that breed in flowing water. Dr. I. B. Tarshis, of the Patuxent Wildlife Research Center, takes notes on his studies of the production of blackflies in water of varying temperatures and turbidity.

Although birds may be hosts to many parasites, both external (such as lice) and internal (such as intestinal worms), most of these are host specific and will not infect man.

Disease is a dynamic—not static—phenomenon. Health, according to the World Health Organization of the United Nations, is a state of complete, physical, mental, and social well-being. We recognize that disease bulks large in the struggle for survival, but constant changes in the nature of disease make the struggle never ending. People who have the broad concept that disease is a part of nature have the greatest opportunities for control of the zoonoses. Our problem is to study the nat-

ural history of such diseases if we are to control them. With the increase in the numbers of people on earth and the competition for the remaining available habitat for both man and birds, the importance of birds as reservoirs of disease will continue to command attention. The diseases of most significance today may not be the important ones tomorrow. Knowledge of those we have today may help us better to understand the problems of zoonoses that will develop in the future.

Malaria has been a major disease and birds have helped us to develop knowledge about it.

Dr. Asa C. Chandler, of Rice Institute, wrote in a textbook in the thirties that malaria "has been

The small specks on this net are blackfly larvae. They will be brought into the laboratory to study the life history of the leucocytozoan parasite they carry and transmit to waterfowl.

estimated to be the direct or indirect cause of over one-half the entire mortality of the human race."

For centuries, malaria was attributed to bad air—as its name implies. People avoided swampy areas, particularly at night, and many prime agricultural regions were not developed because of the fear of malaria.

The discovery in 1880 that a protozoan parasite (*Plasmodium*) lived in red blood cells of patients having malaria turned the tide of battle against the disease, a battle that became a classic of medical conquest. Within a few years after the discovery of the causative organism in man, the parasite was found to occur in the blood of many species of

birds. For some years it was thought that birds were a reservoir, or source, of the infection to man, but findings by many researchers demonstrated that the parasites from birds would not survive in man, and vice versa.

Anopheline mosquitoes, which appear to be standing on their heads in the act of sucking blood, transmit the malarias to man. Culicine mosquitoes, which perch parallel to the surface while feeding, transmit the plasmodial infections in birds.

The first demonstration that mosquitoes carry the parasites was accomplished by Ronald Ross, a British colonial physician who was working with sparrows (species of *Passer*) in India just before

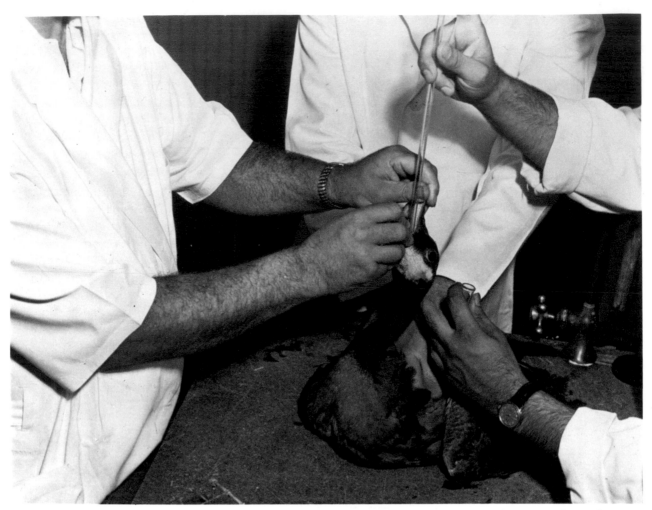

Researchers feed a known number of eggs of a parasite to a Canada goose to learn the dosage level that may be necessary to cause disease.

this century began. It was the key to most of the later developments in the conquest of malaria. For his discovery, Dr. Ross was awarded a Nobel Prize in 1902 and was knighted in 1911.

Little is known of the details of Ross' manipulations, of the trials and tribulations he must have encountered in working with his mosquitoes with the limited knowledge for handling these insects in captivity available at that time.

It was vividly brought home to me in one of my own early experiments. I was attempting to determine whether a small blood-sucking fly (hippoboscid) were involved in the transmission of a malarialike parasite in birds. I confined two naturally infected chipping sparrows in a small screened cage and each day introduced a dozen

flies captured from other trapped birds. After another week elapsed, I decided it was time to retrieve and examine my flies. To my chagrin I could find none. Closer observation of a repetition of the experiment brought to mind a quotation from Lewis Carroll: "And this was scarcely odd, for they'd eaten every one."

Experimental birds in laboratories in the United States and other countries have been the "test tubes" of basic research on malaria. The findings have been interpolated to man and put to use for his benefit.

Many of the investigations on drugs were preceded by laboratory experiments on birds.

Details on the life history of the parasites and other facts basic to a full understanding of the inner workings of the disease were developed from studies of caged canaries, java sparrows, house sparrows, and other birds.

Since the Second World War, great advances in the control of malaria have been made by using insecticides on mosquitoes and drugs for infected persons. Modern control techniques applied with the support of the World Health Organization are continuing to reduce, control, and even eradicate the disease.

In the United States, even in places where the disease was of great economic significance until after the war, malaria is now rare in man.

Birds may be important in the future by providing the only available source of plasmodial parasites to demonstrate living material to students of a disease once of such far-reaching significance to the welfare of man.

Schistosomiasis is another widespread parasitic disease in which birds have had a direct relationship. Its long name derives from the little, flat worms, known as schistosomes, that are responsible for the infection. As a disease, it occurs primarily in the Tropics and subtropics and is particularly prevalent in places where agricultural irrigation is extensive, as the Nile River Valley. As many as 85 percent of the people there are infected. Although the death rate reaches only about 10 percent, the tremendous impact of this infection on the vitality of victims has a drastic influence on the productivity of people in areas where the disease is rampant.

The schistosome parasite develops first in the body of a snail. The stage that is infective to man escapes from the snail and swims in water until it finds a suitable host. The parasite penetrates the skin of people and eventually reaches internal organs, where it can cause extensive tissue damage.

The mature worms produce eggs, which escape with the human excreta and ultimately reach the appropriate habitat to infect more snails.

In this disease of man, birds are not involved. However, birds are hosts to various schistosome parasites. Water birds become infected from stages that escape from infected snails, just as man gets his schistosomiasis from snails.

At the stage when the bird parasites escape from the snail, they are not particular about what sort of creature they attack. Their chief goal apparently is to penetrate the skin of a person or animal, and many an unwary wader or swimmer has become a victim. Where the bird parasite enters the skin, an itching irritation develops. You may know it as swimmer's itch or clam digger's itch. The itch often is accompanied by an allergic reaction that is quite severe in some victims. After penetrating the skin, the parasites develop no further, for they cannot complete their life cycle in man.

Encephalitis, a virus disease, has a complex cycle in which birds may be involved.

Originally it was called equine encephalitis, because it was first recognized as a disease in horses. Today it is a major scourge of people in many countries.

In the thirties, when it was established that a virus caused encephalitis in horses, it was suggested that encephalitis may have been a factor in the reduction of the number of horses in the United States. Indeed, there has been speculation that the disease indirectly stimulated the rapid advance in farm mechanization.

Dr. J. W. Beard, of Duke University, and his associates in 1938 developed a vaccine from infected chick embryo tissues. It is available for horses as a measure of control.

A virus is not visible through the ordinary microscope. It can be seen only with the aid of the powerful electron microscope. It can pass through a filter fine enough to trap microscopic bacteria.

Techniques have been devised for isolation and identification of the viral agent of encephalitis in blood samples. Its presence in the blood is termed viremia.

Another tool available to the scientist is the demonstration of presence of antibodies in the blood. When the body of an animal becomes infected, certain changes take place. They are considered a reaction of the body to combat the infection. By following proper techniques in the examination of blood, it is possible to demonstrate the presence of antibodies, an indication the animal has been exposed to the specific infection.

Encephalitis is called an arbovirus disease because it is transmitted by blood-sucking arthro-

Carlton M. Herman locates documents on wildlife diseases by using a modern punch-card system. Keeping up with progress and results of fellow scientists is a part of the research process.

pods, such as mosquitoes and ticks. The vector—carrier—of the virus of this infection is a mosquito. The mosquito can become a vector only if it consumes the virus. Thus the source animal must be infected and have a viremia at the time the insect feeds on it.

Because the viremia that occurs in sick horses is considered to be insufficient to infect a mosquito, some other source in nature must be involved.

Equine encephalitis acts much like polio. Patients that recover often suffer paralytic effects. Its occurrence in people is comparatively limited, but some persons have contracted it in late summer.

Birds may be a source of the encephalitis virus present in mosquitoes, which in turn they transmit to horses or man. Antibodies have been found in various wild birds; they therefore have been exposed to the infection. Although in most cases the infection that has been observed is of low value and of short duration—a day or two—some kinds of birds, such as pheasants, house sparows, and do-

mestic ducks, are known to die from the disease.

Among pheasants, infection can be transmitted when a susceptible bird pecks an infected one. Although pheasants and some other birds must be considered as a potential source of encephalitis transmitted to man, the true role of birds in maintaining the cycle of this disease is not precisely known and needs further study.

Pheasants in captivity have been known to die from this disease nearly every year since the mid-thirties. Despite evidence of the disease in pheasants in a resort area in New Jersey, no human cases were recognized there until the summer of 1959, when 30 deaths were reported. The resultant publicity caused vacationers to go elsewhere. In addition to the infections that occurred in some people, the community suffered economic losses estimated in millions of dollars from lack of potential visitors at the height of the tourist season. An extensive research program was started in an effort to prevent future outbreaks.

Natural infections have been uncovered in several species of rodents and reptiles. In at least one case, a viremia lasting 28 days was recorded from a snake.

Ornithosis, a newer and broader term for psittacosis and parrot fever, is an airborne respiratory infection. Birds and people become infected by inhaling the contaminated discharges and bits of droppings of infected birds. It is suspected that some persons have been infected simply by walking through a pet shop that had infected parakeets.

Dr. K. F. Meyer, for many years director of the Hooper Foundation of the University of California, has delved extensively into studies on ornithosis. Better than anyone else, he is aware of the precautions research scientists must take to avoid unnecessary exposure to infectious agents and has indeed been a champion of good precautionary procedures.

A story is told that on one occasion he was explaining the proper precautionary procedures in his laboratory to a group of visiting colleagues. He concluded his remarks by stating that anyone working with this agent in the laboratory who contracts the disease is a damn fool. Subsequently one of the colleagues, while visiting Dr. Meyer in a hospital where he was confined as a patient with ornithosis, asked him what happened. Dr. Meyer replied, "I was a damn fool!"

The importation and sale of parrots have been curtailed drastically by State and Federal quarantine regulations adopted in the early thirties.

By the middle of the 19th century, the doctors came to recognize a disease that they believed was contracted from psitticine (parrotlike) birds. Parrot fever was extensively studied at the Pasteur Institute in Paris beginning in 1893.

Dr. Edmond Nocard, of the Institute, isolated a bacterium from infected parrots and man. Nocard's bacillus until 1929 was recognized as the cause of psittacosis, as the disease was then called. Continuing research has demonstrated that the causative agent is actually a viruslike organism. The disease now is known to occur in a variety of birds in many parts of the world, including the United States. A high incidence occurs in domestic pigeons. It also may affect ducks, turkeys, and chickens.

Psittacosis, or ornithosis, probably is the best known example of a disease common in birds to which man is directly susceptible. It is responsive to treatment by antibiotics, and people do not now often die from it.

Salmonella is a name given to an extensive group of bacteria that produce intestinal upsets or typhoidlike disease.

One of the chief sources of salmonella food poisoning in man has been improperly handled poultry and egg products. Despite constant vigilance of health departments, food and drug administrations, and inspectors in the food processing industry, occasional salmonella food poisoning is reported. Improper handling of custards and other egg and poultry products is blamed. A sensible precaution is to cook eggs, rather than eat raw eggs, especially if the shells are dirty or cracked.

Diseases caused by the salmonella bacteria also have been a factor in the health and survival of birds. They are the greatest single disease problem in the entire poultry industry, and millions of dollars and extensive research efforts have been expended toward their control and eradication. Strict regulations have been established by governments and the poultry industry. Tests are made from blood samples of all birds in breeding flocks, and infected birds are destroyed. A system of accreditation has been incorporated into the program to avoid transfer of the infection from one flock, or one hatchery, to another.

Other diseases are common to birds and people. Birds may be involved in the maintenance cycle of many other infectious diseases of man, but the processes, extent, and significance of most of them have not been clearly delineated. Some of them may be rare and incidental.

I have heard it said that crows in Russia carry plague by contamination on their feet. It is now recognized that histoplasmosis (a fungus disease) may have something to do with concentrations of bird droppings, which can serve as a culture medium and source of human infections.

Birds also can serve as temporary hosts of disease vectors, such as ticks, which carry certain viruses and fever-causing agents.

People must rely on their physicians to diagnose and treat their ailments, no matter what the source. Although birds are involved in various relationships in the health of man, the problem remains the concern chiefly of the specialist investigating health problems in wildlife and of trained research personnel in the field of public health. These specialists recognize the many unsolved problems as a challenge and will continue to seek solutions for them.

—CARLTON M. HERMAN.

Birds Kept for Food

THE COMMON BARNYARD FOWL is almost gone from American farms and backyards. In its place, scientific breeding and feeding, automation, punchcards, and chain-belt methods of production have given us highly specialized birds, a highly specialized poultry industry, and a bounty of meat and eggs.

Time was when nearly every farm had **poul-try**, which the farmer's wife and children cared for and which provided extra food and chicken money for a new dress. She saved some eggs for hatching (hoping the roosters had done their job) and placed them in nests under broody hens. Sometimes the hen would refuse all her supervision, make a nest in the haystack, and hatch a brood of chicks all on her own. The poultry (the term we use for birds that are domesticated to produce eggs or meat) roamed the farmstead, foraging for food to piece out the grain thrown out once or twice a day for them.

Most of the males, known as spring chickens, were killed for meat one by one as they got big enough. Extra eggs were sold for "egg" money. A farm family might also have had a few turkeys, several ducks, and some geese and guineafowl.

Modern poultry were developed from breeds and varieties bred for show purposes rather than for economic utility. The first poultry show in America was held in 1849. Poultry shows are still held at county and State fairs, but the birds in them are mostly for display, not for food.

Birds seen in poultry shows represent many sizes, shapes, and colors. More than 200 distinct breeds and varieties are described in the American Standard of Perfection. They range from the tiny, 22-ounce chicken bantam hen to the 36-pound turkey tom; from the agile, upstanding fighting game cock to the squat, heavily muscled Cornish chicken; and from the snow-white plumage of white Leghorns, through the delicate lacings and pencillings of Wyandottes, to the coal-black plumage of Jersey black giant chickens.

Besides the breeds and varieties described in the American Standard of Perfection, many unusual types have been developed. Among them are chickens like the Creeper, which has legs so short it walks like a duck; the Japanese Phoenix, which has tailfeathers 7 to 8 feet long; and the Araucana, which lays blue-shelled eggs.

Now the hatching is done in large, modern hatcheries. The production of hatching eggs has become so specialized that one firm may produce only males, which are used to cross with females produced by another firm. This is particularly true in the broiler industry, in which crossbreeding is common.

It is important that the mothers of broiler chicks be able to produce large numbers of fertile, hatchable eggs; secondary emphasis is given to rapid growth rate and meat type. On the other hand, producers of the sires of broiler chicks can give full time and attention to rapid rate of growth and meat type as long as the roosters provide good fertility for their mates.

The large commercial breeding firms hire geneticists to develop highly productive birds. The breeding program involves many simple and intricate procedures, including trap nesting, testing for disease resistance, blood typing, and pedigree analysis. Data are combined with the aid of electronic computers into programs of inbreeding and hybridization, strain crossing, or other systems of breeding, all of which are designed to produce eggs and meat most efficiently.

In breeding programs involving crosses, the strains or lines used are determined on the basis of their special properties for nicking with each other.

The hatcheries take fertile eggs and change them into newly hatched poultry. Poultry producers then raise the birds either to lay eggs or produce meat—not both.

Instead of being a small sideline on a diversified farm, poultry may be the producer's main or only enterprise. Poultry no longer forage for food. They are kept in large houses from the time they are received from the hatchery to the time they go to market.

Research in agricultural engineering has yielded new designs for well-insulated, well-lighted, and fan-ventilated poultry houses.

Instead of the hit-or-miss feeding of earlier years, poultry are fed highly efficient, well-balanced rations that provide all the nutrient they are known to need. Nutritional research with poultry also has added to our knowledge of vitamins and the other nutrients people need.

The poultry rations are designed with the help of high-speed, electronic computers. Feed is prepared and mixed in large feed mills according to special formulas for different ages and types of poultry and is delivered by truck to the producer's bulk feedbin.

The processing plant takes the eggs or poultry as they come from the producer and clean, grade, inspect, and otherwise change them into the eggs and poultry we buy.

A single organization may finance and direct an entire poultry operation, including the breeding flock, hatchery, feed mill, poultry producer, processing plant, and wholesale or retail outlets.

The total of these developments is that the poultry and eggs that Americans pay more than 5 billion dollars for each year provide 3.9 percent of their food energy, 12.6 percent of the protein,

Hens are fed scientifically devised rations in the large, modern poultry houses, which provide adequate space, ready access to water and feed, and greater freedom from parasites and disease.

9.6 percent of the phosphorus, 9.2 percent of the iron, 9.3 percent of vitamin A, 7.1 percent of niacin, and 10.2 percent of riboflavin.

Chickens have been kept by man for centuries. In China, the domestic fowl is traced to the Chou Dynasty (1122 to 249 B.C.). The chicken was fully domesticated in India as early as 2000 B.C.

The ancestors of chickens lived in the jungles of southeastern Asia. Chickens were first brought to the West Indies, South America, and Mexico by the Spaniards. When Cortez invaded Mexico in 1520, he established a flock of 1,500 chickens.

Fighting cocks have furnished amusement al-

most from the time chickens were domesticated. Many countries have developed special types of fighters. The sport is considered cruel and inhumane in the United States and is illegal, but it flourishes underground in places, and large sums change hands in bets and in trading breeding stock. The sport is practiced openly and legally in many countries.

Most of the broilers marketed in the United States owe their desirable meat type to their well-muscled pit-game ancestors.

The modern chicken used for eggs and meat is a product of many decades of research, selection,

The young daughter of the owner of a poultry farm and hatchery at McAllisterville, Pennsylvania, admires some of the chicks that are ready to leave the hatchery in special shipping boxes.

and breeding by the poultry industry, State agricultural experiment stations, and the United States Department of Agriculture.

Large commercial breeding firms keep thousands of pedigreed breeding birds in a continuing effort to improve the egg-producing and meat-producing potentials of their strains. Computers are used in selecting the best parent stock. As a new improved strain or breeding combination is produced, it is distributed to hatchery-supply flocks, which send the hatching eggs to hatcheries with special authorization to sell baby chicks of that particular strain.

At the hatchery, the eggs are placed in mammoth incubators, where they are kept at about 100° F. and 57 percent relative humidity. The eggs are turned regularly to prevent the developing embryos from sticking to the shell. After 3 weeks in the incubator, the chick embryos are fully developed and begin pecking a hole around the large end of the egg through which the chicks emerge.

The baby chicks then go to poultry producers, who put them into freshly cleaned houses under hovers, which are heated to 95°. The temperature under the hover is reduced about 5° each week for about 5 weeks.

295

The chicks are given plenty of clean water and a starter feed containing a balanced mixture of protein, carbohydrates, fat, minerals, vitamins, and other ingredients designed to get them off to a rapid, healthy beginning.

Later they are vaccinated and given medication at scheduled times to prevent the occurrence of disease.

More than 1.7 billion dollars' worth of eggs for table use were sold in the United States in 1965.

Egg production was 112 eggs per bird in 1925. In 1965, almost 300 million hens averaged about 220 eggs each. Leading in egg production are California, Iowa, and Georgia.

Very popular as an egg maker is the hardy, small-bodied, productive single-comb white Leghorn. The Leghorn originated in Italy, but it has since been improved upon in England, Denmark, and America. This bird is small—the cocks weigh about 6 pounds and the hens 4.5 pounds. The single-comb white Leghorn is noted for the beauty of its sweeping curves of neck, back, and tail and its pure white plumage. A striking feature is the large, red erect comb of the cock with its five regular points. On the hen, the comb lops over to one side at a rakish angle. Leghorns lay white-shelled eggs.

The single-comb white Leghorn is used commercially as pure strains, as "hybrids" when its inbred lines are crossed with inbred lines of other egg-type breeds, and as strain-crosses in which one strain of single-comb white Leghorn is crossed with another to combine desirable traits of both strains.

Only the pullets—females—in egg-type strains are useful commercially as food producers. The males do not produce meat economically. Producers therefore dispose of the young males. But baby chicks all look alike. Most persons cannot tell the males from the females, but skilled persons sex chicks soon after they hatch at a rate of 800 or more chicks an hour with at least 95 percent accuracy.

Pullets often are reared in brooder houses by specialized operators from the time they are baby chicks until they are 18 to 20 weeks old, when they are old enough to start laying eggs and are sold as starter pullets. Other producers raise their own pullets.

The period from hatching time to 20 weeks of

This up-to-date installation near Salisbury, Maryland, shelters 37 thousand broilers for market.

age is critical to later egg production of the hen. Many pullets are put on a diet and their daily quota of light is restricted so that they will not start laying small eggs prematurely.

When the pullets are physically mature and ready to begin laying good-sized eggs, they are placed in large laying houses—egg factories—which have automatic feeders, waterers, egg gatherers, and waste disposal systems. They are given a laying ration designed for maximum production of large eggs. Electric lights are used to stimulate egg production.

Laying houses usually are of two types. In floor operations, the layers are allowed the freedom of the floor of the house. The floor is covered with litter (wood shavings, wheat straw, peanut hulls, or some other inexpensive, moisture-absorbing material), or the hens are on wood-slat platforms about a foot above the floor. Nests usually are placed along the sides of the house and are darkened to encourage the hens to enter to lay their eggs.

Laying houses are 30 to 50 feet wide and 150 to 500 feet long and may be 2 or more stories high. They are divided into pens containing 500 to 1,000 layers. Feeders and waterers are placed over a droppings pit, which is covered by coarse wire netting. The droppings pit is cleaned frequently with a mechanical pit cleaner. Walls and roof of the house are insulated. Ventilation is controlled to help regulate temperature, humidity, and odors inside the house.

In cage operations, the hens are kept in compartments made of coarse wire screen. Small cages may have one or more birds—colony cages 10 to 25. Houses for caged layers are similar to those for floor layers except no nests are required and the droppings are handled differently. The cages are set up in long rows and are suspended from the ceiling for ease of bird handling. The cage floors are slanted so the eggs roll into a trough next to the aisle and are easily gathered in wire baskets or plastic trays. Moving belts are used to make egg gathering automatic. Droppings are permitted to pile up on the floor for several weeks or months before removal or they may drop into a water-filled pit under the cages.

The eggs are taken to cool rooms, where they are cleaned, weighed, graded, and placed in retail cartons or large, 30-dozen cases for storage or transportation to markets. Eggs sometimes go into the housewife's grocery cart within a few hours of production and often within a week.

Egg production was highly seasonal before 1940. A surplus of eggs flooded the market during the spring, and prices dropped. Similarly, egg production dropped in the fall and early winter, and prices went up. Electric lights now are used to create an artificial day length more conducive to optimum egg production the year round. Breeding, nutrition, and management have improved, and fluctuations in production and prices are smaller.

Large commercial egg operations have expanded rapidly. Egg-producing units sometimes exceed 100 thousand layers. At least one operation in the United States has reached about a million layers.

Eggs you buy are graded AA or Fresh Fancy Quality, Grade A, and Grade B. Grade B eggs are not so fresh as Grade A; Grade AA are freshest. Egg size is classified as Jumbo, Extra Large, Large, Medium, Small, and Pewee. Size is not related to quality—Grade A Mediums are just as high in quality as Grade A Large eggs.

The color of eggshells depends on the breed or strain of the hen that laid the eggs. Some people prefer brown eggs; others prefer white eggs. Shell color has no effect on the size, shape, grade, quality, or nutritive value of the egg.

Per capita egg consumption in the United States was about 314 in 1965. It was 393 in 1951. The drop has been ascribed to a habit of eating smaller breakfasts and more competition from prepared cereals.

The prices to American producers averaged 33 cents a dozen in 1965. In 1951, when per capita consumption was highest, the retail price of Grade A Large eggs was 74 cents a dozen, compared to 53 cents in 1965.

Eggs are a well-balanced food. Laboratory rats lived as long as 2 years (a ripe age for a rat) on a diet of whole commercially dried eggs. The protein in eggs is easily digested by most persons and has a good balance of amino acids. Eggs also are good sources of iron, vitamin A, and riboflavin, and are one of the few foods containing vitamin

D. A large egg contains 20 calories in the albumin and 60 in the yolk.

Eggs can be stored for days at room temperature, although their quality is maintained much longer if they are refrigerated.

Eggs are used for many purposes. About 85 percent are marketed as shell eggs and are eaten soft boiled, hard boiled, poached, scrambled, baked, or fried. About 10 percent, mostly in dried or frozen form, are used for industrial purposes. Bakers use about 7 percent of the total supply. Eggs are an important ingredient of prepared cake, doughnut, and pancake mixes, and ice cream, macaroni, noodles, mayonnaise and salad dressing, infant foods, candy, sausage, milkshakes, and eggnog.

Eggs are used in medicine as a source of culture media and as antidotes to certain poisons. The developing chick embryo is used in medical research for testing new drugs, diagnosis of such diseases as spinal meningitis, and the production of vaccines. Nearly 30 different virus vaccines are produced with chick embryos.

Eggs are used in diluting semen for artificial insemination of livestock. They are used in manufacturing such varied articles as artists' paints, cosmetics, fertilizers, photographic supplies, printing ink, leather, textile dyes, soaps, and glues.

Eggs have been used to make egg-shell mosaics and figurines.

Just before Easter the demand increases for eggs for coloring and for egg hunts and egg rolling. The custom of coloring eggs at Easter goes back as far as the fourth century.

The broiler industry has changed faster than any other phase of American agriculture. Chicken meat once was primarily a byproduct of the egg industry, but not now.

Against 34 million broilers in 1934, more than 2 billion broilers valued at a billion dollars were produced in 1965. Georgia, Arkansas, and Alabama were the leaders.

Per capita consumption of chicken meat increased from 13 pounds in 1938 to 38 pounds in 1965.

The American broiler industry has reached an efficiency whereby it can produce, process, and ship broilers overseas at less cost than they can be produced and processed in most foreign countries.

Many of us can remember when chicken for Sunday dinner was a rare treat. Chicken is now readily available at reasonable prices and is a regular constituent of the American diet. The meat is low in calories and is a good source of niacin, the pellegra-preventing vitamin.

Chicks to be grown as broilers once came from large, meaty fowls such as purebred Rhode Island reds, Plymouth rocks, and New Hampshires. These three breeds originated in America and lay brown-shelled eggs.

The Plymouth rock comes in several varieties, the barred Plymouth rock and the white Plymouth rock being most popular. Cocks weigh about 9.5 pounds and hens 7.5. Barred Plymouth rocks are noted for their feathers, which are crossed by alternating white and black bars.

Rhode Island reds have a rich, brilliant-red plumage, except for the main tail and wing feathers, which are mostly black. The two varieties differ only in comb type—single comb and rose comb. Cocks weigh 8.5 pounds and hens 6.5. New Hampshires were developed from Rhode Island reds and have chestnut-red feathers. They weigh the same as Rhode Island reds.

The demand for faster growth led to crossbreeding, and a desire for better meat type led to the use of Cornish as one parent in the cross. Cornish fowl were developed in Cornwall, England, and were noted for their weight. Cocks weighed 10.5 pounds and hens 8 pounds. They laid brown-shelled eggs and had a broad breast, close-fitting feathers, and a small pea comb. They also had poor production, fertility, and hatchability of eggs.

Improved strains of white Cornish were developed later, and now most broiler chicks are sired by roosters of the white Cornish type and are hatched from eggs laid by white Plymouth rock hens. White-plumaged birds predominate among meat-type chickens because they have no dark pinfeathers to detract from the appearance of the dressed chicken.

Broiler chicks of both sexes are raised together in specially designed houses. Broiler houses are 25 to 50 feet wide and 150 to 500 feet long. They are one-story buildings in the South, two stories high in Pennsylvania, and three stories high in Maine. Each house may contain 10 thousand to 100 thousand broilers. Floors are covered with litter. Walls

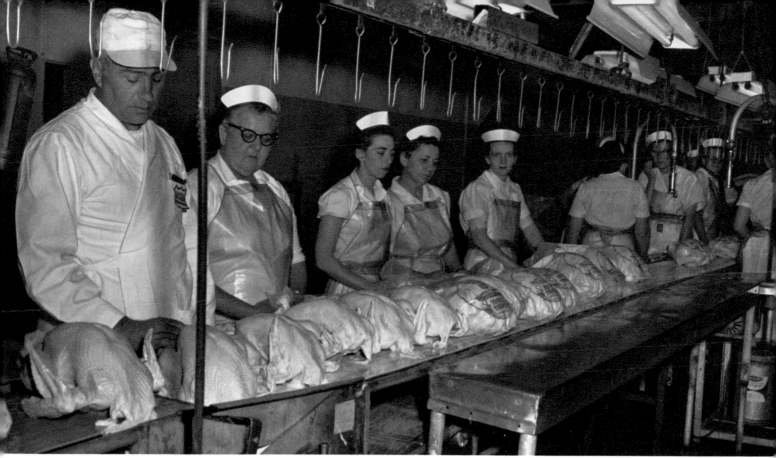

Careful inspection and grading and attractive packaging of poultry products in processing plants are factors in the growth of the industry.

and roofs are insulated and the houses are well ventilated. Feeding and watering are automatic. Houses are completely cleaned and disinfected before each new brood of chicks is received.

About 14 weeks were required to produce a 3-pound broiler in 1941, but in 1965 most broilers were marketed when they were 8 to 10 weeks old and weighed about 3.5 pounds. Only 2.5 pounds of feed were needed to produce a pound of broiler in 1965, compared to almost 4 pounds of feed in 1948.

A grower may have 10 thousand birds or more ready to sell at one time. The broilers are caught, put into crates, loaded on trucks, hauled to processing plants, unloaded, taken from the crates, and attached to a moving line. Within a few minutes they are killed, bled, scalded, picked, singed, eviscerated, cleaned, inspected, graded, weighed, chilled, and packaged. They may be stored for a time before going to a distributor, who may again store them briefly. Then they are trucked to the retail store, where they are placed in refrigerated cases.

Capons are male chickens that have been castrated, usually at 5 to 6 weeks. They are then fed for 6 to 7 months for market. They fatten readily and have tender flesh even if kept beyond the usual market weight of 7 to 8 pounds. Broiler stocks with white plumage and yellow skin, such as white Plymouth rocks or white Cornish crosses, are preferred, although New Hampshires and Rhode Island reds sometimes are used for capon production.

Hens or stewing chickens are mature females no longer useful for egg production. They are widely used in processed products, such as canned soups.

Chicken is sold fresh, canned, smoked, frozen, precooked, cut up, stuffed, or trussed. Chicken may be broiled, fried, roasted, baked, stewed, or made into chicken-and-dumplings.

Chicken of high quality is available in convenient packages with more white meat and less waste than ever before. Yet the average retail price of chickens dropped from 63 cents a pound in 1948 to 38 cents a pound in 1965. The lower prices are due largely to greater production and efficiency of production. The growers' gross income from broilers went up from 100 million dollars in 1941 to 1 billion dollars in 1965.

Federal inspection of meat insures that the poultry meat is pure, safe, and wholesome wherever it is served. About 5.25 billion pounds of ready-to-cook chicken were certified as wholesome by Department of Agriculture inspectors in 1965. Much of this poultry was reinspected as cut-up products and as ingredients in convenience foods. The inspectors remove from food channels any meat that shows signs of disease, spoilage, or contamination.

The turkey is the only truly American bird that has been domesticated to provide sizable amounts of human food.

Turkeys were domesticated by the peoples of ancient Mexico long before the discovery of America by white men. Some of these turkeys were taken to Europe in the early 1500's, where they were further domesticated.

For many decades the domestic turkey was a rangy, narrow-breasted bird much like the wild turkey. People ate turkey mostly at Thanksgiving and Christmas. As time went by, improvements in breeding, nutrition, and management evolved a bird that found favor throughout the year.

The young domestic turkey requires more special care and attention during its first few weeks of life than the young chicken. Also, because of its larger size and different behavior, the housing and equipment for raising turkeys are somewhat different. Otherwise, the breeding, feeding, and management of turkeys bear many resemblances to those of meat-type chickens.

The broad-breasted bronze is the most popular variety. It originated in England. Its plumage is rather similar to that of the North American wild turkey, but it is heavier and more muscular. White-feathered birds are easier to dress to a more attractive carcass, and the broad-breasted large white turkey has been growing in popularity.

Turkeys are marketed as mature roasters at 5 to 6 months, and often are served as roast turkey.

On a turkey ranch in Pender County, North Carolina, automated feeding reduces work and operating costs.

These white pekins, 5 to 6 weeks old, are being raised for sale on a duck farm at Aqueboque, New York.

The average turkey hen weighs 15 pounds when marketed alive or 12 pounds ready for the oven.

Turkey toms average 25 pounds alive or 21 pounds ready to cook and are used primarily by hotels, restaurants, hospitals, schools, and cafeterias. Turkey fryer-roasters are marketed at 3 to 4 months and weigh about 9 pounds alive or 7 pounds oven-dressed.

Turkey producers raise nearly 100 million turkeys for market, for a gross farm income of 377 million dollars. Most of our turkeys are grown in California, Minnesota, Iowa, Missouri, and Wisconsin. Federal inspectors certified about 1.25 billion pounds of ready-to-cook turkey meat as wholesome food in 1965, and 210 million pounds were inspected for canned and other processed foods.

Turkey breeders over the years have constantly endeavored to improve the meat type and quality of their turkeys. Today we have turkeys that have broad breasts and a high percentage of white meat. One undesirable consequence has been a reduction in the ability of the birds to mate properly, and fertility has suffered. To improve fertility, artificial insemination is used to produce hatching eggs from the large meat-type strains.

Turkey prices to United States producers have gone down from 47 cents per pound live weight in 1948 to 21 cents in 1965. Per capita consumption has increased from 3.1 to 7.2 pounds. The average price to the American consumer in 1965 was 47 cents a pound, ready to cook.

All domestic ducks except the muscovy have descended from the wild mallard, which was not domesticated before Roman times. Cortez introduced domestic ducks into Mexico about 1520 and established a flock of 500.

Ducks constitute an important part of the poultry industry in some parts of the country. Almost all the commercially produced ducklings in the United States are white pekins. The pekin originated in China, and most of the pekins in this country are descended from 14 ducks introduced about 1873. The drakes weigh about 9 pounds and the ducks 8 pounds.

Other varieties are raised occasionally, and the smaller Indian runner and khaki Campbell ducks are noted as excellent producers of large eggs, putting some of our best white Leghorn chickens to shame. However, duck eggs are not generally accepted by the American public for eating purposes.

The domesticated muscovy is derived from the wild muscovy of Central America and South

301

America. It is noted for the red, rough, bare skin over much of its head and face and for the large difference in weight of the two sexes. Drakes weigh 10 pounds and the ducks 7 pounds. The meat of the muscovy is distinct and flavorful. When crossed with other domestic ducks, it produces progeny that are usually sterile.

About 11 million ducks were slaughtered under Federal inspection in 1965. They were 7 to 8 weeks old and averaged about 6.5 pounds. About 60 percent of the ducklings marketed in the United States were produced on Long Island, New York, but duckling production has been increasing in the Midwest.

The total production of ducks in the United States has changed little since 1930, but they are raised on only one-tenth as many farms.

Domesticated geese are less numerous than ducks but are raised extensively in some districts.

Geese like grass, and some American farmers use them to keep their cottonfields and strawberry beds free of grass and weeds. They place feed supplements at one end of the crop rows and water at the other. The geese then eat the grass and contribute a bit of fertilizer as they travel up and down the rows for additional feed and water. Because geese do not like young cotton or strawberry plants, the arrangement is acceptable for all concerned.

Geese were domesticated by the ancient Romans several centuries before the Christian era.

The most popular breeds in this country are the Toulouse, Embden, African, and Chinese. The Toulouse comes from southern France and is descended from the wild graylag. It is the largest of domestic geese—the gander weighs 26 pounds and the goose 20. The Embden was one of the first imported into the United States and was first called the Bremen for its city of importation. However, it originated in Hannover, Germany, and also is descended from the wild graylag.

The African goose probably originated in India either from the wild Chinese swan goose or from a cross of this species with the wild graylag. It has a distinctive knob on its head. The Chinese probably was developed in China from the wild Chinese swan goose. The white Chinese is most popular for meat production at an early age because it grows rapidly and tends to deposit smaller amounts of internal fat. The wild Canada goose is amenable to domestication but is of little economic importance for food.

Only 850 thousand geese were sold in 1959. New

Harry Smith, of East Moriches, Long Island, checks on his week-old ducklings in a hot brooder, where the temperature stays at 75° F.

Mexico was the leading State with 260 thousand; most of them were produced by one large pecan and cotton enterprise, which utilized geese for keeping out grass and weeds. California and Minnesota also produce many geese.

Guineafowl provide a small income to farmers. As with squab and pheasant, guineafowl are served as a specialty item in hotels and restaurants. They have a gamy flavor and some people consider them a delicacy.

Guineafowl have a loud cry of alarm and are easily disturbed by anything unusual. Many farmers formerly kept a few guineafowl around the farm to serve as alarm signals. No stranger could approach a farm at night without arousing the guineafowl.

Domestic guineafowl are descended from the wild guineafowl of Guinea, West Africa. Guineafowl have been domesticated for many centuries and were raised as table birds in Greece as early as 500 B.C. They were brought to America by the early settlers. Pearl, white, and lavender varieties are found in the United States.

Pheasants and quail are sometimes raised for meat but do not constitute an important part of the poultry industry. When they are raised as domestic birds, it is usually a sideline, and most of them are released in the fields to be hunted.

The ring-necked pheasant has been associated with man in its native Asia for many thousands of years. The pheasant was familiar to the ancient Greeks and Romans. In recent years, it has been introduced throughout Europe and much of North America. It has had ample opportunity to become domesticated, but has not been tamed to the extent it can be kept unconfined as have domestic fowl and turkeys.

Coturnix quail were kept by the Romans. They were well known in Egypt and were pictured on Egyptian hieroglyphs about 2500 B.C.

The bobwhite quail of the East and the California quail are semidomesticated in that they easily become accustomed to living in orchards and gardens near man's habitations. They are valued for food and for sport.

Japanese quail may come into use as poultry as time goes by. They have been widely used for meat

Guineafowl are a specialty item in poultry farming.

Newly hatched bobwhite chicks.

and egg production in Japan since 1910. They are being used more and more in United States laboratories for experimental projects related to poultry. They mature in 6 weeks, at which time they weigh almost 6 ounces. They lay as well as chickens, and their eggs weigh one-third ounce. The meat is tasty, and the eggs are considered a treat when boiled and served as hors d'oeuvres.

—WILLIAM E. SHAKLEE.

Pigeons and Doves

YOU PROBABLY would not know what to call those birds in my backyard. They are a rich chestnut red with a white tailband. They came from Damascus, Syria, where they are called Shikli Ahmar. They decorate the garden and do not scratch out the flowerbeds. I like them. In fact, I like all kinds of pigeons and doves.

Many boys (but few girls) get "pigeon fever" between the ages of 10 and 15. It usually runs its course in a year or two, but occasionally it becomes chronic.

To those unfamiliar with the affliction, my own case history may be enlightening.

It hit me in 1924, in Austin, Texas. I contracted it from older boys I knew. They used to make intrepid nighttime expeditions to catch wild pigeons in farm barns and city buildings.

The boys kept the birds in makeshift coops. They sold most of the catch to Mexican meat markets at a dime apiece. The prettiest ones they traded among themselves. How I longed to have some! But my parents were not sympathetic, and I had no coop.

Once the catchers got caught, in the attic of the women's dormitory at the University of Texas. They had climbed the fire escape and crawled in a gable window the birds used. Their shirts stuffed with struggling pigeons, the boys were escorted downstairs by police past rows of giggling coeds.

The boys got higher prices for squabs—young pigeons almost ready to leave the nest. One day I went along on a raid of eaves' nests. Monkeylike, the boys scrambled over the roofs and reached into the recesses to drag out their prey.

"This squeaker's too small, still in pinfeathers," called down one of the boys.

"I want it! Give it to me!" I cried. So it was tossed down, and ecstatically I carried it home. My pigeon!

My parents were unhappy about my having this frightened, peeping bundle of dull-colored feathers. But the appealing dark eyes won their hearts. Pidgy was permitted to stay in a box on our back porch.

Like the other boys, I bought some chicken scratch feed at the grocery. But Pidgy did not know how to eat. She had been fed by her parents all her short life. So I had to poke the grain down her throat and push her bill into a cup of water. Pidgy caught on fast. Soon she came running to me for food, waving her wings and squealing happily.

Pidgy became a real pet. She rode on my shoulder and flew to my outstretched arm when I snapped my fingers. She explored neighbors' roofs and one day fell down our chimney. What a mess!

Gradually the dirty plumage moulted, and beautiful, iridescent, purple-green feathers covered her neck. Her wings made a sibilant whistling when she flew. The squealing voice changed to a stuttering coo, and the dark eyes changed to fiery orange. She liked to have her neck feathers tickled, but did not like to have anyone hamper her wings.

Next I obtained a pair of coal-black babies from another eave's nest. My knowing friends informed me that a nest pair are always male and female. These birds had not heard about this fact, however, and both grew up to be males. Pidgy settled on one of them as her mate. I was told that pigeons mate for life.

Our back-porch door was kept partly open during the day, and the birds came and went freely. The male carried in twigs and straws, which Pidgy arranged into a nest. Her mate was extremely jealous and followed her around, not letting her get near the other male. This behavior was called driving.

Soon Pidgy laid two shiny white eggs. She incubated them most of the time, but her mate took a shift between about ten in the morning and four in the afternoon. The birds pecked my hand when I took the eggs out of the nest, as if to say, "These don't belong to you!" They did not hurt me, though.

When I held the eggs up to a light I saw a red network inside—blood vessels. After two and a half weeks they hatched, helpless little beings with closed eyes and long, yellow down. Pidgy took each empty eggshell in her beak and dropped it outdoors. I watched the young ones being fed. Both parents had pigeon milk; they practically swallowed the babies' tiny beaks, then pumped them full. The squabs grew like mushrooms.

When the young were about a week old, Pidgy went into the street one morning and was run over by a milk truck. I picked up the crippled bird and was heartbroken. My parents suggested that a lady we knew might be able to do something. She did. She deftly sewed up the lacerations with needle and thread, touched the seams with iodine tincture, and put little splints on the broken leg. I went home with hope. Pidgy was hospitalized in a ... the porch.

... 's mate took over the chores ... well. One day I was astonished to find a new female pigeon in the porch. The other male was still a bachelor, but Pidgy's mate had been unfaithful. Before Pidgy was back on her feet, a new nest was completed, and the newcomer laid her own eggs.

At this point, my parents laid down the law that a porch should not become a dovecote. One of my pals had a wonderful coop, formerly an outhouse (superseded by indoor plumbing). He had nailed up boxes on the inside walls and had cut a hole near the roof. His pigeons flourished and foraged freely around the country. Lacking an outhouse, I tried to create a substitute out of packing-crate lumber and chicken wire. It was my first serious effort at carpentry. Fortunately, the birds were not critical.

We boys now began to expand horizons. We found that there were other kinds of pigeons.

Pigeons like this carried messages for the U.S. Army during the Second World War and earlier, but electronic devices have taken their place.

As a Christmas present, one received a pair of yellow tumblers, funny little birds with short bills and pearl-colored eyes. When released with the other pigeons, they made quick back-flips in flight.

I bought a pair of white fantails, at a fantastic price. They strutted around like little peacocks, their necks wobbling back and forth. My other pigeons were shocked at these new arrivals, but eventually accepted them. "What beautiful doves!" commented a visitor. Doves? No, I replied, these are pigeons. Different, yes, but not doves. Doves live in trees, not coops, don't they?

A wonderful article in the National Geographic in 1926 greatly intensified my pigeon fever. The author, Elisha Hanson, was a prominent Washington attorney and fantail fancier. His knowledge was spellbinding, and the pictures in color were breathtaking.

Then I obtained a batch of literature from the Plymouth Rock Squab Company of Melrose, Massachusetts. The proprietor, Elmer Rice, gave a glowing picture of profits to be made by raising and selling squabs for the luxury trade. He hap-

pened to have breeding stock and equipment available for shipment. I sent off for two pairs of a fabulous new breed, red carneaux, and some equipment, including a water fountain. How excited I was!

My wonderful red carneaux failed to live up to my commercial hopes. In fact, they failed to live. They must have been accustomed to better things. But I tried selling some squabs from my other pigeons. Picking off the feathers and dressing the plump birds was not so difficult for me as killing them, but I had to outgrow sentimentality, or the flock would eat me out of my allowance.

People in our neighborhood bought my squabs at up to 35 cents each. These people were partial to the special flavor and all-dark meat. But some of my squabs had such dark skin that nobody wanted to buy them. These we had at home for dinner. We also had pigeon pie.

My next infatuation was racing homers, often mistakenly called carriers in the newspaper. Racing homers had been greatly popularized by their heroic service in the First World War. Everybody

306

had heard of Cher Ami. Winged telegraphs, someone called these pigeons, and before the telegraph they were the fastest method of long-distance communication.

There were several racing homer men in Austin, and I soon got a start, again at steep prices. San Antonio and Dallas were hotbeds of the racing sport, and I learned more racing lore from the experts there. One of them put his hand on my shoulder and told me his biggest secret: "Son, take it easy. Don't place all your bets on one bird." Time and again his advice later proved correct, too late.

Racing homers gave me my first experience with pedigrees. Each bird had such a document, as well as a seamless aluminum legband stamped with identification data. I began keeping strict records. One of the revelations of such activities was that a single pedigree might include a particular champion as sire, a grandsire, and also a great-grandsire. Linebreeding, I was told, is strong medicine for success.

Success for some people. My luck didn't seem very good. Although my homers performed magnificently in flying around the neighborhood, I lost a lot of them in training. Some even failed to get back from a 5-mile release. The great depression had struck, and I couldn't afford the sport. Oh, well, at least the squabs from the homers were meatier than those from the common pigeons and sold well.

Unfortunately for my finances, the birds produced poorly. There were all sorts of troubles: Some females stopped laying. Squabs died of "canker" and other maladies or for no apparent reason. Predators dined well at my expense. There were cats, rats, dogs, opossums, snakes, hawks, and little boys with BB guns to contend with, night and day. Weevils riddled the feed, and mice riddled everything else. Louseflies slid among the birds' feathers and sucked their blood.

As a university student, I majored in zoology. The microscope opened a new world for me. I looked at "canker" and saw myriad jiggling microbes, called trichomonads. I looked at prepared smears of squabs' blood and saw malarial parasites in some of the erythrocytes. I looked at bits of droppings from ill pigeons and found eggs of in-

The Capistrano Mission in California is famous for its colony of returning swallows, but these white pigeons remain at the Mission all year.

testinal worms. In the feathers, tiny mites were riding happily between the barbs, like hobos riding the rods.

Experience in dressing squabs was helpful to me in comparative anatomy. I knew, as did Shakespeare, that pigeons have no gall bladder and that squabs have a "bursa of Fabricius," which disappears with maturity. I learned that, unlike our eye, the pigeons' eye has a complex structure inside, called the pecten, whose function is not known.

The university library had pigeons hidden all through the stacks. I ransacked the card catalog, journal indexes, the Readers' Guide, and the encyclopedias. From bird books to zoology journals, new information poured out, and the world seemed a much larger and more amazing affair than ever.

Many of the books and articles were in foreign languages. I studied German, French, and Latin. With a dictionary I could even tackle Dutch, Spanish, and Italian. Now I learned why the words "pigeon" and "dove" were often confused—the

The Palmetto Pigeon Plant at Sumter, South Carolina, raises about 180 thousand squabs annually for food and for use in research laboratories.

Germanic word (*Taube*) was the same for both. The Greeks had several distinct terms, and the Romans also. In English, we follow whim, and only a taxonomist can keep things straight.

Two pigeon authorities in the library impressed me above all others—Charles Darwin and C. O. Whitman. Both were argumentative, not dogmatic, and presented evidence in large amounts to support grand ideas.

Darwin's celebrated observations on "reversion to the wild type" when pure breeds are crossed I verified from my own experience. His reliance on selection as the basis for evolution seemed entirely in accord with what I knew. I began to think of my pigeons as the latest tiny sprouts on a tremendous

tree. Farther over on another limb were the mourning doves; that dead branch over yonder was the passenger pigeon, exterminated by greedy hunters.

I learned that Whitman dreamed of a co-ordinated, comprehensive approach to the biology of pigeons: Embryology, heredity, behavior analysis, and so forth. This ambition I vowed to support. But Whitman's theories sometimes seemed crazy.

I began in 1931 to correspond with Dr. Leon J. Cole, a professor at the University of Wisconsin, where active research along such lines with pigeons was in progress. He offered me several white silky fantails, a type quite rare but known to Darwin. I was elated to get them and proceeded to cross them with my homers. Some of the progeny were silky, others not—no intermediates. I wondered why. As my records accumulated, an explanation jumped out at me. I felt like Gregor Mendel.

My explanation disagreed with what had been published at the University of Wisconsin. Sure of myself now, I challenged the previous work. Also I began picking holes in other published studies, especially in color inheritance, and badly bent Dr. Cole's ear with my criticisms. But in 1933 he generously took me in as a graduate student and even let me bring along my own birds for advanced study. What had been merely piddling now was called research.

Dr. Cole's pigeon lofts were remodeled hog and sheep barns on the Agricultural Campus. For certainty of pedigrees, each pair of birds was in a separate cage. Here I became custodian of dozens of unusual and exotic types—porcupine pigeons, hybrids from pigeons crossed with ringneck doves, turtle doves from England, and many others.

For the first time I faced the mysterious barrier between natural species. The stock dove of Europe is a lot like our common pigeon but prefers to live in trees. The triangular-spotted pigeon of Africa has a bare, red area around the eye, bifurcated neck feathers, and a sirenlike coo. These species were being crossed with domestic pigeons at Wisconsin. The hybrids had very limited fertility. The pigeon x dove hybrids were "mules"—practically sterile. By contrast, fantail x racing homer hybrids were very prolific.

These barriers and breakthroughs provided materials for studies by Dr. M. R. Irwin. His pioneering explorations of blood types in these birds were opening the now important field of immunogenetics.

Dr. Cole tried to get the confidence of the wild birds by feeding them a little hempseed by hand. They were crazy for it, as if it were candy. Even so, most of these imported types remained extremely aloof and suspicious.

The 1934 National Pigeon Show was held in Springfield, Illinois. Never having had the opportunity before, I went there. Some 4 thousand pigeons in a convention hall can be overwhelming. I was in clover. I met influential fanciers and show judges, who guide the development of fancy types. I marveled at the gaudy modenas and swallows, the stately English carriers, the massive giant runts, the Jacobins, and the Russian trumpeters, which I had only heard of before. Monuments to pigeon fever!

Dr. Cole was an avid collector of pigeon literature, especially old books, such as Prideau Selby's *Pigeons* (1835). Most of these seemed to me a proliferation of previous poppycock, much of it tracing to old Greek and Roman writers. But, still, even the most shabby pamphlet usually contained a personal observation of value or kernel of novelty. Gradually I came to appreciate the University of Wisconsin's famous quotation: "The continual and fearless sifting and winnowing by which alone the truth can be found."

To keep track of what I read on pigeons and doves, I kept a bibliographic card catalog. When I got near a thousand cards, I thought the end must be in sight. It wasn't.

The number of scientific reports on pigeons was astonishingly large. Before the day of incubator-hatched millions of baby chicks, pigeons were the birds of choice for laboratory experiments. Literally scores of articles were written just on experiments with vitamin B_1. I learned that a pigeon fed sugar or polished rice without vitamin B_1 would die more quickly than if starved completely. Of course, the persons making such experiments were not victims of "pigeon fever"—they simply used the birds as convenient tools.

It seemed strange to me that practically all the publications on pigeons and doves were from Europe and the United States. Except for ornithological works by outsiders, not a single one was from Asia or Africa. Yet the Middle East, India, and Egypt were reputed to have been the source springs of most domestic breeds. There must be thousands of fanciers in those lands, and clever breeders at that. Didn't they write? Or hadn't their writings reached our libraries? Perhaps the religious aspects of pigeons in Moslem culture had something to do with the matter?

In 1936 Dr. Cole turned over to me a batch of correspondence he had had with Wendell M. Levi, an attorney in South Carolina. He had been president of the National Pigeon Association, and he conducted the questions-and-answers page of the American Pigeon Journal. He also was head

The Palmetto Pigeon Plant has about 31 thousand breeding adults of the white king commercial breed and keeps records of the production of each pair.

of one of the largest squab farms in the country, Palmetto Pigeon Plant. Like so many other pigeon experts, he had set his mind to write a book. Not just a book, but a compendium of all knowledge. He was requesting assistance from Dr. Cole and other scientists.

Here was a man after Whitman's heart, and the venture commanded my loyalty. Off and on for the next 5 years I fielded problems. Accuracy was Mr. Levi's watchword—check, doublecheck, check again. Who analyzed the composition of pigeon milk? How does the pigeon focus its eyes? And so forth. Back to the library, again and again. More pigeon information was squeezed out of books than I had dreamed could have been known.

Meanwhile, back at the barns, the birds were shelling out new data, in spite of various difficulties. Probably the worst trouble was tuberculosis. Second worst were mice. At night I would open cage doors, and the barn cats grabbed mice by the dozen, without ever harming the birds.

As my records piled up, I was able to calculate positions of three genes in a pigeon chromosome. This was my most thrilling accomplishment, and yet such an esoteric concept proved completely incomprehensible to my pigeon-breeding friends.

Finally fledged in 1937, I left my pigeons at Wisconsin and wandered off. Chicago, Boston, New York. I had time to study the park pigeons, dig in the great libraries, visit the museums. I even visited the Plymouth Rock Squab Company, by this time in a state of near-collapse. What the depression and the recession had done to the luxury trade!

The summer of 1938 I spent at the Palmetto Pigeon Plant in South Carolina, with Wendell Levi. Here I found a perpetual battle to keep little troubles from flaring up into big ones. A stopped-up water pipe might make a thousand birds go thirsty. A dog scaring the birds in one pen could excite pandemonium in the entire plant. A few bedbugs carried in on a laborer's clothes could result in a devastating infestation.

Feeding all those thousands of pigeons was entirely by hand, at least twice a day. I thought a self-feeder system might save a lot of labor; so I experimented with various designs. A compartmented feeder, each kind of grain separate, seemed to work. The birds ate what they wanted, and the feeder only needed filling once a week. But labor was cheap, and the ability of the birds to choose the best proportions of grains was not trusted. My "cafeteria" therefore made little impression.

Another problem I tried to solve was the losses of eggs that failed to hatch. Literally bucketfuls were thrown out every day. What was wrong? I became known to the help as "rotten-egg doc." Many of the eggs were simply infertile or cracked, but, surprisingly, these were not the majority. Some eggs seemed merely too small or too large, or had defective shell structure, or were defective internally—perhaps infected before laying? Blind alley. But a bonus came out of this odorous investigation. I found a number of twins and strange monstrosities of scientific interest.

The next few months saw me back in Wisconsin working with Dr. Cole. A new group of graduate students was making history. Ray D. Owen worked out a method of artificial insemination for pigeons and doves. This he put to use in species crosses and in propagating a new freak type, which Dr. Cole had obtained from a racing homer breeder—completely naked pigeons. Without wing or tailfeathers, the birds could not copulate.

Ray and I undertook a study of "pearl" eye color, compared with normal orange. Then we compared the eye colors of chickens and pigeons (chicken heads were obtainable free in large quantity). We were astonished to find totally different chemical pigments making up the superficially identical orange in these birds.

By the summer of 1939 I was home in Texas, and Dr. Cole sent me what was left of my pigeon stocks. A sad remnant; many were in the last stages of tuberculosis. I set up "sanatorium" cages for them and started producing young ones. Happily, with the sunshine and wire floors, they grew up free of the disease.

In the course of further breeding, I made a discovery: With the so-called "faded" color gene, a pure stock could be produced in which the males are white and the females colored, even as babies. Since even experts are unable to tell the sex of squabs in other pure stocks, I felt that this discovery might have commercial possibilities. Mr. Levi was impressed, and we started the project. The now well-known auto-sexing varieties resulted.

In 1940 I persuaded a young woman who also had been a student under Dr. Cole to join me in matrimony. Not only was she immune to "pigeon fever"; she was tolerant of it in others and nursed me through subsequent crises.

Mr. Levi's magnum opus, *The Pigeon,* came off the press in 1941. Reviews were enthusiastic. Dr. Cole, in a long commentary in the Journal of Heredity, called it "a landmark in pigeon literature." Dr. Frank M. Chapman in Natural History (March 1942) wrote: "A call to attention! For Natural History does not often have the privilege of calling the attention of its clientele to so notable a publication."

As the United States war effort took hold, not only young men but also racing homers were drafted for military service. The Army Signal Corps set up "pigeon companies," with training centers at Red Bank, New Jersey, Camp Crowder, Missouri, and elsewhere. The official textbook in the training centers was *The Pigeon.* There were able men in the pigeon service, and ingenious new training methods and mobile loft designs came forth.

The war caused labor shortages at the pigeon farms. Handfeeding became too expensive; cafeteria feeders filled the breach. Automation was on its way.

During the war years, I was employed on Long Island in the laboratory of Dr. Oscar Riddle, at Cold Spring Harbor. This laboratory was part of the Genetics Department of the Carnegie Institution of Washington, and a large research colony of pigeons and doves had been maintained there since about 1910. It was there in 1932 that Dr. Riddle had isolated the hormone prolactin, which controls milk secretion. Production of pigeon milk was the test criterion.

Dr. Riddle had noted a mysterious increase in size of the thyroid glands of the pigeons both from Palmetto and in his own flock after 1940. Soon it became clear that an epidemic of goiter was in progress. A few of the older birds died because the glands grew so huge as to choke them. The birds continued to try to breed, but fewer and fewer eggs hatched.

We experimented with iodine treatment and cured the trouble promptly. But we never found out the basic cause of the epidemic. Pigeon breeders still are plagued sometimes by such trouble if they do not give the birds iodized salt. The poor

This racing homer, equipped with a 1-ounce radio transmitter and trailing antenna, was used in experiments in pigeon navigation conducted by Dr. Louis C. Graue at Bowling Green University.

hatchability of the eggs seems explained by inadequate iodine reserve—the mother's goitrous glands are so greedy for iodine that none gets into the eggs.

We experimented with thyroidectomy and learned that complete removal of the glands resulted in very slow, poor healing of incisions, with bad infections. Many other kinds of operations were routinely performed in this laboratory without such complication. I learned much about anesthesia, stitching, and postoperative care.

Dr. Riddle had a selected stock of pigeons, the males of which had an oviduct on the left side. This was sometimes so large that it could have produced an eggshell, but no ova were released for it to work on. We made crosses of this "hermaphroditic" stock, and deduced that the females were loading their eggs with female hormone, thus feminizing the male embryos.

Whitman had laid a sound foundation for studies of pigeon and dove behavior, but he might have been amazed at some later developments. Dr. Riddle had another type of pigeons with a hereditary brain defect, which caused them to act tipsy. Occasionally this ataxia got so severe that the birds went into violent convulsions, resembling the tetany resulting from removal of the parathyroid glands. How complex the normal controls must be!

You might think that tumblers, pouters, trumpeters, and neckwobbling fantails have coo-coo behavior, but in 1943 my pigeons showed me a new act. In my elegant new cages, where each pair was privately housed to the best of my ability, mates went beserk and fought each other for possession of the nest. Eggs were smashed, babies trampled to death, and a female occasionally was killed. Since such perversion never occurred in flock pens, the only explanation seemed to be that the coop was too small. Modern psychology classes the phenomenon as frustration aggression. Ringneck doves are gentler than pigeons; I have never seen them argue that way, even in a very small breeding coop.

Another perversion appeared. Some of the pigeons, especially the females, plucked out and ate the growing pinfeathers of their own squabs. Once they acquired this habit, they would not reform, even in a flock pen. Cause and cure were both unknown.

After the war, there was quite a hullabaloo of new theories to explain navigation by homers. Men in the British and the American military pigeon service had conducted some experiments and came to contradictory conclusions. New experiments have blossomed, with ever more sophisticated techniques, but even today there is little agreement. Perhaps the sun and biological clock theory of the English psychologist G. V. T. Matthews has the most adherents. Certainly vision is essential for pigeons to navigate. Even night-flying homers have to be able to see. My experience with such types of blindness as microphthalmia and cataracts shows that such birds are totally disoriented. Even gluing the eyelids shut incapacitates a homer.

I have seen some clever magicians' acts with pigeons and doves and a striptease artist, who distracted the audience with pigeons instead of ostrich plumes or balloons. Such stunts seem tame by comparison with those of Dr. B. F. Skinner, a psychologist at Harvard University. The "Skinner box" for analyzing operant conditioning is now a standard prop in many psychological laboratories. A pigeon properly motivated by being half-starved is rewarded with a few grains of food for selected actions. Before long, a trick is learned. Automatic recording and electronic controls may be added. By such methods, the bird's ability to discriminate, to form concepts, can be analyzed. Trained pigeons were seriously considered for cheap computers in antisubmarine guided missiles.

Dr. Riddle retired in 1945, and the Carnegie Institution terminated the research on pigeons and doves. My next position was in New Haven. My pigeons again were private piddling.

Because of Mr. Levi's book, more and more fanciers around the country were eager to correspond about scientific questions, especially heredity. They kept prodding me, showing me new puzzles, asking me to make talks, displays, diagrams. Outstanding among these gadflies were Carl F. Graefe of Cuyahoga Falls, Ohio, and Ray E. Gilbert of Salt Lake City, Utah. Ray became president of the National Pigeon Association and got me appointed chairman of its research committee.

Dr. Cole passed away in 1948, and laboratory research on pigeons reached a nadir. However, I was in the midst of exciting tests of crazy-quilt pigeons obtained from breeders, especially Carl Graefe. These queer birds, properly termed "mosaics," are violations of ordinary laws of heredity. From breeding tests and pedigrees, I concluded that a new cause must be invoked for some cases. In the Journal of Heredity in 1949 I proposed the term "bipaternity," signifying two fathers. Apparently extra or supernumerary sperms can in some cases contribute cells to an embryo. Recognition of such a condition would not be possible in pure stock—it requires varied ancestry. Hail to the mongrel!

About this time, Dr. Clay G. Huff, of the National Naval Medical Research Center, started a pigeon project in his studies of malaria. My services as consultant were requested. The project did not turn up resistance mechanisms that he was looking for, but the search was interesting.

We moved, family, pigeons, cages, and all, to Iowa in 1952. When the birds began breeding in corn country, a new and sometimes fatal disease appeared in some of my squabs. They became anemic, with large blackish liver and spleen. Malaria!

The late parasitologist, Dr. Elery Becker, and his students became interested. We spent a lot of time Sundays getting blood samples from all my birds. Not just one kind of malaria was found, but two: *Plasmodium relictum* and *Haemoproteus sacharovi,* both different from the kind my birds in Texas got from the lousefly. In Iowa the birds had no louseflies. The mourning doves in Iowa commonly have *Haemoproteus sacharovi,* but what insect transmits it to pigeons is still unknown.

At Harvard University, B. F. Skinner's white carneau pigeons play a game for some grains of food.

A demonstration model of a three-pigeon guidance system for an antisubmarine missile was given serious consideration during the Second World War.

Mother and daughter feed the pigeons, a pleasant pastime, in Capital Square, Raleigh, North Carolina.

These were the days of new wonder drugs—sulfa, penicillin, aureomycin. It was hard to remember that quinine had been a specific against malaria long before. And now a magic bullet was found for "canker." Dr. Robert M. Stabler in Colorado had been studying *Trichomonas* of pigeons and how to control it, partly because infected pigeons had given fatal cases to some of his falcons.

All this parasitology stimulated me to review the apparently harmless feather mites. They are still a mysterious group, with strange life histories. For example, why should one kind spend part of its cycle quietly attached to the thyroid gland?

The farm boys of the Midwest catch pigeons just as my boyhood friends used to do. There are buyers if you know where to find them. Hunting clubs sometimes get them for target practice. Falconers train their hunting birds with them. Some people eat them. The Dairy Science Department of the University of Missouri has bought thousands for Dr. C. W. Turner's research—prolactin assays. Another large consumer is the Institute for Enzyme Research at the University of Wisconsin, which uses extracts of fresh-killed pigeons' liver and breast muscle.

Such a bonanza for boys has not occurred in all laboratories using pigeons. Studies on atherosclerosis in pigeons, a clogging of the arteries, at the Bowman Gray Medical School in North Carolina started with Dr. T. B. Clarkson's discovery of a case in the white carneau breed, not the feral barn pigeons.

Many cities have enacted ordinances restricting pigeon fanciers' breeding activities. Usually the racing homers wangle exemption. But the park pigeons are not so easy to restrict and often become such an abundant problem that desperate remedies may be tried. Poisoning, shooting, and trapping have all been temporary palliatives. The seat of the trouble is people with "pigeon fever." They feed the pigeons.

City health departments continually try to do something about these depraved characters. The newspapers cooperate magnificently in scaring—or, educating—the populace. "Noted medical authority finds pigeons carry X disease" is a good headline. A succession of such scares has emanated from the great cities. First there was the *Salmonella*

exposé in the 1930's. Then equine encephalitis, psittacosis-ornithosis, Newcastle disease, toxoplasmosis, and finally cryptococcosis. Health authorities have not yet identified the cause of "pigeon fever," if they are aware of the disease.

Health authorities are handicapped in their cause by the Bible, which is respectful of doves and pigeons. And pigeons just naturally go with temples. That cleanliness is next to holiness is a new concept. And when a popular brand of soap is named "Dove," who's unclean? And the common stereotype of the dove of peace, not to mention slang terms signifying harmlessness (except perhaps "stool pigeon"), do not blacken a reputation.

One of the unwitting promoters of "pigeon fever"—the affliction I caught in Texas—is the Boy Scouts organization. The boys are invited to achieve a merit badge in pigeon raising. More than 32 thousand boys have gained this badge since its innovation in 1933. Incidentally, the guide pamphlet for this merit badge was written by Wendell M. Levi.

In spite of ordinances, scares, and the great mobility of modern populations, it seems that the pigeon fancy and the racing sport continue about as usual. Aviculturists continue to import exotic species of doves and pigeons, and make occasional unusual species hybrids.

There is perhaps an increasing awareness of the significance of mutations as the key to "progress": One needs only to look at the blossoming of new varieties of the budgerigar in the last few decades as an example. In all probability, the domestic pigeon's proliferation of hundreds of breeds and varieties was just such an accumulation of mutations, starting perhaps about 5 thousand years ago with a behavior deviation of the wild blue rock pigeon. Once it traded its wild heritage for a mess of pottage and came to depend on civilized man, "pigeon fever" did the rest.

There is also increasing curiosity concerning varieties of domestic pigeons in those parts of the world which seem so reticent to write about such matters—Asia, the Middle East, and North Africa. We still have little firsthand knowledge. We hope to be able to piece together more of the early history of pigeons before books were first printed.

Searching out the world's varieties of domestic

William A. Smith painted this picture of Bob Smith, who was on leave, in front of St. Mark's in Venice.

pigeons has been the latest endeavor of Mr. Levi. More than 700 color photographs are presented in his new book, *Pigeons in Living Color* (T. F. H. Publications, 1965). Undoubtedly this will intensify "pigeon fever" on an unprecedented scale. The project in part sprouted from the importation of a number of beautiful breeds, never before seen here, from Damascus, Syria, about 1955. A native of that

city, successful in America, wanted to have here the pigeons of his boyhood. From him I obtained my Shikli Ahmar.

Then came accounts of pigeons in Spain, previously insulated from other European pigeon activities. Spaniards are alone in using pouters for the sport of "thieving"—enticing other breeders' birds to one's loft, trapping them, and holding them for ransom. This game, played with other breeds, is enjoyed all around the Mediterranean region. But the Spanish thief pouters are probably the world's most expert seducers.

And finally Chinese indigenous breeds became known, with imports from Hong Kong.

The impact of these "new" types shakes the equanimity of the pigeon fancy. Old favorites may be toppled. Crosses may give rise to still more novel and beautiful varieties and make more victims of "pigeon fever."

And now the case history of my "pigeon fever," with all its side issues, must close. Mine, you will say, obviously is not a typical case. True, it has been severe, with unusual scientific manifestations. But the point of our examination has been to reveal some of the range of the symptoms rather than the mean.

A statistical view may give hope, or perhaps not. Most victims of "pigeon fever" have children (and parents) who are immune. This has been the case in my family. Thus no one can be sure where the lightning will strike next. But I still burn.

Perhaps "pigeon fever" is merely a variant of a basic esthetic drive and allied to the ardor of the artist. Certainly it is ancient. What Pliny wrote of the Romans he knew 2 thousand years ago still sounds fresh: "Many persons have quite a mania for pigeons, building houses for them on the tops of their roofs, and taking delight in relating the pedigree and noble origin of each."

—W. F. HOLLANDER.

316

The Hand of Man

Birds and Pesticides

No ASPECT OF THE EFFECT of people on birdlife has been debated so hotly in recent years as the effect of pesticides on bird populations. On the one hand, it is asserted that mortality of wildlife is extensive; on the other, that counts show bird populations in the United States are increasing or at least are stable. There are claims that large-scale insect-control programs are unjustified and counterassertions that pesticides keep us from the brink of famine.

By some, species like the robin are said to be in danger of extinction; by others, wildlife mortality is regarded as confined to scattered, local examples of the misuse of pesticides or to instances of outright experimentation.

Spokesmen for the chemical industry are accused of trying the hard sell, scientists are alleged to be biased by the source of their funds for research, and conservationists are accused of exaggeration and emotionalism.

Where does the truth really lie?

The truth lies buried under masses of statistics and some thick layers of recent history. It is further obscured by a tendency to quote statements out of context and by tendencies in all of us—including me—to analyze this complex problem against the background of our own training, experience, and scale of values.

Among the difficulties is the breathtaking speed of the chemical revolution. Only a generation ago, the annual report of an agricultural experiment station would mention only four or five pesticides that its staff was studying. Today it is apt to describe contemporary research on about 80. In 20 years, almost 10 thousand different pesticidal formulations have become available in the United States alone—more kinds than there are species of birds in the world. Indeed, a recent report places the total number of brand names or labels at 50 thousand. The end of this chemical revolution is nowhere in sight.

The turning point in this extraordinary development, from our point of view, came during the Second World War when DDT was recognized as a persisting chemical that could kill a wide variety of insect species. The compound became available at a time when military and public-health authorities in many war-torn lands were faced with potentially enormous outbreaks of pestilent diseases. The dramatic success of DDT ignited a research explosion that is still taking place.

By and large, the old-fashioned insect killers had not alarmed conservationists. Insect-control programs before 1940 usually involved neither great acreages nor the use of aircraft. The use of arsenical sprays against the gypsy moth in Massachusetts from 1925 to 1928 went almost unnoticed, although careful census work by Albert A. Cross at that time indicated that nesting in one place he studied was depressed about 40 percent for a 4-year period and that some locally common birds, like the black-billed cuckoo, were practically wiped out. This report by an amateur ornithologist was buried in government files, and its implications received little attention. Local bird populations in Massachusetts appear to have recovered later.

The possibility that DDT might harm birdlife was sensed early in its history as an insecticide. Research on its potential wildlife effects began in 1944, when the Public Health Service became concerned with the effects that DDT and other mosquito larvicides would have on desirable insects, fish, and aquatic birdlife.

Equally important evaluations of DDT were started in 1945 under the auspices of the Fish and Wildlife Service and the former Bureau of Entomology and Plant Quarantine of the Department of Agriculture. This research concentrated chiefly on forest situations and the direct short-term effects of DDT, but it was well planned, imaginative, and well executed. From it emerged some practical conclusions that served us well for more than a decade: Five pounds of DDT per acre kill nesting birdlife; 1 pound per acre does not; 2 pounds per acre applied annually for 5 years eventually will have undesirable effects. These results I call "the 5–2–1 rule."

This pioneer research made DDT our best-studied compound and has saved the United States from making many bad mistakes in its forest-insect and mosquito-control operations. It had two important limitations: Only one insecticide was involved, and only a few broad types of environment were studied.

These Federal research programs were soon engulfed by the new stream of agricultural chemicals that poured into the market. Some were chlorinated hydrocarbons related to DDT. Others belonged to quite different families of chemical compounds. The hazards they posed to wildlife were not at this time systematically subjected to intensive studies in the field. The toxicity of these new chemicals to the laboratory rat, however, was known to vary greatly.

In terms that are called LD_{50}s in technical literature, where 150 milligrams (mg.) of DDT per kilogram (kg.) of body weight will kill 50 percent of the laboratory rats under certain experimental conditions, this statistic was 90 mg. for heptachlor, averaged 69 for toxaphene, and ran about 37–87 for dieldrin, 10–60 for aldrin, and 10–35 for endrin. A few of these particular insecticides were actually

ROBINS

less toxic to rats than DDT: BHC (600), TDE (2,500), and methoxychlor (5,000–7,000). A metabolite (degradation product) of heptachlor later proved to be two to four times as toxic to mice as the original chemical.

Thus the 1950's opened with increasing confidence in the potentialities of the "miracle" chemicals to control insect pests and with a rather limited base on which to evaluate the possible side effects of the new programs of insect control that were now put into effect.

An important research finding of the new decade was the discovery by James B. DeWitt, of the Bureau of Sport Fisheries and Wildlife, that a low but steady intake of chlorinated hydrocarbons under laboratory conditions would affect the reproductive success of game birds. This discovery was promptly confirmed by Richard E. Genelly and Robert L. Rudd, of the University of California, who also worked with game-farm birds. Its implications were to loom large in the thinking of conservation-minded people in the pesticide controversy that developed a few years later.

A severe and critical limitation on these implications should be noticed: No one could truthfully say that the laboratory diet of these captive birds duplicated what wild birds would have in Nature. The research pointed more to a possibility than to a probability.

On the whole, the routine use of insecticides on cropland attracted little attention from conservationists, although grasshopper-control operations did receive some scrutiny in the early fifties. Government-sponsored large-scale aerial applications of insecticides did, however, attract attention, beginning in 1956. Each was a program aimed to exterminate a foreign insect pest that had extended its beachhead over millions of acres in the United States.

The first of these major programs was carried out in the East against the gypsy moth, a leaf-eating insect that had been with us since 1869 and had gotten as far west as Michigan. A Federal-State program was undertaken to "eradicate" this pest with 1 pound of DDT per acre. The project in-

Analyses to discover pesticide residues in tissues of woodcock give indications of the extent of pesticide contamination in forests and fields.

volved spraying more than 677 thousand acres in 1956, more than 3 million acres in 1957, 493 thousand acres in 1958, and 106 thousand acres in 1959. A basic assumption of the control agencies was that the hazards to wildlife on nonforest land would be the same as those to be expected from the spraying of forest lands. No trained ornithologists were assigned to watch for possible bird mortality on farmland and other habitats that were soon involved in this program.

Despite the efforts made to establish safety methods for the conduct of this project, the City of New York restricted the use of DDT over the watershed forests protecting its great reservoir holdings, Connecticut limited applications to spot treatments only, and a group of citizens on Long Island unsuccessfully sought a court injunction to stop the aerial spraying.

The main arguments in the court action pertained to possible losses of wildlife, the threat to human health, and the practicality of trying to eliminate an insect pest on so large an acreage. The plaintiffs received a sympathetic and much-quoted dissent from Mr. Justice William O. Douglas when they were turned down later by the Supreme Court of the United States, but they simply did not have sufficient facts on which to base their case.

A second big program, begun in 1957 in the South, involved a Congressionally authorized attempt to eradicate the imported fire ant, an insect that appears to have been introduced about 1918 at Mobile, Alabama. Dieldrin and heptachlor were selected initially for application rates of 2 pounds per acre over an area stretching from Florida to Texas—an area that was said to encompass 27 million acres. There did not exist at this time any formal administrative channels for wildlife ecologists to advise the Department of Agriculture on the probable effects on wildlife of this eradication project. When one recalls our 5–2–1 rule about the effects of DDT and the LD_{50} statistics for dieldrin and heptachlor given to laboratory animals, it is easy to see that direct mortality to wildlife was inevitable.

It was also spectacular. Wildlife biologists of the Department of the Interior, State conservation departments, and universities soon had solid evidence of direct mortality on the order of at least 80 percent for resident birds in places where detailed studies were conducted. I would say that several million birds and mammals perished as a result of this program. The insecticides now appeared in the tissues of woodcock scattered throughout the United States and Canadian range of this species, and—for the first time under field conditions—the reproductive success of an avian species, in this case some wild turkeys, was reported to have been locally affected.

The repercussions emanating mainly from this colossal blunder have been many. Intensive research on alternative methods of control finally led to reduction of the application rates to one-fourth pound per acre (applied twice to each area) and finally to alternative chemicals posing little hazard to wildlife.

Fortunately for the South, the program did not involve a solid block of 27 million acres, and at least on the smaller areas most of the affected bird populations seem to have recovered within 3 years. Indirect effects of the program on the reproductive success of birds have not been measured adequately. They may possibly persist for some years to come.

Few pesticide programs of municipalities have been evaluated for their effects on wildlife. Formulation and application rates in mosquito control are not standardized nationally, and ecological generalizations about the actual effects of specific mosquito projects seem to be impossible to make at this time.

Spraying to kill larvae of mosquitoes can be effectively carried out with application rates as low as one-tenth of a pound per acre. Repeated applications like these have not been observed to have a direct effect on local bird populations, but by no means are they used universally. The possibilities of long-range indirect effects I shall discuss later.

Resistance of mosquitoes to DDT has been developing at the lower latitudes, and some mosquito-abatement districts are now resorting to other chemicals, like malathion, which fortunately break down soon after they are used in the environment.

The Bureau of Sport Fisheries and Wildlife, in its interest to preserve uncontaminated aquatic habitats for waterbirds, seems to have been successful in encouraging conservative application rates, but the degree to which mosquito-control programs may or may not be seriously contaminating local aquatic-wildlife habitats is still largely unknown—from a wildlife-conservation point of view.

The use of DDT as part of the efforts of cities and towns to combat Dutch elm disease in the Middle West was a significant factor in developing the pesticide controversy in that region.

Dutch elm disease was first discovered in the United States in 1930. Entomologists then lacked the insecticides that could have nipped the first landings of the bark beetles that carry the deadly fungus. Spread of the disease was fairly rapid despite federally subsidized programs to remove and burn diseased trees and so prevent a disaster comparable to that of the chestnut blight.

It was clear by 1940 that the disease could not be confined. Federal subsidies were dropped. Except for research, extension teaching, and lab-identification work, the protection of elm trees was left up to each municipality. Research by the Forest Service and the Fish and Wildlife Service did show in 1947 that DDT was effective in controlling bark beetles but that wildlife mortality would also result.

Many cities in the East continued to rely on sanitation (tree trimming and removal of dead trees or wood), and the local use of DDT seems to have attracted little attention from bird lovers. By 1950, however, the disease had reached Detroit. By 1954 it was in Chicago. By 1957 it had crossed the Mississippi River. It was now in a region where many towns had planted the hardy, fast-growing American elm to temper the hot suns and strong winds of the prairie. When the fungus reached the Middle West, it threatened elms in town after town, a resource valued in millions of dollars and priceless in terms of beauty and shady comfort.

Full-scale control programs to control the beetles with heavy applications of DDT were now started. Application rates varied with the size of the shade trees and with the number of trees sprayed per acre. Some ran as high as 17 and 24 pounds per acre. One operation (presumably very limited in extent) was said to involve 100 pounds.

As one might expect from our 5–2–1 rule on the

effects of DDT, some of the losses represented virtual annihilation of the breeding-bird population. Excessive mortality of songbirds was first noted by G. J. Wallace and his coworkers at Michigan State University. They recorded bird mortality in at least 20 residential communities in Michigan. Comparable losses appear to have taken place in the suburbs of Chicago. In Wisconsin, losses of 90 percent of the nesting birdlife were calculated by L. G. Hunt, of the University of Wisconsin, on two urban areas north of Milwaukee.

In the face of these research reports, the *Silent Spring* described by the late Rachel Carson was said by some to be highly exaggerated. People who protested against spraying were told that they would have to choose between robins and elm trees. This dogmatic assertion was by no means a fair and thoughtful answer to a complex problem in conservation.

Since bird mortality in this campaign to save the elms seems to be directly proportional to the number of trees sprayed per acre, it is possible that some communities with relatively few elms can use DDT and sustain no unusual losses of wildlife.

The great monotypes of shade trees in the Middle West clearly are often at the opposite pole of spraying, and most of the bird mortalities there seem to have differed in magnitude markedly from those in the East. I attribute this difference partly to the fact that sanitation was the sole control technique used throughout the East during the thirties, whereas tons of DDT were used from the very start of control in the Midwest.

The bird mortality occurs almost entirely in spring, regardless of whether DDT is sprayed that spring or the previous fall. I know of no research to support the statement that fall spraying reduces spring mortality of locally nesting species.

The bird kills include breeding birds drawn into the areas because they are partially or almost completely devoid of birdlife. They also include migrant birds, but these seem to be less involved in Wisconsin than in Michigan, where the spraying has been carried out somewhat closer to the peak of the May migration.

There has been no adequate literature to explain carefully to a puzzled public the reasons that should underlie the choice between a sanitation

Yellow-throated warblers about to be fed. It is through food that much pesticide contamination is transferred to birds.

program for one area and spray plus sanitation in another.

Research has shown, however, that the spring use of methoxychlor can protect elm trees and that this compound is not nearly so toxic as DDT to robins and other birdlife. Songbird populations are now recovering in communities that have substituted this compound for DDT. Still other compounds, which can be injected into elm trees and eliminate spraying entirely, are being studied intensively.

The choice between robins and elm trees is thus becoming at least a less distressing dilemma. As in the fire ant problem, society is using research to solve a difficult problem. But methoxychlor is more expensive than DDT, and DDT is still in common usage.

Near the end of the fifties, additional research disclosed an extraordinary phenomenon concerning pesticide-wildlife relationships. This involved the concentration of a pesticide by biological mechanisms in our environment and the gradual transmission of a pesticide through successive "layers" of a biotic community.

An adult and young western grebe. About 100 grebes died at Clear Lake, California, in 1954 following a spraying of TDE to control gnats.

The first inklings of this phenomenon were discovered on the University of Illinois campus by Roy J. Barker of the Illinois Natural History Survey. The insecticide was DDT. The elm disease was phloem necrosis, different from Dutch elm disease in that it requires spraying during the foliar part of the annual cycle of the trees—not during the dormant season, when the bark can be sprayed for beetles carrying Dutch elm disease.

Dr. Barker found that leaves averaged 230 micrograms of DDT immediately after spraying and 31 when they fell to the ground that autumn. Earthworms subsequently ran 33 to 164 parts per million of DDT. Robins that died in numbers in the spring after the initial spraying had 68 to 196 parts per million of DDT in their brains. A delayed but relatively simple chain reaction evidently had taken place.

Chain reactions in lakes in California have been observed, with even more amazing complications. At Clear Lake, an interesting phenomenon has been described by Eldridge G. Hunt and Arthur I. Bischoff, of the California Department of Fish and Game. On this 19-mile-long body of water, 14 thousand gallons of TDE (a close relative of DDT, sometimes called DDD, and known to be low in its toxicity to mammals) were carefully applied in 1949 at an estimated contamination rate of 14 parts per billion to control gnats. Two other treatments ensued in the next 8 years.

When about 100 western grebes died in December 1954, nothing in our knowledge of pesticidal effects pointed to the low application rate of TDE as a possible reason. Examinations of the dead birds failed to disclose evidence of infectious disease. Equally negative findings followed grebe die-offs in 1955 and 1957. Chemical analyses of the 1957 carcasses thereupon showed that the birds had somehow ingested large amounts of TDE.

How could this possibly be?

Further tests disclosed that the food web in Clear Lake was completely contaminated. Plankton had concentrated the chemical about 265 times; small fishes about 500 times; the fish-eating grebes, about 80 thousand times; and the fish-eating game fish, about 85 thousand times. Some of the fish in this pyramid had edible flesh running more than 200 and visceral fat more than 2 thousand parts per million. Even the cooked parts of the game fish had higher levels than those permitted in domestic meat by the Food and Drug Administration.

The Clear Lake die-off of western grebes, it should be noted, came as the result of the deliberate application of an insecticide to the lake by entomologists. The project seems to have been intelligently planned and carried out with caution. The biological concentration of TDE was completely unexpected. So, too, I think, was the persistence of the chemical. Six years after the last application, Mr. Hunt was still finding largemouth bass with 12 parts per million of the insecticide in their fat, white catfish with 16.8, and western grebes with 808. The disappearance of the TDE in this community is still nowhere in sight, and the ability of the grebes to reproduce successfully under these circumstances remains to be ascertained.

Other lakes have now been shown to display this same type of concentration. In one, James O. Keith, of the Bureau of Sport Fisheries and Wildlife, found invertebrate animals to average 73 parts per million of toxaphene (here applied to kill fish); fish had 200 parts per million in their fat; and a white pelican had 1,700 in its fat.

The position of a bird in an animal pyramid seems to determine in significant ways the level of insecticide it will carry. British investigators, who reported on residues in seabird eggs, found 0.3 in the eggs of plankton-feeding kittiwakes, 0.9 in the omnivorous herring gull, 3.5 in fish-eating auks, and 7.8 in cormorants that feed on large fish.

Another British study showed peregrine falcons to contain the highest residue levels of five species of hawks under study. In the small samples of raptorial birds studied thus far, there is the interesting suggestion that bird-feeding hawks are carrying higher levels than mammal-feeding ones. This possibility has not been explored in our country.

In recent years there has been a steady stream of evidence to show that the persisting insecticides are now nearly universal contaminants in natural environments. The British data on seabird eggs were from the North Sea and the North Atlantic. Chemists of the Food and Drug Administration have shown 12 out of 38 marine fish oils to be carrying more than 10 parts per million of these compounds; thus the Gulf of Mexico is contami-

Coturnix quail kept in cages at the Patuxent Wildlife Research Center are used by chemists and biologists to measure the effects of pesticides on birds.

nated, and so, too, is the North Pacific. Fish and Wildlife Service biologists have even found five insecticides in the eggs of whooping cranes held in captivity and trace amounts (parts per billion) of the DDT complex in adelie penguins taken in antarctic waters.

Research on the transport of these insecticides is still in progress. For some years, the Water Quality Network of the Public Health Service has given little hint that any large volume of insecticides was being carried by the Nation's rivers into the sea. But the routine method of sampling such water in the past has paid little attention to the sediments present, and it is these tiny soil particles to which DDT is promptly attached.

Thus when a die-off of the 899 birds occurred on the Tule Lake National Wildlife Refuge in 1960–1962, James O. Keith discovered that the DDT entering the refuge was not so much in the irrigation water but rather in the suspended material that this water carried. Biological concentration had done the rest.

Rivers are not, however, the only mechanism that can transport insecticides. In central England, BHC, dieldrin, and DDT have all been found in

extremely minute quantities in rain water. As to just how much of these chemicals are thus carried about the world throughout the year, we do not know now.

We also know very little, as yet, about the biological significance of low-residue levels of these insecticides in animal tissues. It is well to remember just how small one part per million really is. It is approximately equivalent to one inch on a road that is nearly 158 miles long; or one tablespoon of butter taken from a mass of about 2,800 pounds. Modern methods of chemical analysis are detecting pesticides on a parts-per-trillion basis.

It is also well to recall that birds, fish, and mammals like ourselves store the persisting insecticides differentially in the body's tissues. Visceral fats, liver, and gonadal tissues tend to accumulate the highest concentrations. Levels in the animal brain are important clues to death by the chlorinated hydrocarbons. J. Anthony Keith, of the University of Wisconsin, has collected healthy-appearing herring gulls with an average of 2,441 parts per million of DDT, DDE, and TDE in their body fat but only 20 parts per million in their brains.

Birds that stop feeding will transfer stored DDT into their blood, increase the level of this compound in their central nervous system, and—if sufficient amounts have been stored—die with the typical tremors of DDT poisoning. This sequence took place in an experiment on house sparrows deprived of food for 16 hours. It has also been demonstrated in captive woodcock. It must surely take place at least occasionally in the wild.

Now, in 1966, we know very little about the general level of insecticides in North American birdlife. Virtually all the chemical laboratories initially analyzing pesticide residues in birds were associated in one way or another with research projects involving particular examples of pesticide use or misuse. Hence their statistics on pesticide frequency in bird tissues have tended to be of a nonrandom nature.

Among the seemingly unbiased statistics emerging have been those on American woodcock shot by hunters and those on eagles found dead by law-enforcement officers. One publication of the Fish and Wildlife Service reports 68 percent of 280 woodcocks to be carrying heptachlor epoxide (average 1.6 parts per million) and 71 percent of 210 woodcocks to be carrying DDT (average 1.7 parts per million). Even these figures should not be accepted as representative of the woodcock population until the precise source of the specimens is clarified. Kills at TV towers seem to be a potentially unbiased source of specimens for residue analyses on a population-wide basis.

Fears about depressed rates of the reproductive success of birds have frequently been expressed by conservation-minded people worried by the pesticide problem. In New Brunswick, Bruce S. Wright, of the Northeastern Wildlife Station, reported lowered ratios of juveniles to adults among woodcock sampled on forest-sprayed areas. The evidence that this ratio is influenced by insecticides is circumstantial. A woodcock age-ratio survey has been maintained on a "continental" scale by the Bureau of Sport Fisheries and Wildlife. According to Fant W. Martin, Aelred D. Geis, and William H. Stickel, no overall change in age ratios was evident during the first years of this project.

Age ratios of waterfowl also are closely followed by the bureau and its cooperators. In general, these have been so dominated by environmental factors, like drought, as to be useless indices of potential pesticidal effects. Age ratios have changed markedly in the bald eagle, however. In 1935–1941 at Hawk Mountain, the famous migration-watching station in eastern Pennsylvania, 37 percent of the bald and golden eagles passing the mountain consisted of immature birds. In 1954–1960, according to Maurice Broun, of the Hawk Mountain Sanctuary, this figure dropped to 23 percent for bald eagles and to 26 percent for goldens. In a continental survey of the bald eagle population south of Canada in January 1962, carried out by Alexander Sprunt IV, of the National Audubon Society, 24 percent of 3,807 birds were found to be immature.

Regional nesting failures of our national bird have been reported on both coasts of the Florida peninsula, along the shores of Lake Michigan, and along the Atlantic coast from about New Jersey north to Maine. Nesting populations of this species have decreased markedly in these regions since 1950, and their virtually complete extirpation will take place within the next decade.

On the other hand, populations of the bald eagle in southern Florida, central Minnesota, British Columbia, and Alaska all appear to be prospering. Among 61 bald eagles illegally shot and recovered by the Fish and Wildlife Service, insecticides have been found in all but one specimen. Some of the residue levels in the birds' fat were substantial; others were not. At the present time, the residue levels in these birds have not been related to specific nesting populations, and the role of insecticides in the population decline of this species has not been critically tested.

An equally serious decline in breeding ospreys has taken place from New Jersey to Maine in the past 10 to 20 years. On eastern Long Island, this decline has been about 99 percent since 1945; in New Jersey, 95 percent since 1960; in Maine, 80 percent since 1955. In Chesapeake Bay and estuaries farther south, osprey populations appear to be stable.

Here, as in the research on bald eagles, it has been difficult for scientists to say categorically that the pesticide residues thus far found in the eggs of these birds, or in the fish that they eat, are conclusive evidence of a pesticide cause and effect. A great deal of interesting research on this problem remains to be worked out.

The decline of nesting peregrine falcons since 1950 has been even more spectacular. Between 1950 and 1965, this species became all but extirpated as a breeding bird in the eastern one-third of the United States. It is nearly gone from the Province of Ontario, and is significantly down in numbers in our Western States. In western Europe, the decline is more than 90 percent in Finland, more than 95 percent in northwestern Germany, and about 60 percent in Great Britain. Nesting populations of peregrines in British Columbia and the Canadian Arctic are said to be stable.

Not all birds at or near the top of biotic pyramids seem to be in trouble: Red-tailed hawks, rough-legged hawks, and prairie falcons are said to be examples. These birds tend to be mammal eaters or omnivorous species.

Bird-eating species, like our Cooper's hawk and Europe's sparrow-hawk, are among those that have also exhibited marked population declines in recent years. These declines in both fish-eating and bird-eating species, when they do take place, in-

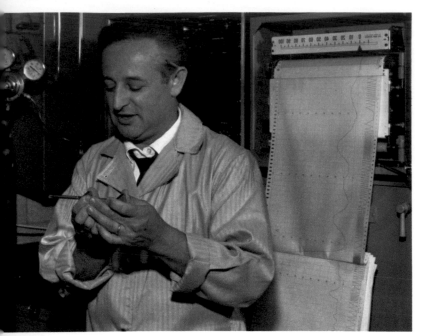

Calvin Menzie, a chemist, uses gas chromatography to measure residues in the tissues of birds to determine the effects of pesticides.

volve a common behavioral pattern. At conspicuous nesting sites, eggs are either not laid for 4 to 6 years or they are eaten by the birds themselves. Young birds do not replace the adults that gradually disappear, and extirpation results.

Only the British seem to have studied this phenomenon with any degree of thoroughness, and they are convinced that the decline of certain raptors in England and southern Scotland is closely associated with the agricultural use of dieldrin. Other insecticidal compounds, however, are being found in these birds, and the possibility of synergistic effects is not excluded.

Synergism is a term used to express the combined action of two or more drugs in a manner that is more than purely additive. Its existence as a pesticidal phenomenon in raptorial birds is neither proved nor understood.

Some Dutch reports of birds dying with heavy convulsions illustrate the degree to which pesticides will accumulate in raptorial birds. Breast-muscle tissue of one such bird, a buzzard, contained 26 parts per million of the DDT complex, 11 of dieldrin, 5 of lindane, and 1 of heptachlor epoxide.

328

Ornithologists have, I think, done a reasonable job in measuring population trends of bald eagles, ospreys, and peregrines, and in measuring reproductive failures in those populations that are declining. Critical tests of the pesticide hypothesis connected with the declines have not, however, been carried out. Nesting birds have not been shot and their residue levels related to those found in their eggs. Geographic variation in the residue levels of food webs remains to be studied.

It is hardly necessary to point out that Federal legislation specifically prohibits the collecting of eagles by scientists and that public sentiment surely frowns on our collecting the relatively few ospreys and peregrines left in the Northeastern States. The whole research approach to these questions is further limited by our inability to breed numbers of these birds in captivity and with controlled diets. A final difficulty centers on the present lack of reproductive data on other species fed very low levels of insecticides in captivity.

These difficulties do throw the arguments of British ornithologists into a compelling focus. The population decline of these raptorial birds has been rapid, synchronized, characterized by reproductive failure, and—for the species involved—historically unique. The environmental factor or factors required to produce such phenomena must be new. Only two really new environmental factors have appeared since the Second World War: Radioactive fallout and persisting pesticides. The fact that some regional populations of raptorial birds are untouched by the decline rules against fallout as a logical factor.

The buildup of residue levels in raptorial and fish-eating birds is a biochemical phenomenon that is by no means understood. There seems to be little doubt that in aquatic and marine ecosystems the pesticidal content of bottom sediments is inexorably transferred from bottom sediments to invertebrate animals to fish and to fisheaters.

In terrestrial ecosystems, the compounds seem to be more rapidly broken down. Although it is difficult to obtain, there is some evidence that predators do indeed tend to select the weakened members of prey populations. Thus toxic chemicals could be channeled to the top of the biotic pyramid where a bird like a peregrine might be affected.

Although our pesticide studies of lakes and estuaries are still relatively new, it now seems quite possible that many of our fish-eating birds are living in dangerous environments.

The full implications of the effect of pesticides upon bird populations are thus by no means yet apparent. Unlike some conservationists, I do not feel that the robin is on the verge of extinction. As the research reports come in—and they come in slowly but surely—I think a clearer picture is emerging. The old 5-2-1 rule of the forties is no longer a safe one. Charles Elton's classic concepts of animal food chains, food webs, and biotic pyramids are taking on new dimensions.

It seems increasingly clear that the use of persisting toxic chemicals on our landscape must be now evaluated in new terms of transport and biological concentration. Ecosystems in the great cottonlands of the South and in the orchard country of our Northwest are among the many that still await study of the effects of insecticides upon bird-life. The biological significance of pesticidal residues in animal tissues also represents a challenging question that may require a decade of research.

Some respected ornithologists, like Roger Tory Peterson, believe that continued use of the persisting chlorinated hydrocarbons in the United States can wipe out bald eagles, ospreys, and other fish-eating birds in many large watersheds and that this use can even extirpate the peregrine falcon as a breeding bird in the United States south of Canada.

This is not a pretty picture. It is perhaps best regarded as a blurred one, made up of an incomplete mosaic of facts that are still being assembled. The trend of ecological research on wildlife and pesticides points not to a waning of fears but rather to an increasing awareness that the effects of persisting insecticides upon birdlife are far more complex and potentially dangerous than most scientists have realized.

—JOSEPH J. HICKEY.

Hunting Versus Vandalism

THEODORE ROOSEVELT drew a distinction between regulated sport shooting and the kind of gunnery that is outdoor vandalism. "True sportsmen, worthy of the name, men who shoot only in season and in moderation," he observed, "do no harm whatever to game." He deplored "the kind of game butcher who simply kills for the sake of the record of slaughter."

We need to note that distinction when we consider hunting and its effects. Hunting today is assumed to be regulated and nondestructive because we, the people, have created Federal and State agencies whose charge it is to study the problems and make rules to that end.

Misunderstanding on this point is widespread.

An example: A suggestion was made that a harvest of mourning doves could be taken in some of the Northern States. It drew violent opposition. People who opposed the proposal assumed that shooting would mean a decline of the dove population. The recommendations of game managers implied there would be no reduction of the breeding stock or annual production of doves. Regardless of who was right, it is evident that the two sides were not arguing from the same premises. Likely enough, this is not a difference in principle as much as a lack of communication.

Shooting abuses are still with us. Insofar as they are legal or permitted, they are chargeable to our entire hunting program. But before we can evaluate sport shooting, we need to examine its biological basis and the theory and practice of keeping it nondestructive.

Our game birds in their wild communities belong to a prey-animal category. Through millions of years they have been fed upon. The fact of their survival means they are prolific. Their subsistence is near the lower end of the food chain, which is to say they feed on plants or the small animal life that lives on plants.

Basically, the seasonal numbers of any animal are determined by the quality of its environment—some combination of climate, soil, water, vegetation, associated animal life, and possibly things unseen and unknown. Our game-prey species commonly are adjusted to an economy of abundance. Being productive, they are likewise expendable. Their lifespan is short. The individual is lost in a massive annual overturn of population.

We human beings are poorly conditioned to think in these terms. The animal world most of us know is made up of individuals: The dog at the back door, the neighbor's cat, the blue jay at the feeder, the dove cooing on the wire. Like the game manager who must rise above his beginnings, we must get oriented to the field of population mechanics if we are to appraise the hunting harvest in its true perspective. (To sidestep major complexities, we consider at the outset in this chapter only resident, nonmigratory species.)

We have to realize first that in life communities there is a teetering balance between production and destruction. The average crop of young turned out during the breeding season must be at least equal to mortality the rest of the year, or the species in question would disappear.

Likewise, breeding output cannot consistently outweigh loss factors, because the population does not go on increasing; it encounters the limits of environmental resources. At this upper level we say numbers have reached the carrying capacity of the habitat, just as stockmen describe the carrying capacity of an acre of pasture or range in terms of the cows or calves or steers it will feed.

Thus, during the thirties, when biologists began exploratory surveys of gun-harvested game birds, they found a simple, natural classification for any

Excess numbers in wild populations of game birds are removed by natural factors if they are not taken by hunters. Cold weather and deep snow in North Dakota caused the death of this pheasant.

fall sample: Birds were either young of the year or old stock, the survivors of the previous breeding season. It probably is true that the lopsided nature of the resulting age ratios was a major revelation in promoting a fuller appreciation of the annual population turnover.

On a tract in southern Michigan, cock pheasants showed a ratio of 10 young of the year to 1 old bird. On another tract, where pheasants were abundant and even more heavily hunted, a common ratio was about 15 to 1. At first sight, this seemed inconceivable, but later it made sense on the basis that the spring production of several hens was being matched against the survivors of a cock population that had been thinned out by hunting.

As figures accumulated on the bobwhite quail, in which both sexes are shot, ratios of near 4:1 were obtained consistently in many States. The work was extended to grouse and ducks. In fact, age-ratio sampling became a recognized elementary need in any wildlife study.

It is a normal expectation for most of our game birds that the fall population will consist of 65 to 80 percent young, as against 20 to 35 percent old birds. If a quail population is 80 percent juveniles in October and this occurs year after year (as it does), then we have an obvious deduction: From one fall season to the next, 8 out of 10 quail are being lost, and they are replaced during the spring and summer breeding season.

This is the yearly waxing and waning of numbers, the production and removal of the annual surplus.

We have abundant evidence that we cannot carry the doomed birds to another year, and there is no point in trying, because a new generation is coming up. This applies principally to resident species; I consider the situation of migratory birds later.

The consistency of age ratios is striking. So also is the consistency of the kill under some conditions. At the Rose Lake Wildlife Experiment Station in Michigan in 3 years out of 4, with pheasant populations remaining about constant, the kill was approximately 10 cocks per hundred acres—although the hunting pressure more than doubled. In a year when pheasants were strikingly abundant, the kill went up to 17 birds per hundred acres. Obviously, the size of the hunting harvest depended on the numbers of pheasants in relation to the cover pattern, rather than the amount of hunting done. Of course, hunting effort had to be above a certain minimum necessary to take the crop, but this was guaranteed by the fact that abundance of birds automatically attracts heavy gun pressure.

It is clear that hunting is a "density dependent" mortality factor: Hunters kill a higher proportion of a dense population than of a sparse population. During the hunting season, as game is thinned out, shooting returns decline, and hunters give up.

This progessive diminishing return was shown by figures on pheasants at Rose Lake. In a 22-day season, about 70 percent of the kill was taken the first week, 20 percent the second week, and 10 percent the last 8 days. It is evident that the hunting of resident game birds has built-in safeguards that make it largely self-regulatory.

The phenomenon of diminishing returns qualifies as a general population principle, since it applies to most mortality factors. Hunting by the fox is subject to the same limitations experienced by a two-legged, gun-bearing predator. Infectious disease, food privations, accidents, and weather extremes (which operate in terms of cover limitations) all tend to lose effect as the population declines. With the progressive reduction of numbers, each surviving animal has more living space and less competition for habitat accommodations. It steadily becomes more comfortable and secure.

Thus we have a basic proposition: Various causes of mortality substitute or compensate for one another.

If you eliminate one factor (such as hunting), the others take up the slack, and that annual population surplus disappears anyway.

Conversely, when any loss factor becomes preponderant (as when you take a heavy hunting crop in a short time), the thinning of numbers makes other types of mortality less effective. In other words, hunting heavily in the fall greatly reduces natural losses during the winter. In that case, we have put to human use a segment of the bird population that would have been wasted otherwise.

Such a weeding out actually is beneficial, because birds that survive the shooting season can enjoy the best of food, cover, and other habitat amenities with minimum competition. They should enter the breeding season in good physical trim.

These relationships, as applied to most nonmigratory species, explain why the closure of local areas to shooting (that is, sanctuaries) or closing the State hunting season for a year or more (formerly done when grouse were down) does not overrun the land with birds. It has not worked, because hunting is not a critical factor that limits the year-to-year population.

It is proper to ask just how large a proportion of the fall population can be taken safely. On that point, game managers have liberalized their thinking as facts accumulated.

It is generally conceded now that most of our small game birds can maintain their numbers under a 50-percent kill. In grouse range, such a harvest is seldom if ever attained over any large area. Quail are more vulnerable in farming areas, and one-half or more may be taken under persistent hunting. It is true of the bobwhite and arid-land quail of the Southwest (California, Gambel's, mountain, and scaled quails), however, that a 20- to 30-percent harvest is common in much of the hunted range.

Cock pheasants probably are the most durable of our game birds in the face of gun pressure. The removal of even 9 out of 10 cocks by hunting probably would not limit breeding productivity in most ranges. This is largely academic, because a kill of this degree is possible only under the highest densities. Authorities now assume that in any reasonable fall season you cannot overshoot the cock pheasant. Some illegal kill of hens always occurs, but that ordinarily is not limiting. In Ohio in recent years, hunting has taken 3 out of 4 cocks and 1 out of 5 hens; that probably is representative of most of our fair-to-good pheasant range.

The natural adjustment that commonly takes place between hunting effort and game density means that the hunting harvest will be high in years of exceptionally high production. Obviously, that is a time when more birds are surplus to the population and therefore can be spared. When birds are down, hunter returns are lean, and hunting pressure declines—only a small proportion of the population is shot.

If overshooting did occur, so that the breeding stock were substantially reduced, still another population principle would give aid and comfort to the game biologist. He calls this one inversity. It means that, other things being equal, an inverse relationship exists between breeding stock density and the productivity of young.

On reflection, this is not especially surprising, because at each season of the year a bird population is under some sort of limitation of carrying capacity. Potentially, a numerous breeding stock could produce a huge crop of young. But a concentration of numbers results in high rates of loss from all causes, and there is a big expenditure of young birds that cannot be accommodated by the habitat.

On the other hand, a small breeding stock has much more leeway in stocking the range to capacity, and a much higher percentage of its output can survive. In practice, this means that a reduced breeding stock may well offset its reduction by increased efficiency.

It should be evident that the meaning of age ratios in autumn is qualified by how plentiful the breeders were and what happened during the nesting and rearing season. So appraised, age ratios are a means of interpreting events during any particular year.

For example, in exceptionally dry years, desert quail of the Southwest may do little nesting at all; then the fall age ratio will be far short on young birds. Similarly, a year of drought on the northern prairies affects age ratios in the kill of waterfowl in the Midwest. When gunners take more adults than young, as has been the case with mallards some years, it means disaster conditions.

It is generally true that weather during the breeding season is the commonest critical factor that determines productivity for our game birds. A cold, wet spring is the most frequent and effective source of disappointment to the hunters of grouse, pheasants, bobwhites, and turkeys—that is, in nonarid regions. In the speculative management of yesteryear, it was assumed that to shoot birds when they were down would be an indignity they could hardly survive. As we have seen, those scattered fowl in a sparse population are highly secure from hunting or anything else. The hunter and his dog may as well get some exercise. When a State has good, workable season dates and bag-limit regulations on its resident game, these seldom need to be changed because of annual fluctuations in the supply of birds.

In large degree, the foregoing discussion has been limited to nonmigratory, upland birds. The situation is complicated for all species that migrate, particularly for those that flock. A migrant essentially starts over with new dynamic relationships in every area it visits. This undoubtedly is true of doves, woodcock, waterfowl, and other birds that shift their ranges with the seasons and may be used as shooting targets. The density factors and population doings that are largely a protection to localized birds become a liability to the travelers.

When a population of resident game birds has lasted out the high kill of opening day, they ordinarily are through the highest loss-rate for the season. They know the cover pattern of the home range, and they get more escape-wise as well as more sparse.

On the other hand, migrant waterfowl that may be shot in September in Alaska and Canada must sustain a succession of opening days as they go south and encounter progressively later hunting seasons. They may still be hearing the boom of guns in February. The thinning out of numbers

Licensing of hunters and basing hunting regulations on actual statistics of game populations are essential in modern management of game.

and the learning about local hazards begin all over again each time the survivors of northern campaigns move to a new concentration point farther south. This gauntlet of guns is run by the bulk of our waterfowl, which are produced in a great region stretching from the Northern States on into the Arctic. Most of the hunting is done on migration routes and on the wintering grounds of Southern States.

Regulating this continentwide game harvest is an international and interstate problem and hence is primarily a Federal responsibility. Within the framework of Federal regulations, the States may restrict shooting further, although they seldom do.

Half a century ago, when brooding and feeding marshes of Northern States had not yet felt the full impact of the draglines, the average annual production of waterfowl was well beyond the demands of a relatively small hunting population. Shooters of ducks and geese were accustomed to abundance. Those who could afford it made investments in club properties, gear, and services at favored points in the traditional staging areas of waterfowl. Even the average guy who held no club membership had access to wetlands and waters where he had little interference or competition. Kills per hunter were high, but total kills were not likely to be excessive.

The trend of changes since the early 1900's has been against the hunter—and the ducks. Headlong agricultural drainage and reclamation of marshes and bottomlands have steadily removed nesting grounds and restricted shooting areas. The annual production of ducks—particularly prairie nesters—has been cut down, and migrants are funneled increasingly through the remaining concentration waters, where private shooting properties hold an advantage over lands used by the general public. The prime example of this is Central Valley in California, a historic wintering ground where less than 10 percent of the pristine marshes remains, and a major part of this remnant is tied up in private clubs. If it were not so tied up, it would be drained at once as high-value cropland.

How do you safeguard an outdoor resource that is being whittled away by environmental deterioration and is at the same time under ever greater levy by an increasing public?

Added to manmade difficulties are the natural and periodically recurring dry years on prairie nesting grounds. In the long haul, drought helps to set plant successions back to early stages, renews fertility, and helps to maintain productive conditions for waterfowl, but low rainfall also means an immediate scarcity of ducks. Aerial surveys of the pothole country through wet years of the midfifties showed a general increase of birds, followed by a decline with the onset of a dry climatic phase in the late fifties. The same trends were evident in decades past.

Migratory waterfowl can be overshot even when their numbers are low. Studies of banding returns amply verify this. The hunting kill, in substantial degree is *added to* (rather than substituted for) natural mortality. Significantly, it is the one cause of duck losses that can be managed on a year-to-year basis.

Time was when our waterfowl were under heavy onslaught by market hunters. It was terminated (legally, at least) by the Migratory Bird Treaty with Great Britain (acting for Canada) in 1916. One by one, certain critical wet areas were rescued and managed as refuges—Horicon in Wisconsin, Malheur in Oregon, Muleshoe in Texas, Tule Lake in California. Not, unfortunately, the Kankakee in Indiana. The national wildlife refuge system was recognized and authorized by the Congress in 1927. But it had no money; so in 1934 the Migratory Bird Hunting Stamp was introduced; it was a time of drought and dizzy decline for the birds. The Federal Aid in Wildlife Restoration Act of 1937 gave the States more money for wetland acquisition and research. Live decoys and spring shooting were outlawed. Later on, shooting over bait was prohibited, and restrictions were placed on guns.

Wet years and war gave the ducks a respite, but in the late forties the dawn of a new era was evident. Its basis: A huge increase in human population. To feed a limitless demand for more business, the development of open spaces and resources of all kinds was pursued with all the ingenious devices of the scientific age. The pioneer, conquer-the-wilderness urge took on new, diesel-powered vigor.

The social functions of open space and recrea-

336

tional land and water were correspondingly submerged. Ears attuned to the symphony of stamping mills do not pick up the wheezing of waxwings. The outdoor aspects of our living standard have been free and taken for granted, and they weigh lightly against the dollars-for-today spirit in political and legislative forums.

If the general needs of the public for outdoor recreation have been little considered, the protests of waterfowl hunters have been heard hardly at all. Expedients to salvage the waning bird resource have been supported mainly by the sportsman's funds, and they necessarily involve all manner of restrictions on the sportsman himself. Aside from the biological problem of saving the ducks, there is the human problem of dividing the harvest.

In recognition of the north-to-south association of certain breeding ranges with travel routes and wintering resorts, Federal biologists developed the concept of management by flyways. Breeding and wintering surveys are taken and regulations are set with some measure of independence in four longitudinal regions across the United States—the Atlantic, Mississippi, Central, and Pacific Flyways. This helps to allow for the varying geographical status of birds and shooting conditions. It also serves to impress the nimrods of Maryland, Arkansas, and California that their ducks are from different sources and that, relative to seasons and bag limits, all men are not created equal.

Birds with relatively undisturbed arctic and subarctic breeding ranges have been more consistently productive than those on the drought and drainage-plagued prairies. Thus the duck supply on the Pacific Flyway (coming to a greater extent from the Arctic) has permitted more liberal bag limits than could be applied farther East. Geese, predominantly northern nesters, have held up comparatively well countrywide. Diving ducks that nest over water—notably the canvasback and redhead—have been particularly hard hit by dry years, and cutting down the kill of these birds, while permitting a greater harvest of other species, has been a frustrating problem.

A primary obstacle to differential regulations and kills—a practical imperative if the waterfowl season is not to be closed entirely in large areas—is the inability of the average gunner to identify ducks. If all ducks were mallard drakes, there would be little cause for concern, for this is the best known of our waterfowl. The high incidence of greenheads in the take-home bag in certain shooting grounds suggests that they have been sorted *post mortem* from a larger kill of females and other species whose legality was unknown or speculative.

Although this kind of loss occurs, there are reasons for thinking that restrictions on species have been effective to some extent. The wood duck has been on and off the protected list through the years, and on the whole it is doing fairly well. The canvasback and redhead seem to be in status-quo jeopardy, but they have hung on despite little visible support from the primary but drought-stricken nesting ranges of Manitoba and Saskatchewan.

Another enigmatic aspect of regulating the kill is Federal-State relationships. Annually, in State hearings, flyway councils, and national meetings there is a free-for-all pulling and hauling for advantageous regulations—season dates, season length, zoning within a State, and bag limits. Particularly in States where a strong political influence has been maintained in conservation affairs, partisan pressures are exerted on game officials and national representatives. In turn, the pressures are transmitted to the Director of the Bureau of Sport Fisheries and Wildlife and other Government administrators (the Secretary of the Interior and ultimately the President are responsible for Federal regulations).

The competitive claims and dissatisfactions before any given hunting season are further complicated during the shooting period by the vicissitudes of weather, which figure importantly in the movements of migrating waterfowl and hence in the quality of hunting in any local area.

There is nothing in the waterfowl situation that could not be improved considerably by more ducks or fewer people. Providence does not seem to have either of these benignities in view for the immediate future. But there are latter-day developments which are refreshing and may even justify some optimism.

The technical and administrative staffs of Canada, the United States, the individual States and Provinces, and several private organizations co-

A hunter uses a well-trained dog to retrieve birds he shoots. To do otherwise is poor sportsmanship.

338

operate closely in surveys of nesting and wintering waterfowl and of the annual kill. Banding programs are soundly organized and are done by a modern punchcard and machine-sorting system. Returns are analyzed and results published by biostatisticians with an efficiency that improves each year. We are building a solid knowledge of our waterfowl. Evidence thereof is in *Waterfowl Tomorrow,* a 770-page book published by the Department of the Interior in 1964.

More broadly, the many volumes of reports filed by the Outdoor Recreation Resources Review Commission have had some attention. An informed leadership in both Houses of the Congress is increasingly heard from on outdoor issues. The Secretaries of Agriculture and Interior have communicated, and there are moves afoot which seem to recognize that the encouragement of all-out drainage is not in the public interest.

It is proper to hope that increasing facts and better information procedures will untangle a snarl of bioeconomic difficulties. But as long as it must be said with each passing year that there has been a further deterioration of our waterfowl range, the resource and those who hunt it have an uncertain future.

Migratory marsh and shore birds, such as rails, gallinules, snipe, and woodcock, are principally the game of specialists. They share a habitat jeopardy with other wetland fauna. There have been occasional pesticide problems and devastating freezes on the winter range, but hunting and regulations have seldom been a major issue.

In large measure, Federal-State regulation of hunting is successful and orderly for the cousins of the passenger pigeon. The band-tailed pigeon is hunted in the three Pacific Coast States. Excessive killing at concentration points was common in earlier days, and the bird was shot as far east as Colorado and New Mexico.

Studies have demonstrated a remarkably low rate of increase for the band-tail—evidently it is normal for adults to outnumber the young in a fall population; that undoubtedly was the case with the passenger pigeon also. The band-tailed pigeon is a species that may be called sensitive to hunting. Natural losses are low, in keeping with a low reproductive rate, and hence hunting is a major mortality factor. But pigeon concentrations evidently occur relative to the abundance or scarcity of food—mast and wild fruits of forest areas or cultivated fruits and grain crops in settled valleys. The birds may be plentiful and heavily shot in one area and hardly touched in another. Local crop damage may be important one year and nonexistent the next. These erratic and unpredictable habits have been a protective factor, as have periods of years in which no hunting was permitted. The precedent of severe restrictions when needed is reassurance that this species can be perpetuated in the presence of hunting.

The white-winged dove is an important shooting species in a narrow region north of the Mexican border extending from southern California to west Texas and along the Rio Grande to the Gulf. It is a less productive breeder than the mourning dove and differs from it in being a gregarious nester. In some respects, though, the management and hunting problems of the two species are similar. The mourning dove is legal game in 30 States, principally in the South and West. From Montana and Wyoming eastward to the Atlantic, most Northern States are closed to dove shooting, Illinois and Pennsylvania being exceptions.

As I noted earlier, in States where the dove has traditionally been on the songbird list, any move to hunt it provokes spirited controversy. Characteristically, the issue becomes a subject of contention in the legislature, with emotions playing a strong part in the choosing up of sides.

Biologically, it probably is true that a crop of doves could be taken in any State which has a reasonably high breeding population. Both State and Federal biologists know this situation reliably, and their knowledge is growing. This is not to say that any particular viewpoint is right or wrong. After the actual facts are made known and given realistic consideration, if the preponderance of public opinion is against dove shooting, then it would seem proper for this opinion to prevail.

There should be no real lack of technical guidance for a hunting program. Dove research is now a national effort involving biologists in many States, with excellent Federal coordination. One of the significant findings has been that, while there are extensive movements, the preponderance

Hunting methods are controlled by regulations to help keep the harvest of birds by hunters within biologically allowable limits.   A hunter uses a duck call and wood decoys.   Live decoys are illegal.

of the kill in a given State tends to be locally reared birds.

It has become evident in latter-day wrangles over dove shooting that more is involved than just the taking of a crop of birds. Much of the opposition is simply opposition to more hunting of any kind. Embittered landowners take any opportunity to express themselves against the rankling evils of trespass, property damage, and other kinds of vandalism by a hoodlum minority of hunters. The issue gives bird enthusiasts and outdoorsmen in general a forum in which to oppose the irresponsible gunnery that has whittled away (legally and illegally) at hawks, owls, eagles, cranes, herons, swans, and even condors—in fact, anything large

and feathered that someone with a low outdoor IQ feels like shooting.

In many States, laws are inadequate.   In many more, the penalties for violation are inadequate. Dove shooting is indeed likely to result in abuses wherever there is no proper control of shooting from roads.   This is elemental in the regulation of hunting. Likewise, there should be a requirement that a gun be broken down or cased in an automobile. The law-enforcement officer needs the advantage of these rules in dealing with poaching and other violations. The legal hunter should support them wholeheartedly.

Most States protect certain birds of prey, but some have attempted to allow general shooting of game-killing species, such as the Cooper's hawk and great horned owl. This poses another problem in identification, and it means that all large birds are shot—including the bald eagle and the almost extinct Everglade kite.

There has been no evidence that any general killing of birds of prey is justified in game management or as a property-damage control measure. This fact is being increasingly recognized, with the result that more than a third of the States now give legal protection to all birds of prey except where they do damage to poultry or other stock. The enforcement of such laws varies from good to none at all.

There are excellent reasons why birds of prey should have effective protection, with the exceptions I noted. The bird hobbyist and many other outdoor-minded people place a premium on the seeing value of hawks and owls. The species involved are not prolific enough to hold up under the shooting they are now getting in many sections. Birds hanging on fences and news pictures of slaughtered "chicken hawks" do much to foster a general and increasing public resentment against hunting of all kinds.

Unless widespread abuses are minimized, we are likely to see the continued growth of opposition to hunting. The true sportsman has every incentive to make his own analysis of the situation and aggressively support measures to curtail the outdoor indecency that abounds around large population centers. Conscientious hunters must do this to preserve their hunting privilege. But it must come about also if the many varied categories of outdoor recreationists are to be brought into a common conservation front. This is long overdue. The fact that the conservation movement is a house divided is a weakening influence in times of crisis. The burgeoning of human populations attests that the crises have only begun.

Most of the important advances in managing game and regulating hunting have come through the initiative and support of organized sportsmen. Local and national groups have exerted leadership that has made all the difference between what we have now and what we might well have lost. Sportsmen stand firm on their American right to bear arms afield and to take a game crop under properly controlled conditions. It is justly due the hunter that the basic soundness of his position be recognized.

Likewise, it behooves all who use a gun to see the preponderant value of birds and other wildlife as a part of the living landscape, to be enjoyed by anyone, at any time, without restriction. This costs the hunter nothing, and the rewards will be great.

—Durward L. Allen.

The Newcomers

MOST OF THE BIRDS new to America were brought in by folk to whom the skylark was a well-remembered song at dawn, the European goldfinch a pleasurable sight on the summer thistles, the pheasant a flashy, toothsome citizen of field and nearby woodland.

In most such instances, it was the emotional attachment to familiar, well-remembered species that provided the incentive. Cage birds probably were the first arrivals. Among favorites were the common canary, 6 thousand of which arrived in one shipment, the European goldfinch, and the black-capped warbler, all brought from Europe, and the Java sparrow. In later years, importations of parrots and parakeets were legion.

With time, many of the cage birds escaped or were liberated, but none succeeded in becoming firmly established in the continental United States.

Beginning about the middle of the 19th century, interest in releasing exotics boomed. Several societies for importing songbirds were formed. Skylarks, wood larks, European robins, nightingales, European blackbirds, song thrushes, starlings, house sparrows, and chaffinches from Europe and crested mynas from southeastern Asia were the most popular species.

Hopes soared, but only a few species found conditions to their liking or were liberated in large enough numbers in the New World. Skylarks, probably totaling well over a thousand, were set free from New York to the Pacific coast. Breeding flocks were reported for some years thereafter. Congratulations were premature, for only in the vicinity of Victoria, British Columbia, are they still to be found in North America. Here, also, is the only successful transplant of the now unwelcome crested myna.

At least as many European nightingales were imported, but the birds seemed seldom to arrive in good health and soon disappeared. The European robins apparently never bred. The European tree sparrow, a favorite in Germany, became established in the vicinity of St. Louis and at Springfield, Illinois.

The increase in three new species has been uncomfortably explosive. The soon-to-be-notorious English, or house, sparrow was released in 1853 in Brooklyn, the following year in Portland, Maine, and later elsewhere. As cocky newcomers, they were soon successful, although three successive plantings were required in Quebec City. Their westward spread had reached the Mississippi by 1886. They are now common coast to coast.

Eugene Schieffelin, a wealthy New York drug manufacturer who loved birds, decided to introduce birds mentioned in Shakespeare's plays. Most of his introductions failed, but 80 pairs of starlings, freed in Central Park, New York, in 1890–1891, thrived. Why earlier attempts failed in Quebec, Cincinnati, Portland, Oregon, and elsewhere remains a mystery that even modern biologists cannot explain. By 1898 the starling had established itself in New York City and spread to Stamford, Connecticut, and Plainfield, New Jersey. Sixty years later, following the pattern of human European immigrants, starlings had crossed the mountains and plains and had become established all the way to the Pacific coast.

One other import made its mark. It is our semi-domesticated pigeon or rock dove, the trusting favorite of park benchers, the litterer of city ledges, and a familiar inhabitant of country barnyards from coast to coast. How rock doves got here is unrecorded, but we do know that only in a few can-

Cattle egrets, migratory birds from the Old World, came to the United States on their own and are increasing in the Southern and Eastern States. They were first seen in Florida in 1942.

yons and cliffs, notably the gorge below Niagara Falls, have they been successful in establishing colonies under truly wild surroundings.

Few nongame species are imported any more, except for sale as cage birds. But before the keen interest subsided, at least 44 different kinds had been released intentionally in the United States and Canada. Only three found conditions over the broad continent to their liking.

Another foreigner, the cattle egret, has attracted attention because of the rapidity with which it is extending its range in the United States. This egret is an Old World species which was introduced into British Guiana early in the 20th century and which, being migratory, found its way into Florida, where it was first observed in 1942. Within 10 years, scattered individuals were seen as far north as New Jersey and Massachusetts. Tens of thousands now nest from Florida north to New Jersey, and additional colonies are becoming established in the interior of the continent. The National Audubon Society's annual Christmas bird count first listed a

single bird in 1953. Only 8 years later, 3,120 cattle egrets were found on the 1961 Christmas count—more of this species than of any of our native herons or ibises. Along the Texas coast these birds increased from 10 pairs in 1959 to more than 20 thousand pairs in 1966.

In an island environment, though, conditions are different. Isolated from continental populations, islands are apt to have a more meager assortment of plant and animal species. Thus they may be particularly susceptible to the invasion of exotic forms.

Hawaii is an example. Of 94 kinds of foreign birds known to have been liberated there, 53 were believed to have established themselves at least locally by 1940, and about 36 were still surviving there in 1965. Most of the songbirds have remained close to civilization, but a few, notably the Pekin nightingale and the Japanese white-eye, penetrated wooded areas. The white-eye is rapidly invading the remote mountain forests, the last stronghold of the native honey-creepers, several

344

species of which are on the verge of extinction.

Game birds from far lands have received their share of attention ever since colonial days. More than 30 kinds have been liberated, but only three have been eminently successful.

The best known is the ring-necked pheasant. Richard Bache, son-in-law of Benjamin Franklin, released a shipment of ring-necked pheasants from England in New Jersey about 1790. They disappeared after a few years. So did subsequent releases, some of them large, in the East and Midwest.

But nearly 100 years later, about 100 pairs, trapped in China and shipped by O. N. Denny, American consul-general in Shanghai, were turned loose in the Willamette Valley of Oregon in 1881. They prospered beyond expectations.

Encouraged by this good fortune, other States redoubled their efforts. Early stock came mainly from England. Later, game farms raised millions of young birds for release. Preferring agricultural lands in Northern States, they thrived where no native species of gallinaceous bird was common.

But again a touch of mystery: Of the hundreds of thousands liberated south of the Mason and Dixon Line, only a handful survived to rear young. We found an explanation a few years ago when pheasants imported from northern Iran took readily to many southern agricultural areas. Early failures also stalked attempts to acclimatize the Hungarian gray partridge. For instance, nearly 40 thousand birds, mostly wild-trapped in Hungary, reached the United States and Canada in 1908 and 1909 alone.

A planting of 207 pairs near Calgary, Alberta, turned out to be astonishingly successful, and releases, some of them large, followed in many States and Provinces. Large grainfields, not too clean-farmed and adjacent to dry grasslands, particularly in northern Iowa, southern Minnesota, and southern Manitoba westwards, provided prime habitat. Both spread and increase were fantastic for a while before declining somewhat to the number that the land could support. Little competition with native species has been reported.

Chukars, partridges native to the Himalayas, have been released in the arid trans-Pecos country of western Texas, where introductions have been sponsored by the Texas Game and Fish Commission.

345

Jungle fowl, ancestors of domestic chickens, were introduced on the Hawaiian Island of Kauai by the early Polynesians and still inhabit mountains there.

Attempts to introduce capercaillie, large grouse native to the coniferous forests of Europe and western Asia, into our Northern States have been unsuccessful.

The third successful species was the chukar partridge. The original stock probably was obtained from the rough uplands and steep, rocky, and dry slopes of the Himalayas. Few who imported the chukar, beginning in 1883, knew this or realized the importance of releasing them in similar habitat. Under the hit-and-miss policy that prevailed, birds were liberated in all but nine States in numbers from a few to 85 thousand birds. By 1954, it is reported that 324 thousand birds had been released. Almost all of these were from game farm stock.

The chukars flourished in Nevada and later in other Western States to the extent that by 1964 open hunting seasons had been declared in eight States, including Hawaii, and in two Provinces of Canada.

Chukars have not become established on the eastern slopes of the Rockies. We do not know why. Between those slopes and the Atlantic, there is little of the rough terrain the birds require, and annual precipitation may exceed the 20 to 25 inches that seem to mark the upper limit of chukar tolerance.

Game birds also have been remarkably successful in Hawaii, sometimes in habitats rather different from their native range. The most prolific colonizers have been the ring-necked pheasant, the Japanese green pheasant, and the spotted dove, all from Asia, the barred dove from Malaysia, and the California quail.

An early introduction was that of the red junglefowl. Domesticated in southeastern Asia from wild stock some 4 thousand years ago, they must have been carried to Hawaii in the canoes of early Polynesians. Once there, some became progenitors of a semiwild strain that today is found in forests on the island of Kauai.

Many game birds were unable to adapt to the New World.

Some were pheasants, among them the long-tailed Reeves' from the mountains of central China, the silver, showy golden, and the Amherst.

Others were species of grouse. Into northern woodlands went the giant capercaillie, the lyre-tailed black grouse, and the smaller hazel grouse, all from Scandinavia, but to no avail.

General Lafayette sent the first live red-legged partridge to George Washington at Mount Vernon in 1786. Others followed, mostly in small numbers. More attempts were undertaken in 1956.

The thicket-loving bamboo partridge, which was acclimatized in Japan from China, was released, mostly in Washington, about 1906 and again some 20 years later, but without success.

The commonly domesticated guineafowl is native to the hot, equatorial western Africa. Good fliers, aggressive, and apt at stealing nests and raising broods far from barnyards, many have escaped or been liberated in the United States; they have not succeeded in establishing a wild strain. They have thrived in Jamaica, Cuba, Hispaniola, and Puerto Rico, but possibly they cannot survive in the wild in much colder climates.

Migratory birds take to new environments less easily than sedentary species. They require one type of habitat for winter and another in which to breed. Sometimes introduced birds lose their urge to migrate. That happened when the Canada goose was brought to New Zealand.

Many nonresident species, including the small migratory quail, may not be so adaptable. The coturnix, as they are often called, are abundant in grasslands and grainfields in Europe, Asia, and Africa. They are easy to catch for shipment and breed at an astonishing rate in captivity.

Thousands were loosed, mostly in the States bordering the Atlantic, between 1875 and 1885. Some bred in the year of release; most of them migrated apparently southwards and did not return. A second round of liberations took place between 1956 and 1960. In spite of the importation and release of close to 500 thousand individuals, the experiment was a failure.

Many kinds of ducks and geese have been imported, mostly for aviaries. Among the commoner have been the Baikal teal, European teal, and the Egyptian goose. Of the waterfowl, only the mute swan, a favorite of European parks, has maintained itself in a semiwild state. From the New York City area it has gradually spread northward into southern New England and southward to Maryland.

Of the reasons we can suggest for the few successes and many failures, the first is that sentiment often triumphed over sound judgment. Eyes did not see nor minds picture the differences between the New World and the Old World in climate and in woods and waters. Birds often were liberated in country quite unlike their native range. Many of the birds, after a trying trip from their point of origin, were not in fit condition to fend for themselves in strange surroundings.

The number of birds released can affect the chances of establishment. They must find cover to their liking, learn to avoid new enemies, and adjust to new foods. Until they know their way around, they are accident prone.

The average lifespan of many of our native birds is less than 2 years after they reach adulthood. The psychological and physical adjustment required of an exotic to a new environment is so much more rigorous that still fewer may be expected to survive. Birds raised on a game farm find adjustment to wild conditions so difficult that losses often are 60 to 80 percent in the 6 months following liberation.

Many of the transplanted birds start to wander, looking perhaps for the fields or forests that were their home before they were trapped. Chukars wearing numbered leg bands were found 3 months later some 40 miles from the spot where they were released. Pheasants have been shot more than 100 miles from the point of liberation only a few months thereafter.

In general, the fewer the number set free the fewer are the chances of establishment.

Even the subspecies chosen may make a difference. Our northern ring-necked pheasant is actually a hybrid involving three races: The black-necked from the Black Sea coast, the Mongolian from central Siberia, and the Chinese ringneck from eastern China. Birds of almost pure Chinese blood have found conditions to their liking mostly in California and parts of Oregon. Farther north and east from the Rockies to the Atlantic, the birds exhibit closer affinities to the blackneck and the Mongolian races.

None of these pure strains nor any of the hybrids have prospered in the Southern States. But other subspecies, introduced from the rice, tobacco, corn, and barley belt along the Caspian Sea in northern Iran have shown promise in the South.

When natural happenings or man upset the general balance and no barriers like oceans, mountains, or deserts intervene, new species that are adapted to the changed conditions move in. Usually under natural conditions, there is time enough for the already established native species to adjust themselves to the invaders.

But when change occurs suddenly, as it often does at the hand of man, the resulting interference or competition with the established plants and animals may be so intense as to reduce the abundance of some native forms and to eliminate others altogether.

The aggressive habits, high breeding potential, and an ability to compete successfully with native hole-nesting species, such as bluebirds and woodpeckers, have made the house sparrow an unwelcome guest. By the middle of this century, the starlings had replaced the house sparrow as the country's most unwelcome immigrant.

Most other introduced songbirds seem not to compete seriously with native species. Among them are several that have been in new homes more than 50 years: The skylark and the crested myna in southwestern British Columbia; the canary on Midway Island in the Pacific; and the European tree sparrow, a close relative of the house sparrow, near St. Louis.

In the early fifties, we might have added to the list the house finch, a species abundant in the Southwestern States, which was liberated on Long Island about 1940. In later years, however, this western finch has spread so rapidly in the East as to cause considerable alarm. It was first noted in New Jersey and Pennsylvania in 1955, in Maryland in 1958, in Virginia in 1962, and North Carolina in 1963. By the midsixties the eastern population numbered in the tens of thousands. In the arid Southwest, the house finch is so abundant as to be considered a problem species in some farming areas. Will it become a similar problem or even a more serious problem in the farming areas of the East that it is just now invading? This raises the question as to whether attempts should be made to control this bird in the East while control is still possible, or whether to let Nature take its course.

We watch with interest the spread of more recently introduced species, such as the spotted-breasted oriole, red-whiskered bulbul, and blue-gray tanager, all in the Miami suburbs. None of

In one century, the wild turkey disappeared from the fauna of 18 States. Gone from the northern parts of its range in the Great Plains, the Great Lakes area, and New England, this fine native species is still common locally in most of the Southern States. It is being reestablished in some States by releases of breeding stock.

them has a closely related native competitor in southern Florida.

So far there seems to be no serious competition in food habits and nesting sites between the cattle egret and other herons. Most cattle egrets nest later than do native herons, whose colony sites they frequent, and the cattle egrets put their nests in smaller crotches.

We see no danger signal at the moment that would cause alarm at the presence of this Old World species upon our continent. Such large numbers should be watched carefully, however.

Few instances of serious competition between exotic and native game birds for food, shelter, nesting sites, or territory have been noted. There have been reports, however, of severe fighting between prairie chickens and pheasants in defense of their territories.

A survey of 2,016 nests of the ruffed grouse in New York State uncovered pheasant eggs in 11 of them.

Competition between pheasants and quail, once feared, is now generally considered to be of minor importance.

It is largely because of the plowing up of once extensive prairie grasslands that the greater prairie chicken has been seriously reduced in numbers; one race, the heath hen, is now extinct, and the others are threatened with extinction. The gray partridge, as well as the pheasant, has adapted well to much of the range that is no longer able to support the greater prairie chicken and sharp-tailed grouse. Competition between the introduced and the native species is not considered a major factor in the precarious status of the greater and lesser prairie chickens.

Hybridization between closely related exotic and native species is a possibility. Many such crosses made by aviculturists have proved to be infertile. Yet in New Zealand, the native grey duck commonly crosses with the introduced mallard. The offspring are fertile, and the hybrid is now common.

The native bobwhite almost disappeared from parts of the northeastern United States during the first quarter of the 20th century. The reason was believed to be a succession of winters in which severe cold followed a heavy, wet snowfall, trapping the roosting birds beneath a hard crust. At the height of the decline, large numbers of a southern race of bobwhite were wild-trapped, mostly in northern Mexico, where the climate is relatively mild, and shipped to the depleted areas for liberation. More than 233 thousand of these birds are said to have entered the United States between 1910 and 1925. It has been suggested, but never proved, that hybridization with the native strain produced a cross less able to withstand northern winters.

No fertile crosses between Old World and New World birds, under wild conditions, have been documented in the United States.

Losses to farm crops and the nuisance caused by birds may be serious.

Exotics are often implicated. Vast flocks of starlings, along with native blackbirds, rank as major pests on corn, rice, other cultivated crops and soft fruits and in many cattle feedlots. Shotguns are no match for them, and biologists have been testing chemicals to discourage feeding or inhibit reproduction. Annual losses from starlings alone are estimated in millions of dollars.

To a lesser degree, a similar situation exists in the case of the house sparrow and the rock dove. Most of the inquiries from the public as to ways to reduce bird nuisances pertain to these three introduced species.

Several species of songbirds were introduced as controls for insect pests. The cocky house sparrow was supposed to combat the dropworm larvae of the snow-white linden moth, which once was an objectionable pest in cities. The European great tit, a close relative of our native chickadees, was highly recommended in the nineties to apple growers in the West as a possible enemy of the common coddling moth.

In no instance, however, has a feathered foreigner proved to be more effective than our native species in controlling insect pests.

Diseases and parasites are normal in wildlife. New diseases, to which our native plants and animals are not resistant, can cause serious problems. Many an infection now common was carried unknowingly into the New World by poultry, pigeons, or livestock. New birds, caged or wild, also can be carriers.

Newcastle disease is widespread in the Old World. It reached the United States in early shipments of poultry. Many strains of it are relatively mild, but particularly vigorous ones have been found in Asia. Before the days of rigid quarantine, many chukar partridges were shipped from India to California. In one such shipment, several birds died. A pathologist identified the cause as a virulent strain of Newcastle disease. The remaining birds were destroyed.

There has been much speculation, but no proof, that disease carried by foreign birds has seriously affected several of our native species. Some au-

The chachalaca, the only representative in the United States of a tropical American family of gallinaceous birds, lives in the lower Rio Grande Valley, notably in the Santa Ana National Wildlife Refuge. Chachalacas of Mexican origin have been introduced on Sapelo and Blackbeard Islands off the coast of Georgia.

thorities believe the introduction of diseased rock doves may have contributed to the extinction of the once-abundant passenger pigeon.

Mild forms of trichomoniasis occur in many native pigeons and doves, but it may be that a more virulent strain was introduced through the importation of diseased rock doves. In the Snake River Canyon of Idaho, for example, golden eagle chicks feeding on rock doves that breed there died from trichomoniasis.

People in Honolulu no longer see any of the native Hawaiian land birds unless they hike the mountain trails. Even along these trails, introduced birds far outnumber the native ones. Only three species of native songbirds persist in any numbers in the higher mountains of the island of Oahu.

If introduced species actually were responsible for the disappearance of native Hawaiian species, very likely it happened through disease rather than by direct competition, as the species that have invaded the mountain forests were not introduced until after the major decline of native birds.

Effective regulation or control of traffic in and release of exotic birds has long been wanting. The Lacey Act of 1900 prohibited the importation of mongoose, fruit bats, house sparrows, starlings, and such other birds and animals as the Secretary of Agriculture may declare injurious to agriculture. Permits were required to make sure that no prohibited species were allowed through Customs.

A few other species have been added by amendment, and the administration of the act has been transferred to the Secretary of the Interior. Revisions under consideration could provide additional protection against the release of harmful species.

There still is a potentially serious problem of unintentional releases. More than a million songbirds are imported annually by the cage bird industry. Except for birds in the parrot family and the mynah, exotic songbirds are admitted without inspection (other than a total count) and with no control over the species that are pests elsewhere. Hundreds or even thousands of them escape each year at ports of entry because of faulty caging, and no penalties are imposed on the shippers. Few of the escaped birds survive, but the possibility exists that pests may become established in this way.

The Department of Agriculture is responsible for preventing the importation of foreign diseases and parasites that might seriously affect native or domestic birds and mammals. Gallinaceous game birds, ducks, geese, and pigeons are placed in quarantine for 60 days before shipment and again for 3 weeks or more following arrival at port of entry. Postmortem examination of sick or dead birds is carried out by pathologists. Entire shipments may be destroyed if infection with important diseases or parasites, not already common in the United States, is found. From January 1961 to May 1964, 14,530 nongame and 8,425 game birds were passed through quarantine.

Despite the large numbers of exotic game birds imported to date, we know of no new disease or parasite that has become established among our native species as a result of such introductions.

Whatever the undesirable economic and social effects of starlings, house sparrows, and rock doves, the successful transplanting of the ring-necked pheasant, gray partridge, and chukar partridge has meant much to outdoor recreation.

Pheasants, now legal game in most Northern States, provide more man-days afield than do any of our native upland game birds. The hunters' gamebags bulge with from 10 to 12 million pheasants a year. Gray partridges, finding conditions to their liking in several Midwestern States and the Prairie Provinces of Canada, provide a harvest in some years equal to that of ruffed grouse and turkey combined. In western North America, hunters now bag about a million chukars a year.

Hunting for small game provided 138 million days of recreation afield in the United States in 1960, when about a billion dollars were spent on hunting. But for the successful exotics, these totals would have been substantially less, and the hunting pressure on our native birds and mammals would have been somewhat greater.

Another aspect of the introduction of exotic birds often is overlooked. Millions of dollars and much labor have been expended in obtaining, caring for, and releasing them. Looking back, we know that money and effort were wasted, not knowingly, but in terms of need and results. As the early fever for exotics subsided, conservationists decided to place major emphasis on improving conditions for the

351

The gray francolin of India often is kept as a pet in its native land.

native and introduced species already at hand. From 1930 to the end of the Second World War, few new birds were considered for trial. Of these, only the chukar has made a place for itself.

During the war, American servicemen came into contact with many new birds overseas. Great interest was expressed in the birds that might make good hunting at home. Money was plentiful and, for a time, it was feared that a new round of hit-and-miss introductions was in the making.

By now conservationists understood better the dangers inherent in casually bringing in new species. Yet no large reservoir of knowledge covering these game birds had been accumulated. Who then was to judge which of the new species now suggested for release were worthy of consideration?

Although wildlife does not recognize political boundaries, nonmigratory species are under State jurisdiction. Joint State-Federal cooperation and control were obviously required. The Fish and Wildlife Service, interested State conservation commissions, and the Wildlife Management Institute reviewed the problem. The International Association of Game, Fish and Conservation Commissioners appointed a committee to recommend action and to consider new species suggested for trial liberation. Working together, a fresh approach based on cooperation arose.

The agencies organized a foreign game introduction program in 1948. One purpose was to discourage actively ill-considered or unwise introductions by providing detailed ecological informa-

352

tion on species being considered. Another was to determine whether a need for new birds existed and, if so, to locate and provide only those most suitable for trial.

Emphasis was placed on game birds that might establish themselves where native species were absent or uncommon. To locate such areas, each State was asked to survey its game-deficient habitats. More than one-fifth of the United States was indicated as being unproductive of native game birds.

Federal biologists analyzed reports of the surveys and reviewed world habitat and climatic niches to uncover similar environment in foreign countries. An on-the-spot study of the local game birds living therein was undertaken then.

Folly, failure, and error were thus minimized by providing a basis of fact against which to judge species suggested for trial: Were they abundant and widely distributed? Were habitat and climatic conditions reasonably similar to those in a State in which new species were desired? What foods did they eat? Where did they find water? What of their habits? Were they fliers or skulkers? Where did they nest and how many eggs were laid? Were there any records of crosses with other species? Were they combative? How successful were they in avoiding enemies and people? What were their diseases and parasites? Were they detrimental to agriculture? Were they pests in other ways? If successfully introduced, might competition, serious to our native birds, arise?

Thus, through field contacts, review of published accounts, consultation with biologists and sportsmen, we were able to choose birds worth further consideration.

Carefully planned trial introductions of the species selected were then carried out in cooperation with State conservation departments.

The plan worked well. Since 1950, more than a hundred varieties of game birds in Europe and Asia have been considered. Of these, 14 species and 4 additional subspecies were selected for intensive study before recommending them for trial release in one or more of the 45 States collaborating with the program.

It is still too early to evaluate results of most of the introductions. Iranian pheasants, black francolins, and gray francolins, however, have demonstrated an ability to survive, reproduce, and increase substantially on a number of release areas.

Indian sandgrouse have disappeared. Reeves' pheasants, though tried in substantial numbers in several States, are barely hanging on. Six other species are maintaining themselves in numbers sufficient to justify guarded optimism. Two others probably have failed.

None of the game bird species introduced has proved detrimental to agricultural crops.

Nor has their presence proved inimical to any native game birds that were in coverts in the general vicinity in which some of the new species were released.

No two persons will reach the same total on the balance sheet for introductions of foreign birds.

Some species have been costly failures. A few have been brilliant successes. Some have become nuisances. Others are much sought after. Each species must be carefully judged on its own merits. None should be brought in except after careful investigation of its characteristics in its native range and a biological evaluation of its probable impact on agriculture and on our own birds. Lastly, one should be reasonably sure that new species, if successful, will not merely add another bird to our fauna but will also serve some important, useful purpose.

The question of introductions is primarily a matter of balance. Every new species that manages to establish itself must change the balance of Nature in some way. Each will leave some impression on the environment and on its plants and animals.

The balance between the interests of birdwatchers, sportsmen, aviculturists, farmers, and ecologists also is to be considered. To each, an introduction spells different promises or problems. All must be given due consideration to the end that man and Nature may coexist even though the interests of both must be modified to meet our known needs for a long time to come.

—GARDINER BUMP and CHANDLER S. ROBBINS.

OIL-SOAKED CANVASBACKS

We Are Warned

CANARIES THAT MINERS used to take down into the pits gave them early warnings of the presence of dangerous gases. Caged birds in the trenches of the First World War gave the same service to soldiers in France. Birds now are warning us of the dangers to them and to us of the gases, grime, poisons, dust, and slime with which we befoul their homes and our communities.

One is carbon dioxide (the chokedamp of which the mine canaries warned), which combustion in motor vehicles and factories adds to the atmosphere at a rate approaching 6 billion tons a year.

Other items and sources of pollution are lead poisoning; sewage lagoons; oil; salt poisoning; acid mine pollution; the discharges of liquids from sewers and industrial plants (the President's Advisory Committee calculated that an expenditure of 20 billion dollars would be required to provide a minimum type of sewage treatment for 80 percent of the country's population by 1975; the cost of cleaning up gaseous and solid wastes is even greater); and other forms of air pollution.

Birds, like people, must breathe clean air to survive. The thin shell of air around the earth is filling rapidly with contaminants. It is receiving greater and greater discharges of dust and gases— a rain of grime, the smudges and stains of an expanding industrialization.

Dust particles that circulate about us include bits of pulverized metals, fallout from nuclear blasts, and mists from innumerable sprays.

Gases in the air include sulphur dioxide from coal fires, oxide of nitrogen from gas fuels, and carbon monoxide from the burning of coal gas and paper.

The effects of neutron-gamma radiation on birds were studied in late summer in 1964 near Savannah, Georgia. No dead birds were found during the studies, but there were disappearances, emigrations from the test areas, and reduction of the singing urge in local birds. There is cause to believe that territorial birds were affected adversely by radiation tests.

We have reports that birds succumb as they fly through volcanic gases or through acrid smoke from chimneys. There is a suggestion in records maintained by zoo veterinarians that the ordinary urban atmosphere is becoming deadlier. A study made in Philadelphia over a 62-year span on 3,306 birds and 1,702 mammals, all zoo residents, revealed lung cancer in three of all the animals that died between 1901 and 1935 and in 20 of the animals that died between 1935 and 1963.

As to lead poisoning: Ducks that feed in shallow water, head submerged and tail pointing skyward, strain out bits of food from the aquatic vegetation and deposits on the bottom. Along with the seeds and sprouts their probing beaks pick up, the ducks sometimes take in pellets of lead shot fired over the marsh in some earlier hunting season. The pellets enter the gizzard and digestive tracts of the birds and remain there a long time.

Frank C. Bellrose, of the State Natural History Survey Division in Illinois, found that mallards are affected most frequently in the Mississippi Valley. Investigations in southern France on nearly 8 thousand ducks once indicated that nearly 25 percent of all birds there contained lead shot. Studies by the Scottish Ministry of Agriculture, Fisheries, and Food of several hundred birds of about 50 species pointed out the seriousness of the problem in a part of the British Isles.

Lead poisoning is a problem in many countries.

British studies do not establish the effects on the fertility of the birds but show that birds dosed experimentally with lead shot appear to have less ability to migrate and higher mortality rates in the first year of the experiment. British investigators reported that 60 to 80 percent of adult mallards having one ingested pellet will die if they continue to feed on wild seeds.

Mr. Bellrose estimated that 1 percent of the deaths of mallards in the Mississippi Flyway each year is caused by lead poisoning.

Many deaths of ducks, geese, and swans in the Coeur d'Alene River area of Idaho since 1925 have been attributed to lead poisoning and to zinc and copper carried in the river and deposited on vegetation.

The loss of eight swans in the Jersey Zoo in England in 1965 brought the discovery that their gizzards were full of lead shot, which gradually had been worn down. It was then learned that the zoo had been established on a marsh that had been used by wild mallard ducks and by hunters. Spent shot accumulated on the bottom was picked up by the swans.

Many investigators, noting high losses of waterfowl in the Detroit River between Lake St. Clair and Lake Erie, examined more than 14 thousand redheads, canvasbacks, lesser scaup, and black ducks between 1948 and 1955. Their reports listed many causes of the mortality, including lead poisoning.

Investigators of the Bureau of Sport Fisheries and Wildlife, manufacturers of ammunition, and private organizations have sought a new kind of shotgun load. Lead coated with a plastic material has not been very effective in reducing the poison effect, but pellets composed of iron or other metal heavy enough to carry well from the gun muzzle may be adequate substitutes. Stopgap measures sometimes taken in heavily hunted marshes include throwing fine gravel over the muddy bottom areas in shallow water to cover derelict shot and increase the probability that birds will pick up the gravel rather than lead.

Measures to correct pollution sometimes are harmful to birdlife.

Among them are sewage lagoons, which are open, rather shallow ponds, to which total sewage

discharges from small communities are piped and pumped. Normal biological processes of decomposition and decay make the discharges relatively inoffensive. Effluents from the ponds are discharged through simple overflow devices into the nearest stream drainage. The process is automatic and economical and is sanctioned by State and Federal health authorities.

Within a short time after construction, the lagoons develop their own plant and animal organisms and attract waterfowl. Plant and animal foods are available, and the ponds make excellent resting areas for the birds.

That the lagoons can be a hazard, however, is pointed out in a report from Regina, Saskatchewan, that dead and dying grebes were found there. The birds had water-soaked plumage and were unable to float on the surface. A thick detergent scum was on top of the water. Living birds that were captured, cleaned, and retained in captivity recovered their waterproof condition within 2 weeks. It is evident that detergents and soaps entering the lagoon were detrimental to the welfare of the birds. In time, it is believed that the use of detergents that will decompose quickly in the lagoon will remove some of their threat to the resting birds.

Widespread losses of birds are due to oil floating on the surface of water. Water birds may set their wings, extend their feet, and glide into the smooth slicks of oil—traps from which few escape. Their feathers are covered immediately with oil. Natural buoyancy and insulation of feathers are quickly lost. The birds soon sink or freeze. If they try to preen and rearrange the feathers, their beaks become clogged with sticky goo, and some suffocate. A few may be able to lift themselves off the oil patches or swim free of them, but very likely the oil makes them sick and weak.

The problem is most acute in heavily traveled sealanes, especially along our east coast, the Atlantic shores of the British Isles, the Great Lakes, and the St. Lawrence. An increase in use of oil as

Air pollution is distasteful and potentially harmful to birds and people alike. This is New York City, lower half of Manhattan Island, in midafternoon of a normally clear day.

357

Visual measurement of air pollution pinpoints offenders and permits enforcement of air-pollution abatement measures.

fuel for ships and the expanding traffic of oil tankers made the problem acute after the First World War. The Congress passed the Oil Pollution Act in 1924 to cover the navigable territorial waters of the United States.

An International Conference on Pollution of the Sea by Oil was held in London in 1954 and again in 1962. The Convention of 1954 was ratified by 28 countries, including the United States, and the amendments of 1962 are accepted by 12 countries. Each country agreed to regulate the oil-handling activities of ships under its control or sailed by its nationals and to confine the shipping activities that may spill oil onto the surface of the ocean to specified areas where spills may be relatively harmless.

Although progress has been made, oil sometimes is handled carelessly, and tons of oil sometimes are released accidentally. One wreck off Canada in 1954 caused the death of 1,500 ducks. Oil jetti-

soned off Newfoundland in the winter of 1960 was reported to have killed 250 thousand razorbills, eiders, murres, and puffins. A collision of tankers off the Cape Cod Canal late in 1965 released enough heavy oil to endanger rafts of sea ducks wintering in the area.

An oil pipe burst on a tank farm at Savage, Minnesota, on the banks of the Minnesota River near its confluence with the Mississippi a few miles upstream from St. Paul. The oil—1.4 million gallons—was trapped by ice and caused no immediate problem. One month later, a tank of soybean oil about 70 miles upstream burst in subzero temperatures, and 3 million gallons oozed into two small tributaries and then into the Minnesota River. Late in March 1963, temperatures rose, the snow and ice melted, the oils thinned, and all the oil moved downstream into the Mississippi just in time to coat the open waters there when northward migrating ducks arrived. Estimates of dead and suffering birds were as high as 10 thousand. The National Guard worked to keep the oil from spreading into protected channels and bays, and citizens began picking up birds for cleaning and rehabilitation in a game refuge. By late June, most of the oil had been buried by new vegetative growth or by sand and wave action, but the public and the oil companies will never forget their losses.

Emulsifiers and detergents are available to help disperse oil lenses and slicks when they appear, but they are costly and are stopgap measures barely able to meet minor emergencies.

Better training of crews that handle oil cargoes, suitable equipment aboard ships and docks, tighter enforcement of existing laws, and the prompt reporting of trouble spots by the public will help to keep the careless disposal of oily substances to a minimum. Under the right conditions of temperature, microbial oxidation of the pollutants then can remove offending oils before they cause harm.

Another hazard to birds is the use of rock salt on highways in winter to control the slippery con-

Oil and oil wastes carelessly or accidentally dumped on the high seas and elsewhere create a problem for birdlife. This oil-soaked gannet on a beach at Nags Head, North Carolina, could not fly and soon died.

Industrial complexes generate immense pollution control problems. Ingenuity, expensive precautions, and constant vigilance are required to minimize contaminants in our rivers.

ditions. Birds attracted to the open highways, including pheasants and quail in search of grain and gravel, also pick up salt crystals or items of food that have become coated with salt.

Evidence of salt poisoning in birds has been recorded in Wisconsin. Pheasants and quail had suffered severe derangement of the central nervous system.

Pollution may not always kill birds directly, but it may lessen their supplies of food and deprive them of places to live.

Pelicans, cormorants, gulls, and some species of

ducks, which eat small fish, may nest near good fishing areas. If the fish are killed by pollution, the birds must leave.

Once in a while, the addition of moderate amounts of nitrogen and phosphorus from sewage effluent or wastes from meatpacking plants raises the fertility level of lakes to the point where additional plants of value to waterfowl may thrive. This condition usually is temporary. It does not persist in a stable pattern, because effluent will be added continually to the point where the lake becomes an open sewage lagoon. Decay of the plants, severe depletion of oxygen, death of fish, odors, and general unattractiveness may result, and the use of the area by waterfowl may be reduced.

The great number and variety of waterfowl, shore birds, and herons on our continent spend much of their winter time in the brackish estuarine waters of our coastlines. These waters also are nursery grounds for food fish, game fish, oysters, crabs, clams, and shrimp.

The coastline waters receive all pollution from a zone that has more than half of the petroleum refining plants of the country, half of the factories that make inorganic chemicals, and two-thirds of the factories that make agricultural pesticides, organic chemicals, and paper pulp. This zone, up to 250 miles deep along the Atlantic, Gulf, and Pacific coasts, also contains about 60 percent of all the people in the United States. Where isolated losses of birds may occur in specific trouble spots throughout the country, entire species and total continental populations of birds can be affected by the growing pollution of tidal marshes, coastal estuaries, and other waters where the rivers meet the sea.

Three case histories were given in 1965 in a Report of the Environmental Pollution Panel of the President's Science Advisory Committee. In Great South Bay and in Moriches Bay, Long Island, New York, a serious pollution problem has reduced the usefulness of the bays to waterfowl and has caused the failure of a shellfish industry, interfered with recreational use, and caused damage to nearby houses. Much of the early pollution came from farms rearing domesticated ducks;

Planned control of pollution benefits industry, people, birds, and fish, all dependent upon clean air and water.

A clean river is a healthy river for men and birds.

later pollution has been from septic tanks in new residential areas.

Barnegat Bay and Raritan Bay in New Jersey are similarly degraded from their early clean and useful conditions. A "red tide" situation in Barnegat Bay during the summer of 1964 at first was blamed on the effluent from a dye factory; later it was found to have been fostered by sewage and septic tank wastes containing organic nitrates and phosphates on which bacteria and algal organisms flourished. Up to 5 million cells per liter were produced in the bay.

In Raritan Bay, an analysis in 1951 showed the presence of many industrial chemicals as well as sewage contamination. Up to 1,087 parts of phenol were found in 1 million parts of water; 1,960 parts per million of formaldehyde; 5.8 parts per million of copper; and 375 parts per million of arsenic. Waters formerly used by people and ducks alike are no longer safe for either.

Information from 20 States in which highly acid waters drain from mines indicated that 5,800 miles of streams and 15 thousand acres of impoundments are damaged seriously by acid mine waters. These areas are mostly in the Ohio River Valley, primarily in bituminous coal fields.

In other parts of the country, mining for copper, zinc, phosphorus, silver, and barium releases additional waste waters into streams.

In West Virginia, 360 million gallons of acid mine waters containing high concentrations of sulphuric acid have been known to enter streams daily. This water is unfit for drinking and bathing and fish cannot live in it. Birds avoid streams and lakes that have high concentrations of such water.

The Detroit River below Detroit, Michigan, and Windsor, Ontario, for much of its distance from Lake St. Clair to Lake Erie is clean and useful to man and waterfowl. Below Detroit, however, the effluents from tremendous industrial complexes and from overloaded municipal sewage treatment facilities contain potent mixtures of chemical and biological wastes.

In winter, great flocks of ducks remain in the open water below Detroit. In the spring of 1960, an estimated 10 thousand ducks died in their sanctuary, some from oils, some from glycerides, and some from metal plating wastes and other poisons flowing through the area. Losses are especially severe because of the open water, the tendency for waterfowl to concentrate in large flocks in winter, and the relative scarcity of other places where the birds might go. State and Federal biologists, if given enough warning, can often drive the birds into cleaner waters and can hold them there by judicious use of grain feed until the more preferred wintering grounds are safe once more.

What to do about pollution?

Sanitary engineers have given us thoughtful, workable recommendations for the construction of necessary cleanup facilities. The cost will be high, but the public seems willing to pay it.

The President's Message on Natural Beauty on February 8, 1965, set forth the problems of pollution in our total environment. It indicated deep concern that entire regional airsheds are heavy with poisonous materials, that every major river system is now polluted, and that the longer we wait to act the greater the danger and the larger the problem of cleaning up wastes.

The Federal Water Quality Act of 1965 was designed to prevent pollution before it occurs rather than to work out cures for chronic illnesses. A vigorous Federal and State enforcement program is bringing pressure where it is most needed on cities and industries to prevent discharge of unsuitable wastes.

Beyond that, we need further research to test the effects of contamination levels in the air and to recommend effective control measures. We have no truly objective measure of the total extent of damage done to birds and wild animals by pollution. Investigations of such effects on living creatures other than people and domestic crops and animals are not the clear responsibility of any Federal agency. We reason that pollution can cause damage, that pollution is increasing, and therefore damage will increase. This documented trend must be stopped.

—RAYMOND E. JOHNSON.

Deathtraps in the Flyways

A PHYSICIAN driving through Eau Claire, Wisconsin, in the predawn hours of September 19, 1963, was startled to see hundreds of dead birds in the beams of his headlights. As he slowed down, he could see many more dead birds strewn on both sides of the highway. Dr. Charles A. Kemper, of Chippewa Falls, Wisconsin, was observing what happens when a massive migration strikes a thousand-foot television tower and its guy wires.

Birds have been flying over the general area of Eau Claire probably for hundreds of centuries on their annual pilgrimages to the South. The steel pylon that pierced the sky for a fifth of a mile is new.

At that height, the top of the tower poked squarely into the ancient migration route of millions of birds when bad weather forced them to lower altitude. Man had failed to inform the birds of the new obstacle in their path and unintentionally had made the obstacle even more inviting to birds on overcast nights by equipping it with aircraft warning lights.

The birds arrived in waves. Milling around the lights, thousands were killed or injured when they hit the tower. Others hit the cables or collided with other birds. Still others were killed on impact with the ground.

Forty-two species were identified among the 5,595 birds picked up on the night of September 18–19. About 11 of every 12 birds killed were vireos or warblers. Magnolia warblers had the highest fatalities—846.

The collision of birds with manmade structures is not a new development.

Shortly after the 555-foot Washington Monument was completed in 1884, birds began hitting it— "thousands probably being killed," one report said. It was not uncommon to find a bushel of dead birds killed during a night.

"Later as the city grew," the report said, "either the birds changed their course of flight or the survivors became educated concerning the dangers of the Washington Monument." Apparently few other birds hit the monument until aviation beacons were installed in 1931.

One of the earliest reports of migration collisions was that of September 21–27, 1887, when more than 40 species crashed into the Old Exposition Building in Milwaukee. The lighted structure stood some 200 feet high.

The Empire State Building (1,472 feet), the new Pan Am Building (808 feet) in New York City, the Statue of Liberty (305 feet), and the Philadelphia Savings Fund Building (491 feet) are among other flyway roadblocks at which migrating birds have been killed.

One of the worst offenders is not a building, tower, or monument, but a powerful searchlight, a ceilometer. Focused on cloud covers, the ceilometer is used to determine the cloud ceiling at airports. Migrating birds often cluster in the ceilometer beam, colliding with one another or swooping downward in confusion to hit the ground and buildings.

The use of filters over ceilometers has proved successful in preventing bird mortality, but not all ceilometers are filtered.

The danger from television towers is greater than ever because of the steady increase in the number of towers. By law they must carry warning lights. The increased heights of the towers also may prove a serious additional hazard.

One of the communication tower systems most

destructive to birdlife is the one maintained for the Navy at Midway Atoll in the Pacific. Interlacing cables and guy wires on 300-foot radar towers on Eastern Island killed 2,901 Laysan albatrosses between November 15, 1964, and May 22, 1965.

Harvey I. Fisher, of Southern Illinois University, reported those figures in November 1965 in an article prepared for Audubon Magazine. Dr. Fisher conducted a study of the Laysan albatross under a contract with the Office of Naval Research since 1961.

"We may be facing the elimination of one-sixth of the world's population of Laysan albatrosses because of one group of antennas on Eastern Island," he said. He estimated that continuation of the antenna mortality rate might reduce Eastern Island's 30 thousand breeding pairs to 500 pairs in 15 to 20 years, not counting whatever other adults of this long-lived species may have survived.

The new 2,063-foot television tower near Blanchard, North Dakota, is the tallest structure in the world. Fairchild, Wisconsin, has a new 2,000-foot tower. Other supertowers stand 1,795 feet at Shreveport, Louisiana; 1,751 feet at Knoxville, Tennessee; 1,749 feet at Columbus, Georgia; 1,676 feet at Cape Girardeau, Missouri; 1,638 feet at Paducah, Kentucky; 1,610 feet at Roswell, New Mexico, and 1,600 feet at Columbia, South Carolina, and Oklahoma City, Oklahoma. Plans for several supertowers have been contested in the courts.

Miles of tower guy wires multiply the hazard. The North Dakota structure has nine guy wires, each a quarter of a mile long. The tower in Shreveport has 7 miles of guy cables. The longest of its 24 guy cables extends close to half a mile. Cables and guy wires of such length on the supertowers may create flyway traps 50 to 100 yards wide in any direction at an altitude of a thousand feet or higher.

The location of most towers in timbered, brushy, or marshy terrain makes it difficult to find birds that might have been killed.

Not all mortality occurs in overcast weather with low cloud cover. Mrs. Amelia Laskey, an ornithologist in Nashville, Tennessee, has observed extensive casualties during clear weather around a tower. She said, however, that overcast and precipitation—

There are more than 500 TV towers in the United States. Some of them are more than 2 thousand feet high. Hundreds of thousands of migrating birds fly into them and are killed.

immediately preceding the good weather or in nearby areas—always are involved.

When Dr. Kemper drove to Eau Claire that day in September 1963, to continue his studies of the mortality of birds at television towers, he had been alerted that a massive migration was taking place. He had arisen at 4 a.m. and headed for the WEAU–TV tower in Eau Claire. He could see its flashing red beacon 12 miles away. The ground was wet, and the cloud ceiling hovered just above the top of the tower. Two days earlier he had found 195 dead birds at the tower.

During the night, Vincent Heig, a graduate stu-

dent in the University of Minnesota, had picked up thousands of birds by the time Dr. Kemper arrived.

"We continued picking up birds till about 8:30," Dr. Kemper reported. "Birds were still striking the tower even at that hour. Then suddenly they stopped."

He counted 464 birds in one parking lot of 8,100 square feet. He estimated a total kill of 15 thousand.

When the overcast continued into the following night, Dr. Kemper returned to the tower soon after sunset. The nocturnal migration again was in full swing.

"To count bird chips [the sounds emitted by birds during migration] would have been impossible," he reported. "It was almost a continuous peep-peep-peep. Birds were falling at the rate of four to six a minute within hearing range. You were lucky if you weren't clunked on the head by a falling bird.

"When a 1,000-candlepower television camera spotlight was aimed at the structure, we could see great masses of birds buzzing or milling around the tower. I made several counts of birds falling, some with the spotlight on and some with it off. The number diminished when the light was on. If the tower were sufficiently illuminated, perhaps more collisions could be prevented."

The 4,600 dead birds (46 species) picked up on the night of September 19–20, 1963, brought the two-night total to 10,195. This figure compared with the 1,525 birds of 40 species Dr. Kemper had picked up at the same tower on September 20, 1957, when thousands of warblers, thrushes, and tanagers were strewn everywhere—one dead bird about every 10 square feet. He estimated the September 20, 1957, toll at 20 thousand dead birds.

David W. Johnston, a biologist at Mercer University, estimated that 50 thousand birds were destroyed October 7–8, 1954, at the ceilometer of the Warner Robins Air Force Base near Macon, Georgia.

His estimate was based on the number of birds actually counted from the roof of the building where the ceilometer is housed and on a calculated density of birds lying on the runways and grass within a radius of a thousand feet from the ceilometer.

With what did the birds collide? With other birds, the ground, and nearby obstructions. Some birds flew on through the light beam, but others apparently were attracted by it.

Although the hazard of ceilometers can be reduced or eliminated by extinguishing or filtering their beams during overcast nights of a cold front period in the migration season, the problems of towers and high buildings remain. Collisions continue, especially if the lights on the structures are not turned off.

The Empire State Building might well be more destructive than it is, but its management douses the stationary searchlight during the migration seasons (September 15 to November 1 and April 15 to June 1). Revolving lights there are not hazardous to birds.

Only 24 hours before the stationary beam was to be turned off for the 1964 migrating season, the Empire State Building was the scene of a large migration kill. On Monday night, September 14, 1964, a heavy migration passed over Manhattan and ran afoul of the stationary beam. Ninety-four percent of the birds were warblers.

On September 15, 1964, Roland C. Clement, staff biologist of the National Audubon Society, collected 497 dead birds of 32 species from streets and rooftops near the Empire State Building.

Most migration casualties at towers and buildings, however, are not reported as fully as that at the Empire State Building—if they are reported at all.

Mrs. Elizabeth D. Velie of Long Lake, Minnesota, attempted in 1963 to tabulate the recorded mortality at towers and buildings. Her report, published September 1963, in The Flicker, official quarterly of the Minnesota Ornithologists' Union, covers as many recorded cases as she could find. Her first record is for September 21, 1887, and her last for September 12, 1961.

Mrs. Velie wrote: "There are about 500 television towers in the United States, and since our survey gives only random reports on 10 to 19, it is easy to imagine the magnitude of the loss in bird life."

To accumulate her data, she relied heavily on the established ornithological journals. She divided the tabulation into television and radio towers, airport ceilometers, and combined obstructions.

Dr. Charles A. Kemper and Daniel Rudahl search the vicinity of TV towers at Eau Claire, Wisconsin, for dead and wounded birds.

There is little uniformity in the source data. Some reports give the actual "size of kill;" some, the estimated figures; some, both actual and estimated figures; and some give no indication of the losses other than to say "large," "tremendous," "negligible," "trunkful," "severe," and so on.

Of 27 reports on bird mortality at television and radio towers (October 6, 1954, to September 14, 1961), 23 reported the number of dead birds picked up. These totaled 26,094. Eleven estimates of kills totaled 36 thousand.

Of 13 reports on airport ceilometers (1948 to September 12, 1961), only 7 listed the number of dead birds picked up, for a total of 5,943. Three

reports estimated total mortality, a combined total of 52,600.

Of 11 reports on combined obstructions (September 21, 1887, to September 12, 1961), 8 listed the number of dead birds picked up, a total of 8,185, after deduction of those counted in the tower and ceilometer lists. The estimated kill was reported in four instances, totaling 57,900 after deduction of duplicated figures.

All but two of the 46 reports that cited weather conditions linked poor weather to the bird losses. Generally the night was overcast, with a low cloud ceiling and rain or drizzle. Some reports cited windy nights. Others said the losses occurred during or following a sudden cold front. A few cited cold, wind, and rain.

One of the two exceptions was the report of bird mortality at the Washington Monument for the 1932, 1933, and 1935 fall migrations. Those losses occurred when the weather was "mostly clear, without moon, some wind."

The other exception involved collisions at four Florida shopping centers May 9–14, 1960, when the weather was bright and clear. Smoke clouds from brush fires may have forced the northbound birds to low altitude, where they flew into the shopping center window glass.

Herbert L. Stoddard, Sr., who supervises daily pickups of birds that have collided with the 673-foot and 1,010-foot TV towers on Tall Timbers Plantation, 20 miles north of Tallahassee, Florida, has noted a possible cause for optimism.

In a recent letter to me, he mentioned that the much larger girders and guy wires required for towers of tremendous height may make it easier for migrating birds to see the structures. The smaller guy wires of 500- to 1,000-foot towers probably are more dangerous, he said.

The presumption, however, that the higher the tower, the more devastating the damage to migrating flocks has been borne out to some extent by Dr. Kemper's studies. He has found no casualties around the 500-foot tower at Eau Claire.

The bird kills at the two Florida towers are

When the Empire State Building in New York is lighted, many birds fly at it and die. When its stationary searchlight is turned off during the migration season, the mortality of birds drops.

368

about equal, but the 1,010-foot tower has killed many more *species* than the 673-footer.

Mr. Stoddard wrote: "We are evidently getting birds from higher levels where many more waterfowl and shore birds and other high flyers are endangered."

While man's deathtraps in the flyways take a deplorable toll, the effects are not totally without benefit. The fallen birds are sent to university laboratories for scientific study.

Mr. Stoddard, who has shipped thousands of specimens to laboratories, has made some interesting findings without leaving the grounds—such as discovering that migrating finches continue flying despite heavy rain.

"Why," he asked, "should the vireos, warblers, and thrushes seek ground cover on the appearance of heavy rain, while finches continue their flight?"

Of the 149 species and 15,251 individual birds handled at the WCTV tower (Tall Timbers) from October 1955 to July 1, 1961, not a single eastern bluebird casualty was recorded.

Roy Anderson, of the Tennessee Game and Fish Commission, examines songbirds killed when they collided with a TV tower.

Even though the bluebird is primarily a day migrant, as Mr. Stoddard observed, it would seem that one or two would collide with the tower occasionally, just by accident. The bluebird is common at Tall Timbers all year.

Other thrushes, and the mockingbird, brown thrasher, and catbird, made up almost 10 percent of the total kill.

We have learned also that fall migrations suffer far higher losses at towers than spring migrations, and that the species killed in greatest numbers in the East and Midwest is probably the red-eyed vireo. This species represented about 20 percent (3 thousand) of all casualties at Tall Timbers in the period cited. The palm warbler was second with 8 percent (1,206).

The Tall Timbers records indicate that some species believed to be exclusively daytime migrants sometimes migrate at night. These include the mockingbird, the cardinal, the brown-headed cowbird, American goldfinch, the red-headed woodpecker, and the purple martin.

The toll of birdlife at towers and other high structures probably is more severe than the statistics show. Cats, dogs, owls, hawks, and other predators quickly dispose of many of the dead birds.

Even persons with experience as professional trappers or wildlife managers may be misled by the absence of dead birds near a tower.

Some mammals eat birds without leaving a trace. Owls may do likewise or carry them off to their young. Rain and winds quickly disperse the feathers.

To ascertain losses to scavengers, Mr. Stoddard places 8 or 10 dead "test birds" on the lawn about once a week. If a third or a half of the test birds disappear by morning, the need for scavenger control is obvious. Otherwise, the research station's study may have little value.

House cats and opossums consume many tower kills, but Mr. Stoddard cited the great horned owl as worse than all other scavengers. Screech owls make inroads on the birds, but the horned owls quickly eliminate their smaller cousins. More than a dozen horned owls were trapped, marked, and released 200 to 500 miles distant. None has been retrapped at Tall Timbers.

While the owl problem has not been solved, Mr. Stoddard believes that the presence of one great horned owl is helpful, since it holds the numbers of cats, opossums, and skunks to a minimum.

Crows are wily and persistent intruders. They search the tower area systematically at sunrise. When Mr. Stoddard tried to beat them to their reconnaissance by patrolling the area just before sunrise, the crows came in 20 minutes earlier. Several flew just in front of his car, picking up small birds that he had headed for.

Rats, herring gulls, and other creatures not present at Tall Timbers are almost certain to make short work of tower-killed birds in other parts of the country. Only an all-night vigil and use of test birds can ascertain the loss to predators at each tower during the migration season, especially in deep grass or marshy country.

Dr. Kemper reported that if the casualty toll at Eau Claire is small, the crows will take most of the dead birds before he can get to them. The thirteen-lined ground squirrel is also a serious interloper at Eau Claire.

"If you arrive at the tower very much after sunrise," Dr. Kemper informed me, "most of the birds will be gone because of crows and ground squirrels. Thus, if less than 200 birds hit the tower, and you come at 8 a.m., you might be misled into thinking few or no birds were killed."

We have no evidence that any of our rare or endangered species have run afoul of towers, buildings, or ceilometers, but the possibility of such a disaster is reason for concern.

Chandler Robbins, an ornithologist in the Bureau of Sport Fisheries and Wildlife, believes that a comparatively small number of towers located in a peculiar geographic pattern may cause excessively high mortality among certain age-sex classes of a given species to the point where its breeding potential over a wide area may be seriously affected. He suggests that more and higher towers may increase casualties a decade from now more than a hundredfold.

He cited the purple sandpiper and Ipswich sparrow as species that may suffer severe losses to supertowers and ceilometer beams.

Most migration collisions probably can be avoided if the tower or ceilometer lights are switched off or filtered.

About 2 a.m. on September 11, 1960, birds began concentrating in the ceilometer beam of Berry Field, the municipal airport at Nashville. A meteorologist placed a filter over the bright ceilometer beam, and the birds dispersed without a casualty.

A ceilometer operating without a shield or filter at Duluth, Minnesota, on October 18, 1963, however, soon was the center of falling birds. Eighty-two birds were killed in half an hour. At 9 p.m. the light was turned off and casualties ceased.

The National Park Service says there is no logical explanation, from its observations, for bird losses at the Washington Monument. The Monument, over the years, has been floodlighted from dusk to midnight. Red aircraft warning lights have flashed throughout the night. In 1959, both the floodlights and aircraft lights were modernized and their candlepower greatly increased.

Migration casualties were numerous before 1959 and for a year or two following installation of the new lighting, but it is now a rare occurrence to find a dead bird in the morning. Can any significance be attributed to the modernization of the floodlighting, or has the migratory bird flight pattern changed relative to the Washington Monument?

The Bureau of Sport Fisheries and Wildlife has tested luminous tapes and other devices intended to make high structures more easily visible and less deadly to birdlife. Eventually we may find a solution to this mortality problem that will match our advances in engineering and electronics.

Until then, those of us who are interested in safer flights for migrating birds will have to rest our hopes on perennial good weather conditions.

—John Vosburgh.

BLUE-WINGED TEAL

Mark What You Leave

TIDAL WAVES OF SETTLERS and fortune-seekers surged across the lush wilderness of North America for a full century after the American Revolution put an end to the Proclamation of 1763, which the British had imposed so as to contain westward expansion.

They were exciting, dangerous, profligate, and productive years for an America that was finding its first strength as a Nation.

They were doleful days for wildlife, which Nature had evolved to help stabilize the plains and forests: Entire populations of some species were reduced to remnants or to extinction. For the stragglers that lived on into the 20th century, the epitaph could have been written by the generations that broke the prairies.

To say that it could have been otherwise is but the wisdom of hindsight. Land-hungry settlers gave little thought to Nature as a community of living things—they even trampled one another as they rushed to occupy the new lands. The wonder is that more species of wildlife were not eliminated.

The history of land use in the Northeastern States illustrates the changes man brings about in wildlife populations in pursuing his own ends. The lesson to learn here is that the axe, the torch, and the plow and dragline can be used constructively only when people understand their long-range effect on the whole environment.

When the first colonists landed, there was the forest primeval—almost overwhelming to a people from more developed countries. It was not, however, the unbroken stand of forest patriarchs Longfellow pictured in his poem, "Evangeline."

The Indians, who had been here at least since the ice of the last great glaciers melted back, had altered parts of the primitive forest by burning to clear underbrush and by cutting trees for sundry uses. Even so, their needs for land were so modest as to leave untouched extensive stands of fine, mature trees. Primitive stands were more diversified in age and size than those we see today, which, in many places, are what they are because of forest management.

As always under natural conditions, the trees of yesteryear grew in communities. In these natural communities grew also an associated group of shrubs, ground flora, soil organisms, mammals, birds, and insects.

Typical of the mixed deciduous forest of the Northeast were such permanent resident species as the pileated and hairy woodpeckers, the white-breasted nuthatch, and the wild turkey. Among the typical summer residents were such small birds as the scarlet tanager, solitary vireo, and hermit thrush.

One of the colonists' first tasks was to clear this forest in order to plant crops, to protect themselves against Indians, who were made unfriendly by the greed of some colonists, and to ward off malaria, for the forests were thought to be malaria ridden. Indeed, settlers in some areas avoided the valleys and used only the hilltops for agriculture and residence.

Now, to convert a forest to pasture or cornfield entails a drastic change in habitat.

Cutting a forest means eliminating a community of organisms that has lived in association a long time. The pileated woodpecker, the scarlet tanager, and other inhabitants of the mature woodland are now made homeless. They do not, cannot go elsewhere because, at least during the nesting season, other forests are already tenanted to capacity.

No, these displaced animals roam about looking for a vacant niche, and a great many of them perish without finding one. They vanish from the landscape.

So, in learning that the destruction of a forest involves the destruction of most of its associated animals and plants, we also learn a principle of conservation. That is that we should retain at least samples—and sizable ones—of all the major vegetation types that Nature has produced in a region. Not only will such forests, or prairies, or marshes help perpetuate many dependent species, they will be of great scientific interest and value to the forester, the botanist, and the zoologist. They can be of esthetic and spiritual value to all perceptive citizens.

But this is only half the story. Cutting the forest has *changed* the habitat; it has not destroyed its potentialities for production. The sun still shines here, rain falls, and the soil, if not allowed to erode, still contains the mineral and organic accumulations of centuries, perhaps millennia. The pastures the colonists developed supplanted the forest and made a different kind of habitat. Its tall redtop grasses and timothy provide a cover that meets the needs of the bobolink and the meadowlark, birds that were confined largely to the natural meadows near streams and marshes when the region was densely forested.

The woodsmen's axe and saw rival the plow in the changes they have produced in bird populations. The clean-cutting of a forest does away with a whole community of living things, including wildlife.

Because the early colonists tilled the land by hand and later with the help of the horses, oxen, and mules, their fields were small, especially in the glaciated part of the Northeast, where boulders left by the melting ice littered the fields and had to be cleared away before a plow could be used. Little draining of fields was done. The corners of fields, whether marked by split-rail fences or stone walls, were left untilled and unweeded. Such farms were ideal for bluebirds and bobwhite, which quickly expanded their populations into the new habitats and became common where they had been uncommon or rare. The ruffed grouse, a bird of the forest edge rather than of deep woods, also found the new patchwork landscape to its liking and prospered—for a while.

Almost species for species, we see a woodland population of birds replaced by another typical of open country, of pasture and hedgerows, and

the borders of second-growth woods. Meanwhile, the forest waits in the wings until allowed to recapture old territory.

American agriculture reached its zenith about 1850, if measured by land in crops.

About that time, the more easily worked lands of the interior began producing in competition with eastern farms, even though the costs of transportation to market were greater. This new competition initiated a great exodue from the difficult, rocky, hill-country farms of the Northeast. Some farmers moved west to work the better lands. Others moved into the growing towns and cities.

It was a dramatic phase of our society's rapid transition to urban life. Throughout the first quarter of the 20th century, this movement from the farm worried many persons. There was talk of agricultural decadence, and everyone knew what this could mean to the Nation. Even today,

374

many mistakenly refer to soil exhaustion as the cause. The myth died hard, but we have finally come to recognize this shift as a form of technological displacement. Between 1850 and 1950, some 13 million acres of agricultural land were allowed to go back to the native vegetation in the New England States, New York, and Pennsylvania.

This reversion from abandoned pasture to native plants is an orderly process. Pasture grasses must be mowed and fertilized if they are to be maintained in regions of high rainfall, such as most wooded regions. The neglect of such husbandry will quickly favor other plants—daisies, goldenrod, dewberry, yarrow. When they dominate, the bobolink, which came to occupy the tall-hay meadow, will abandon the field, and other species, like the field sparrow and the Henslow's sparrow, will move in.

Then comes a shrub stage, with bayberry along the Atlantic coast, chokeberry, shadblows, and others. Anyone who knows that song sparrows prefer this sort of habitat also knows that this phase in the history of the landscape will favor song sparrows for a while, then towhees and brown thrashers. Yellowthroats will move in where the new tangles of weeds and shrubs are moist.

As woody plants return, there is a gradual transition back to forest again. First, in the Northeast, comes a short-lived generation of junipers, thornapples, cherry, gray birch, aspens, sassafras, and others, the pioneers varying with the region and the water relations of the soil.

Birds and mammals have an important role in distributing the seeds of trees and shrubs.

These are soon followed by maples, oaks, and hickories. What appeared to be mere plant succession is soon recognized as plant-animal, or community, succession. We are even becoming aware of the fact that some of the trees have simply "waited" through the agricultural phase. The roots of ancient trees, still alive below the pasture, are sending forth new shoots, which need only the cessation of mowing and grazing to prosper. Not all mighty oaks from little acorns grow.

The early pole-stage forest also has its typical birds. American redstarts supplant yellowthroats and chestnut-sided warblers at this stage. Ovenbirds and wood thrushes come in when a closed canopy has been formed. Animal occupants change in kind and number as one plant community succeeds another in time.

Anyone who has seen stone walls in a New England woodland should have stopped to ponder this seeming anomaly, realizing that stone walls are not built for the fun of it. These walls must once have enclosed pastures or other agricultural openings. Indeed, they testify to the historical sequence of landscape changes we have been discussing.

In many places in the Northeast today, the cycle of forest destruction and recovery is nearly completed. New woodlands now approach maturity on land cleared by the colonists between 1650 and 1750, farmed for a few generations, and abandoned about 1850. The pileated woodpecker and the scarlet tanager have returned to these acres, which once harbored other generations of their kind but which nurtured quite different species for the century or two that man forced change upon the land.

And so it will ever be, provided only that the changes we make are not so drastic as to lead to the extermination of plant and animal species or the depletion or pollution of soil and the water table.

New England will never be quite the same for our having made it over, because the passenger pigeon and the heath hen are gone now. And in New England at least it is a question whether the wild turkey can come back as long as the American chestnut continues to succumb to the attack of the accidentally introduced fungus that has eliminated almost all the mature individuals that once furnished so much valuable food for so many kinds of wildlife.

The relationships between land and birds I have outlined for the northeastern forest apply equally to all wildlife and in every other region of this continent and the world.

Only the actors and the sequences in this natural drama change.

Lands can be managed today so as to attract and favor a particular species. The tall-grass pastures of early New England, so productive of bobolinks, are now almost gone. There are still many good pastures in the Northeast, but most of them—the best of them from the current economic viewpoint—are sown to clovers, which are too low to produce much cover for birds. So the bobolink and another tall-grass species, the upland plover, have both declined in numbers as a result. That, of course, merely returns these two species to precolonial status, but some day, if we decide to value such neighbors above certain other products of the land, we will at least know how to produce the conditions that attract them.

Rotations, or the lack of them, have a similar significance.

Many crops have been planted traditionally only at intervals of years, the length of the interval varying with the crop and the region. That was done to minimize insect attack and permit the soil to regain fertility.

The direct attack on insects made possible by chemical insecticides and fertilizers has tempted many farmers to reduce or give up rotations. In many sections, corn now is sown after corn, year after year. This spreads a festive board for the insect and other enemies of corn, and they thrive to the point where the farmer must use chemical pesticides routinely. And because many of these chemicals have been persistent ones, the soil in places has become poisoned for many desirable forms of life, including the birds that formerly took advantage of the plant diversity the rotations provided.

If the species involved were all local, permanent residents, the damage done by such practices would be local and therefore subject to quick repair. Population pressure from unaffected areas soon would fill the vacuum.

But the threat may be more serious with tran-

Some of man's changes are quite acceptable to some birds. This eastern phoebe nests on a beam of a bridge.

Birds fitted to live in the tall grasses of the prairie fared badly as prairies were plowed.

sient species. A species whose population migrates along narrow pathways in its annual trek up and down the continent may have a large proportion of its total numbers exposed to pesticidal contamination in a relatively few places. Exactly this sort of threat hangs over such species as the shore birds and some of the waterfowl that use a few favorite resting and feeding places in migration. For some of these birds—buff-breasted sandpipers, golden plover, the tenuous population of Eskimo curlews, and some of the geese—fallow fields that lie as inviting as of old have become poisoned by persistent chemicals.

Agricultural demand for land, surprisingly enough, is actually expected to decline by some 50 million acres during the next 20 years. This would be the first major reduction in farm acreage since the white man occupied the continent, because past changes have been shifts in use as new areas have been opened to replace others that were being abandoned.

But the necessary intensification of agriculture on even a reduced acreage brings problems.

It will first (as at present) contribute to a population explosion of such grain-eaters as the blackbirds, and create a demand for their destruction.

Secondarily, as is true already in fruit-producing districts, many species (such as robins, waxwings, orioles, and other colorful migrants, which play an important role in maintaining ecological balance in the landscape) will become increasingly serious competitors with farmers who are caught in the vise of narrowing profit margins.

It is well to recognize that these are problems in land use. It is not the birds that have changed so much as our use of land and our economics. It is therefore proper that careful consideration be given to where the major adjustments should be made.

The pursuit of "efficiency" and short-run economic advantage tends to oversimplify the landscape, favoring monoculture instead of diversity. These practices are poisoning whole food chains. In their effects on birdlife we see a first reason for questioning their long-run social wisdom. Indeed, the very progress of agricultural technology has forced us to take another look at agricultural ecology.

Dr. David Pimentel of Cornell University has suggested that we need to reconsider the commitment to clean farming that has eliminated hedgerows and fence-corner vegetation in this genera-

Men and machines have made vast changes in the use and distribution of surface water—changes that have reduced habitat for marsh and water birds.

tion. His research into the significance of diversity in Nature has begun to document the fact that man needs Nature's help in minimizing insect damage to crops. Some years ago the English ecologist Charles Elton warned that we had better leave some of this job to Nature.

Consider water habitats also. The end link of many an aquatic food chain is often a bird, whether tied to the water surface, like a loon or grebe, or freer to move about, like the bald eagle, which is a fisheater. The herons, ibises, storks, gallinules, rails, ducks, shore birds, and several others are dependent on aquatic habitats. Man's activities, through drainage, diversion, or flooding of land surfaces, have a pronounced effect on the status and distribution of these bird populations.

The blackbird explosion that is so much talked about today, if analyses of censuses bear it out, may well be related in part to our drainage activities of the past century. It is probable that 35 percent or more of our wetlands (marshes, swamps, and small ponds) already have been drained and thus made useless to marsh and aquatic birds and other animals that depended on them.

For most birds, this shrinkage of habitat has meant a corresponding decline in numbers, but not for the red-wing, our commonest blackbird. This species simply shifted to upland nesting sites and prospered, since there is much more upland than there ever was marshland.

Just how this shift in habitat took place is uncertain, for it occurred over several decades and we paid little attention to it until recently. Red-wings have always used a wide variety of nesting sites, however, from the usual—and still used—cattail marsh to tall-grass pastures, and even trees. It is likely that when wetlands were drained or filled, the displaced birds had to join their less orthodox, upland-nesting relatives, and soon learned by imitation that a nestful of young could be produced on dryland.

The duck tribe has not been so fortunate. Some species can and do nest in upland fields and woods borders, but they need wetlands to raise their young to maturity.

Some clue to the importance of wetlands—so often considered wastelands by people brought up in ignorance of Nature's food chains—is evident

378

in the food requirements of a wading bird colony.

The young of the white ibis, for example, are fed about seven times daily during the 50 days of their nestling life. Each nestling is fed an average of 183 items daily. A sample diet was composed of 56 crayfish, 78 grasshoppers, 41 cutworms, and 8 small snakes. Multiplied by three birds per nest and 50 days, and adding the food requirements of the two parents, we find that one family of ibises will consume some 36 thousand items during the nesting season.

Our largest colony of white ibis is at the National Audubon Society's Alafia Banks Sanctuary near Tampa, Florida. It contained 3,750 nesting pairs in 1963. At the rate of consumption I mentioned, this one colony would require 135 million food items. But Alafia Banks is also the nesting site of 7,500 adult cattle egrets, 500 snowy egrets, 500 Louisiana herons, 400 little blue herons, 400 yellow-crowned night herons, 200 glossy ibis, 200 common egrets, and 50 black-crowned night herons!

Philip Kahl, Jr., a research biologist for the National Audubon Society, computed the food requirements in terms of minnows of a 6-thousand pair colony of wood ibis in the Society's Corkscrew Swamp Sanctuary in Florida, as more than 2.5 million pounds per season. That is 1,250 tons of small fish, all of which the birds must gather in shallow waters less than 20 miles from the nesting site.

The importance of permanent surface water becomes obvious in the light of such food requirements for only two among the many wading bird species. And as natural wetlands inevitably diminish as man remakes the landscape, it is equally obvious that we will have to manage waters in order to produce the food required to maintain heronries and other colonies of nesting birds, even where sanctuary has already been provided.

An important part of this task is for the biologist to provide a formula for including these wildlife values in the calculations and programs of the engineering profession, since engineers have the first responsibility in planning water diversion works, which can mean life or death for the water birds and many other forms of wildlife. Wiser planning could do much to make impoundments and diversions contribute greatly to the perpetuation of a variety of habitats that in turn would maintain animals of all sorts.

The new rice culture developed since the Second World War in Arkansas, the Great Valley of California, and in coastal Louisiana and Texas is one of the dramatic changes of land use that illustrates the effect of water on wildlife.

In the early 18th century, when the American population was hemmed in by the mountain barrier of the Appalachians, rice culture flourished in the southeastern lowlands, in the bayou country, and at the mouths of large rivers. With rising labor costs in the 19th century, however, most of these rice farms were abandoned. Old canal systems in lowland South Carolina and Georgia are even today mute testimony to this bygone agricultural era.

The advent of new mechanical tools—notably powersaws to clear swamp timber (in Arkansas) and draglines to ditch swamps and marshes—after the Second World War created new opportunities for the economic development of wetlands. Government subsidies aimed at stimulating growth rather than balancing values, favored the rapid development of a new rice-growing industry. Some 3 million acres were devoted to rice in the mid-South in 1960.

This is intensive, heavily capitalized agriculture. It requires technological competence. The new rice farmers have progressed from the use of farm horses and mules to the airplane in a few years. Nowhere else is the airplane so intimately associated with agriculture. Seeding, fertilization, control of weeds by herbicides, and spraying of chemical insecticides are done by airplane. Pilots and planes are available from specialized agricultural service companies. In practice, 2 years of rice production are rotated with 3 years of use as improved pasture for beef production. Nearly a million acres thus are flooded for rice each year.

This rice-growing region is the winter home of 4.5 million ducks and geese, an important segment of the North American waterfowl population, including the most important part of the blue goose-snow goose population. Millions of other birds, notably shore birds, terns and gulls, herons, ibises, and blackbirds, also use these wetlands at some time of the year.

379

Striking changes have taken place in the distribution and habits of birdlife, but the intensive use of 3 million acres of seasonally wet lands has not really eliminated a like amount of habitat from wildlife use. An interesting and important point, that. The new rice culture, imposed partly on original marshes and partly on the nearby coastal prairie, actually has introduced a more stable environment than existed previously.

The vast coastal marshes of Louisiana, like the primeval forest, were a patchwork of successional stages recovering from the disruptions of fire, hurricane tides, and overgrazing by geese and muskrats. The wintering geese followed wherever appropriate stages of plant succession furnished good conditions of food and cover. Sometimes they did not use large tracts of these marshes intensively for years at a time because of unfavorable feeding conditions.

So, as long as man's management involves secondary benefits to wildlife without direct conflict with the primary objective, it contributes to regional diversity and may actually enhance production of wildlife. Canalization of the marshes, for example, has provided permanent water, which is helpful for broods of young ducks, and furnishes feeding grounds for herons and other wading birds. Even in this region of high annual rainfall (45 to 60 inches), seasonal drought may dry out natural pools.

Hosts of insects and other invertebrates are forced out of hiding when the ricefields are flooded in the spring. They are a great attraction to migrant shore birds, terns, the smaller gulls, herons, gallinules, and others, and this feeding by these big birds, which seldom are thought of as insectivorous, reduces greatly the numbers of insects. Their droppings also improve the fertility of the soil.

Of the birds that use ricefields, farmers have no love for transient red-winged blackbirds and summer-resident purple gallinules and fulvous tree ducks because they eat rice and interfere with its cultivation. A new practice of raising crawfish in ricefields after the harvest may encounter new problems, when the glossy ibis, white ibis, and the herons discover this source of natural food. Unfortunately, also, where rice and cotton have preempted the coastal prairie of Louisiana and Texas, these crops have destroyed much habitat of prairie chickens.

Wildfires in forests are a scourge to wildlife—but controlled fire in the hands of skilled technicians sometimes is a tool of forward-looking management.

380

Everywhere similar changes are going on.

The irrigation of millions of acres in the West has improved habitats here for a variety of birds. However, the precious water sometimes is obtained by impounding strategic lowlands. The total number of birds may have increased, but a number of interesting localized forms may have been eliminated or greatly reduced.

We see this today in the interior valleys of California, where some shallow waters have been canalized or impounded so as to reduce natural wetlands habitat to zero. Because these are the only waters of their kind in the region, the waterfowl have been thrown into conflict with agriculture. Birds like the American avocet and the black-necked stilt also have been much reduced in numbers locally and regionally, because this was their main breeding ground. Only the national wildlife refuge system and other sanctuaries now stand between them and oblivion.

Elsewhere the introduction of small but reliable amounts of water has improved the carrying capacity of arid regions. The "gallinaceous guzzler" of modern wildlife managers is an example. These half-buried (for shade), cement-lined water troughs have been good for quail in places where only a few birds once barely got along.

Large impoundments may or may not enhance regional diversity, depending on whether manipulations of water levels make their margins unproductive. In the Midwest, however, large reservoirs on major streams have become important wintering grounds for ducks, geese, and bald eagles.

The year-round productivity of many of these reservoirs, as also of natural lakes and bays elsewhere, however, is being impaired by the disturbance of the hordes of outboard motorboat enthusiasts, who penetrate every cove that has not been specifically barred to such traffic. Protection from human disturbance is especially important to the survival of colonial birds—pelicans, cormorants, herons, gulls, and terns—which nest on islands in large bodies of water.

So far we have considered only the results of man's necessary remaking of the landscape to satisfy his needs. We have noticed that as long as our activities are not too drastic, as long as we leave oases of natural lands, Nature has means of rebuild-

The stump of a giant cypress in Mingo Swamp, a reminder of the magnificent forest that once graced this part of southeastern Missouri. The swamp was the home of the ivory-billed woodpecker 100 years ago. Logging and drainage did away with the mature forest and the ivorybills, too.

ing her communities once we are through with the land. And our needs do change, from generation to generation and from society to society.

But there have been great abuses also, abuses that have wasted the basic resource, the land itself. These include destructive burning; overgrazing; careless plowing; unwise disturbances of native vegetation in brittle environments; excessive drainage of prairie potholes; the pollution of air, land, and water by industrial and municipal wastes; oil at sea or in coastal waters; and the careless use of persistent chemical pesticides.

It is ironic that our concern for birds and other wildlife has been among the basic causes of our awakening to the Nation's conservation needs. For, ultimately, conservation is not for the birds, but for mankind. We must learn that the power given men by modern technology is particularly susceptible to abusive overuse unless an ecological orientation can be provided all farmers and other land managers.

Today's most disturbing portent is that a new wave of human population has been abuilding with almost frightening momentum and that this population, equipped now with all the powerful appurtenances of technology, is again cresting across the land.

In the wake of this second human remaking of the face of America, several more species—particularly those that have already been reduced to remnant populations—are certain to perish unless our generation sees to it that their needs are met, and their survival insisted upon.

It has taken man a long time to include birds in his world view. Early man was deeply involved with a few large birds through his totemistic view of Nature. The eagle, which symbolized power and freedom, always was respected and honored. Men wore its tailfeathers proudly, and a man might derive courage from eating the heart of an eagle he caught by hand from a pit dug into a hillside.

To the Egyptians, the falcon symbolized a sun god, since it soared through the heavens with the ease of the sun itself.

A totem animal was a bond with Nature, a covenant that would give the families of men the sort of eternal stability they thought they saw in the animal species.

But this totemistic involvement included only the larger, more dramatic, more important wild animals. Smaller birds had little or no sanctity. They were for eating, for boys and women to pursue.

When western civilization developed, we abandoned the totemistic mythology as superstitious but put nothing more sophisticated in its place. For centuries thereafter, wild birds and other animals became mere things, the furniture or decor of Nature, divorced from man—so it was thought and taught.

I hope it is true that, as I believe, we can now see glimmerings of a new, deeper, and more humble realization that man and birds are related "nations" that share the same great adventure in time—evolution.

As our acceptance and appreciation of the evolutionary viewpoint become more central to our orientation, we will look back with awe, with a piety touched with pathos, at those other living things that mark the stages in our progress.

Among all these, birds will continue to please us more than most, and we will pay more heed to their requirements for survival as we make over the planet to satisfy our human needs and aspirations. It is not—as my friend Ian McMillan has pointed out—so much that we need rare species like the California condor, but rather that we need to save them. The attributes of wonder, humility, and selflessness that we must exercise in order to safeguard the existence of other species are the very attributes we will need to exercise in working out our own survival as a civilization, even as a species.

For, ultimately, we must ask this question: Whose is the land? Too often is the Bible quoted by greedy individuals to justify our disregard of the needs of other species: "*. . . and let them [man] have dominion over the fish of the sea, and over the fowl of the air, and over the cattle, and over all the earth, and over every creeping thing that creepeth upon the earth.*" (Genesis 1:26)

What folly it is to assume that so great a privilege should impose no responsibilities to husband these resources wisely!

The Bible, indeed, contains many admonitions to safeguard the earth's productivity, but it is even more important, I suggest, to accept an obligation to be receptive to new revelations.

The new science of ecology has taught us that only in biotic diversity can there be stability. And biology, in elucidating the significance of organic evolution, has once again reminded men that they are indeed their brothers' keepers.

In remaking the earth to suit ourselves we must somehow learn, and quickly, to rid ourselves of that tendency of our civilization to crowd all God's creatures, but man, from the face of the earth.

Edwin Arlington Robinson reworded the injunction that has echoed down the halls of time since we became conscious of our humanity:

> *Whether you will or not*
> *You are a King, Tristram,*
> *For you are one*
> *Of the Time-tested few*
> *That leave the world,*
> *When they are gone,*
> *Not the same place it was.*
> *Mark what you leave.*
>
> —ROLAND C. CLEMENT.

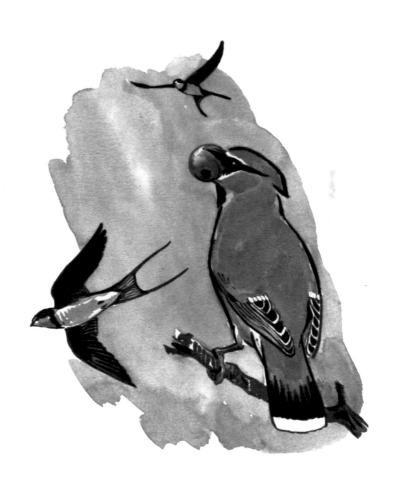

For Better or Worse

Birds at Airports

THE CRASH OF AN AIRPLANE after colliding with a flock of starlings at Logan International Airport in Boston in 1960 made us all aware of two problems long known to pilots. Pilots knew that many kinds of birds gather on runways, but when aircraft were relatively slow and maneuverable, even on takeoff, they counted on being able to lift a wing over the birds that rose in front of them.

Also, in the early days of experimental radars, technicians in the United States and abroad realized that large sea birds were giving them good echoes and confusing images on radar screens.

Since 1960, the amount of air traffic and the speed of aircraft have zoomed, and so has the seriousness of the two problems.

Because of a much greater thrust of a jet engine and high speeds on takeoff and landing, a pilot must concentrate his attention on handling the aircraft so completely that he cannot let himself be diverted by the actions of birds, and he usually is unable to maneuver to avoid them.

Furthermore, the fine tuning and the tremendous speeds of the jet engine make it highly vulnerable to damage from stones, bolts, and other objects it might suck in. Magnetic sweepers now are used to keep runways clean of debris, but the hazard of birds to aircraft has become worse.

An example is the large number of collisions with albatrosses at the U.S. Naval Air Station on Midway Island, near the western end of the Hawaiian chain. There soaring albatrosses, each weighing 4 to 8 pounds, played in the updrafts about 200 feet over the runways just where pilots were least able to maneuver. Some relief was had when ground along the runways was leveled to reduce updrafts and the leveled areas were paved to keep the birds from nesting within 750 feet of the center of the runways.

But Midway is not the only airport with problems. Difficulty has been experienced on our west coast, at Air Force bases in the South, several airports along the Great Lakes, and in Eastern States. Concern with bird hazards at airports is especially high in Europe. Bird hazards do not seem to vary with the volume of air traffic but by location. British Overseas Air Corporation reported its hazards to be most serious east of the Suez Canal.

Although it is albatrosses at Midway, it may be black kites at Dakar or herons in India and the eagle-kites in Malaysia. It may be vultures and snow geese at gulf coast military bases, tree swallows at Kennedy International Airport in New York, starlings at Boston.

It is generally agreed, however, that the most serious hazards almost everywhere are gulls. Crows are next, especially in western Europe. Shore birds are a close third in most countries.

In Europe, the shore birds are primarily golden plovers and lapwings. In the New World, they are primarily black-bellied plovers and some of the sandpipers. Mourning doves and horned larks often are hit in the United States because of their abundance on inland airports. Not hit so frequently but still hazardous because of their large size are the swans and geese. A collision between a jet trainer plane and a snow goose caused the death of an astronaut in Texas.

The Federal Aviation Agency and its equivalents in other countries have requested that damage to aircraft be reported so that the where, when, and why of bird damage can be evaluated.

The Bureau of Sport Fisheries and Wildlife identifies the remains of birds involved in the strikes. Some amazing items have come to light:

A mallard hit at 22 thousand feet, an evening grosbeak high over the Rockies, and an island thrush at 15 thousand feet over the South China Sea.

Such information tells us how frequent the strikes are. It establishes that (despite a few spectacular records at high altitudes) most collisions take place at low levels and at high speeds and that the chief zone of hazard is takeoff and landing.

The information is reassuring, too. It indicates that heavy incidence is measured as one, two, or three collisions per 10 thousand landings and takeoffs and that most collisions do no damage at all.

The chief hazard to military aircraft at a NATO fighter base in The Netherlands is during high-speed, low-level operations. Their experiences are confirmed in Canada and at U.S. Air Force bases in Southeastern States. In fact, military administrators in Europe know that low-level, high-speed training operations may have to be postponed at certain times when many birds are migrating.

Why are there birds at airports?

The answer is clear enough if you look at an airport from a bird's viewpoint. Most airports are so attractive to birds that you may well think they were designed to be wildlife refuges.

Consider Logan International Airport. It was built on many square miles of onetime mudflats and gravel bars, bare at low tide, once a major gathering place for migrating shore birds, and the wintering ground of more than 5 thousand black ducks. Large mussel beds around it are a magnet for herring gulls.

Raised runways were built, but between the runways, to hold costs down and to help drainage, low areas were left; they now are filled with fresh water. Before 1960, the edges of these ponds and most of the low places on the airport were heavily grown up with tall reeds; beyond them, on the edges of the runways, were bushes, including bayberry and sumac.

Thus, although the area had not been planned that way, it provided a maximum amount and variety of habitat and edge. (Edge, the margin between different habitats, is highly attractive to birds and other forms of wildlife.) Ponds, reeds, bushes, and edge altogether make an inviting oasis close to the asphalt and bustle of busy Boston.

At Kennedy International Airport, New York,

Laysan albatrosses at Sand Island, Midway Atoll, are friendly birds, but they have caused problems on runways at the Naval Air Station on Midway.

bayberry bushes were planted to hold the soil at the ends of the runways. Large numbers of tree swallows on their autumn migration from the Northeast gather behind the sand dunes and in the bushes, especially in bad weather when the birds feed on the berries instead of insects.

The bayberry bushes could be removed, of course, but the problem is larger than that: The airport was built on the migration route of hundreds of thousands of swallows. Many say that the airport is more important than the migrating swallows or the ducks that gather in large numbers in a tract into which the airport has been expanding. But as long as there are swallows and ducks, their hazard to aircraft must be faced.

Airports can be planned to avoid such competition. The question is whether the community is willing to pay the price for a better location.

Solutions based on biology no doubt can be worked out and sometimes an easy, temporary solution may be at hand, but in the long run anticipation of the problem is going to be its best solution.

For example, the starlings responsible for the crash of the Electra at Logan had been attracted to roost in the reeds at the edge of the ponds. When the reeds were kept cut, the starlings no longer returned in large numbers. A patrol was started to frighten birds away from places where they might be dangerous.

Gulls are an illustration of a larger biological problem.

In winter, there used to be as many as 25 thousand gulls in Metropolitan Boston. During the breeding season, 3,500 pairs of gulls occupied the islands just east of Boston. More than a thousand pairs bred at Logan Airport itself and near some buildings along the waterfront. Birds moving between dumps, metropolitan and suburban reservoirs, fish piers, pig farms, and the ocean passed over Logan because it was in a central position.

A recent explosion of the gull population is related closely to the availability of garbage and wastes in metropolitan areas. The numbers of gulls would decline considerably if the sewage and garbage were kept from them.

In the 1890's, the herring gulls were in danger of extermination in America, and the National Audubon Society hired wardens during the breeding season to protect the few remaining colonies. By 1900, there were 8 thousand breeding pairs in New England, all on islands east of Penobscot Bay, Maine. By 1965, there were 80 thousand breeding pairs in nearly 200 colonies on the coast of New England and nearby New Brunswick, and more than half of these bred in Massachusetts.

To learn more about the ecology of breeding gulls, the Division of Wildlife Research of the Bureau of Sport Fisheries and Wildlife let a contract to the Massachusetts Audubon Society's research staff, which surveyed the New England breeding islands and colored 4,500 incubating birds and other adults at 6 sites. Interested citizens and staff men who regularly visited gull gathering places from Maine to New York reported they saw colored birds 10 thousand times.

Because we gave each colony area a different color, we could measure the average distance of gull movements and find out which contributed to the population around Logan Airport. We learned that breeding gulls do not go far from their breeding colonies—only 5 miles if there is a convenient fishing port, as at Gloucester, Massachusetts, and up to 25 miles if there is no major source of food nearby, as at the Isles of Shoals, New Hampshire, and Salem Harbor, Massachusetts.

By examining the food regurgitated by the adults we caught at the nest and by the young we handled, we learned that gulls even at the relatively remote colonies depend a lot on remains of bottom fish, hot dogs, french fried potatoes, lobsters, and other items obtained from garbage.

In the course of our 3-year study, three different dumps closed down. In each instance, the number of gulls at each dump dropped from thousands to a few dozen. At Columbia Point, the dump was closed three times and the gulls left; as soon as the dump reopened, the gulls returned by the thousands.

A census by air of the shoreline from New Brunswick to New Jersey one winter helped us locate 110 thousand gulls, of which 80 thousand were in the metropolitan areas of New York, Boston, Portland, and Narragansett Bay; 20 thousand were at dumps and fishing ports away from city complexes (as at Belfast, Maine, dumps at Barn-

Refuse and garbage dumps attract large numbers of gulls. When they are objectionable or a hazard to nearby air traffic, discontinuance of the dump is one of the ways to solve the problem.

387

The future of albatrosses on Sand Island has been said to be precarious. Eugene Kridler, a biologist, prepares to relocate albatross chicks on an experimental basis to a much safer place on Eastern Island.

stable on Cape Cod, Portsmouth, New Hampshire, and so on) but still primarily dependent on man for food. We found only 10 thousand that were making an honest living on what they could scavenge in the tidal zone.

These factors have allowed the gull population to increase and to become a hazard at airports. Authorities can reduce the hazard if they control pollution.

Instead, the military, Federal agencies, and cities have looked for easy remedies, such as repelling devices and shooting the birds.

In nearly all places where shooting has been tried, birds have learned quickly to stay out of shotgun range. Alarm calls have been used to drive birds away; they helped scare starlings from cherry orchards in Europe. Gull alarm calls were unsuccessful in The Netherlands.

Recorded calls that birds give in extreme distress can be effective. Some species, such as pigeons,

normally will not give a distress call. Others, including lapwings, often do not react to it. The normal reaction of gulls is to rise, fly to investigate the sound, circle, and then fly away. In several countries where high-fidelity equipment is used on birds that are shy of people and that have ample space for feeding, the results have been satisfactory. In places where birds are tamer or are confined in their food supply, or where inferior recordings have been used, birds have soon become conditioned so that they do not respond. Then additional stimulation (Very flares or shotgun fire) appears to work.

A combination of devices, supervised by trained persons, may be the solution for birds that gather at airports, although various techniques of habitat management are best.

Falcons have been trained in Canada and Britain to fly at gulls and are successful where they can be used, but falcons are rare, delicate, and expensive to train. In heavy rain and fog, when an airport needs them most, they are of limited use.

Another difficulty is to spot the birds on runways. Men in the control tower cannot see even flocks of birds at the end of a 2-mile runway.

To overcome it, airports may have to turn to regular patrols or closed circuit television, with cameras at many places. Certain types of radars give promise.

Because of the peculiarities of radio waves, certain targets of small or intermediate size may form almost as good an echo as large targets, and some birds may form images similar to those of small fighter aircraft. The radar in its voltage control also tends to make all targets (except those below its threshold) of uniform intensity.

A study at the Massachusetts Institute of Technology established that many "angels"—spurious unidentified echoes—were birds. Experimental confirmation came when electrical circuits were installed in the radar to eliminate small targets having the characteristics of birds. The angel targets disappeared.

The problem arose because the radar systems occasionally were not able to track aircraft through a large migratory movement of birds. The small scale of the map shown on a radar and the large size of the spot made on the screen from an echo

A sound truck broadcasts the distress call of an immature gull at the Moffett Naval Air Station in California to frighten off the herring gulls that frequented the runways, where they have been a hazard to aircraft.

make it possible sometimes for only a few birds to fill the entire screen with targets. As few as six birds, spaced regularly over a square mile, can fill up all the space; on a night of dense migration, when there may be a bird per acre in the sky (or, in terms of total area, 6 million birds over eastern New England) it may be impossible to track aircraft within 30 miles on a large search radar.

Another need is to know whether a pilot is apt to encounter birds in flight.

Investigations at the Zurich Airport in Switzerland (where landing control radar was used), in Great Britain (where high-power, 10-centimeter search radars were used), and in Sweden and North America have told us about migrations and have demonstrated that bird movements are measurable on radar to a certain extent.

Limitations are set on the use of radar in counting birds by its ability to separate targets and the size of its map. Even so, it can indicate when few birds or many are migrating and at what altitude and direction.

The Dutch have used such information to tell military fliers when many small birds are moving between 2,500 and 4,500 feet and to warn them to avoid those altitudes.

At the Salt Lake City Airport in Utah, the land-ing control operator has directed aircraft away from the dense flocks of ducks and blackbirds that occasionally move through the landing pattern.

At eastern airports, commercial flights may be rerouted when radars spot large numbers of starlings and cormorants, ducks, and geese that may be flying along the coast.

A flight of migratory whistling swans was picked up on the radar at Washington National Airport just before an inbound plane collided with one of these great birds and crashed.

Very likely as many as 65 percent of all birds move on in a short span—perhaps 10 percent—of the total period of spring and autumn migration. Interruptions to commercial or military training operations therefore would be less serious than those caused by bad storms.

Let me repeat: The problems created by birds at airports and on radar do not seem insurmountable. They would be quite simple were it not for financial or political limitations and motives. We know or can find the biological and physical factors and take reasonable steps to remove the basic causes. That is, when we are sensible about where we dump our filth and substitute long-range planning for short-term financial gain.

—William H. Drury, Jr.

389

Wires, Poles, and Birds

THE CAROLINA POWER and Light Company was having a series of costly and bothersome interruptions of electric power at one of its installations. The source finally was traced to a city dump. Flocks of gulls, rising from the garbage, were causing momentary short circuits between overhead transmission lines. Now and then the wings of a gull would touch two wires and cause the short. The birds were electrocuted, and the power company had an expensive problem. The solution was to spread the wires farther apart, to a distance exceeding the wingspread of the gulls.

Near Aberdeen, Idaho, possibly 100 eagles are electrocuted on transmission lines each year. Most of them are golden eagles. A few are bald eagles. At several points, as many as six dead eagles have been found beside a single pole. The varying stages of decomposition indicate they are electrocuted one at a time.

Apparently the eagles use the transmission towers as perches and are killed when their spread wings come into contact with two wires. When such contact occurs, there is a flash, and the eagle plummets to earth in a shower of sparks and burning feathers.

The Pacific Gas & Electric Co. of California corrected a similar situation in the High Sierras when eagles used transmission towers as lookout points to scan the landscape in search of prey. Sometimes an eagle would drop far enough when it took off from a tower so that the feathers of its wings spanned two wires.

The solution was to place on top of each tower a 2-inch wooden dowel perch, high enough so the eagle would clear the wires on the takeoff. Electrocution then became a rarity. A small detail like the diameter of the perch was important: It had to be large enough so that it could be readily grasped in the claws of the eagle. Otherwise it would not be used.

Uninsulated, low-voltage lines often used in rural districts also may cause trouble. For example: In south-central North Dakota, where trees are scarce, crows began building nests on short crossarms of pole lines. Because the crossarms allowed limited clearance between conductors and ground wires on the poles, the nests were short-circuiting the line and causing service failure, especially in wet weather.

An engineer who knew that kingbirds are enemies of crows, carved and painted several king-sized kingbirds and mounted them along the powerline. The crows were effectively discouraged, but a simpler way would have been to put the lines farther apart in the first place.

Sometimes birds sit on poles and eject a stream of excrement that short-circuits uninsulated lines. Others defecate as they leave a perch; if the perch happens to be an electric line, anything can happen. The best way to avoid damage to both bird and line is to use insulated wires or at least to alternate insulated and uninsulated wires. Guards made of a few pieces of wire sticking out hedgehog fashion will discourage birds from perching on crossarms.

Phase-to-phase shorts of low-voltage lines may follow a mass takeoff from perches at midspan. The uninsulated wires may then swing enough to touch each other, even though clearances otherwise are adequate. An open telephone line in Iowa had a short circuit every day, but only at sunrise. Inspection by maintenance people at 4 a.m. disclosed that hundreds of roosting swallows were weighing the upper lines down against the lower ones. Tightening of the lines corrected the difficulty.

It seems that more and more birds, especially crows, like to nest on the steel crossarms of utility towers. The shorting hazard mounts when the birds use as nest-building materials pieces of metal scrap and wire that workmen may have failed to pick up.

What to do about the flocks of starlings that roost on poles and wires and towers? What, indeed? Utility companies and others have asked that question for years.

An electric company in Massachusetts used a small, cannonlike machine to keep starlings from roosting in its switchyard. A mixture of acetylene and air in the device gives sharp, loud blasts at intervals, and the watchman sets it off when he sees a flock of starlings starting to settle.

Ospreys on Long Island and in Rhode Island began building nests on top of power poles some years ago when the tall, dead trees they previously used became scarce. When an osprey drags a 10-foot strand of wet seaweed across a powerline, the results may be spectacular and destructive.

To outsmart the birds, the companies put up duplicate poles, on top of which were platforms and sticks for nests. Ospreys liked them better than the powerlines. Another and cheaper way is to put a platform on a bracket that extends 3 or 4 feet from the side of the pole.

As if all that were not enough, woodpeckers have developed a taste for utility poles.

If they dug only nest holes, the situation might be tolerable. Most nest holes are dug near the top of the pole, where the strain is not great, and probably do not weaken the pole enough to be serious. But the woodpeckers, particularly the pileated woodpecker, insist on exercising their high-grade chisels in enlarging cracks in poles. They also dig large holes of uncertain function, sometimes a half-dozen to a pole.

In the Midwest, red-headed woodpeckers do considerable damage. In the Southwest, the golden-fronted and ladder-backed woodpeckers cause most of the trouble. In the Far West, acorn woodpeckers, the major culprits, dig holes in poles and crossarms, into which they stuff acorns for storage.

The utilities have tried various countermoves. Some companies have obtained permits to shoot the marauders, but that offends many people and is not generally successful anyway. One company in Kansas shot 37 red-headed woodpeckers off a pole in a single season, but the damage continued. Others have tried poles of fiber glass and cement,

protective wire mesh, and ropes hanging from poles like snakes.

A project was established at Pennsylvania State University in 1955 to study the problem with special reference to the pileated woodpecker. Although birds in general have a poor sense of smell, it was hoped that some chemical might be found that would send the woodpeckers packing. After 5 years of testing some of the smelliest and stickiest compounds known to man, however, no satisfactory chemical repellant had been found. The woodpeckers hacked happily through everything on the menu and even ruined the aluminum tags used to distinguish which chemical was being used on each pole.

The Koppers Co. started a similar program in 1961 under the direction of John V. Dennis. He announced in 1963 that a successful repellant had been developed. It comes in two forms: A paint for use on new or slightly damaged poles and a thicker product intended for use in filling holes of considerable size.

There is another side to this picture—a more positive side.

Poles and wires are perches from which male birds can broadcast their territorial ambitions and romantic intentions. They are guard posts, where the mate may stand watch over the nest. They are gathering places, where birds assemble in twittering throngs to prepare for migration. They are courting places, resting places, and sites from which to watch for prey. They are storage places for food. They are potential homes.

Hole-nesting and tree-nesting birds may like utility poles as well as they do trees. Where trees are lacking, as in parts of the West, poles may actually extend the range of a species.

The red-headed woodpecker has moved into new areas of New Mexico as utility poles have become available for nesting sites. In Panama, one species of hawk that normally nests on dead trees has become more abundant since utility poles have provided more nesting places.

Many birds have adopted the pole-nesting habit even in places where trees are relatively abundant.

An osprey, also called a fish hawk, makes a nest on the double crossarms on a powerline pole.

Such hole-nesting species as the eastern bluebird, house wren, tree swallow, yellow-shafted flicker, and sparrow hawk often use poles. Branch-nesting birds, such as robins, crows, and scissor-tailed flycatchers, nest on the crossbars and transformer boxes.

In two other places are birds and utilities linked—rights-of-way that are kept clean under utility lines running through fields and woods, and trees along roads where utility lines exist.

The use of selective herbicides to maintain rights-of-way has had interesting results. A relatively permanent shrub vegetation, rather than a high growth that is cut back periodically, thus is maintained. An edge between different types of habitat provides better conditions for wildlife than large stretches of the same vegetation. Since rights-of-way provide such an edge, particularly where they pass through forests, they provide a useful break in the otherwise unbroken habitat of a single type. These breaks are bound to increase the number of species by supplying a greater diversity of habitat.

The narrow bands of utility rights-of-way are indeed important to a variety of birds from the tiny chickadee to the magnificent wild turkey. As feeding grounds, they may provide nuts, fruits, and seeds in abundance and a variety of insects. As breeding grounds, they are well suited to birds that nest on the ground or in low shrubbery. Towhees, field sparrows, indigo buntings, and many other songbirds, as well as such game birds as bobwhite and ring-necked pheasants, thus are benefited by the presence of the utility lines.

Rights-of-way under powerlines must be maintained at a relatively low level of growth so that emergency repairs may be made quickly when required. This is done most easily and economically by selective spraying. Dr. Frank Egler, of Norfolk, Connecticut, recommended these vegetation belts in rights-of-way:

The maintenance trail—under or close to the wires: Low, nonthorny vegetation; in some cases suitable for walking, but generally for trucks and jeeps. Vegetation may be herbaceous, but shrubs, such as blueberries, especially if scattered, are permissible and desirable. In some types of terrain, especially if rocky or mountainous, no maintenance trails are needed.

Under-the-wire vegetation—below the wires and approximately half the width of the right-of-way (except for the maintenance trail): A low, shrubby vegetation of high landscape and conservation value; closed enough to keep out or restrict the growth of tree seedlings and sprouts. Azaleas, viburnums, dogwoods, elders, blueberries, and huckleberries are desirable. There should be no unnecessary destruction of vegetation in this zone.

Side vegetation—the marginal quarters of the right-of-way can be allowed to develop into a dense vegetation of tall shrubs and small trees that will not grow large enough to fall into the wires. Rhododendrons, shadblows, dogwoods, and small magnolias are especially desirable. This belt adds

A new pole replaces one that woodpeckers weakened.

to the combination of edge effect of the total vegetation and thus to productivity of all forms of wildlife.

The chemical herbicides recommended for control of undesirable plants are 2,4–D and 2,4,5–T. They are not known to be harmful to human or animal life as commercially used and if carefully applied according to directions on the container label. Care should be taken that cattle will not graze or browse such plants as chokecherry, which are poisonous when withered. The chemical is not persistent in the soil and disintegrates within weeks or a few months. Other chemical herbicides are generally harmless, although arsenical compounds and new and relatively unknown chemicals should be avoided.

Spraying can be as a weak water mixture or as a relatively strong oil mixture. Water mixtures generally are applied uniformly and are not effective for root kill. Oil mixtures are applied selectively to stubs or to the basal bark of woody plants or as an overall spray to low, woody vegetation (under 3 feet). Caution is essential in spraying with oil mixtures. The season for spraying and the type of application (stub, basal bark, or overall) depend on the type of vegetation.

Shade trees bordering streets along which power-lines pass often must be trimmed and disfigured to prevent outages. Utility arborists have prepared booklets that list trees that are desirable from the esthetic view and interfere the least with wires.

A variety of tree species should be used so that

Tree swallows perch on telephone wires at Cape Hatteras, North Carolina. Wires, poles, and crossarms provide observation sites and resting places for many kinds of birds.

a single epidemic disease will not destroy a community's entire planting. A greater variety of trees also will attract birds.

Many birds are adaptable. In a world managed by man, most species have been able to adapt to man and his works. Less adaptable birds have become rare or extinct.

The wire-pole-bird relationship exemplifies this adaptability. Some people would like to have all utility lines put underground, but many birds would prefer things left the way they are. Imagine the thousands of bank swallows in migration with no wires to perch on. Or sparrow hawks with no wires from which to watch for prey and no utility poles in which to build their nests. Imagine miles and miles of American highways without fly-catchers, blackbirds, and sparrows that delight eye and ear from their roadside perches.

Of course, these interrelationships between birds and people are complex. All ecological relationships are. Our problem is to understand these relationships and then to make a policy of coexistence work—for ourselves and for the birds.

—ALLEN H. BENTON and LEWIS E. DICKINSON.

Farmers and Birds

WE ASKED REPRESENTATIVE farmers in three or four counties in each of 47 States not long ago how they and their fellow ruralists, the birds, were getting along these days. The replies were like a cosy, newsy letter from home.

That the farmers listed 81 species or bird groups by name we took to mean that they are still on intimate terms with the creatures that share their work, homes, and worries.

Most of the farmers noted that the numbers of birds had increased, particularly red-winged blackbirds, pigeons, starlings, common grackles, crows, and house sparrows, about which they were less enthusiastic than the bobwhites and ring-necked pheasants. There were fewer robins and bluebirds, their old friends, and ducks.

About three-fourths of them said they were trying to be good neighbors and hosts by providing food, vegetative cover, and nesting places; regulating water levels for waterfowl; propagating and stocking game birds; and prohibiting hunting.

They liked game birds especially, but farmers almost everywhere paid attention to songbirds, too. Several even said they had helped increase the numbers of birds of prey.

A goodly number said birds paid for their bed and board—bobwhite, pheasant, doves, waterfowl, birds of prey, songbirds—even blackbirds, starlings, and crows. Maybe, we gather, farmers can see some good even in what some of us think are problem species, or perhaps some farmers live and work where they are not a serious problem.

Birds help control insects, almost all the farmers said. Others give them extra income from hunting; have recreational and esthetic value; help them keep down rodents, rabbits, and weeds; do scavenger work; and provide hunting for themselves and their families.

Nearly all, however, said birds had done some economic damage, mostly slight but now and then serious. Losses, including complete crop failures on a few farms in one or two counties, were sufficiently heavy that individual farmers had to discontinue growing sweet corn, sorghum, blueberries, cherries, filberts, or small fruits.

Damage was done to 63 crops. The birds ate grain, small fruit, and tree fruits and nuts; pecked fruit and melons; shook berries to the ground; destroyed the seed or plant of newly planted grain; nipped off the central part of head lettuce; and dropped their manure on plants.

Damage to grains was caused mainly by blackbirds, starlings, and crows. Robins did most harm to fruit. Upland game birds and waterfowl did damage to grain. Upland game birds and doves caused about 25 percent of the damage to vegetables. Songbirds (including the blackbirds, crows, and starlings) caused more than 80 percent of the reported damage.

Producers of cattle, poultry, hogs, and fur and game animals commonly mentioned troubles through transmission of disease and parasites, the eating of feed, predation, nuisance effect, and contamination, but in only 29 percent of counties were more than half of the producers believed to be affected. Most of the complaints of damage to livestock involved starlings, primarily to cattle and hog producers; house sparrows, to producers of poultry, cattle, and hogs; and blackbirds and magpies, to cattle producers. Hawks and owls were mentioned as affecting poultry production, but not nearly so often as starlings or house sparrows.

Some told of damage or contamination of buildings, feedlots, farm equipment, grain elevators, and cattle feeders, but mostly such damage was considered a nuisance more than a financial loss.

We did not get the impression from all this that farmers are unduly exercised about damage by birds, however. When problems became serious, nearly all the farmers used devices to frighten the birds away, poisons, and chemical repellants. Generally they frighten or repel rather than kill birds. We like to think this means the bond between farmers and birds is as strong as ever—they do not hesitate to poison rodents, insects, and other pests.

We thought it interesting that few farmers mentioned crows, which once were unwelcome visitors on farms.

Of the birds commonly controlled, only the robin is a protected species. Most farmers, we learned, understand the Federal Migratory Bird Treaty Act, which gives considerable Federal protection to migratory birds.

Few farmers showed interest in insurance to protect them from their bird losses. In two counties, though, most of the farmers wanted such insurance; perhaps they were high-risk counties, where valuable crops, such as sweet corn, may be damaged by a roving flock of birds and serious loss to an individual might occur in a short period. Federal insurance against duck depredation in Canada is available but is little used.

Most farmers think of hawks and owls as assets in controlling bothersome rodents. No longer are all hawks thought of as "chicken hawks." Quite a number of farmers want to protect owls and hawks.

Most farms are open to hunting. Some farmers forbid hunting on their land because of illegal trespassing, the damaged fences, open gates, and frightened livestock.

Comparatively few farmers seemed interested in selling recreational hunting rights, probably because they do not think the financial returns would be great enough or they value their privacy more highly.

Farmers sometimes band together to sell access rights to their lands to a private club. The profits, though, have not been substantial—seldom as much as a dollar an acre. Some States, notably Pennsylvania, have fostered arrangements whereby farmers allow hunting and the State game officials help police the area, stock it with game birds, and provide shelter and food plants for the birds.

Our poll, in which questionnaires were sent to a 5-percent sample of counties in the coterminous States and brought returns from all except Colo-

Some farmers use houses of gourds to attract purple martins, which feed on many kinds of insects.

rado, underscored several things we have all known. Nowhere do birds and man live closer, nowhere does man affect birds more, nowhere do birds affect man more than on the farm. Much of the farmer's work is in shaping his land, and what he does may determine which birds and how many can live there.

The first farmers were in the fields to see the arrival and passage of the birds in spring. They knew what birds nested where. They watched them raise their young. They saw them eat insects and knew them to be crop protectors. When farms were small and families large, no part of the farm was left unattended for long. Losses from hawks or owls or other birds ordinarily could be controlled.

The farmers considered their birds as a part of the farm, a part of Nature, as much a part of the scheme of things as sun, rain, frost, and wind. In

each hill of corn they planted four kernels: "One for the blackbird; one for the crow; one for the cutworm; and one to grow."

Farming has changed, though, and the change has left few species of birds unaffected. The use of fields of one crop or pastures with one species of animal has meant changes in the varied flora and fauna native to an area.

Grasslands and forests once covered about seven-eighths of our land; marshes and desert, most of the rest. Grassland populations probably averaged about three or four, forest about six or seven, and marsh about five or six breeding birds per acre. By 1950, about 20 percent of these original lands were converted to cropland, 25 percent to farm pasture, 10 percent to farm forest, and 5 percent to farmsteads and the like. Most of the remaining land was used for timber or grazing. The average now is fewer than four birds per acre on most of these lands.

In Michigan, I found that bird population densities on extensive croplands averaged less than 0.5 individuals per acre during the breeding season. Strip-farmed lands with fenceline hedges have much higher densities, but the birds are forest-edge birds rather than field birds.

Pasture and hayfields have a richer number of species and a higher population density than croplands. In Michigan, they averaged about three birds per acre. Some marsh birds, such as the red-winged blackbird, have been able to utilize the new hayfields and have prospered there. Many grassland birds have been able to adapt to managed hayfields, and some have extended their range eastward because of farms.

Although virgin prairie is almost entirely eliminated, the total amount of grassland has not been reduced. Rather, it is the geographic distribution, size of continuous areas, and quality of the habitat that have been changed.

Marsh birds have greatly declined with the loss of most of the habitat. Wildlife refuges, public and private, have concentrated on saving wetlands, but there was a total of 153 million acres of artificially drained lands in 1950 and drainage was progressing at a rate of about 1.5 million acres a year.

Considerably more open savannahlike parks and forest borders were created on the farms. Farmsteads usually have trees and shrubs, sometimes in areas which formerly had none. Orchards of various kinds were established and, before the heavy use of pesticides, they had higher population densities than any other habitat. Shelterbelts and windbreaks are commonly planted or maintained and trees are saved in fencerows and pastures for shelter of stock. Swallows, martins, phoebes, wrens, bluebirds, cardinals, buntings, and various native sparrows nested in or around the farmstead.

I have heard farmers say that a barn with a barn swallow never burns. Such prized game birds as geese, ducks, bobwhite, and mourning doves were able to utilize parts of the new farm environment.

New breeding populations of Canada geese in Maryland, North Carolina, Pennsylvania, Colorado, and Wyoming are being established, partly around the 1,400,000 farm ponds and reservoirs built by 1965.

Once when I was working in the Bureau of Sport Fisheries and Wildlife in Washington, I got a call from a farmer in Pennsylvania who was pleased that a flock of geese had landed in his pasture. He asked, though, how long the apparently testy birds would keep his cattle from drinking at the farm pond.

In California and southern cotton fields, Wisconsin cranberry bogs, and many tree farms, geese are grazed to keep down weeds.

Thousands of young mallards are raised on marshy or swampy ground on farms. In the Dakotas and neighboring Provinces are many glacial potholes, the main production centers for the redhead, canvasback, ruddy duck, and others. Drainage and droughts have so reduced the breeding habitat of these ducks that in 1962 the Federal drainage subsidy to farmers was modified to require approval of the Fish and Wildlife Service.

Farmers are hosts to millions of hunters and most of them ask permission before they go on a farm.

A farmer shares his mailbox with a bluebird, which has built a nest in the rear of the box.

A farmer's fence is a lookout post chosen by a young mockingbird just out of the nest.

The Service must offer to purchase such lands and make payments in lieu of taxes if they prevent subsidized draining. Funds from sale of Federal Duck Stamps, required since 1934 to hunt migratory waterfowl, have helped purchase wetlands. Still, only 3 million acres had been purchased and reserved for waterfowl in 1958.

The bobwhite, the most generally distributed resident game bird, is prized by farmers. Considered a songbird and not hunted in some Northern States, it reaches its peak abundance on farms and plantations from Oklahoma to Georgia. Many farmers gladly leave nesting cover and protect the nest and young. No other species has been the object of so much private management.

The mourning dove is the most widely distributed migratory game species. It, too, is regarded as a songbird in much of the country, but interest in it as a game bird is growing, and lately it has become one of the more hunted species. It is a bird of the open fields. Usually it nests in trees along the edge of a field.

Farm crops are important to doves, and mechanical corn pickers and combines leave much food for them. Weedy, uncultivated patches or parts of harvested fields also are excellent dove habitat.

Many songbirds are a part of the farmers' day. In the more intensively pastured fields are the killdeer and horned lark. Ungrazed hay is the center for many native sparrows: The Henslow's sparrow in the center, the grasshopper and Savannah sparrows on the interior fence posts at the field border, and the field and song sparrows at the forest border where fields meet the farm woodlot where the cardinals and towhees live.

The flicker, red-headed woodpecker, and bluebird feed in fields from fence-post perches, but with the disappearance of wooden posts, most of them nest in the woodlot edge. Killdeers from the pasture and the robins from the farmstead follow the plow as it works through the soil. Overhead swallows and swifts sweep through the air.

In the woodlot, nuthatches, titmice, chickadees, creepers, and hairy and downy woodpeckers search every crevice for insects. Nesting structures for wrens, swallows, martins, and bluebirds are common to many farmsteads.

As the farms change, so do the birds, and farms are still changing. Much of America's history was a period when doing a "land-office business" meant converting 9 or 10 million acres of wildland into farms each year. Since the Second World War, this trend has been reversed, and 4 million acres of depleted farmland have been abandoned each year. The rate was increasing in 1965.

The house wren—a small bird with a big appetite for insects.

The mourning dove is a favorite songbird. It is a prized game bird as well. The harvest over, flocks of mourning doves may move into fields to feed on waste grain and weed seeds.

The American family farm, in early times the home of more than 95 percent of our people and the backbone of Jefferson's democracy, is still going, but today the farmer is a shrinking minority of less than 10 percent. American technology, made possible by our rich farmlands, has enabled us to produce more and more on less and less acreage. Nationally, 150 thousand farms are being abandoned each year. Rural Pennsylvania had three times as many people in 1940 as in 1960.

These abandoned lands have formed a haven for many birds, both forest and forest-edge spe-

The bobwhite builds its nest with vegetation and likes unmowed fencerows and waste places on farms.

cies. At the same time, the highly successful farms have produced such surpluses that millions of acres have had to be converted to grassland reserves. This has helped the grassland species to thrive. These three groups of farm birds now are increasing. More than a million farm ponds have helped wetland species and waterfowl, but they hardly offset the loss of over 150 million acres of valuable marsh and wetlands in drainage districts. This group of birds has also been depleted because of drought.

Renting of additional land, debt financing of costly equipment, and formal business contracts have changed the old independent freeholder into a highly technical entrepreneur. As management of farmlands becomes more efficient, technical, and complete, the farmland birds will become more and more subject to management by the farmer, but our survey shows that he is still sympathetic and wants many bird species around him.

A separate but growing trend for urbanites to buy up old farms as "hundred-acre-homesites" within commuting distance of urban centers or as summer homes is a countertrend to commercial farms. On such homesite farms, management is much less intensive. Pastures are maintained as openings for views and vistas or for riding horses. Gullies are planted in shrubs and trees. Erosion is controlled. Little tilling takes place. Ponds are prized. Birds are a main crop for this new and growing group.

—John L. George.

Birds and Forests

SOME PEOPLE think of a forest as a community in which each woodpecker, each squirrel, each oak has a definite job to do for the welfare of all. It is as if somebody had put each laundryman, doctor, policeman, newspaperman in a prescribed place to perform a special function in the life of a whole city.

Ecologists are more likely to consider that birds, other animals, and trees and other plants have evolved together (as do jobs, services, and sources of livelihood in a city) and that each species has become adapted through thousands of years of evolution to live a normal life with the others in the forest community. The various forest denizens occupy separate and generally satisfactory niches, which are combinations of physical factors and biotic relationships required in the normal course of living.

The kinds of trees, shrubs, and other vegetation in the forest, the special situations created by topography and physiography, and the actions of other animals determine the variety of niches available. These, in turn, directly affect the behavior and distribution of birds.

Birds usually nest in the area where they spend a great deal of time in search of food, the exact location within the niche varying with the kind of bird. Nests may be on the ground, in shrubs or other low-growing vegetation, among the branches of the trees, or in the cavities of standing dead or living trees.

In the average woodland community in our Northern States, birds nest at various places up to the very tops of trees. The ovenbird and ruffed grouse, for example, are typical ground nesters. The hooded and black-throated blue warblers usually favor the undergrowth. The robin, blue jay, wood thrush, and red-eyed vireo utilize the lower branches. The pileated woodpecker, northern three-toed woodpecker, and yellow-bellied sapsucker are associated with cavities in trunks of living or dead trees. Orioles, crows, hawks, owls, eagles, and Blackburnian, black-throated green, and cerulean warblers nest in the higher branches or treetops.

Each kind of bird has its own favorite places for feeding and nesting. Most species stay close to their feeding and nesting places, but some, such as the kingfishers, herons, and hawks, range far.

Nature is never static. She continually exhibits a changing face. One group or community of plants replaces another. The new group, by changing such factors as temperature and moisture, eliminates the community that brought it about and favors a new one, which becomes the next step in what we call plant succession.

Gardeners know how this happens: Crabgrass may crowd out bluegrass; brambles may kill crabgrass; trees may replace the brambles. Along with plant succession there are changes in the kinds and numbers of species of plants, mammals, and birds. The last and highest stage in plant succession we call the climax.

Every experienced birdwatcher recognizes that there is a close relationship between the bird population of a woods and the plant species that comprise it.

Scientists in Minnesota who studied birdlife in two major forest climaxes, the maple-basswood and the spruce-fir, noted some kinds of birds in both, but found other species to be restricted to only one community. The pine warbler, broad-winged hawk, mourning warbler, white-breasted nuthatch, myrtle warbler, and ruby-throated hum-

mingbird tended to inhabit only the maple-basswood forest. The yellowthroat, purple finch, white-throated sparrow, ruby-crowned kinglet, brown creeper, gray jay, and yellow-bellied fly catcher were found only in the spruce-fir community.

All in all, because of adaptation, life in the forest flows rather smoothly. There is a temptation at times to believe that each animal was created for the specific role it plays. We tend to classify the vireo as good, because it consumes insects, and the great horned owl as bad, because it preys on weaker forest denizens.

We need always to bear in mind that birds have no sense of what people call "moral values." Self-preservation is a powerful instinct in all wild creatures. The bird does whatever it can to survive in its particular niche and is unconcerned as to how we classify its acts. The scarlet tanager, for example, consumes myriad caterpillars, many of which are destructive. The tanager, however, is less concerned about the value of his foraging to the forest than he is about the effect in his own digestive system.

Birds affect forests at a point of urgent need. Most foresters are convinced that the worst enemies of forests are insects. Even though fires continue to do heavy damage in forests, modern methods and equipment are more and more effective against them, and fire is generally recognized as secondary to insects in destructiveness in the forest. The damage by spruce budworms, tent caterpillars, leaf miners, and other insects grows increasingly serious, and the problem remains complex and costly.

Make no mistakes about it: Birds are valuable assets in our forests.

German and Soviet foresters regularly install nest boxes for cavity-nesting birds and tack up shelves or nest pockets on trees to attract open-nesting birds. It is one of the ways they use to protect the timber resource. They and other foresters in Europe have satisfied themselves that birds are useful biological agents against destructive insects.

American foresters have been slow in following

A dead tree in a forest is the home of the young family of a yellow-shafted flicker.

this lead, but an increasing number of them recognize that birds constitute a positive force working steadily and effectively against many insect pests.

Natural forests, unimproved by man, usually have plenty of cavities—more than enough to accommodate a normal population of hole-nesters. In intensively managed forests, things are different. A tree with a cavity is considered as not worth its keep and is cut out to make room for one that will pay its way. Most commercial forests therefore have few natural places for cavity-nesting birds.

The installation of nesting devices is an attempt to have both intensive forestry and a somewhat near normal bird population to help in the endless battle against insects.

The Washington State Department of Natural Resources, for example, has issued instructions to Boy Scouts and other groups for the construction of birdhouses for a number of cavity-nesting birds and has encouraged the erection of such nesting facilities in Washington forests in the interest of insect control.

Not that we should measure the worth of birds to forests—or ranges or elsewhere—wholly by economic or practical matters. The question of bird values is largely personal. That makes overall value difficult to measure. Much depends on opinion, your opinion and ours, as to what is important. Each of us has his own value scale into which he places each bird in terms of pleasure, inspiration, beauty, and interest. Some may be impressed if we say the value of birds in forests may be placed at 4 million dollars a year—but is it not true that when we feel the need to attach a price tag to an item we probably are in doubt whether it has any other strong value for us?

Insect-eating birds display so many foraging techniques that it almost seems that some bird is specialized to prey on every forest insect that exists. That is not true, for there are many more kinds of insects than there are birds, yet some birds are specialized so they can take advantage of the special food supply offered by common insects.

These adaptations account for the diversity of species that live in our forests.

From dawn to dusk, the nuthatches and creepers search along main trunks and large branches of trees for scale insects and other quiescent forms.

Kinglets, vireos, titmice, many of the warblers, wrens, and their like search the various parts of the stems and foliage. Each concentrates more or less on a particular area, so that the entire tree or bush is carefully searched for insect life.

Woodpeckers bore beneath the bark or other woody surface in their search for insect larvae.

Thrashers, towhees, and many of the sparrows forage through litter under trees and bushes. They take seeds and many kinds of insects and their larvae.

Flycatchers use the still-hunting technique for a part of their food. They fly out from a perch to capture insects in free flight.

Swallows, swifts, nighthawks, and their allies forage by coursing back and forth through the insect-filled air. Each bird catches masses of insects in a day's collection.

Thus, birds are a spoke in Nature's balance wheel. Undoubtedly they help prevent buildups of many insect populations to the point where they become serious menaces, but birds, by themselves, are not a sufficient force to prevent outbreaks of insects. There is no point in overrating birds as control agents; they need the assistance of cold winters and parasitic and predaceous insects as well as the occasional hand of the forest manager to lessen the explosions of insect numbers.

Some examples: Blackbirds and grackles overcame a host of army worms in Louisiana; woodpeckers suppressed Englemann spruce beetles in Colorado; red-winged blackbirds curbed leaf rollers in Colorado; woodpeckers checked a serious outbreak of the tussock moth in Ohio; and quail, meadowlarks, bobolinks, yellow-headed blackbirds, and other prairie birds overcame a horde of locusts in Nebraska. But, during an outbreak of the forest tent caterpillar in Minnesota, a normal bird population was unable to exert any appreciable amount of control.

These examples indicate that birds, at times, can suppress forest and range insects whose numbers have grown to pest proportions. Ornithologists believe, though, that their greatest service is their constant pressure, which prevents potential insect pests from reaching damaging proportions under normal conditions.

The ecologist approaches the subject of birds and insects with the aim of understanding better the interrelationships between the two components of the ecosystem. He does not believe that the chickadee exists to control caterpillars any more than caterpillars exist to feed the chickadee. He wants to know, however, the relationship between the two: What is the effect of the chickadee on the number of caterpillars? What effect do caterpillars have on the survival of chickadees?

He recognizes a web of food chains in the forest. To him, there is significance in the plants that capture the sun's energy for the formation of food materials, the insects and other animals that eat the plants, the smaller birds and mammals that eat these lower-level consumers, and finally the larger predators that subsist upon the smaller birds and mammals. These creatures together constitute a web of life within the forest that fascinates all students of natural history. The ecologist finds it difficult to hold one member as being less important than another in rounding it out.

The forester's viewpoint is somewhat different. He judges birds according to their contribution to the welfare of the forest. On that basis, the insectivorous birds we have discussed rate high. Most of them commit no damage, and any value derived from their consumption of insects is considered as net gain. We may be justified therefore in saying that the insect-eating birds are the forester's best friends, even though at times he may fail to acknowledge the fact when he fails to give them adequate protection.

Woodpeckers may appear to be an exception to that sweeping statement. Fortunately, however, most of the objections to woodpeckers arise from their activities outside the forest, and the forester gives them a fairly clean bill of health.

Of the 22 species and 72 races of the woodpecker family in the United States, only 2 species and 7 races can be classed as clearly detrimental to forest trees. These are the sapsuckers, which have scarcely a friend among foresters. The other 20 species and 65 races are all good citizens of the forest environment. Some of their acts may be detrimental at times, but the good they do easily offsets the occasional damage.

The sapsuckers differ from the other members of the woodpecker tribe in that they consume relatively few insects—mostly ants and a few wood-boring larvae. The sapsucker's staple diet appears to be the living cambium layer and the sap that flows from the wounds they make on the tree. They often expose such large areas that scars deface the boards that may be later cut from the tree. Dark stains result from fungi and bacteria that gain access through the scars. At times, the tree is weakened seriously or killed by their attacks.

The yellow-bellied sapsucker alone causes an estimated damage of 1.2 million dollars annually to the lumber industry. It attacks 250 kinds of trees, but the loss it causes so far has been less than the expected cost of efforts to control it.

Lest we be accused of failure to recognize any positive value of the sapsucker, we should acknowledge that two Canadian biologists have reported the yellow-bellied sapsucker to be one of the avian predators on the larch sawfly, a serious defoliation pest of the tamarack in Manitoba. Thus, even this forest pest species must be rated as making at least one contribution toward the forester's interests.

The large pileated woodpecker chops holes in timber in search of insect larvae. The excavations often are looked upon as damage to the tree, but usually, we believe, the holes are akin to surgery at periods of serious illness, since the larvae for which the bird is searching very likely would destroy the tree were it not for the woodpecker.

Woodpeckers sometimes are accused of excavating nesting sites in sound trees. We are not sure how true that is. Some ornithologists say woodpeckers only excavate in sound wood if there is dead wood under it. Others believe there must be insects under the surface to induce excavation.

Be that as it may, woodpecker holes occasionally are found in apparently sound trees. The holes may damage timber or weaken the tree because they allow bacteria or fungi, which lead to rotting, to enter. Most of the cavities, however, cause no economic loss. Many of them are used later by other insectivorous birds for nesting.

If these values are insufficient to balance the tables on the woodpecker, surely the plus values for insect control will serve to tip the scales well in his favor. In general, when a woodpecker concentrates on a tree, we can be sure that an insect outbreak impends. Thus, considered as a group, the wood-

A downy woodpecker searches for insects in the trunk of a birch and helps combat forest pests.

409

pecker must be given hearty commendation in the woods. Certainly, the woods would be a less joyful place without them.

Two other values of birds in forests justify a brief mention.

One is that some birds—notably hawks, owls, and shrikes—suppress mice and other small mammals, which at times destroy seedling trees and so thwart the reproduction of trees. This is an example of something we mentioned earlier. The raptors are interested primarily in survival. Their chief concern is to get food. The effect, from the forester's point of view, is control of species that otherwise could become serious forest pests.

In the woods, the ruffed grouse is king among game birds. To get one, the hunter needs stamina, alertness, and a keen eye; the sport he has is not easily matched elsewhere.

Less abundant than the grouse, but more of a trophy, is the wild turkey, the only American game bird to be classed as big game. Once nearly extirpated over most of North America, the turkey has been restored over much of its former range by wise conservation and restocking. Today it is recognized as a game resource in 23 States.

The American woodcock, or "timberdoodle," which nests in the northern forests and winters in the Deep South, also provides fine sport for those who have persistence, knowledge of the bird, and a good shooting eye. Because it depends on earthworms, in which pesticides from the soil may become concentrated, the woodcock may be highly vulnerable to insect-control programs. Biologists have been deeply concerned about the dangers to woodcock of widespread applications of pesticides.

The blue grouse and band-tailed pigeon of the West and the bobwhite of the East and South must be included also as forest game birds. Quail are considered generally as nonforest birds, but they are often found in the pinelands of the Southeast.

As good as their record is, birds are not an unmixed blessing in the forest. We have already mentioned the sapsucker as one forest pest.

Many other birds eat tree seeds and hinder reseeding more than is generally believed. Thirty-seven species feed on seeds of conifers. Most forest birds are insectivorous during the months when insects are active, but many kinds depend primarily on seeds when insects are dormant. Among them are the sparrows and finches, grosbeaks, crossbills, meadowlarks, blackbirds, and quail. Doves eat almost no insects at any time.

Most of the seeds are surplus—our earlier statement about the coadaptation of the members of a community holds true here, also. Plants ordinarily produce such an abundance of seed that those eaten by birds are not missed.

The main difficulty springs from the insistence of the modern forester on efficiency of reproduction. Loggers sometimes remove all but a few seed trees and hope to have the forest regenerated by natural seeding without undue delay. Often birds and small mammals consume so many seeds that reproduction is delayed by several years.

When a forester is managing the forest on a rotation of a hundred years, every year in which reproduction is delayed represents a financial loss of 1 percent of the operation. In such a situation, the detrimental role of the seed-eating bird in the forest often has been assessed a considerable economic figure.

The problem of forest regeneration is not simple, and it is not always possible to assign a positive role to birds. Not every year is a seed year, but enough seeds are produced in good years to feed the birds and rodents and still leave a surplus to reproduce a stand of trees.

After germination, the young seedlings are subjected to many hazards. Rodents, rabbits, and larger animals may nip off the young plant. Cutworms destroy many. The roles of birds in controlling some of these pests are not entirely clear, but they are believed to have some positive part. Drought or the direct rays of the sun may kill young plants in exposed locations. Competition with weeds may prevent others from thriving. Among the many hazards faced by seeds and seedlings, seed-eating birds must be included as potentially unfavorable factors. Doves, meadowlarks, quail, pine siskins, and purple finches are among the species implicated most commonly, but most seed-eating birds may be harmful at times when they are present in large numbers.

In the longleaf pine belt in the South, foresters learned from a survey that mourning doves, bobwhite, meadowlarks, cowbirds, and several kinds of blackbirds were eating sizable amounts of pine seed. They were eating more during years when seed crops were heavy—less during seed-short years. Apparently the seed crop, when abundant, attracted and held larger numbers of birds.

In a forest of jack pine in northern Minnesota, a sampling of four juncos, eight chipping sparrows, eight goldfinches, and one Brewer's blackbird disclosed that all but three had fed on jack pine seeds. Because fair-sized flocks of all were present, they may have eaten a large part of the seed fall.

Before we reach a decision as to the role of birds in regeneration, we need to consider the entire ecological picture. In the first place, birds that eat forest seeds also eat many insects. The young of most such birds are fed an animal diet. Consequently, the bird pays for much of its seed diet by performing a valuable role in insect control.

Most ornithologists therefore believe that only a few seed-eating birds can be considered as unmitigated pests in the forest. They think methods other than control of birds should be sought when it becomes necessary to protect forest seeds.

One way is to coat seeds with a chemical that repels birds and at the same time controls insects and fungi; the coated seed thus receives double or even triple protection. This results in seed protection but leaves the birds for their beneficial role in forest protection.

Some of the seeds birds eat are digested entirely. They mostly are the seeds of what foresters consider preferred species. But some of the seeds have tough seedcoats and pass unchanged through the bird's digestive tract—some actually are in a better condition for germination when the bird voids them. Many such seeds are of trees that foresters consider weed species. The birds, of course, spread them throughout a forest.

Some trees spread by birds, such as flowering dogwood and redcedar, are desirable. In one locality in southern Minnesota, a medium-stocked stand of redcedar was established by seeds eaten and later expelled by birds. Hawthorne and Japanese honeysuckle are examples of plants that easily can become a nuisance in certain places, although in others they are valued as part of a good wildlife habitat.

Blue jays are commonly given credit for planting acorns that grow into prized oaks in widely scattered spots.

Birds also spread some tree diseases and parasites. The seeds of mistletoe stick to their feet and beaks or are eaten and dropped later in excrement at other places. We think birds were responsible for the spread of black spruce dwarf mistletoe in Minnesota, but we are not sure exactly how it came about. Mistletoe, despite its romantic aspects at Christmas parties, is a parasite on the tree, and its spread is not viewed by the forest manager as a beneficial act. Chickadees, nuthatches, and gray jays were accused of being the culprits.

In places, the accumulation of droppings by colony-nesting or roosting species is a nuisance. Sometimes 2 or 3 million starlings and blackbirds may roost in a few acres of woods. Some of the herons and ibises nest in rookeries in trees, and after a few years their droppings may weaken or kill the trees. Usually these gatherings of birds do not involve large areas, and the spectacle of the nesting birds often is of such interest that the losses are overlooked.

So far, what birds do for and to us. What do we do for and to birds?

We have cut down forests and woods and so have removed the homes of some birds. But at the same time we have made room for open-land birds, and can say therefore that our activities have not been altogether detrimental to birds as a group.

We have eliminated a few birds from the scene. We may have reduced others to a rather precarious position. A few species, such as the mourning dove, robin, mockingbird, and cardinal, have prospered from their association with man.

In managing the forest, we would like to encourage certain birds that are especially helpful in control of insects. As we said earlier, Soviet and German foresters have done more in this regard than Americans.

Not all cavity-nesting birds use artificial boxes readily, however, and minor differences in the shape of the box or in its placement may influence its attractiveness for the bird in question. If these boxes are to be used by birds, they must be in the kind of place favored by the appropriate species.

It would be fine if we could encourage more

Edges between forests and fields, if left uncut, may harbor a rich array of birdlife.

by trimming out the top to stimulate a more bushy growth. A species of Russian warbler seemed to like junipers trimmed in this way. Of 22 nests, 12 were in bushes that had been browsed by elk, and 2 were in bushes that the biologists had trimmed. These details are scanty, we know, but they indicate a type of study and management we need if we are to have more insectivorous birds in forests and woodlands. As it is, we can cite a planting of shelterbelts in North Dakota, where 15 mourning doves nested—only one to an acre. We have had some success, though, in getting robins and phoebes to nest on artificial brackets.

In preparing this chapter, we questioned some 20 managers of Federal, State, and private forests in widely separated parts of the United States on their attitude toward birds in the forests and the extent to which birds are favored in silvicultural practices.

As we should expect, there was considerable difference in the attitudes expressed toward birds. Nearly all who responded recognized that birds are of high interest to forest visitors. Well over half gave credit to birds as positive factors in insect control. Most of them did not find birds to be highly destructive in the forest. Only two or three mentioned sapsuckers and seed eaters as constituting special problems.

About half of the forest managers stressed the fact that silvicultural practices are aimed at keeping the forest suitable for a variety of birdlife. Several commented that interest in birds in the forest has greatly increased over the past few years and that this trend probably will continue into the future.

The value of birds in the forest was well summarized by the supervisor of a National Forest of more than a half-million acres in Virginia, as follows: "The value of birds in the modern, recreation-oriented forest is very high. Game bird hunting is very popular on the Jefferson National Forest, and indications are that it will continue to be even more so. Bird watching, photography, as well as interest in artistry is also presently popular with expectations to be even more popular as the surging human population increases and people have more available free time."

We Americans have been giving more and more attention to the multiple use of forests so that they

open-nesting birds to establish homes and families in certain places where they and we would benefit.

The Germans construct "nest pockets" of branches tied to trees so as to attract birds to nest there. German foresters, knowing the value of birds in shelterbelt plantings, use a fairly large number of hardwood trees and shrubs to attract insectivorous species.

Russians have induced flycatchers to nest on shelves attached to trees. Russian biologists have experimented with improving the form of shrubs will yield higher returns in timber, wildlife, grazing, recreation, and water for this and future generations. To the wildlife manager, multiple use means particularly the development of the wildlife resource. To us who are deeply interested in the welfare of birds, multiple use entails two questions: How can we best manage the woods so as to cause the least damage to birds? How can we best encourage beneficial birds in the forest?

Birds differ considerably in the ways they react to changes in the environment.

At one extreme is the robin, which flourishes in a variety of habitats, from open country to dense woods, and tolerates changes in nesting places.

Near the other end of the spectrum is the Kirtland's warbler, a species that nests in stands of jack pine in a certain growth stage in lower Michigan. They are limited by their dependence upon young pine growth of a certain density, and their future is tied to the management of jack pine forests in such manner that adequate nesting habitat is available.

Regardless of the degree of sensitivity, each species of bird has some set of conditions that is optimum for it, and many species are quite sensitive to minor changes.

No two birds have identical requirements of habitat. The density of nesting cover, the kind of tree selected for nesting, the nearness to water, the amount of shade, and many more factors influence each bird in the selection of its nesting site.

Common birds of the boreal spruce-fir forests of the North and on high mountains are the black-throated green warbler, Audubon's warbler, myrtle warbler, golden-crowned kinglet, Swainson's thrush, and various species of juncos. In contrast, those of the eastern deciduous forest are the red-eyed vireo, ovenbird, wood thrush, and scarlet tanager.

We can readily see that variety of habitat is essential if we want a rich birdlife in the forest. Monoculture—the commercial management of a forest to produce a single species of tree—makes for a meager birdlife. On the other hand, fewer birds may mean a greater risk of plant disease in such a forest, for birds, as we have seen, are a factor in maintaining a healthy stand of trees.

Farmers who own woodlots and foresters will do well, then, to bear in mind always the welfare of birds as a vital aspect in deciding on the pattern of timber harvest, just as wildlife biologists are concerned with the effects of different harvest practices on populations of deer and other game.

Furthermore, a forest manager and woodlot owner may be able to improve conditions for birds by encouraging undergrowth on the forest floor. The removal of some undesirable trees, for example, may let more sunlight reach the forest floor and encourage the growth of shrubs, which will improve the habitat of certain birds.

The word "habitat" brings us back to the thoughts we started this chapter with. *Habitat* means *home*. This world is big enough, people are enlightened enough in this day, and birds are sufficiently adaptable, given a reasonable chance, for all living things to have proper homes.

—FRED H. DALE and LAURITS W. KREFTING.

Amid Brick and Asphalt

Birds in cities? Yes, indeed. Glover-Archbold Park, which is 4.75 miles from the White House in Washington as the starling flies, is a natural, untended woodland. The ground is deep in humus and leaves. Fruit-bearing shrubs and understory trees provide nesting sites and food for birds.

It has an abundance of wildlife: Red-shouldered hawks and barred owls, pileated woodpeckers and four of their cousins, bobwhites, chickadees and titmouse, house and Carolina wrens, wood thrushes and veeries, Acadian flycatchers and wood pewees, and a dozen varieties of vireos and warblers.

It supports one of the most varied and dense nesting populations of any woodland area in the country for which population studies have been made.

European ornithologists who visited the park en route to an International Ornithological Congress expressed envy of such an area in the middle of a city. Their parks, they said, are too artificial and manicured.

Another example: A different kind of park is the Wissahickon in Philadelphia. I have visited it early in the morning and late in the afternoon and, particularly when birds are migrating, learned some significant facts with respect to migrants, the length of stopovers for individual birds, and the weather patterns that seemed to influence their flights.

Any city park set amid brick and concrete may be an oasis for a small bird caught at dawn over an extensive city. Then all kinds of unusual visitors may be seen—woodcock and sapsuckers, thrushes and warblers, sparrows and kinglets. Central Park in the middle of New York City is such an over-sized migration trap. Bird observers have enjoyed it for years.

Since rivers often are migration highways for night flyers, birding in the early morning along river banks frequently is rewarding. I have found that the narrow strip of neglected trees and grass between Riverside Drive and the West Side Expressway, between 96th and 125th Streets in New York City, is an excellent place to make a quick appraisal of what migratory movements have occurred on fall nights.

Still another example, but of a different kind—a city park so planted and landscaped as to leave suitable habitats for few birds and so thoroughly sprayed with chemicals that even those few birds may be missing. A biologist recently returned from a tour of duty in the West was walking with me along the Mall in Washington. As we looked over the expanse of grass and shade trees, he asked, "Where are the robins and chipping sparrows? When I was stationed in Washington, there was a robin's nest in every second or third tree."

I had to tell him that for several years we had not found a robin's nest between the Capitol and the

Washington Monument and that many of the migrant robins attracted to the area died in convulsions characteristic of insecticide poisoning.

Birds in parks like these—and in many other examples that come to my mind and yours—are the most visible representatives of the world of Nature. For some, the birds of the city are welcome reminders of childhood days spent in woods and fields or of vacations in the country.

For others, who are indifferent to Nature and country living, the birds of the city may be only a nuisance.

A city and its suburbs may be a hospitable region with a diverse birdlife, or it may be an avian wasteland. In recent years, many cities have become the latter, because green and open spaces have been crowded out and because heavy applications of chemical insecticides have eliminated food resources and killed off the birds.

The time has come when thought should be given to making the city and its environs, the destined habitat for increasing numbers of birdwatchers and other outdoor enthusiasts, a suitable habitation for a wider representation of the birdlife of the region.

The central city, even when no thought is given to attracting them, is often the home of a surprising number of birds, and they are not all house sparrows and starlings.

The flat, gravel roofs of downtown buildings may be nesting sites for nighthawks. Their sharp, nasal *peents* and the *boom* of their steep dives are heard most frequently at dusk. Chimney swifts nest in most sections of every city and fly daytime patrols for winged insects.

Among the most interesting city dwellers, in my experience, are the white-crowned sparrows of San Francisco. They sing from the rooftops of downtown buildings and seem to have vertical foraging territories in the vines that cover the sides of some older buildings.

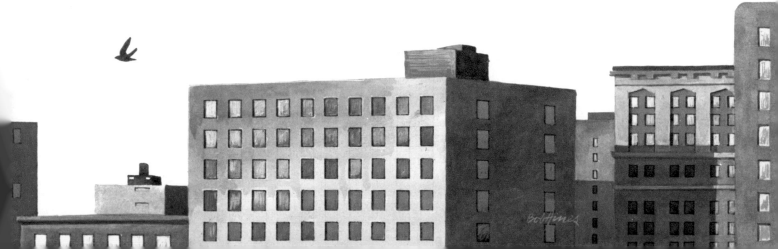

City boys and girls learn about birds and their ways and needs in highschool biology classes.

In downtown Washington, Pennsylvania Avenue has had its nesting sparrow hawks for years. In some winters, a peregrine falcon has used the Willard Hotel and the Old Post Office as lookouts. One tower of the Smithsonian Institution has been home for successive generations of barn owls.

Introduced species are likely to be the most numerous and most conspicuous birds in cities, as well as in small towns and suburbs.

In the horse-and-buggy days, when waste oats and other grains were dropped in the streets, the house sparrow, which built its bulky nests behind blinds, under cornices, and among vines, was a common pest. Today, its numbers reduced, it is hardly more than a minor nuisance.

In many cities, the starling is rated as a major pest, because its communal roosts, in shade trees and on buildings, defile the buildings and bespatter pedestrians and cars.

The domestic pigeons, established as feral birds in nearly every city, have found urban buildings quite comparable to the rock cliffs of their Old World ancestors. Their chief crime seems to be a disposition to nest in crevices provided by the intakes of air conditioners.

In some instances, the accumulated droppings of starlings and pigeons have been identified as a source of the viruslike disease that once was called parrot fever but now more properly is called ornithosis.

These commonly disliked introduced birds have their useful, as well as their interesting, features.

The house sparrows may occupy boxes where bluebirds would be more welcome tenants, but they also eat many garden insects, including the adult Japanese beetles.

Starlings are deplorably aggressive in driving native birds from their nesting cavities, but starlings

416

eat the grubs of the Japanese beetle and so spread the milky white disease, a highly successful biological control for Japanese beetles. Their mass aerial maneuvers at their nightly gatherings are fascinating to observe.

Even the pigeons, in responding to the very young and the old who visit parks with peanuts, are a source of entertainment.

Despite any paucity of birdlife, cities and towns are centers of increasingly active interest in birds and birding. School children have their nature study programs. Adults have their Audubon and ornithological societies. Homeowners and apartment residents maintain feeding stations and birdbaths.

Natural history museums have expanded their old exhibits of "local birds" to include informative displays that trace the evolution of birdlife, relate different birds to their natural habitats, and offer some first insights into the mysteries of migration and bird behavior. The exhibits in some museums have been elaborated to deal with all aspects of birdlife at home and abroad and offer a visual treatise on the birds of the world. Such exhibits afford the stay-at-homes a chance to supplement the fine bird articles that appear in popular and scientific natural history publications and enable the prospective traveler to prepare himself for adventures in distant lands.

In fact, it sometimes seems that there are more opportunities to study birds in the cities than in the country.

Nature centers, as adjuncts of museums of natural history, as projects of ornithological societies or as independent community ventures, are bringing bird study and natural history generally to thousands of urban children and their parents. They are helping city children to understand, as country children may from their first awareness of the world about them, that man is part of the natural world and that people of all ages can find abiding pleasure, excitement, and important insights in learning to enjoy birds and all of Nature.

The better nature center is so located that it is able to preserve some diversity of habitat—woods, fields, and a pond or stream—for visitors to explore, and indoor exhibits are combined with nature trails that use the outdoors as a living museum.

In hundreds of communities across the land, bird clubs, Audubon societies, and natural history associations carry on year-round programs that enable people with both professional and amateur interests to meet and exchange experiences about birds and the natural environment. Visiting lecturers present color films of natural areas and wildlife. The wonders of familiar things and the fascination of the new and the strange are alike effective in providing new dimensions for outdoor enjoyment. Identification classes for birds, flowers, trees, and other aspects of Nature prepare participants for meaningful field trips. Bird and nature walks in

When a robin built a nest on a telephone at White Oak, Maryland, a substitute telephone was put up.

417

George P. Grindle, a member of the Audubon Naturalist Society, takes his son on a birdwatching expedition in Glover-Archbold Park in Washington.

local parks and field trips on weekends to more distant vantage points enable city dwellers to escape from asphalt jungles to more serene and intriguing surroundings.

All these programs have the great virtue that they are being done largely by amateurs for amateurs. As essentially spontaneous responses to new interests, these activities, with experience and some guidance, may become a continuing interest for the participants and can develop articulate and well-informed citizens dedicated to sound conservation policies and programs.

Identification classes can be expanded into an integrated course of study embodying an ecological approach to Nature, beginning with the geology and climate of the region, providing a basic understanding of biology, including an examination of the behavior of animals and the dynamics of wildlife populations, and making each wildlife community characteristic of the region a specific object of appreciation and understanding.

Such an enterprise which combines seminars with field trips to representative natural areas within 150 miles of Washington, D.C., is presented by the Audubon Naturalist Society, under the aegis of the Graduate School of the Department of Agriculture, as a natural history field school program.

Since most birdwatchers are urban residents, it is not surprising that the birdwatching possibilities of cities and their environs are thoroughly exploited. And when they are sought out, a number of birding areas can usually be found—in city parks, in private sanctuaries, at city dumps, and in neglected bits of "waste" land where a few trees and weeds make a stand against the spreading blight of concrete and pollution.

Any city located on a waterway—ocean, bay, river, or lake—has an ecological magnet that will bring a variety of birds to its borders, at least in migration if not as year-round populations. Where sewers empty into river or bay, there is usually a concentration of gulls and other birds that will repay periodic examination. Thus a remarkable number of records for European gulls visiting North America has been established at the sewer outlet at Newburyport, Massachusetts.

Old, established cemeteries may be better birding places than city parks, particularly if they are planted with a variety of evergreen and deciduous trees and flowering and fruiting shrubs. Mount Auburn Cemetery in the center of Cambridge, Massachusetts, is certainly the country's most famous "birding cemetery" because so many significant records have been established there. During the second week in May, at the height of the spring migration of warblers, in no spot in New England can so many varieties of birds be found with so little effort.

Reservoirs are particularly worthwhile for winter birding as long as they remain unfrozen. Two reservoirs in New Haven are frequently visited by European widgeon during the seasons when they are present in southern New England.

The first notice that Washington had of a visitation of red-necked grebes came when one was sighted on McMillan Reservoir; ultimately seven gathered there.

Lakes in city parks where waterfowl are fed occasionally are hosts to unusual visitors that have strayed beyond their normal ranges.

Most interesting, where they exist, are tidal flats where transient shore birds may be found. Any reservoir may have such visitors during periods of low water levels.

Dumps may attract gulls and other scavengers. Hawks and owls may also hunt there for rats.

Airports may attract special bird populations, depending on their location. My favorite is Copenhagen, where oystercatchers may be seen from planes taxiing along the runways.

Since jet aircraft may suffer a power failure if birds are drawn into the jet engines and since any aircraft may be disabled if a large bird strikes a vulnerable part, studies have been undertaken to devise means of keeping birds away from airports and runways.

All birds are not problems at all airports. Where airports are open to birdwatchers, as at the smaller airports and private fields, the airport may be accepted as a substitute for "barren country." Besides horned larks, meadowlarks, and killdeers as nesting birds, airports are visited in winter by northern horned larks, Lapland longspurs, and

A spunky killdeer refuses to be crowded out by suburbia and nests on the doorstep of the Atomic Energy Commission headquarters near Washington.

419

In the still of the night, the mockingbird often bursts out in full song in cities of the South.

snow buntings and in spring possibly by migrating upland plovers and other shore birds. Such small birds, singly or in small numbers, are no threat to the planes that use these airports.

Residents of the suburbs can live surrounded by birds if there is a reasonable degree of neighborhood cooperation. You and your neighbors then will enjoy them during their season of song and nesting, be entertained by their gathering at winter feeding trays, and be able to watch the passage of the semiannual migrations.

Even the most ardent bird observer has relatively little time in which to go afield, but that need not be a handicap if the residential area is attractive for birds as well as for people.

If you are taken with status symbols (a new car, a large house, stylish clothes, a fine lawn), there is one status symbol that is not in the advertisements but may mean more than all the rest in terms of an enjoyable, livable community—the birds that choose to reside with you.

420

Ecologists recognize various plants and animals, singly or in combination, as indicators of the character of a forest, field, farm, or other natural or man-altered area. Birds are among the most useful indicators. They are among the best of Nature's status symbols. Have you considered what your present bird neighbors indicate about the status of your community? Are you privileged or underprivileged, congested or spacious, urban or suburban?

To illustrate the avian status scale, we might consider the summer residents available to an eastern city:

If your only birds are chimney swifts circling in the sky by day and nighthawks zooming down at dusk, then you are a cliffdweller in the center of town. Chimney swifts are satisfied with old chimneys, which provide sites for their nests. The nighthawks find that flat gravel roofs of apartments are secure places in which to raise their young.

The house sparrow, as the sole or dominant nesting bird, is indicative of crowded houses and pavements, little or no open space, and few or no grassy areas or shrubs.

A song sparrow or a chipping sparrow would represent an improvement in the environment—pleasant lawns of some size and at least a sprinkling of small shrubs to provide nesting cover.

A cardinal or a mockingbird would be a higher status symbol for a city or urban neighborhood. Either would indicate more spacious lawns and more landscaping. The cardinal would be satisfied with a few trees and some dense shrubs. The mockingbird would insist on small trees as well, such as dogwoods or hawthorns, for they like to nest higher than the cardinal.

Young robins surviving to feed on the lawn in summer would advertise a neighborhood of grassy lawns and shade trees. Their survival would signify that the neighbors had not doused their grounds with lethal sprays and that lawns had not been poisoned with massive applications of chlorinated hydrocarbons. Robins and bluebirds are reminiscent of old-fashioned orchards. The bluebird would be the higher status symbol, for it requires not only trees and open areas but also the presence of old woodpecker holes or nesting boxes.

Chickadees and titmice would similarly reflect

a community where older trees provide natural nesting cavities or where people are providing nest boxes.

The presence of red-eyed vireos and yellow-throated vireos would proclaim a fine old neighborhood with fully grown shade trees lining the streets or scattered through the yards.

The scarlet tanager is a rather special symbol, indicative of the presence of a substantial number of mature oak trees.

The top status symbols for a suburban neighborhood would be wood thrushes, catbirds, or brown thrashers. All require an area of gracious shade trees, naturalistic plantings of smaller trees (dogwoods, thorns, and the like), and many shrubs, preferably with a mulch or litter around them. Such a neighborhood would enjoy the finest of bird songs, a vocal advertisement of a place for pleasant living.

The birdlife of a neighborhood can be transformed by wise planting.

How much can be accomplished in residential areas was demonstrated to me when I found 15 species nesting in one season in a single residential yard in the Chevy Chase section of Washington. Sixteen bird families included mourning dove, downy woodpecker, wood pewee, blue jay, white-breasted nuthatch, house wren, mockingbird, catbird, brown thrasher, robin, wood thrush (two pairs), red-eyed vireo, scarlet tanager, cardinal, and song sparrow. And the yard was visited throughout the year by a variety of other birds.

What kind of residential area could produce such abundance and variety of birds? The area had once been wooded, and mature trees were left standing when the houses were built. Not all of the neighbors had planted trees and shrubs that were specifically attractive to birds, but none of them at that time was using highly toxic insecticides or herbicides.

Few of the neighbors operated feeding stations or birdbaths, and there were a number of cats. If proper cover is provided for birds, cats are unlikely to affect seriously the bird population. Birds have many more young than the habitat can support, having become adjusted to the normal high incidence of nestling mortality in the wild.

The successful attraction of birds depends upon meeting their minimum requirements for food, water, and cover. Cover is most important during the nesting season to provide protection from weather and enemies and to afford nesting sites.

The residence to which I refer was well planted, with the general objectives of shade, foundation planting, border planting, and screening accomplished through the use of trees and shrubs attractive to birds. The canopy trees consisted of red oak, tulip tree, silver maple, American elm, apple, eastern white pine, and eastern hemlock. These trees were planted around the borders of the yard. The oaks were between the sidewalk and the street. Between the larger trees, there was an understory of smaller trees, of which flowering dogwood was the most numerous, and all around the yard was a border of low shrubs, including various azaleas, rhododendrons, and bush honeysuckles. This pattern of planting duplicates the woodland-edge effect that is so attractive to birds and provides suitable niches for canopy, understory, and ground species.

Planting may be adapted to the characteristics of the residential lot and to the other interests of the homeowner.

The basic requirements of cover and food can be provided in many ways. If the yard is small, the emphasis should be on cover, depending on natural foods to supply the few birds that can be attracted. If the yard is large, it may be possible to indulge in the luxury of a jungle of briers and vines in a back corner.

Trees and shrubs of various kinds attract different birds, but not every yard in the neighborhood needs to duplicate each species. A few evergreens (hemlocks, spruces, pines) will draw northern visitors, such as the red-breasted nuthatch. Where variety is possible, it may be desirable to select trees and shrubs that ripen their fruits at different times in order to prolong the season for the birds.

Fruits, berries, seeds, and mast are all sought by some birds. All may be easily provided by a variety of trees.

The following recommendations are offered for the eastern section of the country. The red mulberry is sought out by some 50 kinds of birds; the white mulberry does almost as well. The native cherries are eagerly eaten by some 70 birds. According to the section of the country, the available species may be chokecherry, black cherry, wild red cherry, and others.

The buds of various birch trees are eaten by northern finches in winter. Tulip tree and box-elder retain their seeds into the winter, when they are a favorite food of evening grosbeaks, purple finches, and goldfinches.

The early seeds of the American elm are eaten by the finches and by white-crowned sparrows in migration.

The black gum, planted in the open, develops into a beautiful shade tree. It is unsurpassed in the brilliant beauty of its fall foliage, and its late summer fruits are eaten by scores of birds, including tanagers, orioles, thrushes, and other songbirds.

The spiny balls of the sweet gum contain seeds that are taken by the finches and other small birds. They are, however, a nuisance to rake up from the lawn.

The pines, especially the white pine, hemlock, and spruces, furnish good cover at all seasons, nesting sites in summer, and food reserves for northern visitors in winter.

Few people would think of planting a hackberry, but its persistent fruit provides winter fare for 40 species of birds.

Mast (nuts and acorns) is a staple food for some birds and, of course, for squirrels. Those who are annoyed by squirrels at feeding stations may choose to omit such trees.

Other trees appear to be highly attractive to insect-eating birds. Among them are the silver, or cut-leafed, maple, which is continuously visited by brown creepers and nuthatches in winter, the willows, and the mimosa. Mimosa always receives studious attention from migrant warblers in the fall and hummingbirds during the blooming period.

Smaller trees, some of which provide the understory in mixed and deciduous woodlands, are particularly attractive for home plantings. The spectacular red berries of the flowering dogwood seldom last long after the leaves fall; some 100 kinds of birds compete for them. Flowering crabapples are desirable because they hold their fruits into the winter, when they are used by the mockingbirds and others.

The thorns are doubly useful because they afford secure nest sites in summer and decorative winter fruits, which are ultimately eaten by the birds. The Washington hawthorn is perhaps the best known, but the thicket thorn has fruit that is eaten by 80 birds. The cockspur thorn is used sometimes to divert birds from other fruit trees.

The American holly gives good nesting cover and has berries that are used by thrushes and other wintering birds.

All trees and shrubs appear to require a reasonable amount of direct sunlight if they are to bear good quantities of fruit.

Many shrubs, native and exotic, have attractive fruiting habits, colorful fall foliage, and growth patterns that make them suitable either for specimen planting or mass use. Both migrant and resident birds, more than fourscore strong, seek the berries of the shrub dogwoods—gray dogwood, silky dogwood, red osier, and alternate-leaf dogwood. Spicebush, so common in bottomland woods, is most attractive to thrushes and vireos.

All the fruiting viburnums are highly desirable for their fall fruits: maple-leaf, arrow-wood, highbush cranberry, withe-red, black-haw, nannyberry, and others.

The bush honeysuckles, particularly *Lonicera tatarica,* are attractive in flower or fruit, and the berries are much sought after by birds.

Anyone who has raised small fruits and berries in a home garden knows how birds enjoy them. Some 100 birds are drawn to wild and cultivated raspberries, blackberries, blueberries, and huckleberries. Competition of birds may be reduced somewhat by providing a birdbath or fountain. Common buckthorn is eaten even before the raspberries, and the elderberries also provide diversionary attraction.

Cotoneaster and multiflora rose, often used as wildlife hedges, make good screen plantings and provide valuable food reserves. The deciduous hollies, particularly inkberry and winterberry, are attractive shrubs and hold their berries for winter use.

Many of the trees and shrubs I have recommended are native species and, with the landowner's permission, can frequently be had for the transplanting. You get the best results if you select small specimens, transplant only when the ground is wet, and mulch and water abundantly for the first season. The easiest and surest course is to use nursery stock; order by mail from a nursery specializing in native plants if the local nurseries do not stock the desired varieties.

You can attract birds to your lawn or garden by feeding them and by providing birdbaths and nesting boxes.

Those devices seldom are successful, though, unless the neighborhood is so planted that birds naturally visit the vicinity. If plantings attract the birds, nesting boxes and birdbaths, as well as feeding, can persuade them to stay.

A birdbath is useful in attracting birds at all seasons but is particularly successful in summer, when natural sources of water may be lacking in residential neighborhoods. It will be irresistible if the surface can be kept dappled by a tiny inflow of water or by drops falling occasionally on the surface.

Bird boxes should be designed for specific species—with small holes for wrens and chickadees, deep boxes for nuthatches and woodpeckers, wide but narrow openings for tree swallows. Carefully measured holes can avoid the competition of starlings where small birds are sought.

Also, it is necessary to consider the location requirements for the species that are sought: Low locations for bluebirds, high sites for crested flycatchers, sheltered overhangs for the shelf of the phoebe, very open locations for the apartments of purple martins, shaded locations if boxes are made of metal, sunny locations for the wood boxes of early nesting species.

Feeding stations attract birds chiefly in the winter when resources of natural foods are limited. "Wild bird seeds" and grain may be fed on the ground, on a tray, or from a hopper.

Whatever method you use, supply only limited amounts of feed at a time so that the grain is clean and dry. Be sure to clean off the trays after a rain or snow. Do not let a moldy condition develop, as the spores from some molds may become a source of a fatal pneumonia to birds.

Dried fruit (or perhaps pieces of fresh fruit) are necessary if mockingbirds, thrushes, waxwings, or other fruit-eating birds come to the feeders.

Nuts and "peanut hearts" appeal to all kinds of birds.

Suet is taken by woodpeckers and other wintering birds that naturally feed on insects and insect grubs during the winter.

Water also is appreciated at the winter feeding station and can be kept from freezing with an automatic electric heater of the kind used on poultry farms.

I think more urban and suburban residents enjoy birdwatching through the window during the winter months than manage to find time for field trips when spring and summer come.

A final word of warning on attracting birds to the home. Because nearly all birds eat insects during the spring and summer, no one who makes intensive use of sprays and reduces his insect populations can expect to have many bird neighbors.

Moreover, no one who makes use of chemical insecticides or applies chlorinated hydrocarbons, such as chlordane, to his lawn, or whose neighbors do so, should attempt to attract birds to the area. To do so is to condemn them and their nestlings to death.

Urban and suburban residents who are interested in birds and Nature generally should have an opportunity to enjoy their recreations more frequently than is possible only by making long trips.

Those who have made any progress with birding have discovered that birds are associated with particular kinds of habitats, each species having its special niche in the economy of Nature. Birding then takes on a new fascination, for birds become the keys to different types of habitats and the best fun in birding comes with observing the bird in its natural environment. The fuller, more significant experience of birding with an ecological insight requires facilities, just as baseball, golf, and other recreations require suitable facilities.

Every city, I think, should have within easy distance a variety of natural areas that collectively represent all the different types of natural areas and wildlife communities that are indigenous to the region. These natural areas should be extensive enough to support reasonable populations of the kinds of wildlife that are associated with the habitat.

Thus, there might be a marsh, a woodland lake,

a bottomland forest and swamp, an upland pine woods growing up on an abandoned field, a bog that is perhaps a relict of glaciation, and as many more as the diversity of the surroundings of a city permit.

These natural areas should be living museums, preserved in their natural state, altered only to provide access for people under conditions which would not disturb the wildlife. They could serve also as outdoor study areas for children who are studying biology and for college students engaged in research.

The natural areas, or living museums, would replace the natural areas that earlier generations found within walking distance of city limits. They could be established as private sanctuaries, as public areas administered by natural history societies under a trust arrangement, or as special-status parks. They should not be "developed," but should be left in a natural state and administered only to the extent necessary to prevent abuse.

City dwellers also should have access to country places where they may observe at first hand the significance of different patterns of land use and the meaning of conservation practices as applied to our basic resources of soil and water, of farm land and forest.

Sound public policies in the management of our renewable resources depend upon a realization by our citizens that people are a part of the world of Nature.

This realization can hardly come as an abstract intellectual exercise. It can come through increasing opportunities for individuals to experience Nature.

In terms of these larger goals of making the individual a citizen of the universal natural world, as well as a citizen of his city and nation, birding and natural history studies are of more than private concern. They should be encouraged by preserving many unspoiled examples of natural areas for the enjoyment and the self-education of urban and suburban residents.

—Irston R. Barnes.

424

Answers To Conflicts

STARLINGS IN THE CITY

A Conservationist's View

IN NATURE, birds are neither good nor bad. Each species is a part of the web of life, in which in the long run each has a chance to thrive and survive. In man's world, the situation may be different. We judge each thing on the basis of what it does to and for us here and now.

We consider some birds good because they give us food, or feed on harmful insects, or furnish recreation and inspiration. We label some birds bad because they feed on our ripening grain and fruit and endanger our economic security, or because we think some species interfere with our sport by capturing some fish or game, or because they foul buildings, shade trees, and the water supply.

The debate will go on, maybe forever: Should

426

we kill the birds, as some persons recommend, that interfere with our immediate well-being or our pleasure?

We like clear-cut answers to all questions. Is a bird beneficial or harmful to us? Is it a "good" or a "bad" bird? How can we control it?

But for most species of birds, it is hard to reach simple, clear-cut judgments that stand up very long. Like us, birds may mix some good and some bad behavior. Few birds (and few men) have habits and traits that are all black or all white. The shadings of gray vary among individuals and species, depending on many local conditions.

A few examples:

That friendly and welcome announcer of spring, the robin, is admired and loved by many of us. Who can be against the robin? Night workers who must sleep days justly complain the early-morning springtime songs of even a few robins keep them awake. Growers of strawberries, raspberries, cherries, and grapes may lose enough to robins to put them out of business.

Who can be against the Canada geese?—those majestic birds whose honking and V-shaped flights in fall thrill us and which are eagerly sought by hunters. Still, this favorite of the naturalist and prize of the hunter can be a pest to farmers, when it feeds on the tender shoots of fall-planted crops and puddles the fields after rain or irrigation. In fact, Canada geese, introduced into New Zealand in 1905, did such damage to farm crops that the species was declared a pest, and a continuous open season was established for a number of years in an effort to keep their numbers in line with natural food and habitat available and prevent depredations upon crops and ranches.

Who can be against our common dabbling ducks, such as mallards and pintails, which are the backbone of America's waterfowl hunting, with all its economic, sporting, recreational, and social implications and for which millions of Americans go afield each year just to see and study? Still, these shallow-water or surface feeders almost every year do serious damage on grain farms in the prairie pothole region of Canada and the nearby prairies of the United States.

Again: Our American warblers are valued because they feed on destructive insects and so help protect our crops and forests. Their bright colors, nervous flight, and cheery songs make them a general favorite. Yet, occasionally, under unusual conditions and in late summer and during fall migration, flocks of some species descend on vineyards and orchards and inflict damage by puncturing ripened crops and drinking the sweet fruit juices.

Red-winged blackbirds were estimated to have caused damage of 110 thousand dollars to corn on 555 farms in Ottawa County, Ohio, in 1957, despite considerable effort to protect the crop.

Two Federal research workers estimated losses of 460 thousand dollars by blackbirds to the rice crop in Arkansas in 1953. The farmers themselves put the damage at 1.4 million dollars. I assume the

A typical fall scene at the Horicon National Wildlife Refuge, Mayville, Wisconsin. Here Canada geese are feeding contentedly on food grown especially for them. Migratory waterfowl refuges help the sport of hunting; they curb crop depredations; and they delight millions of visitors who come to see the birds.

first estimate was reasonably accurate; the farmers' estimate would be an example of how objectivity may be lost when personal interests are at stake.

A House of Representatives Agricultural Committee in 1960 prepared a list based largely on farmers' estimates which showed that depredations of birds in the United States inflict about 100 million dollars' worth of damage to agriculture each year. About 30 species of birds at times are involved in these losses, and nearly all the damage is to 20 crops. The Arkansas figures I cited may indicate that the congressional figure may be somewhat too high. Even so, evidence is clear that the losses sometimes are serious.

The overall public good, in my opinion, would be served if the numbers of red-winged blackbirds and the likewise widespread and often pesky brown-headed cowbirds and starlings could be safely and humanely reduced to levels that would make their presence in rural America more tolerable to farmers, even though they also can be of service to agriculture and Americans generally.

I like to think of bird control as an aspect of bird management rather than an isolated activity. Our overall objective should be to manage bird populations so as to perpetuate and enhance their values and at the same time prevent or lessen losses. Bird conservation and bird control must be balanced to

428

serve the greatest good for the greatest number of people. Prevention wherever possible is better than corrective measures.

When we plant a cornfield next to a large, attractive marsh, we invite depredations from great concentrations of blackbirds, cowbirds, and starlings. Planning of fields and crops may forestall the visits of birds.

Let us examine some of the points we should consider in order to harmonize bird preservation and bird control.

First, let us regard birds as innocent until they are proved guilty.

We may not see birds feeding on destructive insect pests 50 weeks in the year but we easily can see (and magnify out of proportion) the few peaches or cherries birds take. How easy it is to overlook the greater service the birds give in preventing insect outbreaks!

Red-winged blackbirds were held guilty of reducing yields of sorghum in Virginia in 1961. Investigations by scientists of the Virginia Polytechnic Institute, however, disclosed that the poor yields were largely due to a plant disease, anthracnose, and to insects that commonly attack disease-weakened plants.

Arkansas farmers ascribed poor stands of lespedeza to blackbirds feeding on newly sown seed. Federal biologists collected 200 blackbirds in the fields where damage was said to be highest. Laboratory analysis of contents of the birds' stomachs showed not a single seed of lespedeza. Cage tests later with red-winged blackbirds, common grackles, and cowbirds showed that those birds (at least in captivity) would not feed on lespedeza seed. The conclusion was that the poor stands resulted from natural flooding, severe wind action, killing frost, and poor germination of seed.

In southern Louisiana, yellow-crowned night herons, known locally as grobecks, and a few related species were charged with hurting the bullfrog industry. Examinations of the stomachs of 100 herons taken from the area proved that the birds were guiltless. Not a single bird had taken a frog. These waders had fed almost entirely on crawfish, which at times do considerable damage to the shallow lakes, ponds, and marshes by bur-

Brooke Meanley, a biologist, bands red-winged black-birds at a winter roost in Arkansas. Such bandings have disclosed that many wintering blackbirds in the State are not involved in depredations on rice because they are on northern breeding grounds when damage occurs.

rowing into the dikes and causing leaks and run-off of the water, thus reducing the habitat required for the successful commercial production of frogs.

From the national and overall view, there obviously is full justification for protecting a species and engaging at the same time in limited control—not everywhere or at all seasons but in

The robin is a highly respected bird, but it likes strawberries and cherries and sometimes eats away the grower's profits.

local situations and at times when depredation may be expected.

Actually, complete protection of birds is advisable in an agricultural and industrial Nation like ours only to a limited extent. With few exceptions, complete protection may be accomplished on private bird preserves, inviolate sanctuaries, and on Government refuges and parks where birds are not in close competition with man for food, living space, effective use of land, the economics of making a living, and so on.

We can control the numbers of birds by several practices that prevent or deter birds from committing depredations or causing damage. They include managerial practices that attract, increase, disperse, frighten, or reduce specific species for a

particular time or place or otherwise prevent depredations. The manipulations of habitat is a major means of doing that.

Maintaining an even keel in management of migratory birds so as to reconcile the conflicting values of birds and the conflicting wishes of the public in regard to them is no easy task. I speak from experience. I know the contradictions in a combination program of bird conservation and bird control, but I know of no better way to provide balance and coordination and to prevent extremes in either direction—of going too far or not going far enough.

It is not easy to determine in a clear-cut fashion where reasonable programs of bird protection and bird control should begin and end or where, to what extent, and under what conditions reductional control should be approved.

To be consistent and fair to all segments of the public, the administrator of the programs must be guided by a clear, constructive, dynamic philosophy, a policy mature enough to serve the people now and for generations to come.

We need always in programs a high degree of coordination, cooperation, and communication among participants, the Government, and the public.

It is basically a problem of using resources; perhaps the only permanent solution will be one of philosophy and policy. The actual problems of control likely are as permanent as people and agriculture. The nature and magnitude of the problems will vary with the season and circumstances, and any successful solution must prevent or remove the cause of the problem. Frequently, this will require some adjustments in agricultural and land-use practices and policies that will help us avoid some of the conflicts with birds.

Always, too, let us remember the position birds have in the minds and hearts of millions of Americans.

Remember, for example, the time the District of Columbia sought congressional authority to kill starlings in downtown Washington. Hearings brought out that there were too many starlings and they were a great nuisance but also that they were helping to keep in check the Japanese beetle, a pest in parks, lawns, and gardens. The Congress turned down the request.

These compensatory activities of birds are among the reasons why the Federal and State Governments usually keep to the middle of the road in such matters.

I submit, then, a number of precepts and suggestions:

Because there is much overlapping in the distribution of locally desirable and undesirable bird species, every effort is called for to protect the desirable species whenever control is directed against offending species.

Most depredations are characteristic of individual species, local in scope, and usually last a relatively short time.

Extermination of a native species must not be allowed to occur as a result of any program of control. Control actions must be tempered by esthetic, recreational, scientific, and economic considerations. They must be based on biological knowledge so as to reduce interference with other birds and with other animal or plant life.

Control methods must be humane and selective.

We should avoid methods that reduce populations of birds when adequate control can be effected by nonlethal means.

Control methods should not be permitted that endanger people, their property, or desirable wildlife.

The control of protected species should be legally possible only under authorization of the Federal and State services.

Control always should be held to a reasonable minimum.

All procedures should be based on research designed to disclose whether and to what extent control may be needed and the procedures most likely to give the desired results with the least harm.

The problem is urgent. It is not a question as to whether America can afford to support the research I recommend, but whether we can afford not to support it.

—CLARENCE COTTAM.

The Legal Basis

WE SIGNED A TREATY in 1916 for the protection of migratory birds because we and the Canadians had become alarmed at the rapid decline of birds, particularly waterfowl. It said:

"Whereas, Many species of birds in the course of their annual migrations traverse certain parts of the United States and the Dominion of Canada; and

"Whereas, Many of these species are of great value as a source of food or in destroying insects which are injurious to forests and forage plants on the public domain, as well as to agricultural crops, in both the United States and Canada, but are nevertheless in danger of extermination through lack of adequate protection during the nesting season or while on their way to and from their breeding grounds;

"The United States of America and His Majesty the King of the United Kingdom of Great Britain . . . being desirous of saving from indiscriminate slaughter and of insuring the preservation of such migratory birds as are either useful to man or are harmless, have resolved to adopt some uniform system of protection which shall effectively accomplish such objects and to the end of concluding a Convention for this purpose. . . ."

The treaty recognizes three classes of birds—migratory game birds, migratory insectivorous birds, and other migratory nongame birds. Some are named by families, and others by common names.

"Permits to kill any of the above-named birds,"

the treaty said, "which under extraordinary conditions may become seriously injurious to the agricultural or other interests in any particular community, may be issued by the proper authorities of the High Contracting Powers under suitable regulations prescribed therefor by them respectively . . . ."

Not all that have migratory habits are included. All of the order *Falconiformes*, or birds of prey, and the "aliens," including the house sparrow, rock dove or feral pigeon, and the starling, are omitted.

The United States Government implemented the treaty in 1918 by the passage of the Migratory Bird Treaty Act.

A similar agreement was promulgated in 1936 with the Government of the United Mexican States.

One difference between the two treaties is that in the Mexican-United States document the birds are included by using the scientific name of the family. Thus all species of the listed families are given protection.

Another is that only two classes are recognized—migratory game birds and migratory nongame birds. Since a number of species of birds occur in Mexico and the United States but not in Canada, these are included in the Mexican treaty but are not mentioned in the Canadian convention.

The chief omissions from the Mexican treaty were the birds of prey and fish-eating species. An interpretation of the law by the Solicitor of the Department of the Interior gives protection to many species if they belong to families of birds included in the Canadian treaty. This is the basis for protecting the Hawaiian goose or nene, which occurs in neither Canada nor Mexico but does occur in Hawaii.

By independent, unilateral action, the Congress has given protection to bald and golden eagles.

The Federal Government has put teeth into the treaties. Many forms of management are carried on, with emphasis on migratory game birds, particularly waterfowl. Refuges have been established. A staff of law-enforcement officers watches over the welfare of the birds. Biologists conduct studies to add knowledge needed for management, including techniques to lessen damage by birds.

Interested conservation groups and organizations give counsel on policies relating to management of migratory game birds and advice on programs to rescue rare or endangered species.

Generally speaking, nearly everyone recognizes the desirability of perpetuating these feathered creatures in increasing numbers, if this is possible. Yet there are times and places when there are too many birds, at least for the good of man's interests. And, unfortunately, the times and places are becoming more frequent as man intensifies use of lands or alters habitats occupied by birds. It is a fact, however regrettable, that birds become misplaced as wildlife habitat becomes "people habitat." Thus we have situations where birds are not welcomed because danger to human life or serious economic losses will result if their activities are permitted to continue without restriction.

Most damage by birds is local and transitory, although the rice farmer of Arkansas or the Idaho cattle feedlot owner may feel the blackbirds and starlings concentrate too early and stay too late. It would seem that the farmer suffering damage should assume the responsibility to protect his interests.

But public agencies, particularly the Federal Government, cannot ignore the problem. Laws enacted by the Congress require Federal attention to the matter. Remember, the treaties give continual protection to most migratory nongame birds and provide that they can be destroyed if they are causing damage. At least the Federal Government, therefore, must give permission to kill the offending birds if killing them is necessary to protect farm and forest crops. Procedures to that end have been established.

By order of the Secretary of the Interior (Part 16, Title 50 of Code of Federal Regulations), a person may destroy blackbirds, cowbirds, and grackles without a permit when they are committing serious depredations or are about to do so to ornamental and shade trees and agricultural crops.

The Director of the Bureau of Sport Fisheries and Wildlife has like authority to issue depredation orders to permit the killing of migratory game birds that cause or are about to cause serious damage to agricultural, horticultural, or fish-cultural interests.

As long as the farmer is permitted legally to kill blackbirds to protect his interests, has not the Government gone as far as it can to resolve the problem? Not quite.

When he kills offending blackbirds, the farmer may unwittingly destroy some mourning doves or robins—species that are protected. He would then violate the Migratory Bird Treaty Act and would subject himself to prosecution.

Under certain circumstances and after inspecting the conditions of the bird depredation, the enforcement officers of the Bureau may issue individual permits to cover the accidental destruction of protected birds when a farmer engages in a campaign against blackbirds.

The Bureau of Sport Fisheries and Wildlife has a many-sided responsibility.

It conducts research on the food habits, life histories, and populations of the species that cause damage or nuisance.

It develops damage-control methods, like frightening devices, repellants, alteration of habitat, and reduction of population, and encourages development of damage-resistant strains of crops.

Blackbirds darken the sky at a large winter roost in the rice belt at Grand Prairie, Arkansas.

It participates in studies and surveys to determine the kind and extent of bird damage, the need for control, and the techniques to be used.

It disseminates research findings on the effective methods and on how to conduct repellent, frightening, and control programs and demonstrates effective methods.

Under certain conditions, it takes part in direct reduction of bird populations. In this sensitive situation, men of the Bureau are keenly aware of public attitudes for and against Federal participation—that is, through the Bureau of Sport Fisheries and Wildlife. They must sift out the biological facts

from the tempests of emotion, however, and make decisions that protect the resources as much as possible and yet relieve the damage situation.

Obviously, their efforts to control unwanted birds must assure the safety of other species that may intermingle with the pests or are attracted to places where control programs are carried out.

For example, the mourning doves that feed in the same feedlots where hordes of starlings are consuming and defiling livestock feed must be protected when action is taken against the starlings. For that, expert knowledge and extreme care are necessary if the job is to be done successfully

Growers of holly in Oregon cannot market the foliage and berries that droppings of starlings ruin.

435

and economically and without undue risk to other birds, animals, and people.

Some persons hold that there should be no direct, planned attempts to reduce numbers of birds because they already are subject to normal mortality factors. Some fear that once the Federal Government embarks on such activities the pressure will be great to expand them to the point where it will handle all such problems even though most such damage is of local concern. Many persons condemn the use of poison.

Through the years, the Bureau of Sport Fisheries and Wildlife and its predecessor agencies have been in the middle of two strongly divergent currents of opinion on what the position of the Government should be.

The policy has been one of moderation, but as time passed and the problems of bird and man relationships have taken on more safety and economic significance, the guidelines have been modified to permit greater flexibility of action.

The guiding principles of the Bureau are that no indigenous species shall be threatened with extinction as a result of control actions.

Any control must consider humane, esthetic, recreational, and economic aspects.

All activities shall be carried out in accordance with State and local laws, ordinances, and regulations and must be cosponsored by political subdivisions represented by elected officials.

Permission must be obtained from the owner, occupant, or administrator of land and water areas before control of birds is undertaken.

Only methods that safeguard desirable birds, other animals, and persons and their property shall be used.

The least possible interference with other animal and plant life is permitted.

No direct population reduction program on migratory game birds shall be carried out by the Bureau. Rather, the reductions, when necessary, are achieved by hunting regulations, permits, or special depredation orders.

The population-control programs recognize different courses of action for migratory game birds, migratory nongame birds, and those not offered Federal protection.

For the first group, which includes waterfowl,

doves, pigeons, and cranes, the Bureau's programs include the use of frightening devices and herding, the purchase and management of habitat to lure and to keep the birds from private lands, the distribution of grain to draw them from depredation areas, and the issuance of killing permits and special orders to allow hunting by the general public.

No direct reduction is practiced by Bureau personnel.

The programs for the migratory nongame birds follow a different course. Because blackbirds, grackles, and cowbirds may be killed without a permit, under a Secretarial order, whenever they are doing or about to do damage to crops, their control normally is left to the person who suffers the damage. Where robins raid a cherry orchard or gulls become a safety hazard around airports, the Bureau investigates the complaint and may issue a special killing permit if conditions warrant.

When other methods will not relieve the problem, the Bureau may resort to direct methods on its own lands and on other Federal lands if the administering agency assumes a substantial part of the costs.

On private lands, the Bureau provides technical advice, guidance, and demonstration of the methods that generally can be used by individuals without risk to other forms of life. However, there must be a cooperative agreement with State agencies or political subdivisions that establishes the cooperating agencies as the sponsors and outlines their responsibility for the program and its costs.

On occasion, the Bureau may directly engage in a program of reducing bird numbers if the only satisfactory method is one that requires professional direction to avoid dangers to other birds or animals or to man. The damage caused by the nuisance species must be significant and the dangers of the method to our living resources must be potentially serious.

The policies on the control of unprotected birds—that is, those not specified in laws—such as starlings and house sparrows, are somewhat different, because the Federal Government does not have responsibility for their management and many States do not mention them in their laws.

They occupy a limbo insofar as they concern the Government unless it is necessary to protect Government property from them. The Bureau uses whatever methods are best suited to protect its property and carries out similar programs for other Federal agencies if they pay most of the costs.

As to private property, any reductional program on unprotected birds is the responsibility of persons who suffer damage as long as protection methods present no hazard to federally protected species.

If a State agency or a legal governmental subdivision has executed a cooperative agreement dealing with bird damage problems and will pay much of the costs, the Bureau furnishes technical assistance to demonstrate proper methods. It may also engage in a population reduction program if the damage is significant and if protected and unprotected species are intermingled or if protected birds will be exposed to serious danger if the control is not done by bird specialists.

To sum up: Any direct Bureau participation to reduce bird numbers rests on the policy of avoiding accidental damage to nontarget birds protected by the treaties or Federal statute.

We believe it is essential that bird control be guided by those who have a direct responsibility to protect this valuable resource. To do otherwise is to endanger these creatures by overcontrol.

Most of the control techniques we now have are so risky that only professional persons should apply them. Actually, we have few satisfactory methods of achieving reduction of large numbers of birds. The chemical, electronic, and other scientific tools that we have and may develop will provide no one method that will correct all situations. We look less for a method, though, than for a wider understanding of the problems.

—Lansing A. Parker.

Scaring Makes a Difference

MAKE A BETTER DEVICE to scare birds away from your cherry trees or strawberry patch, and a grateful world will beat a path to your door. It must meet two specifications. It must be effective. It must not be dangerous to you, your children, other people, and property.

Otherwise, anything goes—and has, from time beyond ken.

If you think it's too easy to be worthy of your best efforts, consider this list of bright ideas other people have had: Smacking sticks or boards together and other hand-made noises; horns; fire and smoke; scarecrows like men, monsters, hawks, and owls; firecrackers; shiny, wind-moved twirling objects; patrols with rifles and shotguns; roman candles; flares and revolving lights; automatic exploders; projectile bombs; delayed-action shotgun shells; pressure horns; airplanes; amplified distress and alarm calls of the birds themselves; chemical repellants; ammonia sprays; narcotizing agents; and electronic shocking devices.

In simpler times than now, when farmers thought the birds were getting a little too gluttonous, one of the kids in the family had fun, earned his keep, and scared the birds away at the same time. Many a farm boy developed a good

STARLINGS AT FEEDLOT

pitching arm and eyesight by throwing rocks and sticks at birds and improved markmanship through the use of rifles and shotguns. In those days, almost any kind of scaring device or technique turned the trick.

But times have changed, and so have we. Small farms have grown into big farms. Single-crop farming is commonplace. There are more machines, chemicals, specialization, and competition.

Birds, though, still have strong urges to eat well, avoid problems, and multiply, and many have been doing that better than ever in our expansive fields of grain and seed crops, orchards and vineyards, feedlots, irrigated desert farmlands, prickly fields of safflower—even on lands once dotted with saguaro cactus and in soil-conserving fallow and stubble fields.

Hence the need for new, better scaring devices. The main types of problems now involve relatively few kinds of birds but more individual birds in more places.

Fire, one of man's earliest devices for managing night-feeding animals, has been used successfully against waterfowl in grain crops at night. Smoke alone was tried, but chemicals in the smoke hurt the crops.

Oil-burning highway signal flares have been of value.

Somebody thought of putting an electric hand lantern on a bicycle wheel in a field. Wind wings on the wheel caused it to turn and shine over the field. An improvement was larger spotlights powered by small electric motors operated by batteries. Large, 24- or 30-inch spotlights powered by gasoline generators have made 160-acre grainfields in Canada off limits for ducks.

Bright strips of metal and cloth twirled or fluttered by the wind and scarecrows made in the image of men and hawks and owls are pretty good in some places. They are effective, however, for only short distances and for short periods, because birds, particularly the resident species, get used to the gadgets rather quickly and after that pay them little mind.

All these visual deterrents (except powerful rotating spotlights) do little to stop bird damage over extensive cropland. Their main help seems to be in the short-term protection of gardens, nurseries, and small orchards where few birds are doing damage. That's not to say, though, that there are no possibilities of perfecting something better for large concentrations of birds.

Devices that transmit the sound of explosions or other impulses to the ears of depredating birds, when properly used, have given excellent results. They are best if they are not applied at the same places consistently, if the interval of use is not constant or rhythmic, and if they are used in combination.

Firecrackers, rockets, and such may cause fires. If you plan to use them, check your State, county, and city laws first.

The Chinese long ago began using firecrackers to scare birds. We have modernized the idea. We use firecrackers at varying intervals on fuse rope; make bigger salutes and bombs; manufacture shell-crackers that can be fired from a conventional shotgun.

Various kinds of mortars fire or project a delayed-action explosive missile over a field. For use at night, the projectiles have flares of light besides explosives.

In some States, the experimental use of these devices has been so successful that legislatures have amended their explosives laws to permit their legal use in farming districts. Enough men to apply

A farmer at Lewes, Delaware, uses shiny foil plates to scare blackbirds away from his sweet corn. Such devices are impractical in most large-scale farming.

Automatic exploders, which make a sound like a gunshot, frighten blackbirds out of ripening cornfields.

them properly can make them effective over large areas. When people or livestock are nearby, it's best not to use these explosive devices.

Firearms have been used successfully for generations to protect valuable crops. The .22-caliber rifle, perhaps, is the most effective single instrument against most kinds of depredating birds in extensive fields of grain or corn. The pinglike sound of a rifle slug traveling at high speed frightens birds out of fields. One man with a rifle on a platform can keep birds off about 160 acres. Some farmers have put a shooting platform on the bed of a pickup truck. As they drive in the fields, they stop now and then to shoot.

The man behind the rifle must know the capabilities of his weapon, else it becomes hazardous, for a .22 rifle is effective up to a mile or so. A shotgun has only a short range and ammunition for it is costly. Birds soon become conditioned to the sound and move safely out of range. Adequate protection of the field with a shotgun requires constant movement from place to place.

A new way is to amplify and broadcast the distress and alarm calls of the marauders themselves. Tape recordings are made of the signals birds give each other when they sense danger. Loud speakers carry the recordings for all the birds to hear—and act on.

This method has produced some fine results in its experimental stage. The electronic equipment needed is rather costly, and maybe experienced operators are needed for it. Over extensive areas, amplified calls played from aircraft appear promising.

People have suggested the use of high-frequency sound above the human hearing range. The widest reported hearing range in wild birds appears to be that of the starling, ranging from 700 to 15 thousand cycles per second. All the experiments we have heard of, however, have failed to indicate that birds actually receive or react to frequencies inaudible to man, say from 18 thousand cycles upward.

Automatic exploders were used 50 years ago in the ricefields of the Southeastern States against bobolinks and blackbirds. Forty years later other exploders, using bottled acetylene gas or carbide, appeared on the market. All of them however, seemed to need frequent repairs. When trouble-free models do become available, however, they will offer one of the most effective and economical means of protecting crops from birds. Even now, the less-than-perfect models are regarded as valuable tools by many farmers and some airport managers.

Birds do become adjusted to them, however, and the explosions must be staggered, and the exploders must be moved occasionally. They may not be advisable near residential areas and farms where milk, meat, or eggs are produced. Continued harassment is reported to result in lower production of these foods.

Bird repellants are chemicals that act through the senses of sight, smell, or taste and deter birds from doing damage. Some of the compounds are poisonous.

Sticky pastes have been used to keep roosting birds off sheltered ledges of building. After a trial or two, the birds find a more comfortable roost elsewhere. Sometimes the compounds deface buildings more than the birds do. One such product, sprayed on the trees, was used effectively in 1965 to keep starlings from roosting along the route of the Presidential inaugural parade in Washington.

Somewhat similar paste compounds, applied to telephone poles and the like, reduce woodpecker damage, which is heavy in some parts of the country.

A reasonably effective way to discourage red-winged blackbirds, cowbirds, starlings, grackles, purple martins, and others from roosting in trees in large numbers in late summer and winter is to apply dilute ammonia sprays at night after the birds have settled into the roost. High-powered spraying machines are necessary. Wind and weather must be right. It must not be applied close to buildings and people.

To keep birds from eating tree seeds in refores-

Bird calls are being recorded for later broadcasting. Birds can be frightened from places where they are not wanted by broadcasting amplified alarm or distress calls of the offending species.

tation projects in several parts of the country, scientists at the Denver Wildlife Research Center some years ago began studies to find bird-repellent compounds. While this research is still in its infancy, such compounds as Anthraquinone and Arasan, with satisfactory sticker coverings of latex or asphalt emulsion, provide good protection for seeds of loblolly, slash, and longleaf pines from birds. Direct seeding now may proceed with more confidence that the seeds will survive bird damage and sprout.

Finding a chemical repellant that will protect farm crops is more difficult. Some compounds give varying degrees of protection, but the best of them leave residues above tolerance limits set by the Food and Drug Administration.

Chemical repellants may be useful on such crops as corn, grapes, lettuce, and forest trees, but they appear to be unsuitable for use in feedlots, roosts in holly groves, and around airports.

Soporifics are chemicals that are mixed in bait material and immobilize the birds that eat enough treated bait. They put the birds to sleep or produce flutterings, floppings, and other distress symptoms, which cause other birds to leave the baited area and stay away for long periods.

Certain toxic compounds produce similar effects, but usually kill the birds. Soporifics have value at cattle and poultry feedlots, on vineyards, and at airports. They also have good application in protecting grain and other crops if the depredating birds can be made to take the bait instead of the field crops.

The birds that take the soporific-treated bait suffer little pain and are incapacitated for only a short time. Acceptable to even ardent bird lovers, the use of soporifics in controlling bird damage has a high potential.

Of the electronic shocking devices, one of the first was developed and tested in 1955. Called a

Airplanes are used to herd flocks of waterfowl out of fields where they are damaging crops.

bird snapper, it consisted of two bare parallel wires, about 2 inches apart and suspended on poles above the crop to be protected. Standard 110-volt current was transformed to 15 thousand volts; as pressure built up within the system, intermittent random arcing between the wires produced loud snapping noises. The idea was that the noises produced would send birds packing.

Variations have been tried, but none has been very effective. Many have had other drawbacks. Birds alighting on the wires were severely shocked, burned, or electrocuted without regard to species. Costs of construction were high. Interference with radio and television reception was common. Though the charged wires are well above human reach, the system is dangerous.

Other bird shocker systems now on the market were designed primarily for installation on building ledges at roost sites of pigeons, sparrows, and starlings.

The units consist of a generator for producing a pulsating current of several hundred volts having low amperage. The current passes through an uninsulated wire strung in parallel about 2.5 inches from two ground wires. When activated, there is a magnetic shock field for several inches around the wires. The birds need not come in contact with the wires to receive a shock. After one or two such experiences, the birds of a flock—especially starlings—quickly learn to avoid the installations, although pigeons may perch on ledges just beyond the shock range of the wires.

Costs of the electrical shocking system may be many thousands of dollars on tall buildings, where steeplejacks and licensed electricians have to install them. Maintenance costs generally are quite low. The system occasionally is short-circuited through breakage of wires by window washers and repairmen. When that happens birds may still stay away for several weeks or months.

Properly installed, these electrical wiring systems are scarcely visible from street level. They are not hazardous to people and create no risk of fire. They are used on several buildings in Washington.

Some of us had high hopes that radar might be adapted in some way to control nuisance birds. So far, however, no proved, practical application of radar in bird management has been developed.

Municipalities across the country have used many frightening devices in attempts to end the objectionable roosting of starlings. Dummy owls are effective deterrents for only a short time—the birds quickly discover they are harmless.

Problems of costs, hazards, and technicalities are great but, we think, not insurmountable.

The response of birds to electrical fields has never been studied adequately, but there seems to be enough evidence to conclude that birds in flight receive and respond in some degree to radiations of electrical energy. For example, perching birds seem to avoid the wires of powerlines carrying very high voltages. In what manner and to what degree such radiations affect birds certainly should be given careful study; it may lead to the use of

Starlings used to roost on the frieze of a public building in Washington, but (below) an electrical wiring system now keeps them away.

444

static electricity and other forms of electrical radiations to solve some vexations.

The matter does not end with perfecting some device, whether chemical, electrical, visual, or audible, or a combination. There still will be factors of space and place, whether a small garden, a small building, a small farm, or farms and orchards that cover an entire valley or even a large part of a State.

That entails matters of effectiveness of the devices, costs, an adequate supply of devices, the availability of labor to install and operate them properly, and the economics of protecting the crop or building or orchard, or whatever.

For example, if a given combination of scare devices is effective at a cost of 50 dollars an acre, its use on a crop of head lettuce having a net profit potential of, say, a thousand dollars an acre, likely would be good business. Its use to protect a grain crop with a net profit potential of 50 dollars an acre, however, would seem to be a quick way to bankruptcy.

Even the best of scaring devices for a given problem is not apt to give the protection desired unless it is used properly. That requires an understanding of the capabilities of the equipment and technique and of the birds themselves and their habits, and the exercise of good judgment, reliability, and persistence in applying the technique.

—CECIL S. WILLIAMS and JOHNSON A. NEFF.

To Kill a Bird

SOME OF THE PEOPLE to whom birds are a trouble and nothing else offer what they think is a simple cure: Kill the birds. It's not that simple. Even if we had ways (which we do not) to reduce the total number of blackbirds and not harm others when we do so, just what effect would killing a hundred, or a thousand, or a million have on the total damage they do?

Female red-winged blackbirds lay an average of four eggs, of which about 60 percent hatch. If all those young birds lived until the following spring and produced young, and so on, blackbirds would overrun the continent before long. That won't happen, because there is not enough blackbird food to support expanding populations indefinitely. Also, there finally would not be enough suitable places to nest. We know that the combined effect of all depressing influences—food, bad weather, natural mortality, reproductive difficulties, and such—increases progressively as populations approach the limits of food and shelter requirements. Any species is limited by the factors of its environment. When times are good, more will survive.

What does "kill the birds" really mean? Nothing much, unless we add details as to when, where, and which birds.

Resident, local flocks of such birds as house sparrows offer fair targets for effective control measures of several kinds. Birds that gather into large flocks and migrant flocks that combine into enormous seasonal roosts—blackbirds, for example—are quite another matter.

Those who say, "Kill the birds!" usually think of reducing the hemisphere's populations of blackbirds to the point that their total damage will abate noticeably. This is advocating an absurdity. Any significant long-range effect from reducing artificially the continental blackbird population means that at least 60 percent must be removed and be kept removed.

Let's assume the continental population of blackbirds totals 500 million, although it has probably reached more than that. We would have to remove more than 300 million and repeat the process every few years.

Most damage and most nuisances are relatively local in terms of time and place. Efforts to control damage must be pinpointed to a specific, local situation to be worth doing. When they are, the efforts can be concentrated and are surer of success.

There are exceptions. Some of the tremendous migrant and wintering flocks become intolerable because of their numbers or their feeding habits, but most of these flocks are so located they do not interfere beyond being a tolerable and often interesting nuisance. Examples of the intolerable situations are the "million-class" flocks that gather in cattle feedyards, consuming tons of cattle feed daily and contaminating the remainder by their excrement.

Another is the "million-class" flocks that take up winter quarters around such places as a city water supply reservoir. If flocks of this size cannot be moved out of those areas (and usually they cannot be), killing out such a flock or a substantial portion may (and only may) be a possible solution. Killing methods that can be safely used around such places as a city water supply are limited in kind and effect.

Now some partial prescriptions and some promising leads.

Nuisance birds have been studied ever since the Federal Government took an interest in their control in 1889. Indeed, the origin of the Fish and Wildlife Service is partly due to recognition of the need to study the problem. So it is not a new problem and, logically, answers by the score should be available. They are, but most solutions have employed frightening or repellent devices.

To one aware of the economic and esthetic value of birds and the dynamics of populations, reductional control is justified only as a last resort. Those who have suffered serious damage are quick to reply that frightening just moves the problem to someone else. Sometimes that is true, but

not always. In one place in South Dakota, for example, flocks frightened from a cornfield moved into nearby fields to feed extensively on weed seeds.

Strychnine-treated grain has been used widely. Often it is effective, but its quick action brings about early warning symptoms. Only some of the birds in a flock ingest killing amounts of the treated bait before the onset of effects. All birds then usually stop feeding, and the birds that survive seldom are enticed to eat treated baits a second time. The uneaten baits left in the field remain a hazard to some other innocent seed-eating birds, although gallinaceous species, such as quail and pheasants, are highly resistant to strychnine. The carcasses of the poisoned birds may contain enough strychnine to poison animals that eat them.

Some slow-acting poisons have been used. Several hours may elapse between the time of feeding and death. Thus, starlings baited during a late winter afternoon at feedlots may die during the night at a roost several miles away. Collecting and burying the carcasses there is relatively simple, and the danger of the accidental poisoning of other animals is lessened.

Because blackbirds eat many things, attractive foods are available to them in midsummer, and they seldom are tempted by poisoned baits. But farmers see the damage they do, and, understandably, they want to try the most readily available lethal agent to destroy the birds. "Readily available" means a host of toxic chemicals waiting to be misused. The victims may be many species of innocent birds and other animal life.

When those lethal agents are taken in by mouth, the problem is to get the nuisance birds (and only them if possible) to ingest the chemical. When we know more about the feeding habits and seasonal movements of depredating species, it may be possible to develop selective baiting techniques. Like the selective weedkillers, which affect some plants and not others, we may also find species-specific lethal agents for birds.

Other ingenious techniques for destroying large numbers of birds have been tried. To destroy huge concentrations of crows that at times gather for the winter in Oklahoma and forage on grain, a device patterned after military fragmentation bombs was used. Sections of stove pipe were loaded with shot, bolts, stones, bits of iron, and sticks of dynamite and placed in roost trees. All were wired in series to be detonated at once when the crows had settled for the night. Large number of crows were killed. Many others were mangled.

In northeastern Africa, flamethrowers destroyed more than 3 million weaver birds. The operation did not stop the damage to crops, but it started brush fires.

Contact poisons sprayed on roost sites usually are highly toxic to nearly all living things, including people. The spray may be hazardous for months.

Starlings may enter feedlots by the hundreds of thousands, as they did when this picture was taken near Collinsville, California, and cause great losses.

Fruit growers by and large would be happy if there were no starlings, which may get at bunches of high-quality, ready-to-market seedless grapes (above) and ruin them (below) in a very short time.

In Africa, when other methods were useless against weaver birds, authorities treated roost and nest sites with parathion, an insecticide, by aircraft shortly after dark. Native drums warned villagers to stay away from the treated areas. Seventy million weaver birds were reported destroyed in this one operation.

Similar treatments have been carried out by olive growers in Tunisia and by rice growers in the United States.

Poison gases have been considered as a quick and humane way to kill large numbers of birds, which are highly sensitive to gases. Many problems must be solved before any workable method

Some farmers build traps to capture blackbirds that forage in crops. The birds in the trap are decoys for others, which are caught and destroyed. This trap is near a ricefield in Arkansas.

can be developed, however. Since they are poisonous to all animals, the first problem is how to control drift of the gas with air currents. Aside from an occasional use as fumigants to destroy roosting pigeons, sparrows, and starlings in buildings, gases have not been applied successfully in bird control.

Shotguns and rifles have been used against the pigeons, sparrows, and blackbirds around farm buildings, corn plantings, grain elevators, and food processing plants. In many parts of the country,

Great horned owls, which are a natural foe of the crow, are used as decoys to attract crows within gun range. The hunting of crows is welcomed by the farmers who suffer heavy crop damage from them.

these methods for solving bird problems are now prohibited by State and local laws.

It has been suggested that blackbirds be taken off the protected list to afford sportsmen an opportunity for target practice, but I doubt whether many would be killed because of the high cost of ammunition and the reluctance of many farmers to permit hunters on their land.

Even before gunpowder was invented, man used his ingenuity to develop animal-catching devices. Modifications of these early inventions still are effective sometimes. The decoy and modified Australian crow traps have been used effectively in cherry orchards in Washington to control local starling damage. They are being employed on blackbirds in the ricefields of Arkansas and other parts of the country.

A pest-control operator sets a trap to remove pigeons from a site where they are not wanted.

The light trap, a large funnel-shaped enclosure equipped with spotlights, was developed by Bureau of Sport Fisheries and Wildlife biologists to catch large numbers of roosting birds for banding. When used on concentrations of 1 million to 5 million starlings or blackbirds, spectacular catches may be obtained. Numbers as high as 100 thousand have been taken in a single night. We must interpret the catch in terms of the total concentration, however; then the total effect is not large.

Since predation is one of the means by which Nature exercises control over animal populations, the application of this technique to bird problems is under study by the Bureau. In one situation, raccoons and foxes were introduced on several small islands off the Massachusetts coast that herring gulls used as nesting sites. Large numbers of gulls in the vicinity of Logan Airport in Boston are a hazard to aircraft and a reduction in their numbers was deemed essential.

Predation by the raccoons and foxes eliminated about 90 percent of the eggs and young gulls and thus proved to be an effective control measure. The technique cannot be applied to many situations where the presence of predators might be objectionable or where other species of desirable birds and mammals are present.

The manipulation of population levels through controlling the birth rate is preferable to the destruction of large numbers of birds by the use of lethal agents. Research has begun at the University of Massachusetts to find substances that alter the reproduction of birds. Many materials have been tested. One is Sudan Black B, a nontoxic dye. Birds that ingest the chemical are not affected, but more than 90 percent of the eggs laid by treated birds do not hatch. If substances of this type can be incorporated into the daily diets of local flocks of nuisance species, such as pigeons, sparrows, and starlings, before their breeding seasons, a reduc-

452

tion in population levels may be achieved provided repopulation by flocks from adjoining areas does not occur. Here again, the application of a control technique would depend on the development of methods that restrict the exposure of the treated baits to only the target species.

It is the task of the research biologist assigned to study lethal agents to explore all mechanisms by which bird populations can be reduced. He must appraise their effectiveness, determine hazards, devise application techniques to minimize such dangers, and make recommendations as to their conditions of use.

Since no two bird problems are alike, he cannot guarantee the degree of success that will be achieved in the field. Nor can he be expected to serve as the judge and jury in deciding when and where lethal controls shall be applied. Because bird problems are local and mostly affect the individual landowner directly, it seems right that he should make these decisions.

But society has a stake in the decisions, for birds belong to all of the people and migratory birds may be under the jurisdiction of two or more countries.

Furthermore—to repeat what has been said before—there is danger that other valuable birds may become innocent victims of control efforts and there is also the matter of selecting the best time and location to conduct a bird-control program. Selective lethal control will require considerable knowledge to decide what to use and how to apply it.

Those who embrace the balance of nature theory believe in letting the situation alone and relying upon natural forces to exercise necessary control.

I question that, however: Man has already so altered the environment that "natural" enemies of the pioneer era no longer exist or can no longer cope with the situation. Furthermore, some of the foremost pests are foreigners that did not bring their diseases and other enemies when they came to this country. Few persons who suffer losses are willing to wait for the development of natural controls.

However, biological control, with a big assist from scientific research, holds promise of reducing bird populations. A possibility may be the sterilization of birds so they cannot reproduce. If it can be developed for birds, it would have the merit of not being offensive to persons who do not want to kill birds—among whom are most of us.

—WALTER W. DYKSTRA.

An Ounce of Prevention

JUST AS WE CAN ratproof buildings against rodents and treat marshes to combat mosquitoes, we can use an ounce of prevention to cure a pound of damage some birds do in some places. The three main ways to avoid the damage are to alter farming practices so as to reduce or eliminate situations that invite damage; to change a habitat, so that birds are less likely to cause trouble; and to exclude birds from places where they cause damage.

At some times and places it may be easier for a farmer to change his farming practices than it is for the birds to change their habits. Rice-growers in southwestern Louisiana and east Texas for years battled the depredations of blackbirds (chiefly red-winged blackbirds) without making much headway against them. They finally converted their ricelands to pastures, and now many raise cattle.

But that is an action of last resort. As a rule, far less drastic adjustments to birds may involve alterations in time and method of planting and harvesting crops, in varieties of crops grown, and in cultural practices.

454

Planting either before or after most of the migrating birds have passed north may be possible. In parts of the Southeast, however, March and April planting of rice means little loss to bobolinks but considerable loss to red-winged blackbirds. Conversely, planting in May avoids most of the red-wings, but bobolinks exact a toll on sprouts. Some ricegrowers in this region consider the red-wing the lesser of two evils and therefore plant in March and April.

During the summer and early fall, the main roosting place of blackbirds (chiefly red-winged blackbirds) in the extensive Arkansas rice belt is in ricefields. When the ripened ricefield is drained for harvesting, which is done to dry it up enough so that the combine can operate without bogging down, most birds leave and seek an undrained ricefield, because they like to roost over water. Fields are drained about 10 days before harvest.

Some farmers have learned that fields sometimes can be drained 2 to 3 weeks before harvest; that reduces bird-caused stem breakage, rice depredations, and shattering of the grain. When the roosting populations comprise thousands of birds, damage to the crop can be great.

Sometimes in southern Louisiana ricefields are planted early to permit harvest in July in order to produce a second crop, known as a stubble crop (from rice seed left in the stubble from the original harvest operation). The practice increases production in a given field and at the same time gets around the major bird problem, because the first or main crop is harvested before the birds have concentrated in huge numbers. Many of the birds that cause damage to rice are migrants from breeding grounds in northern United States and southern Canada.

Corn that becomes vulnerable to attack by blackbirds at the middle of the growing season—in the milky-dough or roasting-ear stage in the Middle Atlantic States—is damaged less than comparable corn maturing earlier or later. That is because in midseason the blackbirds turn to feeding on other attractive foods, chiefly wildrice, and they are not so active during this postbreeding, premigratory period. By planting corn in this area so that it comes into the milky-dough stage in midseason, farmers can avoid much damage.

Another example: Farmers who raise hogs in northwestern Nebraska, to save on overhead in fattening hogs, used to turn the animals loose to feed on corn grown for the purpose. Flocks of migratory waterfowl then were attracted to the feedlots at night. Sometimes they consumed more of the grain than the hogs did. Farmers who went back to the usual way of harvesting, storing, and feeding the grain to the hogs found their savings far exceeded the expected advantage of self-feeding the hogs in the field.

Some farmers plant sorghums, millet, and other crops for the express purpose of diverting birds from their main commercial crops. The plantings offer an alternative feeding area and a place for the birds to go. In some situations, however, the practice may draw more birds into the region and so defeat the objective of protecting the main crops.

Soybeans, which do not attract blackbirds, often are grown in conjunction with field corn and rice.

Experience in New Jersey and Delaware indicates that farmers can expect almost twice as much damage in cornfields next to marshland as to corn grown 800 yards from the marshland. It makes sense to grow crops less vulnerable to depredations on acres close to marshes.

Varieties of corn that withstand attack by blackbirds are grown in sections where bird damage is severe. This "resistant" corn usually has a heavy, tight husk that extends well beyond the tip of the ear. When most of the farmers in one township in New Jersey agreed to switch to such corn in 1964, the total estimated damage was gratifyingly less than that in nearby areas.

Certain varieties of rice are less subject to damage than others. Johnson Neff and Brooke Meanley, of the Bureau of Sport Fisheries and Wildlife, in their bulletin, "Blackbirds and the Arkansas Rice Crop," published by the University of Arkansas, wrote:

"Although Zenith is the most widely grown variety [of rice] in eastern Arkansas and is frequently severely attacked by birds, it is a variety that, given free choice, birds do not like as well as some others; its hull is very rough, with a high percentage of silicon content. It is frequently eaten mainly because it is the most widely grown variety.

A grower of blueberries near Troutdale, Oregon, tries out plastic exclosures to keep birds away.

Ornate architecture provides ideal roosting places for starlings and pigeons.

456

"Some farmers intentionally leave their rice stubble unplowed until spring; others would find the practice profitable. When stubble fields are left undisturbed through the winter, the immense wintering blackbird population performs a great sanitation service, removing literally tons of waste seed and many insects, possibly lessening the insect and weed problems of the next growing season."

Some types of wheat are more susceptible to bird depredations than others. Varieties that must be swathed before threshing are vulnerable to bird depredations for longer periods than those that can be combined without swathing. As a result, they are subject normally to much damage.

Shortening the time that a crop is subject to attack saves trouble and damage.

Peanuts dried in shocks, especially in wet seasons, are available to birds for weeks. The use of artificial dryers eliminates shocking and almost completely eliminates losses to birds.

Corngrowers who have dryers can harvest their crops earlier and thus lessen the duration of depredations in the field. Drying artificially has another advantage; it reduces development of mold on the grain, which becomes especially bad in damp and cool autumns and particularly on ears that have been opened by birds.

Dryers are gaining favor among ricegrowers, too. Besides lessening the period of exposure to damage, less grain is shattered and lost before and during harvest. Shattering losses sometimes are blamed on birds when other factors are more responsible.

The introduction of combines and dryers to harvest rice in Arkansas had the advantage of reducing materially the damage previously inflicted by migratory waterfowl on shocked grain. In bad weather shocked rice is exposed to depredations for long periods.

The method of planting makes a difference. For example, planting rice seed from airplanes in shallowly flooded fields reduces losses of seed to blackbirds. But any ducks that are around may be attracted to such fields which, from the air, look like ponds—instead of blackbird damage, there will be duck damage. Most damage by ducks can be avoided if the rice is planted by machines, rolled, and then flooded.

A modern office building, designed for efficiency in maintenance, has few places where birds can roost.

457

Aerial seeding in shallow water instead of on moist soil can reduce depredations of blackbirds and other birds on newly planted ricefields.

To lessen pulling of sprouts and scratching out of seed by birds, some farmers plant corn and other seed the maximum depth that growing requirements permit. Tests with such birds as robins, meadowlarks, and boat-tailed grackles held in large enclosures indicate that deeply planted seed is less likely to be destroyed than shallow-planted seed.

The golden eagle is a predator in much of the sheep and goat country of the Southwest, particularly in western Texas and New Mexico.

While reports of damage are often exaggerated—losses due to malnutrition, poor herding, stillbirths, and diseases often are charged to depredation by eagles—there is no doubt that losses to eagles do occur at times. It is rare, indeed, that the problem is acute, except in places where serious overgrazing occurs and the range is in poor condition. The solution lies in better range management (in which all grazing is held within the carrying capacity of the land), better herding and management procedures, and lambing under sheds.

Depredations by migratory waterfowl are serious in many places, all the more because of excessive drainage of marshes, potholes, and lakes for crop production.

Part of the answer is in the system of Federal migratory waterfowl refuges, which provide homes for several million waterfowl that might otherwise be forced to feed in farmers' fields. The development of more refuges in regions where food and habitat for the birds are deficient is a practical way of relieving damage to commercial crops.

In sections of the Prairie Provinces and adjacent States where the waterfowl concentrate, a feeding program is necessary to save the birds and to protect the farmers from excessive losses.

The farm is not the only place where there is opportunity to avoid problems that birds cause.

At Moody Air Force Base in Georgia, for example, blackbirds that move to and from a 4-million bird roost fly across runways during training flights. The main evening movement to the roost near sunset and the main morning exodus near sunrise each takes about an hour. Air strikes can be avoided by suspending the training flights for about an hour in the morning and evening.

In cities where flocking birds, like starlings, are a nuisance, it helps to give the trees where the birds are accustomed to roost a heavy trimming. This reduces the attractiveness of the trees to the birds and they then seek more acceptable quarters.

Some eastern cities have been bothered by large winter roosts of starlings and blackbirds in pine trees near reservoirs: Their droppings may kill trees and create health problems. Presently known harassment measures have had little effect. The only practical solution we know lies in changing watershed management practices to make the area unattractive. A selective thinning of such roosting sites opens up these dense areas without adversely affecting the watershed. These thinned evergreen stands become unsuitable to the birds and so they seek other shelter. The new site they choose, as likely as not, could be in an area where they would not be a problem. At any rate, it is poor planning to establish an ideal roosting habitat for birds in a place where they will cause serious damage.

The design of buildings has something to do with the presence of pigeons, sparrows, and starlings, which like to roost on wide ledges over windows and doors.

A way to avoid problems of roosting birds is to use tile, aluminum, stainless steel, and structural glass and to favor exterior designs of buildings so that the birds cannot roost there. The Federal Triangle in Washington, for instance, is an impressive place of classical architecture and—before extensive combative measures were invoked—a costly roost of starlings. New Government buildings in the District of Columbia are less ornate and to some beholders far less inspiring, but they also are far less attractive to birds.

In the Northern States, starlings, pigeons, and sparrows often become a nuisance by their roosting in towers, ventilators, and church belfries. This objectionable roosting often can be prevented by closing the entrances with 1-inch galvanized or rustproof wire.

Problems with birds (and rodents, too) around homes, grain elevators, loading platforms, storage barns, and warehouses and commercial establishments where grain is handled can be minimized by practicing good sanitation and meticulous housekeeping. That calls for the daily cleanup of premises and the careful handling of grain sacks to avoid spillage. One cannot lay out a banquet for birds and rodents anywhere and not expect them to use it.

Just as scare devices and lethal measures do not solve all problems caused by birds, so, too, there are limits to the steps that can be taken to avoid bird problems. A combination of practices may be necessary to keep peace between troublesome birds and men engaged in commercial enterprises.

—John L. Buckley and Clarence Cottam.

BLACK-BILLED MAGPIES

We Need To Know

THE BIOLOGIST centers his thinking on four questions as he continues his search for better ways to manage nuisance and destructive birds.

What makes a bird a bird?

How can I exploit its singular traits to perfect a specific control?

What makes the species I am interested in different from any other?

How can I capitalize on its peculiarities?

Everyone knows that birds have the monopoly on feathers. They and bats are the only vertebrate creatures capable of flight. A biologist knows that birds have a sky-high pulse, high metabolism, high respiration, and high body temperature. Birds are oviparous. Their gut and digestion are unique. The herring gull is large and has webbed feet; the sanderling is small, and its toes are not webbed. Starlings roost in trees. Quail roost on the ground. Blackbirds love rice in the milk and dough stage; robins pick cherries and pull up angleworms. The crow nests on high and hatches helpless young;

460

the pheasant incubates on the ground and its chicks are precocial. Many differences set one off from the other.

Persistent probing for exclusive characteristics and traits is the means by which the biologist finds the thin spot in the protective armor of a problem species. It is the grand scheme to selective management of bird populations, in which the main goal is to achieve the desired measure of control with the least possible sacrifice of birdlife and other environmental coinhabitants.

Anyone who has studied the complexities of ecological communities and knows the interdependence of organisms, one group to the other, senses the difficulties. Techniques that will forestall the development of an undesirable situation, prevent access, or repel, divert, or relocate nuisance flocks are preferred to killing them. Sometimes there is no alternative, and research on lethal methods has to go on.

Ornithologists have learned a great deal about the distinguishing features of birds. Our knowledge of taxonomy and ecology is well advanced. Gaps exist, though, in our information on the fine points of behavior and physiology of the individual species and the races within species.

An example or two will indicate how filling in the voids may help us attain the goal. Herring gulls, a menace at some airports, can vomit at will. This makes it difficult to give them a dose of chemicals. Having taken readings on the chemistry of the entire digestive tract, physiologists at the University of North Carolina judge that it is practicable to select a pill coating that will not dissolve until the active ingredient gets way down into the intestine, beyond the point of no return.

The scientists also say that the high metabolism in birds may make them vulnerable to interruptions in their normal intake of food and water. They speculate that a chemical that depresses the appetite, if it remains effective through several feeding periods, may have significant consequences, such as the bird's inability to maintain adequate body temperature on a cold night. Daily and seasonal habits of feeding, resting, breeding, and traveling will reveal where, when, and how to place baits, set traps, operate frightening devices, or apply repellants.

Entomologists have compounded a sex attractant which will pull male gypsy moths to a central location, where they may be conveniently dispatched; thus there may be no need to spray large scopes of woodland. In a related way, biologists are using the attraction principle. Birds of a feather flock together; that old saying is the basis of the decoy trap. Lured by their noisy relatives, starlings, grackles, and blackbirds are themselves caught.

Bird-resistant crop varieties, while probably not in the same league with rust-resistant wheat and virus-resistant tomatoes, are proving to be of some value, especially corn and grain sorghums. Plant breeders are best qualified to carry on this research, but biologists can provide technical assistance and encouragement.

Another lead that ought to be pursued is the effect of changes in cultural practices. Farmers in Arizona, for example, time the planting of grain sorghum so that the crop matures after early October, by which time the white-winged doves will have departed for their wintering grounds in Mexico. Field combining instead of shocking or swathing has eliminated many duck depredations in the northern small-grain farming areas and has reduced rice depredations by red-winged blackbirds.

We can make frightening devices more and more effective if we learn how to exploit better the keen senses of sight and hearing of birds.

Many of the techniques devised to scare away depredating flocks bring timely relief and by themselves have saved valuable crops from heavy damage. They may provide no lasting solution and sometimes merely chase the vandals to neighboring fields. The harassment, however, if it does not drive birds to other types of food, usually will lessen the damage sustained by an individual grower. Often we find that the crop is vulnerable for only a matter of days. If protection can be provided during this small fraction of the year, the despoilers may be a prime asset during the off-season. They can do a great good by consuming weed seeds and insects.

The novel idea of Hubert Frings, a zoologist formerly of the Pennsylvania State University, to use amplified playbacks of recorded bird calls—alarm and distress notes to repel them and feeding

A farmer in southern Maryland inspects damage by blackbirds to his corn. Red-winged blackbirds, the major offenders, feed on the grain chiefly when it is in the milk or soft-dough stage.

462

and mating calls to attract them—has opened a new province of inquiry for the researcher. It would be a mistake if a part of the research effort did not continue to be centered around physical repellants and attractants.

As far as we know now, birds (except some species of the vultures) do not have a well-developed sense of smell. That may explain why we have few chemical repellants for birds.

Chemists of a private company hit upon a substance that causes distress symptoms when individuals ingest it. The squalls and squawks and erratic flights of affected birds panic their companions. Scientists in the Bureau of Sport Fisheries and Wildlife screened out another compound that evokes similar reactions. These discoveries may give greater dimensions to ways of using chemicals to repel birds.

The research carried out by Morley Kare at the University of North Carolina heightens our appreciation of a bird's sense of taste. A complicated but fascinating business, this probing of how, why, and what birds taste! Although the horny beak does not seem to be of much use as a sensing organ, a bird's tongue, mouth, and throat serve the purpose.

We know that bobwhites will not eat seeds of rattlebox and coffeeweed. How do they detect toxic and undesirable properties in these seeds which to us, at least, appear as savory as lespedeza and partridge pea? And do the properties, whatever they are, offer any prospects as bird deterrents if we isolate and apply them to other foods? Deep digging into the fundamentals of taste may hasten our progress in the development of chemical repellants.

We fence foxes out of the henyard and cows out of the corn. Why not fence birds out of the vineyard? The answer is simple. Costs, using our present methods and materials, ordinarily are prohibitive, except for small acreages of high-value produce. There is a possibility of adapting fine-mesh, lightweight netting for this purpose, but the general outlook for bird fences is not rosy. Perhaps we need to turn our thoughts away from nets and fences and seek a completely new protective principle of some kind.

Ultrasonics, as far as we have gone, have been a disappointment, but it is doubtful that all the re-

Ripe Kadota figs look like this after starlings have feasted on them.

cent advances in the physical sciences have been considered fully. One day, a high-energy source, such as laser, may provide the foundation of an effective damage control instrument.

Another field for exploration is the use of tranquillizing drugs. A problem of bird damage often is compounded by the numbers of songsters, whom no one wishes to see destroyed, among the culprits. Or, it may be a flock has taken up residence in the wrong location, as too many pigeons in a park. The solution may simply be relocation.

One possible way of getting the birds in the hand for this purpose is through the use of soporific—sleep producing—or tranquillizing drugs. Ideally, the chemical should enable one to capture an entire unwanted population and remove it, or any part of it, unharmed and unruffled to distant reaches, where it will be out of trouble.

The mobility and homing ability of some birds, however, may bring them back to the scene in a short time. Such was the case of the goldfinches at the Agricultural Research Center at Beltsville, Maryland. Mist nets, constructed of fine, almost invisible threads, were erected across their flight paths to valuable seed plots. When the entrapped individuals were translocated, they soon returned.

The main obstacle in the use of drugs generally is the rather narrow margin between an effective dose and a lethal one and how to get just the right amount—no more, no less—to the bird.

Other technicalities revolve around the knockdown time and the period of immobilization or unconsciousness. If they cannot be captured before the flock finishes feeding, the ones who have ingested a dose may be miles away and out of reach before the ingredient takes hold. Should the sleep period be too long, the birds may be prime targets for pneumonia or some such illness.

Intensive explorations to ascertain the rather exacting limits are warranted. With our burgeoning knowledge of chemistry and physiology, there are prospects in this approach.

Up to this point, we have been discussing ways and means of controlling birds without sacrificing their numbers. But in some circumstances the only solution is to reduce or eliminate a population.

Reductions of populations can be effected directly through the use of lethal weapons or indirectly through the inhibition of reproductive success.

An intriguing and potentially effective route of investigation lies in the field of chemosterilants—substances that prevent conception or birth of young. Think of a "birth control pill" for birds!

The approach is humane. The principle is effective. Dr. E. F. Knipling and fellow entomologists of the Department of Agriculture have successfully battled the screw-worm by a sterilization technique and appear to have the control of other insect pests within grasp. Their calculations seem to prove that a large number of sterile individuals alive and active in the environment will create a greater drain on a population than if the same number were killed outright. The reason is that the sterile animals are competing with the normal ones for mates, space, food, and position in the peck order.

Since 60 percent or more of a small bird population ordinarily is replaced annually in what is called "population turnover", it is apparent that a large reduction in reproductive capacity of a species should cause a precipitous decline in the numbers of the succeeding generation.

Biologists in the Bureau of Sport Fisheries and Wildlife have tested a number of reproduction inhibitors in the laboratory. Early indications are that the scheme will work for birds. The surface of possibilities has scarcely been scratched, however, and a number of problems must be worked out before we have a dependable management tool. Considerably more effort should be devoted to the screening of chemosterilants.

We need to find material that in a single exposure will render either sex sterile but will not affect courtship behavior.

Then we need to find ways and means of getting the compound of choice to a large segment of the target population without contaminating desirable birds or other organisms.

Here again we see the need to reinforce our knowledge of the behavior and physiology of species. Painstaking work is involved, to be sure, but the need is incontestable.

When numbers of birds must be cut down forthwith, such as at cattle feedlots where large concentrations often eat and befoul feed, lethal chemicals are a direct solution.

Some effective toxicants are available, but I doubt whether the search for selective avicides will ever be finished, because various species differ greatly in acceptance and vulnerability. For example, an excellent avicide, which scientists in the Bureau have tested and analyzed, works well on starlings, but sparrows and raptors are quite resistant to it.

Reaction time also is to be considered. Sometimes a situation calls for quick manifestations. In other instances, the first signs of distress would frighten away most of the flock.

Perhaps, when we reach the point of being able to pick and choose, we shall ask the specialist to deliver a substance that is undetectable when ingested by a bird and the effects are not evident for several hours, so that the bait site remains attractive. In this fashion, the ones that escape a lethal dose today can be expected to return to the scene tomorrow and go down the same path to oblivion. We should be able to regulate the time of mortality with precision, so that it occurs when the birds are congregated in a resting or staging area or on a roost. In this way, the carcasses can be disposed of easily when necessary. We would hope, too, that the chemist will tailor the substance so that it will degrade to a harmless residue as soon as the specific job is done.

It may be desirable in some situations to use a contact poison rather than an ingested one. This might be distributed on an artificial perch or the roost vegetation. It must not be hazardous to non-target wildlife, food-chain organisms, domestic animals, or people. More than one promising toxicant has been discarded because of its danger to other forms of life.

Biologists experimented with one lethal spray that was quite effective on roosting birds. Large numbers dropped at the site. Others, however, managed to fly several miles before succumbing. Since these carried an unacceptable residue on their plumage, the chemical was abandoned. Tests of another one revealed that some animals sharing the same environment were 5 to 10 times more susceptible than the target species. It also was quickly discarded.

And so it goes—endless screening and disappointments to wind up with a few compounds that will do the job safely and effectively.

We have used mirrors, cannons, live decoys, and lights with traps, but we have not yet reached the ultimate of finesse in the ancient art of capturing animals. It is doubtful whether we have run our string on lures and enticements. Are avian sex attractants limited to the senses of sight and hearing? Maybe we can discover new food enticements or flocking behaviorisms that will enable us to lead our quarry right into the snare.

Traps have the advantage that they can be made just as selective as we want. The captured can be sorted one by one if need be. Experience in the cherry orchards of Washington and Michigan leads us to believe that traps can be effective damage controllers for some crops. Trapping methods will be improved as we continue to acquire knowledge of sight, taste, and sound reflexes of the target species.

Among the biological and ecological means of reducing bird populations, the stress of disease comes to mind. We recall from history the plagues that decimated wildlife and the use of myxomatosis—a host-specific virus disease—in solving the rabbit problem (at least for a while) in Australia after all other ways had failed. It would be good if we could find a disease entity that would do the same thing to the starling—as long as it did not in any way damage other kinds of birds.

Therein, of course, lies the danger in employing a disease. In Nature, a lethal agent may adapt itself to a new victim when the preferred host becomes scarce. This is not at all an uncommon occurrence in predator-prey relationships. Many will recall what happened when the mongoose was introduced into the Hawaiian and Caribbean Islands in the hope of ending their infestations of rats. The rascal soon turned to wild birds and poultry, which were easier to catch than rats.

Researchers in the Bureau may have discovered the nearly ideal situation in which to introduce a predator to control nuisance birds. It is the seasonal introduction of foxes and raccoons onto the offshore islands of New England where colonies of herring gulls regularly nest. The first tests were successful in reducing the numbers of young birds produced. The island fauna did not include other species that the foxes and raccoons could prey on. Such pat situations are rare, though. A point to bear in mind in making a choice of predators is to choose one that can be easily recaptured or arrested when the initial objective is reached.

Finally, we should explore further opportunities of manipulating the habitat. The problem bird may have a narrow range of adaptability to its environment. If a requirement is destroyed, the population may just fade away.

For example: Biologists eliminated a hazardous concentration of blackbirds at the end of one of the busiest runways at Stapleton Airfield, Denver, by burning down the vegetation in which they roosted. In the United States and Canada, concentrations of gulls at garbage dumps on or near airports have been dispersed by closing down the dump or burning the refuse.

As with all techniques I have mentioned, habitat manipulation has limits. It is not a panacea.

None of the methods can be applied to every situation. Some may have an exceedingly limited utility. Nevertheless, all merit consideration and exploration because there are so many kinds of problems before us. The effectiveness of any measure is governed by how well it fits the object

Farmers of yesteryear used scarecrows to reduce crop depredations by birds. Farmers of today look to research to give them better methods to do this job.

species of bird. Each is unique in one or more aspects, which can be defined only by intensive biological studies of populations, year-round habits and behavior, and ecological relationships. Species uniqueness is the common denominator of selective management.

Problems of bird damage of today and tomorrow will not be solved by a single magic formula.

Rather, the successful manager will have to write the right prescription for the particular ill. He will keep the side effects confined within allowable bounds. He will have to understand the environmental interplay and know the traits and characteristics of the problem species in much greater detail than he does now.

—C. Edward Carlson.

466

Working for Their Survival

Laws That Protect

JUST 50 YEARS AGO, grocers stocked iced barrels of wild ducks, geese, quail, and shore birds and strings of robins, meadowlarks, and cedar waxwings. And 50 years ago, every milliner offered handsome birdfeathers, and shop windows displayed ladies' hats adorned with nuptial plumes of the snowy egret and breastfeathers of pelicans and grebes.

Such commercialization of wildlife was the job of the market hunters, and they worked hard at it. Their business was to shoot, kill, and sell—6 days a week, year in and year out. Between 1840 and 1910, they eliminated for all time five kinds of birds. Several more were reduced to the brink of extinction.

They were the deadliest professional hunters the world has ever produced. One of them boasted he had killed more than 139 thousand birds and other animals. They knew their hunting areas like the palms of their hands. They quickly located game concentrations. For decades they used nets, decoys, bait traps, winged floating sink boxes, and big-bore guns mounted like cannons on boats to kill ducks and geese.

468

The ducks sold at 50 cents or so a pair; the annual income of 400 market hunters in one locality amounted to more than 100 thousand dollars for years. One poultry dealer in New York received 20 tons of prairie chickens in one consignment. Some big poultry dealers sold 200 thousand game birds in 6 months.

All told, our program of bird protection has been 250 years in the making. But it was the work of the market hunter that so shocked the sensibilities of the public as to stimulate prompt and sweeping action. And so, really effective legislation in behalf of wildlife is of recent enactment, most of it having occurred during the lifetime of people still living.

Today almost all of the 850-odd species of birds that inhabit the United States and Canada receive protection under Federal and State laws.

Hunting regulations are established annually to permit the taking of surplus supplies of game birds—as quail, pheasants, waterfowl, and doves—without endangering the basic breeding stock.

Birds whose diets comprise mostly insects, weed seeds, or rodents injurious to farmers—among them cardinals, mockingbirds, meadowlarks, orioles, robins, and certain birds of prey—are afforded complete protection.

Other birds, such as gulls, the scavengers of the sea, and birds that may not be particularly useful but are not injurious, also receive protection.

Species that are considered injurious—crows, house sparrows, starlings, anhingas, cormorants, hawks, ibises, jays, kingfishers, magpies, owls, pelicans, and ravens—are outside Federal laws, but State laws protect all of them except crows, goshawks, Cooper's and sharpshinned hawks, great horned owls, house sparrows, and starlings.

Under our present laws, anyone who unlawfully takes wild migratory birds for the purpose of commercialization is deemed to be guilty of a felony and upon conviction may be fined not more than 2 thousand dollars or imprisoned not more than 2 years, or both. In addition, all equipment and accessories used for such an illegal purpose are subject to forfeiture to the United States. The States also regard market hunting as a serious offense, and persons convicted of taking resident game birds such as wild turkeys, quail, and pheasants for the purpose of sale are subject to severe penalties in State courts, including the confiscation of vehicles and other equipment used in the commission of the offense.

Sportsmen in New York in 1791 were responsible for one of the early pieces of protective legislation. It was through their effort that a closed season was established on certain game birds between April 1 and October 5.

Not long afterwards Massachusetts enacted a more enlightened law to close the hunting season on several game birds during their nesting period and protect "birds which are useful and profitable to citizens . . . as instruments in the hands of Providence to destroy noxious insects, grubs and caterpillars, which are prejudicial or destructive to vegetation, fruits and grain."

A growing realization that many nongame birds, long labeled a menace to the farmer, were in fact of great value led to the first legislation specifically drafted to protect them. Connecticut in 1850 passed a law protecting insectivorous birds. New Jersey enacted a law "to prevent the destruction of small and harmless birds," including the small owl. The following year Vermont acted to protect nongame birds throughout the year and prohibit the destruction of their eggs and nests.

In the seventies and eighties, concern over the alarming slaughter of game prompted the formation of the Boone and Crockett Club, and the killing of vast numbers of birds for the plume trade was a reason for the rise of the Audubon movement. But the mistaken idea that migratory game birds, especially waterfowl, were inexhaustible still prevailed. Some States passed laws prohibiting the killing of song and plumage birds and the destruction of nests, but the States continued to compete for their share of waterfowl, were jealous of their rights, and looked askance at any Federal intervention. They still do to some degree.

The slaughter of game for commercial purposes had become so appalling by the nineties as to become a national scandal. By the turn of the century, 32 States had outlawed the sale of game, and 11 more prohibited its export. These restrictions were ineffectual: As long as a market for game existed, the resourceful violator, abetted by common carriers, managed to move it from where it

Enforcement of regulations for the hunting of migratory birds is an important part of the job of Federal game management agents. Here hunter and agent are happy the law has been obeyed.

was taken to where it could be sold. Once the contraband crossed the State line, the aggrieved State lost its jurisdiction and evidence. Action by the Federal Government was needed and requested. Finally it came.

The Congress in 1900 enacted the Lacey Act, which was named after active, prescient John F. Lacey of Iowa, and was based on the interstate commerce clause of the Constitution. It imposed controls on the importation of foreign birds and animals, prohibited the entry of certain species known to be injurious to agriculture and horticulture, and made illegal the shipment in interstate commerce of animals and birds taken contrary to State or Territorial law. The act meant the beginning of the end of market hunting in the organized, big-business sense of the past.

The act curtailed illegal activities after game had been killed, but more uniform legislation was needed to protect and manage migratory birds—the ones that breed in one section of the continent, winter in another, and traverse one or more States in passing to and from their breeding grounds.

Until about 1910, the States confined most of their protective legislation to resident upland game birds and animals that stayed in one State the whole year. By prohibiting shooting during the breeding season, restricting the methods and means by which game could be taken legally, prohibiting the sale or export of game, and establishing bag and possession limits, the States assured their citizens of reasonable hunting opportunities as far as resident species were concerned.

But the States were little concerned with providing protection to birds not "belonging" to them. In most States the season opened when the birds arrived in a State and closed when they left. The senseless extermination of the passenger pigeon shows the result of the provincial attitude toward resident v. migratory species.

If migratory birds were to be saved from oblivion, a national law, equally applicable to all States, was needed. So George Shiras III, a Congressman from Pennsylvania, in 1904 introduced a bill to protect the migratory game birds of the United States. It failed to pass, but it planted a seed.

The seed was the thought that the responsibility for determining migration routes and the distribution and population status of waterfowl was not within the scope of the individual States and that Federal administration of laws and management practices as to migratory birds would be in the best interests of the birds and the public alike.

The Congress in 1913 passed a migratory-bird law, which gave the United States Department of Agriculture the authority to adopt regulations fixing closed seasons. The Department's regulations of that same year initiated a great change in our conservation of migratory birds.

Shortly afterward, negotiations were started for an international agreement to protect birds that migrate between Canada and the United States. The treaty was signed on August 16, 1916. On its authority, the Congress enacted the Migratory Bird Treaty Act to implement the provisions of the convention, and the law was approved by President Wilson on July 3, 1918.

The wholesale slaughter of egrets for their ornamental plumes, or aigrettes, used on ladies' hats, helped arouse Americans and Canadians a half century ago to the need for measures to protect the lovely birds.

Game Management Agent Lawrence M. Thurman and Guy Willy, staff officer of the Blackwater National Wildlife Refuge, at Cambridge, Maryland, check maps and prepare to make a survey of waterfowl on the refuge. Agents use airplanes also to spot illegal hunting and trapping of waterfowl.

The Migratory Bird Treaty Act, which implemented the treaty, establishes a perpetual closed season on songbirds; prohibits the sale or purchase of any wild migratory birds, their parts, nests, or eggs; prohibits the interstate transportation of birds taken contrary to law; provides for the establishment of regulations governing the hunting, possession, transportation, and importation of migratory game birds; provides for the taking of wild migratory birds for propagating, scientific, and educational purposes; and provides for their destruction under controlled conditions to protect agricultural and other interests.

Violations of the Migratory Bird Treaty Act, with the exception of unlawfully taking migratory birds with intent to sell, are classified as misdemeanors. Any person who violates or fails to comply with any regulation made pursuant to the act and is convicted of the offense is subject to a fine of not more than 500 dollars or imprisonment not to exceed 6 months, or both.

The United States and Mexico entered into a similar convention on February 7, 1936. The two treaties extended the foundation for migratory bird protection to all of North America.

A number of later laws broadened the Federal role for wildlife protection and provided new authority for the improved management of the overall resource. Among them were the Upper Mississippi River Wildlife and Fish Refuge Act of June 7, 1924; the Migratory Bird Conservation Act of February 18, 1929; the Waterfowl Hunting

Stamp Act of March 16, 1934; the amended Migratory Bird Treaty Act of June 20, 1936; and the Bald Eagle Act of June 8, 1940, which was amended October 24, 1962, to provide protection to the golden eagle as well.

Although the migratory bird conventions are outstanding examples of international agreements in the cause of conservation, it is unfortunate that their protective coverage has not been extended to include most of the North American birds of prey, which also are in need of protection.

An example is the golden eagle. For many years it has been looked upon as a predator and therefore a fair target. And for many years, ranchers who attributed losses of stock to the golden eagle carried on organized campaigns against it. Later the killing of eagles from aircraft became first a sport, then a business. Ranchers who were losing lambs and other stock to golden eagles hired pilots to reduce the eagle population near their properties.

As frequently occurs in wildlife control programs, the campaign against the golden eagle developed to an extreme not justified by the birds' habits as predators. Public indignation followed on the reports of wanton and indiscriminate slaughter, and the demand grew for protective legislation. In 1962, an amendment to the act protecting bald eagles gave protection to golden eagles as well. At the same time it provided for discriminate control under regulation by the Secretary of the Interior where the golden eagle was causing unquestionable damage to livestock.

State and Federal laws covering hunting are composed of two types of regulations. A set of basic restrictions covers the manner and means by which game may be taken. These remain relatively constant year after year. A second portion of the game laws governs when, where, and how much game may be taken, and these regulations are subject to change, depending on the amount of the harvestable surplus available in any particular year. In those years in which game reproduction is good, the regulations reflect the condition in longer seasons and larger bag limits. In years when reproduction has been poor, the opposite is true.

Annual hunting regulations are widely publicized, and they are generally well known to the

An agent of the North Dakota State Fish and Game Department is on a mission of mercy—to rescue a weakened mallard that had failed to migrate south.

public. However, nongame species of birds far outnumber by kinds and total number those that are hunted. These birds likewise come under the protection of the law. And, aside from hunting regulations, there are other laws covering both game and nongame birds.

473

The following are some situations and questions that appear regularly with reference to legislation on birds:

If I find an injured robin, can I nurse it back to health without violating the law?

Yes. To obtain temporary legal possession of the bird, promptly write the regional office of the Bureau of Sport Fisheries and Wildlife nearest you and request a permit to retain the bird in your possession. These permits are issued free of charge. Permittees are required to release the bird to the wild if and when it recovers sufficiently to fend for itself. If the bird is permanently crippled, it must be turned over to a public zoo for exhibition.

May I use the feathers of lawfully acquired migratory game birds to make fishing flies?

Yes. Federal regulations governing the use of plumage of migratory game birds are: "Any person, without a permit, may possess and transport for his own use the plumage and skins of lawfully taken migratory game birds and any person, without a permit, may possess, dispose of, and transport for the making of fishing flies, bed pillows, and mattresses, and for similar commercial uses, but not for millinery or ornamental use, feathers of wild ducks and wild geese lawfully killed, or seized and condemned by Federal or State game authorities." Information concerning State regulations governing the use of resident game bird plumage can be obtained from State conservation department authorities.

Who must have a duck stamp when hunting ducks and geese?

Everyone 16 years of age or older, including landowners who hunt on their own lands. The stamp, validated by the hunter's signature in ink across the face of the stamp, must be carried on the person while hunting.

Do you have to have a duck stamp to hunt other migratory game birds other than waterfowl?

No. A stamp is not required for hunting mourning and white-winged doves, band-tailed pigeons, woodcock, snipe, rails, gallinules, and coots. The coots referred to are members of the rail family,

Federal and State game management agents help to teach youngsters good sportsmanship and safety.

not the scoters or sea ducks that are sometimes called coots.

Can I recover damages from the Federal Government for losses to my crops caused by migratory birds?

No. Although the Federal Government, in pursuance of international treaties, undertakes the protection of migratory birds, it has been held by the courts not to be responsible for damage done to private property by such wildlife.

Can I obtain Government-owned grain to feed birds frequenting my backyard feeder?

No. Federal agencies are without statutory authority to furnish grain purchased under the Government's price-support program for the purpose you mention.

If I know of protected birds being shot, to whom should I report this?

Report violations as promptly as possible to your local State conservation officer or the United States Game Management Agent (Federal Warden) nearest you. The latter's name, address, and telephone number can be obtained from your State conservation officer.

Why are mourning doves permitted to be hunted?

Mourning doves are the most abundant and widely distributed game birds in our country. Of all the doves frequenting our country in August, 70 percent will die before spring because of disease, accident, or predation, or at the hands of the hunter. Of the millions of doves that die each year from all causes, hunters harvest only 20 percent. In view of the present status of the resource, the lack of evidence that hunting has an adverse effect on dove populations, and the great amount of recreation afforded by hunting, prohibiting dove hunting is not only unnecessary but is not in the public interest.

Laws and regulations are inclined to be meaningless unless provision is made to see to their proper enforcement. And so, State and Federal conservation laws are administered by a force of 4,500 State conservation officers and 165 United States game management agents.

Like most police officers, the Federal game agent may be on call 24 hours a day. His assigned district may be a part of a State or an entire State, and he is subject to temporary assignment anywhere on the North American Continent. It is not unusual, for example, for an agent who operates a waterfowl banding station in northern Canada during July and August to be sent to band wintering birds in Mexico the following January and February. Agents assigned to the Northern States during the waterfowl season may report for duty a thousand miles from home to help protect birds on the wintering grounds.

The duties of State and Federal conservation officers may be as variable as the total conservation program requires and include technical and semitechnical activities in determining the current status of wildlife populations; the annual production; the status of wildlife habitat; the extent and effects of pollution on wildlife resources, the tagging of animals, and the banding of birds; and the teaching of safety and the use of wildlife damage-control methods. They also attend public meetings to explain and discuss game management practices, the regulations, and conservation education.

Human nature being what it is, game law violations can be expected to continue to occur, committed by small boys with BB guns, who have never been told by their parents not to kill non-game birds; by men who shoot or trap game for sale; and by the hunter who makes a practice of poor sportsmanship by taking more than his limit or hunting out of season.

Nevertheless, there is evidence everywhere across the land that more and more people are aware of their responsibilities for the survival of wildlife.

This evidence takes various forms. One of them is that in some communities there is a marked improvement in game law observance. Those who have brought it about are those who have come to realize that the observance of game laws is essential if enough wildlife is to survive to meet the needs of the hunter and nonhunter alike.

—ERNEST SWIFT and CHARLES H. LAWRENCE.

Men and an Idea

THIS IS THE STORY of an idea and how it grew. The idea is that one person's enjoyment of birds and his wish to protect them and know more about them can be multiplied by sharing. We tell the story in terms of a few men, whose faith moved mountains. They were not the first surely to think of bird clubs, and the organizations they helped found were not the first ones.

But one of the first to leave records and influence the course of subsequent events was the Nuttall Ornithological Club, which was born in the early seventies in Cambridge, Massachusetts. William Brewster was its guiding light.

Brewster was born in Wakefield, Massachusetts, in 1851 and educated in the public schools of Cambridge. Introduced at the age of 12 to the then mystic art of taxidermy, he soon became an enthusiastic bird collector. As his collection of skins, nests, and eggs grew, so did his knowledge and appreciation of the natural world around him.

476

Almost entirely self-taught, since few books on American birds were available in those days, Brewster nevertheless soon became recognized as the leading authority on birds in New England. At the time of his death in 1919, he was curator of birds at the Cambridge Museum of Comparative Zoology. He wrote several books and hundreds of scientific papers.

He was more than a scientist. His love for the land and its living creatures was deep and sensitive. When he learned that Davis Hill in Concord was to be sold for its timber, he bought the property to protect a grove of stately pines from the woodman's ax. Later he expanded his rural holdings to 300 acres, which he called "October Farms." He converted them into a nature reserve and sanctuary, where, although he loved hunting and collecting, all birds were safe from the gun.

He organized a group of young friends with allied interests into the Nuttall Ornithological Club. Under his leadership, the club developed into an influential society.

Brewster and several associates in the Nuttall Club conceived the idea in 1883 of forming a national society to promote the study of ornithology. J. A. Allen, Elliott Coues, and Brewster invited 48 leading ornithologists to attend a meeting to form an American Ornithologists' Union. Their model was the highly respected British Ornithologists' Union.

Twenty-one persons met in New York on September 26, 1883, and formed the union. Its stated objectives are: "The advancement of its members in Ornithological Science; the publication of a journal of ornithology and other works relating to that science; the acquisition of a library; and the care and collection of materials relating to the above objects."

In the second annual meeting of the union, Brewster moved that a committee be formed to work "for the protection of North American Birds and their eggs, against wanton and indiscriminate destruction." The resolution was aimed at the millinery trade. At that time market hunters were killing millions of birds each year for their plumage. Because the choicest plumes were produced by breeding birds, the slaughter usually was carried out while the victims were nesting.

The union published two bulletins on bird protection in 1886 and prepared a model law to protect nongame birds. The law was adopted almost immediately by New York and 3 years later by Pennsylvania.

The AOU has been active in bird conservation ever since.

It publishes The Auk, a quarterly. Among the books it has published are *The Check-List of North American Birds, Handbook of North American Birds,* and *Ornithological Monographs.* Its dues, 5 dollars a year, include a subscription to The Auk. Its address is the American Museum of Natural History, Central Park West at 79th Street, New York, 10024.

The union persuaded the Congress in 1885 to appropriate money to establish an Office of Economic Ornithology in the Department of Agriculture. Its secretary, C. Hart Merriam, became director of the baby bureau.

The baby was eventually to grow into the Bureau of Biological Survey in 1905 and into half of the Fish and Wildlife Service when, in 1946, the Bureau of Fisheries was transferred from the Department of Commerce to the Department of the Interior, and the two bureaus were merged. The Service was reorganized in 1956, and most of its functions were divided into two bureaus—the Bureau of Sport Fisheries and Wildlife, which now handles all work relating to birds (except certain informational services) and the Bureau of Commercial Fisheries.

By the eighties, a sizable number of scientists and writers had begun to stir public concern about the needless destruction and waste of American wildlife.

One of the more effective voices was that of George Bird Grinnell, writer, scientist, explorer, hunter, crusader, and editor and publisher of Forest and Stream, a magazine of note between 1873 and 1930.

Except for a common love of Nature, Dr. Grinnell in many ways was the opposite of William Brewster. Brewster concentrated on a limited field; Grinnell's interests were cosmopolitan. Brewster rarely strayed far from Massachusetts; Grinnell probed the wild, unexplored regions of the continent.

Rock Creek Nature Center in Washington is operated by the National Park Service. Natural history displays, hikes, and lectures are featured in programs here and at national parks.

George Bird Grinnell was born in 1849. When he was a small child his family moved to Audubon Park, New York. His first schooling was from Lucy Audubon, the widow of John James Audubon, who operated a small private school for her grandchildren and the children of neighbors. It was through her that George Grinnell developed his lifetime interest in birds.

After graduation from Yale in 1870, he spent 6 months with the party of O. N. Marsh collecting fossils in hostile Indian country. This was the first of almost annual visits to the West, on some of which he lived among Indians and hunted with them.

His career could have ended in 1876 when the press of official duties forced him to decline an invitation from General Custer to accompany him on his last expedition. On a later trip to the West, Dr. Grinnell explored and mapped the region now embraced by Glacier National Park. His writings resulted in the establishment of the park.

Dr. Grinnell was active in the establishment of nearly every national conservation organization between 1883 and his death in 1938.

Dr. Grinnell had been elected fellow of the American Ornithologists' Union at the 1883 meeting. The next year he was one of the five members selected to serve with William Brewster on the committee for bird protection.

It was Dr. Grinnell who drafted the model State law for the protection of nongame birds. Through his magazine he became an influential force for its enactment.

While campaigning for the model law, Dr. Grinnell coined the term "Audubon Society." He had a special feeling for the great naturalist and painter of birds because of his early association with Lucy Audubon.

Through the columns of his magazine, he began to enroll members who would sign a pledge not to kill the nongame birds or wear their feathers. Most of the signers were schoolchildren. No fees were asked. By November 30, 1888, the membership was 48,518.

The correspondence became too burdensome for Dr. Grinnell and his magazine staff, and Forest and Stream dropped the Audubon Society in 1889 and did not mention it again for 7 years.

The idea, however, did not die.

A group in Philadelphia organized a Pennsylvania Audubon Society in 1886, but it, too, became inactive. In 1896, the Massachusetts Audubon Society was formed. Its leader was William Brewster, of the Massachusetts State Sportsmen's Association. The Massachusetts example soon inspired the revival of the Pennsylvania Society and the organization of similar societies in several other States.

The principal activity of the Bird Protection Committee became the organization of Audubon groups in the belief that a broader base of public support than the scientific groups was needed to pass bird protective laws and to obtain appropriations for government research and law enforcement.

The National Association of Audubon Societies was organized and incorporated by the State of New York in 1905. It is now the National Audubon Society.

T. Gilbert Pearson, a young teacher of biology at Guilford College in North Carolina, became its first secretary. He was elected its chief executive officer in 1911. Like Brewster, Dr. Pearson's original interest was in the scientific aspects of bird study. This soon blossomed into a broader interest that left an indelible mark in conservation.

Pearson, an affable, friendly, and likable man with a keen sense of humor, was born in Tuscola, Illinois, in 1873. He was graduated from the University of North Carolina in 1899. As a student and as a teacher at Guilford, he devoted much of his time to the collection and study of birds.

This interest inspired him to organize the Audubon Society of North Carolina in 1903. He served as its secretary until 1905, when he was asked to serve as the secretary of the new National Association of Audubon Societies. In 1922, during conferences with leading ornithologists in Europe, Dr. Pearson organized the International Committee for Bird Preservation, the first such international conservation group.

He died in 1943 in New York City. At that time, he was president emeritus of the National Audubon Society.

The headquarters of the Society are at 1130 Fifth Avenue, New York, 10028.

At National Audubon Camp, Greenwich, Connecticut, classes are held outdoors and consider many aspects of natural history, including soil resources.

Its publications include: Audubon Magazine, a bimonthly; Audubon Field Notes, a bimonthly published in cooperation with the Bureau of Sport Fisheries and Wildlife; Audubon Leader's Conservation Guide, a semimonthly; Audubon Nature Bulletins and Charts; Audubon Junior Program materials and leaders' guides on birds, trees, mammals, plants and wildflowers; and *The Story of Ecology*.

Audubon Research Reports include *The Ivory-Billed Woodpecker*, by James T. Tanner; *The Roseate Spoonbill*, by Robert Porter Allen; *The Whooping Crane*, by Robert Porter Allen; *The California Condor*, by Carl B. Koford; *The Flamingoes: Their Life History and Survival*, by Robert Porter Allen; *The Current Status and Welfare of the California Condor*, by Alden H. Miller, Ian I. McMillan, and Eben McMillan; and Audubon Conservation Reports, a new series: *The Golden Eagle in the Trans-Pecos and Edwards Plateau of Texas*, by Walter R. Spofford.

The society maintains wildlife sanctuaries to protect unusual ecological communities, the breeding grounds of colony-nesting birds, and waterfowl wintering habitat. Some sanctuaries are used chiefly for educational purposes, as at Audubon camps, where summer short courses in field natural history are offered to adults, and at Audubon centers for year-round instruction of children. Other educational activities include the Audubon Junior Program (since 1910) and Audubon wildlife film lectures, which have local sponsors.

In its early decades, the society campaigned against the "plume hunters" and the commercial trade in feathers of wild birds, a fight it eventually won through public education and enactment of protective laws. Current campaigns seek protection for the birds of prey and involve research and conservation projects on the California condor, bald eagle, and other rare and endangered species.

The society sponsors the annual Christmas bird count, an activity participated in by more than 750 local groups in the United States and Canada. The results are published in Audubon Field Notes.

Local branches, which numbered 96 in 1965, have joint members with the National Society. Some 200 affiliates include State Audubon societies, other local Audubon groups, bird clubs, ornithological and naturalist societies, garden clubs, and conservation clubs.

A class in North Tarboro Elementary School, North Carolina, is learning about the birdlife of the State from Mrs. Carrie S. Clary.

Many State and local Audubon societies themselves maintain sanctuaries, operate nature centers, conduct educational field trips, and engage in research. Dues are 8 dollars and 50 cents a year.

Many regional, State, and local ornithological societies and bird clubs have been organized. Many are active today.

Besides the American Ornithologists' Union, two of national significance are the Wilson Ornithological Society, organized in 1888 and named in honor of Alexander Wilson, the father of American ornithology and author of the first comprehensive work on California birds, and the Cooper Ornithological Club, which has members throughout the Nation, although most of them are on the west coast and in the Rocky Mountain States.

The Cooper Ornithological Society was founded in 1893. Its objectives: "The Observational and cooperative study of birds; the spread of interest in bird study; the conservation of birds and wildlife in general; the publication of ornithological knowledge."

Its publications include The Condor, a bimonthly; *Pacific Coast Avifauna;* and *The C. O. C. 1893–1928, A Systematic Study of the Cooper Ornithological Club,* by Harry S. Swarth.

The society has concerned itself with conservation issues as well as the advancement of ornithological knowledge and, at annual meetings, often has discussions of conservation matters and takes an official position. Its interests extend to wilderness resources and wildlife habitat as well as to the animals themselves. Dues are 5 dollars a year.

The Wilson Ornithological Society began in 1888. Its objectives are: "To advance the science of ornithology, particularly field ornithology as related to the birds of North America, and to secure cooperation in measures tending to this end by uniting in a group such persons as are interested therein, facilitating personal intercourse among them, and providing for the publication of the information that they secure."

Its president in 1965 was Roger Tory Peterson, Neck Road, Old Lyme, Connecticut. It publishes the Wilson Bulletin, a quarterly.

Its Josselyn Van Tyne Memorial Library, established in 1930, is housed in the University of

Miss Dorothy Treet welcomes Carl W. Buchheister, author of this chapter, and Charles H. Callison to the Aullwood Audubon Center near Dayton, Ohio.

Michigan Museum of Zoology, Ann Arbor. Members may borrow material in the library by mail.

The annual reports of the Wilson Society's Conservation Committee have become noted and widely used statements of social, economic, legislative, and administrative factors affecting the populations, habitats, and ecology of birds and other wildlife. Dues are 5 dollars a year.

Many sportsmen's clubs were organized during the 19th century. Some were short lived; others existed a long time. Some, whose leaders were broadly interested in natural history, paid attention to nongame species as well as those hunted for sport.

The first such organization of national scope was the League of American Sportsmen. It was formed in 1898 in New York City by G. O. Shields, editor and publisher of the magazine Recreation, who attracted wide attention by a vigorous editorial campaigning against "game hogs."

The purpose of the league was to protect "game and game fish, the song, insectivorous, and other interesting birds not classed as game birds; enforce game laws where such exist and to secure and enforce such laws which are not now existent; promote good fellowship among good sportsmen; foster a love of Nature; encourage propagation of game and game fish; and to work for reasonable

Ira N. Gabrielson, President of the Wildlife Management Institute, discusses problems and needs of wildlife at the White House Conference on Conservation of Natural Resources.

Daniel A. Poole is editor of the Outdoor News Bulletin, published biweekly by the Wildlife Management Institute as a report to the Nation on important events in the management of natural resources.

bags and gun-license laws." The league survived until 1908.

Another group of nationwide purposes and support, the American Game Protective and Propagation Association, was formed in 1911. Its name was changed later to American Game Protective Association and in 1931 to American Game Association. It began with the support of the sporting arms and ammunition industry, which continued until the association was disbanded in 1935, and its purposes and leadership were regrouped in the American Wildlife Institute, now the Wildlife Management Institute. From 1915 to 1935 it sponsored the annual American Game Conference, meetings that were the forerunners of the North American Wildlife and Natural Resources Conference now sponsored by the Wildlife Management Institute.

The aim of the Wildlife Management Institute is "to contribute to the nation's welfare by promoting the better management and wise utilization of all renewable natural resources." Its president is Ira N. Gabrielson, 709 Wire Building, Washington, D.C. 20005.

Among its publications are: Transactions of the annual North American Wildlife and Natural Resources Conference; Outdoor News Bulletin, a biweekly; a number of books, including *Ducks, Geese and Swans of North America,* by F. H. Kortright, 1942; *Birds of Alaska,* Ira N. Gabrielson and Frederick C. Lincoln, 1959; *Prairie Ducks,* Lyle K. Sowls, 1955; *Hawks, Owls, and Wildlife,* Frank and John Craighead, 1956; *The Canvasback on a Prairie Marsh,* H. Albert Hochbaum, 1959; *Pheasants in North America,* Edited by Durward L. Allen, 1956; *High Tide and an East Wind* (The Story of the Black Duck), Bruce S. Wright, 1954; and leaflets and booklets.

The institute provides consultant services for Government natural resources agencies, private groups, and individuals, and maintains a staff of field extension specialists. It assists research by financial contributions to Cooperative Wildlife Research Units at 18 land-grant colleges in the United States and at one Canadian university and by grants and fellowships for special studies. It finances and administers the Delta Waterfowl Research Station in Manitoba in cooperation with the North American Wildlife Foundation. The institute is supported by industries, groups, and individuals. It has no set schedule of membership fees.

A militant sportsmen's organization, the Izaak Walton League of America, was born in Chicago in 1922. Its early accomplishments included the successful sponsorship of legislation establishing the Upper Mississippi National Wildlife Refuge in 1923 and 1924, rescue of the Horicon Marsh in Wisconsin, the purchase through a private fund-raising campaign of elk refuge lands in Wyoming, and the preservation of wilderness-canoe country of the Superior National Forest in Minnesota.

Although its name indicates to some persons an organization of anglers—just as they think of the Audubon Society as involving only birds and birdwatchers—the league has pursued a broad conservation program. It has devoted proportionate attention to birdlife. It has been a leader in the campaign to control water pollution.

The stated objectives of the Izaak Walton League of America are: "To support the protection and restoration of America's soil, woods, waters and wildlife; to help increase opportunities for outdoor recreation and safeguard public health; to hunt and fish in accordance with the law and

to respect the property rights of others; and . . . to foster the wise use of all natural resources."

Its headquarters are at 1326 Waukegan Road, Glenview, Illinois. Its publications include the Izaak Walton Magazine, Outdoor America, a monthly, and miscellaneous books, bulletins, educational pamphlets, and leaflets.

The league maintains an office and staff in Washington. Its program is carried out through State divisions and local chapters. The organization emphasizes sportsmanship, responsibility in resource use, and educational work with youth groups. It has sponsored Federal and State legislation for water pollution control, helped establish national and State wildlife refuges, defended national parks, and strongly supported wilderness preservation.

League of America are: "To support the protection of the Outdoor Recreation Resources Review Commission, a congressionally created study group whose report in 1962 led to creation of the Federal Bureau of Outdoor Recreation and passage of the Land and Water Conservation Fund Act of 1964. Dues are 3 dollars and 50 cents a year.

An ambitious plan to federate all citizen con-

Headquarters of the National Wildlife Federation in Washington is the center of a foresighted program to help arouse all citizens to a keener appreciation of all our natural assets.

483

Jay Johnson, of the North Carolina State Museum, prepares a specimen of the fulvous tree duck for public display. Through exhibits and lectures on birds, natural history museums help people learn about the creatures that share the earth with them.

servation groups was conceived by the late J. N. Darling, a noted cartoonist known as "Ding."

Darling entered the conservation field by a roundabout route. Born in Norwood, Michigan, in 1876, he received a degree in biology from Beloit College in 1900. On graduation from college, he became a reporter on the Sioux City Tribune. His skill with the sketching pen, however, soon caused his employers to assign him as a full-time political cartoonist. In this field he won two Pulitzer prizes.

As an avid sportsman with a particular fondness for duck hunting, Darling was appointed to the Iowa State Fish and Game Commission. His concern for the future of waterfowl during the severe drought of the early thirties was reflected in his cartoons on this subject. They brought him national recognition as a conservationist and led to his appointment as a member of a three-man commission appointed by President Franklin D. Roosevelt to develop a wildlife program.

President Roosevelt asked him to become the chief of the Bureau of Biological Survey in 1934. Through dynamic leadership, tough-mindedness, and hard work, he laid the foundations of the modern United States Fish and Wildlife Service and expanded the Federal wildlife refuge system. Many people feel that his vigorous and energetic administration, which lasted only 2 years, saved more than one species of waterfowl from extermination.

One of Darling's dreams was of a national organization to unify all conservation interest in the United States into a single coordinated force.

He proposed that all local groups interested in the out-of-doors would belong to State wildlife federations, which in turn would make up the General Wildlife Federation, as it was first called. He and other conservationists persuaded President Roosevelt to call the first North American Wildlife Conference, which was held in Washington in 1936. An outgrowth was the National Wildlife Federation, formed in 1937.

Eventually the federation achieved representation in all the States, although most of the State federations were primarily organizations of sportsmen's clubs. Today the National Wildlife Federation is active in many phases of national conservation.

The 1936 conference in Washington was financed and directed largely by the American Wildlife Institute, which, as the Wildlife Management Institute, has continued to sponsor the annual North American Wildlife and Natural Resources Conference.

Ding Darling's dream of an all-embracing federation of wildlife and outdoor interests fell short, but in 1946 a mechanism was devised to provide a continuing exchange of information and cooperation among the citizen organizations and the scientific societies concerned with the renewable natural resources. It is the Natural Resources Council of America.

The National Wildlife Federation has headquarters at 1412 Sixteenth Street, N.W., Washington, D.C., 20036.

Its publications are National Wildlife, a bimonthly; Conservation News, a semimonthly; and Conservation Report (on legislation), approximately weekly during sessions of the Congress. It prints wildlife conservation stamps and albums and publishes numerous educational leaflets and booklets.

While the federation's activities broadly encompass all wildlife and wildlife habitat, birds are accorded proportionate attention. Federation-sponsored National Wildlife Week programs have featured "Save the Prairie Chicken" (1953), "Save America's Wetlands" (1955), threatened birds along with other "Endangered Wildlife" (1956), and "Waterfowl for the Future" (1962).

The federation organized a National Prairie Chicken Committee in 1953 and has continued to sponsor annual meetings of its successor, the National Prairie Chicken Technical Council. Activities have included special surveys and studies of waterfowl conditions in the United States and Canada.

Voting members are State wildlife federations or associations, of which there is one in a State. Most of them are federations of sportsmen's or conservation clubs. Some are council-type organizations encompassing other groups. All have the primary purpose of conservation, wise use, and restoration of wildlife and other natural resources. All are encouraged to maintain close working relationships with Federal and State conservation agencies and individual buyers of hunting and fishing licenses. Dues are 5 dollars a year.

A number of bird banding associations has been formed to assist banders in standardizing methods and equipment; promote cooperation between individuals and Government agencies engaged in banding and other scientific work with birds; publish the findings of banding studies and other material of special interest to banders; and to promote conservation.

Among them are the Eastern Bird Banding Association, which was established in 1923. It publishes EBBA News, a bimonthly whose editor is Frank P. Frazier, 424 Highland Avenue, Upper Montclair, New Jersey. Dues are 4 dollars a year.

Inland Bird Banding Association was organized in 1929. The IBBA News, a bimonthly, is edited by Terrence N. Ingram, Apple River, Illinois. Dues are 2 dollars a year.

Northeastern Bird Banding Association was organized in 1922. Bird Banding—A Journal of

Thomas L. Kimball, Executive Director of the National Wildlife Federation, examines a sheet from the wildlife conservation stamp series, which the federation issues to help support its work in conservation.

Ornithological Investigation, a quarterly, is published with the cooperation of the Eastern and Inland Bird-Banding Associations. Its editor is E. Alexander Bergstrom, 37 Old Brook Road, West Hartford, Connecticut. The association's dues are 5 dollars a year.

Western Bird Banding Association was organized in 1925. Its Western Bird Bander is a quarterly edited by William K. Kirsher, 340 Elm Street, Menlo Park, California. Dues are 2 dollars and 50 cents a year.

Ducks Unlimited was organized in 1936.

Headquarters are at 165 Broadway, New York 10006. Its publications include: Ducks Unlimited Quarterly; Duckological, a monthly published by Ducks Unlimited, Canada, at 389 Main Street, Winnipeg, Manitoba; *Crisis on the Flyways,* and other pamphlets and circulars.

Ducks Unlimited set out to preserve, restore, and manage waterfowl habitat, particularly in the "duck factory" breeding areas of the Canadian Prairie Provinces. Beginning with an initial appropriation of 100 thousand dollars in 1938, through 1965 it had raised about 13 million dollars through subscriptions from members and other contribu-

485

Private conservation organizations are at the forefront in the struggle to save from destruction some significant samples of the natural world. This sandhill crane was nesting on the Camas National Wildlife Refuge, Idaho.

tors. The money was spent on some 750 "duck factory" projects, which encompassed more than a million acres of water-controlled lakes and marshes with some 6 thousand miles of shoreline.

Ducks Unlimited, Canada, maintains an engineering and construction department, a production department, and an ecological department. The last cooperates in research and management practices with United States, Dominion, and Provincial wildlife agencies. Annual dues are 5 dollars.

The Wildlife Society was organized in 1937 for persons engaged professionally in wildlife management, research, and administration. Its interests are the establishment and maintenance of the highest possible professional standards, development of all phases of wildlife management along sound biological lines, and publication of research findings.

Headquarters are at 3900 Wisconsin Avenue, N.W., Washington, D.C., 20016. Its publications include: The Journal of Wildlife Management, a quarterly; Wildlife Monographs, some of whose titles are *Field Feeding by Waterfowl in Southeastern Manitoba, A Study of Waterfowl Ecology on Small Impoundments in Southeastern Alberta, Ecology of the Scaled Quail in the Oklahoma Panhandle;* and Wildlife Society News, a bimonthly.

Papers published in The Journal of Wildlife Management include studies of mammals, fish, amphibians, reptiles, birds, and general ecology. Annual dues are 10 dollars.

The World Wildlife Fund was established in 1961 as an international organization to save threatened species of wildlife. It has affiliated "appeals" in various countries. An important number of its projects concerns American birds and animals. It acquires important habitat and transfers it to suitable agencies to manage. It also issues grants for scientific studies. Among the species that the fund has helped are Attwater's greater prairie chicken,

486

the bald eagle, the Hawaiian goose, the white-winged dove, and the masked bobwhite of Mexico.

The American branch of the World Wildlife Fund maintains offices at 1816 Jefferson Place, N.W., Washington, D.C. It is supported by contributions and has no set dues. It issues circulars and leaflets on specific projects.

There are several organizations that, while not concerned primarily with birds, still contribute directly to bird conservation because they preserve vital local habitat.

One of these is the Nature Conservancy, with offices at 2039 K Street, N.W., Washington, D.C. It was founded in 1950 to preserve natural areas of outstanding beauty or scientific importance. Samples of virgin forest, virgin prairie, marshland, and swamp ranging in area from 1 acre to nearly 4 thousand acres have been saved through its efforts. When an area is acquired, it is usually turned over to a university, scientific organization, or State or Federal agency for management. The Nature Conservancy publishes the Nature Conservancy News, a quarterly. Its annual dues are 5 dollars.

The Wilderness Society has a similar goal on a broader scale, although it does not acquire land. Its purpose is to promote the establishment and preservation of publicly owned wilderness areas.

On September 3, 1964, a National Wilderness Preservation System was established by Act of Congress, largely through its efforts. This law assures the preservation of 9 million acres in its natural unspoiled state. They are set aside for educational, scientific, and recreational use compatible with such areas. Mechanized transportation and permanent developments are barred. These areas provide habitat for many species that require unspoiled wilderness to survive.

The Wilderness Society has offices at 729 15th Street, N.W., Washington, D.C. It publishes a monthly magazine, the Living Wilderness. Its annual dues are 5 dollars for regular members.

These national conservation organizations, and there are others, represent democracy in action. Each, in a more or less specialized field, supplements and complements the actions of the Federal and State Governments in conservation. Many operate where the public agencies cannot act because of legal restrictions. Some own and operate sanctuary areas. All perform valuable educational services. Together, they serve as a heavy counterweight against exploitative commercial and political forces that are often exerted against wildlife today.

—CARL BUCHHEISTER.

KIRTLAND'S WARBLER

Before It Is Too Late

No MORE CAN YOU HEAR the loud call of the passenger pigeon in American forests. It is gone forever. In your great-grandfather's day, millions of these gentle, delicately fleshed, pink-breasted, gray birds lived and bred and had their being in the nut-bearing woodlands that stretched westward from the coast.

Early settlers savored their meat, which could be had with little effort in the crowded nesting grounds and during their concentrated migrations, and shot and netted them wholesale.

Passenger pigeons could flourish in the days of the Indians and first colonists, who changed the forests very little. Their doom came when more people arrived, cleared large tracts for farms, and turned their fine, new guns against the almost-helpless birds.

Overspecialized in their dependence on nut-bearing forest trees, the pigeons could not adapt themselves to the changes or avoid the new dangers. They disappeared rather quickly. By 1880, they were beyond saving.

You can see a stuffed relict of this once proud species in the National Museum in Washington. Alongside is a plaque, like a tombstone, that reads: "Martha, last of her species, died at 1:00 p.m., 1 September 1914, age 29, in the Cincinnati Zoological Gardens. EXTINCT."

No more does the great auk enliven the bleak islands of the storm-swept North Atlantic. It is gone forever.

Once thousands of them provided eggs, feathers, oil, and meat for sailors and countless hunters who ruthlessly pursued and killed them for more than 300 years. Black and white, penguinlike, and of the size of a goose, the great auk could not fly because of its small wings, although it was a good underwater swimmer in pursuit of fish. Masses of great auks nested on a few flat-topped islands, and so were accessible to hunters and easy to kill.

It was the first bird in the Western Hemisphere to be recorded as extinct. A breeding pair, the last known survivors of relentless hunting and their own natural shortcomings, was killed in Iceland in 1844.

There is no monument to the great auk.

No monument—only regret and a memory.

No more does the heath hen sound its booming mating calls around New York, in southern New England, and elsewhere along the Atlantic seaboard. It is gone forever. It is the latest American bird to become extinct.

Once it was fairly common along the northern Atlantic seaboard, a plump, brownish, barred, chickenlike bird. Wholesale shooting for the market and the destruction of its habitat when the land was settled removed uncounted numbers of heath hens two generations ago.

Aroused as to its plight, conservation-minded Americans spent considerable sums in efforts to save this race of the prairie chicken, but the last heath hen, a mateless male, died on Martha's Vineyard, Massachusetts, in 1932.

But, although I regret the loss of the passenger pigeon, the great auk, the heath hen, and the 76-odd other species of birds in the world that have gone out of existence in the past three centuries, whether by natural processes or man's depredations, I am more concerned about the future.

LEAST CHIPMUNK

The Attwater's prairie chicken is fast losing its ancestral prairie home along the Texas coast and needs help from man to survive.

Still, their passing points up several types of weaknesses to note for the future and puts us on guard for the 36 kinds of birds within the United States whose existence is in danger now.

One weakness is specialized adaptation for a particular mode of life. The flightless great auk, well adapted to a life at sea without man, could not evade the human marauders, but the related razor-billed auk, which retains its power to fly and nests on inaccessible oceanic cliffs, still is numerous in the same general area where the great auk once lived.

Passenger pigeons died out, but the mourning dove, another member of the pigeon family and a popular game bird, not only survived but increased in numbers. It has a less restricted diet, thrives in manmade environments, and does not nest and flock in mass, as did the passenger pigeon.

Another point, a happier one, is that people have become more aware of the problem. The passing

of the great auk cast hardly a ripple anywhere, and that among naturalists and the fishermen who ate the meat of the helpless birds. Martha's death aroused considerable public concern. Intensive measures—too late, alas!—were tried to save the heath hen.

Now many, many Americans ask for and read—as eagerly and soberly as they read physicians bulletins from the bedside of a great man who is dying—regular reports on how the few remaining whooping cranes fare in their struggle for life.

But who knows of the plight of Attwater's greater prairie chicken, except ornithologists and conservationists? And do even they know the exact status of Bachman's warbler and the ivory-billed woodpecker, which may even now be making their last stand, unobserved?

The greatest danger to our birdlife today is not public apathy or greedy exploitation but ignorance

490

of the status of certain species and lack of understanding of the requirements of the species and the reasons for the decline.

A species declines and becomes extinct if its habits, physiology, or body structure have become highly specialized for efficiency in a certain environment, and then conditions change so that the specialization becomes a handicap; it cannot adapt itself to the change.

The fate of the great auk, passenger pigeon, and heath hen (and also the Labrador duck, Carolina parakeet, and Louisiana parakeet, all of which are North American species and subspecies that flourished when European man first arrived on our continent but now are gone forever) warns us to be alert for signs in other species that may be similarly handicapped by adaptation to special, but now changing, conditions.

Such danger signals are flashing for a number of species.

One signal is that a rare subspecies is not well known. It is difficult therefore to distinguish it from commoner forms and to single out individuals for selective protection.

That signal applies to the tule white-fronted goose. We know little about this gray goose with black-speckled belly and white face, but it is encountered so seldom we believe it probably is endangered. Its nesting grounds were unknown until the summer of 1964, when a small colony of white-fronted geese breeding at Old Crow Flats in Yukon Territory was identified as this larger and darker colored race.

We have evidence that it winters in small groups, generally close to (but somewhat separated from) other white-fronted geese in Sacramento Valley and the marshes on the north side of San Francisco and Suisun Bays in California.

An occasional specimen turns up now and then in the interior south to Louisiana and Texas. This subspecies is so uncommon and so hard to distinguish in life from the common forms of white-fronted geese that it would be difficult to give it separate treatment. Hunters shoot it un-

The millerbird nests only on Nihoa Island, a part of the Hawaiian Island National Wildlife Refuge.

knowingly along with other white-fronted geese. In fact, it may be shot disproportionately often because it has a relatively trusting nature.

A search for examples of tule white-fronted geese to determine where the remaining population is at all times and what conditions may be limiting its increase or threatening its survival was begun in California in 1963 by the Bureau of Sport Fisheries and Wildlife.

Artificial propagation may be the best way to save it. Captive flocks are being developed by the Bureau and a few aviculturists. Stock thus can be perpetuated until it is learned where it can be used most effectively for starting new colonies in the wild.

Another endangered form, about which we know much more, is the Aleutian Canada goose. This small, dark, white-collared subspecies of the well-known honker once nested on a number of the Aleutian Islands, but now it is known to breed only on tiny, precipitous, remote Buldir, near the very end of the Aleutian chain.

Presumably it winters scattered thinly and unrecognized among individuals of other, commoner subspecies of Canada geese in its former wintering areas in the interior valleys of California. It has all but disappeared from former wintering areas in Japan.

The rapid decline of the Aleutian goose was due to the destruction of eggs and young by arctic foxes, which were introduced to supplement the fur harvest and which became overly abundant when the market for fox fur declined. Since the Buldir Island breeding colony (about 300 individuals) was discovered in 1962, however, there is a fair chance that the race can be reestablished in its former nesting places on other islands after the foxes have been eliminated. The only reason they have survived on Buldir is that this island was bypassed in the fox introduction program. The Bureau of Sport Fisheries and Wildlife has undertaken to eliminate these foreign foxes from Amchitka, Kiska, and Agattu, which the geese once favored as breeding grounds.

A California condor teeters on the edge of a cliff. Fewer than 40 individuals of this giant among birds survived into the sixties.

Sixteen young Aleutian Canada geese were removed from Buldir Island in 1963 to the Bureau's propagation station in Colorado to serve as breeding stock for liberation later when the foxes had been removed.

These geese were doing well in 1965 but at that time had not reproduced. Other subspecies of Canada geese breed readily in captivity, however, and there is no reason to believe the Aleutians will not do likewise.

To return the captive-reared offspring into the wild again is another aspect to consider carefully. A method of conditioning to wild existence applied successfully with other species is to use blinds, so that the birds can be tended without seeing the persons who supply their needs.

Among the unique and extraordinary birdlife of the Hawaiian Islands is a strange, land-going waterfowl, the Hawaiian goose, which Polynesians call nene (pronounced nay-nay). Its closest relative probably is the Canada goose. It has become adapted to existence on dry land to the extent that the webs between its toes are small.

Until a few years ago it lived only on the barren lava flows of the great volcanoes of Mauna Loa and Hualalai, largely within the boundaries of the Hawaii Volcanoes National Park. Their numbers had been reduced to about 50 by 1950.

The Congress appropriated funds for work to restore the nene—to study its requirements and to begin a propagation program at Pohakuloa, Hawaii. Since 1962, several lots of breeding stock have been shipped from the Severn Wildfowl Trust at Slimbridge, England, where more than 100 Hawaiian geese have been reared in captivity, to Maui Island, once a part of the nene's natural range.

With others from the Hawaiian propagation center at Pohakuloa, they were liberated in the crater of Haleakala volcano on Maui, where the habitat was deemed suitable. Others of the Pohakuloa stock have been released on breeding grounds on the island of Hawaii. Some of these geese have mated with wild birds and have nested. If initial successes are continued, these experiments will supply further evidence of the value of avicultural methods in managing endangered species.

The breeding grounds are patrolled, and goats, dogs, mongooses, and feral pigs are controlled to

493

some extent. Those animals, brought to Hawaii in recent times, are a hazard to the nene and a number of other native bird species that evolved on these oceanic islands, which at that time had no predatory mammals.

The Mexican duck, like most members of its family, must have water to survive. A close relative of our common mallard, it adapted itself to the Southwest and the Mexican highlands, where supplies of water are scanty. The already limited habitat of the Mexican duck began to dry up rapidly when growing cities and irrigation farms drew heavily on the water.

Hardest hit is the northernmost population, which has been considered a subspecies, the northern Mexican duck. It has nearly disappeared from the United States parts of its range, primarily because marshes have been drained for agriculture and grazing. Even worse, in its northern range, the normally dark-streaked, brown Mexican ducks are losing identity through hybridization with the aggressively expanding mallard.

Our latest count, in 1965, indicated that fewer than 150 wild Mexican ducks were left in the United States; they were confined to restricted areas in southwestern New Mexico and central-western Texas.

Others have been reared in captivity by the New Mexico State Department of Game and Fish, which has distributed several pairs to private waterfowl breeders and the Bosque Del Apache National Wildlife Refuge.

The hope is to keep a pure breeding stock of northern Mexican ducks going and available for reintroduction into the wild when—if ever—suitable habitat can be supplied again. But its future in the wild is not bright, because more and more of the relatively few marshes are being drained. Channelization of the Rio Grande and drainage of the San Simon marshes in southeastern Arizona and southwestern New Mexico have removed thousands of acres of its habitat. Even farther south in Mexico, where this duck is more numerous, its future is jeopardized by the increasing drainage of wetlands.

The tiny, sandy coral island of Laysan, in the leeward chain of the Hawaiian Islands, once harbored five species of birds that lived nowhere else in the world: A duck, a rail, a millerbird, and two Hawaiian honey-creepers.

Today only the duck and one of the honey-creepers are left.

The others were victims of rabbits, the first of which a guano-digging crew brought in about 60 years ago. They multiplied so fast they ate nearly all the vegetation, destroyed thereby the habitat for the birds, and finally ate themselves out of existence. Much of the vegetaion has now come back.

The two surviving species, the tiny, white masked, brown Laysan duck and the brown and yellow, sparrowlike Hawaiian honey-creeper, known as the Laysan finchbill, increased with it from near extinction to fairly dense populations.

The Laysan finchbill is particularly abundant and, barring complete loss of habitat or introduction of predators or disease, seems to have a fairly secure future.

The extinction of the three species and the near loss of the others exemplify how tenuous is the existence of land-dependent birds on small oceanic islands.

Members of the Tanager Expedition, sent by the Biological Survey in 1922, found only 10 Laysan ducks still living. A landing party estimated about 500 on Laysan Island in 1964. More than 100 others are nurtured by aviculturists who cooperate with the Bureau of Sport Fisheries and Wildlife in maintaining a reservoir of breeding stock.

The Laysan duck thus seems now to be in relatively good contition, but it still is vulnerable—the wild birds are limited to one small island, whose central lagoon is filling with windblown sand. There also is the possibility that rats, cats, and other predators, which would be fatal to ground-nesting birds, may be introduced accidentally.

We can be sure of the safety of the Laysan duck only when numbers of them are established on other islands where habitat is suitable. That we are planning to do.

The southern population of the American bald eagle is in trouble, if not in immediate danger of extinction.

This southern subspecies of our big, brown and white national bird nests only near coasts and larger inland bodies of water, mostly in the southeast. It winters throughout its breeding range, but some of them wander northward after the breeding season to the Northeastern States and southeastern Canada.

Observations of nests and counts during migration testify to an alarming decline in the numbers of southern bald eagles and the production of young in northern Florida and along the Atlantic seaboard. The only exception seems to be in the Everglades National Park in southern Florida, where natural conditions still prevail in their habitat.

A reassuring augury is the concern and efforts of many Americans in behalf of this noble bird.

The National Audubon Society has undertaken an intensive investigation to learn more about its changing status and to determine the possibilities for remedial action.

The Bureau of Sport Fisheries and Wildlife conducts studies on the effects of insecticides the eagles may ingest with food—primarily dead fish.

Conservation organizations keep track of nests to ascertain breeding success. The Florida Audubon Society has obtained agreements with landowners to treat as sanctuaries more than 2 million acres where nests are located. Members make annual inspections of these nesting sites.

The bald eagle is protected by the Federal Bald Eagle Act. As amended by the Congress in 1962, the act also protects the golden eagle, and so gives additional protection to the bald eagle, the dark-colored young of which might easily be mistaken for golden eagles.

Still, to assure the survival of the southern bald eagle, several measures are needed.

We need continued but discreet surveillance of nest sites to determine success of production and to learn reasons for failures.

We need continuing research on the effects of pesticides and other presumed limiting factors.

More Americans need to know about the plight of the eagles. Contacts must be made with local residents and landowners in bald eagle nesting areas to obtain maximum interest and cooperation in protecting these birds, particularly those who own land and live where the birds nest so they will know how vital is their cooperation in protecting them.

Vital also is that we set aside sizable acreage around active nests near bays, lakes, and rivers as refuges. Public purchase of the land so that there can be adequate control seems to me the best way to do that.

Great herds of large plant-eating animals roamed the grasslands of this continent long ago. With them were large scavengers, which lived on the carcasses of the creatures that died from one cause or another.

The California condor is a relict of those days. This big, dusky-plumaged, orange-headed vulture with a 9–10-foot wingspread now is confined chiefly to the mountains at the southern end of the San Joaquin Valley in California. It nests mostly in the Los Padres National Forest. It has come upon hard times.

More roads and reservoirs are being built in the mountains. More people are using them for recreation. More exploration for oil and development is going on. More arid land is brought under cultivation and out of livestock production.

Very likely fewer than 40 California condors exist today. To protect them, the National Audubon Society, the United States Forest Service, and the California Department of Fish and Game have established a year-round patrol on the Los Padres National Forest. Protection is not easy; the condors make far-ranging flights in search of their ever-diminishing food.

Illegal shooting is still one of the chief hazards, despite policing. Placement of carcasses on the Los Padres National Forest sanctuary to encourage them to stay out of unprotected areas, where there is more danger of being shot by irresponsible gunners, may be one approach to their conservation. Even more rigid protection of the few remaining nesting sites is essential. Certainly there must be much greater effort in public education and law enforcement if the condor is to survive.

Once, over the open savannas of waving, tall marsh grass of southern Florida soared and swooped graceful Everglade kites, picturesque, dark-colored hawks with slender, hooked bills and blood-red eyes.

Now they are probably the closest to extinction of any North American bird. Only 15 of them were alive in 1964, and they produced only 2

An Everglade kite at Loxahatchee National Wildlife Refuge in Florida.

John J. Lynch, of the Bureau of Sport Fisheries and Wildlife, treats an injured sandhill crane, which is being raised in captivity in Louisiana. Sandhill cranes are cousins of the whooping crane, and biologists think procedures learned in raising them may be useful in continuing efforts to save the whooping crane.

young. Ten birds were counted in 1965, and no young were produced.

They do not breed when the rains fail, as in 1962 and 1965, the normally high water levels of south Florida drop, and there is less marsh vegetation they need for nesting and smaller numbers of the one species of snail on which the kites depend for food.

Their chances for survival are poor. A dispute over water supplies in southern Florida, and diking and draining of wetlands for grazing and agriculture near Lake Okeechobee worsen the effects of severe droughts. They make two strikes already against the Everglade kite.

The third strike may come soon. The kite is a hawk, and some hunters consider all hawks vermin: "The only good hawk is a dead hawk." How dangerous can be a little knowledge without comprehension of the total picture!

We are doing little to save the Everglade kite. We try to discourage indiscriminate shooting. We lift feeble voices now and then to say these birds need protection. Audubon societies conduct tours to Lake Okeechobee, and the leaders plead for understanding of the kite and its dangers—but their eloquence is for people already sympathetic.

Fortunately, the Loxahatchee National Wildlife Refuge contains considerable good habitat for kites, and the few remaining birds have concentrated there. A nesting area on the refuge has been closed to the public during the breeding season.

What really is needed—and needed at once, before it is too late—is action to set up more refuges in the best tracts of the remaining habitat and to patrol diligently the places where the birds nest. Maybe it is too late already.

I mentioned earlier the heath hen, now gone. Another subspecies of the greater prairie chicken, Attwater's greater prairie chicken, also is in danger because of loss of the habitat it needs.

It is a race confined to the coastal prairie of Texas. Its numbers are small numbers—probably not more than 750 in 1965. It is protected from hunting, but its habitat is being plowed up for crops, overgrazed, and being developed for oil.

A spark of hope was kindled in 1965, when laudable efforts on the part of the World Wildlife Fund and Nature Conservancy, two leading conservation fund-raising organizations, produced the 365 thousand dollars for a down payment on 3,500 acres in Colorado County, Texas, most of it in original prairie that supported 300 or 400 Attwater's prairie chickens. It is an encouraging start, but several preserves of at least 5 thousand acres each are needed to save this bird.

Every time Crip and Josephine produced an egg, the event got as much attention as the birth of a royal heir. They were a pair of captive whooping cranes at Audubon Park Zoo in New Orleans. Josephine, the last surviving member of the Louisiana wild population, died from heart failure following a severe hurricane in October 1965. Her history in captivity goes back to 1941 when she was picked up in a ricefield—injured and unable to fly. "Crip," short for cripple, was found wounded on the gulf coast wintering grounds in 1949. When brought together this pair formed a union, which had lasted for 10 years. They were members of the best known of our endangered species, whose comings and goings were carefully reported in our newspapers.

As far as we know, this great, white crane, one of two species in North America, breeds only in Wood Buffalo National Park in central-southern Mackenzie District in Canada. There the Canadian Wildlife Service makes counts of nesting pairs and young and gives all possible protection to them.

The Canadian Wildlife Service and the Audubon Society of Canada were successful recently in bringing about a change in plans to construct a railroad line through the area in which the whooping cranes breed.

In recent years, whooping cranes have been found in winter only on the gulf coast of Texas in or close to the Aransas National Wildlife Refuge.

The small numbers of whooping cranes had been increasing slowly until 1962. The 14 wild whoopers in existence in 1938 had increased to 38 in 1961, and 7 more were in zoological parks in New Orleans and San Antonio.

We felt some optimism then about their prospects for survival. Their breeding area evidently was subject to occasional adverse weather, but it was remote and safe from human interference.

Silky bantam hens have been used successfully to incubate the eggs of the rare nene goose, whooping crane, and sandhill crane. As foster parents, they have a part in efforts to save our endangered species.

A family of feeding whooping cranes at the Aransas Refuge includes a mottled youngster, a bird of the year.

These whooping cranes were photographed in January 1964 at the Aransas National Wildlife Refuge, near Austwell, Texas. Sights like this would not be possible even now if it were not for the special protection these birds receive in the United States and Canada.

Many conservation groups, newspapers, television, and radio had kept the public informed about the status of the whooping crane and emphasized the need for strict protection.

Furthermore, the residence of the birds during the winter in the Aransas Refuge and nearby seemed to have reduced greatly the hazards at that season. The chief losses had been of young nonbreeding birds, which occasionally summer away from remote breeding grounds, in more populated districts where the hazards are greater.

But we were optimistic too soon. After 38 birds migrated north in the spring of 1962, everything seemed to go wrong.

For the first time in a number of years and the second time in the 25 years of recordkeeping, no young birds were reared. Six of the 38 failed to appear on their wintering grounds in the fall of 1962. Four more cranes disappeared during the winter of 1962–1963.

The loss in a year of 10 older birds and the lack of reproduction was a shocking setback.

In the summer of 1963, however, the cranes produced 7 young. That fall, 32 whoopers came south to their wintering area. In 1965, the most successful year of all, 44 cranes, including 8 young, appeared on the wintering grounds.

This fluctuation in breeding success in just 3 years points up that great variation in production is characteristic of the cranes and teaches us that we cannot relax our vigilance because of favorable years.

Therefore the Bureau of Sport Fisheries and Wildlife has intensified efforts to keep track of the numbers, to protect the cranes at Aransas, to increase the size of the refuge, thus placing under protection more of the land the birds require in winter, and to plant grain on this land to induce the cranes to spend more time within its protective boundaries.

Research has been started by the Bureau looking toward a possible expansion of efforts to rear whooping cranes. Studies of captive sandhill cranes, which are close relatives of whooping cranes, are underway. The aim is to learn more about the problems involved in capturing, rearing, and liberating cranes; how to meet the difficulties; and to train personnel in such techniques against the

time we begin to rear whooping cranes in captivity.

Hawaii seems to have more than its share of endangered birds.

One of these with a very doubtful future is the gray and white Hawaiian dark-rumped petrel. It is a seabird that comes to land only to nest, for which it chooses sites only in mountainous cliffs on Hawaii and Maui. Feral dogs, cats, and perhaps mongooses may be their worst enemies.

Another endangered bird, the chickenlike, dusky, red-billed Hawaiian common gallinule frequents fresh-water marshes. It and two other rapidly disappearing forms, the diminutive, brown Hawaiian duck or koloa and the black and white, long-legged Hawaiian stilt suffer from the progressive drainage of wetlands.

The Hawaiian common gallinule is resident on the islands of Kauai, Molokai, and Oahu. Its numbers have declined greatly since 1952, particularly on Oahu, where the greatest demand for agricultural land has hastened the drainage of the galli-

Victor Olson carries a young, injured whooping crane into an airplane for a trip to Monte Vista, Colorado, where it can receive proper treatment.

nule's wetland habitat. It is believed to be most numerous on Kauai, where it has an estimated population of 100 to 150 birds.

Attempts to transplant this species to the islands of Hawaii and Maui have been unsuccessful.

Its prospects are not good, in view of the trend in land use. Little has been done in its behalf. It seems to me that the best we can do is to make every effort to preserve and create all of the wetlands possible and to propagate the bird in captivity until new habitat can be established or developed for it.

The Hawaii Division of Fish and Game has set up a project for breeding the Hawaiian duck in captivity and carrying out an ecological study of it.

Also among Hawaii's vulnerable birds are several small forest-inhabiting species: The Kauai oo, akiapolaau, Kauai akialoa, Kauai nukupuu, ou, palila, the crested honey-creeper, Maui parrotbill, and the small Kauai thrush.

Several had been considered extinct for many years but were rediscovered by diligent search. At best, the population of these remaining must be very small. Their continued existence depends on keeping undisturbed the forest habitat they need,

preventing further introduction of competing foreign species, and protecting them from already imported disease and predators.

Other Hawaiian species that seem to be in danger are the Hawaiian hawk and the Hawaiian crow. They, however, are less dependent on undisturbed habitat and more on direct protection from shooting by irresponsible persons.

Old accounts of the tremendous slaughter of game by market hunters often mentioned the Eskimo curlew, which traveled in dense flocks and so was exceptionally easy to shoot during its migrations from the arctic coast to the pampas of Argentina.

Like the great auk and passenger pigeon, the gregarious nature of this curve-billed, brownish streaked shore bird made it susceptible to mass shooting, particularly on its northward flights in spring over the midwestern prairies. It became almost extinct before the enactment of conservation laws put an end to this type of hunting.

For more than two decades it was in truth thought to be gone. But one bird was seen at Galveston Island, Texas, in March of 1959, 1960, and

Few individuals remain of the rare Hawaiian goose.

1961. Two birds were seen there in the spring of 1962, but none in 1963 or since. They were indentified by experienced ornithologists from personal sightings and photographs. But in 1963 came the first record of fall migration in many years. A specimen was discovered in the freezer of a resident of Barbados, West Indies.

We cannot say from observation of a few individuals in migration and without knowledge of their breeding and wintering grounds what their prospects of survival are.

It is encouraging, however, that the species has survived the period of greatest hazard from excessive hunting to a time when the remaining individuals are relatively safe from the gun, at least in the North American parts of their range, where the greatest slaughter formerly occurred.

Federal laws in the United States and Canada prohibit the shooting at any time of all shore birds that may be confused with the Eskimo curlew.

The Texas Game and Fish Commission has prohibited collecting, even for scientific or educational purposes, of all migratory birds in Galveston County, where the recent observations occurred. Game wardens and the Federal game management agents patrol the area during the time Eskimo curlews may be expected to be there.

Strict protection in the places where it is known to occur seems to be all that can be done for it at present. Special efforts should be made to find its present breeding and wintering areas so that we can seek other ways to succor it.

The Carolina parakeet became extinct in the United States many years ago. Another member of the parrot family, the Puerto Rican parrot, seems to be close to extinction. Its other subspecies, which occurred on Culebra Island, Puerto Rico, has been considered extinct, although we have had unconfirmed reports of sightings in 1965. This endangered remnant of a formerly common West Indian parrot is restricted chiefly to the Luquillo National Forest of 3,200 acres in eastern Puerto Rico, 1,600 to 2,700 feet above sea level.

A survey in 1959 disclosed that about 200 of these medium-sized green parrots with red foreheads remained, and their number was declining. Predation by rats, insufficient suitable habitat at lower elevations, and possible shortage of cavities for

An Eskimo curlew at Galveston Island in 1962. The future of these shore birds is uncertain.

A young ivory-billed woodpecker perches on the cap of J. J. Kuhn in Louisiana.

nesting sites may be factors adverse to the survival of Puerto Rican parrots.

The control of rats, acquisition of additional habitat, and the construction of nesting boxes have been suggested as helpful practices. The Forest Service and World Wildlife Fund have planned studies of the requirements of the parrots and ways to put recommended procedures into effect.

Woodpeckers we all know and enjoy. They are extraordinarily adapted to their environment. Their bills are effective axes for chopping wood. Their tongues are like harpoons for spearing grubs in woody tunnels. It seems that they should be able to get along well in almost any wooded place.

But one of them, one of the largest and most powerful of this remarkable group, the great red, white, and black American ivory-billed woodpecker, is in danger. The distribution of this giant among woodpeckers is extremely limited and is known to a few persons. They prefer not to tell where the birds are for fear of further endangering the species.

No authentic reports of occurrence of ivory-billed woodpeckers have been published since those for northern Florida in 1952, but persistent mention of sightings by qualified observers in the Southeastern States keeps hope alive that a few indivduals may have survived.

Even if remnants of breeding stock still exist, however, the comeback of the species is extremely doubtful because of its dependence on large tracts of overmature pines and hardwoods for its food supply and the scarcity of such forest types of sufficient size and maturity within its native range today.

If tracts are known that still harbor ivory-bills, we should try hard to protect them by preventing logging and other activities that destroy the virgin nature of the forest and make it uninhabitable for these highly specialized birds.

The possible loss of our ivory-bill is all the more serious because an intensive search in 1962 and 1963 for its close relative, the imperial ivory-billed woodpecker of Mexico, failed to turn up a single bird.

The Kirtland's warbler in summer has a special forest home—stands of young jack pine in Michigan.

One of the best known of our endangered birds is the little gray, black, and yellow Kirtland's warbler. Years of study by Josselyn Van Tyne and Harold Mayfield, leading American ornithologists, and observations of countless birders have made it the subject of a book by Mayfield and many published notes and papers at ornithological meetings.

Kirtland's warbler has a very small breeding area—only 12 counties in the lower peninsula of Michigan. Its very low population comprises only about a thousand individuals. It has this advantage though: It is the only endangered songbird in America for which something substantial is being done.

One reason for its precarious existence is its restrictive habitat requirements—a fire-initiated combination of young jack pine stands with undergrowth of a special density. The Michigan State Conservation Department and the Forest Service have set aside as refuges land on which this type of habitat can be maintained through sylvicultural manipulation, including the judicious use of fire.

Other factors may militate against Kirtland's warblers in their only known wintering areas in the Bahama Islands, but we do not know what they are. We need to make a careful study of the wintering situation and to take whatever remedial action is necessary.

We do know that nest parasitism by the brown-headed cowbird is getting worse and, unless checked, may work against their survival.

All in all, however, prospects look relatively bright for Kirtland's warbler.

A great mystery of American birdlife is the status of Bachman's warbler.

We know so little about it that we are not sure whether it is an endangered species or not. It seems that it must be, because with all the birdwatching in the United States, only two Bachman's warblers have been seen in two localities in many years—at Lorton, Virginia, and near Charleston, South Carolina. In neither place was the bird nesting.

Although never abundant, this species was noted much oftener in the early part of this century, even though far fewer bird observers were afield than now.

This mysterious species has always been ex-

Men of the Bureau of Sport Fisheries and Wildlife and the U.S. Coast Guard remove goslings of the rare Aleutian goose from Buldir Island, Alaska, for shipment to the States. They are being raised to start captive flocks. Birds from this stock will be reintroduced to islands where they once flourished.

tremely local in distribution, even in migration. Although the nonbreeding Bachman's warbler near Charleston was seen in dry upland second growth, and the one near Lorton in immature swampwoods, the normal breeding habitat of the species has been assumed to be the extensive swamp forest along the lower channels of the large rivers of the Southeast.

This type of habitat is not scarce, but possibly most of it is not mature enough. Since Bachman's warbler became rare before thorough analysis of its habitat requirements could be made, however, it may be that we do not have an accurate understanding of them.

It may well be that harmful factors exist in Cuba, its only known winter range. We do know that other species of wildlife have suffered in Cuba because of drainage of swamps, cutting of timber, and other changes in the use of land; perhaps

Bachman's warbler is affected by the same conditions, which would contribute to its extinction just as quickly as loss of its breeding habitat.

Unfortunately, we know even less about its distribution in its winter range than we do in its breeding area.

Without much more knowledge of the total requirements of Bachman's warbler and the factors that affect its survival, we cannot assess the prospects for its continued existence. Complete legal protection, as with all songbirds in the United States, presumably benefits this warbler to some extent.

Two other little-known songbirds that are at the borderline of survival are the Cape Sable sparrow and dusky seaside sparrow.

They inhabit marshes of southern Florida. They suffer from water deficiencies in their habitat, but for different reasons.

504

The Cape Sable sparrow, which lives in fresh marshes on the western border of the Everglades, is suffering from the general water shortage characteristic of southern Florida in recent years.

The dusky seaside sparrow, which is confined to salt marshes near Cape Kennedy, is endangered by habitat changes brought about by introduction of fresh water into the marshes to control mosquitoes.

So, by way of summary, I say we know some facts about the endangered species but not nearly enough: Our ignorance may be the beginning of wisdom.

As to those about which we have fairly complete information, I would say that direct killing by man is of relatively little consequence today, but it still must be considered in the case of some of the larger, more conspicuous species, such as the California condor, whooping crane, and Florida Everglade kite, which have been reduced to so few individuals that the loss of even one is significant.

Loss of required habitat seems to be the most important hazard facing most of the endangered birds. Usually it is a result of the utilization of the land for other purposes. Particularly damaging has been the severe reduction in amount of tall grass prairie in the Midwest, the virgin forests of the East, and the loss of wetlands by draining everywhere.

Predation, competition, and disease from introduced birds and mammals have been particularly severe in Hawaii.

The breaking of food chains by elimination of vital links (as by pesticides) is an ever-present hazard to the endangered species.

A complication is that some species migrate out of the United States into other countries. The problem therefore is international.

I must not end on too discouraging a note. I do not believe man has started an irreversible trend down the slippery plank to extinction for species in general. Other species will become extinct eventually; that is the way of Nature: Old species die, and new ones are born, just as with individuals. But the rate of species loss has been accelerated in the past 200 years.

If we knew more and if we wanted badly enough to do so, we could do much to arrest the decline.

Wildlife research biologists can acquire or supply information on management methods needed to protect endangered species. For that they need public and financial support. The support, that is, of interested, concerned people.

—JOHN W. ALDRICH.

Refuges and Sanctuaries

THIS IS A CORDIAL INVITATION to attend open house at the places birds live. There are hundreds of them in the United States. They have various sizes from a city lot to 11 million acres and various names—bird refuges, sanctuaries, wildlife management areas. We are proud of them. You will be, too.

Come as you are. Come to have fun. Come prepared to be awed, inspired, and enlightened. Come to learn, to share in an experience you will not have in cities or world's fairs or Disneylands or Coney Island.

Come, for example, to the 65-thousand-acre Bear River Migratory Bird Refuge in Utah. It is 15 miles west of Brigham City near the center of Bear River Valley. It is on the delta where the Bear River empties into Great Salt Lake. The Promontory Mountains are on the west. The Wasatch Range is on the east. A perfect setting, that, for the photographs you will want to take of the constantly changing panorama (except in January, February, and March) of birdlife.

Canada geese are among the first to arrive in April. They begin to nest shortly thereafter. Hundreds of thousands of ducks are next, accompanied by white-faced ibises, snowy egrets, grebes, and thousands of shore birds. If you have never seen an acre of dowitchers, avocets, and black-necked stilts by the hundreds, or western and eared grebes everywhere, Bear River gives you a chance to do so.

Bear River, one of the few refuges established by an act of the Congress, came into being in 1928, before the 1929 Migratory Bird Conservation Act became law.

One reason for its establishment was that botulism, a form of food poisoning, had become rampant in the area. Land was purchased, studies of the nature and probable causes of the disease were intensified, and five fresh-water pools were developed to regulate water levels. Some details are still unclear about this form of botulism—but an index of the success of the work at Bear River is that mortality of birds from botulism has dropped nearly to zero. Previously, as many as 100

LONG-BILLED DOWITCHERS
AVOCETS

thousand waterfowl were stricken in a single year.

Very likely you will not be aware of botulism and other problems of management—housekeeping, so to speak—as you drive or stroll, with other birdwatchers, along the 12-mile loop road on the broad, gently sloped dikes of Unit 2, but I think an awareness that refuges exist for more purposes than pleasure alone will add to your appreciation of their place in our national life.

The campaign against botulism was justification enough for the development of Bear River by the Bureau of Biological Survey, but an extra dividend is its use by people.

The State of Utah, in approving the establishment of the refuge, specified that a part of it be open each year to the public. Thus 17 thousand visitors were welcomed in 1964. One-fourth of them hunted waterfowl. One thousand fishermen came for black bullheads, carp, and, occasionally, channel catfish. More than 10 thousand studied or photographed the birds.

Brigham City constructed a massive overhead sign across Main Street and U.S. 30–S. It welcomes visitors and proclaims Bear River as the "Gateway—World's Greatest Game Bird Refuge." Maybe it is.

Or come to Lake Merritt in Oakland, California, which was established as a wildlife sanctuary by the State Legislature in 1870. High-rise apartments surround the lake now, but it continues to attract a sizable number of wintering ducks—canvasbacks, pintails, American widgeons, coots. Between November and April the widgeons and coots feed on

the extensive green lawns. At that time, all wildlife photographers become experts.

Sometimes a European widgeon visits the 155-acre, tide-replenished, salt-water lake in the heart of Oakland. Word of it spreads rapidly among the birdwatchers in the San Francisco Bay area. Visitors buy packets of grain for 10 cents at the park and feed the wildlings, which soon lose their normal suspicion of people. Children take to it gleefully, as they do to the exhibit panels, 3 by 4 feet, which have pictures of birds to be seen and introduce them—maybe for the first time—to the wonders of wildlife.

Lake Merritt, a municipal sanctuary or preserve, is owned by the City of Oakland. Other well-known municipal sanctuaries include the Tinicum Swamp at Philadelphia; the heron rookery in Stone Harbor, New Jersey; and the 37-thousand acre Cook County Forest Preserve, which adjoins Chicago on the west.

Inconsistencies in designations need not bother us. Private and municipal preserves generally are known as sanctuaries. State and Federal areas are called refuges or management areas. On true sanctuaries, generally established to protect wild birds or animals, all forms of disturbance are prohibited; public entry generally is restricted or prohibited; bird sanctuaries of the National Audubon Society are of this type.

National Parks contain great acreages of sanctuaries. Wildlife rarely is disturbed. Beautiful Yellowstone Park became the first National Park in 1872 and probably the second wildlife sanctuary following Lake Merritt. Hunting is prohibited in the 191 natural and historical areas in the national park system, which areas cover more than 23 million acres.

One of them is Crater Lake National Park in Oregon. It was established in 1902 and is a place of superlative scenery—cobalt-blue waters, chastely white mountaintops, somber green forests, and evidence of earlier volcanic action. Wildlife is

At the Lower Klamath National Wildlife Refuge in California, as on many national wildlife refuges, one can see flocks of white-fronted geese, snow geese, and other birds in fall and spring.

508

Brigham, Utah, proclaims it is the gateway to the Bear River National Wildlife Refuge, where spectacular flights of migratory waterfowl are common in late summer and fall.

abundant. No sign says you must not feed the golden-mantled ground squirrels and Clark's nutcrackers. A crowd usually gathers whenever anyone starts tumbling shelled peanuts down the long volcanic ash slope in front of the lodge. The ground squirrels seem to have unlimited storage capacity in their cheek pouches, and the nutcrackers fly away to cache each peanut against the winter. The nutcrackers are bold. The squirrels are fast and leave only when their cheeks are bulging.

The National Forests provide excellent opportunities for wildlife production. About 25 percent of all big-game animals in the United States live in them. Except in refuges established to protect certain species, such as the California condor refuge of 35 thousand acres in the Los Padres National Forest in California, the National Forests provide hunting in accordance with laws of the State in

Pelicans and other birds abound at the Anaho Island National Wildlife Refuge in Nevada.

which they are located. The forests are actually the most extensive public shooting preserves in the United States. The 173 National Forests and national grassland areas cover 186 million acres.

Another unusual refuge of the Forest Service is one to protect the Kirtland's warbler in the Lower Peninsula of Michigan. Units are burned according to specific schedules to produce new growth of jack pine at a height that the birds like. The refuge is considered an outstanding example of progressive species management.

Pennsylvania has developed an extensive system of State game preserves that range from 1,200 acres to 3 thousand acres. Fire lanes are cleared, and each refuge is marked by a single strand of wire high enough to permit free access of game. The surplus animals from the protected area restock the surrounding region. Habitat that attracts turkeys, deer, and bears is insured by controlled burning, which brings an immediate response in the growth of berry- and other fruit-producing shrubs.

Extensive tracts within National Forests have

Winter is closing in at the Bear River Refuge. Ice is thickening. Snow covers the Wasatch Range. The large birds in the foreground are whistling swans.

The National Audubon Society maintains a number of bird sanctuaries, such as this one on Galveston Bay, Texas. In the foreground are one common egret and a group of roseate spoonbills.

been designated as State game refuges in Wyoming, Montana, Idaho, Utah, and California. The Federal Government has authority to locate refuges only on the public domain and specially acquired lands, but a number of States may give their State game officials authority to establish refuges, including those on private lands; refuges then are created by law or by regulation. Hunting may be forbidden or limited to certain kinds of game. These refuges do not involve Government ownership; often their main aim is to prevent public hunting.

Since 1937, the States have received funds from the Federal excise tax on sporting arms and ammunition. They can acquire projects to benefit wildlife, which may be used in part for public hunting and are combination game preserves and public shooting grounds. The funds also have gone into the restoration of several famous waterfowl marshes, among them the Horicon Marsh in Wisconsin, Ogden Bay in Utah, Cheyenne Bottoms in Kansas, and the Roseau Unit in Minnesota.

You will be welcome, too, at refuges and sanctuaries developed by private organizations or individuals.

One such is the Paul J. Rainey Wildlife Sanctuary, which the National Audubon Society established in 1924 on 26 thousand acres in Louisiana. The land had been the magnificent shooting preserve of Mr. Rainey, world-renowned big-game hunter and photographer. It was deeded to the Society after Mr. Rainey's death by his sister, Mrs. Grace Rainey Rogers.

The sanctuary lies along the gulf coast in the midst of wintering grounds of blue and snow geese. For many years it was inviolate; muskrats increased to a point where they threatened to eat out the vegetation. Now the regulated trapping of muskrats maintains a balance of open water and protective vegetation birds need for food and nesting. The income from muskrat pelts provides some revenue for operating the sanctuary.

The Corkscrew Swamp Sanctuary, 35 miles southeast of Fort Myers, Florida, covers 6 thousand acres and includes our largest remaining stand of bald cypress. It is the most important sanctuary of the National Audubon Society. The largest nesting colony of wood ibis in the United States finds protection there. It is ideal as a nesting ground, but extreme drought made it practically deserted for 2 years. Before the drought, regular tours were conducted in the sanctuary. A raised boardwalk into the heart of the swamp permits you to see this magnificent wildlife wonderland.

Other sanctuaries of the National Audubon Society in Florida include the Alafia Banks Rookery and Green Key in Tampa Bay; and small islands for great white herons in Florida Bay near Everglades National Park.

At the society's Vingt'un Islands Sanctuary in Galveston Bay, Texas, you can see the Nation's largest nesting colony of roseate spoonbills. This bird was snatched from the brink of extinction in the United States shortly after 1900.

Another group of islands the society leases lies near the Aransas National Wildlife Refuge on the gulf coast above Rockport, Texas. There you will see the major population of reddish egrets in the United States.

Within easy reach of many Americans is Hawk Mountain Sanctuary, a haven for thousands of migrating hawks and a living monument to the late Mrs. Rosalie Edge, its founder and benefactor. Her interest was not limited to hawks. Mrs. Edge had studied birds in all parts of the country. She was well prepared for her determined efforts to stop the useless slaughter of birds of prey. In eastern Pennsylvania, near Hamburg, the narrow Kittatinny Ridge, easternmost chain in the Appalachians, has a slight break or saddle. It was at this break hunters shot thousands of hawks during each fall migration. The birds, mostly from the Maritime Provinces and New England, follow the ridges. They glide many miles, seemingly without effort, on the updrafts of air.

Mrs. Edge and a small group of dedicated conservationists formed an emergency conservation committee and later the Hawk Mountain Sanctuary Association to raise money to acquire the 2-square-mile tract on Hawk Mountain in which the Lookout, at 1,540 feet, is centered. Any weekend from late September into November you will find someone parked on each of the massive sandstone boulders that comprise the Lookout. It is an ideal spot for hawkwatching.

Maurice Broun, biologist, ardent conservationist,

On a warm fall day at Hawk Mountain Sanctuary, Kempton, Pennsylvania, visitors scan the skies for the red-tailed hawks, like the one at the right.

and lecturer, was hired by Mrs. Edge as Hawk Mountain's only protector. He has conducted educational programs for more than 30 years not only at the sanctuary, where he and his family reside, but through Pennsylvania and adjoining States. The programs encompass more than the protection of hawks; the need for the conservation of all wildlife resources is shown in illustrated lectures.

When rain or fog engulfs the Lookout, as sometimes happens, the hundreds of visitors may adjourn to an assembly hall to view exhibits and slide and film presentations.

Mr. Broun described his experiences at Hawk Mountain in a book, *Hawks Aloft,* first published by Dodd, Mead Company in 1949.

When you visit Hawk Mountain, plan to use one of the open Adirondack shelters, if you are of the rugged type, available for camping near headquarters. Each one has 12 bunks, and a stone fireplace. Tables, spring water, and latrines are available. You will need to bring your food, charcoal, and necessary equipment. Requests for reservations for use of the shelters must be made by mail—Hawk Mountain Sanctuary, Route 2, Kempton, Pennsylvania—in advance and must be accompanied by a deposit of a dollar per person per night.

Visitors to Hawk Mountain come from all parts of the United States and other countries. On one beautiful October morning, for example, 30 Boy Scouts and their leaders perched themselves on rocks at the Lookout, hoping to be the first to spot a hawk. By 9:00 a.m., most of them had finished eating their lunches.

For the first hour or so no hawks were flying. Finally a single, immature red-tailed hawk appeared as a dot, glided ever closer, and then went by the observers at near eye level. It was pointed out, and its field marks were described. The veteran observers, who now were sure this was the beginning of a big flight, were shocked to hear one Boy Scout announce, "Well, we've seen a hawk. Let's go home!"

Private preserves or sanctuaries may range from the premises of a farmer or landowner who posts his land against public hunting to tracts where developments and improvements have been made to attract and protect birds and animals.

Some are famous.

Bird City, on 5-thousand-acre Avery Island, Louisiana, was established by E. A. McIlhenny, whose interests included the manufacturing of tabasco sauce, mining for salt, and bird banding. Bird City, seen by thousands of visitors each year, is a nesting ground for snowy egrets and other herons.

The W. H. Kellogg Bird Sanctuary near Battle Creek, Michigan, since 1927 has sponsored many studies on waterfowl. Trumpeter swans, the only ones for many years in captivity in this country, were imported from a dealer in Holland. He had obtained the parent birds from Canada.

The Lockhart Gaddy Wild Goose Refuge, near Ansonville, North Carolina, started in 1934 as a

fishpond, was enlarged to 4.5 acres. It has attracted 7 thousand Canada geese, and many times that number of human visitors. Geese soon became dependent upon grain packets, purchased by visitors. You can easily spot banded geese as they feed about you.

The Jack Miner Bird Sanctuary, Kingsville, Ontario, established in 1904, has attracted as many as 25 thousand Canada geese and is a conservation-education center. Banding has shown that these birds migrate chiefly east of the Mississippi River.

Many persons ask us for information on how to develop their properties into wildlife sanctuaries. Their holdings may be an acre to 300 acres. Some may have a stream, a pool, a marsh, woods, and other prepossessing features.

We tell them how easy and rewarding such projects are. We give details about planting and caring for shrubs and trees that produce seeds and fruits birds like. Ponds should have submerged weeds or other plants like wild millet, smartweeds, and bulrushes. A landowner can post his premises against public hunting and so establish a sanctuary.

We recommend Farmers' Bulletin No. 2035, "Making Land Produce Useful Wildlife," which was prepared by the Department of Agriculture and can be had from the Superintendent of Documents, Government Printing Office, Washington, D.C., 20402, for 15 cents or from the Office of Information, the Department of Agriculture, Washington, D.C., 20250 without charge.

A helpful book, *The New Handbook of Attracting Birds,* by Thomas P. McElroy, Jr., published by Alfred A. Knopf, Inc., New York, was revised in 1961.

One of its chapters, on sanctuaries for birds, gives information on articles of association, which have been used extensively by cities in the Southeast in establishing their entire communities as sanctuaries.

Organizations of sportsmen and conservationists also establish and maintain sanctuaries for wildlife. Some duck clubs have set aside parts of their holdings as management units.

An example is the Bean Patch on a club between the Sacramento National Wildlife Refuge and the Gray Lodge Waterfowl Management Area, owned by California. Once when I flew over this flooded field, the water was black with pintails and widgeons—maybe as many as 500 thousand birds were present.

At some clubs, gamekeepers operate hatcheries that produce and liberate more birds than are annually taken. Private quail-shooting preserves, ranging from 10 thousand to 20 thousand acres, chiefly on leased lands, are maintained in some Southern States.

Our national wildlife refuge system—with 304 areas, totaling 28.5 million acres in 1965—includes extensive tracts of land and water selected for their usefulness to wildlife, particularly migratory birds and the rarer mammals. Perhaps you have seen one of the boundary markers—the sign of the flying goose.

The system began in 1903, when Theodore Roosevelt set aside a small island in the Indian River in Florida for the protection of a colony of brown pelicans and herons that nested there—the Pelican Island National Wildlife Refuge.

For a long time it was assumed that the refuge

In Virginia and other Southern States, it is a practice to establish estates as bird sanctuaries. This sign is at the entrance to Stratford, the birthplace of Robert E. Lee in Virginia.

At a private Canada goose sanctuary at Ansonville, North Carolina, a visitor feeds the geese shelled corn.

was only a 3-acre mangrove island, but later surveys disclosed the land area designated in the Executive order actually totaled 616 acres and included the island, large mangrove stands, and nearby salt marshes.

The refuge was designated a Registered National Historic Landmark in 1963. The first Federal wildlife warden, Paul Kroegel, who protected Pelican Island from 1903 to 1920, was honored at dedication ceremonies.

After Pelican Island, 36 more small islands were set aside primarily for the protection of colonial birds.

Among them were Three Arch Rocks, Copalis, Flattery Rocks, and Quillayute Needles National Wildlife Refuges off the coasts of Oregon and Washington. These rocky islands are almost inaccessible and people have not disturbed the birds on them—common murres, tufted puffins, rhinoceros and Cassin's auklets, pigeon guillemots, western and glaucous-winged gulls, fork-tailed and Leach's petrels, pelagic, Brandt's and double-crested cormorants, and black oystercatchers.

A number of national refuges for migratory waterfowl were established on reclamation reservoirs and drainange sumps between 1908 and 1930. Executive orders established such units as Malheur and Upper Klamath Lakes in Oregon, Tule Lake and Lower Klamath in California, and Deer Flat and Minidoka in Idaho. Concentrations of 8 million ducks and geese have been recorded on the Klamath Basin refuges.

A few big-game refuges were brought under Federal protection during this period by special acts of the Congress and through donations by conservation organizations.

The Congress in 1924 authorized an appropriation of 1.5 million dollars to buy bottom lands for the Upper Mississippi River Wild Life and Fish Refuge. It covers 194 thousand acres and extends 284 miles from Wabasha, Minnesota, nearly to Rock Island, Illinois. This first congressional recognition of the needs of migratory waterfowl was followed in 1928 by an appropriation of 350 thousand dollars to establish the Bear River Migratory Bird Refuge.

Under the authority of the Norbeck-Andresen Migratory Bird Conservation Act of 1929, a few national wildlife refuges were acquired, including St. Marks in Florida; Salton Sea in California; Swanquarter, North Carolina; and Crescent Lake, Nebraska.

A great drought and the economic depression in the thirties slowed the program of acquiring refuges, but in 1934 President Franklin D. Roosevelt appointed Jay N. Darling, a cartoonist; Thomas Beck, a magazine editor; and Aldo Leopold, a biologist, to a committee that immediately set a goal of 50 million dollars for the purchase and restoration of submarginal and other lands for wildlife, especially migratory waterfowl.

The move fired the enthusiasm of conservationists everywhere. "Ding" Darling later became Chief of the Biological Survey. He changed the course of refuge history. He aroused Americans to the plight of drought-stricken and overshot ducks with his eloquent tongue, his facile pen, and his pungent cartoons.

In a short time, he obtained 8.5 million dollars of emergency funds to buy lands and construct dikes, dams, fences, and buildings. An additional 6 million dollars were provided through a resolution that Senator Peter Norbeck attached to the Duck Stamp Act of 1934.

As Mr. Darling recounted it, the measure "was probably the only one in history passed by the Congress because the Gentleman from South Dakota had left his false teeth in the washroom of the U.S. Senate Office Building." Passage of the Duck Stamp Act was assured, and the roll call was a mere formality. As it was about to start, Senator Norbeck, minus his teeth, arose and asked for unanimous consent to add as a rider a Senate Resolution, which he proceeded to read from a speech in a voice vibrant with emotion, but with indistinguishable articulation. The rider passed, although no one understood a word he said.

During the 20 months Mr. Darling served as Chief of the Bureau of Biological Survey, accepting no paychecks and foregoing the income from his cartooning, then syndicated to 130 daily newspapers, he initiated the acquisition and development of 62 waterfowl refuges that are now the backbone of the national wildlife refuge system.

The 1934 Migratory Bird Hunting Stamp Act made it mandatory that a duck stamp (which now costs 3 dollars) be in possession of anyone over 16 years of age when hunting migratory waterfowl. Mr. Darling drew the design for the first stamp—a pair of mallards dropping to a landing in a wind-swept marsh.

A new design is used for each year's stamp. More than 160 designs are submitted annually, and selection is made by a committee composed of representatives of the Division of Philately and Postal History in the Smithsonian Institution, the Bureau of Engraving and Printing, and two national conservation organizations.

The winning artist receives no direct compensation except an album containing a sheet of the stamp he designed.

The duck stamps are a continuing source of funds for waterfowl restoration. Revenue received from the sale of duck stamps from the time the act became effective in 1934 through 1964, totaled more than 84 million dollars.

The funds were used to acquire more than 440 thousand acres of refuge lands for migratory birds and to purchase more than 66 thousand acres and obtain easements prohibiting drainage of nearly 94 thousand additional acres of small wetlands for waterfowl production. Before 1960, about 50 percent of the fund was used to develop and maintain migratory bird refuges.

An amendment to the act in 1960 specified that all money (except the actual expenses connected with the sale of the stamps by the Post Office Department) must be used to acquire land for these birds.

Between 1960 and 1964, about 250 thousand acres have been acquired for new migratory bird refuges and additions to existing ones. That is almost as much acreage as was acquired in the first three decades the migratory bird legislation was in operation.

Some form of hunting is permitted on parts of 109 refuges; hunters had a total of 462 thousand days of hunting in 1964. That was about 3 percent of all public use on the refuge system. Besides, hunting on land within a mile of refuge boundaries furnished an estimated 656 thousand days of sport.

Forty-six of the refuges are for the protection of migratory birds other than waterfowl. They have large nesting colonies of pelicans, herons, egrets, ibises, spoonbills, and seabirds.

One, the 1,980-acre Santa Ana National Wildlife Refuge on the Texas-Mexico border in a large bend of the Rio Grande, is about 35 miles west of San Benito, headquarters for this and the 44-thousand-acre Laguna Atascosa National Wildlife Refuge.

Experienced birdwatchers have seen more "life birds"—those that they identify for the first time—on the Santa Ana Refuge than on any similar area in the country. Unless you have birded in Mexico or along the Mexican border in Arizona, these all may be new birds for you to watch for on your first late spring or early summer trip to Santa Ana: Least grebe, black-bellied tree duck, gray hawk, jacana, chachalaca, red-billed pigeon, white-fronted dove, groove-billed ani, pauraque, buff-bellied hummingbird, rose-throated becard, kiskadee flycatcher, green jay, black-crested titmouse, long-billed and curve-billed thrashers, black-headed oriole, Lichtenstein's oriole, white-collared seedeater, and olive sparrow.

Equally exciting are the general wildlife refuges in Alaska and Hawaii. Almost unbelievable bird populations visit Bogoslof, just north of Unmak Island in the Aleutians; Semidi, on the south side of the Alaska Peninsula; and Tuxedni, on the northwest shore of Cook Inlet. Here you will see kittiwakes, puffins, fulmars, murres, auklets, cormorants, and gulls. On many islands in the 1,200-mile Aleutian Islands National Wildlife Refuge chain you also may encounter sea otters wherever there are kelp beds.

Eighteen national wildlife refuges are primarily managed for big game. Four favor American bison; five, bighorns; and one, the muskox. Three large tracts in Alaska and one in Montana have the special classification of wildlife range. They were established to conserve a variety of wild birds and animals.

Wetland areas in the wildlife refuge system include numerous waterfowl production areas—small pothole marshes in North Dakota, South Dakota, and Minnesota that have special duck-producing qualities. Emphasis has been placed on their preservation to prevent their imminent destruction by drainage and conversion to agricultural uses. Nearly 10 thousand of these small wetland

The sign of the flying goose marks the boundaries of national areas dedicated to the preservation of wildlife resources for the enjoyment and enrichment of the lives of people everywhere.

areas have been scheduled for purchase, lease, or easement. More than 66 thousand acres had been acquired by 1965.

The national wildlife refuges often are thought of as pristine, self-operating wildlife paradises. Oftener than not, they have been created from areas abused by drainage, lumbering, burning, overgrazing, and soil erosion. Almost always they must be restored to first-class wildlife habitat through sound management practices. That means the construction of dams, dikes, and fences. Roads and trails are needed to provide access and a means of fire control.

The planting of aquatic and other food plants for waterfowl and other wildlife is becoming an important management feature of the refuge program. Management may also involve the construction of irrigation systems, regulating livestock grazing to create habitat for more successful waterfowl nesting, soil conservation practices, pest control, forestry programs, and eradication of rough fish.

About 160 national wildlife refuges have permanent staffs. They may be responsible also for the management of nearby unstaffed refuges. A typical refuge staff has a refuge manager, an assistant, maintenance men and equipment operators, and a clerk. The manager and his assistant generally have college training in wildlife management.

Many refuges contribute substantially to the income of the county in which they are located. By law, the local government shares in revenues of the refuge from farming, grazing, haying, sale of timber products, and other economic uses necessary for the best management of wildlife habitat.

Refuges further add to the economic base of the community through local expenditures for food, supplies, and lodgings by people visiting the refuge for recreational purposes, through local purchase by the refuge of supplies and services, and through the payrolls of refuge employees.

For years, refuges had signs: "National Wildlife Refuge. Hunting, trapping, trespassing prohibited. $500 fine, six months imprisonment or both for molesting wildlife or damaging property on this refuge." Gates were locked, and persons who were allowed within the refuge usually had to carry permits.

All that has been changed.

Recreation facilities on refuges scarcely existed before the depression days of the Civilian Conservation Corps camps. Little or no money was appropriated for the purpose. The cost of cleaning up recreation sites came from operational funds, which had been appropriated to improve refuges for wildlife. In recent years, everybody has become aware of the need for recreational maintenance.

The Congress in 1962 enacted Public Law 87–714 "to assure continued fish and wildlife benefits from the national fish and wildlife conservation areas by authorizing their appropriate incidental or secondary use for public recreation to the extent that such use is compatible with the primary purposes of such areas."

Congressman Dingell of Michigan, who supplied most of the language of the act, no less than

520

10 times included the admonition that recreation on the refuges must be secondary and that the protection of wildlife must be the primary objective.

Passage of the act was opportune, for the Land and Water Conservation Fund Act of 1965 provided funds for acquiring small parcels of lands adjacent to refuges that may be developed for recreation and refuges for endangered species of wildlife.

Public use on the national wildlife refuges has increased threefold—from 3.4 million visitors in 1951 to 14 million in 1965. About 70 percent of the 1965 visitors were sightseers, birdwatchers, picnickers, and users of the water areas for swimming and boating.

The refuges are unexcelled for birdwatching. Many are covered during the Christmas bird counts sponsored by the National Audubon Society. Counts on the Laguna Atascosa Refuge in the southern tip of Texas and the Sabine Refuge in coastal Louisiana have exceeded 150 species.

The Christmas counts on the Chincoteague National Wildlife Refuge on the Delmarva Peninsula, Virginia, are an index of enthusiasm: None of the 20 or more participants lives within 100 miles of the refuge. Total counts have reached 130 species, among them nearly 20 kinds of shore birds. For many years, I covered the extensive tidal bay at the south end of the refuge. This boat trip presented some problems in bad weather. The variety of birds was not great, but the total of individuals was astounding. In 1964, the 378 horned grebes and 317 common loons were the highest totals for these species among the 723 counts throughout the country.

The Chincoteague participants also recorded top counts in the Nation of white-winged and common scoters, and hooded mergansers.

Many films have been made on the national wildlife refuges. An extensive footage of Disney films has been made on these areas. Many lecturers on the Audubon Screen Tours have shown the dramatic courtship performance of the western grebes on the Des Lacs National Wildlife Refuge, North Dakota. These swanlike grebes actually run side by side on top of the water, wings extended, necks sharply arched. With no visible signal, they terminate their run by swooshing into the water. You need no special permit to photograph birds on most refuges. With a few days' advance notice, a manager usually can offer suggestions where bird concentrations are to be found and where temporary blinds can be placed.

More and more blinds are being built for wildlife photographers. At Malheur Refuge, the Oregon Audubon Society constructed a permanent stone blind and dedicated it to two early wildlife photographers, William L. Finley and Herman T. Bohlman. The blind allows photographing of the trumpeter swans at Sod House Springs, which has open water the whole year.

The Garden Club of America in 1965 presented

If you take a boat from Rockport, Texas, up the Intracoastal Canal through part of the Aransas National Wildlife Refuge in Texas, you may see the rare whooping cranes that winter there.

a Founder's Fund Award of 3 thousand dollars to the Garden Club of Somerset Hills, New Jersey, to construct an elevated blind in the Great Swamp National Wildlife Refuge. This observation and photographic shelter, elevated 10 to 12 feet, has viewing portals on three sides. Great Swamp is less than 30 miles from New York City.

Visitor centers have now been developed on national wildlife refuges for the first time. The purpose and function of refuges are presented at these centers through exhibits, films, and slides. Auditoriums will accommodate 65 persons—two busloads of students. Nature trails, both guided and self-guided, are provided.

With funds from the Accelerated Public Works Program, visitor centers have been built on the Moosehorn Refuge in Maine, Seney Refuge on the Upper Peninsula of Michigan, and the Blackwater Refuge on the Eastern Shore of Maryland.

At Blackwater Refuge, the center is in the midst of an area formerly closed because most of the 85 thousand geese fed there. Now you can watch these birds through picture windows without disturbing them.

The refuge managers and staff conduct tours of the refuges, prepare information pamphlets, and participate in community activities. In 1964 they welcomed 3,014 groups, comprising 172 thousand visitors, and presented programs concerning refuge operations to 2,030 groups (104 thousand persons) at gatherings elsewhere.

The visitors were mainly members of sportsmen's clubs, bird and garden clubs, service clubs, school and youth groups, professional and scientific organizations, and religious groups.

Refuge managers also prepared 1,300 releases for 1,050 newspapers and presented 72 television and 760 radio programs. They constructed 62 exhibits, which an estimated 183,600 persons saw at open houses, meetings, and parades.

They sponsor a number of annual events. For instance, the daily guided tours on the National Bison Range in Montana and the Seney National Wildlife Refuge, Michigan, have become traditional. The 3-day meeting of the Order of the Antelope is equally famous on the Hart Mountain National Antelope Refuge in Oregon. Paid tours by qualified leaders are encouraged. Boat tours have been inaugurated from Rockport, Texas, up the Intracoastal Waterway in order that persons may see the whooping cranes wintering on the Aransas Refuge. Several guided auto trips are made each week to the Brigantine National Wildlife Refuge from a hotel in Atlantic City, New Jersey.

Each October on the Horicon National Wildlife Refuge in Wisconsin concentrations of more than 100 thousand Canada geese feed along State Highway 49. On one Sunday afternoon, an estimated 30 thousand persons jammed the highway to watch them. The State Highway Department widened the highway to six lanes, but traffic continues to be halted while people observe and photograph these birds. Some make tape recordings of the honking birds.

In the midthirties, the entire population of trumpeter swans in the United States was within a 60-square-mile area centered around Red Rock Lakes National Wildlife Refuge, Montana, and Yellowstone National Park, Wyoming. Management programs, including the prohibition against shooting any white waterfowl along the Snake River, have saved the birds to the point that they are no longer considered on the endangered list. The breeding population at Red Rock Lakes reached the saturation point chiefly because of the territorial requirements of each pair of swans. A program was started to transplant trumpeter swans to the National Elk Refuge in Wyoming, Malheur in Oregon, Ruby Lake in Nevada, and Lacreek in South Dakota. The swans have nested successfully on these four national areas, the most recent, on Lacreek, being the first time in 80 years these birds have nested east of the Rocky Mountains.

Transplants have been made to the Turnbull National Wildlife Refuge in eastern Washington. So that you and other Americans may enjoy the birds and become more familiar with their habitat and biological requirements, a program was inaugurated to lend mated pairs of the swans to publicly administered zoological parks. Pairs of these birds have been supplied to 33 zoos.

The plight of the Key deer led to the acquisition of an area for its protection. National Key Deer Refuge is the center of an administrative unit which includes the Great White Heron and the Key West National Wildlife Refuges. Collectively these three areas in the southern half of the Florida Keys have benefited such birds as the white-crowned pigeon, roseate spoonbill, great white heron, reddish egret, mangrove cuckoo, the gray kingbird, and the black-whiskered vireo. The plant life of these keys is equally interesting. At least 300 species of plants have been found on Big Pine Key. An estimated 100 thousand persons visited these refuges in 1964.

One of the oldest refuges and probably the least visited is the Hawaiian Islands National Wildlife Refuge. This chain of small Pacific Islands and reefs extends for more than a thousand miles between the main inhabited islands of Hawaii and Midway Islands.

Laysan Island, largest in the chain, contains about 2 square miles. It has more than 164 thousand nesting pairs of Laysan and black-footed albatrosses, both of which are known as gooney birds. Sooty terns occur in numbers far larger than for albatrosses. There are three species of boobies, several terns, red-tailed tropicbirds, shearwaters and petrels, and several kinds of shore birds. The refuge is the only home of the Laysan duck, Laysan finch, and Nihoa millerbird. The total breeding area of the world's population of Hawaiian monk seals is limited to the Leeward Islands, including the Midway Islands and Kure, which are not a part of the refuge.

The Clarence Rhode National Wildlife Range, bordering Bering Sea between the Yukon and Kuskokwim Rivers, has been described as the finest waterfowl area in North America.

I saw this entire 1,870,000-acre area during an aerial reconnaissance flight in 1962. The flight from Bethel was direct to Hooper Bay, which was described so dramatically in Herbert Brandt's *Alaska Bird Trails*. More than 90 percent of all black brant in the world nest along the coastal area of this range, occupying a strip averaging no more than 2 to 3 miles in width. The emperor geese and cackling Canada geese nest in the tundra for the next few miles. The intermixture of ptarmigans, sandhill cranes, whistling swans, and myriads of ducks makes this a waterfowl paradise. It was low tide at the time of our flight and shore birds by the thousands were feeding on the mudflats, which extended for 2 to 3 miles offshore. Two native

villages are within the range, and Eskimos use much of the area for hunting and fishing. Air transportation will continue to be the only means by which you can visit this area for quite a number of years to come.

The annual migrations of blue and snow geese have continued to intrigue birdwatchers everywhere. That segment of the population which winters on the gulf coast, principally in Louisiana, leaves in late February for the North. Many stop en route at the Squaw Creek National Wildlife Refuge along the Missouri River, north of St. Joseph, Missouri.

By short flights, the quarter-million birds move northward and reach Onawa, Iowa, in mid-March and Sand Lake National Wildlife Refuge, where I was the manager for 3 years, toward the end of the month.

Sometimes they make a nonstop flight to the gulf coast in the fall. At other times a considerable part of the population stops at the national wildlife refuges in Wisconsin, Illinois, Kentucky, and States to the South. Some years, their flight lines have been east of the Mississippi. More than 100 thousand of these geese can be seen regularly on the Squaw Creek Refuge in mid-November.

You can join the hundreds of birdwatchers and photographers in western Iowa and Missouri during March and November who observe this annual spectacle.

Bird lists have been prepared for about 120 of the refuges. On at least 9 of the areas nearly 300 or more species of birds have been recorded—Parker River and Monomy in Massachusetts; Brigantine in New Jersey; Bombay Hook in Delaware; St. Marks in Florida; Sabine in Louisiana; Aransas and Laguna Atascosa in Texas; and Havasu Lake, Arizona-California.

With all these tremendous concentrations of birds, one would expect visitors to be completely satisfied. C. J. Henry, while manager of the Lower Souris National Wildlife Refuge in North Dakota, told of birdwatchers who had traveled across the entire country to visit that refuge. With geese, ducks, and water birds everywhere they inevitably would ask, "Where can we see a Baird's sparrow and the McCown's longspur?"

—Philip A. DuMont.

523

A Look Ahead

HEN I WAS A BOY in northwestern Iowa, there were still great tracts of virgin grassland, and greater prairie chickens were fairly plentiful. They made good hunting.

As the grasslands that provided the needed nesting habitat were broken up for farms, the birds disappeared gradually. The last prairie chicken nests I found on our farm were in the fencerows, and none of those that I watched succeeded in bringing off a brood.

Every dog and coyote in the neighborhood soon learned to hunt the fencerows, and whenever one found a prairie chicken nest, he quickly disposed of the eggs and often the brooding hen as well.

By reducing the grasslands that were so vital to the species, the farmers doomed the prairie chicken over great tracts, and they would have done so if no one had fired a single shot at the birds.

This story, with variations, can be told of many other species and many other habitats between the Atlantic and the Pacific.

Now, as I write 60 years later, I sit near a win-

524

dow from which I can see a little natural amphi-theater that a few years ago supported three or four coveys of bobwhite quail. It has been permitted to revert largely to brush, and only a single covey remains. The meadowlarks have disappeared with the quail, indigo buntings, and field sparrows, which are hedge birds and prefer some brush. All four require open lands next to the brushlands.

I think of what may happen to birds in the next 40 years. As our population and need for living space and food grow, shall we reach a point where we will see little birdlife except house sparrows, starlings, and domestic pigeons?

Some pessimists foresee just that. Some optimists see little or no threat to birdlife in our varied activities.

I agree with neither, and I should like to tell you why.

Some clues to the future I read in the lessons of the past.

We have lost a number of species, and other once-abundant species are threatened. Why?

The Eskimo curlew and possibly the Carolina parakeet were victims of overshooting. The parakeet was a nuisance to agriculture. The curlew apparently was a victim of unrestrained market hunting, a practice that extended into and sometimes through the breeding seasons of many species and was a factor in the decline of shore birds, many of the herons, and possibly some of the game birds.

Market hunting has practically been eliminated. Recreational hunting has been placed under rigid control. As long as these controls are maintained, it is unlikely that the gun will ever again be a major factor in the decimation of any species that exists now in satisfactory number. It is quite different, though, with a few species, such as the California condor and Florida Everglade kite, which are in such small numbers that even occasional loss to an irresponsible, law-violating gunner results in a relatively high percentage decline in the population. For them shooting still is a serious factor.

Many things people do harm birds much more than hunting.

The worst is to destroy habitat. Earth-moving and land-clearing machinery can alter large tracts in a few days and drain prairie marshlands, the nesting places of waterfowl, like the redhead and

canvasback. The more adaptable species, like the mallard, have been able to find substitute foods by feeding on waste grain in agricultural fields, but those with more rigidly fixed habits have fared badly.

The practice of bulldozing all vegetation from the landscape to make way for homes eliminates the habitat for nearly all native species of birds. The lawns, shrubbery, and shade trees of a developed suburban community provide a type of habitat quite different from the woodlands and fields they replace.

Curiously enough, the prevailing pattern of suburban development often provides a temporary, favorable influence on birdlife. Developers may buy large blocks of land and permit them to lie idle for years before actually starting to build on them. Then we actually may see more quail, pheasants, and other birds that like mixed weedy and brushy cover near suburban developments than exist in farmland farther from the cities. Eventually suburbia overflows these areas, and their bird populations are lost.

Another major threat to birdlife is the highways that have been burying a million acres of land under concrete every year. They and the industrial and residential development that inevitably follows the new throughways and turnpikes take a heavy toll of birds. The end is not in sight. The highway lobby is powerful. The truckers, contractors, suppliers of cement and other materials, and motorists that comprise it began pushing for additional construction even before the present national highway system is finished.

On the debit side also is the cutting of forests and woodlots that we have been doing for two centuries. One probable reason for the decline of the ivory-billed woodpecker was the cutting of the old forests in the South. On the other hand, as many of the forests were replaced by farms, the bobwhite quail and mourning dove increased in numbers and others, such as towhees, catbirds, and brown thrashers, were helped by the development of brush and sprout growth on cutover lands.

Changes wrought by changes in highways and woodlands are plain enough. Other influences are more subtle.

For many years, I have watched the summer

fluctuations in birdlife in an area at Blue Sea Lake in Quebec. The relative abundance of some species has changed markedly. Some have increased in places where there has been no apparent change. Others have dropped; I do not know why.

Indigo buntings, field sparrows, and chestnut-sided warblers are still present there, but they have abandoned the formerly open fields and hedgerows as the forest closed in on the bush-studded clearings where they were abundant during the late thirties. The red-eyed vireo, black-and-white warbler, black-throated blue warbler, myrtle warbler, and redstart have also declined, although there have been no obvious changes in the vegetation they have occupied or in the condition of their territories.

In places where the conifers have been cut, the black-throated green warbler and other species that prefer evergreen woods have declined, although they remain as abundant as ever in the remaining stands of conifers.

I also have noted increases that have been difficult to relate to changing local conditions. Herring and ring-billed gulls, black ducks, and hooded mergansers, for instance, have increased in the past decade without noticeable changes in the local marshes or water areas and despite a greater use of the shorelines and islands by summer residents. Loons and the common merganser have declined, probably because of the encroachment of human influences on their nesting sites.

Local changes like these have taken place for centuries in response to changing conditions.

One new development which may significantly influence birdlife during the next four decades is the use of highly toxic and stable pesticides. No one knows yet what their ultimate effect will be, but I fear that it will be much greater than many persons care to admit but probably somewhat less than the exaggerated fears of some naturalists.

It is still too early to determine the long-range cumulative effects of these substances on the environment, the food chains, and the individual birds and mammals themselves. Evidence is growing that some of the chlorinated hydrocarbons, for example, reduce the reproductive capacity of birds and cause weak or deformed offspring in some species. We have evidence also that points to pesti-

cides as a factor in the decline of bald eagles. Probably simliar effects are taking place in the osprey and other birds of prey.

A major difficulty the research biologist has is to find specimens of mammals or birds whose tissues are free of some traces of the chlorinated hydrocarbons. Such specimens are prerequisites of any controlled experiment.

These chemicals alter food chains and local environments wherever they are applied. Such effects are quickly apparent in water. While the total volume of insect fauna and microplankton in streams or ponds may recover rapidly, the composition of the fauna almost always is altered drastically. The renewed life often is made up of species that are a much smaller part in the food chains of birds than those that existed before.

Chemical herbicides will continue to alter habitat. Brush areas in some sections are being eliminated. The effect has been to reduce some of the once-abundant inhabitants of the brushlands.

In western Texas, brush-eradication programs, employing chemical spraying and bulldozing on a broad scale, are eliminating much of the remaining habitat of the lesser prairie chicken and species associated with it. In southern Texas, similar programs are eliminating the habitat of a complex of tropical and semitropical birds that are found nowhere else in the United States. If this work is carried to its obvious conclusion, many of these birds will become rarities, especially since lands on the Mexican side of the Rio Grande are being subjected to the same treatment.

It makes no difference whether clearing is done by chemical or mechanical means—the result is the destruction of habitat, but the application of chemical brush killers through aerial spraying acccelerates the rate of destruction.

In areas cleared for grazing and farming along the Texas coast, I have noticed an interesting response by the small coastal form of the horned lark. As more of the land becomes heavily grazed or cultivated for crops, these birds have become increasingly common. At the same time, the Attwater's prairie chicken, for this reason, is coming closer to extinction, and nearly all other grassland species there have declined.

It may well be that if the clearing of land for

crops that are not particularly needed is not checked, many of the common and spectacular birds of this and other parts of the country will become locally scarce or nonexistent.

These, as I see it, are the major threats to the birdlife of America. Most of them are altering for the worse or destroying habitat of some of our more interesting and valuable forms of birdlife.

It is probable that some of the very rare species that we have been struggling to save will disappear in the next 40 years. The ivory-billed woodpecker may already have passed the point of no return. The California condor now numbers about 40 and the whooping crane about 50, including 7 in captivity. Both are slow breeders. The recovery of a slow-breeding and slow-maturing species is an extremely slow process once its numbers are reduced to such pitiful remnants.

The plight of the whooping crane is complicated further by the fact that its breeding and wintering grounds are separated by 3 thousand miles. Each year, each of the birds must undergo the hazards of a 6-thousand mile round-trip migration in order to survive. The condor in recent times has declined by one-third; the whooping crane has held its own over the last 10 years, but whether or not either can exist for 40 more years remains in doubt.

Some of the hawks and owls may disappear in this century. To habitat destruction, influences of pesticides, and the interference of human activity with food chains and nesting activity, we must add a prejudice held by many people against these species.

I take hope, though, in what seems to me to be a more enlightened public opinion toward predatory species. Many States have enacted laws, patterned after the model law of the National Audubon Society, that provide legal protection for these spectacular and generally beneficial birds. There has been an improvement in general attitudes toward these species by farmers, sportsmen, and the public. Although these laws and attitudes are strengthened with passing time, as they are likely to be, however, an intensification of adverse factors that influence predatory populations will probably result in a decline in hawks and owls.

I perceive some heartening developments. The trumpeter swan, for example, has increased from a dangerously small remnant to a point where the restricted breeding ground that the species occupied at its lowest ebb has become fully stocked, permitting the transplanting of swans to establish nesting colonies on other Federal wildlife refuges. Sizable breeding populations also exist in Alaska and Canada. It seems to me that, with the relatively wide distribution that the somewhat limited numbers of swans enjoy, the species is on its way toward rebuilding its population and toward filling all the habitat suitable for it.

The prospects for saving Kirtland's warbler are improved. Its population for a number of years has remained at around a thousand. Now that some 12 thousand acres of Federal and State forest land are being managed primarily for its benefit in Michigan, this small bird has a chance not only to survive but to expand its numbers.

It is another species that must undergo the hazards of a long migration, between its winter home in the Bahamas and its breeding grounds in the pine barrens of Michigan. Without the minutely detailed knowedge that we have of the requirements and habitat needs of the Kirtland's warbler, the work that is now being done in Michigan would be impossible.

The future of birds as well as other forms of wildlife will depend in large measure upon increasing knowledge that can come only from intensive research. There are more people interested in wildlife today than ever before, and I believe that research activities eventually will be expanded as far as necessary to obtain the needed information. But in a few cases the emergency is great and there is considerable question whether the knowledge will be obtained in time!

Changes in habitat caused by agricultural or residential development are not detrimental to all species. Grackles, red-winged blackbirds, cowbirds, and starlings have increased tremendously coincidentally with these changes. An increasingly accelerated change may reverse the situation, and these birds may once again become scarce. It is almost certain, however, that the numbers of red-winged blackbirds and grackles are many times those which existed when most of the Eastern States were almost totally forested.

One way to analyze the future of birds is to

discuss them under the major habitat types—forests, grasslands, human habitations, and wetlands.

The forest land species, after suffering the most from lumbering of pioneer America, as a group appear to have a better chance to thrive in future years than most other species. Great blocks of Federal and State forests are being managed primarily on a multiple-use basis, and privately owned commercial forests operated on comparable principles are increasing each year.

Some species that require overmature timber to thrive may be eliminated, but such losses may be offset slightly by gains on lands where the forests are managed under longer cutting rotations for the development of sawlogs, veneer, and other products that require mature types of timber.

The abandonment of farmland and its natural reversion to brushland and forest are providing large blocks of habitat in many Eastern States for brushland and woodland birds. I can remember many farms that formerly supported good populations of quail that now contain only forest species. Quail have given way to ruffed grouse, and the meadowlarks, vesper sparrows, and other field birds have been replaced by thrushes, woodpeckers, warblers, and vireos.

There has been a marked increase in privately owned forest lands that are managed for the production of pulpwood and similar short-term forest products. They usually are cut in blocks in regular cycles that provide cover in all stages of development from newly planted clearings to mature trees.

But forest birds will not escape the Juggernaut of civilization. The rapid encroachment of residential, highway, and industrial development into the countryside surrounding all towns and cities will continue to take its local toll of the habitat of forest birds. The farm woodlots that dot the landscape today are falling before the blades of bulldozers as farmers turn to fuels other than wood and as mechanized corporate farms absorb whole blocks of family homesteads.

The future of this brown pelican is in the hands of Frank Johnson, Refuge Manager of the Cape Romain National Wildlife Refuge. He is shown moving it to higher ground as it was in danger of being flooded out. Brown pelicans are declining in numbers.

The current practice of growing softwoods, mainly pines, for pulp in the Southeast, has become a form of monoculture like the growing of corn or wheat on larger acreages. Some birds can live in the young growth produced by growing cycles of 15 to 20 years, but plantations of these kinds usually replace more varied cover that supported a greater wealth of birdlife.

In recent years, however, the tendency of some companies has been to alter their forest-cultural practices to permit a greater production of saw timber. If the tendency continues, it should offset some of the losses caused by the expansion of pine-pulp farming.

A major fly in the ointment of my generally optimistic outlook for forest birds is the increased use of chemical pesticides, primarily chlorinated hydrocarbons, for controlling forest insects. A continuation of the trend could affect the reproductive cycles of some species or destroy the foods on which they depend. But I am confident that growing public concern over the side effects of chemicals will bring about changes, and new methods of pest control that will serve the purpose without endangering other forms of life.

The future of most forest birds seems quite secure. Even in the unlikely event that we should develop a form of economy that does not require forest products, forest lands will be perpetuated for their value in watershed protection and for their growing importance to recreation.

The plowing and cultivation of the virgin prairies west of the Mississippi have had a profound influence on the composition of their birdlife. Many species required extensive areas of unbroken prairie for their welfare. As long as the individual farms were small, scattered, and cultivated by horse-drawn machinery, the prairie farms contained an abundance of habitat for wildlife. The corners of the hedgerows and brush-grown fencerows were not easily cultivated and usually were permitted to grow into undisturbed havens for birds and small mammals. Small marshes, rock outcroppings, and similar areas that could not be tilled were left in their original state to provide islands of undisturbed habitat in the fields and pastures.

As farm machinery improved and permitted one

man to cultivate a farm ten or more times the size of his father's homestead, most of the hedgerows and field corners were eliminated. The stump and rail fences were replaced by sterile barbed wire. Wetlands were drained.

Such species as the greater prairie chicken, sharp-tailed grouse, upland plover, and long-billed curlew, to mention only a few, were greatly decreased in numbers with the destruction of their habitat, which was a more important factor in their decline than the more spectacular market hunting that prevailed at the same time.

Many of the smaller species of birds that were of no interest to the hunters declined with the game birds.

Improved weed control has eliminated much of the foxtail, pokeweed, and other plants that provided food for birds in many cropfields. Vast local areas of farmland therefore have become nearly devoid of birdlife.

When I was a small boy in Iowa, the only birds that nested regularly in our cornfields were killdeers and horned larks. All others left as soon as a piece of prairie was broken and placed under cultivation. Some persisted nearby along the weedy fencerows, in the clover fields, and in odd bits of suitable cover at the edges of the potholes and ponds that then dotted the countryside.

Fortunately, none of these species entirely disappeared, and all are found today on the growing acreages of the Federal and State wildlife areas, which perpetuate their habitat even in many heavily cultivated areas. Some are more abundant than they were 25 years ago. It is not difficult to find most of the grassland species in some abundance if one seeks out the spots that have been preserved in a relatively natural state.

As long as the Federal and State governments and some private individuals and organizations maintain tracts of grassland in refuges and sanctuaries or for other purposes, there is little question but that the grassland birds will survive.

If agricultural practices change again to provide conditions more generally favorable to birdlife, these areas will hold enough seed stock to permit the birds to rebuild their numbers.

The outlook for birdlife on intensively cropped agricultural lands right now is far from bright.

Most are so heavily sprayed with toxic chemicals that very little birdlife remains. I know of nothing more barren of breeding birds than the average cottonfield. Many grain and cornfields are little better, although they do provide food for large numbers of migrating birds in the spring and fall. With use of large machines for cultivating fields, a condition that is unlikely to be reversed, the birds in agricultural communities will be limited.

My hope is that the trend toward using deadlier and heavier applications of weed killers and insecticides in croplands will be reversed and replaced by the use of specific pesticides or preferably some forms of biological control.

On the other hand, many marginal farms are being abandoned and are reverting to grasses and herbs where the climate and soil characteristics are such that brush and forest do not invade the area. With these ecological changes, the birdlife returns.

Birds that are adaptable enough to live in the shade trees, shrubs, and lawns around human habitations should continue to exist in the same numbers in which they are found today, if problem insects can be controlled without poisoning birds.

Robins, cardinals, mourning doves, some of the thrashers, mockingbirds, and catbirds, the chipping sparrows, song sparrows, the grackles, and many others have found it possible to thrive and to reproduce their kind near human habitations. In many parts of the country, some are more numerous than they were 20 years ago because of the increased interest of people in maintaining feeding stations, nesting boxes, and other bird attractants.

There are innumerable feeding stations around every major city where chickadees, titmice, various sparrows and finches, woodpeckers, and other family groups avail themselves of free meals of suet and sunflower seeds. This is particularly help-

A symbol of changes in a changing world. This launch of a powerful Atlas-Agena rocket at Cape Kennedy, Florida, contrasts sharply with the slow, easy flight of these common egrets. Thousands of birds live in the security area around the Cape. While they are often seen by authorized personnel during launches, seldom are they photographed at liftoff.

ful to some species during the winter, when natural food supplies may be depleted or not available because of ice and snow.

As some of the new, sprawling suburban communities of today gain maturity, their now spindly shade trees and shrubbery will grow into useful nesting habitat for such species as can exist in an area completely dominated by man.

I have left until the last the category—wetlands—that causes the greatest concern to most ornithologists.

The spectacular and interesting birds whose numbers are limited by their preference for marshlands are among those that are most gravely threatened today. Their habitat has been greatly reduced, and the alarming pace of its destruction has not been checked.

Despite all of the efforts of State and Federal wildlife agencies and many private individuals and organizations, more wetlands are being drained each year than are being restored. The pot of gold at the end of the rainbow promised by the drainage promoters holds more allure to most people than the facts of life.

A few drainage schemes have been based on careful appraisals of soils, climate, and soil fertility. But many, if not most, of these projects produce lands that are almost worthless for crop production. Often the soils remain waterlogged even after the surface waters are removed, or drainage exposes marsh bottoms that are too alkaline or too acid to produce crops.

Our most spectacular concentrations of birds are found around marshes and small lakes. Herons, gulls, terns, grebes, loons, ducks, geese, swans, and a great variety of other birds must have wetlands and water to reproduce. Many have feeding habits so circumscribed that they can feed only in well-watered areas.

In the Northern States, drainage programs destroy nesting habitat for these migratory birds and feeding and resting areas for those that nest farther north.

In the South, drainage and the intrusion of salt water into brackish and fresh water marshes of the Gulf and Atlantic coasts, are impairing the food-producing capabilities of many prime wintering areas for the same species.

The species that have suffered most obviously are those that nest and breed on the southern edges of the great northern breeding grounds into which agriculture has penetrated. Those that nest farther north are still relatively abundant.

The arctic-nesting geese, for example, still come south in locally spectacular numbers in the average year. Unless man develops some intensive use of the arctic regions that produce these flights, these geese will thrive as long as winter habitat is provided them in the South so that they can rest and feed.

I do not foresee the extermination of any of these wetland species within the next 40 years, except possibly of the whooping crane, whose present status is too precarious to make prediction possible. Several of the less common species of the present undoubtedly will be in the "rare" category by the year 2000.

On the other hand, I doubt that any youngster now living will ever see the great masses of migrating ducks and some other waterfowl that provided an awe-inspiring spectacle for those of my generation. The habitat that produced and maintained those massive flights no longer exists.

Sample populations of most of these birds, however, should always be available, at least in limited numbers, to those who wish to see and enjoy them. The gradually spreading system of publicly owned water, marsh, and lake areas is insurance of their continued survival.

One possibility is that the growing efficiency of agriculture, which is now working against the maintenance of birdlife, will permit the retirement of many acres that are now being cultivated.

If so, it will be possible to restore many of the wetlands that constitute the most rapidly vanishing form of habitat today. This would provide a material boost to many upland species as well, since the margins of marshes and lakes are heavily used by many species, such as song sparrows, yellowthroats, yellow warblers, and kingbirds, not classified as marsh birds or waterfowl.

The conservation of migratory birds is peculiarly dependent on international goodwill and cooperation for success. But the whole job of international political action in behalf of birds has not been finished. It will not be until the countries of South

America and Central America have the opportunity to join their neighbors in North America in a common effort to preserve species that range between North America and South America in annual migrations.

As an example, I cite the golden plover, blackpoll warbler, gray-cheeked thrush, black-bellied plover, white-rumped sandpiper. These birds nest in Canada, migrate through the United States and Mexico, and then finally spend their winters in Central America or South America. No one country alone can do the job of preserving these birds and others like them.

Perhaps this unfinished task will be completed in the next two or three decades.

My prediction is that by the year 2000 we may have lost some of the exceedingly rare species that we have been trying desperately to save. But as far as I can foresee under present conditions and trends, I do not believe that the species composition of our birdlife will change greatly in the next 40 years. Numerically there will be substantial changes in abundance; losses in some areas offset by gains elsewhere. Because the majority of species require natural habitats, they will probably decline, while the minority that thrive in man-made habitats will increase.

Unforeseen developments could alter the present picture materially, but I confidently expect that birdwatchers at the turn of the century will be able to go afield in the United States and see most, if not all, of the species of birds that are found here today.

—Ira N. Gabrielson.

CANADA GEESE
BLACK-CROWNED NIGHT HERON
BELTED KINGFISHER
PINTAILS

We, the People

WHEN ALL IS SAID AND DONE, it is what we Americans think and do today as individuals that determines what place birds will have in our lives tomorrow. What we think about birds is the sum of our information and understanding of birds, our experiences with them, and our appreciation of them as part and parcel, like air and light and trees, of our lives.

What we do grows out of what we think: The laws we ask our representatives in legislatures, councils, and the Congress to pass, the support we give them, the protective zoning ordinances we ask our city and county governments to adopt, the birdhouses and feeding stations we put up, the parks and refuges and sanctuaries our communities and States and groups of dedicated citizens establish with our foresight and help.

We. Not *they;* not somebody else; *we.*

We, for instance, are the 700 residents of Stone Harbor, a village on the root of the cape that New Jersey thrusts between Delaware Bay and the Atlantic Ocean and a locality that abounds in people, resorts, sand, cedars, hollies, and birds. Within our town limits in 1947 we set aside a 21-acre wooded tract as a sanctuary for herons, egrets, and ibises, whose nesting places were endangered by the relentless megalopolis of the eastern seaboard.

Now, at the peak of the season, we have more than 5 thousand birds as friends and neighbors, a treasure of beauty, inspiration, and interest to us and the 12 thousand persons from nearly all States and many other countries who sign each year the visitors' register. (We estimate that 75 thousand persons stop at the sanctuary but do not sign the register.) During the nesting season, which starts shortly after the birds arrive from the South in mid-March and lasts until early August, we can see many birds flying out to the feeding places and back to the sanctuary throughout the day.

After the nesting season, the birds, except the night herons, leave for the feeding grounds at daybreak and return just before sunset. The night herons leave for the feeding places at dusk and return in the morning. A detail like that is a minor matter in the totality of life, but the purpose of the sanctuary is just that: To remind us of the totality of all kinds of life on earth.

We, too, include a group of Philadelphians (about 800 in 1966), who in 1953 organized Philadelphia Conservationists, Inc., to acquire and preserve natural areas that usually are within 100 miles of Philadelphia and so are easily accessible by automobile to city people who want to enjoy wildlife. We have regional interests, though, that embrace eastern Pennsylvania, New Jersey, Delaware, and, sometimes, beyond.

Of the nine major land acquisition and preservation projects the Conservationists have completed since 1954, the first and probably best known is the Tinicum Marshes, a tract of 205 acres in the industrialized southwestern corner of Philadelphia. Overhead, airliners roar to and from nearby International Airport. Not far off is crowded Industrial Highway.

But inside Tinicum Wildlife Preserve are, in their times, many thousands of pintails, baldpates, shovelers, greater scaup, and other kinds of migratory ducks; occasional egrets, herons, and glossy ibis; bald eagles and hawks; pheasants, bobolinks, kingbirds, and other land birds; mink, muskrats,

and turtles; wildrice that may reach 13 feet; 150 kinds of plants, and 230 species of birds. All within a city!

And people. Tinicum is more than vacant space or a breeding and resting ground for birds and animals. It is a living biological museum that more than 40 thousand persons a year like to visit. Many of them are schoolchildren, exploring a universe they could not otherwise know and adding to their perspective of life.

We also are members of the Great Swamp Committee of the North American Wildlife Foundation and the nearly 20 thousand persons who contributed to buy 2,900 acres for presentation to the Department of the Interior as the start of the preservation of the Great Swamp, whose final boundaries as a national wildlife refuge will include 6 thousand acres of meadow, marsh, forest, and ponds.

At the dedication of the Great Swamp National Wildlife Refuge in New Jersey, Stewart L. Udall, Secretary of the Interior, said:

"We are gathered here today to celebrate a successful and very meaningful battle to save the American countryside. But it is the distinctive nature of this battle that makes the Great Swamp victory so important, for we applaud here this afternoon, not action by the Federal Government, or by some public spirited philanthropist or foundation, but disciplined, tough-minded action by voluntary citizen groups who were determined that the outdoors need not be sacrificed to the demands of development.

"I am hopeful that this will serve as a memorable example for the whole country, because we can win the 'battle for the countryside' only if more individuals and organizations are ready to put sweat and devotion and dollars into the fighting for Nature's scenic treasures, where they are hardest to preserve—on the edge and in the center of urban America."

We, as another example, are citizens of Hempstead, a township on Long Island, New York. Dismayed by years of official disregard for the extensive bays and marshes within the town boundaries, *we* organized the Hempstead Town Lands Resources Committee. The committee leads an educational campaign to alert town residents to

Richardson Dilworth, former mayor of Philadelphia, inspects the Tinicum Wildlife Preserve located in the southwest tip of the city. Preservation of this 250-acre tract of marsh has contributed thousands of hours of healthy outdoor recreation to Philadelphians who come to see waterfowl, to fish, or to study Nature.

the danger of the imminent loss of the recreational, economic, and esthetic values of the town's salt meadows and bays, which support extensive shell and fin fisheries and a large and diverse bird population. As a result, in 1965, the town board moved to have 10 thousand acres of tidal wetlands the township owns dedicated permanently for fish, wildlife, and other conservation purposes.

The action supplanted one in 1963 that put 2,500 acres of the holdings in a conservation plan and was taken after a long battle to keep the lands from being ruined for fish and wildlife by dredging, filling, pollution, and channeling.

Plans were made to have the prized wetlands

administered jointly by the Hempstead Conservation and Waterways Department and the New York State Division of Fish and Game, which will pay all of the costs of developing the marsh and half of the costs of maintenance.

So much interest was generated that the local Congressman introduced legislation in the Federal Congress to preserve the region as a "National Wetlands Recreation Area" under control of the Secretary of the Interior.

We are the directors of the Cedar Point Club, a hunting preserve located on the south shore of Lake Erie between Toledo and Sandusky. Unable to use the club as in former years, and fearful that

536

its prized marshes might be destroyed, *we* conveyed the million-dollar property to the North American Wildlife Foundation, which, in turn, gave it to the Department of the Interior. It is now and will always be a part of the national wildlife refuge system—the Cedar Point National Wildlife Refuge, haven for many kinds of wildlife and ultimately the center for nature appreciation programs in this heavily populated part of the Midwest.

We also are the conservation-minded citizens of Massachusetts and Rhode Island, who were the first to secure passage of State laws to insure the protection of coastal marshes. The Rhode Island Coastal Wetlands Act permits the State Department of Agriculture and Conservation to zone areas where the ecology should not be disturbed as a matter of public policy and lays the burden on the owner to establish any monetary losses that may result from the zoning.

In Massachusetts, similar zoning or classification powers are established, but they authorize that the State may acquire wetlands by eminent domain when the courts might construe the zoning to have been a taking without just compensation.

We, again, are the concerned residents of the San Francisco Bay area, who could see that great estuary gradually becoming a sump for the effluents of the rapidly developing cities around it. Working through civic groups, Audubon societies, and a score of interested agencies, *we* succeeded in securing the passage of a State law establishing the San Francisco Bay Commission. The Commission is empowered to study the resource problems of the bay and to develop a comprehensive plan for preserving its essential values, while guiding shore development into directions that may augment, rather than erode, the natural values of the Bay.

We also are the 41 thousand people of Rochester, a city of medicine, science, clinics, hospitals, hotels, and some industry among the farms of southern Minnesota.

In a city park within a mile of the famous Mayo Clinic in 1936, *we* dammed the Zumbro River (which, against such as the mighty Mississippi, is hardly more than a country creek) to form 20-acre Silver Lake. The warm water a power plant discharges into it keeps it partly open, even during cold weather. It was a good home at first for the 15 Canada geese that Dr. Charles Mayo, Sr., had bought in North Dakota for his nearby estate, Mayowood, and a dozen large, pinioned geese from Nebraska that a patient of the Mayo Clinic had willed the city.

Our flock grew fast. Within a year, 500 to 600 wintering birds came to the little lake, attracted by the warm water, the food we put out, the pinioned geese, and the relatively undisturbed feeding area on the 800-acre State hospital farm nearby. Silver Lake now shelters as many as 8 thousand wild geese every winter. We like them, and our visitors like them, too, and we think there is therapeutic value to the ill and infirm, as well as to the rest of us, in the presence of the healthy creatures of another world.

When Dr. Harold C. Hanson, of the Illinois State Natural History Survey Division, came to

Farmers can be and often are important contributors to bird conservation. At Eagle Lake, Texas, flocks of geese (mostly snow geese) come into a harvested rice field to feed on weed seeds and waste grain.

Rochester in 1962 to band some of the geese, he found that they averaged nearly twice the weight of the usual Canada geese. Dr. Hanson finally decided they were examples of the supposedly extinct giant Canada goose, *Branta canadensis maxima.*

We who live in Green Bay, Wisconsin, are grateful to Chester Cole, a citizen who noticed in 1935 that our migrating waterfowl were becoming scarcer, and set in motion the activities that gave our city the Bay Beach Wildlife Sanctuary, whose 215 acres (80 of them water) in 1966 attracted a wintering population of 1,500 mallards and black ducks and 275 Canada geese.

He and a few associates first dug by hand a small pond and put out some feed to see if birds could be lured back to the Bay Beach marsh, which once teemed with wildlife but which, because of drainage and development, was no longer providing breeding sites and natural food for birds. That first venture was promising.

Then they got advice from wildlife experts, started digging lagoons, begged funds, embarked on a feeding program, cleared away undesirable vegetation, moved dirt where necessary, and, when it was a going project, turned it over to the Green Bay City Park Board for the enjoyment of all citizens. Many persons, civic organizations, city and county governments, and business and industrial firms had a part in the work, and the sanctuary is a monument to citizens' cooperation, participation, and enterprise.

Harold E. Shine, District Game Manager, once wrote: "Those of us who are acquainted with the value and importance of the Bay Beach sanctuary to the community can visualize the need for more areas of this nature. It is a prime example of what can be accomplished by many enterprising communities. Natural areas adjacent to some of our cities and villages provide wonderful opportunities for development. The actual value cannot be measured in dollars and cents, but they can be priceless to any community for educational and recreational purposes."

Priceless, beyond a doubt, are the pleasures the 300 visitors a day (109,500 visitor-days a year) derive from the Bay Beach Wildlife Sanctuary, the knowledge gained by the schoolchildren who come from distances up to 100 miles, and the increase in the numbers of ducks, geese, and other migratory birds that visit the project.

To most of us, the Cook County Forest Preserve System seems to be a highly organized, well-financed, county enterprise. It is all of that—but it is much more. It is the product of the imagination and determination of a small group of Chicagoans who 50 years ago decided that they were "the people." They did not wait for history; they made it. They were people who said, *"We* will do it!"

Their preserve system is not a park, in the usual sense, but a natural reservation and a forested sanctuary, with facilities for picnicking and similar forms of intensive use on the fringes. Most of the holdings are kept in a primitive state. The system is organized as a district and is governed by 15 commissioners, has a staff and advisory committee, and is supported by taxes. It was authorized by the Illinois State Legislature in 1913 and was established in 1915.

Pressures have been great to divert some of the lands for various purposes, such as flood control and utilities, highways, and real-estate developments, but the commissioners of the system have pursued steadfastly a policy of providing the greatest good for the greatest number.

Every year, approximately 15 million persons visit the preserves. They come in family groups, organized picnics, youth groups, classes with their teachers, conservation or nature-study groups, and as participants in many forms of outdoor recreation.

Cook County teachers and school systems use the forest preserves as outdoor laboratories to give reality to their classroom and textbook instruction. The preserves are the only large areas in Cook County in which a natural landscape may be studied at first hand. Workshops and summer courses in the techniques of outdoor education are conducted for teachers.

Each year, during the summer vacation period, many thousands of children enjoy outings in the preserves as members of day camps, most of them conducted by youth and welfare organizations.

I have recited here a few examples—there are many more just as good or better—of what people have done on their own initiative for the preservation of birdlife and for their own enjoyment. Let me give two examples of problems about which conservation-minded citizens have become increasingly worried. One is in Fairfax County, Virginia, not far from the District of Columbia. The other is in Florida.

In Fairfax, plans were announced to develop a high-density residential community on Mason's Neck, a peninsula of 13.5 square miles projecting into the estuary of the Potomac River at the county's southernmost point. Mason's Neck has been labeled the finest open space remaining in the Washington metropolitan area.

Conservation interests were mobilized by a citizens' committee from interested residents and neighbors of the area. The fight for the preserva-

tion of Mason's Neck began with hearings before the zoning board and the county supervisors.

Secretary Udall urged county officials to reject plans for the subdivision so that Mason's Neck could be used in ways to enhance the conservation potential of the entire region. A federally managed wildlife preserve, a State park, and a locally managed area under the control of the Northern Virginia Regional Park Authority were among the many suggestions offered.

The Northern Virginia Regional Park Authority is unique as a political instrument for conservation. The history and functions of the authority may be of interest to other communities that face similar problems of land use and planning.

Under the Virginia law, cities or counties may

Pintails, mallards, other wild waterfowl, pigeons, and people enjoy Lake Merritt in Oakland, California.

join a regional planning group, and if action is deemed necessary, may form an authority—a quasi-independent political entity with the power of eminent domain for land acquisition, development and management of acquired areas, and issuance of revenue bonds for financing the work of the authority. Late in 1961, the Counties of Fairfax and Arlington and the City of Falls Church entered into an agreement that created the Northern Virginia Regional Park Authority. Later, the City of Fairfax joined.

Each of the participating jurisdictions appoints two members to the overall board of the Regional Park Authority, and the terms run for 4 years. Ira N. Gabrielson, president of the Wildlife Management Institute, has been chairman since the beginning of this organization.

The Northern Virginia Park Authority has acquired approximately 2 thousand acres of land, mostly in Fairfax County or in adjoining Prince Williams County, along Bull Run. About 400 acres are on Mason's Neck. The rest is on Cub Run and Bull Run. The acquisition program contemplates the purchasing of 10 thousand to 15 thousand acres, including more on Mason's Neck and the entire valley of Bull Run.

The authority has undertaken the development of two recreational units to provide camping space and facilities for school classes and youth organizations for instruction in conservation and outdoor values.

Its development plans contemplate concentrating public use areas at suitable points within the park and leaving as much land as possible in wilderness, open woodland, and countryside to provide the complete range of environments needed for open space for hiking and riding trails and for Nature preservation and interpretation, where people can go to enjoy the out-of-doors.

Here, indeed, it has been a case of *we, the people*

In mid-November 1965, there were 7,400 Canada geese at Silver Lake, which is one-half mile long and three blocks wide, in Rochester, Minnesota.

540

at work. Recognition of need, followed successively by enactment of the necessary statutes, organization of the authority, mapping of the master plan, and finally realization of the first acquisition and development goals—all these have come about as the outgrowth of the interest of a few persons willing to devote their time to an enduring conservation achievement.

I have called Florida the Nation's "conservation battleground," for nowhere in our land is the conflict between exploitation and conservation more apparent. The vast influx of people seeking a life in Florida's balmy weather has turned the State into a developer's paradise. Unfortunately, much of the development is at the expense of the living resources, which historically have been a major facet of Florida's attractions. Swamps are drained and filled to make places for the facilities needed by the thousands of new residents and vacationers who have been flocking to the Sunshine State.

The very extent and diversity of Florida's natural riches and the variety of human interests concerned with them make a host of problems inevitable. Change in land-use patterns concurrent with the State's tremendous increase in population is the major problem as far as fish and wildlife habitat is concerned. For example, a decrease of almost 1.5 million acres of forest and woodland is expected by 1975.

Extensive destruction has occurred in very valuable estuaries and bays, and fresh-water areas, as well. The significance of these losses is just now being recognized.

Spoil from navigation channels creates biological deserts in coastal waters because it is harmful to shellfish and indirectly to the whole life chain of the coastal marine environment. Beach erosion is a serious problem on many shores. Yet the beach restoration projects may be more destructive of the essential resources of an area than erosion itself.

Three current projects have become controversial—the proposal to convert Old Tampa Bay to a fresh-water lake, the construction of the Cross-Florida Barge Canal, and the reduction of the water supply for Everglades National Park. The Old Tampa Bay project will cause marine fishery losses, while numerous other related questions are unresolved. The Cross-Florida Barge Canal will flood about 45 miles of the Oklawaha River and adjoining swamps. The problem of adequate water for Everglades National Park has been aggravated by severe drought, but the basic problem lies in the manmade alterations to the natural drainage systems and water level regimes of central and southern Florida.

With all these problems, the people of Florida are experiencing a growing realization of the coming crisis in conservation and are doing something about it.

The 1965 session of the Florida Legislature passed 68 acts dealing with water resources and related activities. Among these are five progressive acts dealing with beach and shore erosion. An amendment to the Water Resources Law provides for plugging wild-flowing wells to prevent waste.

The Bulkhead Act of 1957 was a major step toward best utilization of the State's coastal water bottoms. This act provides that submerged land sales to private interests be made only if the trustees of the Internal Improvement Fund find such sales to be in the public interest. It also requires that a bulkhead line be established before fill permits can be issued.

As a further example, there is Marco Island, a demonstration of what can be expected from coordinated, constructive planning. Private, concerned citizens stimulated close coordination and careful planning by State and Federal agencies and the developers. As a result of the mutual interest, cooperation, and compromises which were reached, this development boasts areas dedicated to fish and wildlife, including eagle nest sanctuaries and special dredging procedures to minimize siltation.

When Florida passed the Outdoor Recreation and Conservation Act of 1963, it became one of the few States to establish a specific tax and definite funding for land acquisition and other conservation purposes.

From all this, it is obvious that from earliest times the wealth and abundance of Florida's natural resources have excited visitors and residents alike. Conflicts and divergent interests inevitably came into being, so that Florida has been the scene of conservation struggles since before the turn of the century.

These conflicts will inevitably continue, but

Florida has the resources to provide a future with a conservation foundation. The most important of these resources is people—informed, energetic, and interested citizens. In Florida, concerned citizens *are* becoming acquainted with projects and programs affecting their magnificent fish and wildlife resources; they are becoming informed on the issues involved; they are demanding thorough explanation from all parties concerned. The machinery exists in our democratic processes to give voice and vote. It's up to *us, the people* to use it.

People who want to do something for birds, other wildlife, Nature, and themselves can get advice and help from many Federal and State agencies and private institutions and organizations.

The Departments of the Interior, Agriculture, Health, Education and Welfare, and Housing and Urban Affairs are among the major Federal agencies with programs that might apply in certain local situations.

Usually the agencies are limited to proferring advice and consultative services, but several provide some measure of financial support to local units of government. The same may be said for the national and regional conservation organizations. Most of them can give advice, since the national conservation leaders have had much experience in guiding conservation campaigns to successful conclusions. There are, however, many foundations established to aid in meritorious public-service activities. Their funds may be limited to educational projects and land acquisition or on occasion may be granted without any limitation as long as funds support project objectives.

Throughout this book we have seen how inevitably and inextricably in America there are birds in our lives. They grace the landscape, enliven the sky, waken the day; a silent world yields to their melodies and their occasional clatter. They serve as the basis for sport and recreation; they are an unadvertised control over weeds and insects. They occasionally (usually because of what man himself has done to the environment) become overly abundant, and we call them pests.

However (and wherever) birds *are* in our lives. To keep them there throughout all the tomorrows is at once the challenge and the burden we today must face and accept. Across America we have been doing a part of the job.

As Americans continue to grow in appreciation—appreciation of the place of the out-of-doors and its creatures in the enrichment of our lives and appreciation of the fact that we will preserve these treasures only if we wish to preserve them—the outlook for birds in our lives also continues to improve.

But whether we succeed or fail will depend on the extent to which we ourselves accept the responsibility to help.

We must be willing to make that extra effort that will help to preserve some special bit of habitat.

We must be the ones willing to serve on a park board and gain a place for people to enjoy birds along with boardwalks, bandstands, and ball diamonds.

We must join with other conservation-oriented people across our country to support the national organizations and programs.

We, all of us, must be the responsible stewards of birds in our lives.

Then, *we* shall have birds in our lives.

We, the people.

—JOHN S. GOTTSCHALK.

Contributors

Authors

John W. Aldrich, an ornithologist in the Bureau of Sport Fisheries and Wildlife since 1941, specializes in the classification and distribution of birds and mammals. Dr. Aldrich formerly was curator of birds in the Cleveland Museum of Natural History. He is a Fellow of the American Ornithologists' Union.

Durward L. Allen, professor of wildlife management at Purdue University, formerly was Assistant Chief of the Branch of Wildlife Research of the Fish and Wildlife Service. He is the author of *Our Wildlife Legacy.* He received the Wildlife Society award in 1944 and 1955.

Winston E. Banko, a research biologist in the Bureau of Sport Fisheries and Wildlife, has had more than 15 years of experience in ornithology. He is the author of *The Trumpeter Swan,* which was cited by the Wildlife Society as an outstanding book on terrestrial wildlife in 1960.

Will Barker, a writer and editorial consultant, formerly was a writer-editor in the Fish and Wildlife Service. His articles have appeared in many magazines and an encyclopedia. His books are *Familiar Animals of America, Familiar Insects of America, Familiar Reptiles and Amphibians of America, Winter-Sleeping Wildlife,* and *Wildlife in America's History.* He has been cited twice for his work in conservation education by the National Wildlife Federation.

Irston R. Barnes, a practicing economic consultant in New York, is a former professor at Yale University and Columbia University. His weekly column, The Naturalist, has appeared for a number of years in the Washington Post. He has been active in the affairs of the Audubon Naturalist Society of the Central Atlantic States as president and chairman of the board of directors.

Allen H. Benton, professor of biology, State University College, Fredonia, New York, is co-author of *Field Biology and Ecology, Manual of Field Biology and Ecology,* and *Keys to the Vertebrates of the Northeastern States, Excluding Birds.* Dr. Benton is president of the Federation of New York State Bird Clubs.

Shirley A. Briggs is editor of the Atlantic Naturalist, a magazine published by the Audubon Naturalist Society of the Central Atlantic States, Inc. She also does freelance writing, illustrating, and museum exhibit work.

Carl Buchheister, president of the National Audubon Society, joined that organization in 1936 as director of the Audubon camp in Maine. He was vice president of the society for a number of years before he was elected president in 1959. He has written and lectured on the major conservation issues for more than 30 years.

John L. Buckley is ecological research coordinator on the Science Adviser's staff, Office of the Secretary of the Interior. Formerly he was technical assistant, Office of Science and Technology, Executive Office of the President, and Chief, Office of Pesticides Coordination, Bureau of Sport Fisheries and Wildlife. His services with the Bureau began in 1951 in Alaska. Formerly he was Director of the Patuxent Wildlife Research Center.

Gardiner Bump, Biologist in Charge of Foreign Game Introduction Program, Bureau of Sport Fisheries and Wildlife, has written and lectured extensively on game birds. For a number of years Dr. Bump was superintendent, Bureau of Game, New York State Conservation Department; he directed the production of its book, *The*

Ruffed Grouse, Life History, Propagation, and Management.

C. EDWARD CARLSON is Chief, Division of Wildlife Research, Bureau of Sport Fisheries and Wildlife. He has been in wildlife work in the Federal service since 1948. He has administrative responsibility for a wide range of research on the management and ecology of bird populations.

ROLAND C. CLEMENT has been Staff Biologist, National Audubon Society, New York, since 1958. He previously was executive secretary of the Audubon Society of Rhode Island and an editor for the New England Museum of Science and worked in business for several years. He edited *A Gathering of Shore Birds* and contributed chapters to *The Warblers of North America* and *Waterfowl Tomorrow.*

HENRY B. COLLINS, an anthropologist on the staff of the Smithsonian Institution, has specialized in archaeology and anthropology of the Arctic. Dr. Collins is the author of more than 80 papers and monographs in his field. For his *The Archaeology of St. Lawrence Island, Alaska,* he was awarded the Gold Medal of the Royal Academy of Sciences and Letters of Denmark.

CLARENCE D. CONE, JR., is biophysicist in the Space Radiation Biology Laboratory of the Langley Research Center, National Aeronautics and Space Administration at Hampton, Virginia. He is also an associate research scientist at the Virginia Institute of Marine Science at Gloucester Point.

WILLIAM G. CONWAY is curator of birds and director of the New York Zoological Park, New York. He was formerly curator of birds, St. Louis Zoological Park. He has traveled to many parts of the world to find interesting new birds for public exhibition.

CLARENCE COTTAM is Director, Welder Wildlife Foundation, Sinton, Texas. He is a former Assistant Director, Fish and Wildlife Service. Dr. Cottam has received several national awards and honors, including the Aldo Leopold and Audubon medals. He is a fellow of the National Academy of Sciences.

FRANK C. CRAIGHEAD, JR., is president of the Environmental Research Institute, Boiling Springs, Pennsylvania; wildlife research consultant for the National Geographic Society; consultant for the Bureau of Land Management, Department of the Interior; and research associate, Montana State University. His main field of interest is resource management and wildlife research.

JOHN J. CRAIGHEAD is leader, Montana Cooperative Wildlife Research Unit, and professor of forestry and zoology, University of Montana. John and Frank Craighead, brothers, have collaborated on several projects, including radio tracking of grizzly bears. They have coauthored papers and books, such as *Field Guide to Rocky Mountain Wildflowers, Hawks, Owls, and Wildlife,* and a Navy training text, *How to Survive on Land and Sea.* John Craighead is a former president of the Montana Wilderness Association and a vice president of the Wildlife Society. He is a Fellow of the American Association for the Advancement of Science and vice president of the Environmental Research Institute.

ALLAN D. CRUICKSHANK has been on the staff of the National Audubon Society for more than 28 years. He is well known for his photographs of birds and his contributions to public education in bird conservation as lecturer, instructor in ornithology, and editor. He has written six books, among them *1001 Questions Answered About Birds, Birds Around New York City,* and *Hunting With the Camera.*

FRED H. DALE is Director, Pesticides Review Staff, Bureau of Sport Fisheries and Wildlife. Dr. Dale has 30 years' experience in wildlife research and game management.

LEWIS E. DICKINSON is a nature columnist for the Barrington Times in Barrington, Rhode Island. He has been active in the field of conservation for more than 40 years. He has written several articles and a book on conservation, *Along Nature's Trails.* He is a past president of the Audubon Society of Rhode Island.

PHILIP B. DOWDEN was Assistant Chief, Insect Identification and Parasite Introduction Research Branch, of the Entomology Research Division in the Department of Agriculture and specialist in biological control of insects in the Forest Service. He has written many articles on the biological control of insects.

WILLIAM H. DRURY, JR., is director of research, Massachusetts Audubon Society, and lecturer at

544

Harvard University. Dr. Drury has written many papers on population biology in birds and on factors that stimulate migration, energy consumption, and orientation of birds.

PHILIP A. DuMONT heads the Branch of Interpretation, Division of Wildlife Refuges, Bureau of Sport Fisheries and Wildlife. During his more than 30 years in wildlife refuge work, he has managed Sand Lake National Wildlife Refuge, South Dakota, and served as biologist at Malheur National Wildlife Refuge in Oregon. He has written many leaflets about the birds and mammals in national wildlife refuges.

ALLEN J. DUVALL is an ornithologist in the Bureau of Sport Fisheries and Wildlife. He has had more than 30 years of experience in this field, including 10 years as Chief of the Bureau's Bird Banding Laboratory.

WALTER W. DYKSTRA is Research Staff Specialist with the Bureau of Sport Fisheries and Wildlife. He assists in the administration of Bureau research on the biological effects of pesticides and on control of bird and other wildlife depredations. He is a member of the Committee on Plant and Animal Pests of the National Academy of Sciences, National Research Council and alternate member of the Federal Committee on Pest Control.

TOM EVANS is Public Affairs Assistant in the Department of the Interior. He has worked for Voice of America and as a reporter for various newspapers.

IRA N. GABRIELSON is president, Wildlife Management Institute and a former Director of the Fish and Wildlife Service. He has received several national honors, including the Aldo Leopold and Audubon medals and the Distinguished Service Medal of the Department of the Interior. Among his books are *Wildlife Refuges* and *Wildlife Conservation*.

JOHN L. GEORGE is professor of Wildlife Management in the School of Forest Resources at The Pennsylvania State University. He was formerly a research staff specialist for the Bureau of Sport Fisheries and Wildlife; curator of mammals for the New York Zoological Society; and coordinator of graduate conservation programs at Vassar College. He is the chairman of the Committee on Ecological Effects of Chemical Controls for the International Union for the Conservation of Nature.

JOHN S. GOTTSCHALK is Director of the Bureau of Sport Fisheries and Wildlife. Previously he was Regional Director of the Bureau's Northeast Region and President of the American Fisheries Society. He has had more than 30 years of experience in fisheries and wildlife management. He is a winner of the American Motors Conservation Award.

CARLTON M. HERMAN is Chief, Wildlife Disease and Parasite Studies, at the Patuxent Wildlife Research Center. Before joining the Federal service in 1950, he was in charge of wildlife disease investigations for the California Department of Fish and Game.

JOSEPH J. HICKEY is professor of Wildlife Management at the University of Wisconsin. He was formerly editor of the Journal of Wildlife Management and is the author of *A Guide to Bird Watching*.

W. F. HOLLANDER, professor of genetics at Iowa State University, has written more than 50 papers in his field and is widely known for his scientific work on pigeons and doves.

RAYMOND E. JOHNSON, Assistant Director, Bureau of Sport Fisheries and Wildlife, joined the Bureau in 1952. Before that, Dr. Johnson spent 7 years with the Michigan Department of Conservation.

JOHN KIERAN for many years wrote a column in the New York Times and participated in the radio and television program "Information, Please." He is the author of several books, including *Introduction to Nature* and *Natural History of New York City*. He received the John Burroughs Medal in 1960.

JOSEPH E. KING, a biologist and ornithologist, is Chief, Branch of Marine Fisheries, Bureau of Commercial Fisheries. He has done extensive research on marine ecology in the central Pacific area and the Gulf of Mexico.

JACK M. KIRACOFE, an aviculturist by avocation, edits and publishes Modern Game Breeding magazine. He is president of the Whooping Crane Conservation Association, vice president of the International Wild Waterfowl Association, and a director of the American Pheasant and Waterfowl Society.

LAURITS W. KREFTING is a wildlife research biologist in the Bureau of Sport Fisheries and Wildlife. His 30 years of experience in wildlife research have been devoted mostly to wildlife on public lands.

CHARLES H. LAWRENCE is Assistant Chief, Division of Management and Enforcement, Bureau of Sport Fisheries and Wildlife. He was formerly a United States game management agent and has had extensive experience in law enforcement.

JOSEPH P. LINDUSKA, a wildlife biologist, is Associate Director of the Bureau of Sport Fisheries and Wildlife. He was previously director of public relations and wildlife management for Remington Arms Company. Dr. Linduska in 1963 received an award of the Outdoor Writers Association of America for distinguished service to conservation. The Wildlife Society awarded him its conservation education award in 1963, and the Department of the Interior awarded him a Conservation Service Award in 1964 for his contribution to *Waterfowl Tomorrow*.

E. MAYR is director, Museum of Comparative Zoology, Cambridge, Massachusetts. He is author of *Animal Species and Evolution*. He is a former president of the American Ornithologists' Union and the International Ornithological Congress.

ROBERT T. MITCHELL, an entomologist and wildlife biologist, is engaged in research for the Bureau of Sport Fisheries and Wildlife on control of bird depredations to crops. His experience includes research on biological control of insects and food habits of birds and mammals.

WILLIAM MORRIS is an editor on the staff of American Heritage and author of a newspaper column, "Words, Wit and Wisdom." He is coauthor (with Mary D. Morris) of *A Dictionary of Word and Phrase Origins*.

JOHNSON A. NEFF, a wildlife biologist, has had 34 years of experience in economic ornithology with the Bureau of Sport Fisheries and Wildlife. He has written numerous papers on bird depredations and methods for their control. He received the Distinguished Service Award of the Department of the Interior in 1965.

ALVA G. NYE, JR., is an Industrial Specialist (Aircraft) in the Office of the Secretary of Defense. He is a former vice president of the Falconry Club of America and an honorary member of the Deutscher Falkenorden, a falconry society in Germany. He has practiced falconry for more than 40 years.

LANSING A. PARKER was Associate Director of the Bureau of Sport Fisheries and Wildlife at the time of his death in 1965. He was active in wildlife management and administration for many years, holding positions of Assistant Director, Bureau of Sport Fisheries and Wildlife and Assistant Chief, Branch of Federal Aid to Wildlife. He was a charter member of the Wildlife Society; became a member of the Society of American Foresters in 1938; and was Associate Editor, Forest-Wildlife Management Division, Journal of Forestry, from 1960 to 1965.

ROGER TORY PETERSON is an ornithologist, explorer, artist, writer, lecturer, and photographer. His books on birds include *A Field Guide to the Birds, A Field Guide to Western Birds,* and (with James Fisher) *The World of Birds*.

OLIN SEWALL PETTINGILL, JR., an ornithologist, is director of the Laboratory of Ornithology, Cornell University, and author of *A Laboratory and Field Manual of Ornithology, A Guide to Bird Finding East of the Mississippi,* and *West of the Mississippi*. He was editor of *The Bird Watchers' America* and is a contributing editor and columnist of Audubon Magazine, secretary of the National Audubon Society, and formerly president, Wilson Ornithological Society.

ROBERT L. PYLE is Technical Assistant to the Director, National Environmental Satellite Center, Environmental Science Services Administration, Suitland, Maryland. His previous employment was as oceanographer with the Bureau of Commercial Fisheries. He is an active bird bander, a member of the Council of the Eastern Bird Banding Association, and a past president of the Hawaii Audubon Society.

WALTER W. RISTOW is Associate Chief, Geography and Map Division, the Library of Congress. He has been its representative on the United States Board on Geographical Names for more than 15 years and is a former chairman of the board. Dr. Ristow is the author of several monographs and has contributed papers to a number of professional journals.

CHANDLER S. ROBBINS is Chief, Migratory Non-game Bird Studies, the Bureau of Sport Fisheries and Wildlife. He has conducted research on bird migration and populations for the Bureau for more than 20 years. He is coauthor of *Birds of Maryland and the District of Columbia* and senior author of *Birds of North America*. He is technical editor of Audubon Field Notes and editor of Maryland Birdlife.

REX GARY SCHMIDT has been employed as an audiovisual specialist in the Fish and Wildlife Service and the Bureau of Sport Fisheries and Wildlife since 1950. He is a former art and photography editor of the magazine Missouri Conservationist. His motion picture on the whooping crane has been widely shown in the United States and abroad.

WILLIAM E. SHAKLEE is Principal Poultry Geneticist, the Cooperative State Research Service, Department of Agriculture. Formerly he was engaged in poultry genetics research at the University of Illinois and at the Agricultural Research Center, Beltsville, Maryland.

EDWARD A. SHERMAN is engaged in conservation education work for the Northeast Region of the Bureau of Sport Fisheries and Wildlife. His writings on wildlife have been published in many newspapers and in magazines.

KENNETH E. STAGER is senior curator of ornithology at the Los Angeles County Museum, where he has been active in ornithology since 1940. He has conducted intensive research on the sense of smell in birds. Dr. Stager is an adjunct professor of biology at the University of California. He is a fellow and past president of the Southern California Academy of Sciences and a member of the Board of Directors of the Cooper Ornithological Society.

WILLARD F. STANLEY is chairman of the Biology Department, State University College, Fredonia, New York. His chief activities are in the fields of biology and genetics. He is a member of the American Topical Association and one of seven men who organized the Biology Unit of the association. He is secretary-treasurer of the unit and editor-publisher of Bio-Philately. He received the American Topical Association's Distinguished Philatelist Award in 1955.

VLADIMIR CLAIN-STEFANELLI is Curator of the Division of Numismatics, U.S. National Museum. He is a fellow of the American Numismatic Society and of the Royal Numismatic Society (London), and honorary life member of the American Numismatic Association. Dr. Stefanelli is an advisor to the Department of the Treasury on the status of gold coins and has been a contributor to many numismatic publications and periodicals.

ERNEST SWIFT is conservation advisor to the National Wildlife Federation. He served previously as executive director of the National Wildlife Federation, Assistant Director of the Fish and Wildlife Service, and Director of the Wisconsin Conservation Department. He has written many essays on conservation.

BARBARA M. VAYO is a freelance writer and public relations consultant to the R. T. French Co., Pet Bird Food Division, Rochester, New York.

JOHN VOSBURGH is editor and general manager of Audubon Magazine. Mr. Vosburgh has been a writer for the Washington Post, city editor of the Key West (Florida) Citizen, and assistant Sunday editor of the Miami (Florida) Herald, for which he wrote a nature and conservation column. He helped to organize the Monroe County Audubon Society, Key West, Florida, and was president and a 10-year member of the board of directors of Tropical Audubon Society in Miami.

CECIL S. WILLIAMS is Director, Denver Wildlife Research Center, Bureau of Sport Fisheries and Wildlife. The Center's activities include research on methods for controlling damage caused by birds. Mr. Williams has more than 35 years' experience in research on wildlife management.

Editors

ALFRED STEFFERUD from 1945 to 1965 was editor of the Yearbook of Agriculture and before that was on the foreign staff of the Associated Press. He is the author of several books, including *How to Know the Wildflowers* and *The Wonders of Seeds*. He was consulting editor of *Waterfowl Tomorrow*.

ARNOLD L. NELSON is Special Assistant to the Director, Bureau of Sport Fisheries and Wildlife. He is a former Director of the Patuxent Wildlife

Research Center and Assistant Chief, Division of Wildlife Research. He is the author (with A. C. Martin and Herbert Zim) of *American Wildlife and Plants* and was managing editor of *Waterfowl Tomorrow*.

Artist

BOB HINES is an artist-illustrator in the Bureau of Sport Fisheries and Wildlife. Formerly he was an artist for the Ohio Division of Conservation and Natural Resources. He designed the 1946 Migratory Bird Hunting Stamp and four Wildlife Conservation Postage Stamps, which featured the wild turkey, king salmon, prong-horned antelope, and whooping crane. His illustrations have appeared in many books and magazines. He wrote and illustrated Ducks at a Distance, for which he received the Conservation-Education Award of the Wildlife Society.

Photographers

GRATEFUL ACKNOWLEDGEMENT is made of the several thousand photographs submitted for consideration. We list below the sources of the photographs in this book and (when they were given) the names of the photographers.

Agriculture, United States Department of: 294, 295, 296, 299, 301; Peter Killian 30; (Soil Conservation Service) W. B. Forney 6

Alabama Department of Conservation: 346 (upper)

Allen, Garner: 429

Armand Denis Productions: Des Bartlett 116, 528

Associated Press: 444 (upper)

Balser, D.: 448

Bauer, Erwin A.: 124

Benson, Frank: 40

Benton, Allen H.: 84, 86

Blakeslee-Lane Photographers: David Hamilton 109

Bleitz, Don: 17, 501 (upper)

Boehm, Edward Marshall: 103 (upper left)

Boston Public Library: 60, 62, 64 (right)

Bowling Green State University Photo Service: Louis Graue 312

Canadian Government Travel Bureau: 76

Carley, Curtis: 456 (upper)

Childress, Richard: 443, 456 (lower)

Chinn, Jack: 539

Colorado Game, Fish and Parks Department: 126; George D. Andrews 275

Contor, Roger: 75

Cornell University: David G. Allen 143 (upper)

Craighead, John and Frank: 202

Cruickshank, Allan D.: 26, 52, 72, 137, 138, 139, 140, 143 (lower), 146 (lower), 234, 409, 512 (lower)

Defense, United States Department of: 452; S.

Gatti 166 (upper); (U.S. Army) 306; (U.S. Navy) 176, 389; David C. Armstrong 18; (National Aeronautics and Space Administration) 260

Dermid, Jack: 9, 16, 117, 118, 128, 142 (lower), 149, 152 (upper), 161, 227, 242, 244, 246, 253, 261, 268, 300, 303 (lower), 308, 310, 314 (lower), 340, 344, 359, 376, 380, 393, 394, 398, 400, 402, 406, 420, 430, 450, 466, 516

Du Pont: 358, 360, 361

Fischer, Robert J.: 377

Florida News and Photo Service, Inc.: Joseph J. Steinmetz 255

Garnett, John: 153

General Dynamics: 531

Hawaii Visitor's Bureau: 281 (upper)

Hawk Mountain Sanctuary: Maurice Broun 514

Hialeah Race Track: 181 (lower)

Interior, United States Department of the: (Fish and Wildlife Service) 41 (lower), 83; Dan Chapman 288; C. G. Fairchild 243; Rex Gary Schmidt 14, 80, 81 (lower), 82, 85, 87, 88, 89, 92, 93, 94, 95, 99, 100 (lower left), 102, 103 (lower), 107, 110, 112, 113, 125, 127, 159, 188, 192 (lower), 237, 239, 264, 265, 266, 267, 285, 290, 326, 328, 362, 381, 412, 444 (lower), 457, 470, 478, 482, 483, 485, 497, 500; (Geological Survey) 70; (Bureau of Indian Affairs) Jim Aycock 279, 280; (Bureau of Land Management) 374; (Bureau of Reclamation) 378; (Bureau of Sport Fisheries and Wildlife) Winston E. Banko 386; Charles Cadieux 278 (lower right); John W. De Grazio 441; Vern Erickson 515; Charles Gibbons 182, 509; Luther Goldman 50, 100 (upper right), 101 (lower), 119, 130, 148 (upper), 151 (lower), 152 (lower), 156, 157, 166 (lower), 192 (upper), 223, 226, 232, 286, 303 (upper), 350, 401, 418, 440, 472, 490, 498,

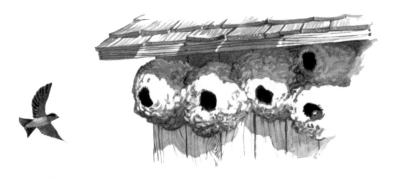

Appendix

FEW SCIENTIFIC NAMES of plants and animals have been used in the text of this book. Most of the vernacular names that appear are of North American species of birds; for their scientific names the reader is referred to *The A.O.U. Check-list of North American Birds,* Fifth Edition, 1957, published by the American Ornithologists' Union. It can be purchased by writing to the Union's Treasurer Burt L. Monroe, Sr., Post Office Box 23447, Anchorage, Kentucky 40223. The price is 8 dollars.

The following list gives the vernacular name and a scientific name of all other species of plants and animals and a few subspecies of North American birds. The list is restricted almost entirely to names that refer to definite species or subspecies. In a few instances, scientific names are provided for genera or families to which a more generalized vernacular name applies.

Authorities for both vernacular and scientific names, other than the A.O.U. *Check-list,* are *Gray's Manual of Botany,* Eighth Edition, 1950, by Merritt L. Fernald, and the most recent works available on the fauna of the various parts of the world to which the named species is native.

African ostrich, *Struthio camelus*
akiapolaau, *Hemignathus wilsoni*
Aleutian Canada goose, *Branta canadensis leucopareia*
alligator gar, *Lepisosteus spatula*
alternate-leaf dogwood, *Cornus alternifolia*
American bison, *Bison bison*
American eagle (bald eagle), *Haliaeetus leucocephalus*
American elm, *Ulmus americana*
American holly, *Ilex opaca*

Amherst pheasant (Lady Amherst pheasant), *Chrysolophus amherstiae*
anchoveta, *Engraulis ringens*
Andean flamingo, *Phoenicoparrus andinus*
Archaeopteryx, *Archaeopteryx lithographica*
arctic fox, *Alopex lagopus*
arrow-wood, *Viburnum dentatum*
Attwater's greater prairie chicken, *Tympanuchus cupido attwateri*
Australian radjah shelduck, *Tadorna radjah rufitergum*
Baikal teal, *Nettion formosa*
bamboo partridge, *Bambusicola thoracica*
bar-headed goose, *Anser indicus*
barred dove, *Geopelia striata*
bighorn (bighorn sheep), *Ovis canadensis*
black bullhead, *Ictalurus melas*
black cherry, *Prunus serotina*
black francolin, *Francolinus francolinus*
black grouse, *Lyrurus tetrix*
black gum, *Nyssa sylvatica*
black kite, *Milvus migrans*
black swan, *Cygnus atratus*
black-billed tree duck, *Dendrocygna arborea*
black-capped warbler, *Sylvia atricapilla*
black-haw, *Viburnum prunifolium*
black-necked pheasant, *Phasianus c. colchicus*
black-necked swan, *Cygnus melanocoryphus*
black-shouldered peafowl (color phase of peafowl), *Pavo cristatus*
bluegill, *Lepomis macrochirus*
blue-gray tanager, *Thraupis virens*
blue-naped coly (mousebird), *Colius m. macrourus*
box elder, *Acer negundo*
brush turkey, *Alectura lathami*
budgerigar, *Melopsittacus undulatus*
bullfrog, *Rana catesbeiana*

bullhead, *Ictalurus* sp.
bush honeysuckle, *Lonicera* sp.
Cabot's tragopan pheasant, *Tragopan caboti*
cackling Canada goose, *Branta canadensis minima*
canary, *Serinus canaria*
Cape Barren goose, *Chloephaga novae-hollandiae*
cape cormorant, *Phalacrocorax capensis*
cape gannet, *Morus capensis*
cape penguin, *Spheniscus demersus*
capercaillie, *Tetrao urogallus*
carp, *Cyprinus carpio*
cave swiftlet, *Collocalia* sp.
chaffinch, *Fringilla coelebs*
channel catfish, *Ictalurus punctatus*
Chilean pintail, *Anas georgica spinicauda*
Chinese ring-necked pheasant, *Phasianus c. torquatus*
chokeberry, *Aronia* sp.
chokecherry, *Prunus virginiana*
cockspur thorn, *Crataegus crusgalli*
coffeeweed, *Cassia tora*
common buckthorn, *Rhamnus cathartica*
common shelduck, *Tadorna tadorna*
Congo peacock, *Afropavo congensis*
cotton rat, *Sigmodon hispidus*
Coturnix quail, *Coturnix coturnix*
crested eagle (symbolic), probably based on *Aquila chrysaetos*
crested honey-creeper, *Palmeria dolei*
crowned crane, *Balearica pavonina*
Cuban bee hummer (bee hummingbird), *Mellisuga helenae*
deer mouse, *Peromyscus maniculatus*
demoiselle crane, *Anthropoides virgo*
dodo, *Raphus cucullatus*
eastern hemlock, *Tsuga canadensis*
eastern white pine, *Pinus strobus*
Egyptian goose, *Alopochen aegyptiaca*
elk (wapiti), *Cervus canadensis*
Emperor penguin, *Aptenodytes forsteri*
emu, *Dromaius novae-hollandiae*
English rabbit, *Oryctolagus cuniculus*
Eurasian golden plover, *Charadrius apricarius*
European bison, *Bison bonasus*
European blackbird, *Turdus merula*
European great tit, *Parus major*
European goldfinch, *Carduelis carduelis*
European robin, *Erithaeus rubecula*

European sparrow hawk, *Accipiter nisus*
European tree sparrow, *Passer montanus*
five-spined stickleback, *Eucalia inconstans*
flowering dogwood, *Cornus florida*
fox squirrel, *Sciurus niger*
freshwater snail (apple snail), *Pomacea palludosa*
gizzard shad, *Dorosoma cepedianum*
golden pheasant, *Chrysolophus pictus*
golden-mantled ground squirrel, *Citellus lateralis*
goosefish, *Lophius americanus*
gray dogwood, *Cornus racemosa*
gray francolin, *Francolinus pondicerianus*
gray duck, *Anas superciliosa*
gray parrot, *Psittacus erithacus*
gray sea eagle, *Haliaeetus albicilla*
graylag goose, *Anser anser*
great moa, *Dinornis maximus*
great titmouse, *Parus major*
guanay (Peruvian cormorant), *Phalacrocorax bougainvillii*
guineafowl, *Numida meleagris*
hackberry, *Celtis occidentalis*
hammerhead, *Scopus umbretta*
harpy, *Harpia harpyja*
Hartlaub's duck, *Cairina hartlaubi*
Hawaiian common gallinule, *Gallinula chloropus sandvicensis*
Hawaiian crow, *Corvus tropicus*
Hawaiian dark-rumped petrel, *Pterodroma phaeopygia sandwichensis*
Hawaiian duck (koloa), *Anas wyvilliana*
Hawaiian goose (nene), *Branta sandvicensis*
Hawaiian hawk, *Buteo solitarius*
Hawaiian noddy (white-capped or black noddy), *Anous minutus*
Hawaiian stilt, *Himantopus himantopus knudseni*
hazel grouse, *Tetrastes bonasia*
heath hen (race of greater prairie chicken), *Tympanuchus c. cupido*
herring (alewife), *Alosa pseudoharengus*
herring (Pacific herring), *Chipea harengus pallasi*
highbush cranberry, *Viburnum trilobum*
Himalayan monal (pheasant), *Lophophorus impeyanus*
hoopoe, *Upupa epops*
horned screamer, *Anhima cornuta*
huiabird (huia), *Heteralocha acutirostris*
hyacinthine macaw, *Anodorhynchus hyacinthinus*

Illiger's macaw (red and blue macaw), *Ara maracana*
imperial ivory-billed woodpecker, *Campephilus imperialis*
imperial pheasant, *Lophura imperialis*
Indian blue peafowl, *Pavo cristatus*
Indian mynah bird, *Acridotheres tristis*
Indian sandgrouse, *Pterocles exustus hindustan*
inkberry, *Ilex glabra*
Iranian pheasant, *Phasianus colchicus talischensis*
island thrush, *Turdus poliocephalus*
James's flamingo, *Phoenicoparrus jamesi*
Japanese green pheasant, *Phasianus versicolor*
Japanese quail, *Coturnix japonica*
Japanese white-eye, *Zosterops japonica*
Java sparrow, *Munia oryzivora*
jewelweed, *Impatiens biflora*
jungle myna, *Acridotheres fuscus*
kagu, *Rhynochetos jubatus*
kalij pheasant, *Lophura leucomelana*
Kauai akialoa, *Hemignathus procerus*
Kauai nukupuu, *Hemignathus lucidus hanapepe*
Kauai oo, *Moho braccatus*
Kauai thrush, *Phaeornis palmeri*
king salmon, *Oncorhynchus tshawytscha*
kiwi, Family Apterygidae
koloa (Hawaiian duck), *Anas wyvilliana*
kookaburra, *Dacelo novaeguineae*
lammergeier, *Gypaetus barbatus*
lapwing, *Vanellus vanellus*
largemouth bass, *Micropterus salmoides*
lavender finch, *Lagonosticta caerulescens*
Laysan duck, *Anas laysanensis*
Laysan finchbill, *Psittirostra c. cantans*
least chipmunk, *Eutamias minimus*
Lilford crane, *Grus grus lilfordi*
long-tailed cuckoo, *Eudynamis taitensis*
Louisiana parakeet (race of Carolina parakeet), *Conuropsis carolinensis ludoviciana*
lovebird, *Agapornis* sp.
lyre-bird, Family Menuridae
lyre-tailed black grouse, *Lyrurus tetrix*
magpie-jay, *Calocitta formosa*
mahi-mahi (dolphin), *Coryphaena hippurus*
maned wood duck, *Chenonetta jubata*
maple-leafed viburnum, *Viburnum acerifolium*
maasbunker, *Trachurus trachurus*
mandarin duck, *Aix galericulata*

masked bobwhite, *Colinus virginianus ridgwayi*
Masai ostrich, *Struthio camelus massaicus*
Maui parrotbill, *Pseudonestor xanthophrys*
meadow vole, *Microtus pennsylvanicus*
migratory quail, *Coturnix coturnix*
moa (Order Dinornithiformes)
Mongolian pheasant, *Phasianus colchicus mongolicus*
muscovy, *Cairina moschata*
muskox, *Ovibos moschatus*
muskrat, *Ondatra zibethica*
nannyberry, *Viburnum lentago*
nene (Hawaiian goose), *Branta sandvicensis*
nightingale, *Luscinia megarhynchos*
nightjar, *Caprimulgus europaeus*
northern pike, *Esox lucius*
ocellated turkey, *Agriocharis ocellata*
opossum (Virginia opossum), *Didelphis virginiana*
ostrich, *Struthio camelus*
ou, *Psittirostra psittacea*
ousel cock (ring ouzel), *Turdus torquatus*
palila, *Psittirostra bailleui*
peafowl, *Pavo cristatus*
Pekin nightingale, *Leiothrix lutea*
Peruvian booby, *Sula variegata*
Peruvian cormorant (guanay), *Phalacrocorax bougainvillii*
Peruvian pelican, *Pelecanus thagus*
pied flycatcher, *Ficedula hypoleuca*
pilchard, *Sardinops ocellata*
pollock, *Pollachius virens*
Prjevalski's horse, *Equus przewalskii*
pronghorn antelope, *Antilocapra americana*
Puerto Rican parrot, *Amazona v. vittata*
quetzal, *Pharomachrus mocino*
rattlebox, *Crotalaria spectabilis*
razor-billed auk (razorbill), *Alca torda*
red bishop, *Euplectes orix*
red-crested pochard, *Netta rufina*
redear sunfish, *Lepomis microlophus*
red junglefowl, *Gallus gallus*
red-billed blue magpie, *Urocissa erythrorhyncha*
red-legged partridge, *Alectoris rufa*
red mulberry, *Morus rubra*
red oak, *Quercus rubra*
red-osier, *Cornus stolonifera*
redstart, *Phoenicurus phoenicurus*
red-whiskered bulbul, *Pycnonotus jocosus*

Reeves' pheasant, *Syrmaticus reevesi*
rhea, *Rhea americana*
rock dove, *Columba livia*
rosy-billed pochard, *Netta peposaca*
ruddy-headed goose, *Chloephaga rubidiceps*
sacred ibis, *Threskiornis aethiopicus*
salmon, *Salmo* sp.
sarus crane, *Grus antigone*
scarlet macaw, *Ara macao*
shadblow, *Amelanchier canadensis*
shoe-bill stork (shoebill), *Balaeniceps rex*
sika deer, *Cervus nippon*
silky dogwood, *Cornus amomum*
silver maple, *Acer saccharinum*
silver pheasant, *Gennaeus nycthemerus*
skipjack (tuna), *Katsuwonus pelamis*
skylark, *Alauda arvensis*
slender-billed cockatoo, *Kakatoe tenuirostris*
smallmouth bass, *Micropterus dolomieui*
song thrush, *Turdus ericetorum*
South American condor, *Vultur gryphus*
South African shelduck, *Tadorna cana*
spicebush, *Benzoin aestivale*
spotted dove, *Streptopelia chinensis*
stock dove, *Columba oenas*
sunbittern, *Eurypyga helias*
swan goose, *Anser cygnoides*
sweet gum, *Liquidambar styraciflua*
swinhoe pheasant, *Lophura swinhoei*

tamarack (American larch), *Larix laricina*
thicket thorn, *Crataegus intricata coccinea*
thirteen-lined ground squirrel, *Citellus tridecem-lineatus*
thorns, *Crataegus*
tiger salamander, *Ambystoma tigrinum*
triangular-spotted pigeon, *Columba guinea*
trumpet-creeper, *Bigonia radicans*
tui bird (tui), *Posthemadera novaeseelandiae*
tule white-fronted goose, *Anser albifrons gambelli*
tuliptree, *Liriodendron tulipifera*
Washington hawthorn, *Crataegus phaenopyrum cordata*
whale-headed stork (shoebill), *Balaeniceps rex*
white-footed mouse, *Peromyscus leucopus*
white mulberry, *Morus alba*
white-naped crane, *Grus vipio*
white spoonbill, *Platalea leucorodia*
wild millet, *Echinochloa* sp.
wild red cherry, *Prunus pennsylvanica*
willows, *Salix*
winterberry, *Ilex verticillata*
withe-rod, *Viburnum cassinoides*
wood lark, *Lullula arborea*
yellowfin tuna, *Thunnus albacares*
yellow-naped Amazon parrot, *Amazona auropalliata*
Zanzibar red bishop, *Euplectes nigroventris*

Index

Shearwater, 25, 218, 230; guide for locating tuna, 238; Manx, illus., 24; 26; slender-billed, 279; sooty, 283
Shelley, Percy Bysshe, 46
Sherman, Edward A., 58–65, 547
Sherman, Roger, 105
Shields, G. O., 481
Shikli Ahmer, 304
Shine, Harold E., 538
Shoveler, 84
Shrike, northern, illus., 122
Sign of the flying goose, illus., 520
Sims, John, 75
Sinnock, J. R., 93
Skinner, B. F., 313
Skua, 218, 224
Sleeping sickness, illus., 30
Smith, Harry, checks on his week-old duck-lings, illus., 302
Smith, Margaret Chase, 267
Smith, S. Percy, 283
Smith, William A., illus., 316
Snail, water, food, 18
Snipe, 162, 474; common, 131, 162
Songbirds killed by TV towers, illus., 369
Soporifics, 463
Sora rail, 131
Sparrow, 97, 244; Cape Sable, 504; chipping, 411; dusky seaside, 504; European tree, introduced, 348; field, 526; fox, 282; golden-crowned, illus., 262; 264; grass-hopper, 17, 401; Henslow's, 400; house, 16, 162, 218, 229, 289, 326, 350, 397, 416, 420; illus., 446; 469; Ipswich, 268, 370; Java, illus., 284; 289; olive, 519; Savannah, 401; song, 46, 401, 420, 532; swamp, 46; vesper, 46; white-crowned, 17, 264; white throated, 406
Spoonbill, roseate, illus., 512; 513, 523
Sporting firearms industry, 133
Squirrel, fox, 206
Stabler, Robert M., 315
Stager, Kenneth E., 218–229, 547
Stamps, Israeli, illus., 89
Stanley, Willard F., 78–89; illus., 84; 547
Starling, 162, 240; introduced, 247, 263, 348; **385**, 391, 396, 397, 416; illus., 426, **435**, 439, 440; 441; illus., 456; 459; illus., 463; roosting, illus., 443, 444; 469; 526
Starling in feedlot, illus., 448
State hunting licenses, sale, 133
Stearns, Stanley, illus., 83
Clain-Stefanelli, Vladimir, 90–97; illus., 94; 547
Stefferud, Alfred, 547
Stewart, George, 69
Stewart, Robert E., 159
Stiles, Edmund W., illus., 157
Stilt, black-necked, 381, 506; long-legged Hawaiian, 499
Stoddard, Herbert L., Sr., 205, 368
Stone, Witmer, 158
Stravinsky, Igor, 42
Strigel, Bernhard, illus., 61
Stuart, Jesse, 45
Study on raptors versus food species, 208
Sunflower seeds on feeding station, illus., 146
Superstitions, 49–57
Swallow, 16, 46, 49, 54; bank, colony, illus., 39; 385; barn, 272; cliff, 272; tree, 153, 246, 385; illus., 394
Swan, 34, 42; illus., 72, 277, 355; mute, introduced, 347; trumpeter, 84; illus., 182; hatched at Philadelphia Zoo, illus., 197;

515, 522, 526; whistling, illus., 83; 183, 279; illus., 512; 523; whooper, 42
Swan Lake, Minn., a painting, illus., 73
Swanton, John R., 57
Swarth, Harry S., 481
Swift, Ernest, 468–475, 547
Swift, chimney, illus., 414; white-throated, 272
Swiftlets, cave, 5

Tanager, 366; blue-gray, introduced, 348; scarlet, 373
Tape recordings, 440
Tarshis, I. B., illus., 286
Tattler, wandering, 279
Taverner, P. A., 263
Teal, blue-winged, 84, 274; illus., 372; green-winged, 84
Television towers detrimental to migration, 364
Television towers searched for dead and wounded birds, illus., 367
Tennyson, Alfred, 34, 46
Tern, 74, 224, 230, 233, 235; concentration of, illus., 237; guide for locating tuna, 238, 263; arctic, 271; common, illus., 261; least, illus., 268; Royal, illus., 253, 270; sooty, seasonal cycle, 24, 523
Thomson, Charles, 107
Thoreau, Henry David, 8, 71
Thrasher, 16; brown, State emblem, 120; illus., 144; curve-billed, 519; long billed, 519
Thrush, 14, 46, 244, 366, 369; gray-cheeked, 282, 533; hermit, State bird, 120; 373; Swainson's 264; wood, State bird, 120; 405
Thurman, Lawrence M., illus., 472
Tiercel, 167
Tinicum Wildlife Preserve, Philadelphia, 535; illus., 536
Titmouse, 16, 97, 240, 246; black-crested, 519
Todd Wildlife Sanctuary, Maine, illus., 138
Tomtit, 120
Toucan, 30
Towhee, 401
Trap, illus., 450, 451; 465
Treaties, 433
Treet, Dorothy, illus., 481
Trichomonas of pigeons, 315
Trichomoniasis, 351
Troels-Smith, Denmark, J., 277
Tropicbird, 97, 230; red-tailed, 523
Tropical rain forest, 30
Tui bird, 97
Tule Lake National Wildlife Refuge, 326
Tumbler, yellow, 306
Tumblers, illus., 304
Turkey, 4, 15; illus., 72, 79, 404; domesti-cated by ancient Mexicans, 300; ocel-lated, 180; wild, 78; illus., 81; 124; illus., 125; 322; illus., 349, 351, 373; illus., 404; 469
Turkey ranch in Pender County, N.C., illus., 300
Turkey stamp, illus., 79
Turner, C. W., 315
Turnstone, ruddy, 269

Udall, Stewart L., 535
Upland game birds, 205
Upper Mississippi River Wildlife and Fish Refuge Act, 472
Use of dogs to retrieve birds, illus., 338

Vaccine, 285
Vaccines developed in eggs, illus., 30

Vayo, Barbara M., 184–189, 547
Vegetation belts in telephone right-of-way, 393
Velie, Elizabeth D., 367
Veteran hunter instructs boy, illus., 133
Vinci, Leonardo da, 34
Violations, 475
Vireo, 16, 365, 369; black-whiskered, 523; red-eyed, 17, 19, 262, 272, 405, 526; solitary, 373
Vole, meadow, 206; irruption, 213
Vosburgh, John, 364–371, 547
Vulture, 61, 218, 219, 229; American, 203; black, 221, 222; illus., 223, 250; Old World, 203; turkey, 221, 222, 223; illus., 225; 259

Wagner, Richard, 42
Wallace, G. J., 323
Warbler, 366, 369; American, 427; Audu-bon's, illus., 404; Bachman's, 504; bay-breasted, 272; blackburnian, 46, 405; black-capped, import, 343; black-poll, 533; black and white, 526; black-throated blue, 405, 526; black-throated green, 405, 526; cerulean, 405; chest-nut-sided, 526; hooded, 405; Kirtland's, 7, 15, 18; illus., 488, 502; 511; magnolia, 365; mourn-ing, 405; myrtle, 405, 526; palm, 246; parula, illus., 138; pine, 272, 405; pro-thonotary, illus., 244; wood, 16; yellow, 272, 532
Washington, George, 107
Wasted basic resource, 381
Water management, 381
Waterfowl, 7, 205; illus., 278; 336, 396, 436, 439; illus., 442, 472; 475; migratory, illus., 85; 458; wild, illus., 539
Waterfowl Hunting Stamp Act, 472
Waterthrush, 46, 262; northern, 264
Waxwing, 16; Bohemian, 37; cedar, 18, 244
Weaver bird, 448
Weber, Walter A., 84
Weevil, alfalfa, 241
Wendelin, Rudolph, 78
Wetlands, 532
Wetmore, Alexander, 158
Whale, 224
Wheatear, 282
Whip-poor-will, illus., 48; 49, 53
White, Elmo, 79
White, H. C., 232
White-eye, Japanese, 344
Whitman, C. O., 308
Whitman, Walt, 46
Widgeon, 517; American, 84, 507; European, 418
Wilderness Society, 486
Wild horse, Prjevalski's, 198
Wild turkey, see turkey
Wildlife conservation stamp, 485
Wildlife Management Institute, publications, 482
Wildlife Society, publications, 486
Williams, Cecil S., 438–445, 547
Willy, Guy, illus., 472
Wilson, Alexander, 8, 40, 481
Wilson Ornithological Society, 481
Wing, Leonard, 162
Wing prints of a crow, illus., 142
Winged victory of Samothrace, illus., 35
Wireworm, 241
Woodcock, 97, 268, 474; American, 131, 326; illus., 330
Woodcock vs. pesticide, illus., 320
Woodhewer, 30